The Enemy of My Enemy

Galaeron heard Melegaunt Tanthul before he saw him. The human's deep voice came from the shadowy side of the moonlit cairn, growling out the arcane syllables of a bizarre spell. The incantation was unlike anything Galaeron had ever heard, even among the corpse-stealing drow who occasionally worked their evil in the isolated crypts of the Desert Border. The words were booming and raspy, loaded with power and danger, but also intricate and enigmatic, full of cleverness and deception.

When he rounded the corner, Galaeron found Melegaunt working the shadows into an impassable maze of moonlight and darkness, swirling them into dead-end spirals, folding them into meandering corridors that rounded a hundred corners and came back to their own beginning. The wizard himself was nearly impossible to find, his black robes and swarthy complexion blending into the night the same way wood elves melted into the forest.

Though Galaeron did not think he made any noise as he approached, Melegaunt glanced in his direction and nodded. He finished his maze by feeding its only exit into a hole of fuming darkness, then simply melted into the shadows beneath his feet.

"We have until tomorrow dusk, no longer."

The voice came from the ground beside Galaeron. In spite of himself, he hopped away and looked down. The wizard's body was rising out of the shadow, peeling itself up like a turning page.

"We?" Galaeron said. "To do, what?"

"To set things right of course."

Is Not Always My Friend

FORGOTTEN REALMS

More Books by *The New York Times*
Best-selling Author

TROY DENNING

RETURN OF THE ARCHWIZARDS

The Summoning

The Siege

The Sorcerer

THE AVATAR SERIES

Waterdeep

Crucible: The Trial of Cyric the Mad

LOST EMPIRES

Faces of Deception

THE TWILIGHT GIANTS

The Ogre's Pact

The Giant Among Us

The Titan of Twilight

THE CORMYR SAGA

Beyond the High Road

Death of the Dragon
(with Ed Greenwood)

FORGOTTEN REALMS®

TROY DENNING
RETURN OF THE ARCHWIZARDS

THE SUMMONING

THE SIEGE

THE SORCERER

Wizards of the Coast®

Return of the Archwizards Omnibus

Published by Wizards of the Coast LLC

Forgotten Realms, Wizards of the Coast, and their respective logos are trademarks of Wizards of the Coast LLC in the U.S.A. and other countries.

Printed in the U.S.A.

Cover art by Kekai Kotaki
Map by Dennis Kauth

The Summoning originally published March 2001
The Seige originally published December 2001
The Sorcerer originally published December 2002

First Printing: December 2009

9 8 7 6 5 4 3 2 1

ISBN: 978-0-7869-5365-3
620-25129000-001-EN

U.S., CANADA,
ASIA, PACIFIC, & LATIN AMERICA
Wizards of the Coast LLC
P.O. Box 707
Renton, WA 98057-0707
+1-800-324-6496

EUROPEAN HEADQUARTERS
Hasbro UK Ltd
Caswell Way
Newport, Gwent NP9 0YH
GREAT BRITAIN
Save this address for your records.

Visit our web site at www.wizards.com

THE SUMMONING *For Eric Boyd. With many thanks.*

This book would not have been possible without the help of many people; thanks to you all! Some who deserve special mention: Eric Boyd, for guiding me through the forest and pointing out just how much reading I still had to do—and for providing it when no other source was available. Ed Greenwood, for the loan of a very special character—I hope he finds his way home! Skip Williams and Jeff Grubb for talks both shadowy and magical. Jim Butler and Rich Baker for their invaluable comments on both outline and manuscript, and for making the 3e coordination as painless as possible. Rich, again, for his excellent work on *The Shadow Stone,* and to Clayton Emery for reasons that should be apparent by the end of the book. Phil Athans, my editor, for his usual patience, good humor, and insight. Mary Kirchoff for turning me loose on the Realms again. Sean K. Reynolds, Rob Heinsoo, and James Wyatt for their give and take; Duane Maxwell, Julia Martin, Anthony Valterra, Roger Moore, Steven Schend, Michele Carter, Dale Donovan, and the entire Forgotten Realms 3e board and product group for their many ideas and insightful suggestions. As always, thanks to Andria for support, patience, and encouragement.

And thanks to the Forgotten Realms readers, without whom there wouldn't be a Forgotten Realms first edition—much less a third!

THE SIEGE *To Phil Athans. For service beyond the call.*

I would like to thank Eric Boyd for his many contributions to the series, the entire WotC book department for their extra effort on this one, and Andria Hayday for her extraordinary patience and support.

THE SORCERER *To Ed Greenwood. For sharing his world with so many.*

I would like to thank my editor, Phil Athans, for his patience, good humor, and valuable insight; Eric Boyd for his many contributions to the series, and Andria Hayday for her usual extraordinary patience and support.

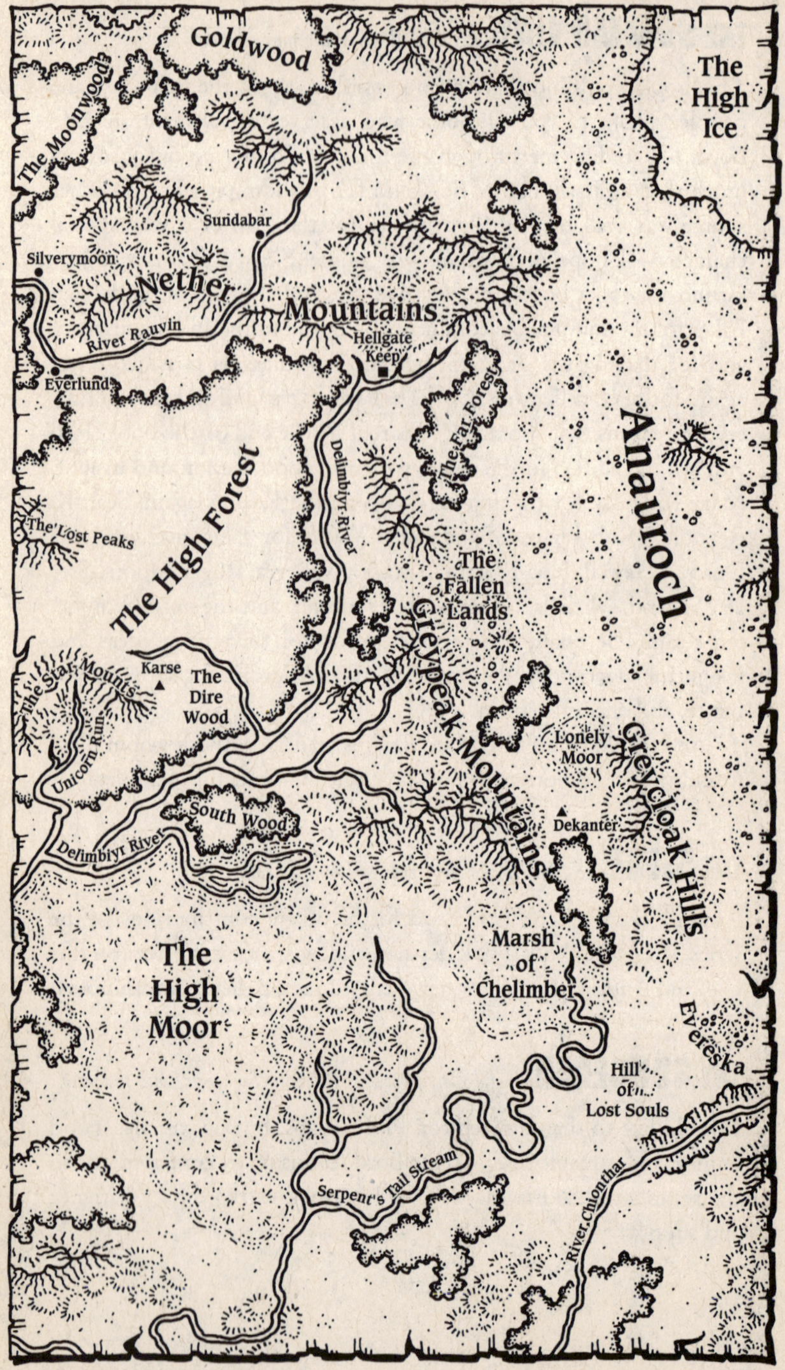
Goldwood
The High Ice
The Moonwood
Sundabar
Silverymoon
Nether
Mountains
River Rauvin
Hellgate Keep
Everlund
The Far Forest
Anauroch
Delimbiyr River
The High Forest
The Lost Peaks
The Fallen Lands
Greypeak Mountains
Karse
The Dire Wood
The Star Mounts
Unicorn Run
Lonely Moor
Greycloak Hills
South Wood
Dekanter
Delimbiyr River
The High Moor
Marsh of Chelimber
Evereska
Hill of Lost Souls
Serpent's Tail Stream
River Chionthar

THE SUMMONING RETURN OF THE ARCHWIZARDS

CHAPTER ONE

20 Nightal, the Year of the Unstrung Harp (1371 DR)

Like every burial cairn Galaeron Nihmedu had ever entered, this one stank of the bodies and breath of those who had opened it. The air was permeated by the odor of saddle soap and camp smoke, and the reek of musty human armpits and sour human breath. What Galaeron did not smell was blood, which meant these crypt breakers were more skillful than most. Usually at least three fell to traps and magic during the entranceway excavation.

As Galaeron led his patrol deeper into the cairn, his dark sight began to illuminate the passage walls in shades of cool blue. Inscribed into the flat wall stones were ancient elven glyphs recounting the lives and deeds of the ones buried within. Like most entrance tunnels, this one was low and narrow, with just enough height to stand upright and barely enough room for an elf's slender shoulders. How the burly humans had found room in the cramped space to clear the corridor he could not imagine, but they had deftly spanned the death pits with rough hewn planks and braced the deadfalls with oak posts.

Galaeron followed the tunnel to the burial chamber. He was surprised to find the room both quiet and dark, given that a pair of his elves were outside guarding twenty shaggy horses and three red-faced sentries. Nor could there be any doubt the humans had reached the crypt. The bronze shield that had once served as a door had been melted almost into nothingness, a crude but effective entry that hinted at plenty of magic.

Galaeron slipped cautiously into the chamber. Seven elf dead lay undisturbed on their ancient biers, their flesh and hair perfectly preserved by the crypt's now shattered magic. Their bejeweled weapons and gold-trimmed armor were lying untouched beneath a thick layer of dust. By their amber skin and ornate bronze armor, Galaeron knew these to be Aryvandaaran nobles, high lords of the aggressive Vyshaan clan who had touched off the First Crown War and plunged the entire elf race into three thousand years of carnage. Though he wished them no peace in their sleep, he would bring their crypt breakers to justice. As a tomb guard, he had sworn to protect all elven burials.

In the tomb's far corner, Galaeron found a knotted rope leading down into a freshly opened hole. The shaft had been excavated by the same magic that destroyed the bronze door, for there was no dirt or rubble heaped around the collar. Trying to imagine what the greedy humans might be seeking down there more valuable than the priceless armor and enchanted weapons of the Vyshaan lords, he led the patrol down the rope.

Thirty feet later, the shaft opened into a labyrinth of low, square-cut dwarven tunnels. By the looks of the working, it had been old when Evereska was young. Dust clung to the walls two fingers thick and lay on the floor a foot deep. The humans' path twined its way eastward through the powder, looking for all the world like a trail through snow.

Galaeron sent two scouts ahead, then, as the last faint light from outside faded, he took a pinch of stardust from his pocket and flung it into the corridor ahead. Though the phosphorescent dust was too faint to be seen by humans, it provided light enough for the sensitive eyes of elves. Recalling the care his quarry had displayed in defeating the crypt traps, he ordered a three-elf rear guard to follow behind. Stooping almost double beneath the low dwarven ceiling, the patrol moved into blackness. Galaeron left his sword in its scabbard and took his customary position three places back from the leader. Though all tomb guards could fight with both spell and steel, he usually served as the patrol's primary magic-user. Not only was his magic more versatile than that of most elves, he had learned in his few battles that crypt breakers often targeted spell-flingers first, and he preferred to shoulder that burden himself.

The human trail ran eastward for a thousand yards, circling past a dozen ancient cave-ins. Narrow seams of sand began to appear in the ceiling, suggesting to Galaeron's experienced eye that they had crossed under Anauroch itself. Not long after, the distant clatter of falling rock started to echo through the tunnels, and his favorite scout returned to report.

We must be careful with these spiders. They look to have venom. A svelte wood elf with a cupid's bow smile and brown eyes the size of a doe's, Takari Moonsnow's slender hands streaked through the near darkness in finger talk. *And their pet has fangs of its own.*

Pet? Galaeron's fingers weaved a basket of lines before him. *What kind of pet?*

Takari smiled coyly. *Better you should see for yourself.*

She spun away and started up the passage, leaving Galaeron knowing little more than he had before her report. He shook his head and followed. If he wanted a Wood elf for a scout, Takari had to be allowed her fun.

Aragath, the second scout—a moon elf—lay near the inside wall of a gentle curve, his head silhouetted against a flickering blue glow that filled the tunnel ahead. The clatter of falling rock was louder, punctuated by the gruff talk of men at work. Galaeron lay on his belly and crawled up beside Aragath. After stooping so long, it was a relief to stretch out on the floor—even if it did mean breathing through his fingers so the dust did not make him sneeze.

Galaeron peered around the corner and almost cried out in shock. Less than ten paces away hovered a leathery orb of gray-green flesh, nearly three feet in diameter and shaped more or less like a head. A huge eye bulged out from the center of its face, and beneath that gaped an enormous mouth filled with sharp teeth. Atop its pate writhed ten thick tentacles, each ending in a single bulbous eye. Nine of these tentacles had been folded over a small length of wood and bound so that the eyes could look only at the top of the gruesome head. The tenth tentacle was sweeping back and forth, spraying a brilliant blue beam across a four foot width of stone wall. Wherever the light touched, six inches of stone deteriorated into yellow smoke.

Galaeron swallowed, hardly able to believe what he saw. The creature was an eye tyrant, one of the rarest and most feared killers of the Underdark. Galaeron had never fought one himself, but he had seen a trophy specimen in the Evereskan Academy of Magic. According to the Histories, the monster had taken possession of King Sileron's crypt in the Greycloak Hills, then gorged itself on two patrols of tomb guards before the great Kiinyon Colbathin finally killed it.

So stunned was Galaeron that he barely noticed the creature's companions until a section of roof collapsed and several men crawled forward to clear the rubble. All were heavy-boned and huge, with thighs as large as an elf's waist and dark braids of hair swinging about their shoulders. Their high boots and battle-worn scale mail were trimmed in black sable, while the belts that girded their thick middles were made from white dragon scales.

As the men worked, the eye tyrant's blue gaze drifted downward, cutting a swath of smoking emptiness inches above their backs. They dropped to their bellies and grunted something in a harsh, rasping language, then a small fist appeared on the other side of the monster and clasped one of its bound eyestalks. Though the hand was hairless and smooth, it was also strong, pulling so hard Galaeron thought the tentacle would pop off.

"Shatevar!" a voice called.

A female face appeared in the narrow gap between the ceiling and eye tyrant's head. Her features were heavy and rough by elven standards, yet striking and surprisingly beautiful, with hair the color of honey and eyes as blue as tourmalines.

Her second hand came into view and pressed a dagger to the trapped eyestalk, then she said in Common, "Try that again, and I'll make a cyclops of you."

"Then keep your oafs out of my way." The eye tyrant's voice was deep and gurgling. "I'm too tired to watch them."

"Tired or dead, your choice."

As the two argued, Galaeron tried to take count of the humans. Behind the eye tyrant stood two men holding what appeared to be glassy black swords. The weapons might have been obsidian, save that they were perfectly molded, with shadow-smooth blades and none of the conchoidal flaking marks he would have expected. Four more men squatted along the near wall, their scabbards resting across their knees. Judging by their shimmering pommels, these weapons were also made of black glass. It was impossible to see how many men might be lurking beyond the eye tyrant, for the brilliance of its disintegration beam washed out Galaeron's dark sight. Still he did not think his patrol too badly outnumbered. There had only been twenty horses outside.

Galaeron backed away from the corner then issued his orders in finger talk. He did not relish trying to capture someone who made slaves of eye tyrants but had little choice in the matter. Word of such a strange encounter was bound to circulate through Evereska, and any leeway given the humans would reflect badly on the entire patrol. The matter would not trouble Galaeron overmuch. It was his reputation as a malcontent that had landed him a posting along the Desert Border in the first place, but there were some among his elves who still hoped to make names for themselves in the Tomb Guard.

Once his warriors had readied themselves, Galaeron used a spell to turn himself and four more tomb guards invisible. Trusting the rest of the patrol to follow, he led the way around the corner, the magic of his boots smothering all sound as he skulked along opposite the crouching humans.

Unfortunately, even magic spells and elven boots could not keep dust from billowing when someone walked through it. Two paces from the eye tyrant, one of the humans pointed at the gray cloud around Galaeron's feet and spoke in his harsh language. When the warrior started to rise, the heavy pulse of bow strings throbbed through the passage. Four white arrows streaked out of the empty air and struck their targets in the unarmored calves, the heads sinking only to the depth of a fingertip. The astonished humans leaped up, banging their skullcaps on the low ceiling, then their eyelids rolled down and they collapsed facedown into the dust.

Rendered visible by their attacks, Takari and three more elves rushed forward, exchanging bows for swords and pausing to turn the heads of the sleeping warriors sideways so they would not smother in the thick dust. Behind them, another half dozen elf archers appeared in the low tunnel, three kneeling in front and three standing hunched behind them.

"Elves!" hissed the female human, still the only woman Galaeron saw in the band. A trio of threatening arrow tips appeared out of the darkness to each side of her broad shoulders, and she glared over the eye tyrant at Takari. "My men better be alive."

"They are only sleeping—as are the sentries you left outside," Galaeron said. Trying not to let the woman's apparent lack of alarm worry him, he annulled his invisibility spell. He signaled Takari and the three elves with her to wait against the opposite wall, then waved at the sleeping men. "These are now our prisoners—as are you. Lay down your weapons and explain—"

"No."

The interruption took Galaeron by surprise. "What?"

"I said no." The woman spun the eye tyrant so that its largest eye faced Galaeron. "We will not lay down our weapons, and we have no need to explain anything to you."

"You have broken a crypt," he said. "In these lands, that gives you much to explain. Surrender now, or you will be the first to fall."

The woman merely looked past Galaeron's archers and called, "Sterad?"

"Here."

A trio of muffled thumps sounded from the rear of the tunnel. Galaeron glanced back and was relieved to see his archers still standing. He was not so relieved to see a pair of burly human warriors standing behind them, looming over the unconscious bodies of the rear guard he had assigned to watch the patrol's back.

"Your rear guard will have a few lumps when they wake," said the woman. "Their headaches will trouble them no more than the wounds in the legs of my men."

As she spoke, the front rank of elf archers spun on their knees to aim at the newcomers. The rear rank ignored the peril at their backs and continued to train their arrows on the woman. If she noticed, she did not seem to care. She said something in her own language to the two men who had delivered

Galaeron's rear guard, and they laid their black swords across their breasts. Though the move was not overtly threatening, Galaeron noticed that it placed their weapons at a good height for hacking his archers in the neck.

The woman looked back to Galaeron. "You've no idea what you've blundered into here, elf, but know I mean no harm to you or your people. You may leave while that remains so."

"Pay her no heed, my prince," said Louenghris, one of the archers in the rear rank and the patrol's only Gold elf. "Let them cut my throat. My aim will still be true."

"Thank you, Louenghris, but it won't come to that," said Galaeron, hiding his annoyance. At only a hundred and ten, Louenghris was the youngest of the patrol's elves and still foolish enough to put the humans on their guard by inviting such things. Allowing a nugget of coal to drop from his sleeve into his palm, Galaeron looked back to the woman. "Perhaps you meant no harm, but in breaking the tomb's seal, you have caused it. Now you must come before the *erlagh aneghwai gilthrum!*"

Slipping smoothly into a spell incantation, he crushed the coal nugget and brought his hand forward. A fan of pink radiance shot from the eye tyrant's huge central eye, speckling Galaeron's vision with pale light. Even through the red spots in his eyes, he could see that the tunnel remained as bright as before.

The woman tapped her dagger above the monster's huge central eye. "Haven't fought many beholders, have you? Magic's not much good around Shatevar."

"I am aware of an eye tyrant's power." Galaeron lowered his gaze to address the creature directly. "But I had not heard they were such faithful slaves. We have no quarrel with you, Shatevar."

Shatevar twisted his toothy maw into a sheepish grin. "Sadly, your warriors are not the ones holding darkswords to my back. Should that change, rest assured I will serve you as loyally as I have Vala."

"Vala?" Galaeron repeated, guessing the reason the eye tyrant had spoken her name. Charm spells were much easier to use when a caster knew his quarry's name, and they did not require anything so clunky as hurling coal dust at someone. "What kind of name is Vala? *Meshim deri—*"

"Enough!" Vala pricked her dagger into the eye tyrant's head, drawing a single bubble of brownish blood.

Shatevar's central eye widened, and again the pink flash filled the corridor. Galaeron's spell died on his lips.

"Try that again, elf, and there will be blood." Still keeping the eye tyrant's largest eye pointed at Galaeron, Vala cut another eyestalk loose from its bonds and aimed it at a fist-sized hole the creature had inadvertently drilled into the wall. "You've eleven eyes. Back to work."

"As you command, mistress."

The eye tyrant began to sweep its blue beam across the wall again, revealing a strange square of glimmering radiance deep inside the hole it had created. Content with a standoff for now, Galaeron dropped his hand and used a pair of curt finger gestures to issue two instructions, the most important being to wait. With a little patience, he might learn what the humans were doing and—more importantly—not get anyone killed.

The eye tyrant continued to melt the rock away, shaping something that looked ominously like a doorway. As the opening grew, so did the shimmering square of radiance, though it seemed little more than a sheet of silvery light. Shatevar's blue beam passed through undisturbed, continuing to disintegrate stone on the other side, while the rocks that occasionally fell from the ceiling tumbled back through into the chamber. Given their location, Galaeron wondered if he might be looking at the fabled Sharn Wall, a barrier of ancient magic rumored to lie buried along the perimeter of Anauroch. If so, he could not imagine what the humans wanted on the other side. The few veteran tomb guards who gossiped about such things claimed the hell beyond was rivaled only by the slave pits of Carceri.

Vala kept a wary watch while Shatevar worked, and the patrol was still awaiting Galaeron's signal when the blue beam began to leave black nothingness in its wake.

"We've broken through," reported a human.

Vala's eyes shifted, and Galaeron knew this to be the best chance he would have. He curled the tip of his index finger, signaling the attack, and a trio of white arrows flashed past. He was already diving as the shafts struck home, two above Shatevar's central eye and the third in Vala's cheek. Though the arrows sank only fingertip deep, that did not prevent the victims from crying out.

To Galaeron's surprise, no human arrows clattered off the wall behind him, and no elf voices cried out in pain. As he rolled, he glimpsed Louenghris falling beneath the blow of a human sword's lustrous pommel and saw two more archers lying in the dust unconscious but unbloodied, then Takari and her companions swept past him, flinging sand and uttering spells of sleeping.

Galaeron came up face-to-eye with Shatevar. Though the lid of its central eye was drooping, the eye tyrant had not yet fallen to the sleep arrows and was swinging around two unfettered eyestalks to attack. The blue beam swept past above Galaeron and tore a six inch hole across Aragath's chest. The scout did not scream; he simply dropped his chin and stared at the red mess spilling down his stomach, then he fell into the dust.

Galaeron was already raising his hand to spray magic at the eye tyrant when a black sword fell on it from behind. The shadowy blade slid through the leathery head almost effortlessly, splitting the skull down the back and spilling the ghastly contents onto the floor. Shatevar's many eyes grew foggy and vacant, then the blue disintegration beam died and left the tunnel in darkness.

"You fool," growled a gravelly voice.

Galaeron looked up, struggling to see. The silvery radiance was still glimmering in Shatevar's door but did not seem to *cast* light so much as *be* light. As his dark sight returned, he found a mustachioed human staring across the eye tyrant's deflated orb at him. By the look of utter contempt on the man's face, it was clear he could see in the dark as well as any elf.

"You have no—"

Takari interrupted the human by catching him across the jaw with the dull side of her blade. He staggered backward, then stumbled over Vala's legs, protruding from beneath Shatevar's cleaved skull, and landed on his back. Takari placed a boot across the back of his neck and kicked his sword away, but the precaution was hardly necessary. The man was sleeping as soundly as his commander.

"Don't break his neck." Galaeron rose. "They aren't killing, so neither should we."

Takari glanced at Aragath's body, then said, "The beholder was theirs."

Despite the bitterness in her voice, she scuttled off to join the hunched battle at the head of the tunnel. It was a strange fight, with stooped figures on both sides striking with hilt pommels and flat blades, the walls echoing with the ferocious yelling of any combat, but no one wailing in fear or grief. Galaeron was not pleased to see that his elves were winning only by dint of magic and numbers—and had the humans been willing to kill, even these advantages would have failed to achieve victory. Determined to end the fight before someone made a mistake and turned it into a mortal brawl, Galaeron summoned to mind the incantation of his sleep spell.

"Can you fools not be silent out there?" The voice was wispy and dark and as deep as the tunnel itself. Galaeron stopped and looked to the hole in Shatevar's doorway, but the voice seemed to be coming from everywhere around him. *"You have led the devils straight to me!"*

The remaining humans fell silent and lowered their swords. Takari knocked one unconscious, and two moon elves slipped quickly forward to take charge of the prisoners and prevent them from restarting the fray. Galaeron used finger talk to divide his patrol between caring for his fallen archers and binding the humans, but he kept Takari at his side. He did not want the unpredictable Wood elf venting her grief over Aragath's death on their prisoners.

Turning to the nearest of three humans still standing, he asked, "Who did that voice belong to?"

The humans looked blindly about, uncertain as to who Galaeron had asked, and he realized they could see in the dark only with their swords in hand. He touched one on the chest.

"Who was that voice? What are you doing down here?"

"No harm to Evereska," answered the man. "That's all—"

The last few words were lost to the crack of a magic blast, then the cavern vanished into an instant of murk thick enough to feel. The clatter of falling stones echoed through the tunnel, almost inaudible to Galaeron's ringing ears, and his vision slowly returned, spotty and filled with strings of spidery darkness. He motioned the guards to continue watching the prisoners then turned toward the source of the explosion.

The head and shoulders of a burly human protruded through a saddle-sized cavity in the back of Shatevar's doorway. Behind the screen of silvery radiance, he looked pale and ghostly, despite what Galaeron guessed to be a swarthy complexion and hair as black as jet.

"Melegaunt?" called one of the prisoners. "Melegaunt Tanthul?"

The figure nodded, then thrust a beefy arm through the hole and shouted, "Help!"

The humans started forward at once, trying to bull their way forward despite their bound hands. It was a bad mistake. Takari laid one out with an elbow to the nose, and the other two fell to their guards' pommel strikes. Fortunately for Melegaunt Tanthul, half a dozen elves were rushing forward in the humans' place. They slowed as they passed through the silvery barrier, then caught hold of his arms and began to pull. The human slipped forward, then abruptly stuck and screamed for them to stop.

The shocked elves obeyed, and the human vanished back through the hole. There was a muffled thump but no scream.

Takari looked to Galaeron for orders, as did the elves inside the silver barrier.

Galaeron shook his head uncertainly but started toward the doorway. "I guess we should see what—"

Something that looked like a mouth surrounded by four arms shot through the hole and began to slam itself around, catching elves between its scaly head and the doorway's rocky walls. One elf tried to scream but instead poured forth a torrent of frothing blood. Another fell with her flattened helmet still on her head. The survivors tried to draw weapons and back away. The creature lashed out with its four arms, catching two of the elves by their throats and arms, then came slithering the rest of the way out of the hole.

With a spiked, slug-shaped body tapering back from its huge mouth to a thin tail, the creature was the strangest living thing Galaeron had ever seen. It had no eyes or ears but was aware enough of its foes to jerk its captives away from the two elves who had escaped its grasp. As they moved to help their comrades, a black bolt materialized out of thin air and struck one down. The second warrior fell when the thing hurled one of its prisoners into her head. Both elves fell with broken necks.

"What hell did these human bastards open?" Takari yelled, reaching down for a second sword. When her palm closed around the leather-wrapped hilt of the human's sword, she hissed and dropped the black blade then displayed a welt of frozen skin. "By the Night Hunter, even their weapons are profane!"

On the other side of the wall, Melegaunt's muffled voice rose up, sounding pained and quivery as it growled out a string of arcane syllables. Something long and spike-covered floated past the hole, then the bearded wizard finished his spell. The only effect Galaeron could see was a set of scintillating shadows.

"Bows—choice of arrows!" Galaeron yelled.

"What of Ehamond?" Takari asked, referring to the elf still struggling in the creature's grasp.

Galaeron started forward without bothering to answer. Of all the elves in his patrol, Takari had been with him the longest, and they shared an almost instinctive rapport. He nudged her toward Ehamond, indicating he would attack and she should rescue.

"When wolves mount porcupines!" she snapped.

Pushing Galaeron behind her, Takari snatched up the human sword and hurled it at the strange beast then sprang forward behind the tumbling blade. Galaeron followed close behind, his spell ready on the tip of his tongue.

The human sword passed through the silver barrier and buried itself to the hilt in the creature's squirming torso, then Takari pushed through the light and was on the creature, slashing and slicing. Galaeron danced through behind her—the barrier dragged at him like a curtain of cold spider silk—and slid over behind Ehamond. The elf was coated in blood, screaming, hacking wildly at the thing's teeth.

"Calm yourself, guard!" Galaeron dodged a claw, then caught a free ankle. "We can't help you like this."

Takari parried a claw, dodged the creature's snapping mouth, then brought her blade down on an arm holding Ehamond. The sharp elven steel bit deep, nearly slicing the limb off at the elbow, and Galaeron pulled Ehamond's right side free. Crying out in elation, Ehamond brought his own blade around and lopped off the hand still holding him. Galaeron stumbled back through the silvery barrier, dragging Ehamond after him, and saw the monster's barbed tail arc around behind Takari.

"Behind—"

The barb struck her between the shoulder blades, piercing Takari's leather armor as though it were parchment. Her arms dropped and her body arched forward. The tail began to pulse, pumping its contents into her body. Galaeron dropped Ehamond's leg and leveled his hands at the tail then cried out an incantation. Four bolts of golden magic shot from his fingers and blasted the barb off the tail, freeing Takari to collapse back through the silver barrier.

She had not even touched ground before a flight of black arrows sizzled past Galaeron to strike the creature. The first three bounced off the thing's thorny hide, but the final stuck deep in its midsection. The archer who had fired it spoke a command word, activating its death magic.

A puckered white ulcer appeared around the wound, but the strange creature did not fall. It did not even sag.

Leaving Ehamond to scramble off on his own, Galaeron grabbed Takari and dragged her away. Her eyes were open but glazed, more shocked than frightened. Another flight of arrows hissed past, but the creature's hide turned gray and stony, and all four bounced off harmlessly. The small number of shafts filled Galaeron with despair, but with Ehamond and Takari wounded and three more elves unconscious from the fray with the humans, only four warriors remained to him.

Much to Galaeron's relief, the creature stayed in the cramped cavity between the silvery barrier and the hole at its back. It snapped the single arrow that had wounded it and tossed the ends at the elf who had fired the shaft.

Galaeron rolled Takari to her side and plucked the creature's barb from her back. The wound was already swollen and pestilent. Deep in the puncture was something small and round, glowing hot scarlet in Galaeron's dark sight. Knowing better than to attempt removing the thing now, he called Ehamond over and pushed Takari into the arms of the battered elf.

"Take her and go. If we don't follow, make a report."

"You'll follow," said Ehamond, glancing toward the strange creature. "You'd better—who'd believe this if you don't?"

With that, he pulled Takari into a cross-shoulder carry and vanished up the tunnel. Galaeron started to toss the tail barb aside, but thought of what Takari would do and threw the spike contemptuously across the silvery barrier. The creature caught it, then rose a few inches and floated to Galaeron's end of the cavity. Though it was impossible to perceive anything resembling emotion on the faceless thing, Galaeron had no doubt that were it able to attack across the silver barrier, he would be dead.

The creature was still hovering in front of Galaeron when a beam of purple magic crackled through the hole, catching the thing in the back and slamming it against the barrier. It writhed madly, loosing an ear-piercing squeal that sounded like it would bring the roof down.

"Now!" It was the same voice that had filled the tunnel earlier. *"Take up my swords and kill it now!"*

The remaining elves reached for their weapons and started forward, but Galaeron did not want them anywhere near the creature. "Not swords! Magic bolts." He raised his hand. "On my count . . . now!"

Shafts of golden magic began to converge on the creature. Some sank into its stony hide with no effect whatsoever, but most struck powerfully, hurling the thing back into the purple beam, blasting off thorns and pieces of hide. Galaeron's first spell had barely left his hand before he repeated it, firing another flurry of raw magic even as the creature tumbled away from the first. His bolts flashed through the silver curtain and met the beam of purple magic coming from the other side.

The result was not exactly an explosion. There was a flash of a thousand colors and the roaring silence of the void, then a horrid prickling and the bewildering realization that he now lay slumped against the tunnel wall. The air reeked of burning iron, and everything ached. There was a crimson ring on the silvery barrier, flickering and steadily growing dimmer as it expanded outward. On the other side of the curtain lay the strange creature, its body pocked and pitted with blast marks, strips of peeled hide showing long strips of green flesh. As Galaeron struggled to comprehend what he was seeing, the thing rose off the ground and floated over to the barrier, then stuck its head through the smoldering hole.

Galaeron's stomach grew hollow, and his stunned elves began to fill the tunnel with low groans. The huge mouth seemed to smile, then the creature floated the rest of the way through the hole. It plucked an unconscious human off the floor, then delicately pulled off his helmet.

Galaeron forced himself to his feet. "Stand if you are awake!" he yelled, reaching for his sword. "Defend yourselves!"

Only a handful of figures stirred, but it was enough to make the creature drop the human. The thing's mouth swung toward Galaeron, shooting a plume of black fog out between its teeth.

There was no time to shout a warning. Galaeron barely managed to close his mouth before the cloud rolled over him, burning his eyes and nostrils and making his lungs cry out for air. The sound of coughing and retching filled the tunnel, anguished and frightened and all too brief. By the time Galaeron could summon to mind the words of a wind spell, half the voices had fallen silent. By the time he actually uttered it and sent the deadly fog whirling down an empty side passage, the rest of the voices were also quiet.

Knowing he would be the next to fall, Galaeron did not fight the terrible rage rising up inside him. Anger bred folly, but it also bred desperate courage and mad strength, and he had seen enough of this devil-creature to know what he needed most. He charged after the receding edge of the black cloud, still holding his breath and swinging his sword blindly into the murk. He felt the edge bite once, then inverted his grip and lunged, driving forward with all his strength.

The blade sank perhaps a foot before slowing to a stop. Galaeron dropped to a squat and heard two arms whistle past his head, then he jumped back and saw two more come slicing out of the swirling cloud. He pulled a glass rod from his sleeve. The fog spun away and left the creature's body floating not five paces away, his sword lodged up near its mouth. Hoping a lightning bolt would prove more effective than the rest of his magic, he leveled the rod at the thing's body and started his incantation.

"Not magic," boomed the deep voice. "I said swords!"

Galaeron glanced over and saw the swarthy wizard stepping through the barrier, dark robes swirling around him like shadow. The creature whirled toward the human, twenty tiny tongues of flame already crackling on its fingertips. Melegaunt circled his hand, creating a wheel of cold blackness in the air before him, and stepped confidently forward. The flames shot straight from the monster's hands into the shadowy wheel and vanished.

Galaeron was already moving, snatching a black sword from the hands of a fallen human and leaping to the attack. Even with the leather wrapped around the hilt, it was so cold it burned his flesh, instantly turning his fingers numb and stiff. He attacked anyway, bringing the edge down two feet from the creature's tail.

The dark blade sliced through effortlessly, cleaving the tail off cleanly.

The creature shuddered in pain and whirled on Galaeron but stopped when it nearly impaled itself on the dark blade. Galaeron lunged for its throat, nearly dropping his weapon when the thing pulled back and his frozen fingers could not adjust.

Galaeron changed hands. In that instant, his armor grew so hot it began to glow, filling the tunnel with eerie pink shadows and washing out his dark sight. He screamed in agony but rushed forward slashing wildly. The creature had no choice except to fall back—straight into Melegaunt Tanthul.

The wizard pushed forward, driving the thing onto Galaeron's blade. It gave the same pained squeal it had earlier, but he could hardly hear it over his own wail. He found the strength to twist the blade and drag it along as he fell.

A pile of green entrails landed on the dust before him, and the creature drifted slowly to the floor at his side. Galaeron screamed and rolled away, fumbling for his dagger.

Melegaunt Tanthul placed a restraining foot on his stomach, then kneeled at his side. "It's dead. Well done, young fellow. Now hold still." The wizard passed his hand over Galaeron and spoke some strange magic, and the armor cooled. "Better?"

Galaeron nodded. "What—"

"No time for talking. There are another dozen on the way." The man pulled Galaeron to his feet, then gestured at the hole in the silvery curtain. "And now they can get at us."

Biting back a scream of pain, Galaeron asked, "They?"

"Later, or we'll be as dead as everyone else."

The wizard started to pick his way through the bodies. Elf and human alike, their faces were contorted into masks of anguish, their chins covered with beards of red froth.

Melegaunt stopped beside Shatevar's deflated body and pointed at Vala's legs. "That one's still alive. Bring her."

Though the wizard looked capable of carrying his own wounded, Galaeron pulled Vala from beneath the eye tyrant. Much to his astonishment, her chest was rising and falling with breath, just as the wizard had said it would be. Galaeron loaded her over his shoulder and started after the wizard, paying no attention as her black sword dropped silently into the dust.

Melegaunt spun on his heel and pointed at the weapon. "Her darksword, you fool."

"I can't carry it." Galaeron displayed his frozen palms.

The wizard stepped closer, running his gaze over Galaeron's face. "What are you doing here?" he asked, seeming to notice Galaeron's pointed ears for the first time. "You can't be of the Granite Tower . . ."

CHAPTER TWO

20 Nightal, the Year of the Unstrung Harp

In the month of Nightal, the sand winds turned wild and bitter, sweeping in from Anauroch full of stinging grit and stabbing cold. At night, no elf in uncloaked armor could long abide their frigid blasts, yet Galaeron's scalded flesh raged at the extra weight of his thkaerth wool cloak. His hands, still dead and white from touching the black sword, had moved beyond pain to agony, and even that did not seem punishment enough. Takari sat slumped on a big human horse, so weak and delirious that Ehamond had to sit with her. Ehamond himself was webbed with claw slashes and puncture wounds. Nimieye and Dynod remained uninjured, having stayed outside the cairn to guard the prisoners, but they would have to scout ahead, and one or both might yet fall to some dragon or griffon drawn by the smell of so much blood. The rest were gone. Of the seventeen elves who had entrusted their lives to Galaeron's command, he had lost thirteen. For such a failure, he deserved more punishment than a simple scalding—far more.

Galaeron fumbled the last binding over Vala's foot and jerked the loop tight then wrapped the end around her boot and stirrup. When he pronounced a mystic word, the line snaked up her ankle, fastening her into the saddle. He did not realize how hard he had tugged until the magic line, taking a cue from his angry yank, cinched itself down so tightly that boot leather bubbled between its coils.

"The line will tighten if you pull." Galaeron normally preferred to let captives discover this for themselves, but he feared the line would crush

Vala's ankle if it grew any tighter. "It can be removed only by the one who put it on."

"Is that so?" Though the binding had to hurt, Vala's pale eyes betrayed no hint of pain, only cold ire. "Then I suppose I mustn't try to escape."

The edge in her voice suggested she had no intention of escaping, not until she repaid Galaeron for the deaths of her men. Though it was a vengeance she would never have, she could at least take consolation in the price he would pay to his own masters. Not since the days of Kiinyon Colbathin had a patrol of tomb guards taken such losses—and never along the Desert Border South, the quietest of any area the tomb guard patrolled.

Galaeron started to walk away, then thought better of it. Without turning around, he said, "We are sorry for the deaths of your men. Know that we would have saved them, had it been in our power."

"But it wasn't, elf." Vala's voice remained unforgiving. "As I said then, you have no idea what you're dealing with."

Galaeron bit back the urge to make a sharp retort. "Then why don't you tell me?"

Vala looked away. "It is not my place."

"Very well," Galaeron said. "Then what about yourself? Where is the Granite Tower?"

Vala's eyes flashed, whether in alarm or anger was impossible to say. "That is not for you to know, elf. We are hardly friends."

"No, I suppose we aren't."

Galaeron turned and walked away. It hardly mattered where the woman and her three sentries were from. In all likelihood, they would soon be joining their fallen companions. The Hill Elders rarely made hasty decisions, but when a tomb guard brought captives before the council, there was seldom much to decide. The sentence for crypt breaking was as certain as it was harsh.

Galaeron heard Melegaunt Tanthul before he saw him. The human's deep voice came from the shadowy side of the moonlit cairn, growling out the arcane syllables of a bizarre spell. The incantation was unlike anything Galaeron had ever heard, even among the corpse-stealing drow who occasionally worked their evil in the isolated crypts of the Desert Border. The words were booming and raspy, loaded with power and danger, but also intricate and enigmatic, full of cleverness and deception. Though it was the third enchantment of caging the wizard had cast since leaving the battle site, Galaeron, who usually had an instinctual feel for all things magic, had yet to grasp this wizard's art.

When he rounded the corner, Galaeron found Melegaunt working the shadows into an impassable maze of moonlight and darkness, swirling them into dead-end spirals, folding them into meandering corridors that rounded a hundred corners and came back to their own beginning. The wizard himself was nearly impossible to find, his black robes and swarthy complexion blending into the night the same way Wood elves melted into the forest.

Though Galaeron did not think he had made any noise as he approached, Melegaunt glanced in his direction and nodded. He finished his maze by feeding its only exit into a hole of fuming darkness, then simply melted into the shadows beneath his feet.

Galaeron stood outside the maze feeling perplexed and foolish. Before his indifference to the ritual tedium of the Academy of Magic had landed him across the glen at the Academy of Arms, he had spent more than two decades studying the basics of every known spellcasting system, and he could not even guess how Melegaunt had vanished. There had been no gestures or words to trigger the spell, nor even a twitch or sharp breath to activate a ring or magic pendant. The wizard had dissolved into the shadows as though by an act of will.

"The umbral maze should hold until dawn."

The voice came from the ground beside Galaeron. In spite of himself, he hopped away and looked down. The wizard's body was rising out of the shadow, peeling itself up like a turning page.

"And they won't like the daylight at first."

Melegaunt braced on the ground then brought his feet beneath him in a practiced motion. As he stood, his body resumed its shape, filling out like a glove inflated with breath.

"We have until tomorrow dusk, no longer."

"We?" Galaeron had to scurry after the wizard, who was already rounding the corner of the cairn. "To do what?"

"To set things right, of course. I'll need at least one company of good wizards and a trio of high mages." The human spun on Galaeron, bushy brows furrowed in concern. "Evereska does have three?"

"I—I couldn't say." Galaeron assumed the city had at least that many, but high mages were not something Evereskans discussed openly and certainly not with humans. "First, we must talk about—"

"We'll talk while we ride." The wizard whirled away and rounded the corner. When he came upon Nimieye and Dynod standing guard over Vala and the other three prisoners, he stopped. "What's this?"

"Your friends are crypt breakers." Though Galaeron had been dreading this moment since coming to realize how powerful the wizard was, his duty was clear. "They must be taken before the Hill Elders, but you were not with them. You are free to do as you please."

"Of course I am." Melegaunt's black beard twitched as though he might laugh. "But this won't do, elf. I was the one who told them to break the crypt. Do you intend to tie me, too?"

Galaeron swallowed and reached for a binding rope. "I have sworn—"

"What you have sworn makes no difference."

Melegaunt gestured at the ground, and icy ribbons of shadow spiraled up Galaeron's legs, squeezing his bones and numbing his flesh. The wizard glanced down and shook his head in an expression of dismay then turned toward the horses. Galaeron tried to go after him and found his feet rooted in place. He flashed a finger command to Nimieye and Dynod, ordering them not to engage the human in what would certainly be a futile attack.

Melegaunt stopped next to the horse carrying the humans' confiscated weapons. "We have unleashed a terrible foe on your people," he said, drawing a black sword from its scabbard. "You will either work with me to return it to its place, or you will wait here until it kills you."

The wizard stepped over to the first of Vala's captured sentries and touched the sword to his binding. Galaeron was not really surprised to see the shadowy edge slicing through the magic cord. Melegaunt handed the weapon to the man and motioned for him to continue then turned back to Galaeron.

"Which shall it be?"

"Death or battle? What choice is there?" asked Galaeron. "But you must promise to do no harm to my people. Otherwise, I choose death."

"No harm I can prevent—and that's the best promise you'll get, given the circumstances." The wizard gestured, and Galaeron's shadow bindings dissolved. "You've chosen wisely, elf. These devils have already laid low an empire, and I would not like to see the same fate befall Evereska."

"You keep calling them devils." Galaeron walked over to undo Vala's bindings, touching each one and whispering a command word. "Is that what they are?"

"Close enough," said the wizard. "Do you know what that silver curtain was down there?"

"The Sharn Wall?"

"Is that what you elves call it? An apt name. Then you must know what lies on the other side."

Galaeron hazarded a guess. "The sharn?"

"I see your high mages have kept their knowledge to themselves." Melegaunt snorted, half amused. "Perhaps I should honor their wisdom until I know why."

"I hardly think it a secret." Galaeron released Vala's last bond. "Most tomb guards know the legend of the Sharn Wall."

The wizard cocked a brow. "Brazen for an elf, aren't you?" He plucked Vala's bare sword from the pack horse and brought it over. "Very well. The sharn are not the trapped ones—they are the ones who made the wall."

"Then what were—"

"Phaerimm," said Vala, taking her sword. "You do know what they are?"

"I do now." Like the Sharn Wall itself, they were the stuff of Tomb Guard legend, mysterious killers who could wipe out whole patrols. From what Galaeron had seen, the description fit. He looked back to Melegaunt. "You were lost in their tunnels?"

"Not lost." As he answered, the wizard turned his attention to Vala. "You are the master of this company?"

"What's left." She cast an angry glance at Galaeron, then dismounted and dropped to a knee before the wizard. "Vala Thorsdotter, daughter to Bodvar's grandson, at your service."

"We've no time for such silliness," Melegaunt said, motioning her up. "But a great-granddaughter to Bodvar! It does my heart good to see his line so long continued."

Vala laid a hand to her scabbard. "A blessing of your gifts, Mighty One."

"No doubt—and call me Melegaunt. You'll find I answer to it more often." Melegaunt waved her to her saddle, then looked down the line of big human horses and frowned. "I don't see Sable."

Vala's jaw dropped. "Milord, Sable has been dead these eighty years." She pointed to a husky black stallion near the end of the line. "But Raven there is of her line."

A flash of grief filled Melegaunt's dark eyes. "Of course. I should have realized." He motioned a human to bring Raven forward, then turned to Galaeron and pointed westward, where a jagged wall of shadows marked the impassable peaks of the Shaeradim. "I trust you elves have a quick way across those?"

"There is a pass," said Galaeron, "but it is watched and warded. You'll have to wear blindfolds and bindings, or none of us will reach Evereska alive."

"Be careful, Mighty—er, Melegaunt," Vala said. "Once he has us bound and blindfolded, we'll be at his mercy, and this elf is a sly one."

"You have a better way?" Melegaunt asked.

"I have heard stories of shadowalking."

"I'd need to know the way, and there is no time to find it."

"Nor would it work," said Galaeron. "Evereska is well-warded against such magic."

The look that passed between Vala and Melegaunt was as quick as it was knowing, but Galaeron pretended not to notice. Whatever they believed—and whatever the truth about these phaerimm—the humans would be under his control when they entered the city.

"The only other way is to circle around and enter through the Halfway Inn. That would take a tenday by horse." He looked to Melegaunt and added, "Only three if you can fly us."

"Still too long." The smile that came to Melegaunt's lips might have been knowing or confident. "We will wear the elven bindings."

CHAPTER THREE

21 Nightal, the Year of the Unstrung Harp

The scent of spruce resin filled the darkness, and Galaeron knew they had completed the Passing. His dark sight began to function again, and the human horses snorted as they sensed the ponies' joy in returning to Evereska. Even Takari perked up, leaning back in Ehamond's arms to draw a breath of crisp air.

Though Galaeron knew that a hundred elf archers watched from the hidden galleries high above, he did not look up. Any sign of acknowledgement would bring a flurry of spells and arrows down on his prisoners, a precaution contrived to keep secret the defenses of the Secret Gate.

The path rounded a curve then arched over a smoky-bottomed abyss on a marble bridge. Galaeron spoke a word of passing and led his companions across, then stopped in a cramped vestibule sealed by a thin sheet of muscovite mica. A stern-faced moon elf in the silver-gilded plate mail of a Vale Guard *kanqat* stepped into view and touched his fingertips to his heart.

"Glad homeagain, Nihmedu." Though the kanqat stood on the other side of the mica, his voice was as clear as his image. He was Orem Arvaeyn, a classmate from the Academy of Arms who—like nearly everyone else—was rising much faster than Galaeron. Orem looked past Galaeron to sneer at the humans. "I see you have crypt breakers. Shall we expect the rest of your patrol soon?"

"No, Kanqat. They won't . . ." The words caught in Galaeron's throat, but he forced himself to meet Orem's gaze. "I couldn't recover their bodies."

The kanqat's face grew even paler. "I see." He studied the prisoners, clearly trying to reconcile the fact that they were mere humans with Galaeron's loss, then asked, "This happened in the Desert Border South?"

Galaeron nodded, confident any account he gave would only make him look worse. "If you please, my scout needs care."

"Of course." The kanqat looked away and nodded, then he stepped aside as the mica barrier rose out of sight. As Galaeron's pony passed by, Orem said quietly, "No need to be short, Galaeron. Not that you'll get one now, but I always thought you merited a better assignment."

Surprised by the kanqat's unexpected kindness, Galaeron pulled aside and let Ehamond lead the others ahead. "My thanks, Orem. Your words may be the only kind ones I hear tonight."

"You were the best of our regiform, Galaeron." Orem shook his head. "You just shouldn't have been so arrogant. There's more to this business than spell and steel."

"Arrogant? What is true is not . . ." Galaeron caught himself then nodded his agreement. "Good advice given too late, I'm afraid."

"It may serve you tonight, if you keep it in mind," said Orem. "Nothing would take the tomb master more by surprise."

"This is a matter for more than the tomb master." Galaeron glanced at Vala and Melegaunt, who were sitting on their horses bound, blindfolded, but far from frightened. "The humans play only a small part in this, and none at all in the deaths of my guards. I'll need to speak with the Hill Elders at once."

"At once? This morning?"

Galaeron nodded.

Orem studied the empty saddles behind Dynod and Nimieye then said, "I'll arrange it."

Galaeron offered his thanks and resumed his place then led the column down a hanging gorge into the forests of the Upper Vale. The trees were ancient and enormous, mostly spear spruce tall enough to scratch the sky. The trail descended sharply, winding through ravines and around craggy outcroppings where the treetops grew thin enough to show streaks of distant cliff.

Though Galaeron was free to remove the humans' blindfolds at any time, he did not. He was convinced that Melegaunt had some way of seeing other than eyes. The wizard sat in his saddle easily, holding his body upright and still even when his black mount slipped or stumbled. In contrast, the other humans rode comfortably but loosely, swaying to every twist in the trail. Vala's jaw remained clenched and tense, her red lip raised in an indignant sneer.

Her patience lasted only a quarter hour, until the trail left the steep slopes of the Upper Vale and descended into the terraces of the Vine Vale.

"How about these blinders and bindings, elf?" she demanded. "I can tell by the wind we're out of the Passing."

"The blinders, yes." Galaeron stopped and motioned Nimieye forward to remove the blindfolds—actually leather half-hoods enchanted to confuse the wearer's sense of direction. "The bindings remain."

"What?" Despite the question, Vala did not seem overly surprised. "I should have known not to trust an elf."

"I promised nothing."

"It was implied," Vala snarled.

"Careful, child. We are in no position to lecture Galaeron about his ethics," said Melegaunt. He let Nimieye remove his hood then locked gazes with Galaeron. "Much will depend on whether he blames us or simple accident for the loss of his patrol."

"Then we are lost," said Vala. "Men make better scapegoats than misfortune."

" 'Tis so, but I think our friend smarter than that." Melegaunt continued to watch Galaeron. "What say you, elf? Will you call us crypt breakers and thieves, or victims like yourself?"

"That's for the Hill Elders to decide," said Galaeron. "My duty is only to tell what happened."

The answer was a dodge, for the truth lay somewhere between the extremes laid out by the wizard. The humans had broken an elven crypt, but the ones inside had been nobles of the much despised Vyshaan clan, and even then nothing had been stolen. And while the humans had resisted the patrol's attempt to capture them, they had risked their own lives to avoid injuring elves. Given these facts, Galaeron's attitude would carry more than a little weight with the Elders.

What Galaeron did not know was how much to trust the humans. There was an undeniable aura of darkness about Melegaunt, and it had crossed Galaeron's mind that the battle in the Vyshaan crypt might be no more than an elaborate ruse to sneak a powerful and evil wizard into Evereska.

Melegaunt smiled crookedly at Galaeron's response then watched as Nimieye removed the hoods from Vala's followers. The three men—Vala had introduced them as Burlen, Kuhl, and Dexon—blinked and glowered at Galaeron, portending the black look Vala shot him when her own hood came off.

"Mind how you tell your tale, elf," she said. "Helm has a memory for word breakers."

"That might concern me, were I a word breaker or a human." Galaeron was beginning to feel a very humanlike anger at the woman. "As it is, I'm a tomb guard holding a band of crypt breakers in custody, with no reason to trust them."

The woman opened her mouth to retort, but Galaeron cut her off by glancing over to check on Takari. The scout was still slouched in front of Ehamond, not quite slumbering, but in some state far deeper than Reverie. It was a bad sign; for elves did not sleep unless they were ill or badly wounded. Galaeron started down the trail at a trot, determined to have Takari in a healer's hands before Eastpeak's shadow left Moondark Hill.

Despite the many concerns facing him—or perhaps because of them—Galaeron found himself bitterly disappointed by the humans' indifference when Nimieye removed their blindfolds. This section of the trail was the most striking part of the return to Evereska, with a vast staircase of vineyards descending toward the city in a series of mist-shrouded terraces, and not one human had stopped glowering at him long enough to notice the view.

In the bottom of the valley lay a rolling patchwork of fields both gold and black. From Galaeron's perspective high in the Vine Vale, these farmlands formed a deep crescent in the bottom of the valley, with the thousand foot cliffs of the High Shaeradim ringing it on the exterior and Evereska looming up in the center. Though the city was often described as walled—usually by bombastic humans who based their "eyewitness" accounts on tales bribed from elves half drunk on the Halfway Inn's potent elquesstria—the walls were in fact the smooth-polished cliffs of the Three Sisters, the largest of the dozen hills upon which Evereska rested.

Behind the cliff tops rose hundreds of towers, soaring up out of a thick bluetop forest to make the city look like a many-spired crown. Most spires rose to twice the height of the surrounding trees, some even higher than the peaks of the High Shaeradim. Their exteriors swarmed with lines of antlike figures, residents of the city going about their daily business with no thought as to how strange it looked from below.

Such was the magic of Evereska, jewel of the mountains, and Galaeron considered anyone who failed to gasp at its wonders worthy of doubt. He led his prisoners down the Vine Vale terraces via a series of gentle switchbacks, then traveled down a narrow lane to the walled pasturelands that surrounded Evereska. As they approached the boundary, Galaeron spoke a word of passing. The gilded gate swung open, admitting the column into a rolling meadow dotted with boulders and bigcone firs. Like many of Evereska's defenses, the gate's purpose was not obvious. While it was not magical, it marked the perimeter of the city's most priceless treasure and best-kept secret, the mythal.

As intangible as it was invincible, the mythal was a mantle of living magic woven by the high mages of old. Galaeron did not fully understand its nature—when the masters spoke of it at all, it was only to claim that no elf alive could comprehend a mythal's intricacies—but most elves believed it to be a mesh of mystic energies spun from the life-forces of its ancient casters, the favor of Corellon Larethian, and the fabric of Faerûn's magic Weave. What Galaeron did know was that first and foremost, the mythal was Evereska's most potent defense, capable of plaguing foes with a dazzling array of assaults—including the famous gold bolts so often attributed to Corellon's guardianship. The mythal also provided other blessings, such as the ability of the city's inhabitants to climb vertical walls. In return, it required only that the elves maintain the health of its sustaining lands.

As the rest of the column crossed the mythal's perimeter, Galaeron glanced over his shoulder to look for any sign that Melegaunt perceived the magic field. The wizard's eyes remained as dusky and unreadable as ever, exhibiting neither curiosity nor surprise as they scrutinized the meadow's green grass and the butterflies still bobbing along in the breeze. Vala and the other humans were a stark contrast to Melegaunt's nonchalance, gawking about with fallen jaws and craning their necks to stare up Evereska's thousand-foot cliffs.

Satisfied that neither Melegaunt nor any of the humans sensed the mythal, Galaeron led the column across the meadow to the Tomb Guard Livery. A simple three-walled shed with a station for each patrol to store its harness and tack, there were no pens or stalls, nor even any mangers or watering troughs. Galaeron dismounted and made his assignments then unbound the humans' feet and helped them dismount as well.

"Nimieye will unsaddle and curry your mounts." He slung the humans' sword belts over his shoulder, taking care not to let the glassy pommels touch his skin. "But we don't corral our beasts."

"It is no bother," said Melegaunt. His hands remained bound like those of the other humans; unlike the others, he did not seem irritated or particularly worried by it. "Raven will bring our mounts when I send for him—though I trust we won't be returning to the Desert Border on horses."

"That much we are safe in assuming, yes," said Galaeron.

Vala gave him a dark look, then stepped out from beneath the livery shed and tipped her head back to stare up the cliff. "How do we get up there?"

"Dynod will lead the way."

Galaeron nodded to Dynod, who took Takari from Ehamond's arms and entered a small, irregular chamber hewn into the cliff base. He vanished from sight, as did Ehamond when he followed. Galaeron motioned Vala and the other humans to follow, then stepped through himself. There was a golden flash and a brief feeling of falling, and when he put his foot down again, it was onto a marble-paved lane filled with the zesty scent of dusktop blossoms.

Vala and her men stood at the edge of the street, silently gawking at the wondrous forest around them. White-paved paths curved off in every direction, twisting through an eye-boggling tangle of towers and trunks. In the sylvan shade, it was difficult even for Galaeron to tell which was which. The trees were uniformly as large around as castle towers, with cross-striped bark ranging from white to gray, and branches so high overhead it was not unusual for mist to form *beneath* the leaf canopy. The towers were sometimes smaller than the tree boles and sometimes larger, but most were almost indistinguishable from the mighty bluetops that dominated the outer rim of the city.

With the sun just rising above Eastpeak's craggy shoulder, it was the busiest time of day. Elves were everywhere, gliding along the ground paths, popping out of high doorways to clamber headfirst down the tower exterior, sometimes even soaring from one building to another like flying squirrels. Even with the unpleasantness to come, Galaeron found himself feeling more content and peaceful than even the calmiest desert afternoon lounging naked in a pool of cool canyon water. This was Evereska, Lasthaven to all the elves of Faerûn, sanctuary to Galaeron and all *Tel'Quess* who would hold some home for their race against the relentless tide of human expansion.

"I believe we are to follow Dynod and Ehamond," said Melegaunt, nudging Vala and the others up the lane. "Galaeron will inform us when we should turn off."

"Follow them all the way." The long ride had fatigued Galaeron more than he thought. Though he always enjoyed his return to Evereska, he usually did not come so close to slipping into Reverie the instant he entered it. He shook himself alert and started up the lane. "We will see Takari to the Hall of the High Hunt."

Melegaunt stopped, finally seeming to take exception to Galaeron's instructions. "Do you think that wise? We wouldn't want to keep the Hill Elders waiting."

"You will do as I say, human." Galaeron pushed Melegaunt after the others but quickly regretted his tone. His anger had more to do with the danger he had unleashed on the city than anything Melegaunt had done. In a gentler voice, he added, "We'll be speaking with the elders sooner than you think, Melegaunt. In Evereska, we have our own ways of doing things."

The path ascended along the bank of a small stream, passing several waterfalls artfully arranged to spill from the mouths of deep emerald pools. As they walked, elves young and old paused to stare at Galaeron's prisoners in open disgust, in part because some had never before seen a human, in part because they knew by the captives' bound hands and Galaeron's Tomb Guard cape that these were crypt breakers. Vala and her warriors did their best to fulfill expectations by sneering and glowering, but no one seemed to take these threats seriously. Galaeron wondered how that might have changed had they witnessed what he had beneath the tomb of the Vyshaan.

By the time they began to traverse Moondark Hill toward the Hall of the High Hunt, a small band of elderly elves had completely encircled the humans. Though none rose any higher than the chest of Vala's shortest man, they did not hesitate to laugh at the captives and make fun of their barbaric appearance, often in languages they knew the prisoners could understand. Though Galaeron could see the humans chafing under this abuse and would certainly have been insulted by it himself, he did nothing to prevent it. To Vala's great credit, she had only to issue one stern command to rivet the eyes of her men straight ahead and render them unresponsive to the mockery.

Finally, the tallest of the elves pulled back his hood and stepped to Galaeron's side. "Glad homeagain, young Nihmedu," he said in Elvish. "I see you've brought us some crypt breakers."

Galaeron looked over to find himself looking at a moon elf with silver hair and a dignified bearing borne of great age and long service.

He bowed without stopping and answered in Elvish, "Lord Duirsar."

The elf lord nodded to someone behind him, then the tomb master, Kiinyon Colbathin, stepped up on the other side. His expression was far easier to read than High Lord Duirsar's—and Galaeron had good reason to wish it was not.

"We've been given to understand that in addition to losing your patrol, you could not wait to make your excuses," the tomb master said, sneering at Melegaunt's back and speaking in Common. "I hope it took more than these five."

Allowing herself a luxury she denied her men, Vala spun on the elf. "It wouldn't have taken that many, had I intended them harm."

"That's enough, child." Melegaunt forced Vala up the path. "Let the fools have their fun. We will make our case to the elders."

Galaeron had to restrain a smile. Whether Melegaunt knew it or not, he and the other humans were already making their case. The elves abusing them *were* the Hill Elders, and they had already begun the trial that would determine whether the crypt breakers lived or died. Kiinyon Colbathin reached out and shoved Melegaunt hard, causing him to trip and stumble into Vala.

Melegaunt merely raised his chin and continued on without speaking, as did Vala. Kiinyon shoved the wizard once more. When Melegaunt made no response except to catch himself before he stumbled into Vala, the tomb master turned his acerbic tongue on Galaeron.

"So, how did the great Galaeron Nihmedu lose his patrol to a band of thieving human murderers? Tell us."

"Be careful who you call thieves and murderers." Vala did not look back as she spoke. "We took nothing and killed no one."

Lord Duirsar cocked a querying brow, and Galaeron nodded.

"That much is true," he said. "We tracked them through an opened tomb, but they left the bodies and treasure untouched."

Galaeron went on to recount how he followed the crypt breakers into the dwarven working beneath the tomb and found them using a beholder to disintegrate a section of wall. Kiinyon Colbathin raised his brow and regarded the humans with newfound respect, for he knew himself how difficult the creatures were to destroy, much less enslave. Galaeron went on to describe how the beholder had killed Aragath and how the humans had refused to surrender but avoided fatal attacks. Vala could not help pointing out here that had she not restrained her men, the matter would have ended with the death of Galaeron's patrol, which would have been a much better outcome for everyone concerned.

Noting the look of condemnation that flashed through Kiinyon's eyes, Galaeron found himself wondering if the woman was trying to get herself killed. He went on to explain how he had heard Melegaunt calling for help then ruptured the Sharn Wall by ordering his patrol to attack the phaerimm with magic missiles.

"You, Galaeron? Puncturing the Sharn Wall?" scoffed Kiinyon. "You've always had a high opinion of your talents, but this is a bit much even for you."

Lord Duirsar was not so quick to dismiss the account. "Kiinyon, if he didn't rupture the Sharn Wall, how do you explain the phaerimm?" The high lord shook his head in despair. "Galaeron, how did you do this thing?"

Melegaunt turned to address them. "Not that Galaeron has any need to explain himself to you, but the fault wasn't his. It was an unfortunate, ah, *blending* of magic that ruptured the Sharn Wall. If there is any blame, it belongs on my shoulders, not his. I should have foreseen the possibility. Now, if you will excuse us, good lords, we really must be on our way."

Melegaunt grabbed Galaeron by the elbow and pulled him up the trail, and it was only then that Galaeron realized they had reached their destination. The Hall of the High Hunt was a great colonnade of soaring shadowtops that enclosed the Singing Spring of Solonor Thelandira, a gurgling fountain of silver waters whose sacred melodies could cure any wound. Dynod and Ehamond were already disappearing between the trunks of two shadowtops, holding Takari aloft between them and calling for High Huntsman Trueshot.

"I know all elves share a special bond, but we must alert the Hill Elders," Melegaunt said, still unaware of who had been tormenting him. "Remember, we have only until nightfall."

"Until nightfall?" echoed Kiinyon. "Why until nightfall?"

"In good time," said Melegaunt. "Now, as I said—"

"It is only a guess." Galaeron ignored the wizard's insistent tugging and continued to address the tomb master. "In truth, they may be free already, but this human laid some spells that he hopes will delay them until this evening."

"This *evening?"* Lord Duirsar cast an uneasy glance at Kiinyon. "That is no time at all."

Melegaunt glanced thoughtfully from Galaeron to Lord Duirsar then finally seemed to realize to whom he was talking and stepped forward to address the elf lord. "Milord, I know the time is but an instant by elven measures, but I assure you that if you can spare me only a small company of wizards and three high mages, I will have the situation under control before then."

Lord Duirsar stared at Melegaunt as though he were mad. *"You,* human? I should say you have done quite enough." He turned to Kiinyon. "Gather what forces you need, Tomb Master, though I agree with the crypt breaker in this much: a high mage or two may be in order, if their studies can be interrupted."

"If?" Melegaunt growled. "Milord, perhaps I did not explain clearly enough. You will need me and three high mages—"

"Do not presume to tell me what I need," said Duirsar. "Evereska was old before your ancestors left their caves. I think us more than capable of cleaning up any mess you can make."

"It is a wonder your head is not as pointed as your ears!" Vala snapped. She stepped toward the elf lord and instantly found herself facing the tips of a dozen sharp swords, Galaeron's among them. She stopped but seemed completely nonplussed. "You have no idea who you—"

"That is enough, my dear." Melegaunt raised his hand to silence her. "If the elves will not accept our help, there are others who will."

"Perhaps so, but they will be difficult to reach from the inside of a bone cage," said Kiinyon. "Evereska is not in the habit of freeing crypt breakers."

Kiinyon glanced around the crowd, and Galaeron realized he was already calling for the Hill Elders' verdict.

"If it pleases the council, I should point out that the tomb they broke was Vyshaan," said Galaeron. While Melegaunt was being both presumptuous and rude in assuming the ancient magic of elves to be less than his own, his only intention was to help, which bound Galaeron in honor to speak on behalf of the humans. "The humans stole nothing. They meant no harm, and in truth the only harm they did was to a clan reviled of gods and elves alike."

Kiinyon Colbathin regarded Galaeron coldly. "And what of the lives lost? The lives of *your* patrol?"

"That was fate's doing," said Galaeron. "And if not fate's, then my own."

This drew a soft whistle from Vala, who said softly, "The worm grows a spine. . . ."

Galaeron ignored her and gestured at Melegaunt. "All the humans save this one were our captives when the phaerimm attacked, and I owe it to him that any of us survived."

"So you say the humans committed no crime?" asked Duirsar.

"The council should not rush to judgment." As a tomb guard, Galaeron could hardly contend that crypt breaking was not a crime. "There is much to consider here."

Lord Duirsar studied those around him. Though no human could have read the indecision in their expressions, it was plain enough to Galaeron. Elves were neither cruel nor hasty, and they would not sentence even a human to death without all due consideration.

At length, Duirsar turned to Galaeron. "Until the Hill Elders come to a decision, we will leave our guests in the care of your family." He turned to Kiinyon Colbathin and added, "Unless the Tomb Guard has more pressing duties for him?"

"Nothing that will interfere." The tomb master glared at Galaeron and tipped his slender chin toward the Hall of the High Hunt. "See to Takari and Ehamond. We'll talk about the lost ones when I return."

Kiinyon turned and the other Hill Elders left without another word, leaving the humans to look after them in puzzlement. The captives' expressions grew even more bewildered when Galaeron began to undo their bindings.

"They have freed us?" Melegaunt asked.

Galaeron shook his head. "You are my guests."

"But the phaerimm . . ."

"Are Evereska's concern," said Galaeron. "You have warned the Hill Elders, and now you must await their decision on the matter of the crypt breaking."

The humans looked at their unbound hands and seemed more confused than ever.

"My family does not treat its guests as prisoners," Galaeron clarified.

"And if we leave?" asked Melegaunt.

"You must not," Galaeron said. "My family has guaranteed your conduct."

"It has?" Vala asked. "When did you do that?"

"I didn't." Galaeron returned her sword. "You did, when you reacted to the Taunting with both honor and restraint. Those are virtues held in much esteem by the Hill Elders."

Vala's eyes lit with sudden understanding. "But you spoke for us." She gave him a rugged smile. "You surprise me, elf. I take back half the bad things I've ever said about you."

CHAPTER FOUR

21 Nightal, the Year of the Unstrung Harp

By the time Galaeron slipped into the leaf-shadowed Hall of the High Hunt, Takari lay naked in the Singing Spring, her complexion returned to its normal bronze and her eyes lucid for the first time since being wounded. Behind her stood an aged moon elf wearing no more clothes than she, his arms hooked beneath hers to hold her above the shimmering surface. The air smelled of moss and sweet water, and the song of the silver fountain trilled through the woody pavilion in gay melodies. Ehamond sat beneath the lilting spray as naked as the others, his cuts and bruises already fading. Dynod stood on the bank with two minor priests, describing the destruction of the patrol.

As Galaeron entered the grove, one of the priests nodded in his direction. There was no hint of embarrassment as Dynod turned toward him. Elves seldom relished the failures of others and therefore had few misgivings about discussing them. Having suffered more than his share of pitying looks and sympathetic encouragement, it was one of the few traits Galaeron wished he could change about the Fair Folk.

Dynod's eyes slid past Galaeron toward the edge of the pavilion, where the humans stood waiting, Melegaunt looking tentative and the others even more awestruck than usual. Knowing the glade of Solonor Thelandira to be the one temple in Evereska where humans would not be an intrusion, Galaeron motioned them forward and turned back to Dynod.

"Then the humans were absolved?" asked Dynod.

"Closer to it than I," answered Galaeron.

Dynod and the priests exchanged knowing looks, then one of the priests offered one of those compassionate little comments Galaeron had learned to loathe early in his studies at the Academy of Magic. "You mustn't worry. Tomb Master Colbathin is a stern commander, but a fair one."

Dynod rolled his eyes and looked away, and Galaeron said, "Had we spent the last two decades in the Greycloaks instead of the Desert Border South, I'd be more inclined to believe that." Ignoring the surprise on the faces of the two priests, he kneeled beside the water and called to Takari. "How do you feel?"

"Like a moth with a fang hole in its back." Her voice was cheerful, if rather weak. "Sick, but happy to be alive."

"I have healed the wound," said Pleufan Trueshot, the aged huntsman holding her. He rolled the scout over to display an inflamed lump where the hole once was. "But I can't rid her of the pestilence."

"It may not be an infection," said Melegaunt, stepping to the bank beside Galaeron. "May I have a look?"

Pleufan nodded. "You are welcome in the Singing Spring."

Much to Galaeron's astonishment, Melegaunt stepped into the water without removing so much as his boots. Dynod and Ehamond also raised their brows, but the high huntsman and his two assistants, who often numbered humans among their worshipers during the monthly Ceremonies, showed no surprise.

Galaeron glanced over at Vala to see if she found the behavior odd, but her expression was one of such total astonishment he could not tell what she was thinking. Her men, however, were staring at Takari with such a look of feral hunger that he began to worry the Hill Elders had misread the humans' reaction during the Taunting. This puzzled him even more than Melegaunt's odd behavior, since the humans had known Takari only as an incoherent battle casualty. Under the circumstances, they could hardly have developed any feelings of love for her, so it was hard for an elf to understand why the mere sight of her naked body should inflame their passions.

Trailing a murky cloud of mud from his trail-worn clothes, Melegaunt waded to the center of the pool and stopped beside Takari. He prodded the sore then looked back to Galaeron.

"The phaerimm did this with its tail, did it not?" Without waiting for a reply, he continued, "Did you see it inject anything?"

"The tail pulsed," said Galaeron. "Later, I saw something small and hot at the bottom of the wound."

Pleufan looked up. "I've tried every poison antidote I know."

Melegaunt shook his head. "Phaerimm don't inject poison," he said. "They inject eggs."

"Eggs?" Takari craned her head around so hard she twisted free of Pleufan's grasp. "What do you mean 'eggs'?"

"Only one at a time," said Melegaunt. He looked to the high hunter. "This is how they reproduce."

"Like caterpillar wasps?" Takari paled to a sickly saffron. "Kill me now! I want nothing eating me from the inside."

"It won't come to that." Melegaunt turned to the high hunter. "Cut out the egg and treat her as for an ague. If she rests, she'll be fine in a tenday."

Takari did not look convinced. "Easy for you to say—"

"Yes, it is. I've cut out six—and no healer to see me through the fever." Melegaunt patted the scout on the cheek, then nodded to the high hunter and waded back to shore.

"Dynod, you'll see that she does as instructed." Galaeron looked to Takari and added, "Then you are to return to your own people for a year."

"Thank you," Takari said, her eyes turning sad, "but I'll wait until after Kiinyon—"

"No, go as soon as you are able," said Galaeron. "Even if he has not spoken it, Kiinyon has already made his decision. I want you gone while the order is mine to give. It has been too long since you walked the High Forest."

Takari's eyes grew liquid. "I will—"

Galaeron raised his hand. "We'll talk before you go," he said. "See me when you're able."

Takari nodded then allowed herself to sink back into Pleufan's arms. "Till next."

"Till next."

Galaeron told the priests to thank the high hunter for him and gave them a gold lion for their goddess, then waited as Melegaunt climbed out of the water. The human rubbed his fingers together, running through the gestures of a minor drying spell, but nothing happened. He frowned and tried it again.

His clothes remained as wet as before.

"Allow me," said Galaeron, more than a little puzzled by the wizard's failure. The mythal would turn back the spell of any non-elf attempting harmful magic within Evereska. But a drying spell was hardly harmful, and Melegaunt would have suffered some adverse effect, had he meant to cause injury. Instead, the enchantment had simply failed. "Is there an incantation?"

Melegaunt raised his bushy brow but shook his head. Galaeron ran his fingers through the same gestures as the wizard then felt the Weave's magic course through him. There was a sizzle and a small flash, then Melegaunt's clothes were dry and smoking.

Melegaunt patted out a small flame. "Did you copy my spell?"

"It's a small talent I have," said Galaeron, glossing over the long explanation of his enrollment in, then expulsion from the Academy of Magic. "It wasn't as strange as your other spells."

"Amazing," said Melegaunt. "You could learn a little control, but amazing nonetheless."

"Would that you were a master in the Academy of Magic," Galaeron laughed.

He turned and led the humans out of the grove. As they returned to the marble-paved lanes outside, Vala came to his side.

"You should have kissed her," she said.

Galaeron nearly stumbled. "Takari? Why would I do that?"

"Isn't that what elf lovers do when they part?" asked Vala. "Or do only humans kiss?"

"We kiss—though not as often as humans, judging by how you breed," said Galaeron, "but Takari and I are not lovers."

"I take back the twelve nice words I've said about you," said Vala. "Only a tusker would treat a woman in love so badly."

"Tusker?"

"Orc," explained Melegaunt. "And Vala, it's hardly a guest's place to interrogate her host about such matters."

Vala lowered her eyes at once. "Of course. I apologize." She fell a step behind and allowed Melegaunt to take her place.

Galaeron glanced back, a little troubled by how quickly her spirit vanished at any hint of the wizard's disapproval. He had been trying to puzzle out their relationship since departing the Vyshaan crypt, but whenever he mentioned the Granite Tower or their past, Melegaunt always changed the subject. Vala told him to mind his own business.

Deciding the best way to win Vala's confidence was to be open himself, Galaeron said, "There's no need to apologize, Vala, but we have never been lovers." He could tell by the look in her eyes that she knew there was more to the story. "We could have been, but such things always come to bad end between moon elves and Wood elves."

"Really?" It was Melegaunt who asked this. "I wasn't aware of that."

"Perhaps because you are not an elf," Galaeron replied.

Ignoring the curious—and sometimes hostile—looks of the pedestrians they passed, Galaeron led the way across the great sunning meadow at the base of Bellcrest Hill and started up Goldmorn Knoll. Apparently sensing the melancholy that had come over him, Melegaunt allowed Galaeron a few minutes of introspection before speaking again.

"They're going to get killed, you know."

Galaeron did not need to ask who the wizard meant. "It would be a mistake to judge our high mages by my skills." He spoke in a low voice, and even then only when they were near no other elves. "Lord Duirsar was not exaggerating when he told you how old Evereska's magic is."

"Old yes, and powerful as well, I'm sure," said Melegaunt. "But how much do your high mages know of the phaerimm? You didn't even know what they were, and your priest wouldn't have realized what was wrong with Takari until the hatchling ate its way through her entrails."

"And how do you know so much about them?" asked Galaeron.

Without answering the question, Melegaunt said, "The phaerimm have spent the last thousand years starving beneath Anauroch, barely sustaining themselves on the few Bedine their slaves can kidnap or lure through the Sharn Wall. And now we—you and I, Galaeron—have given them a chance to escape. I promise you, they will be quick to seize it."

"Which still does not answer my question. Why do you know so much about them?"

"Because I have spent the last century studying them," said Melegaunt. When Galaeron remained silent, he added, "That's all you need know."

"And all you need know is that I won't break my word to Lord Duirsar," said Galaeron. "Not on your say-so. Not on my own life."

"It is not your life I'm worried about."

"Then tell me why," said Galaeron. "If I'm convinced, we will speak again with the Hill Elders—"

"Who would rather see Evereska fall than accept help from a human."

"Who have dealt with enough humans to know their help is never free," said Galaeron. "I'm not a fifth their age, and I have learned that for myself."

They rounded the corner and came to the granite bank of Dawnsglory Pond, where two dozen laughing elves were availing themselves of the morning light to bathe and play in the steaming waters. Galaeron led his companions along to a quiet corner, where a pair of winsome Sun elf sisters were washing the tangles from their hair.

The eldest, a stunning beauty with violet flecks in her eyes, looked up. "Glad homeagain, Galaeron. We heard about Louenghris and your silvers. He will be missed."

Galaeron winced at how fast the news was spreading. It would arrive at his father's before he did. "As will they all, Zharilee." He gestured behind him, where he could almost feel the heat rising off the humans at the sight of the naked sisters. "These are in my care until the Hill Elders decide their fate, and I'm sorry to say they have need of a bath before I take them to my father's."

The youngest wrinkled her nose. "Keep a close watch on them." She rolled onto her back and started toward the center of the pool. "I don't like how that crooked nosed one looks at me."

There was the sound of a heavy blow, then Vala growled, "Close 'em or lose 'em, Kuhl."

Galaeron gave the sisters a moment to retreat, then waved his guests into the pool. "If you please." He glanced toward Melegaunt and added, "It's customary to remove your clothes."

The men's expressions changed from hungry to nervous, and they looked to Vala for instruction.

Vala shrugged and said, "Why not?"

She unbuckled her sword belt, then sat down and began to unlace her high boots. Her men reluctantly followed her example, and ten minutes later they were splashing in the water like pup otters. The men all looked like rothé, with thick tangles of dark hair across their massive backs and huge barrel chests. Vala was stout but much smaller, with rounder curves than an elf woman and—thankfully—only small tufts of hair growing in the appropriate places, but her idea of sport was as rough as that of her men. When they began to play keep-away with one of her boots, she did not hesitate to yank things most elves would have considered it impolite for even good friends to touch. The men responded in kind, grabbing whatever they could in order to keep her at bay. They even tried to include Galaeron in their games, tossing her boot—and Vala herself—at him. So surprised was he to see her eyeing him with the same hungry look he had noticed in the men that he forgot to defend himself and let her hand dart past his guard—and he was even more surprised by what she grabbed. She bowled him over backward and, burying his face in her soft chest, snatched her boot from his grasp.

Galaeron came up coughing, and found Vala holding her boot coyly in one hand. "What's the matter, elf?" She gave him one of those hungry human smiles, then tossed the boot on the bank. "Still too dirty?"

"Not at all." Suddenly feeling very self-conscious, Galaeron turned toward the bank. "My house is not far. We'll break our fast and see to cleaning your clothes and armor later."

They all climbed out of the water and bundled their armor inside their cloaks. Without their clothes, the humans looked a lot less intimidating and drew far fewer sneers, and it was not long before they reached the summit of Goldmorn Knoll. Located well into the interior of Evereska, the knoll was not as high as the Three Sisters nor as large, but it was home to a sizable grove of rare sycamore trees that had left Cormyr during the Time of Troubles and sought refuge in Evereska. Galaeron could not help smiling when he recalled the sight of that endless line of trees marching past his camp along the Desert Border and vanishing into the Shaeradim. He came to the base of Starmeadow Tower—before the sycamores arrived, it had stood in the heart of a favorite meadow for stargazing—and pointed at a hole-shaped doorway seventy feet above.

"There is my home. If you are ever lost in the city, ask for Treetop in Starmeadow, and you will be returned here."

"Treetop," repeated Dexon. The burly human craned his neck, watching a pair of elves crawl past the doorway head-down. "Where's the ladder?"

Galaeron smiled. "There is no need for ladders in Evereska."

He tucked his armor under one arm, then pressed one palm and the sole of the opposite foot to the wall. Thanks to the magic of the mythal, they held fast to the stone, and he began to climb.

"Always use bare skin. Never wear gloves or shoes."

Vala and the others watched him warily for a few moments, then finally pressed their own palms to the wall and started to follow. They were even more delighted than at the pond, and it was not long before they were embarrassing Galaeron with excited whoops and yodels.

Only Melegaunt, who in truth looked like he needed to use more muscle and less magic, did not seem to relish the experience. He stood on the ground for several moments trying to cast a flying spell, which failed as utterly as had his drying magic, then he finally gave up and clambered up the wall. By the time he joined Galaeron and the others beside the door, he was huffing and puffing so heavily he could hardly speak. Galaeron showed the humans the safest way to enter and leave a door hole, which was to approach it from the side rather than clamber over the bottom, and entered.

Inside Treetop was airy and light, all smooth curves and softly glowing walls. A staircase swirled down from the upper floors, rounded a corner in the foyer before them, and flowed into the lower house. Along the walls sat benches of white marble and tables of translucent alabaster, often with a delicately embossed vase or ethereal statuette placed carefully on top.

Galaeron's youngest sister, eighty-year-old Keya, appeared in the doorway.

"Galaeron!" She rushed across the room in a streak of long blue hair and gold-threaded gown and embraced him. "Glad homeagain! This past year has seemed a tenwinter!"

Happy for a change to hear nothing about his lost patrol or how his chances with the tomb master are better than he thinks, Galaeron dropped his armor and hugged her to his chest.

"Keya! More the lady each time I see you." He held the embrace for a moment, then disengaged himself and turned to present his companions. "The Hill Elders have asked me to care for these guests."

"I know." Keya took one look at the looming mounds of hairy flesh and said, "I'm sure one of your tunics will fit the woman."

"Vala," said Vala. She offered her free hand and studied Keya as though sizing up an object of prey. "Well met."

Keya retreated from the stocky appendage in confusion.

"You're to clasp it," Galaeron explained. "A human gesture of friendship."

Keya looked up at Galaeron, her gold-flecked eyes clearly asking if such a thing were truly necessary.

Galaeron took her hand and placed it in Vala's. "You'll have to forgive Keya," he said, laughing. "I'm afraid my sister has never heard humans called anything but thieves and murderers."

"Sister?" Vala's expression softened, and she pumped Keya's hand warmly. "Don't you believe everything Galaeron says about us. I hope you and I will be great friends."

"I'm sure that would be, um, interesting. I've never had a human friend before."

Keya turned to the men and reluctantly offered her hand to each in turn, looking slightly puzzled as they blushed and struggled to cover themselves. Even Melegaunt seemed embarrassed, though he did a better job of hiding it than most.

"I can probably find a cloak that will fit the plump one, but these others . . ." Keya shook her head. "I doubt our blankets are large enough to go around their shoulders."

"Their waists will do, I think," said Galaeron. "Is Father here?"

"In the contemplation." Keya gestured through an archway toward the back of the house, then looked to Melegaunt. "He asks you and Melegaunt to attend him at once. A messenger has arrived from Lord Duirsar."

"From Duirsar?" Melegaunt allowed himself a superior smile, then started for the archway. "Come to his senses, no doubt."

"If you would be so kind, Keya. . . ." Galaeron said.

He motioned to Vala and her men, then went after Melegaunt. He steered the wizard through the circular great room, where the family took its meals on the rare occasions when there were enough of them to fill it, then stepped through a broad archway into the contemplation. His father was standing at the back of the tome-filled chamber, staring over the treetops through a theurglass window. A white snow finch sat on his outstretched finger, chirping and tweeting rapidly—no doubt passing along the latest gossip from Cloudcrown Hill, where the palaces of Lord Duirsar and the great nobles sat scattered among the trees.

Galaeron cleared his throat. "Father? We've arrived."

His father turned at once, a broad grin bringing a little light to his morose eyes. With silver hair and sagging shoulders, he seemed older and smaller than he had the last time Galaeron had been home.

"My son. Glad homeagain."

The bird chirped a greeting as well, though Galaeron was not versed in peeptalk and could only return it with a polite bob of his head.

Galaeron gestured to Melegaunt. "Meet Melegaunt Tanthul, a human wizard of strange magic and no small power."

Galaeron's father inclined his head. "Welcome to Treetop, uh, *Wizard* Tanthul."

"I am a prince in my own city," said Melegaunt, noting the elder Nihmedu's uncertainty about how to address him. "But in truth I've been away so long I have all but forgotten the fact. Call me Melegaunt."

"And I am Aubric."

"Well met, Aubric, and my thanks for opening your home to us." Melegaunt peered around the contemplation, his eyes sliding past the Reverie couch and reading stand as he searched for another person. "I was given to understand there is a messenger?"

Galaeron's father raised the snow finch on his finger. "This is Manynests, attendant to Lord Duirsar."

Manynests chirped in greeting, then launched into a long series of tweets and whistles.

"Lord Duirsar sends his greetings and salutations," translated Galaeron's father. "He reports that Evereska's wizards—" A peep from Manynests prompted him to correct himself. "—that our *high mages* required over an hour to solve your shadow maze."

Melegaunt's eyes widened. "Only an hour?"

The bird began twittering again, and Galaeron's father translated, "Lord Duirsar was surprised that it took them that long. He sends his compliments and inquires whether you would be willing to supply them with the passwords for the traps in the dwarven workings. As entertaining as the high mages find your work, there is a certain element of time involved."

"Yes, of course." So shocked was Melegaunt that he dropped onto the Reverie couch, drawing a wince from both Nihmedus as his hairy rear touched the pristine marble. "The first is purpledusk, the second darkmorn."

"Purpledusk and darkmorn?" Galaeron's father repeated, translating for Manynests.

When Melegaunt nodded, the bird peeped its thanks and took wing, darting through the theurglass window almost before the elder Nihmedu could utter the command word rendering it permeable.

Galaeron went to Melegaunt's side and said, "You surprised me, but it's good that you did not try to use the passwords to coerce your way into battle."

Melegaunt's eyes were still round with shock. "It wouldn't have been much of a coercion. If it only took an hour to break the shadow maze, they would have been through the other spells by midmorn."

"Still, it speaks well of your intentions that you did not hesitate," said the elder Nihmedu. "Manynests will report your cooperation, and that will count for much when the Hill Elders discuss the matter of your crypt breaking."

"I hope it will count for as much as Lord Imesfor's anger," said Galaeron. "I happened across Zharilee and Gvendor when we bathed, and the Golds have already begun to discuss Louenghris's death."

A cloud came over his father's eyes. "I doubt Louenghris's death will count against the humans. Manynests tells me that Lord Duirsar is already thinking of suspending Lord Imesfor from any deliberation related to his son's death. Your fate is a different matter. Kiinyon sent young Imesfor to the Desert Border for a reason, and he'll blame you for any ill will that befalls the tomb guards because of the lad's death."

"He'll blame me for any trouble he can," said Galaeron. "He's already made that much clear—and perhaps I deserve it. I *did* lose two thirds of my patrol."

"And did more good than you will ever know." Melegaunt stood. "I don't mean to speak immodestly, but had you left me to the phaerimm, it would have been a great loss to the world."

"Because?" asked the elder Nihmedu.

"Because it would have been a cowardly thing to do," Melegaunt dodged, no more eager to reveal himself to Lord Nihmedu than to Galaeron. "And your son is no coward. Under the circumstances, he did all that could be asked and more. Kiinyon Colbathin will come to understand that, if he and the others are lucky enough to survive."

"Then we have nothing to worry about." Galaeron's father clasped both Melegaunt and Galaeron on the shoulders and steered them toward the great room. "Kiinyon Colbathin always survives. Now perhaps we should break our fast. With the passwords in hand, the high mages are likely to have the phaerimm destroyed by midmorn, and I don't want you facing the Hill Elders on an empty stomach."

CHAPTER FIVE

23 Nightal, the Year of the Unstrung Harp

The high mages did not have the Sharn Wall patched by highsun of the twenty-first. They did not have it repaired by dusk, nor even deepnight. Grateful for Melegaunt's earlier aid, Lord Duirsar kept the Nihmedus informed via his bird messengers. Kiinyon lost a company of tomb guards when they bypassed Melegaunt's second trap and surprised a pair of phaerimm. The high mages slew the two monsters in a flurry of lightning and fire, but the battle left them so exhausted they had to retire to the surface.

Melegaunt sent word to avoid attacking the phaerimm directly, as they could often absorb magic and fling it back at the caster, or use its energy to heal themselves. Lord Duirsar thanked him for the advice and said he would pass it along.

By the time more high mages and another company of tomb guards teleported from Evereska, half a dozen phaerimm had slipped into the dwarven workings and vanished. Two more companies of tomb guards were teleported in from the Greycloak Hills to track these down. One company was never heard from again. The survivors of the other returned with the good news that they had wounded one of the creatures.

Melegaunt offered to bring Vala and her men and join the battle. Lord Duirsar thanked him for his interest, but said it would be better for them to remain in Evereska. All Evereskan tomb guards were told to report to the College of Magic and Arms. Galaeron was not included in the alert, and Takari had already left for the High Forest. Ehamond and the others were attached to someone else's patrol.

Kiinyon Colbathin reached the Sharn Wall with ten tomb guards and two of his three high mages. After examining the hole, the mages concluded they needed a third to repair it. Kiinyon, who understood the intricacies of high magic no better than any non-mage, flew into a rage. While he screamed, two phaerimm emerged from beneath Anauroch. During the battle, Kiinyon stumbled across a darksword and used it to slay both phaerimm, freezing his hand but saving one high mage. Before retreating, he had the four survivors of his patrol search the tunnel for more darkswords. They recovered sixteen, which Vala requested be returned to her, as they were family heirlooms passed down for five generations.

Unimpressed by the pedigree, Lord Duirsar nevertheless promised to return the weapons after the battle. Until then, he hoped she would not mind if Tomb Master Colbathin put them to use—and was there any way to keep the hilts from freezing the hands of those who wielded them? Sadly, there was not. The magic was attuned to the family that owned it. Melegaunt offered again to join the battle with Vala and her men. Lord Duirsar thanked him for the offer and noted he had suggested the same thing to Kiinyon and the Highest Mage, whose name was never revealed to a human. After much discussion, it was agreed they would keep the offer in mind, though for now they feared a mixture of fighting methods would cause more problems than it cured. The Vale Guard, the Feather Cavalry, and the Army of Evereska were all placed on alert. All tomb guards capable of teleporting themselves were ordered to report to the Vyshaan cairn at once, and the remainder were ordered to ride for it. There were no longer enough wizards to transport them by spell.

Galaeron tried to relieve his frustration by taking Vala and her humans on walks through Evereska. They visited the Floating Gardens of Aerdrie Faenya, the Groaning Cave, the Tower Higher than Eastpeak—from the top of which they could see the Vyshaan cairn and the elf army encamped around it, or so they fancied. Finding Vala much more open around him, Galaeron asked again where her home was and what her relationship to Melegaunt was. She went so far as reassuring him that his people had nothing to fear from hers. The Granite Tower was far, far away and hardly strong enough to pose a threat to Evereska—and that was all she was going to say on the matter while she remained a prisoner. Galaeron decided it would have to be enough.

By highsun of the twenty-first, Galaeron began to notice as many glares directed at him as at the humans. By dusk, people were rebuking him for endangering Evereska through his poor judgement. For one elf to be the object of so much public scorn was unheard of. Galaeron fell into a depression and no longer wished to leave Treetop. Vala told him to get over it. She wanted to see the statue of Hanali Celanil.

On the twenty-third day of Nightal, the phaerimm claimed the dwarven working, forcing Kiinyon and his last tomb guards to the surface. Reports circulated of strange monsters appearing in remote locations. Galaeron snapped at Keya, then realized she and Vala had become good friends indeed when Vala drew her dagger and threatened to geld him. He apologized, and the giant eagles of the Feather Cavalry darkened the skies for a quarter hour as they departed to reconnoiter the phaerimm breakout.

Melegaunt suggested to Lord Duirsar that the Hill Elders command Kiinyon and the unnamed Highest Mage to accept his help. Lord Duirsar responded rather tersely that the Hill Elders had no more right to interfere with the field commanders than a human had to interfere with the governing of Evereska. After that, no more messages came for a while, though Aubric Nihmedu learned from other sources that the Army of Evereska was being dispatched to all corners of the Shaeradim, the Vale Guard had been ordered to establish a perimeter in the mountains around the vale, and the senior regiforms of both academies of the College of Magic and Arms had been ordered to stand ready. Melegaunt approached Galaeron to broach the idea of joining the battle without permission, and Galaeron was so frightened he almost agreed.

It was late that day when Vala came to Galaeron with puffy cheeks and tears in her eyes. At first, he thought Melegaunt had broken his word and left, but he dismissed that notion when she took his hands and held them to her lips.

"Galaeron, I'm so sorry to be the one to tell you."

"Tell me what?" Galaeron could not imagine anything that would make Vala cry. "Have the phaerimm broken through?"

She shook her head. "It's Aubric."

"My father?" Galaeron did not understand. He had seen no sign that his father was preparing to journey west. "There's nothing wrong with my father."

"No." Tears spilled down Vala's cheeks. "No longer."

Pulling Galaeron by the hand, she entered the contemplation, where Aubric Nihmedu lay on the marble Reverie couch, his eyes open wide and a tome spread across his chest. He looked happier than Galaeron had seen him in decades, his lips curled into a slight smile and the furrows gone from his forehead.

No longer puzzled, Galaeron folded his hands over Vala's and backed into the great room. When he judged they would not be overheard, he whispered, "Thank you."

Vala frowned. "Is that all? Don't elves cry?"

"When there is cause."

"A father's death isn't cause?"

"Dying?" The statement was so absurd that Galaeron guffawed, drawing a startled cry from the other room.

Vala glanced through the arch and grew as pale as a moon elf. "He's back!"

"Back?" Galaeron's father appeared in the archway. "Where was I?"

"D-d-dead!" Vala's knees buckled, and Galaeron caught her.

"Dead?"

Aubric looked to Galaeron for an explanation, but Galaeron was laughing too hard to explain.

"Your eyes were open," Vala said. "I thought you were . . . gone."

"Gone?" Finally, Aubric seemed to understand. "Oh, the eyes. You thought I was—"

"Dead," Vala confirmed. "You weren't moving."

"The Reverie," Galaeron said, still laughing. "Haven't you wondered why we have no beds? Elves don't sleep."

Vala looked wary. "Everyone sleeps."

"Not everyone," said Aubric. "Though I suppose the Reverie could be considered a kind of sleep."

"A little, perhaps." Galaeron did not want to confuse the poor human.

"It's a waking dream?" Vala asked.

"Not a dream, exactly," Galaeron said. "We revisit the events in our lives."

"Or we join with the community," his father added.

Vala looked confused.

"To share our feelings," said Galaeron. "It's restful."

Vala narrowed her eyes. "You all thoughtspeak?"

"It's not speech, but we share." Galaeron tried to think of how he could describe the Reverie. "You must have a family."

Vala frowned, insulted. "Do I look like I was *spawned?*"

"Do you ever feel what they feel? Do you ever know what they need without asking them, or experience their pain from afar?"

Vala's eyes lit. "Sometimes with my son. You feel that with all elves?"

"You have a son?" Galaeron was so surprised he did not register her last question.

"Yes, I have a son." Vala ran her fingers down her sides. "You've seen me naked. Did you think this body could be barren?"

Galaeron felt the heat in his cheeks. "Of course not, but elf women—"

"Have no hips. Giving birth must feel like a gut stab." Vala narrowed her eyes, then said, "Maybe that's why you have such slim heads."

"Without doubt!" Galaeron's father clapped a hand on Vala's shoulder. "You've a tongue on you like a Wood elf, my dear."

Vala's expression changed to self-reproach. "I'm sorry. I forgot myself."

"Not at all." The elder Nihmedu shook his head in mirth. "I haven't enjoyed an argument so much since Morgwais was here."

"Morgwais?" asked Vala.

The gaiety vanished from the old elf's eyes as suddenly as it had appeared. "Galaeron's mother. You won't be meeting her."

When no explanation was forthcoming, Vala looked to Galaeron, and a moment of awkward silence followed. Galaeron was spared the trouble of changing the subject by the sudden flutter of wings. A streak of white circled the room three times before Manynests grew calm enough to perch on the elder Nihmedu's outstretched finger.

"I was in here." Aubric had to speak through the snow finch's warbling. "Was it so much trouble to use the door?"

This quieted the bird somewhat. He continued to *zeee* and chirp, and even Galaeron's father had to concentrate to keep up.

"When did Lord Duirsar last hear from them?"

The bird peeped, then continued for another twenty seconds. Finally, Manynests cocked his head, his wings twitching as he awaited a reply.

"Tell Lord Duirsar that the Swords of Evereska will leave within the hour," said Aubric. "I took the liberty of planning for such a summons."

The bird launched itself into the contemplation and was nearly at the window before Aubric could speak the command word to render the theurglass passable.

"That finch is going to break his neck," said Melegaunt, entering the room ahead of Keya and the other humans. "Why so excited?"

"The Hill Elders lost contact with Kiinyon and the high mages an hour ago."

"An *hour* ago?" Melegaunt fumed. "And they're only telling us now?"

Galaeron's father raised his hand. "There's more. They can no longer contact anyone outside the Shaeradim."

"What do you mean?" Keya frowned. "That can't be right."

"I doubt Lord Duirsar is mistaken," said her father. "There is no response to his sendings, and those using the gates never return."

"So any help Evermeet sends won't arrive through Evereska," surmised Melegaunt. "They'll have to fight their way in from outside, with the troops sent by your other allies."

"Other allies?" asked Aubric. "What allies would those be?"

"I've heard Evereska holds a special place in the heart of Khelben Arunsun," said Melegaunt. "Surely he is already mobilizing Waterdeep's forces."

"You are well informed," said Aubric. "Khelben was the first human to visit Evereska, but we elves are a proud people."

"He hasn't been told?" Melegaunt closed his eyes. "What about Evermeet?"

"They were told, but no help was requested. Lord Duirsar has ordered the remnants of the Feather Cavalry to inform all elf-friends of our peril."

"They'll fail," said Melegaunt. "The phaerimm would not overlook such an obvious thing."

"Then it may be some time before Evermeet sends help," said Aubric. "In the meantime, I must excuse myself. Duty calls."

"Duty?" asked Vala.

"Father is the Blademajor of the Swords of Evereska." Keya's voice was as frightened as it was proud.

The elder Nihmedu nodded. "Lord Duirsar has asked us to scout and report."

A look of relief crossed Melegaunt's face. "Good. We're coming with you."

Galaeron's father smiled warmly. "Would that you could, my human friend." He shook his head.

"But as the commander, surely Lord Duirsar will listen to your wishes," Melegaunt objected.

"No doubt, Lord Duirsar would," said Galaeron. "But the Swords of Evereska are a noble militia. The title of blademajor rotates, and it could easily be rotated to someone else through the scheming of a few high nobles."

"My command is tenuous enough." The elder Nihmedu made no mention of why, but they all knew it was because of the blame being heaped on his son's shoulders. He turned to Galaeron. "Manynests mentioned twice that the spell-guard is watching the city exits. You and your friends would do nobody any good hanging in bone cages."

Galaeron studied his father. "You have nothing to fear on our account. I only wish we had nothing to fear on yours." He clasped his father to his breast. "Remember what you have learned from Melegaunt about these devils. No one knows them better."

"I have marked every word." Galaeron's father returned the embrace, then separated himself and turned to Keya. "I am sorry to leave you alone, my daughter. Will you care for Treetop until next I return?"

"Of course." Keya buried herself in her father's chest. "And you won't be leaving me alone. Galaeron and his friends will keep me company."

Galaeron and his father exchanged a look over Keya's head, then the elder Nihmedu turned to Vala. "It may be that we do not meet again, human. Should it prove so, know that your wit and beauty will be a treasure to me always." He nodded toward Galaeron. "And it would do an old elf's heart good to know you will watch after his son."

"Then I'll be glad to be of some use to an old elf." Vala gave the blademajor a hearty embrace, but the bewilderment in her eyes suggested she did not yet fully understand what he was saying. "Sweet water and light laughter, my friend."

The traditional parting caused Galaeron's father to raise his arched brows. "Another day in Evereska, and there'd be no telling you from an elf." He laughed and turned to the other humans. "Sweet water and light laughter to you all."

Aubric was barely out of the room before Keya turned to Galaeron. "That was a strange thing to say. Where does he think you're going?"

"He doesn't know—and that's how it must remain," surmised Melegaunt. Not waiting for a confirming nod from Galaeron, he plucked at Vala's silky green shift. "Get out of this and into your armor."

"Armor?" Keya's jaw dropped, and she turned to Galaeron. "You mustn't let them."

Galaeron took his sister's hands. "Keya, I'm not letting them. I'm *taking* them."

CHAPTER SIX

23 Nightal, the Year of the Unstrung Harp

Once they had descended Starmeadow Tower, the humans moved with surprising stealth, considering their armor and the difficulty of traveling in an invisible group. At times, Galaeron and Keya could not even tell the warriors were behind them. They descended Goldmorn Knoll and slipped past Dawnsglory Pond without drawing a second glance, and Galaeron grew confident their plan would work. They had to stop once and listen to a silver-haired matron assure Galaeron that no one blamed him for freeing the phaerimm and only Golds listened to Lord Imesfor anyway, but even she did not seem to sense the invisible humans.

The forest ended abruptly at the edge of Moondark Hill, where a low stone wall was all that separated them from the empty air. A crescent of green pastureland lay far below, flecked with gray boulders, brown ponies, and emerald stands of fir. Beyond the pasture, the rolling patchwork of black-and-gold winter fields rose toward the mist-shrouded vineyards. The Swords of Evereska were visible on the highest terraces, their long column of ponies wagging like a tail as they rounded the last switchbacks into the forests of the High Vale. There were no other companies in sight, though Galaeron knew there would be a handful of spell-guards posted at the livery stations and the other entrances to the city.

"Now is as good a time as any, unless we want to wait until dusk," he said.

"We dare not wait." Melegaunt's voice came from the air behind Keya. "With the phaerimm, every hour is an eternity."

Galaeron extended his hand. "I'll need the rope."

An invisible hand laid a thin coil of elven rope in his palm. Galaeron looped it over his shoulder and climbed a big duskwood, then crawled out on a sturdy limb well past the wall. He secured the line and fed the bottom out until it touched the pasture. No human rope—at least not that one person could carry—would have stretched so many hundreds of feet, but enough elven cord remained to create a large coil on the ground.

Galaeron returned to his companions and climbed down next to Keya. "All is ready. Stay away from the cliff. If you touch it, Evereska's defensive magic will cancel my spell."

"We're all going at once?" asked Vala.

"We must all stay within ten feet of you or become visible," explained Melegaunt.

"That thread won't hold five of us," objected Kuhl.

"It would hold five stone giants." Keya's tone was anything but patient. "That's an *elven* rope."

The explanation was met with a wary silence, then Vala said, "On with you, Kuhl." There was a lot of scuffing and grunting, then the thick branch sagged dangerously. "We'll be waiting at the bottom, Galaeron."

"I'll be along directly."

Galaeron allowed the humans a few moments to begin their descent, then embraced his sister.

"Too long away," he said, "too quick gone."

"Next time." She smiled bravely and touched her long fingers to his cheek. "Bring me no phaerimm eggs."

"Of that, little sister, you may be assured." He stepped onto the low wall, then glanced at the duskwood branch. "You'll retrieve the rope?"

She nodded. "They'll never know of your leaving. Sweet water and light laughter."

"Back soon for soft songs and bright wine."

Galaeron cast a spell to turn himself invisible, then fixed his gaze on the coil of rope far below and stepped off the wall. His plunge was at first a breathtaking blur of wind and color, but the mythal's magic prevented any native of Evereska from being injured by a plummet from the cliff tops. As he neared the bottom, his fall slowed to a mere descent. He landed lightly on his feet and was there waiting when the invisible humans stepped onto the ground.

Keya pulled the cord up. Galaeron had the humans link hands, then he led them across the pasture to the perimeter of the mythal. He climbed over the wall into a field of winter wheat and stopped in a corner shade bower.

"Melegaunt?"

"Here."

"The spell-guards will be watching the Secret Gate, and we can't pass through unnoticed. Now would be a good time to use your shadowalk to move us to the other side of Eastpeak."

"I'd be happy to, but I think you have noticed my magic doesn't work in Evereska."

"It will now," Galaeron said.

"Really?" There was a pause, then Melegaunt asked, "I wonder why would that be?"

Though he knew the wizard could not see it, Galaeron shrugged. "You have your secrets, I have mine."

"So it seems." The wizard chuckled, low and foreboding, then added, "Very well. I suppose what the master claims cannot be denied the novice. Everyone find me and grab hold."

Though it had been more than forty years since Galaeron had considered any wizard his master, he did as instructed and took hold of an arm. Melegaunt's gravelly voice rose in an incantation, and the world turned dark and indistinct. Five blurry silhouettes appeared around him, then one of the smaller shapes separated itself from the others and started forward.

"We are walking the border between the world of light and the world of the dark," said Melegaunt. "It is easy to lose your way, so you must not release me. Time and distance have no meaning here. If you lose sight of me for even the blink of an eye, I may never find you."

Galaeron found himself clinging to a small arm that could only belong to Vala. She was holding hands with one of her huge warriors, and the warrior's other hand was clamped to Melegaunt's collarbone as tightly as a vise. Though every hand between Galaeron and the wizard possessed at least twice the strength of his own, his eyes soon began to burn for fear of blinking. To one side loomed flat purple shapes. Sometimes they were as high as mountains, with jagged profiles that suggested peaks and ridges. Other times, they were slender trunks with scarecrow arms, swaying in an unfelt wind, reaching down to clutch at Galaeron with fingers of darkness that could not touch.

Opposite the shadows shimmered a vast horizon of yellow radiance, blinding and bright and as hot as the Anauroch sun. Despite Melegaunt's warning, Galaeron found himself longing to walk into the light. Its familiar warmth was an enticing contrast to the cold eeriness of the shadows, and there was something young and frightened inside him that longed to be away from the darkness. He fixed his gaze ahead, forcing himself to concentrate on Vala's back.

Finally, slivers of radiance began to break off the horizon and tumble along to both sides of the companions. Some rolled completely by and passed out of sight. Others landed flat on the ground or lodged themselves between shoulders of purple darkness, creating a ghostly landscape of gullies and hills. Despite the cascade of splinters, the light never grew smaller. The yellow horizon merely flattened out and spread itself into a rolling plain that Galaeron soon recognized as the sands of Anauroch.

Instead of continuing toward the desert, Melegaunt dropped to his knees and tipped forward. Galaeron thought the wizard would fall, but his body merely extended itself at a slant and hung over the ground until the rest of the party followed his example. When they were all leaning forward at the same angle, Melegaunt had Galaeron cancel his invisibility spells, then led them downward into darkness as black as coal. The sensation of descent vanished within a dozen steps. A few minutes later, they stopped, and Galaeron's dark sight began to function.

"Your shadow vision will work now," Melegaunt whispered to the humans.

Vala and her men briefly touched the hilts of their swords, then blinked the sight back into their eyes. The group was standing in a small chamber hewn from solid rock. The walls had been cut so smoothly they seemed almost polished. Along one side of the room lay a sleeping berth, covered with a billowy black mattress of shadow made solid. On the other side sat a small stone desk.

From the front of the chamber came the sound of grunting and scuffling. Galaeron turned and found himself looking through a foot-wide crevice, where a haggard human was scuttling past in a high squat. The man's hair and beard were long and unkempt, his gaunt body coated in sweat-streaked filth. He was dragging a wooden chest crammed so full of parchments, books, and scrolls that the lid would close only partially.

Melegaunt motioned for quiet and stepped to the crevice. He ran through a series of mystic gestures, both cupping his hand to his ear and rubbing the tips of his fingers on his forehead. Galaeron and the others cast puzzled looks at each other and wondered where they were. Their answer came a moment later, when a huge-toothed maw surrounded by arms floated into view. Galaeron raised his hands to summon a bolt of magic, and the humans reached for their black swords.

Melegaunt stepped away from the crevice. "No!" He pushed Galaeron's hands down. "Your magic would have them on us like crows on a battlefield."

Galaeron glanced toward the crevice, but the creature floated past with no hint that it had seen them, its thorny body writhing through the air in a motion part fish and part serpent.

"It's angry with its slaves for being so slow," whispered Melegaunt. "It's complaining that the best holes will be taken. They'll be faster next move, or they'll be egg bags."

As the barbed tail rippled out of view, Galaeron asked, "Where's it going?"

"And where are we?" added Vala.

Melegaunt answered Galaeron first. "I think you know where it's going."

"The dwarven workings?"

"Somewhere in the Shaeradim," Melegaunt corrected. "They must consider it safe haven now."

"Safe haven!" Galaeron could not keep the outrage from his voice. "Never!"

Melegaunt touched a finger to his lips. "Quietly. This cloaking magic was meant to muffle snores, not shouts." He answered Vala's question next. "We're in my last refuge, not far from our rendezvous point in the dwarven workings. The phaerimm will place their WarGather at the breach in the Sharn Wall, to make sure it stays well guarded."

"So we came to *their* side of the wall?" she asked.

Melegaunt nodded. "The phaerimm are as intelligent as they are evil. They'll be ready for scouts. With luck, they won't expect them from this direction."

Galaeron thought of his father, riding out of Evereska on the mission Melegaunt described. "But the Swords—"

"Are still in the Secret Gate," said Melegaunt. "Time is different in the Shadow. If we are lucky, we will have discovered everything Evereska must know before the Swords leave the High Peaks. If we are not lucky . . . In that case, I fear your father must face the risk."

Galaeron nodded. Evereska had to learn the extent of the enemy's victory. If he and his human companions failed, then it fell to the Swords of Evereska to win the information themselves—no matter how poor their chance of success. Seeing that the phaerimm was gone, Galaeron motioned to the crevice.

"Shall we?"

"In a minute," said Melegaunt. "The phaerimm have spells to detect intruders . . . and it would be good if you were able to understand the phaerimm for yourself. Can you copy the spell I just cast?"

"Perhaps . . . a simple combination of eavesdropping and thoughtspeech?"

Melegaunt cocked his brow. "You are a truly gifted *innatoth.*"

"Innatoth?"

"Innate one," said Melegaunt. "What my own people would have called an ArcNatural, but which is better translated in most of Faerûn as 'sorcerer.' "

"What's the difference?" asked Vala.

"Not much to you, but a great deal to me," said Melegaunt. "Even to the best wizards, magic comes slowly and with difficulty. Not so to sorcerers. For them, it is a gift, a natural talent that can be improved with time and practice, but a gift nonetheless. Needless to say, all those wizards who must work at their art tend to be suspicious of those who don't."

"That's an apt description, if ever I heard one," said Galaeron. "Are you an innatoth?"

"Would that I were!" Melegaunt laughed. "I take it you found your Academy of Magic less than accepting?"

"Far less." Galaeron tried to keep the bitterness from his voice. "My father used every political favor he was owed to secure me a place in my regiform, and a more terrible waste I've never seen. I never fit in. Eventually, they accused me of dark magics and demanded to see my spellbook. Unfortunately, I had never kept one."

"Now you're making *me* jealous," Melegaunt said.

Galaeron smiled sadly. "No need. It took Lord Imesfor's intervention to win me a place in the Tomb Guard." He fell silent, recalling the bad end that the high noble's patronage had wrought for his son. In truth, the Gold lord could hardly be blamed for the things he had been saying. "And even that favor has had its price."

"No need to feel sorry for yourself." Melegaunt's voice was at once reproachful and consoling. "It will be your magic that saves Evereska, or I've never cast a spell."

"Did you not say that his magic would draw the phaerimm's attention?" Vala's tone was respectful but concerned. "This is the last place I'd want one of those things to trap me."

Melegaunt smiled. "It would be a better place than you think, but you're right about what I said." He looked to Galaeron. "We must teach our friend to cast magic differently."

"Differently?" Galaeron asked. "That will take time."

"Not for you, I think," said Melegaunt. "Not if you are as brave as you are talented."

"I'm here now."

"Yes." Melegaunt's eyes turned as black as obsidian, so dark that even Vala gasped. "You're brave enough when you meet the monsters outside. Let us see if you have the courage to face the one within."

Melegaunt's face became strangely elflike, his bushy brows rising into arches, his brow becoming high and smooth. His ears grew longer, pushing their sharp tips out through his dusky hair, and his eyes assumed the malevolent gleam of a drow demon.

"Corellon's lute!" Galaeron's head whirled in confusion. This could not be the human who had told him he would be the savior of Evereska—but then again, ever were demons the deceivers of mortals. "What are you?"

"More than you think, I am sure," came the answer.

Knowing he would never have time to cast a spell—and that even if he did, he could not hope to best Melegaunt in a duel of magic—he dropped a hand to his sword. The demon's own hand lashed out as quickly as a jumping spider, caught Galaeron by the throat, and slammed him against the stone wall. A pair of ivory fang tips jutted out beneath Melegaunt's lip, and his shadowy beard changed into a grotesque chin. The humans gasped and murmured, but seemed too bewildered to act. Galaeron tried to draw his sword, but the demon pinned his wrist to the wall.

Vala was the first to recover even a little. "Mighty One!" She freed her blade and stepped forward. "What are you—"

"Stand clear!" Melegaunt glanced over his shoulder. "By the Oath of Bodvar, I charge you obey!"

Vala ground her teeth, but stopped and lowered her sword, then signaled her men to stand fast. When Melegaunt looked back to Galaeron, his eyes were glowing purple, and his fangs were as long as a viper's.

"Do you know what I am, elf? Are you brave now?"

"Y-y-yes." Galaeron could barely choke out the word. Like most surface elves, he feared the drow as much as he hated them, and he could imagine no fate worse than becoming the undead servant of a drow vampire-demon. "Let me have my sword—"

Melegaunt slammed Galaeron against the wall. "I think not." He smiled. "But I give you a choice."

Melegaunt thrust his palm out behind him. "Darksword!"

Vala flipped her hilt around, but hesitated before handing it over. "What are you going to do?"

Melegaunt glared at her, his neck filling the room with unnatural cracking sounds as it turned farther than it should. "Nothing that is not my right by the Granite Tower."

Vala's face fell, and she laid the hilt in his palm. Melegaunt glared at her a moment, then pressed the icy hilt into Galaeron's left hand.

"I give you the choice, elf." He grabbed the weapon by its blade and set the tip beneath Galaeron's jaw. "Serve me or not—your choice."

Galaeron knew no vampire would give him the chance to slay it—but he also knew it would be just like a drow to give him the opportunity then taunt him with his cowardice through the rest of time. He lifted his chin and flipped the black blade forward, drawing the edge across Melegaunt's throat and chest.

The glass passed through the wizard as though his body were smoke. Melegaunt smiled, then plucked the sword from Galaeron's hand.

"Coward." He returned the weapon to Vala, then pinned his captive's head against the wall.

Galaeron struggled, but the drow-demon was too strong. Melegaunt lowered his head, and Galaeron felt two cold pangs in his throat.

"No!"

He brought his knee up into Melegaunt's groin, but even that did not drive the demon away. An icy numbness spread through Galaeron's neck, then Melegaunt raised his head. There were a pair of slowly cooling blood runnels on his chin, and his eyes were glowing damson with mad hunger.

"Do you feel the fear?" he demanded. "Open yourself to it, Galaeron. Embrace it."

Galaeron had no need to open himself to anything. His fear was coursing through him. He could feel it in his hollow stomach, in his heaving chest and hot huffing breath, hear it in his pounding pulse and the wail rising in his throat.

The scream did not quite reach his lips before Melegaunt covered his mouth. "You can't scream, Galaeron." The wizard's face was returning to normal, his pointed ears vanishing into his dusky hair, his arched eyebrows growing straight and bushy. "You mustn't, or the phaerimm will give us all something to fear."

Galaeron pushed Melegaunt away. The wizard sailed across the chamber and slammed into the opposite wall, now looking completely human.

When Galaeron managed not to scream, Melegaunt nodded encouragingly. "Good. Now use it, Galaeron. Use that power inside to cast your spell."

"You're mad! The only thing I'll use it for is to kill you."

Galaeron drew his sword and was instantly separated from Melegaunt by Vala and her men.

"Not like that, elf!" Melegaunt's voice grew stern and commanding. "Will you master your fear, or be its slave?"

Something in the wizard's tone reached Galaeron. He touched his neck where the demon had bit him and felt smooth skin.

"Now, Galaeron!" urged Melegaunt. "Cast the spell!"

Finally beginning to understand, Galaeron let the sword fall and ran his fingers through a series of mystic gestures, then finished by cupping his palm to his ear. His fear did not evaporate as expected, but burned down through him, branding him with raw ribbons of pain that trailed through his body and vanished into the darkness beneath his feet.

Galaeron rolled his hands through the second half of the spell. When he began to rub his brow, the ragged ribbons of pain turned cold, filling him with a biting numbness that started in his feet and shot up through him like icy lightning.

Then Galaeron's mind was filled with wispy voices, all talking at once in half-formed sentences. He let out a groan and covered his ears. Melegaunt stepped past Vala and the others, then took Galaeron by the shoulders and looked into his eyes.

It's a bit confusing. The words sounded inside Galaeron's head, reverberating above a dozen other voices. *You're hearing the thoughts in all of our minds. Think of them as wind, and pay attention only to what you want. It helps to talk until you're accustomed to it.*

Galaeron removed his hands from his ears. "What did you *do* to me?"

"I showed you your shadow self." As Melegaunt had promised, the other voices faded into the background. "Think of it as the wellhead tapping another kind of magic."

"What kind of magic? Vampire? Or drow?"

"Neither—and don't blame me for that thing," chuckled Melegaunt. "What you saw, you made."

Galaeron glared at him. "I didn't make that."

"Not consciously," said Melegaunt, "but whatever a man—or elf—makes, he also makes the shadow of. If he makes himself brave and honest, then he makes a shadow of himself that is not."

"So a man makes a shadow of himself that's a woman?" Vala asked.

"No, that would be the opposite," Melegaunt explained. "A shadow is not opposite, only absence. In the day, it is the absence of the light that your body blocks. In a man, it is the absence of the male, not the presence of the female. In the case of Galaeron's shadow self, it is the absence of kindness and loyalty."

"That thing wasn't part of me," Galaeron insisted.

"No, it wasn't," agreed Melegaunt, "but you created it, and through it, you touched a new magic."

"Then it must be an evil magic." Galaeron retrieved his sword. He could still feel the strange ribbon of coldness that connected him to the ground. "I would that you had never shown it to me."

"Do not let the guardian frighten you." Melegaunt laid a hairy human hand on Galaeron's shoulder. "The greatest treasures are always protected, and this one is key to defeating the phaerimm. It is the only magic they do not understand. If we are to save Evereska, you will need to wield it well, and wield it often."

CHAPTER SEVEN

23 Nightal, the Year of the Unstrung Harp

The phaerimm WarGather lay exactly where Melegaunt had said it would, in the dwarven workings just beyond the breach in the Sharn Wall. A green spell glow hung in the air, barely bright enough to illuminate the room and render Galaeron's dark sight unnecessary. The tiny chamber was packed with phaerimm, the last two feet of their tails dragging on the floor so they could float upright beneath the low ceiling. They were surrounded by swirling clouds of dust, stirred up by a cacophony of strange whistling winds similar to the sand devils he occasionally saw spinning across the sands of Anauroch.

In the back of the room, barely visible through jostling phaerimm and swirling dust clouds, a cage of polished bones barricaded the entrance to a side passage. The vertical bars were made of sturdy human thigh bones, stacked one atop another and fused together with magic. With a lighter color and generally more delicate form, the crossbars were probably elf. The door was a grillwork of ribs interlaced around four skulls, two human and two elf, with sad eyes still floating in the sockets.

The door was hanging ajar, and the attention of the phaerimm seemed to be centered on the tunnel wall beside it, where a pair of elves sat against the stony wall. Through the forest of phaerimm bodies, Galaeron recognized the gilded seams of Kiinyon Colbathin's plate armor. The other figure Galaeron could not identify, though the glimpses of gold thread and red silk suggested it was a high mage.

It was difficult to see more. He and Melegaunt were on the far side of the Sharn Wall, squatting opposite each other to peer through the hole that had been opened by the beholder Shatevar. Vala and her men were a hundred paces away, keeping watch in case any more phaerimm appeared. Even at that distance, their thoughts poured through Galaeron's mind in a constant stream. He tried to focus on the three phaerimm nearest the two prisoners.

Your crudeness has given us nothing but corpses, Tha, said the one nearest Kiinyon. Though it seemed to be addressing its fellow through the swirling winds, Galaeron could understand it only by concentrating on its thoughts. The effort made his head ache, for the message itself was often lost in an emotional muddle of jealousy and contempt. *It is time to let someone more skillful rack them.*

Perhaps, Zay—if there were one more skillful, responded Tha.

The others have screamed their throats raw and told you nothing, countered Zay. *First we must break their will. Only then they will tell us the words.*

Melegaunt tapped Galaeron's arm. *Words?* The wizard did not speak, but only thought the question.

Probably words of passing. Galaeron intentionally avoided any mention of the mythal.

I should have known, Melegaunt responded. *There's a mythal.*

Galaeron scowled. *I said nothing about a mythal.*

Melegaunt shrugged. *Words have shadows, too.*

So I've noticed, Galaeron thought. *But what would Evereska's mythal explain—if there was one, that is?*

Melegaunt smiled knowingly. *Phaerimm need magic in their environment to survive, just as you and I need air. Without it, they starve.*

Then why are they still alive? Galaeron asked. *There can't be much magic in Anauroch.*

More than you think. What do you imagine the Sharn Wall is?

The barrier that imprisons them sustains them? surmised Galaeron. *Cruel.*

Perhaps, but not as cruel as what will they will do to Evereska—if it has a mythal, said Melegaunt. *Phaerimm are solitary, contentious creatures, but there are almost forty of them living close together in the ruins of Myth Drannor.*

Galaeron nodded, already taking the wizard's meaning. The ancient mythal that had once protected Myth Drannor had not perished with the city. Though it had deteriorated over the ages, it was still very powerful—powerful enough, apparently, to nourish a colony of phaerimm. And if the deteriorating magic of Myth Drannor's mythal was enough to sustain forty of the creatures, he could only shudder at the thought of how many Evereska's far stronger mythal might support.

Galaeron shook his head at the thought of the evil he had unleashed.

Melegaunt tapped Galaeron's knee. *You did not unleash this. You were executing a sworn duty. If the blame lies anywhere, it lies with me.*

Galaeron shook his head. *I knew we were in above our heads the instant I saw Vala's beholder, and she warned me so. Had I listened—*

You would have violated your oath to protect the crypts of your ancestors, which is not something Galaeron Nihmedu would do, Melegaunt said. *And had I not been so eager to escape, I would not have instructed Vala to break even a Vyshaan crypt in order to find the dwarven mine. At the least, the fault is ours together, and there is no use second-guessing ourselves. Know that had you been a coward and turned your back on me, the evil you did would have been far greater than this. We are going to set things right, you and I together, but this matter is bigger than Evereska—much bigger. Even were we to fail and Evereska to fall, what you did would still be worth it.*

To a human, perhaps, Galaeron thought.

Though he did not think it consciously, he knew that if Evereska fell, his name would be vilified in the coming ages as terribly as that of the Vyshaan or the drow. On Faerûn, at least, Evereska was the last haven of elven civilization—all that remained of the empires that had founded mighty cities such as Cormanthor and Siluvanede. More determined than ever to find a way to stop the phaerimm—to destroy their entire race, if need be—he turned back to the WarGather.

Having won the argument about the best way to proceed with the interrogation, Zay was holding Kiinyon Colbathin spread-eagled above its—his—toothy maw, flicking his barbed tail across the bloody rents in the tomb master's battered armor.

Would you like that, elf? The phaerimm was using thoughtspeech alone to talk to his prisoner, for the wind language of the phaerimm was clearly not one most elves were likely to speak. *It would be an honor to carry my egg.*

The barbed tail arced down to touch Kiinyon's lips, then the creature motioned to several fellows. They leveled themselves horizontally and ran their own tails over the elf's body, probing for holes and seams in his armor.

Perhaps I will let you carry eggs for all my friends, taunted Zay.

Kiinyon seemed barely conscious enough to notice. His eyes were swollen half shut, his broken nose spread across both cheeks, his lip split so badly that the tip of his tongue showed where there should have been teeth. It was more difficult to tell the condition of the body beneath the armor, save that the deep creases and puckers bespoke plenty of bruises.

Would you like that, slave? All those larva growing inside, slithering through your entrails, eating the food from your stomach?

Impossibly, Kiinyon shook his head and said, "No."

The word was so garbled that Galaeron barely understood it. He was surprised to discover he felt none of the tomb master's pain. Elves who lived even in reasonably close contact were so connected to each other—through the Reverie and the Weave—that they shared at least some shadow of each other's emotional experiences. Instead, Galaeron sensed Kiinyon's anguish and fear only through Melegaunt's eavesdropping spell. There was even—he was ashamed to admit—some small part of him that actually took pleasure in the tomb master's pain.

Galaeron found the strange emotion as puzzling as he did frightening. Elves were not spiteful, for their emotional bonds tended to curb such low passions. In a very real sense, to wish pain on another was to wish it on oneself, and not even the most arrogant Gold was foolish enough to do that. The vile sentiments Galaeron was experiencing seemed all too human.

The phaerimm continued to hold Kiinyon a long time, allowing his fellows to run their barbed tails over the elf's body, until a strange, rhythmic moaning rose from the tomb master's lips. Galaeron did not recognize the sound until the other captive, the elf in the high mage's robes, began to say the Prayer for the Dying.

"Behold, there in the West. There I see my comrades and my lovers, my childhood friends, those who have gone before me and those still to come. There I see them in the tall oaks, high in the limbs where the golden sun lights their faces.

"They are calling my name. They are calling my name. They are calling me West, and there I am going."

The voice was unmistakable. It had not only the clear articulation and eloquent intonation so typical of the Sun elves, it had the same plumy timbre Galaeron had come to know so well over his last two years of duty. The voice belonged, undoubtedly, to Louenghris's father, Lord Imesfor.

One of the phaerimm backhanded the high mage, silencing him, then Zay raised his tail and brought it down hard on Kiinyon's breastplate. The barb penetrated the mithral steel and sank to its base, but Galaeron saw no convulsing muscles as he had when Takari was implanted.

No? Then you must give me a reason, said the phaerimm. *Tell me the first word, and I will let you die without eggs.*

"Goldheart," Kiinyon whispered. "The word is Goldheart."

Liar!

Zay motioned to his fellows, and a dozen barbs pinged through Kiinyon's armor. A couple of the tails began to convulse, but the spasms seemed weaker and more sluggish than the ones that had implanted the egg in Takari. The tomb master screamed, and his body grew puffy and rose toward the ceiling. Only the phaerimm's grasp prevented it from floating all the way.

As astonished as Galaeron was by the strange effect, he was even more astonished to discover he could actually stand to keep watching. By all rights, he should have felt so sickened that he found himself either attacking madly or cowering in fear.

My congratulations, Zay, said Tha, now speaking in the phaerimm's wind language. *The same false answer.*

Zay pushed Kiinyon into the bone cage, where the tomb master floated to the ceiling and hovered helplessly, pinned in place by the strange magic with which the phaerimm had injected him.

The answer cannot be false, said Zay, *only our understanding of it.*

All the same, it has not opened the portal. Tha plucked Lord Imesfor off the floor. *There is only one thing we have not tried. Perhaps the dead can be made to tell what the living cannot.*

Galaeron's heart sank. The phaerimm could be talking about any of several portals into Evereska, but it seemed most likely they meant the Secret Gate, the only way through the mountains from this side. It was also the route by which the Swords of Evereska were leaving the Vale, and Galaeron did not care to think of what might happen when his father emerged from the portal into the arms of a band of phaerimm.

Lord Imesfor began to recite the Prayer for the Dying, this time for himself. Galaeron retreated and turned away. With so many phaerimm in the chamber, he saw no way to effect a rescue, and given the strange, vengeful emotions he had been experiencing, he was not sure he wanted to find out how he would feel when the high mage was killed.

Galaeron felt a tap on his knee and looked up to see Melegaunt. *Come along. We don't have long to plan.*

The wizard slipped past Galaeron, moving down the tunnel to where Vala and her men were gathering. He had to scuttle along like the slave they had glimpsed earlier, for the passage was only four feet in diameter and shaped like a tube—much more comfortable for floating phaerimm than walking humans. Galaeron joined the others and kneeled, his back sore from hunching.

Melegaunt drew a hand across the ceiling and uttered a quiet incantation, creating a curtain of shadow between themselves and the passage into the WarGather. He assigned Dexon to keep a watch on the other side, then turned to the others and motioned for them to speak softly.

"We could slay two or three, but not seventeen," said Melegaunt. "That rules out fighting, so we'll have to do this another way."

Galaeron raised his brow. "If you are thinking of a rescue, you should know that it is Evereskan tenet never to risk many lives in the desperate hope of saving a few."

"And how often is that tenet followed?" asked Melegaunt.

Galaeron smiled. "Not very often."

"I thought so," the wizard said. "Did you see how I opened the shadow path?"

"It was a bit above me," Galaeron admitted. "Though if you took a few moments to teach—"

"No!" Melegaunt's hiss came near to a yell. "That way lies ruin. It is well and good to test yourself with the tame magic of elves, but do not try such a thing with what I have shown you. You will be consumed by your own shadow. Do you understand?"

Somewhat taken aback by Melegaunt's sternness, Galaeron nodded. "I'll use only spells I can handle easily."

"And never mix the two magics." Melegaunt motioned vaguely toward the hole in the Sharn Wall. "We have seen what comes of that."

Again, Galaeron nodded.

"Good. Now, here is what we'll do." He explained his plan, then finished by looking to Vala. "I've seen enough of Kiinyon Colbathin to know he'd hesitate before trusting a human, and there's little reason to imagine a Sun elf high mage would be any less prejudiced. I'm afraid Galaeron must go with you."

Vala studied Galaeron for a moment, then glanced at his scabbard. "Can you handle that thing?"

Suspecting she would be unimpressed by his third place regiform steel-ranking, Galaeron simply nodded. "I can, but the blade wasn't much good against the phaerimm last time."

"Their magic," Melegaunt explained. "Even enchanted steel won't bite."

Vala turned to Dexon. "Will you trade with him until this is over?"

A corner of the human's mustache rose as though he'd rather not, but he nodded. "As long as he understands."

"Understands?"

"If you lose the weapon, his son's name will be lost," said Vala. "In our valley, the noble's title goes with his sword."

Melegaunt frowned at this. "That was never my intention."

"You have been gone a long time," said Vala. "That is how matters have come to be."

"It doesn't matter." Galaeron raised his palms to decline the sword. "I can't hold the sword. The last time I tried, my fingers nearly froze off."

"You will not feel the cold this time," said Melegaunt.

He nodded to Vala, who removed her scabbard and leaned it against the wall, then kneeled facing Galaeron. He removed his own scabbard and passed it to Dexon, and took his own place across from Vala. Melegaunt struck a torch. He had both Galaeron and Vala bound and gagged and stationed a warrior behind each. He took his glassy dagger from its sheath, and kneeling alongside Vala, began his incantation.

A pall of shadow darkened Vala's eyes, and her expression changed instantly to one of vanity and suspicion. Still uttering the syllables of his spell, Melegaunt ran his glassy dagger along the floor beside her, cutting free the shadow cast by the lit torch. Vala's eyes grew instantly feral and angry. She spun on Melegaunt, hurling herself into the air sideways and slamming her knees into his ribs despite her bound feet. Kuhl threw himself over her, pinning her to the floor beneath his big body and holding her there motionless.

Now separated from its body, Vala's shadow rose to its feet and stood upright, bending along the tunnel's curved wall in a way her body never could have. The shadow retrieved the scabbard from where Vala had leaned it, then turned to wait for Galaeron.

Galaeron could not tear his gaze from the thrashing body pinned beneath Kuhl. As Melegaunt kneeled beside him and began the incantation, Galaeron's heart pounded wildly. The thought that he would go as mad as Vala terrified him. Elf spirits were, after all, different than human souls, and he was not at all certain he would find his way back to his body. Still, he forced himself to remain calm and motionless, for he was troubled by the vengeful emotions he had experienced earlier and determined to redeem himself—in his own eyes, if no one else's.

Galaeron had the feeling of being drawn into the stone, then found himself looking up at his own body, trying to peer past Melegaunt as he drew the glassy knife along the ground beside his leg. He could actually feel the blade, icy and sharp, cutting him free of his body. As the wizard finished, Galaeron was seized by a terrible coldness. His body became a wild thing, whirling around at the waist in a mad effort to slam its head into Melegaunt.

Dexon hurled himself onto Galaeron's body, slamming it to the ground and pinning it there. Galaeron felt a pang of concern for the wild thrashing thing, but put it out of his mind and lifted Dexon's scabbard off the man's belt. He hung it where the hooks would have been on his own belt, as Melegaunt had instructed, and the scabbard melted into his form. Galaeron reached down and felt the hilt beneath his palm, but sensed no weight on his hip. Nor did he notice anything particularly cold about the weapon. Rather, it seemed to him that the whole world—the tunnel walls, the darksword, his own form—had become the very substance of cold.

"Ready?" Vala's voice was wispy and deep.

Galaeron nodded and followed her up the tunnel, not walking so much as flowing along the walls. He suffered a moment of disorientation as he slipped through the shadow curtain Melegaunt had hung across the passage, then continued toward the phaerimm's spell glow. Vala glided across the ceiling as he slid across the floor, and together they streamed through the opening into the dwarven workings.

Zay was clutching Lord Imesfor in two hands, holding a third hand over the elf's mouth to keep him from uttering any unexpected enchantments, and using a fourth hand to tug at the high mage's golden rings. Because many of the rings were too small to fit over the elf's broken fingers, the phaerimm was carefully popping each digit off at the appropriate knuckle. Lord Imesfor accepted this with remarkable calm, glaring at his torturer more in anger than pain.

Beneath Lord Imesfor lay a veritable pile of amulets, bracers, girdles, and other magic items Zay had already removed from the high mage's body. A half dozen of the other phaerimm were floating inches off the dusty floor, pawing through the treasure and arguing about who had the right to claim what. Tha already held the high mage's book of war spells in one hand, but that did not prevent the monster from snatching a silver diadem from one of his fellows. Galaeron hoped the greed fest was enough of a display to hold the attention of the others. Without knowing where their eyes were located, he had the constant feeling that they were watching him.

Vala drifted into the shadows on the ceiling and started toward Lord Imesfor. Galaeron slid along the wall, creeping along in small, flickering motions that he hoped would look like normal shadow movements. Melegaunt had assured him that while the monsters could see normal magic as easily as an elf saw at night, the creatures had never detected any spell he cast using his "other source of magic." The wizard had been unable to tell Galaeron whether they could see normal things—like shadows.

Galaeron made his way along the edge of the chamber, then entered the darkness in order to cross the tunnel. As he did so, he felt something cold pulling at him, trying to draw him deeper into the darkness. The spell glow became a green sphere in the far distance, and it took him a moment to realize it was growing smaller. He bit back a cry of alarm and concentrated on moving toward the green light. It grew as large as before, filling the chamber in front of him. Deciding he would rather be discovered by the phaerimm than dragged into the darkness by whatever had grabbed him, he crossed to the other side at the edge of the light and slipped between the bone bars.

The cage was cluttered with listless elves, all with an inflamed puncture wound somewhere on their torsos. They were in various states of ague, and many had fallen into a sort of comatose trance beyond all hope of recovery. The worst had arm-sized snakes writhing beneath their skin, usually along the path of their intestines, but sometimes coiled over their hearts or girding their ribs.

In the center of the cage floated the great Kiinyon Colbathin, stripped naked and clawing at his wounds. Unlike the wounds of the other prisoners, his punctures showed no sign of inflammation or infection. Recalling how Takari had immediately fallen into a stupor and how her wound had swollen, it seemed unlikely that the tomb master had been injected with an egg. Galaeron streamed across the ceiling and pressed himself to the tomb master's far side.

Kiinyon shuddered and cried out. Galaeron slipped a shadowy hand over the elf's mouth and felt it sink into flesh. The tomb master's voice shrieked through it unmuffled.

Several nearby phaerimm turned their open mouths toward the cage. Galaeron wrapped himself around Kiinyon's body and hoped he was truly as unnoticeable as Melegaunt had promised. The tomb master began to shiver. The phaerimm kept their mouths pointed toward the cage. Finally, Kiinyon could no longer contain himself and let out a single groan of fear.

The phaerimm swung their heads away, chuckling in their strange wind language. Galaeron waited until they had turned back to the pile of magic treasure, then pressed his shadowy lips to Kiinyon's ear.

"Master Colbathin, hold your tongue or I swear by the Black Arrow I'll leave you here," whispered Galaeron. "Understand?"

Kiinyon's eyes grew round as plates.

"Do you know who this is?"

Kiinyon nodded, though his eyes held a thousand questions.

"Good. I won't waste time asking whether you are happy to see me," said Galaeron, "but if you want to live, you must comfort Lord Imesfor with the Prayer for the Dying."

The tomb master remained silent, looking first to his own wounds, then to the inflamed punctures of an elf lying nearby.

"Whatever the phaerimm injected you with, it wasn't eggs, or you'd be as sick as everyone else," said Galaeron. "Now, say the prayer if you wish to live."

Instead of obeying, Kiinyon whispered, "What of the others?"

Galaeron looked at their listless forms, and his heart grew as heavy as gold. "They're not going to move themselves, and you felt what happened when I tried to cover your mouth. Do you have a way to carry them?"

"No." Kiinyon closed his eyes, no doubt coming to the same conclusion as Galaeron. Their only choice was whether to leave and let the others die alone, or stay and die with them. "This isn't right."

"No, it isn't, but we'll do what we can." On the ceiling outside, Galaeron saw a shadow flicker back and forth and realized Vala was signaling him. "We're out of time. Speak if you wish to live."

Kiinyon shook his head at the awfulness of the decision, but said, "I *must* live." A cry of fear sounded around the corner, and Kiinyon looked toward the door. "Have strength, Imesfor. Behold, there in the West—"

The prayer was interrupted by the deafening trill of an anguished phaerimm. Galaeron slipped to the front of the cage, then took a position on the wall. On the floor beyond the door lay a crooked phaerimm arm, severed cleanly at the biceps and resting in a pool of rusty blood. Lord Imesfor lay on the chamber floor, holding his mangled hands to his chest, his neck craned back to stare up in shock at the stump of Zay's amputated arm.

Zay shrieked something too fast for Galaeron to understand even with Melegaunt's eavesdropping spell, then reached for Imesfor again. Vala's darksword drove down from the ceiling, appearing out of the shadows as though wielded by the rock itself, and buried itself in Zay's thorny back.

Zay screeched and spun in the air, pulling Vala half off the ceiling. For an instant, her torso hung stretched between the ceiling and the writhing phaerimm, a vaguely female silhouette holding a very three-dimensional glassy black sword. Then she turned the blade into the roll, and the shadowy edge began to cut again. Zay's body opened around the middle and spilled steaming gore into the dust. Vala barely had time to pull herself back onto the rock before a storm of fire and lightning blasted the ceiling.

Galaeron slipped around the corner, then spoke in High Elvish. "Into the cage with you!" He had to shout to make himself heard. "To Kiinyon's side, and into the tunnel of shadow!"

The high mage's eyes went wide, but he rolled to his knees and, using his mangled hands like forepaws, scrambled for the cage.

It's the yellow one! trilled Tha, pointing at Lord Imesfor. *It's his*—

Galaeron drew his borrowed darksword and saw it appear in the air. He silenced Tha with a vicious slash across both jaw hinges, and the phaerimm's mouth fell open gurgling blood. Galaeron sheathed his sword and continued across the floor, streaming safely away even as the stone behind him erupted into a spray of molten magic.

Melegaunt's deep voice rose briefly from the direction of the Sharn Wall. A shaft of spinning shadow shot from the breach across the chamber, knocking shocked phaerimm aside like a battering ram. It extended through the cage door and stopped. Tiny tendrils of shadow twirled off the end like threads off a fraying sweater cuff, weaving themselves through the bone bars of the cage.

This time, the phaerimm were quicker to recover—far too quick for Galaeron's liking. A dozen whirled around, flinging every manner of magic at Melegaunt. Whether the attacks troubled the wizard was impossible to say, for the instant the spells touched the Sharn Wall, they exploded into searing heat. Those attacks aimed into the breach simply vanished into the whirling shaft of shadow, then came spinning back out a few seconds later.

The remaining phaerimm turned their attention to Galaeron's side of the chamber, flinging meteor swarms and ice storms toward the bone cage. The brunt of the attack vanished into the shadow net spinning off the end of the shadow column, but enough of the spells penetrated to fill the air with the stench of scorched flesh and half-lucid elf screams.

Galaeron flowed across the floor and took a position on the wall opposite the door, ready to attack when the phaerimm tried to pass through the net of shadow. Through the mesh of dark tendrils, he could just make out the figure of Lord Imesfor struggling with his fingerless hands to shove sick elves into the mouth of the shadow tunnel. Kiinyon was helping as much as possible, but trapped as he was against the ceiling, he was even less efficient than the high mage.

Galaeron started to wonder where Vala's humans were, but his question was answered when he saw a pair of thick hands pulling a sick elf into the mouth of the tunnel. The other two men were, of course, continuing to wrestle with his body and Vala's.

Realizing their magic was no more able to pass through the Sharn Wall from the outside than the inside, the phaerimm on Melegaunt's side of the chamber concentrated on the whirling column of shadow. As before, their spells simply vanished into the blackness, then came spinning back out. One of the phaerimm even tried to break into the shaft. He lost two arms to the whirling darkness. Another created a blazing orb that illuminated the whole chamber in brilliant silver light, but of course where there was light, there was shadow. The shaft became a writhing, snakelike thing weaving along through the dark corners of the cavern, bowing up behind the moving phaerimm, then disappearing into the dust beneath their floating bodies.

The phaerimm on Galaeron's side of the chamber were more successful. A pair floated alongside the shaft and paused before the cage. The polished bones fell away from each other, collapsing into a heap on the floor and leaving only the shadowy mesh that had spun off the end of Melegaunt's tunnel. One dared push a finger through the mesh. When it passed through without being torn off, the creature pushed an entire hand through—and promptly lost it to Vala's darksword.

The phaerimm's reactions were far quicker than they should have been, at least by elf standards. The creature simply lashed out with its remaining hands and caught hold of the sword hilt, easily jerking it free of Vala's shadowy grasp. The creature trilled at the weapon's icy touch, but held on as its companion blasted the wall with lightning and magic.

Galaeron was on the thing in an instant, flowing across the tunnel ceiling and slashing his own blade across the width of its body. The phaerimm all but exploded, spraying the tunnel with a green ichor and dropping to the floor in a heap of thorny flesh.

It was harder to kill than that. The thing rolled to its back, spraying the ceiling with a long stream of fire. Galaeron shrieked as the heat struck his leg. He flowed down the wall and along the floor, placing the other phaerimm between himself and the one he had just wounded.

Whistling in anguish, the creature on the floor dragged itself away through the dust. Galaeron searched the walls and floor for Vala, but she was as hidden to him as to the phaerimm.

Coward! accused the phaerimm he was hiding behind. Switching Vala's sword from one hand to the other, the creature pushed through the icy net toward the fleeing elves. *They're just shades!*

Galaeron brought his darksword up and severed the hand holding Vala's weapon, then caught the darksword as it fell. He whipped the blade around and plunged it deep into the yelling phaerimm. The creature reacted by spraying the floor with raw magic. Galaeron flowed up the wall, screaming at Kiinyon and Imesfor in High Elvish.

"That's it! We've saved all we can."

The wounded phaerimm turned toward his voice and blasted the wall with lightning, but Galaeron was already back on the floor, slashing at the thing's underside with both swords to hold its attention. Kiinyon and Imesfor did not make things any easier. There were only three elves left in the cage, and the high mage paused to snatch one up in his dismembered hands before hurling himself into the shadow tunnel. Kiinyon grabbed the other two by their collars and slowly kicked his way across the ceiling, dragging them along behind him.

Galaeron escaped another flurry of fire and ice by flowing onto the ceiling, then glanced back to see half a dozen phaerimm floating through the shadow net. Realizing he would never stop them all with his swords, he slipped the weapons into his belt—or, rather, where his belt would have been—then plucked off a lock of his shadowy hair. Moving along the ceiling to avoid being impaled by a spear of golden light, he opened himself to his fear as Melegaunt had taught him.

With so many phaerimm approaching, fear was an easy commodity to come by. It flooded into him, bringing with it that eerie, cold energy he had felt earlier. He tossed the tress of hair at the phaerimm and uttered an improvised wind spell.

A howling gale tore through the cage, blasting the phaerimm with a solid wall of dust. The spell was hardly enough to injure them, but it made them pause in a moment of caution. That was all Kiinyon needed. Carried along by the gust, he floated past the blindly slashing claw of the last phaerimm and vanished into the shadow tunnel.

Thinking to make the best of the opportunity, Galaeron drew his swords again and swung around to finish off his wounded enemy—then felt a shadowy hand grab his wrist.

"Time to go, elf," Vala called. She jerked him into the shadow tunnel. "And give me my sword!"

CHAPTER EIGHT

24 Nightal, the Year of the Unstrung Harp

Galaeron's body hung on him like human armor, heavy and hot and painfully ill-fitted. His shoulders ached, his head throbbed, his neck wouldn't turn. The hand holding his corner of the floating litter was so frozen he doubted the fingers would unbend, and still he counted himself lucky. Dexon, who had been holding him down, had two black eyes, a missing tooth, and so many bruises that they looked like camouflage in the dusky realm.

A gurgling shriek rose from the center of the litter. Galaeron and the other stretcher bearers—Kiinyon, Vala, and her three men—stopped and spun toward the sound. A catatonic elf was thrashing about, coughing, choking, and clubbing fellow patients. Even from the edge of the platform, an arm-sized phaerimm larva could be seen writhing about under his skin, flickering across his breast as it worked its way up into the elf's throat. Galaeron instinctively stretched out a hand, as did Kiinyon on the other side, but the victim was surrounded by a dozen fellow patients and well beyond reach.

"Keep him quiet!" Melegaunt rushed back and vaulted onto the litter, paying no attention to those he stepped on, then slapped a hand over the elf's mouth. "Put us down."

Galaeron and the others obeyed. By the time Melegaunt dragged the warrior off the litter, only the larva tail remained visible, a fingerlike cord worming up toward the gullet. The wizard dropped a knee across the elf's chest, then slipped his dagger tip under the skin and exposed a spine-covered tentacle as big around as Galaeron's arm. He pulled the thing out of its victim and pinned it down while he sliced off the tiny mouth atop its body.

The wizard was not quite finished when the elf's foot swung into the murk alongside their path. He started to slide into the darkness, but was too weak to do more about it than whimper. Galaeron lunged for his arm—then was nearly knocked off his feet by one of Melegaunt's huge arms.

"Don't!"

"Something has him!" Galaeron tried to push past.

Melegaunt held him back. "And it will have you, if you're fool enough to challenge it!"

As the warrior was dragged off, his glassy eyes rolled toward the wizard's face and remained there until he vanished into the shadows. The wizard turned away, his own expression as hard as it was unreadable.

"Take up your friends and keep moving." He motioned to the big shadow stretcher. "We must go before more *shadator* come."

Only Kiinyon did not reach for his corner. "We can't leave him."

"We can and we must." Melegaunt started forward again. "Shadator seldom come alone."

Kiinyon did not move. "Elves are not cowards. We do not abandon the spirits of our dead to places such as this."

Melegaunt turned, this time with an expression of genuine sorrow. "I am sorry for your friend, but there is truly nothing we can do. When the rest of the shadator arrive, they will strike at more capable prey. They'll attack from below, at first taking only one or two of us. But the feeding frenzy will start quickly, and all our spirits will be left to the dark. Is that what you want?"

"Of course not." Kiinyon's face was silver with rage. "But I've seen enough of your magic to know you can do something."

Melegaunt's eyes went dark. "Sadly, you are mistaken." The wizard started to walk again. "You may stay if you wish. It is all the same to me."

Eyes bulging, Kiinyon started after him. "You . . . will . . . not!"

Realizing the tomb master had been robbed of self-control—and perhaps even his wits—by the past few days of death and defeat, Galaeron blocked his way.

"Master Colbathin, if Melegaunt says he has done everything possible, he has. It's only because of him that you are here at all. I was ready to give you up for dead, but he insisted it was possible to rescue you."

Kiinyon's fiery gaze shifted to Galaeron—a definite improvement, since Galaeron was not likely to grow impatient and blast the tomb master into shadows.

"Why am I not surprised?" Kiinyon said. "You and your lazy magic—I should've known you were a coward, too."

"That's enough." Vala stepped to Galaeron's side.

Though her tone was calm, the blow that followed was not. The tomb master was rocked back into Burlen's waiting grasp, where his arms were pinned to his side. Vala produced a black cord and tied his hands.

"Galaeron deserves this abuse no more than does Melegaunt." Whether she was speaking to Kiinyon or Lord Imesfor was unclear. She was looking past the tomb master toward the high mage, whose glassy eyes barely seemed to notice the confrontation. "Nor do we have time for it."

"Do as you must." Lord Imesfor held his arms crossed in front of him, his mangled hands pressed to his chest. "The tomb master will understand when he returns to his senses."

The high mage inclined his head toward their backtrail.

Galaeron looked and saw a ghostly silhouette crossing the light between two shadow hills, four short tentacles where there should have been a nose. He looked away casually, then asked, "Illithids?"

"They've been following us for some time," said the high mage. "I was wondering if they're native to this plane."

"No." Despite the softness of his voice, Melegaunt sounded angry. "They're servitors to our enemy. The phaerimm, I fear, have figured out how to track us."

He gestured in Burlen's direction. The warrior gasped in surprise, then blinked in confusion.

"You will grow accustomed to it soon enough," said Melegaunt. "Someone must keep watch behind us."

Burlen waved a cautious hand behind his helmet. "You might have warned me. This is . . . unnatural."

Melegaunt waved at the maze of shadow and light around them. "Four eyes are as natural as anything here."

The wizard nodded to Vala, then started to walk away. She tossed Kiinyon onto the shadow litter with the patients, then Galaeron and the others took up their positions and followed.

Lord Imesfor scurried to catch Melegaunt. "Perhaps we should tarry. If the shadators are attracted by sound, we might use them to spare ourselves the trouble of ambushing the illithids later."

Melegaunt continued to walk, and quickly. "A good plan, but one we've no time for. Now that the phaerimm have finally discovered where we are, they'll move to cut us off."

"Finally?" asked Lord Imesfor. "The high mages *did* try shadowalking."

Earlier in the journey, Imesfor had related how Evereska's army had stumbled into a phaerimm ambush, then been unable to escape via teleport spells, magical gates, or dimension doors. Each time, they ran headlong into another trap, until all that remained were handfuls of scattered survivors. The final blow came when Imesfor attempted to planewalk to Evermeet, only to emerge where they had found him.

"I'm sorry," said Imesfor. "We won't escape through the shadows."

"If we hurry," said Melegaunt. "The shadows are a big place, and there are only two ways to track someone through them."

"Of course. One is to follow physically." Lord Imesfor craned his neck meaningfully toward the rear. "The other is far easier. Track their magic."

"Exactly." Melegaunt's smile managed to be both patient and condescending. "Tracking elven magic is easy, but mine is another story."

Galaeron resisted the urge to look back, for he saw what the wizard was planning. As long as they believed themselves unobserved, the illithids would bide their time and wait for the phaerimm to attack. If Melegaunt and the others could slip away before then, they could reach Evereska unmolested.

Lord Imesfor did not share Galaeron's faith. "You're telling me the phaerimm cannot see your magic?"

"It's true," Galaeron said, speaking from his place near the front of the litter. "Nor can they defend themselves from it. You saw how the darkswords cut through their shieldings."

Imesfor glanced at Galaeron, then back to Melegaunt. "How?" His tone was not as disbelieving as thoughtful, but there was a hint of condemnation to it. "I don't understand."

Melegaunt's voice grew harsh. "What is there to understand? All you need know is that I can get you past the phaerimm. Do you wish that, or not?"

"Of course." Lord Imesfor kept his voice carefully level. "But there is no sense returning to Evereska. Perhaps you could guide us to Waterdeep?"

"Waterdeep?" This from Kiinyon. "You would ask humans for help?"

Imesfor looked back, sneaking a glance toward their pursuers. A flash of concern suggested he had seen one.

"I mean to ask help of whoever will give it," said the high mage.

"Human help comes at a dear price," Kiinyon said.

Imesfor's eyes narrowed. "I am sure our companions—no, our *rescuers*—understand the strain you have been under."

"We do," said Melegaunt. "Regardless, we cannot take you to Waterdeep."

"I thought as much," said Kiinyon. "Just like a human to open the floodgates of hell and run for high ground."

Finally losing patience, Melegaunt wagged a crooked finger back at the tomb master. "The place I am running is to call the only help that will save your miserable kingdom, which is more than your kind . . ." Melegaunt let the sentence trail off, then his face turned as dark as his hair. "Elves! You are too full of tricks for your own good."

"Perhaps so," said Lord Imesfor. "But then again, your kind have always seemed to measure what is good for others by what is best for yourselves."

Melegaunt's bushy brows came together. "*My* kind?"

Now it was Imesfor's turn to smirk. "Whatever that may be. No normal human would have the power—or reason—to live so long in the caverns of the phaerimm."

Melegaunt studied the high mage a moment longer, then glanced at Kiinyon, and finally looked to Vala. "You may as well cut Master Colbathin free and let him pull his share. He and Lord Imesfor have been playing us a little bit for fools, I think."

Vala drew her darksword, and without breaking stride, slashed the tomb master's bonds off. "We have a saying in my home," she said darkly. "The fur of the clever fox is the finest."

Kiinyon smiled and jumped off the litter. "Then I shall have to take care you don't skin me."

Melegaunt turned to Lord Imesfor. "I'll see you safely out of the Shaeradim, then you can teleport to Waterdeep or wherever you like to ask for help."

"I see." Imesfor's golden eyes betrayed his disappointment. "I thank you for that much, at least."

"Thank me later, when I return to Evereska with the only help that will save it," said Melegaunt.

"Very well, I will thank you then." The high mage still did not sound convinced. "Unfortunately, there are a few minor complications . . ."

The complications were anything but minor. First, there was the matter of teleporting. Even with his fingers torn off, Lord Imesfor was capable of casting the spell, as it required nothing more than a complicated string of mystic syllables. Unfortunately, he had used all such enchantments in the attempt to save Evereska's army and could not teleport himself or anyone else until he studied the spell again.

Melegaunt solved this problem—rather reluctantly—by lending his own spellbook to the high mage. This occasioned hard feelings when he caught the elf puzzling over other spells, especially since Imesfor's accusatory manner in defending his actions suggested the enchantments were of a dangerous—if not outright corrupting—nature. Melegaunt's only response was to nod curtly and turn back to the spell Imesfor was supposed to be studying.

The second problem proved more difficult. Even at his best, Imesfor could not teleport all of the wounded elves to Waterdeep. Galaeron suggested a detour to drop them off at Evereska, but when they turned in that direction, the illithids rushed to catch up. Melegaunt veered away from the vale. When the illithids fell back, he gave Kiinyon a small light, telling him to take Vala's men and the litter and follow the light to safety in the Secret Gate. Eager to look after Keya and find out how his father and the Swords of Evereska were faring, Galaeron volunteered to accompany Kiinyon on the perilous journey back to the Vale. Melegaunt had other ideas, asking for Galaeron to accompany him so he would be able to reenter the Vale when he returned with help. This arrangement did much to reassure Lord Imesfor, who approved the plan wholeheartedly, sternly announcing that if he could sacrifice a son to the war, Galaeron could stand not knowing the fate of his father and sister for a few tendays.

Galaeron stayed. Melegaunt masked Kiinyon's departure with a shadow illusion, and the illithids did not seem to notice until much later, when the illusory shapes of the missing party members finally faded into wisps of black fog. Even then, the creatures seemed rather confused, sending a trio of scouts to search for their missing quarry. Two of the scouts vanished into the shadows and never returned. The third met some horrible end, as evidenced by the hissing screech that came from the direction it had gone.

The sound was more than enough to convince the rest of the illithids that the time for stealth was past. More than a dozen tentacle-faced silhouettes materialized out of the darkness, seeming to float forward in their long robes. Neither Galaeron nor Imesfor needed to be told to run. The creatures considered thousand-year-old elf corpses something of a delicacy, and the tomb guard was always having to fight them off.

Vala, on the other hand, did not seem to understand what the creatures could do if she allowed them to see her eyes. She drew her darksword and turned to face them—then screamed, grabbed her ears, and collapsed in a quivering heap.

Melegaunt spun and attacked without looking at the creatures, spraying a long chain of ebony bolts in every direction. "Get her!"

Galaeron was already scooping the woman into his arms. In her heavy scale armor, she weighed half again as much as he did, but there was no time to cast a spell to levitate her. Once the creatures were close enough, they could blast the thoughts from a victim's mind without making eye contact.

As Galaeron hefted Vala over his shoulder, the darksword slipped from her grasp and disappeared on the dark ground. Knowing what she would do to him if he rescued her but not her sword, he dropped to a knee and ran his hand through the shadow mist until he hit something and felt his fingers go cold.

"What are you doing?" Melegaunt let loose with a long chain of black lightning bolts. Something hissed and fell, and he growled, "Hurry!"

Galaeron grasped the sword by the blade and lifted it out of shadows. Trying not to notice he had just sliced the pads off two fingertips, he tossed the weapon into the air and managed to catch it by the hilt. His palm began to sting with cold.

"Got it!"

He turned to flee toward Lord Imesfor, who stood a dozen paces ahead shaking his useless hands in anger. Melegaunt caught Galaeron by the shoulder and guided him past the high mage.

"This way!"

Melegaunt paused to make certain Lord Imesfor was keeping up with them, then ducked down a corridor of shadow. They ran no more than twenty paces before the first illithid rounded the corner behind them, its breath hissing down the dark gorge. Melegaunt flung a finger over his shoulder and unleashed a storm of black meteors behind them.

Burdened as Galaeron was with Vala's armored body, he was breathing so hard he barely heard the illithids' strangled shrieks. Melegaunt led the way around a bend in the dark passage and came to an intersection, one route veering off between two hill shapes toward a distant wedge of light, the other snaking deeper into the darkness.

Melegaunt pushed Lord Imesfor toward the light. "That way, no more than a hundred paces! You'll come out near the Marsh of Chelimber."

The lord's eyes grew wide. "We've come that far?"

"Yes!" The soft sound of hissing began to sound around the corner behind them. Melegaunt pushed the high mage toward the light. "Run, and cast your spell the instant you see the marsh."

Lord Imesfor sprinted for the light, groaning in pain as he pumped his mangled hands. Galaeron turned to flee in the opposite direction, but was surprised to feel a beefy hand catch him by the shoulder. He turned to see Melegaunt holding a finger to his lips, then watched in growing puzzlement as the wizard drew a veil of shadow down in front of them.

The illithids reached the intersection a moment later. Galaeron was so frightened he barely noticed the icy numbness creeping up the hand that held Vala's sword, but the creatures turned away and rushed after Lord Imesfor.

As Galaeron listened to the procession hiss past, he began to feel steadily sicker and more revolted. He kept waiting for Melegaunt to spring his trap, to step from behind the shadowy screen and spray the horrid creatures with some immensely powerful spell that would slay them all instantly. Melegaunt remained silent and motionless, save that he reached over to take Vala's sword when he noticed how white Galaeron's hand was growing.

Finally, Galaeron's shock gave way to the realization that the wizard had no intention of ambushing the illithids, that he had simply been using Lord Imesfor as a decoy. He dumped Vala's limp form onto the shadow-misted ground, then drew his own sword and started past Melegaunt.

The wizard planted a hand in the middle of Galaeron's chest, stopping him short. "Pick her up. You'll attract a shadator."

Galaeron shook his head. "I see how it is with you humans." He pressed the edge of his blade to Melegaunt's throat. "Save yourselves and sacrifice us!"

"You see less than I thought." Melegaunt wrapped his free hand around Galaeron's sword. Such were the wizard's protective enchantments that even its magic blade did not cut him. "Lord Imesfor will survive, so long as he does what I told him to do."

"You can't know that."

"Can't I?" He pushed Galaeron's sword away. "Even if I could not, would Lord Imesfor hesitate to use you as a decoy? Would you *want* him to, if it meant saving Evereska?"

Galaeron lowered his sword. "You should have warned him."

"Would he have trusted me?" Melegaunt returned Vala's sword to its scabbard, then picked her up himself. "Whatever you think, *we* are the ones who must reach our destination. Any help Imesfor finds in Waterdeep—or even in Evermeet—will do no more to stop the phaerimm than Kiinyon and his tomb guards. You, at least, have seen enough to know that is true."

✡✡✡✡✡

It was one those rare moments that were growing ever rarer, when Khelben "Blackstaff" Arunsun was both idle enough to join his lady Laeral for her highsun "nap" and relaxed enough to enjoy it—when his troubles were far from mind and no worldly problems weighed on his shoulders, and so he was most decidedly *un*happy to hear the boots of an apprentice pounding up the stairs.

"Master Blackstaff!" It was young Ransford, the most excitable of the novices and—at that moment, at least—the most reckless. "Lady Silverhand!"

"Ouch." Laeral turned her head and raised a dreamy green eye toward Khelben. "Gently, my dear."

Khelben looked down and saw that the knuckles of his hands—the hands that had, until two seconds ago, been gently kneading Laeral's shoulders—had gone white. He forced them open, then forced out a calming breath, then forced his voice to remain calm.

"Sorry, love."

"Awake, my lord!" Ransford's cry grew more urgent as he drew nearer. "My lady, awake!"

Listening to crunch of his own grinding teeth, Khelben swung his knee over Laeral's back and placed both feet heavily on the floor. "If this is about three-legged frogs again, I'll have that lad's tongue for a potion of ventriloquism."

He pulled on his black robe, then tossed Laeral's silver shift to her.

Ransford reached the landing and pounded on the door. "My lord, *wake—*"

"Quiet, lad!" Khelben jerked the door open so quickly that Ransford came stumbling across the threshold all elbows and knees. "Don't you know what 'nap' means?"

"I'm sorry, Master Blackstaff, but—" Ransford caught a flash of pale skin as Laeral slipped into her shift, then blushed and fell into a fit of stuttering. "B-b-but—"

"What?" Khelben grabbed the boy's ear. "Out with it."

"Th-th-there's an e-e-elf," he stammered. "A-a-and an, an ill-ill-illillill . . . just come and see!"

Ransford took Khelben by the hand and led him over to the window, but the boy was so excited that Khelben had to speak the word of transparency himself. When he did, he was so surprised he nearly began to stutter himself.

In the courtyard outside, a mangled elf with no fingers was kicking and flailing at a single mind flayer, trying in grim desperation to pull one of the thing's tentacles out of a small round hole in his skull.

"By the Weave, Laeral!" Khelben thrust a hand toward his namesake staff and, in the same instant, felt the familiar comfort of its polished wood. "I think that's Gervas Imesfor down there!"

CHAPTER NINE

24 Nightal, the Year of the Unstrung Harp

It seemed a lifetime since Galaeron had last felt the glaring sun of the Desert Border on his face, or bathed in the moon's milky light, or glimpsed even a star's blue twinkle, and he felt hungry for light—not the flat, toneless white radiance of these endless shadowlands, but real light. Light he could feel, hot and stinging against his skin, light that would make him thirsty and burn the musty smell of sweat from his cloak. Light that would give him some sense of direction, that would mark the passing time by its ebbing and flowing.

They had been marching for what seemed hours, but might have been mere minutes or days unending, winding through a labyrinth of sinuous shapes and sharp-edged silhouettes. Galaeron's mind had long since stopped trying to make sense of the patterns and merely classified them as passing forms. If the lack of light troubled Melegaunt, he showed no sign of it. He simply marched along, leading the way ever onward at the same brisk pace.

Vala, now recovered from her brush with the illithid, followed close on the wizard's heels. Though she never complained, Galaeron could tell by the weariness of her stride and the way she craned her neck skyward that she missed the light as much as he did.

They seemed to be approaching some sort of shadow border, a curtain of utter darkness that Galaeron kept glimpsing at the far end of long shadowy channels, or looming up beyond hill shapes. Whenever the curtain came into view, the stretch he saw was longer. Sometimes he saw two stretches at once, one spanning a broad shadowbed, the other rising behind a nearby slope. Each time, the curtain seemed higher and darker and somehow deeper, as though it were not so much a barrier, but a vast expanse of pure, unlit darkness.

Finally, they rounded a corner and saw nothing but black curtain in any direction, its billowing crown silhouetted against the lighter purple of the shadow sky, its dark feet rooted in the swirling black ground mists. Vala's shoulders slumped, and a sigh almost too faint to hear slipped her lips, and Galaeron knew he had to say something to Melegaunt before he and Vala went mad.

"Melegaunt, wait."

The wizard spun on his heel, his dark eyes searching the dusky landscape behind his two charges. "What's wrong?"

"Nothing, except I'm about to lose my mind," said Galaeron. "Doesn't this bother you?"

"This?" Melegaunt looked around. "After the Phaerlin? You must be joking."

The wizard started toward the shadowy curtain ahead. Vala started after him, but stopped and looked back when she realized Galaeron was not following.

"Are you coming, elf?" she asked.

"Not in there." Galaeron gestured at the blackness ahead. "I'm not going any deeper until I've had a few minutes of sunshine."

Melegaunt turned. "Deeper?"

"Into the shadow." Again, Galaeron pointed at the dark curtain. "Just a few minutes in the light—please?"

Vala nodded her agreement. "In truth, this gloom wears on the nerves. I could use a little sunshine myself—especially if we're going deeper."

"Deeper?" Melegaunt scowled and looked into the darkness ahead. "Deeper into what?"

"Shadow," Galaeron said. "Even I can see that—"

"It's a forest," Melegaunt growled.

Galaeron frowned. Now that the wizard mentioned it, the curtain did resemble the gloomy edge of a deep wood, and the billowing crown was shaped like a forest's outer canopy.

"The Forgotten Forest, to be exact," said Melegaunt. "I'd never take you beyond the Fringe."

"The Fringe?" asked Galaeron.

"The boundary between the worlds of light and the Shadow Deep." Melegaunt waved his arm at the surrounding terrain. "Neither of you would last a hundred steps beyond the Fringe."

Vala scowled and started to object, but Galaeron cut her off by asking, "*Worlds* of light?"

"There are many worlds, young elf. The Shadow Deep connects them all. It's the one mirror that shapes their many lights." Melegaunt started forward again. "And now, if you'd please start walking again, you will see your precious light again in Dekanter. I'd like to be there before the Shifting."

Galaeron raised a questioning brow to Vala, who shrugged and started after the wizard, grumbling, "Better not to be left behind."

Feeling no less distressed for the explanation, Galaeron started after his companions. Once they had formed a neat line again, Melegaunt turned his head a little so it would be easier for Galaeron and Vala to hear him.

"You have noticed how the shadows change as the sun crosses the sky?" Melegaunt asked. "And how they dance in the light of a candle?"

"Of course," said Galaeron.

"What happens when the sun sets?"

"There is darkness." It was Vala who said this.

"There is *shadow,*" corrected Melegaunt. "The sun has not vanished, only sunk out of sight. Its light is blocked by the horizon."

"A fine distinction," noted Galaeron.

"But an important one," said Melegaunt. "On Faerûn, there is only shadow. Everything that people call 'dark' or 'night' is nothing more than light blocked by the world itself."

"Even in caves?" asked Vala.

"Even caves. If they weren't surrounded by rock, the sun would light them," the wizard explained. "But there are places—other planes—where there is no sun or any light. There, no shadow exists, only darkness—true, black, darkness."

"And this has *what* to do with the Shifting?" asked Vala.

"Only this," said Melegaunt. "Darkness is by nature motionless and without life, but shadows are all motion and vigor. They dance and swirl and flicker and continually beget strange creatures, and only light ever fixes them in place."

"So when the sun goes down, they lose form and go into motion," surmised Galaeron. "The Shifting."

Melegaunt nodded. "One could almost say they *become* motion." He craned his neck around to smile at Galaeron. "We'll make a shadow shaper of you yet, elf."

"I'm sure the Hill Elders will like *that,*" said Vala.

Though she made no complaint, Galaeron could tell by how she dogged Melegaunt's heels that she had realized the same thing he did. If they wanted to feel any sunlight on their faces in Dekanter, they had to hurry.

As they approached the forest, the darkness resolved itself into a fence of charcoal depths, laced by black tangles of undergrowth, striped by the ebony columns of impossibly thin tree trunks. Knowing it to be the forest, or more accurately the absence of one, Galaeron began to feel a little more at ease. Elves, even those who dwelled in cities, were at home in the woods. If he could feel safe any place in the Fringe, it would be there. He moved closer behind Vala and spoke to Melegaunt over her shoulder.

"Is Dekanter where we'll find the help you promised?"

"Sadly, no," said Melegaunt "My, uh, friends are a few days farther north—and west, I believe. But I've always wanted to see Dekanter, and as it happens to be on our way, I thought it would be a good place to rest for the night."

Dekanter was the last place in Faerûn—that Galaeron knew of, at least—where the ruins of ancient Netheril could still be visited. Little more than a few towers and dozens upon dozens of holes in the ground, the city was not much to see and even less of a camping spot, but Galaeron suspected the goblins and gargoyles who normally plagued visitors there would quickly see the wisdom in giving any camp of Melegaunt's a wide berth.

"It would ease my mind to know who these friends of yours are, Melegaunt," said Galaeron. "What makes you so certain they can stop the phaerimm when Evereska's high mages could not?"

"Have you heard nothing I've told you?" snapped Melegaunt. "I'm certain because ridding Faerûn of this evil is what they have prepared themselves to do. It's unfortunate they will have to do it in Evereska instead of Anauroch, but they will succeed nonetheless."

"Unfortunate?" Galaeron had visions of his beloved vale being reduced to a ruin of shadow and smoke. "How?"

Melegaunt's voice grew impatient. "How do you think? The phaerimm have already killed hundreds of *Tel'Quess* and may well kill thousands more." The wizard reached the forest edge and continued forward, then suddenly began to grow translucent. "But there is no need to fear for Evereska itself. We will not allow . . ."

The wizard's voice grew softer as his body grew more transparent, then finally faded altogether when he vanished.

Vala pulled up short, and Galaeron stumbled into her from behind, nearly knocking her into the forest after Melegaunt.

"Mighty One?" she called.

Galaeron shouted, "Melegaunt?"

When no answer came, they drew their swords. Galaeron's first instinct was to look for shadators—as though he could actually see one—and illithids and beholders or any of the other deadly creatures of wickedness he was beginning to associate with Melegaunt and their phaerimm enemies. Vala's reaction was more direct and to the point. She grabbed Galaeron and started forward into the forest.

"Vala! Are you . . ." Galaeron made it only that far before he realized she was doing exactly the right thing. "All right, I'm coming!"

A cold afternoon wind began to whip his hair about his ears, then he found himself standing ankle deep in cold Nightal snow, staring at the winter skeletons of a thick forest of oak, walnut, and shadowtop. Melegaunt was no more than three paces ahead, surrounded by a semicircle of eight trees, all still holding their leaves. The largest of the trees, a twenty-foot oak, was blocking their path, shaking a gnarled branch at Melegaunt and rumbling at him in a voice as deep as thunder.

"Through my wood, Melegaunt Tanthul, you do not go!"

"But it is the shortest path, Great Fuorn," Melegaunt protested, "and the only one I know."

"Matters not," said the tree.

Now that he had recovered from his astonishment, Galaeron could make out the twisted bark faces of the eight trees. They had knotholes for eyes, jagged hollows for mouths, crooked limb stubs for noses. Their lips and brows were formed of gathered bark, their cheeks by lumpy burls. Galaeron's mother had once introduced him to a treant in the High Forest, and he recognized these plants as creatures of the same kind.

"Your magic is a thing cold and dark," said Fuorn, "and this wood it shall not enter."

"If my magic feels strange to you, it is because you have never seen its like or power before." Melegaunt pointed east toward Anauroch. "I employ it in a good cause, against the wicked creatures that turned the old forests into barren sand."

Fuorn looked east. "Yes, I recall the magicgrubs." His crown of scarlet leaves swayed back and forth in a sort of nod. "Little larger than men, but with a bite like dragons. We have seen a pair sniffing around our forest, peering into the shadows beneath our branches."

Melegaunt's shoulders squared. "The very ones. The phaerimm. I have come to undo what they have done."

Again, Fuorn seemed to nod. "Then well I wish you—but not here. I will have no battles in my forest."

"I thank you for the warning, tree," said Melegaunt. "You have my promise that no harm will come to your forest."

The wizard lowered his arm and cupped his hand beneath his sleeve, and Galaeron knew something terrible was about to happen. He clipped Vala's heel with the arch of his foot and knocked her to the ground with a sweep of his arm, then slipped forward and used the same technique to knock the wizard off his feet.

Melegaunt bellowed and started to raise the suspicious hand, but stopped when Galaeron's foot pinned his arm to his chest.

"No, my human friend," said Galaeron, "not even for Evereska."

Though he still held his sword, Galaeron was careful to hold the blade away from Melegaunt—and not only because he knew it would never pierce the wizard's magic. Vala had already leaped to her feet and was stepping toward him, darksword ready to strike.

"Have you lost your mind, elf?" Though there was a hint of grief in her expression, the set of her jaw and the hardness in her eyes left no doubt of her intentions. "You know I'm sworn to defend him."

"A little late for that, my dear," chuckled Melegaunt, "but no harm done."

The wizard motioned her to stand down, then brought his hand out of his sleeve and displayed a large black kernel.

"To help the treants protect their wood in the battles to come." Melegaunt handed it to Galaeron, then his voice grew pained. "You couldn't have thought I meant to attack them."

"I didn't know what to think." Noting that the treants were watching them with expressions ranging from bewilderment to suspicion, Galaeron sheathed his sword and examined the seed. It was about the size of an acorn, but as shiny as coal and full of swirling darkness. "I apologize. What is this?"

"Shadowstorm seed." Melegaunt heaved himself up and faced Fuorn. "Hurl it down, and any being not rooted to the ground will be swept into the Shadow Deep. There will be wind and lightning, but any battle likely to be waged near your forest would be stopped at once—or at least moved to where it could do no harm."

Fuorn considered this, then asked, "And rain?"

"If you throw it into the air," said Melegaunt. "But do so only in great desperation. The deluge it brings will quench even the fiercest fire, but the waters will be black and cold—far colder than any ice storm."

This drew a leafy shudder from the treants, for only burning was considered a more awful death than being split down the trunk by the weight of an ice-crusted crown. Fuorn lowered a twisted bough, and Galaeron laid the seed in the cusp of his woody palm.

"With your gift, I will be very careful." Fuorn tucked the kernel into a fold of bark. "And in return give you the favor of a warning word. Of late, the northern shadows have often taken the shape of great wings and long tails."

"Shadow dragons," surmised Melegaunt. "Shimmergloom?"

Fuorn's leafy crown quivered in a contrary sign. "It is sung on the winds that the longbeard Battlehammer slew the great wyrm when he reclaimed Mithral Hall, but it may be that Shimmergloom's seeds have begun to sprout and show themselves. You would do well to walk the shadow way carefully after you round the forest."

"Round the forest?" echoed Melegaunt. "You still refuse us?"

"We thank you for the Shadowstorm seed," said Fuorn, "but what did you risk in its giving?"

Without waiting for an answer, Fuorn stepped back among his fellows. He stretched upright and stood motionless, not so much staring at the travelers as waiting for them to make their decision. Not wishing Melegaunt to come to the wrong one, Galaeron reached for his arm—and felt Vala's strong grasp on his own.

"You surprise me once," she said.

"Don't be ridiculous," Galaeron said. "I mean him no harm."

"Good." She smiled artificially. "I'd miss you."

Melegaunt spun away from the treants and started eastward along the edge of the forest. Vala motioned Galaeron ahead of her, then slipped in behind him, and they both had to scurry to keep pace with the wizard's long strides.

Galaeron was not sure when Vala finally sheathed her sword, but it was in its scabbard when they reached the Lonely Moor just before dusk. Galaeron and Vala took a minute to bask in the sun's fading radiance, then set up camp and cooked a meal of marsh voles over a black-flamed fire Melegaunt had struck. Despite the glyphs and wards the wizard set around the perimeter of the camp, they divided the watch into three shifts and settled in for a wet night.

As it turned out, Galaeron could have taken all three watches himself. Whether it was because of Vala's distrust or worry for his father and Takari back in Evereska, he was never able to slip into the Reverie. He spent the whole night huddled in his cloak, staring at the stars and wrestling with feelings of guilt so vague and ambiguous he could only guess at their source. Of course, he was troubled by the part he had played in releasing the phaerimm, but his regret over that was real and tangible, an emotion so manifest he could almost touch it. The thing bothering him was much more subtle, a queasy hollowness that smacked of disloyalty and betrayal, though he was left to wonder just who he had betrayed. Had he been wrong to distrust Melegaunt? Or to accept so easily the wizard's explanation for the casual betrayal of Imesfor? Whatever the answer, Galaeron feared he would not enjoy a revitalizing Reverie until he had it.

Dawn found them all cold and awake, ready to warm themselves with a brisk prebreakfast march. Before departing, Melegaunt insisted on kneeling between Galaeron and Vala, holding his hands in their shadows, peering first into one, then the other, from the moment the sun broke the horizon until the moment the bottom edge no longer touched it. Only then did he rise.

"Come along, sun lovers. There will be no shadowalking for us today."

"Not that I'm complaining, but why?" asked Galaeron.

"Because I have read the day to come and have no desire to fight shadow dragons. The bugbears will be much easier."

"Bugbears?" Galaeron gasped. "The phaerimm have bugbears?"

Melegaunt shrugged. "Perhaps. The phaerimm control many creatures, most who do not even know it, but I cannot tell everything. I'm only reading shadows." He started northward, motioning Galaeron and Vala to follow. "Keep a sharp watch. We should be all right as long as we don't let them surprise us."

This proved much easier said than done, of course. They slogged northward across a few miles of peat moor, then slipped around the northern tip of the Forgotten Forest and started northwest across the Forsaken Dale. As they crossed the snowy flats, Galaeron kept a watchful eye on the birds, but knew they would not have much to worry about until they reached the Greypeaks in the distance.

Just after highsun, the foothills drew near enough to make out individual gullies, and the pinnacles of the snowcapped mountains themselves began to show above the horizon. Galaeron's thoughts kept returning to his inability to enter the Reverie the night before. The explanation Melegaunt had given for using Imesfor as a decoy was sensible enough, but it still smacked of deceit, and it occurred to Galaeron that he was placing a great deal of trust in a human he really did not know very well. He allowed Melegaunt to drift a short distance out of earshot, then spoke over his shoulder to Vala.

"If I offended you by doubting Melegaunt, I apologize," he said. "Perhaps if I knew more about him . . ."

"You know he is trying to save Evereska." Vala said, prodding Galaeron in the back, urging him to catch up to Melegaunt. "You know he is trying to undo a mistake you made. How much more do you need to know?"

"How much do *you* know?" asked Galaeron, doing his best to ignore the barb about his "mistake." "He claims much, but reveals little."

"He is a good man."

"From where?" asked Galaeron. "I have never seen the likes of his magic before."

"That does not mean it is evil." Vala's voice was sharp enough that it caused Melegaunt to cock his head to one side. "The Melegaunt Tanthul I know is not evil."

"But *I* do not know him," Galaeron said. "I might find it easier to trust him if I knew more about your relationship. Now that you are no longer Evereska's prisoner, perhaps—"

"Very well," Vala sighed. "A hundred years ago, my ancestors were living in log longhouses roofed in thatch and chinked with mud, battling the orc hordes with weapons of cold-forged iron and losing children to worgs and gnolls faster than our women could birth them."

"And I suppose Melegaunt changed that?"

"He did," said Vala. Twenty paces ahead, the wizard seemed to nod smugly to himself. "In return for a pittance of service, he offered to build my great grandfather an impregnable keep of black granite, and to arm twenty warriors with black swords that would cleave any enemy's armor."

"A bargain your ancestor obviously accepted," said Galaeron.

"Not as quick as you believe, for we Vaasans have always been hard bargainers," said Vala. "The debt would be called at some time in the future, when a company of warriors armed with those same black swords would be summoned to service. Bodvar agreed, providing only that all of the swords remained unbroken and the granite keep was never breached."

"I take it the conditions were fulfilled."

Vala nodded. "My own father heard the voice less than a year ago, but he was too old and sick to lead the men. It was left to me to take up the sword."

"And that's all you know of Melegaunt?" asked Galaeron.

"It's all I need to know." Vala's tone was almost soft. "The service of twenty warriors for the kindness he has done my clan? You elves are too distrustful."

"Perhaps so," allowed Galaeron. "We weren't always distrustful. That we learned from humans."

He spied the long valley that led to Dekanter and began to angle toward it, his thoughts consumed by questions of why Melegaunt would want to visit the ruins if the help he sought wasn't there—and what kind of help he might be seeking if it was.

They caught up to Melegaunt and entered the gulch together, and Galaeron was instantly too busy looking for bugbears to concern himself with anything else. The gully was perfect for an ambush, with an abundance of cliff-flanked narrows and blind corners, but they resisted the temptation to climb to higher ground for fear of making themselves more visible to phaerimm searchers. Twice, they were actually ambushed by goblin tribes, but a simple display of magic was enough to send the creatures skittering away.

When they reached the head of the gulch without meeting any bugbears and climbed into the hills themselves, Galaeron began to think Melegaunt was not as infallible as he appeared. The ruined towers of Dekanter were just visible in the distance, a short row of absurdly twisted and impossibly leaning spires silhouetted against snow-blanketed slopes, and the sun was already sinking into the narrow rift of the Bleached Bones Pass.

The sight of the towers seemed to invigorate Melegaunt. Abandoning all effort at keeping a low profile, he clambered along a boulder-strewn ridge toward the sunken roadbed that had once connected Dekanter to the rest of the Netherese empire. Vala scurried after him, apparently abandoning her resolve to never again let Galaeron behind her.

"Melegaunt, what about the bugbears?" she asked.

"Yes, yes, I'm sure they're here somewhere," he said. "But the ruins are still a good mile away, and I must be there when the sun goes down."

The wizard continued forward at a near run, giving Vala and Galaeron no choice except to keep a watchful eye and hope for the best. Soon enough, the towers resolved themselves into jewel-colored oddities of architectural corruption, grotesque forms that arced and twisted in impossible directions with no thought of form or function. Some had no doors or windows, one seemed to be a single warped door spiraling into the sky, another looked to be a huge window with no interior depth at all.

The towers were scattered among the great mines that had been the reason for Dekanter's existence in the days of Netheril. Now long played out, all that remained of the ancient workings were snowy dumps of waste rock and the yawning portals and abysmal shafts of the holes themselves. Even Melegaunt seemed to sense the melancholy insanity of the place. He walked among the ruins silently, inspecting each warped spire like a wandering son returned home to find his house occupied by another family.

When the bottom curve of the sun finally touched the distant saddle of Bleached Bones Pass, he kneeled in the shadow of the door tower and pressed his brow to the dark ground. He spoke a few syllables in some tongue Galaeron did not understand, then lifted his body and shook his head slowly.

"The folly," he said. "The unbelievable folly."

When the tears began to roll down his cheeks, Vala went to his side and slipped a hand under his arm. "Is there time to try another tower?" she asked. "Every story can't be the same."

The thought seemed to cheer Melegaunt. He allowed her to pull him up, then started along a boulder-lined trail toward the window tower. "Yes, another tower would be good."

They had taken no more than a dozen steps when Galaeron noticed a trio of crows circling overhead. Instead of calling to each other in their usual raucous voices, the birds were unusually silent, like anglers afraid their voices might frighten the fish.

"Stop."

Galaeron had barely spoken the word before Vala had her darksword in hand and Melegaunt behind her.

"Where?"

"I don't know," Galaeron said. "Here."

A half dozen paces up the trail, a pair of pointed ears appeared over the top of a horse-sized boulder. Vala spotted them instantly and gestured silently with her sword. Grousing under his breath, Melegaunt fetched something from his robe pocket, and Galaeron realized the emergence of the ears had been too convenient. Bugbears rarely made such foolish mistakes.

"Melegaunt, wa—"

He was too late. The wizard pointed a finger and spoke a single word, and a shadowy bolt of darkness drilled straight through the boulder. There was no thud or anguished roar or any other sound to suggest the attack had hit anything living. Rather, a slimy mauve face with a snout of tentacles rose up behind the adjacent snow bank, fixing Melegaunt with a white-eyed stare.

The wizard screamed once, then clutched at his eyes and crumpled to the ground.

"An illithid?" Even as Vala shrieked the question, she was flinging her darksword at the creature in a backhand flip. "Melegaunt said nothing about illithids!"

The blade pirouetted through the air and took the illithid's head off cleanly.

In the next instant, a dozen bugbears sprang from behind boulders, rock dumps, and snowdrifts to both sides of the trail. Galaeron pulled his sword from its scabbard with one hand and reached into his cloak pocket with the other.

"Vala," the elf shouted, "sword!"

He tossed the sword toward her hilt-first, then pulled his other hand from his pocket and flung a pair of green leaves in the direction of the nearest bugbears. The brutes were huge, a full head taller than Vala's burly men and far broader across the shoulders, but with ugly batlike snouts and gleaming red eyes. Vala caught Galaeron's sword with her off hand and whirled the blade around to point at the charging beasts.

Galaeron uttered his incantation, but instead of feeling the magic flow into his body from the all-encompassing Weave, it surged up through his legs in a cold bolt. With a dozen screaming bugbears on the way, there was no time to be shocked. He simply waved his hand across the hillside, and a cloud of putrid brown miasma filled the air around the bugbears' heads. Four out of the first five creatures collapsed gagging. The fifth perished when Vala dived at its feet, then somersaulted between its legs and slashed Galaeron's magic blade across the front of its belly.

Galaeron slowed the remaining beasts with a pinch of sand and a quick word of magic, sending two into a deep slumber. Vala toppled another with a knee slash, then caught a heavy axe swing against the flat of Galaeron's blade. The bugbear continued to push, confident its strength would simply collapse Vala's guard.

She thrust a hand out in the direction of the dead illithid, and her darksword came flying back into her grasp. She brought the black blade beneath her attacker's big belly, driving the point clear to its heart. Galaeron pointed at the bugbear nearest Vala. Again, the magic shot into him from the cold ground, and the shaft that leaped from his finger to tear open the bugbear's chest was as black as night.

Seeing they were still three paces away from Vala and unlikely to get any closer, the last two beasts turned to flee. There was no question of letting them escape, for their illithid companion made plain the identity of their masters. Galaeron blasted one down from behind with another magic bolt. Vala sprang after the other as it bounded over the edge of the hill, and a strangled howl echoed up the slope.

Galaeron used a pair of lightning bolts and a fireball to finish the bugbears he had incapacitated with his earlier spells. He felt the same surge of cold magic when he cast the first lightning bolt, but found that by concentrating on the living Weave all around him, he could create spells normally. Still, Vala returned from her trip down the hill to find him shivering with cold; it seemed to be welling up inside him, as though the marrow in his bones had turned to shadow.

"Something wrong?" She returned his sword. "You look like that's the first time you ever killed anything."

"Would that it were." Galaeron pulled his cloak more tightly around him. He turned to face Melegaunt, who was lying glassy eyed and drooling on the ground. "I'm fine, but what about him?"

Vala considered him for a moment, then shrugged. "Well, at least he saw his towers."

CHAPTER TEN

25 Nightal, the Year of the Unstrung Harp

When Galaeron climbed down into the rocky basin where they had made camp the previous night, he found Vala lying next to her unsheathed sword, staring into its glassy blade with a vacant expression. On an elf's visage, her arched brow and wistful smile would have suggested a not-altogether-unhappy loneliness, but he was not sure what the look signified on a human face. His first reaction was one of envy, as he himself had again passed the entire night without a moment of Reverie. Then he remembered: humans did not have the Reverie.

"Vala?" Galaeron reached out to shake her.

Her hand came up and caught his wrist in a lightning-fast trap block. He barely managed to pull free and fling himself backward before her darksword cleaved the air where he had been kneeling. Galaeron somersaulted over a shoulder and pulled his own sword to block.

Vala rolled to her hip, her pale eyes vacant and dangerous.

"Vala!" Galaeron called. "It's me—the elf . . ."

Her brow knitted, then reason returned to her eyes. She scowled at the weapon in Galaeron's hand.

"What's that for?" If Vala noticed that she was pointing with her own sword, her face showed no sign. "Trying to kill me in my sleep?"

"You weren't sleeping. Your eyes were open."

This seemed to stir her memory. "That's right . . . I was visiting." Now she scowled. "And you interrupted me?"

"Visiting?"

"The Granite Tower." She jammed the darksword into its scabbard. "Dream walking. You know."

Galaeron shook his head. "Is this like the Reverie?"

"Not really." Vala glanced eastward, where a brightening band of gray horizon foretold the coming dawn. "You didn't wake me for my watch."

Galaeron shrugged. "I couldn't rest. I thought you might as well."

"Thanks, but you should have tried. You look like hell." More gently, she explained, " 'Visiting' is my word for it. Over the years, every darksword seems to inherit a few foibles from its family. Burlen's hums in combat, Dexon's talks in its sleep."

"And yours 'visits'?"

"Spying might be a better term." Vala's cheeks darkened. "It likes to, uh, show me what's happening in the bedchambers of the Granite Tower."

Galaeron raised his brow.

"It's not something I like."

"Of course not," Galaeron said, enjoying a rare opportunity to bait her. "Though you did seem to be smiling."

"I was watching Sheldon sleep." Though there was no indignation in Vala's voice, her tone grew solemn enough that Galaeron regretted chiding her. "He's my son."

"Can you two not be quiet?" rumbled Melegaunt. The wizard sat up, palms pressed to his eyes. "What happened to my head?"

"Illithid," Vala said. "With the bugbears."

Melegaunt pulled his hands away. "Then the phaerimm are a step ahead." He ran his fingers through his dusky hair and hefted himself to his feet. "We'll leave as soon as I've read the day."

They gathered their gear, then climbed to the rim of their campsite and stood in the light of the rising sun. Melegaunt kneeled between Vala and Galaeron as before.

"A day of meetings," he announced, "but nothing to fear. So long as we are cautious."

"How cautious?" asked Galaeron.

"Bad things in the mountains." Melegaunt gestured westward toward Bleached Bones Pass. "But the shadow way looked clear to the north. Good news, is it not?"

Vala and Galaeron eyed each other with looks of dread, then Vala asked, "How bad were the things in the pass?"

"Shadow dragons are fearsome creatures, even in a world of light," said Melegaunt. "More importantly, though, there is speed to consider. The phaerimm will not find it easy to breach Evereska's mythal, but if we give them too long, they will discover a way."

Galaeron gestured the wizard forward.

Melegaunt cast a last, wistful look at the twisted towers of Dekanter, then spoke the words of his shadowalking spell. The world around them grew dull and featureless, with a jagged ridge of purple mountain shapes to the left and a subdued morning glare to the right. Galaeron felt instantly cold and isolated, and saw by the disquiet in Vala's eyes she felt the same.

Melegaunt donned the cold gloom like a favored cloak, letting out a sigh of satisfaction and setting off at a near dash. Vala motioned Galaeron to follow, then fell into position behind him.

"How did you two manage the battle without my help?" Melegaunt's voice was overly innocent. "With a mind flayer present, I imagine the fight was a difficult one."

"Not particularly," said Vala. "I killed it first. Galaeron took care of the rest with his magic."

"Truly?" Melegaunt peered back over his shoulder. "And all your spells worked well?"

"I'm hardly a magic-user of your caliber," he answered carefully. The wizard's interest seemed to suggest certain expectations, and Galaeron found himself less than eager to confirm them. "They worked as well as usual."

"They did the job." Melegaunt looked forward again, his brow lowered in disappointment. "That's what counts."

Galaeron resisted the urge to keep from demanding an explanation of exactly what the wizard had done to him. The question would give away more than he cared to, and he had already seen that Melegaunt was not someone who yielded his own secrets easily. They traveled onward in silence, twisting and winding their way through a maze of hill shapes. The jagged silhouettes of the mountains always remained to their left, but otherwise Galaeron saw no rhyme or reason to their route. Melegaunt turned into the light as often as he turned away, followed shadow troughs as often as he walked through hill shapes, went down as often as up. As the day passed—or what passed for day in the Fringe—the band of radiance to the right rose higher in the sky, then divided into irregular shapes and scattered itself across the landscape.

When mountain shapes started to rise on all sides, Galaeron realized they were climbing into the Greypeaks. He quickly lost all sense of direction. In the Fringe, everything felt flat beneath his feet. When he thought they were ascending, they were descending, and when he thought they were going around, they were going through.

Soon, the shapes turned ghostly and blue, and Melegaunt began to hesitate before picking directions. When the silhouettes grew transparent and gray, Melegaunt started to mumble and backtrack. Finally, the shadows vanished altogether, and Melegaunt stopped and began to turn in circles.

"What's wrong?" Galaeron asked. "Are we lost?"

"Lost?" Melegaunt spun in a slow circle, his eyes scanning the featureless gray fog around them. "I'm afraid so."

Galaeron groaned. "And you can't cancel the spell."

"It wouldn't be wise," said Melegaunt. "We'd probably return to our own Faerûn, but if I took a wrong turn somewhere . . ."

"What if we just went toward that campfire?" asked Vala.

"Fire?" Melegaunt asked. "Where?"

She pointed into the gray distance, but Galaeron could see no sign of fire.

Melegaunt slipped past him and peered over her shoulder, then smiled and clapped her back. "Well done."

Galaeron retreated two steps and peered over Vala's shoulder, then saw two tiny ribbons of yellow and white flickering around each other. "You're sure that's fire?"

"That's what it looks like from the Fringe," said Melegaunt.

Within half a dozen steps, the ribbons expanded into a small circle of flames surrounded by a whirling gray haze. Melegaunt motioned for Vala and Galaeron to ready their swords, then led them into the radiance of the campfire.

The flames turned instantly to their proper orange, and a mewling voice cried out in surprise.

"By the One!" On the other side of the fire rose a pudgy little man in a snow-blanketed cloak and hood, his pink hands held high to demonstrate they held no weapons. "Cause me no harm, and you shall have all I own . . . little as that may be!"

Melegaunt motioned the fellow to lower his hands. "You have nothing to fear from us, so long as we have nothing to fear from you."

The little man glanced from the husky wizard to his two well-armored companions and did not lower his hands. "Why would three so mighty need fear a humble beggar like myself?"

Though the man's cloak was travel worn and his beard disheveled, he hardly looked the part of a beggar. His face was round and soft, his belly ample, his eyes shifty. He had made his camp in a small side gulch high in the Greypeaks, where a tangled thicket of black spruce offered at least some protection from a driving snowstorm blowing in from the east—the cause, Galaeron suspected, of the strange paling that had forced Melegaunt to abandon the shadow way. A single sad-eyed mount stood tied behind a lean-to of dead logs, its saddle and bags tossed carelessly inside the shelter. The horse's expression seemed as downtrodden as that of its master, but its coat gleamed from daily currycombing, and—if anything—it looked overfed. Melegaunt studied the camp, his eye running from the fire to the lean-to to the horse as though everything were exactly where he expected.

Continuing to hold his hands over his head, the little man gestured to the log he had been sitting on. "You are more than welcome to share my fire." He started to close his mouth as though he were finished speaking, then suddenly looked surprised and added, "I couldn't stop you anyway."

"We wouldn't want to impose on you." Melegaunt looked around. "I'm a little turned around in this snow. If you'll point the way to Thousand Faces, we'll be on our way."

"Over the pass?" The little man shook his head vigorously. "You can't, not here."

This drew a scowl from Vala. "You think to stop us?"

The little man's eyes widened. "I d-don't—but even you three are no match for so many b-beholders."

"Beholders?" Melegaunt sounded less surprised than disappointed. "How many?"

"Enough." The little man shook his hooded head in despair. "My luck has been a curse all my life. First it was the mind flayers at Bleached Bones, then the Zhentarim at Dawn Pass, and now it is the beholders. Who knows what it will be at the High Gap? I tell you, we are not going to find a safe place to cross until we are past the Far Forest!"

"Perhaps not," said Melegaunt. "Let me have a look at these beholders. I sometimes have a way with them."

The little man raised his brow. "Truly? If you can get us across these accursed mountains, I would be forever in your debt—no doubt because I seldom repay a favor." A frown of dismay flashed across his face, but he cautiously lowered his hands and bowed to the companions. "Malik el Sami yn Nasser at your service."

✡✡✡✡✡

Khelben paced at the foot of Imesfor's bed, two steps then turn, two steps then look, two steps then turn. To the mage's eye, the elf looked no better than the day he had arrived, save that he no longer had an illithid tentacle probing the hole in his skull. The lord's gaze was glassy and vacant, with a raccoon's mask of purple bruises ringing his eyes, and his sunken cheeks were as pallid as ivory. An inert tongue lolled out of his mouth with no indication it would ever speak again, much less soon.

Khelben took two impatient steps, turned, stopped, then looked to the aradoness leaning over the stricken lord. "You've been with him for nearly two days. When will he speak?"

The elf priestess fixed Khelben with a black-eyed glare. "Your concern for your friend is touching. Bear in mind that it is just that concern that will keep his spirit in his body."

"Lord Imesfor and I have been friends nearly five centuries," growled Khelben. "He knows how I feel about him—and I know how he feels about Evereska. If he knew what was happening there—"

"He does know," said the priestess, Angharad Odaeyns. "Isn't that why you're trying to wake him?"

Khelben gave her a black look. "You know what I mean. If he knew we couldn't get near the place. . . ." He let the sentence trail off, then ran his palm into the canopy post so hard he shook the whole bed. "Cloudblast!"

Laeral slipped a hand through the crook of his arm. "Perhaps we should try another tact, Khelben." She pulled him to the side of the bed opposite Angharad, then used a cantrip to pull a chair across the room for him. "It was you Gervas came to see. Perhaps if you—"

"Lady Blackstaff, I don't think that wise." Angharad started around the bed. "A human touch is not the same. There is no emotional tie."

"Really?" Laeral fixed the elf with an icy stare. "Then why did he come to Khelben instead of Queen Amlaruil?"

The question staggered the proud Gold elf as no blow could have. "I'm sure there was a reason." She stopped at the foot of the bed to think of one. "Perhaps the mind flayer—"

"All we know is that he came to see Lord Blackstaff," Laeral interrupted. She looked to Khelben. "I see no harm in letting him know you're here. Speak to him as though he were awake. Tell him what's been happening."

Khelben's first thought was that Laeral was proposing a monumental waste of time, but he didn't say so. Laeral was the one person he never snapped at—well, that he *tried* never to snap at—and he was accomplishing little enough otherwise. He had tried to teleport into the Shaeradim a dozen times, only to find himself hip-deep in some stinking marsh or sliding down a searing sand dune, so far from his goal he could not even see the mountains, much less find out what was happening in Evereska.

Khelben took Lord Imesfor's hand. "Old friend, it's not going well. In truth, it's going damn poorly. I know you came here in need of help, but you've got to help *me*. I can't seem to get anywhere near Evereska—"

"Fie . . . ream." The word slipped from Imesfor's lips so faint and wispy that Khelben thought he had imagined it.

Angharad gasped, then rushed to the far side of the bed and looked into Imesfor's eyes. His gaze seemed to focus on her, then went glassy again.

Khelben felt Laeral's hand push him toward the elf. "Keep talking."

Khelben leaned over his old friend. "Fie who? What's wrong in Evereska?"

Imesfor's eyes came back into focus. "Fieream!"

"Fieream?" Khelben repeated, then it hit him. *"They* did this to you?"

Imesfor shook his head. "Not phaerimm . . . to me. Illithid."

"We know about the illithid." Khelben glanced to Laeral. "Do a sending."

Laeral nodded. "Already done. Elminster will be here—" She was interrupted by the soft crack of a teleport spell. "Now."

Still stinking of the pipe smoke in his study, Elminster stood in the center of the room, blinking and wobbling as he struggled to reorient himself to his new surroundings. Suppressing the irritation he felt at the showy display of power (Elminster being the only wizard on Toril who could defeat Khelben's wards and teleport directly into Blackstaff Tower), Khelben motioned the wizard over.

"Over here. He's just coming around."

The sound of Khelben's voice helped the wizard orient himself, and he stepped to the bed. "Gervas, ye look like something a carrion worm spit out."

Laeral slapped Elminster on the shoulder. "Be nice. Lord Imesfor isn't alert enough for raw wit."

"I'm alert enough to know . . . that awful fireweed smell." Imesfor tried to push himself into a sitting position, then winced and settled for keeping his eyes open. "My thanks for coming, Stinkbeard."

"My thanks for being alive when I arrived," Elminster said. "Now why don't ye tell us how that hole in your head came to be?"

"We were fleeing the phaerimm—"

"The phaerimm?"

Elminster looked to Khelben, who could only shrug and say, "It's the first I've heard about it, but who else could ward the entire Shaeradim against transport magic?"

"I can think of a few—any two of which would be preferable to the phaerimm," Elminster said darkly.

Gervas's eyes grew concerned. "You don't know?" He looked to Angharad. "How is that possible?"

The priestess looked away. "It wasn't my decision."

"But you *are* from Evermeet?" the elf pressed.

Angharad nodded. "I was told this is an elf problem." She cast an uneasy glance toward Khelben and Elminster, then leaned closer to Imesfor. "Evereska is our last bulwark on the continent. The Island Council feared that the humans would seize this opportunity to claim it for their own."

"What?" Khelben was so angry he nearly teleported over to strangle the priestess. At least that explained the stream of mages and warriors that had been emerging from the basement of Blackstaff Tower all day. There was an elf gate down there that allowed elves to pass freely between Waterdeep and Evermeet, and it had been in nearly constant use since he had asked Queen Amlaruil to send a healer for Lord Imesfor. "Evereska is being overrun by phaerimm, and your people are worried about humans?"

"Evereska is hardly being overrun," said Angharad.

"It is!" Imesfor said. "Not yet the vale, but our armies are gone." He turned from the priestess, who had gone nearly as pale as he, to Khelben. "They took us from behind, and when we tried to flee . . . it was unthinkable. I would have been dead, save for Melegaunt and his humans."

"Melegaunt?" asked Khelben.

"A shadow-shaper, involved in breaching the Sharn Wall," explained Imesfor. He looked to Angharad. "Surely, the council passed that much along?"

The priestess shook her head. "They did not even tell me."

"Then perhaps ye would be kind enough to tell them something for me." Elminster rounded the bed to place himself between Lord Imesfor and the priestess. "Tell them the council would do well to recall how many friends the elves truly have among men—lest they chase them *all* off with their boneheadedness!"

Angharad's eyes widened. "I couldn't possibly—"

"Ye could and ye shall." Elminster shooed her toward the door. "And be quick about it, before I make a caryatid of ye!"

Laeral held the door. "I suggest you hurry. You know how rash and impatient we humans can be."

Angharad glanced toward Lord Imesfor, but before she could ask what he wished, there came a knock at the door.

"Speak!" Khelben commanded.

"Milord Blackstaff," came young Ransford's nervous voice. "Lord Piergeiron seeks a word with you about the unusual number of elves that seem to be gathering in the city."

"Send word that I will attend him the moment I am free."

"I would rather discuss the matter *now*, Khelben," came the warden's deep voice. The door opened, and the towering form of Piergeiron Paladinson ducked beneath the lintel. "They are threatening to buy up every last horse in the city."

The warden's sharp eyes wandered once around the room, lingering just long enough on Elminster and Lord Imesfor to make plain his feelings about being left uninformed of such a gathering.

Laeral was the first to recover, ushering Angharad into Ransford's arms. "See the aradoness to the elf gate, Ransford, and see to it that she uses it—she has an important message to deliver to Evermeet."

Piergeiron stepped aside to let the elf leave, then scowled at Khelben. "Will someone tell me what the devil is going on here?"

"An excellent idea." Elminster summoned a pair of chairs out of thin air and levitated them into place on his side of the bed, then sat down and patted the seat beside him. "Why don't ye come and sit with me, and we'll hear the tale together."

Khelben nodded, grateful to his old friend for diffusing the situation so effortlessly. "Why don't you start from the beginning, Lord Imesfor?"

The elf nodded, then told them the whole story, starting with Galaeron Nihmedu's discovery of the crypt-breaking on the Desert Border, his capture of Vala Thorsdotter and her warriors, then proceeding to the subsequent appearance of the phaerimm and its advertent release. Here, he paused a moment to collect himself as he related the death of his son Louenghris, then went on to describe Evereska's disastrous efforts to reach the Sharn Wall and repair the breach. He finished with a description of how Galaeron Nihmedu had defied the Hill Elders to rescue him and Kiinyon Colbathin, and of how Melegaunt Tanthul had helped him escape through the shadow way.

When the elf finished, everyone in the room sat silently contemplating the story they had just heard and trying to come to terms with the horrible evil that had been unleashed on the world. Finally, Khelben patted his friend's hand.

"Evereska isn't alone in this, Gervas," Khelben said.

The elf nodded. "I know."

"It makes no sense." Elminster was looking at the ceiling as he said this. "I don't care how talented or careless this Galaeron Nihmedu is, he's not going to breach the Sharn Wall—and certainly not by accident."

Khelben frowned. "What are you saying? That the shadow shaper did it on purpose?"

"That would make more sense than some accident, would it not?" asked Elminster. "Think on it. The Netherese have been dead and gone for these fifteen hundred years—"

"Save for Shade," Khelben pointed out. Shade was an ancient Netherese city that had reputedly escaped the fall of Netheril by transporting itself into the plane of shadow. "No one knows what happened to Shade, but if this shadow-shaper is Netherese. . . ."

"My point exactly," said Elminster. "Whether he is a lone survivor—which would make him an archwizard of truly awe-inspiring might—or an expatriate seeking revenge, would it not make sense for him to make the phaerimm *our* problem?"

No one needed to ask what Melegaunt might be seeking vengeance for. The Netherese Empire had consisted primarily of floating cities, built upon the upturned bottoms of truncated mountaintops and kept aloft by the incredible magic of the empire's archwizards. Unbeknownst to them, their profligate abuse of magic was destroying the underground home of the entire phaerimm race, which depended on the inherent magic of nature for survival. To save themselves, the phaerimm had developed a powerful spell that drained the life from Netherese lands, turning their fields to sand dunes and their lakes to arid flats of cracked mud.

As the farms grew less fertile, the empire found it difficult to feed its people, and eventually the stress led to a strange series of wars. Some were fought for sport to keep the restless populace entertained, and some were fought to claim the remaining patches of arable land. The result was an ever-escalating magic arms race that culminated in the mad attempt of the empire's greatest archwizard, Karsus, to steal the mantle of divinity from the goddess of magic, Mystryl herself.

Sadly for all, Karsus was not up to the job. The sudden influx of godly knowledge left him too stunned to perform the most important role entrusted to the deity of magic—that of constantly reworking the Weave of life and mystic power that was the source of Faerûn's magic. The Weave began to unravel.

To save it, the goddess—Mystryl—was forced to sacrifice herself, temporarily severing the link between Faerûn and its magic Weave. Without magic to keep them afloat, the cities of Netheril plummeted to the ground. Karsus himself died imbued with the knowledge of what he had done, plummeting to the ground in the form of a huge red butte. Save for Shade, which had somehow foreseen the disaster in time to withdraw into the plane of shadow, the rest of the empire perished with him. By the time Mystryl could reincarnate herself as Mystra, the new goddess of magic, the empire was gone.

All were silent as they contemplated Elminster's suggestion, until Laeral voiced the question on all their minds.

"Surely, not even a Netherese—survivor or descendant—would unleash the phaerimm merely to have his revenge."

To Khelben's surprise, it was Imesfor who shook his head. "That would not be my sense of it all. This Melegaunt risked much to save my life and Kiinyon's, and his determination seems not to be in destroying the phaerimm, but to set right what he and Galaeron did wrong."

"And this Galaeron?" asked Khelben. "Forgive me, but it is not entirely unheard of for an elf to betray his own kind."

"I know," agreed Imesfor. "I have given the matter no little thought, but I have known father and son for more than a century. Though the Nihmedu family is noble more by name than rank or power, Aubric is thought of so well that he has served the Swords of Evereska as blademajor for five decades now."

"It is the son we are speaking of here," said Elminster.

"That I know," said Imesfor. "Galaeron was known for his arrogance and stubbornness in both academies of the College of Magic and Arms, but he has served on the Desert Border without complaint for twenty years. Were he the betraying kind, he would have done it before now. I thought enough of his integrity to entrust my own Louenghris to his patrol, and even now I blame him for my son's death no more than any father would."

Elminster looked back to Imesfor. "If ye can tell me one thing, then will I rest easy this night."

Imesfor nodded. "I'll try."

"How was it that this Melegaunt could snatch ye and the others from beneath the phaerimm's very noses? They see magic the way dwarves see body heat. And how was it that he shadow-walked ye right out of the Shaeradim, when neither Khelben nor myself nor any of the Chosen can so much as set foot inside its borders?"

Imesfor could only shake his head. "I wish I knew."

Khelben began to have a queasy feeling. "Then we must consider at least one other possibility." He felt Laeral's hand slip into his and was suddenly glad for its warmth. "When the illithid attacked you, where was Melegaunt?"

Imesfor frowned. "We had just parted ways. I was leaving the shadow way to teleport here, and he . . ." The elf let his sentence trail off. "The human bastard!"

"He sent it after ye, did he?" asked Elminster.

"Not *it*," said Imesfor. "Them."

CHAPTER ELEVEN

26 Nightal, the Year of the Unstrung Harp

Even with a veil of storm clouds sliding along the cliff tops and a snow squall blasting through the gorge, Thousand Faces was more museum than pass. At the entrance stood the statues of two stone giant warriors, so lifelike that their chests seemed to rise and fall with breath. Beyond these guardians stretched the sculpture of an entire stone giant steading, carved into the canyon wall in high relief. There was a smith hammering an axe blank, a hunter carrying a pair of mountain elk by their ankles, a mother watching two sons wrestle, and a hundred other figures farther in, increasingly obscured by the howling blizzard. Above the giants wheeled sculpted snow finches and boulder hawks, the finches darting through a breathtaking maze of tree limbs, the hawks soaring across sublime mountain peaks. There were no beholders in sight, but neither were there any stone giants—at least none of flesh and bone.

"Where did you see these beholders?" whispered Melegaunt.

The wizard was lying between Galaeron and Malik, peering into the canyon from beneath the ground-hugging branches of a spruce tree. Vala was on Galaeron's other side, her body touching his at shoulder and hip.

"Find the law keeper," said Malik. "Look into the door on the right."

Galaeron searched the canyon until he came to an elderly stone giant holding a tablet in one hand and a dagger in the other. Next to him stood a doorway flanked by two columns. It ran only a couple of paces before ending in a wall at the same depth as the rest of the sculpture background, cleverly concealing the portal as a relief of itself. So convincing was the effect that had

Galaeron not noticed a swarm of tiny eye-shaped reflections gleaming out of one shadowy corner, he would never have guessed the entrance to be real.

Armed with this insight into the wonder of the giants' art, he reexamined the canyon wall and spotted several other openings. There were two more doorways—one actually disguised as a door and another as the hollow between two trees—and half a dozen windows. A swarm of beholder eyes peered from most of them.

"Malik, you saved our lives," said Galaeron. "Thank you."

"I don't know that he saved our lives," grumbled Melegaunt, "but he did save us some trouble. There are more beholders than I expected."

"How can there be so many?" asked Vala. "All the beholders I have fought were solitary."

"You live far from beholder civilization," said Melegaunt. "The phaerimm have enslaved a whole city."

"Phaerimm?" gasped Malik. The little man backed out from beneath the tree. "Perhaps it is not so far around the mountains after all."

Melegaunt grabbed the newcomer's cloak. "There aren't any phaerimm here, and I can sneak us past the beholders."

He started to back out from beneath the tree, and Vala said, "You're just going to abandon the stone giants?"

Melegaunt did not stop. "They're dead or gone."

"Not all of them."

Vala pointed near the cliff top, where a distant pair of gray legs extended down out of the clouds to balance on the stone wing of a sculpted eagle. As the companions watched, one foot moved up the cliff in search of a foothold, but found none and reluctantly returned to its former place.

"That complicates things." Melegaunt pushed himself out from beneath the tree. "We'll have to hurry, if we are to save him."

"I beg a thousand pardons, but you have clearly lost your mind." Malik crawled after the wizard. "Dead men save no lives!"

"You're free to try another way, of course." Melegaunt stood and started around the shoulder of a small hill. "But there's nothing to worry about. You and the others will go through as I planned. I'll just take a small detour and help the giant off the mountain."

Galaeron found himself racing both Malik and Vala as he scrambled after the wizard into a sheltered draw where they had left their gear and Malik's horse.

"You can't do that," Galaeron said.

Melegaunt faced him frowning. "I'll not abandon anyone to become a beholder's plaything, not when it's within my power to prevent it."

"Granted, but you're the only one who knows where we're going and who we're looking for," said Vala, all but taking the words out of Galaeron's mouth. "If something should go wrong. . . ."

Melegaunt looked insulted. "We're only talking about a few beholders."

"I can't let you take that chance, not when the fate of Evereska hangs in the balance," said Galaeron. Despite the objection, Melegaunt's determination to rescue the giant quelled many of the doubts the elf had been having about the wizard. "I'll rescue the giant, unless you'd rather tell me how to find whoever it is we're looking for."

The wizard's expression turned darker than usual. "Be careful what you wish for, young elf." He looked from Galaeron to Vala, then back to Galaeron again. "Very well, we'll do it your way, provided you can still use the other magic I showed you."

Malik's ears perked up at this. "What do you mean, 'other magic?' "

"It doesn't concern you." Melegaunt turned his back on the little man. "And even if it did, there's no time to explain now."

"I understand completely." Malik slipped around to place himself directly between Galaeron and Melegaunt. "Only, I have always been given to believe that the Weave is the only source of magic."

Melegaunt scowled at him. "Why should this interest you? Are you a wizard?"

"I am a man of many interests," said Malik. "And magic is among them, for my master—"

"We'll talk later," interrupted Melegaunt.

He glanced in Vala's direction. She grabbed Malik by the collar and, even as he tried to explain his interest, dragged him away. Her treatment was rough enough to draw a low whinny of warning from the sad-eyed horse.

Melegaunt turned back to Galaeron. "About the other magic—"

"Still available to me," said Galaeron, deciding to keep to himself for the moment just *how* available. "Here's what I was thinking."

Galaeron outlined his plan.

When he finished, Malik called, "You can cast the same spells twice?" He asked this from near his horse, where Vala had dragged him. "How did you know to study those spells more than once? Or can you do this because of the 'other' magic?"

"Quiet!" Melegaunt hissed.

He turned to glower, but Vala was already locking an arm around Malik's neck. She slapped her other hand over the newcomer's mouth and deftly put him between herself and his horse when the beast turned to nip at her.

"Are you *trying* to give us away?" she asked.

Malik's face paled, and he shook his head.

Melegaunt returned to Galaeron. "Remember, the beholders are less able to detect your shadow magic than the phaerimm, but they can still dispel it. If they notice your presence, stay clear of the rays from their central eyes."

"That lesson I learned from the first one we fought," said Galaeron.

"Good." Melegaunt reached into his sleeve and produced a small wisp of what looked like black fog. "This is shadowsilk, the primary element of much shadow-shaping magic. Let me show you a spell that may prove useful, and we'll be on our way."

The wizard started to run through the gestures, then noticed Malik watching. He turned his back to the little man, confiding to Galaeron, "There's something about him I just don't trust."

"Yes, mysterious humans *do* have a way of raising suspicions," said Galaeron, resisting the temptation to comment on his own uneasiness with the wizard. "You were showing me a variation on a web spell?"

Melegaunt cocked his brow. "I hadn't really thought of it as a web, but yes, I suppose that's the heart of the matter."

The wizard finished his demonstration. Galaeron repeated the words and gestures to make certain he understood them correctly.

"Amazing." Melegaunt could only shake his head. "Magic shouldn't be that easy for anyone."

"It isn't, really," Galaeron confided. "I must practice like anyone else to learn something new. But when it's basically a spell I already know, it's no big trouble to understand a few changes and what they do."

"A few changes?" Melegaunt shook his head incredulously. "No big trouble indeed!"

He went over to Malik and Vala, then circled his hand over the ground, creating a floating shadow disk similar to the one they had used to transport the wounded elves. Malik watched with interest, then undid the girth strap and placed the saddle in the center of the floating circle.

When the little man removed the bit from her mouth, Melegaunt said, "It's not necessary to leave your horse behind. If we cover her eyes, she'll never know we're moving."

"You misunderstand. Kelda needs no blinders." Malik grabbed the mare by the soft halter and had no trouble convincing her to jump onto the disk. "But she has always been a faithful horse, and if you madmen are determined to see us all dead on account of one cowardly giant lacking the courage to die with the rest of his tribe, then I will not have her starving in these mountains because I was too stupid to remove her saddle and bit."

The little man clambered onto the disk and kissed his horse full on the snout. Galaeron looked to the other humans and saw by their expressions that they found this behavior as puzzling as he did. Melegaunt and Vala climbed up with Malik, and the wizard cast another spell, turning the platform and everything on it invisible. There was a startled whinny, followed by a whispered request from Malik to please be silent and not get them all killed. A puff of wind stirred the blowing snow into a white eddy, which started down the draw toward the trail and vanished into the general blizzard.

"We'll see you on the other side, Galaeron," called Vala. "And be careful."

"You may count on it," said Galaeron. "But if something happens—"

"You'll be on your own," said Melegaunt. "Don't worry."

"And that is the most sensible thing any of you have said since I saved you with my fire," added Malik.

Galaeron allowed them another minute to drift safely ahead, then cast two spells on himself. To his surprise, he discovered that the cold magic did not rush into him as it had during the bugbear attack. To make it come, he had to think of his shadow self—to embrace it, really—and open himself to the cold magic's presence. Whether this sluggishness was due to the lack of shadows in the blizzard or because he was not presently overcome by the heat of battle, he did not know. He was just happy to discover he retained more control over his magic than he had thought.

Galaeron launched himself over the spruce tree with a gentle leap, then swung toward Thousand Faces well above the heads of the two stone giant guard statues. To avert the possibility of colliding with each other, they had agreed that Galaeron would fly higher than a giant and Melegaunt would stay lower. This put the wizard and the others more directly in the area watched by the beholders, but there was no avoiding it. The platform would float no more than a dozen feet off the ground.

Galaeron paused at the canyon entrance and used a spell to search for magic wards. He could see a dozen beholders lurking in the grotto's shadowy portals, the reflections of their eyes flitting about like swarms of golden fireflies. With so many eyes turned in his direction, Galaeron was nervous enough that the cold magic came to him very easily. Though the presence of two sculpted guardians would suggest defensive wards in most elf communities, not so with stone giants. The statues were just that, decorative artworks designed to greet—or perhaps intimidate—anyone entering the canyon.

Galaeron flew on, climbing toward the rim of the gorge. The giant's legs were completely hidden behind a low cloud sliding along the cliff tops, but the elf could still see the stony eagle his feet stood upon. Twenty paces from the great bird, Galaeron was astonished to see a swarm of eyes peering out from a window hidden beneath the bird's great wing. Perhaps the little human had been right, after all. By Tomb Guard doctrine, at least, Galaeron should not even try to rescue the giant. The saving of one life simply did not justify the risking of four.

It was a good thing no one followed that particular precept.

Galaeron reached the wall and ascended into the clouds, running a hand along the cliff to orient himself in the gray haze. He felt the eagle's wing pass beneath his fingertips, then rose past the blurry silhouette of a foot as long as his forearm. How the enormous toes could cling to such a small ledge he could not imagine, but the huge ankle was trembling with fatigue. Galaeron ascended alongside the giant leg to a giant waist, where he had to swing around a tool belt hung with steel hammers of various sizes, then continued up the giant's flank. He circled away from a cavernous armpit, looped over gnarled biceps, passed a neck as thick as a pillar, and found himself staring into a pair of eyes as big as dinner plates.

Galaeron took a piece of copper filament from his pocket and rubbed it between his thumb and forefinger. The shadow magic flooded into him, then he pointed at the giant's head and began to whisper.

"Don't cry out, giant. You have nothing to fear."

The giant flinched, lost a toe hold, and groaned. Galaeron cursed the big fellow's lack of self-discipline, then slipped a few arm lengths across the cliff and grabbed the shadowsilk Melegaunt had given him. A glimmer of hope appeared in the giant's face, and his big eyes roved about in search of his savior.

"Be careful!" Though the giant's whisper seemed as loud as rushing wind, Galaeron did not worry about it being overheard. The spell he had cast would prevent that. "Where are you?"

Before Galaeron could answer, a beholder floated up between him and the giant. The thing was close enough to kick, with several of the small eyestalks waving in the elf's direction, but the creature did not seem to notice Galaeron's invisible presence.

A cone of blue light shot from its huge central eye and began to sweep over the stone giant's body. Galaeron raised his hands to cast the spell Melegaunt had taught him, but stopped when the giant continued to cling to the cliff and showed no more fear than previously. Clearly, neither the giant nor the eye tyrant were surprised to see each other, and Galaeron realized their foes knew Melegaunt better than the wizard thought.

The beholder shifted its beam to the cliff and swept it back and forth at random. Keeping a careful watch on the creature's many eyes, Galaeron floated around behind it. By all rights, he should have left instantly, for he knew better than to think he could escape any trap designed to capture Melegaunt. But it was too late. He had already seen the hope in the giant's eyes.

The beholder finished its scan of the cliff face and spun around, flashing its beam back and forth through the cloud. Galaeron tucked in the other side of the giant's torso.

Finally, the beholder gave up and turned to the giant. "What was that groan for?"

"I slipped," the giant said.

"You wouldn't lie to poor Kanabar would you?" As the beholder spoke, one of its smaller eyes swung toward the giant. "Not when Kanabar told the others he had a use for you? You wouldn't lie to Kanabar when he saved your life, would you?"

"No, I wouldn't lie."

The giant's body tensed as he tried to resist the eye tyrant's charm magic, and Galaeron began to worry. Vala's beholder had slain one of his best scouts with nine eyes cloaked. What hope did he have against one able to use all eleven?

The giant spoke again, this time in a higher, almost singsong voice. "Aris would never lie to his friend Kanabar."

Galaeron pushed away from the cliff, then looked across the giant's broad back in time to see a crooked smile come to the beholder's toothy mouth.

"That's right," the beholder said. "So, why did Aris groan?"

The giant's body trembled visibly. "B-b-because his foot slipped."

"And why did his foot slip?" asked the beholder. "Tell your friend Kanabar."

As the eye tyrant said this, Galaeron flung a strand of shadowsilk in its direction and spoke the incantation Melegaunt had taught him. The beholder's eyes swung toward the sound of his voice, but the spell was a quick one, and in an instant, Kanabar was cloaked in a gummy mass of shadow.

"Hey!" Aris thundered. He turned his head and looked directly at Galaeron, who had turned visible the instant he attacked. "What'd you do to my friend, you stupid elf?"

"He's not your friend," Galaeron said, trying to figure out how he would rescue a becharmed giant. "I am."

Galaeron started to reach for his sword, then had a better idea when he saw the beholder's magic-destroying ray burn through the gummy shadow over its central eye. He rattled off a series of vaguely mystic syllables and tucked in behind the giant's body. Desperate to interrupt Galaeron's spell, the beholder swung toward him and ran its blue beam across the giant's back.

The beam flashed across Galaeron's shoulder. He began to fall, but spared himself a long plummet by catching hold of Aris's tool belt. The beholder tried to cry the alarm, but, with its mouth full of shadow gum, managed only a garbled babble.

Looping one arm through the giant's belt, Galaeron drew his sword and braced himself to fight the monster—then gasped as Aris's far hand descended out of the haze and grabbed Kanabar. The beholder looked like a riys melon in the giant's palm.

"Friend indeed!" growled the giant.

The beholder mumbled something unintelligible as Aris smashed it into the cliff.

"Thank the leaflord!" Galaeron gasped. "I didn't know if his ray would work on his own charm magic."

"It did," said Aris. "But I fear you have doomed yourself for naught, elf."

The giant pointed to a trio of round forms drifting toward them out of the haze. Galaeron looked behind him and saw another pair, and yet two more rising into the cloud beneath them. He sheathed his sword, then plucked two more threads off the shadowsilk Melegaunt had given him.

"This seemed like a better idea from down there."

"I imagine so," said Aris. "Should they becharm me again. . . ."

"No offense taken," said Galaeron. "Do as I say, and it won't come to that."

He dropped first one, then two shadow threads and repeated Melegaunt's spell twice in rapid succession. Though he had learned to do multiple castings at the Academy of Magic, it was the one technique that had not come easily for him—and that had prompted him to practice it until it came even more naturally than everything else. The two enchantments worked perfectly, though he was starting to grow tired and felt like the coldness of the new magic would crack his bones.

An alarmed gurgle rose from the beholders as they were engulfed in shadow morass, then they collided with each other and stuck fast. Without waiting to see what effect this would have on the others—though he prayed it would give them pause—Galaeron pointed toward the far end of the pass and cast his most powerful spell. A numbing wave of cold magic rushed through his bones, then a black square appeared just below him and to the side.

"Through the door!" he ordered.

Aris peered down. "I can't fit—"

"Now!" Still holding onto the belt, Galaeron leaped for the square and hoped the giant would follow. "Jump!"

With a deep bellow, Aris released the cliff and obeyed. Galaeron glimpsed a blue ray sweeping through the clouds toward his magic door, then they plummeted into darkness.

A sudden chill bit at his flesh, and there was a dark eternity of falling. Galaeron grew queasy and weak, heard the stillness of his own heart. His head reeled, his thoughts dissolved into a jumble of ill-defined fears, and he was back in the world, plunging through a howling tempest of white. A deafening bellow filled the air behind him. Galaeron glanced back to find a huge gray figure plummeting alongside him, then a circle of treetops flashed past and the world erupted into a cacophony of cracking and snapping. They tumbled groundward, flipping first one way, then another as they were snagged by passing branches. Galaeron tried to push away from the mountainous figure and found he could not.

In the next instant, he crashed down on the giant and lay in a daze, struggling to recall where he was and where he had come from. A low groan shook the air around him, then he started to swing groundward as the enormous body rolled to its back.

The spell's afterdaze vanished in a flash, and Galaeron knew instantly where he was—and who he was with. "Aris, wait!"

The giant gave a startled cry and stopped midroll. "Elf?"

"The very one." Galaeron pulled his arm free and dropped into the snow. "Are you all right?"

"For now." The giant pointed into the storm.

Galaeron scrambled up and peered over Aris's hip. The moon-shaped silhouette of a beholder was careening toward them through the storm, coming so fast it was bouncing into tree trunks.

"Do something!" Aris urged. "Another spell!"

"I don't think I can." Galaeron was so exhausted from the cold magic that had already passed through him that he could not stop shivering. "I'm too tired."

"Tired?" Aris boomed, clawing through the snow in search of a boulder. "Rest when you're dead!"

Seeing the wisdom in the giant's argument, Galaeron plucked another thread off his ribbon of shadowsilk. He tossed it in the beholder's direction and started the spell—then cried out in shock as the cold magic gushed into him. His entire body went icy numb and puffed up to half-again its normal size. When he continued the spell, his skin went as rigid as marble and turned as pale as snow. He choked out another word, and his lips grew so stiff and cold that he could barely utter the last syllable.

The beholder instantly became a massive ball of gummy black

shadow—then returned to normal when a cone of blue light shot through the blizzard to engulf it from behind.

"There!" Aris pointed at a smaller, more indistinct silhouette trailing the first. "Do two, like you did before!"

"I-I can't."

Even as Galaeron said it, he was pulling two more strands off the shadowsilk. This time, when he opened himself to the new magic, it blasted straight through him, and his body erupted into molten pain. Galaeron hurled himself screaming into the snow and rolled back and forth. There was no sizzle of melting snow nor hiss of rising steam, but the world suddenly turned very gray and dark, as though he were looking at it through a veil of smoke.

"Elf?" Aris glanced back and gave a bewildered frown, then rolled to his knees with a boulder in his hand. "Elf, do you have a friend here?"

Fighting through the pain, Galaeron pushed himself up and looked in the direction of the beholders. His smoky vision made everything look doubly hazy in the blizzard, but even given that, the first eye tyrant was so close the eyestalks were visibly writhing atop its head. The second was close enough that he could make out the shape of its big central eye, and behind it—*far* behind—was a figure on horseback. It was hardly a ghost, too faint to tell whether it was Vala or Melegaunt, but one of them.

"The fool!" He struggled to his feet and drew his sword. "Yes, that would be my friend—a friend who shouldn't be here, but a truer one for it."

"What very good news." The giant sounded less exhilarated than he might have. "Then all we must do is survive until he arrives."

Aris hurled his boulder, which soared through the woods and arced down toward the lead beholder. An eye swiveled on the top of its head, then a ray of silver light shot up to intercept the attack. The rock exploded into a spray of pebbles. Judging that they had about two seconds until the creature was close enough to use the ray on them, Galaeron lurched over behind a tree. His legs were numb and sluggish, and the sword in his hand felt more like an awkward orc blade than one forged in elven fire.

"Keep attacking!" said Galaeron. "Keep their attention focused on us."

"That shouldn't be hard."

The giant hurled another boulder, only to have it demolished by another silver ray. Galaeron dashed forward and took shelter behind a slender canyon spruce, then nearly lost his head as a silver beam slashed through the trunk. The top crashed down in front of the beholders, creating a small camouflage barrier. Galaeron hurled himself beneath the boughs and lay very still, relying on the camouflaging magic of his cloak to conceal him until he could attack.

"Elf!" Aris sounded panicked. "What are you doing?"

Galaeron didn't answer, until the blue light of an antimagic ray washed over his shoulder and neutralized his cloak's concealing magic. He rolled out on Aris's side of the fallen tree just as the large beholder sank down on the other side, now using its silver ray to disintegrate a ten-foot swath of boughs.

Galaeron sprang back at the beholder, crashing through the boughs atop the trunk, touching down long enough to spring over and come down on top of the beholder. He brought his sword around and cut half a dozen eyestalks off the head, then whipped the blade around in an arc and drove it into the eye tyrant's skull.

The blade sank to the depth of his thumb, then stopped cold.

"Elf!" Aris let out a sharp huff as he hurled another boulder, then bellowed, "Are you mad?"

Galaeron felt more than saw the boulder sailing past his head, then heard it crackle into a thousand pieces and realized the second beholder was close on him. He flung himself off the first, pulling his weapon free as he dived. His arm skipped over a rock, then he landed headfirst, rolled, came up beneath a big spruce, and found both beholders facing him. If the big one was troubled by the green gore pumping from its severed eyestalks, it showed no sign.

Galaeron raised his sword—and promptly found his view blocked by Melegaunt's broad back. There was just enough time to notice how strange it seemed that the wizard had a dark, well-defined shadow in the flat blizzard light before both beholders blasted the dusky man with their silver rays.

"No!" Galaeron raised his sword and sprang forward to avenge what he knew would be the end of Evereska. Something snagged his foot as he tried to cross Melegaunt's shadow, and he fell flat on his face. "By the Red Moon!"

Quite certain the next instant would be his last, he looked down and found the wizard's shadow holding his ankle.

"You've done your part," said Melegaunt's familiar voice.

No sooner had the wizard spoken than a set of muffled hoofbeats came pounding through the forest. Instead of attacking Galaeron, the big beholder spun to face the sound—then died without a shriek as Vala's black sword came flying from the opposite direction and cleaved it down the center.

The smaller beholder spun all ten eye tentacles in the direction from which the sword had come, only to be driven to the ground when Malik came flying off his horse from behind and began slashing eyestalks with his dagger. Galaeron scrambled to his feet and rushed to help, but by then Vala was already on the creature. She extended one hand to summon her sword, used the other to crush an eye when the stalk swung in her direction, then caught the weapon and drove the tip through the beholder's skull. Unlike Galaeron's blade, hers sank to the hilt.

"Elf?" Aris's looming figure peered over the fallen tree, a big boulder grasped in each hand. "Elf, are you alive?"

"For now."

Galaeron turned to see Melegaunt's mangled body dissolving into shadow, and his shadow coalescing into a healthy body.

"Melegaunt, you were not to risk your life," Galaeron said. "We agreed for the sake of Evereska."

"Aye," said the wizard. "But after you troubled yourself so dearly to save him, how could I let the giant die?"

CHAPTER TWELVE

27 Nightal, the Year of the Unstrung Harp

Galaeron felt himself jerk, then felt the hand clamped over his shoulder and knew that—impossibly—an intruder had crept up on him during his own watch. He rolled away from the tree he had been leaning against and tangled in a heavy cloak in which he did not recall covering himself.

"To your weapons!" Even as he yelled the alarm, he feared he was too late. "They're on us!"

Despite the entangling cloak, Galaeron somehow rolled to his knees and faced his attacker. He found himself looking at three bewildered humans and a very concerned stone giant.

"It's only us, Galaeron," said Vala. "That must have been some dream."

"Dream?" Galaeron threw off the cloak and, searching the woods behind them, reached for his sword. "I wasn't dreaming. How could I have been dreaming?"

Vala rolled her eyes. "That's what people do when they sleep."

"That's what *humans* do when they sleep," Galaeron corrected. He was not sure which implication he resented more, that humans were *Tel'Quess*—of the People—or that he had neglected his duty by sleeping on his watch. "And I was not sleeping!"

"No?" It was the little round-faced man with the bulging eyes who asked this. Galaeron needed a moment to recall what he was doing with them. "Then what are you doing when you close your eyes and snore?"

The night did seem oddly bright, Galaeron realized. He frowned and looked eastward, where an amorphous sphere of light hung just above the Greypeak Mountains. Even through the thick mantle of concealing snow clouds, there could be little doubt that the glowing pearl was the morning sun.

"I fell asleep?" The alarm in Galaeron's voice was unmistakable. "In the middle of my watch?"

"Don't feel bad." Vala gathered his cloak off the snow and offered it to him. "Malik took over, and you needed the rest."

Galaeron accepted the cloak and dropped to his haunches. After two days without a Reverie, there was no denying he needed rest. But to fall asleep—by *accident*? He suddenly began to feel lost and hollow, as though something inside had vanished.

"Why so worried?" Melegaunt came to his side. "Elves *do* sleep. I've seen them."

"Occasionally," said Galaeron. "When we're sick or wounded, sometimes when we're despondent or fall prey to the Gloom, more often as we grow older and the time to go West draws near."

Vala nodded. "When you need to escape your pain and rest. Not so different from humans."

"Much the same," allowed Galaeron, "except that we never *fall* asleep. It's a purposeful act."

"What a joy that must be," exclaimed Malik. "Me, I am always lying awake when I should be sleeping and sleeping when I should be awake. This year alone, it has nearly cost me my life a dozen times." He hesitated a moment, his mouth contorting oddly as he struggled not to say more, then he blurted, "I hardly dare close my eyes for fear of having my throat cut by that Harper witch Ruha!"

Galaeron frowned. The Harpers were among the few humans generally accorded admittance to Evereska, and the mere fact that one of them counted Malik an enemy was reason to be suspicious of him. On the other hand, the little man *had* risked his own life to save Galaeron and Aris from the beholders, and any trouble between humans was no business of the tomb guard's or Evereska's.

Vala and Melegaunt seemed even less interested in Malik's revelation than Galaeron. Vala pursed her lips as though wondering why the little man thought they should care, and Melegaunt merely tugged his beard and studied Galaeron.

Finally, he said, "Things didn't go exactly as we planned with Aris's rescue. How much did you strain yourself with the magic I showed you?"

"I think of it as the cold magic," said Galaeron. "A lot. There was no choice."

Melegaunt's face turned instantly stormy. "Fool! Did I not warn you against testing yourself with this magic?"

"I wasn't testing," said Galaeron. "There was no other choice."

"There is always another choice," said Melegaunt. "It would be better to surrender your body to the beholders than to surrender your spirit to your shadow."

Melegaunt came forward and grabbed Galaeron's head, then tipped it back and pulled his eyelids open.

"There it is. You've let your shadow inside."

Galaeron's stomach turned to ice. "Then get it out!"

"I can't." Melegaunt released Galaeron's eyelids and stepped back. "You must learn to control it, before it learns to control you."

"Control it? How?"

"Carefully—very carefully," said Melegaunt. "Shadows are subtle things. It will try to subvert your nature, to make you see the dark in everything around you."

"See the dark?" asked Galaeron. "You mean dark motives?"

"In a way, yes. For every light, there is a shadow. It will make you look at the shadow instead of the light, to see how every noble act might be selfish. Gradually, you will come to see the darkness before the light. When that happens, you are your shadow."

Galaeron's throat went dry, and he could not bring himself to speak again.

"Galaeron, you must learn to do the hardest thing of all," said Melegaunt. "You must always make sure you see the light before you see the shadow."

"That will be hard." Galaeron thought of the suspicions that had been plaguing him the past few days, and of his decision to keep secret the way the cold magic had rushed into him during the battle against the bugbears. "Why did you ever show me this magic, Melegaunt?"

"Are you that weak?" Melegaunt grabbed his arm and pulled him to his feet. "I give you the most precious gift in the world, and you call it poison? Your shadow is winning already, elf."

The words hit Galaeron like a blow, for his trouble entering the Reverie had come with his doubts about Melegaunt's character. Had the shadow been inside even then? Despite the cold, he felt flushed and sweaty.

"There's something I should have told you about the bugbear battle," Galaeron said.

"The new magic came to you?"

"Unbidden," Galaeron replied. "When I cast my spells, it rushed in of its own accord. I had to concentrate to keep it out."

Melegaunt nodded. "Looming death has a way of bringing you closer to your shadow self." The wizard stared at him. "It is more troubling that you kept it from me."

"You keep so many secrets of your own." Even to Galaeron, his tone sounded defensive. "And after you sicked the illithids on Lord Imesfor, I *did* have reason to doubt you."

"We talked about that. If you were not satisfied with my explanation, you should have said so." Melegaunt's voice lacked its usual patience. "This will be a struggle, elf, and I don't know that you will win."

Galaeron's heart sank. "I don't want this magic. There must be something you can do."

"There is." Melegaunt glanced meaningfully toward Vala's sword. "And should you fail, I will."

"It would be that bad?"

"It would," said Melegaunt. "And I am not here to release yet another evil on this world."

"Nor would I want that. I will take your word as a promise." Galaeron turned to Vala. "And one from you, as well."

She raised her brow and glanced at Melegaunt. When the wizard nodded grimly, she shrugged and seemed a little sad. "I hope you know what you're asking."

"He is only asking what is right," said Melegaunt. He cast a wary eye eastward, where Thousand Faces stood hidden by snow and trees and far fewer miles than any of them would have liked. "We must be on our way. The beholders will come looking for us—"

"I will show you a safe way." It was the first Aris had spoken. "You are going to the Delimbyr River?"

"A little beyond, yes," said Melegaunt, "but that would be a good start."

"Then follow."

Aris turned up the narrow side gulch where they had made camp and started through the blizzard. Melegaunt led the way after him through knee-deep snow. With Malik's horse breaking trail, they were just able to keep the giant's looming silhouette from vanishing into the storm.

As they climbed, Galaeron barely noticed the slope growing steeper. He could not help being frightened—frightened of what he might become, more frightened of what he might cease being. Elves who could not enter the Reverie soon became something else altogether. Unable to share in a communion of like hearts, they grew immeasurably sad and lonely. Eventually, such lone wolves withered of despair or abandoned their home, preferring a life alone—or even among humans—to the constant reminder of the bliss they could no longer share.

Without that connection to his fellows, Galaeron did not know if he would have the strength to control his shadow. Even now, it seemed reasonable to be wary of Melegaunt. Humans were well known for treachery, and the wizard's furtiveness certainly invited misgivings. Why wouldn't he say who he hoped to find, or why he had been studying the phaerimm, or where this new magic came from?

It occurred to Galaeron that Melegaunt's warning might be a scheme to make him doubt his own misgivings. Certainly, there could be no better way to quell a person's suspicions than to make them an object of fear. Hardly had this thought flashed through the elf's mind before another followed suggesting his shadow had planted the previous one. Galaeron had entered a maze of spirals, where every idea turned back on itself and no opinion could be trusted. He felt as though the ground had vanished from beneath the snow, leaving him to flail around helplessly until he grew tired of struggling and simply let the blizzard take him.

After a time, they crossed a high white meadow and came to a steep gully packed full of snow. Aris instructed them to stand well off to one side, then cupped his hands and gave a booming yell. There was a soft rumble so quiet and low Galaeron felt it more than heard it. In the next instant, a tremendous avalanche swept out of the gully and spread across the meadow.

Aris waited a few minutes for the snow to stabilize, then pointed up the chute. "The ridge on top descends into the Delimbyr Valley. Stay on the crest and follow it to the river. The trees are tall and thick, so you won't be seen by any but a few stone giants traveling the same path. Don't hide from them, and tell them what you did for me, and they will do you no harm."

"And what of you, Aris?" asked Galaeron. "Will you be all right?"

"I think not." Aris's voice was so angry and low that it felt like another avalanche barreling down the chute. He snapped the top off a thirty-foot pine, then began to strip away the branches. "The massacre of my steading was a terrible thing, but what those eyes did to the Saga Caves . . . for destroying the work of two thousand years, I will make them pay."

"Sadly, you will not," said Melegaunt. "At least not alone. Will others of your kind help?"

The giant shook his head. "I would not ask such a thing. The responsibility is not theirs."

"No, but it is ours," said Melegaunt. "Perhaps even more than it is yours."

Malik's eyes grew wide. "Think what you are saying—and who you are saying it to!" He craned his neck up at the giant. "The wizard speaks for himself."

The giant paid no attention to the little man and kneeled down over Melegaunt. "Explain."

"Do you know of the phaerimm?" asked the wizard.

Aris nodded. "I have seen their shapes in some of the old murals. A fell and powerful race, by the hewn stories."

"And a cunning race," said the wizard. "Though the beholders may not realize it themselves, the phaerimm are their masters. The phaerimm sent them to Thousand Faces to find us."

"There is no fool like an honest one!" exclaimed Malik, clambering onto his horse. "I pray you have not killed us all!"

Neither Aris nor anyone else paid any attention to the little man. The giant merely considered the wizard's words for a time, then rubbed his long chin and turned to Galaeron.

"And even knowing they were looking for you, you risked all your lives to save mine?"

Galaeron nodded. "I could not have left you and lived with myself."

"You nearly did not survive saving me," said the giant. "That was not a wise thing to do."

"It was wiser than you returning alone to face the beholders," said Melegaunt. "We would join you if we could, but there is greater evil afoot, and we must continue on our way."

The giant nodded. "It is enough that you rescued me."

"You would be doing us a service not to waste our efforts by attacking so many beholders alone," said Melegaunt. "You would be lucky to kill one or two."

"Then that would be justice to one or two." Aris glanced in Galaeron's direction, then rose. "How could I live with myself, were I to fail my steading even in the little I could do to avenge its loss?"

"By doing more," said Galaeron. He knew what the giant was feeling, for he had felt much the same thing as the phaerimm encircled Evereska. "Would it not serve your steading better to strike a blow against the ones responsible for what happened to Thousand Faces?"

The stone giant furrowed his heavy brow. "How can I do that?"

"By coming with us," said Melegaunt, following Galaeron's lead. "We are sworn to destroy the phaerimm—the same phaerimm who sent their beholders to Thousand Faces."

Aris considered this for no more than ten minutes, a very short time for a stone giant, then said, "You must give me a promise in return."

"If it's within my power," said Melegaunt.

"I think it is," said the giant. "You must promise to accept my help until the end. If Thousand Faces is to be avenged, I must be part of it."

"Done," said Melegaunt. "And I promise you this as well, that the beholders who have taken your home are not long for this world. Before all is done, they will rue the day they laid eyes on your steading."

"Then it is a pact." Aris stooped down to pluck Malik out of his saddle.

"What are you doing?" Malik pulled a tiny dagger from inside his cloak and flourished it. "I must warn you—"

"The hill is a steep one," said Aris. Paying no attention to the tiny dagger, he placed Malik on the ground and scooped up the little man's horse. "I will carry this for you."

Aris tucked the mare under his arm and started up the chute, not seeming to notice the beast's flailing hooves and terrified whinnies. Malik scrambled after them, alternating warning the giant not to harm his Kelda and cooing words of comfort to the horse.

Galaeron and the others followed, and soon they were descending a snowy ridge toward the vast Delimbyr Valley. With Aris breaking trail, travel was fast. It required only a day and a half of solid walking to reach the base of the mountains, and the journey would have taken no more than a day had they not made two "brief" stops so Aris could warn giants coming in the opposite direction about the beholders.

As Galaeron listened to Aris's sorrowful descriptions of the fate of Thousand Faces, he found himself thinking of Evereska. Surely, his own city remained untouched. Even the phaerimm could not breach the magic of the mythal—at least not so quickly. Or could they? According to Melegaunt, the phaerimm of Myth Drannor were drawn to the area because of the mythal, and they were great magic users in their own right. What if they knew how to unweave its defenses? Once they entered the city, even the spell-guard would be unable to turn them back. Galaeron would become like Aris, a lone survivor with nothing to live for except vengeance. In a stone giant, such an existence was sad beyond words. In an elf, especially one struggling with his own shadow, it would become an unspeakable evil.

Galaeron longed to move faster, to insist that Melegaunt use his magic to speed them along—even to journey into the Shadow Fringe again—but he knew better than to suggest such a thing. After the battle at Thousand Faces, the phaerimm would be scouring the area for any hint of spell use, and even Melegaunt's strange magic would leave subtle incongruities in the world that would attract the attention of a careful searcher. Better to avoid magic altogether and let the blizzard conceal them.

The trip through the valley proved more trying. They were about halfway across when the blizzard blew itself out, catching them in the open a mile short of the river. Without a steady wind to fill their tracks, a party of bugbears soon spotted their trail and began to pursue. Instead of using magic to eliminate the threat, the companions rushed to the river and crossed the ice. When the bugbears followed, Aris hurled a few boulders into their midst, shattering the ice and plunging the entire band into the cold waters.

The companions were not so lucky the next afternoon, when two gray circles appeared just above the horizon. At first, the companions pretended not to notice their pursuers, hoping the pair would be foolish enough to catch up and attack. When the eye tyrants refused to take the bait, Melegaunt turned to cast a spell. The beholders vanished from sight. Later, Galaeron glimpsed one creature still trailing them. The other was nowhere to be seen.

"He's gone for help," Vala surmised.

Galaeron nodded. "With luck, it will only be beholders."

"*Only* beholders?" Malik gasped. "You are as mad as a cuckold in his harem!"

"Beholders would be better than phaerimm," said Melegaunt. "Unless you intend to make our fight your own, now would be a good time to part ways."

"So you can send your foes after me?" Malik's dark eyes shined with indignation. "I am hardly the fool I look, old man."

Melegaunt shrugged. "You were warned."

The wizard pulled a scrap of shadowsilk from his cloak and traced a shadowy maze on the snow. When he finished, he and Galaeron cast flying spells on everyone in the group—including Malik's astonished horse—and the companions streaked off toward the High Forest. The beholder avoided Melegaunt's shadow maze by circling wide, then became an ominous presence that appeared on the horizon now and again to remind them of their approaching danger.

Finally, they reached the High Forest and slipped into the woods. The beholder stopped behind a hill and hovered there with one eyestalk peering over the summit. Several of the other stalks flitted in and out of view, looking in all directions in search of help.

"Now we have them," said Melegaunt. He pulled a piece of shadowsilk from his cloak and tore off a strand, then strung it between two trees. "We're almost to Karse."

"Karse?" gasped Malik. "Why are we going there?"

"We are not." Melegaunt handed Galaeron a second piece of shadowsilk and motioned for him to begin stringing strands. "Once we have finished

here, it will be safe to part ways. I'm sure you're as eager to be about your business as we are ours."

"I have no business." Malik paused as though that was all he meant to say, then slowly cocked his head to one side and added, "Except you."

"Us?" Melegaunt continued to string shadow strands between trees. "And what would your business be with us?"

Malik paled and said, "Nothing . . . except—"

The rest of the explanation was lost to a tremendous crashing from the forest behind them. Galaeron spun around to see an enormous oak stomping up, its branches waving madly and a huge trunk cavity twisted in an angry snarl.

"No!" the tree boomed. It swept a branch down past Galaeron's head at the strands he had been stringing between tree trunks. The limb passed through the shadowy fibers without effect. A fierce shudder ran through the oak's crown of golden leaves, and it shook a bough in Galaeron's face. "Not in my wood!"

"We mean no harm to the f-forest," Galaeron stammered. Now that he had recovered from his surprise, he recognized the oak as the oldest treant he had ever seen, with a long beard of green moss and a trunk easily a dozen feet around. Realizing the creature would view Aris's wooden club with a dim eye, Galaeron motioned the giant to keep watch at the edge of the forest, then turned back to the treant. "We must take measures to protect ourselves. We're being pursued by beholders."

"By *one* beholder. Eyes I have." To prove it, the treant blinked a pair of knotholes more than fifteen feet up his trunk. "And your welfare is no concern of mine. There is a wrongness to your magic, and in my wood I will not have it."

"It is, indeed, magic of a different sort," said Melegaunt, "but that does not make it wrong."

"That makes it wrong for the High Forest." The treant tried again to drag down the shadow web, then turned to Galaeron when he failed. "Take this down."

Galaeron began to gather the shadowsilk into a ball, drawing a disapproving scowl from Melegaunt.

"What are you doing?"

"This is Turlang's home," said Galaeron, guessing at the treant's identity. Only Turlang, the renowned ruler of the High Forest, could be so huge and old. "We must respect his wishes."

Melegaunt rolled his eyes. "You do know that means they'll catch us?" He glanced at Turlang, then added, "And there would be a battle."

"Fuorn's whispers spoke of your gift to the Forgotten Forest, Duskbeard, so one threat I will forgive." The treant creaked down to peer into Melegaunt's eyes. "His whispers also spoke of the trouble that hunts you, and I will have no magicgrubs in my forest."

"Then you would do well to help us." Melegaunt waved his hand at Galaeron and the others. "We have all sworn to return the phaerimm to their prison, and the help we need lies inside your forest, in the temple of Karse."

Turlang drew himself to his full height. "What help can you need from Wulgreth? That you count a lich your friend only proves the evil I taste in your air."

A chill ran down Galaeron's spine. "Lich?" he echoed, finally understanding the reason Melegaunt had been so secretive about the help they were seeking. "What other lies have you been telling us?"

Melegaunt wagged a finger at Galaeron. "Be careful of that shadow, my friend." Looking back to Turlang, the wizard said, "Wulgreth is no friend of mine, but every treasure has its guardian, and I do mean to deal with him—though not in the way you believe."

Turlang fell silent and motionless, presumably weighing Melegaunt's words against the evil "taste" of their party. As suspicious as Galaeron was of Melegaunt, he feared the malevolence the treant sensed lay in his own dark spirit. Try as he might, the elf could not help attributing the most selfish motives to every action. Melegaunt hoped to strike a bargain with an evil lich. Malik wanted to steal the secret of shadow magic. Turlang refused to help them because he feared the wrath of the phaerimm. Galaeron was losing the fight against his shadow.

He stepped forward and placed himself squarely in front of the treant. "The Turlang my mother speaks of would never turn away a tree-friend."

"Nor would the one standing before you," said the treant. "Were he certain they were tree-friends."

"Then you will not turn us away." When Galaeron waved a hand at his companions, he found only Melegaunt, Vala, and, still standing watch at the edge of the forest, Aris. Malik and his horse were nowhere to be seen, apparently having decided to accept Melegaunt's advice and depart. "On my life, I promise no one here will harm the High Forest, nor allow any harm to come to it through anything he does or does not do."

Turlang regarded him for a long time, then said, "Your life means nothing to me. I know you for an Evereskan by your dress and speech, but there is a darkness in you I do not trust."

"There are more eye-devils coming," Aris called from the edge of the forest.

"How many?" Vala called back, ever the battle chief.

"Too far to say," said the giant. "They are only specks, but there's also something that resembles a dust devil."

Galaeron and Vala exchanged nervous glances, and Melegaunt ran out of patience.

"We're out of time, tree," the wizard growled. "There is more at risk than your forest, and we *will* pass through—"

"What we will do is abide by Turlang's will," Galaeron interrupted. Even were Melegaunt powerful enough to defeat Turlang and his many allies—and Galaeron suspected the battle would be closer than the wizard knew—for an elf to defy a treant in his own forest would be an act of wickedness as terrible as treason. Galaeron turned back to the treant. "If the great Turlang places no value in my promise, I am certain he will value my mother's."

"You would offer your mother's life in place of your own?" Turlang's voice was condemning. "Who is this lucky elf?"

Galaeron had to bite back a wave of anger. "Morgwais Nightmeadow."

The burls above Turlang's eyes rose. "Morgwais?"

Galaeron nodded. "Known to the people of the High Forest as Morgwais the Red."

Vala and Melegaunt looked to each other with expressions of surprise. The treant considered Galaeron's claim for a long time, during which Aris kept up a running account of what he saw.

"They're tiny circles . . . six of them, and something like a funnel with a tail. The one behind the hill is flying back to join them . . ."

Finally, Turlang spoke. "If you are lying about this, your lives are forfeit." He glanced to Vala and Melegaunt, then added, "All of them."

"Agreed," said Galaeron.

Vala and Melegaunt were quick to nod their own agreement, and Aris said, "My life is Galaeron's to pledge."

"Then we have a bargain." Turlang lowered two branches. "I will need your weapons . . . and your pledge not to use your dark magic until you enter the Dire Wood."

Galaeron removed his scabbard and laid it into a tangle of gnarled sticks. "As you wish."

Vala removed her belt and wrapped it around the hilt of the weapon to prevent the black blade from slipping free, then laid it next to Galaeron's sword. Melegaunt pulled his sheathed dagger from its place, but hesitated before laying it alongside the other weapons.

"The dagger I'll yield happily," said the wizard, "but the magic I may need to confuse our foes."

"They will be confused," said Turlang. "I will see to that."

"These are no ordinary beings," Melegaunt warned. "The phaerimm will not be fooled by normal magic, and the beholders can dispel it with a glance."

"It will not be magic that misleads them." Turlang's tone was uncharacteristically peevish for a treant. "Will you promise or not?"

Melegaunt gave Galaeron a hesitant look.

"Decide now," said Galaeron. "It will mean my mother's life if you lie."

At the edge of the forest, Aris called out, "They're spreading out, and turning invisible—the cowards!"

Melegaunt continued to look at Galaeron. "You're sure?"

"It's the only way," Galaeron answered.

Melegaunt shrugged. "Very well, I promise."

Turlang studied the wizard for nearly a minute before shifting his gaze to Aris. "Are you ready, giant?"

For a moment, Aris continued to stare across the valley, his lip curled into a hateful snarl. When he finally nodded and stepped into the forest, his gray eyes were as cold as ice.

"Let's go."

Turlang stretched a branch toward the giant's wooden club. "Your weapon."

Aris passed the club over. The treant held it at limb's length and inspected it for a moment, then he seemed to realize that it had been fashioned from an entire tree trunk. His face twisted into a strange expression of sadness and revulsion, and he dropped the weapon into the snow. The wood grew instantly brown and soft and crumbled into humus.

"Now we may go."

Turlang started into the dark forest, his enormous bulk gliding through trees as gracefully as any elf. Galaeron motioned the others after him, then took a place beside Vala at the end of the line.

She leaned close to him. "Did you see what became of Malik?"

"Not a hoof print," Galaeron replied. He glanced back and was not surprised to see a dozen trees arranging themselves into a boscage, while a like number of druids slipped quietly to and fro, eradicating all trace of the group's passing and laying a false trail in the opposite direction. "But I do hope he didn't go south."

CHAPTER THIRTEEN

28 Nightal, the Year of the Unstrung Harp

The scout and his hippogriff wheeled down out of the gray sky, a ghostly rider on a ghostly mount, almost impossible to see against the steely clouds even with detection magics fully raised. Khelben glanced over at Laerm Ryence, his counterpart and co-commander of the Swift Cavalry, and found the elf's silver eyes fixed on the trail ahead. Here they were, racing toward an army of phaerimm as fast as their spell-driven mounts could gallop, and the fool still had not bothered to cast his detection magic. Such negligence did not speak well for Evermeet's expeditionary company.

The scout swept up alongside the column, his hippogriff's wings thrumming air as he slowed. Lord Ryence jumped visibly, his free hand dropping to his belt of wands, his neck craning to look over the wrong shoulder.

"No need for alarm," Khelben yelled, his voice falling into the rhythm of his galloping mount. He wrapped his reins around his saddle's pommel, then worked a spell to mute the thundering hooves of the four hundred horses behind him. "It's my scout."

Ryence's fingers finally flashed through a detection spell. "So . . . I . . . see." Like most of the elves, he seemed ill at ease on the powerful chargers Lord Piergeiron had selected for their journey. "I am not blind."

Ignoring the testy reply, Khelben turned to his scout. "What is your report?"

The rider, a long-faced man with a two-day growth of beard, said, "About two miles ahead, the Winding Water bends within an arrow's flight of the High Moor. Not a thousand paces beyond, the Serpent's Tail forks north and blocks your way."

"A good place for an ambush?"

"The best. You'd be trapped against the Winding Water, with the Serpent's Tail blocking the way ahead."

Khelben glanced at the steep slope flanking them to the north. Though the escarpment rose only a hundred feet to the High Moor, its face was soggy and slick—difficult climbing under the best of circumstances, impossible with arrows and lightning bolts raining down from above. Opposite the moor lay the Winding Water, easily two hundred paces across, with a dark central channel purling between two banks of solid ice.

"We'll need to cross." Khelben nodded toward the river. "I can bridge the distance with a space-folding door, but we'd have to feed riders through one at a time. It might be faster for your Selu'taar to fashion a good-sized bridge."

Ryence tried to look surprised. "What makes you think there are high mages here?"

"You try my patience, Lord Ryence," Khelben said darkly. Were Laeral there, she would have been proud of him for not calling the elf a liar. "Now is a poor time to insist on polite little secrets."

It was Ryence's aide, a venerable Gold male named Bladuid, who answered, "A bridging spell would not be difficult. Half an hour would be sufficient."

"Too much time," grouched Ryence, annoyed that Bladuid had betrayed his identity. The elf commander pointed his chin toward the wall of snow-caked trees along the river's southern bank. "And we would only have to cross again, or have the Forest of Wyrms to worry us for the next hundred miles."

"Better to lose an hour or two crossing rivers than half a company fighting an ambush."

Ryence's eyes flashed white, and he looked to Khelben's scout. "Did you see any ambushers atop the moor?"

Somewhat reluctantly, the rider shook his head.

"He wouldn't," said Khelben. "Not if the phaerimm are using their magic."

"I'm willing to take that chance."

"I'm not," said Khelben. "There must be enough of us left to hold after we raise our end of the gate. If the phaerimm destroy it, it will take a month for the army to reach Evereska."

"I am not surprised to hear such talk from a human," said Ryence. "The phaerimm are not threatening one of your cities."

"It may not be a human city they are attacking, but plenty of human blood will be spilled defending it." Khelben struggled to conceal the full depth of his contempt for this elf. He had witnessed enough noble ambition to recognize a lord trying to make a name for himself, and he knew that such fools rarely had the good taste to get only themselves killed. "You'd do well not to waste it."

"No elf has asked you to waste anything," said Bladuid, urging his horse alongside Ryence's. "As far as we are concerned, this is an elf matter."

Though Khelben was well aware of the disdain in which most Gold elves held humans, he was unaccustomed to feeling its sting himself. Drawing himself to his full height, he glared past Ryence at the high mage.

"Perhaps you have forgotten who I am. My father was Arun Maerdrym, noble son to House Maerdrym of Myth Drannor." What Khelben did not add—though it was obvious by his entirely human appearance—was that Arun had been a half-elf, and as such the first son of mixed race to be acknowledged by a noble house. "And I, personally, am one of the few—human, elf, or otherwise—who actually recalls living in Myth Drannor."

"Then you should know what happens when elves and humans mix," the high mage replied. "How long ago was it that Myth Drannor fell?"

"More recently than Aryvandar," Khelben shot back. "And you can hardly blame humans for that."

The gibe drew an angry snarl from Ryence and a black glare from Bladuid. No elf—especially no Gold elf—liked to be reminded of how the Crown Wars had shattered the golden age of elven civilization.

Khelben softened his tone. "Fortunately, the spirit of Myth Drannor still lives in some—even in Evereska. I myself have always found a warm welcome in the vale."

"Yes. Perhaps if more humans risked their lives *helping* elves instead of robbing their tombs, they would receive the same welcome you did." The high mage was referring to the time—nearly a thousand years earlier—that Khelben had almost died saving three Evereskans from a phaerimm ambush. When the grateful elves took him home to recover from his wounds, he became the first human ever allowed to see Evereska.

"If I may be so bold," said Khelben's scout, still flying just above his shoulder, "we are trying to help *now.*"

"How very noble of you," Bladuid said. "And your generosity has nothing to do with what will become of human lands if the phaerimm succeed?"

"Waterdeep is a long way from Evereska, mage." The scout looked back to Khelben and pointed up the trail. "There's the bend, milord. If you're going to cross, you'd better do it soon."

Khelben looked over to Ryence. "What say you? Will you humor me this once?"

The elf lord considered his request only a second. "There's no need. We must be two hundred miles from Evereska. The phaerimm are not going to ambush us here."

"Then I wish you well," said Khelben, pulling his horse out of line.

Ryence's eyes widened. "What are you . . ."

That was all Khelben heard before Ryence was carried out of earshot. He raised his hand to call Waterdeep's riders to him, then watched with a heavy heart as the elf warriors streaked past, their heads swinging around to look in his direction. He would have felt better, had their expressions had been less indignant and more perplexed.

The scout landed beside Khelben, keeping a tight rein on his hippogriff so it did not try to snack on the gathering horses.

"A wise choice, milord." In the thickening cloud of steaming horse breath, the scout's invisible form was barely discernible even to Khelben. "That elf is too eager to find his death."

"Let us hope he finds it later rather than sooner. Ryence may be a fool and Bladuid a bigot, but their warriors are brave and worthy, else they would not have traveled so far to fight someone else's battle." Khelben looked away from the elves and fixed his attention on the scout. "Shantar, is it not?"

"An excellent memory, Lord Blackstaff."

"There are only a dozen of you," said Khelben, dismissing the compliment with a wave of his hand. "Tell me how the moor looked when you flew over it. Can a horse cross it?"

"The ground looked frozen enough, but it was too broken. I fear we'd cripple as many as we didn't."

The last of the elf riders passed by, leaving the archmage alone with his company of volunteers—barely a hundred warriors and a quarter that many battle mages. The men looked nervously from one to another, waiting in silence for their commander to explain why he had divided the Swift Cavalry. Khelben paid them no attention, convinced they would learn the reason soon enough, but hoping they would not.

Shantar finally grew impatient. "Lord Blackstaff? The river?"

Khelben looked across the Winding Water to the barren trees, knowing how difficult it would be to return across the river if the elves were ambushed.

"We can't chance the river." Khelben dismounted and passed his reins to a nearby rider, then drew his staff from its holster and started up the slope. "We'll have need of those elves."

✡✡✡✡✡

The first hint of the village was the fruity reek of fireweed smoke, a stench that had led Galaeron to the camp of more than one shiftless, tomb-robbing wizard unable to forgo his indulgence for a few nights. This particular smoke happened to be especially foul, and he had a sudden vision of his mother and her friends squatting in the snow outside their storm-lodge, their hands cupped around white meerschaum bowls and their heads swaddled in clouds of brown fume. Wood elves were the most capricious of *Tel'Quess,* ever ready to test some new delight or enliven a party with a touch of intemperance, and he could easily imagine them becoming slaves to the pipe after seeing some human wizard blow smoke rings through a yellow-stained beard.

As Turlang led the small company deeper into the village, they heard a male voice singing a bawdy tale of one night love. A rush of laughter punctuated each verse, and it was not long before Galaeron could identify his own mother's voice among them. As always, it stirred in him a youthful longing he had long thought past—and also deeper, angrier emotions upon which he dared not dwell if he meant to keep his shadow at bay.

Like most *sy Tel'Quess* settlements, the winter village of Rheitheillaethor was more of a camp than a town. On the ground stood rough huts of log and mud meant only to deceive intruders, while the elves' true homes sat high among the trees. Modest both in size and construction, the nestings were usually no more than a waxed leather tent covering a platform of dead-fall logs. Often, the walls were decorated with elaborate dye-work grisaille depicting winter scenes, usually rendered so that the art enhanced the camouflage. To spare the residents the effort of descending to the forest floor when they wanted to go somewhere, the entire hamlet was linked by an intricate network of catwalks and swing-ropes, all cleverly disguised as crisscrossing limbs and draping vines. With a fresh twilight snow on the ground, as there was now, a careless observer might easily cross all of Rheitheillaethor and never see the real village.

Galaeron's companions were not careless observers. Vala and Melegaunt pretended not to notice the eyes peering down from the sentry hollows, but the care they took to avoid fields of fire suggested they knew exactly where Rheitheillaethor stationed its archers. Aris was not so subtle. The stone giant simply stomped from one tree to another, studying the grisaille and mumbling to himself as he admired the most inspiring of the works. If he noticed the startled elf mothers herding their wide-eyed children out the opposite sides of the nestings, he showed no sign.

At last, they reached the village center. Turlang stepped aside, revealing Rheitheillaethor's only permanent building, a white marble longhouse. Aris was instantly on his hands and knees, studying the sculpted frieze work ringing the building.

Fifty paces beyond the longhouse, a hundred Wood elves sat on snow-cushioned deadfall logs, swilling triplewild mead and listening to the bawdy song the companions had been hearing. The lyrics were being sung by a throaty-voiced human seated on the Honor Chair—a flat-topped boulder nestled in a crook along the bank of the Heartblood River. The fellow's face was thin and weathered, with dancing eyes and a flowing beard stained yellow around the mouth. One hand held a long-stemmed pipe that had single-handedly covered the clearing with a cloud of turquoise smoke, while the other was cupping the fanny of the laughing Wood elf woman who sat on his lap.

With amber eyes, waist-length hair as richly golden as honey, and a face so deeply copper it could only be called red, the Lady of the Wood looked as strikingly beautiful as ever, and it took Galaeron a moment to accept that it was actually his mother on the human's lap. Though Morgwais scorned humans even more than did most Wood elves—and the Wood elf abhorrence of humans was legendary—she did not seem to dislike this man. She had one arm wrapped around his neck and her bosom pressed to his cheek, and if she was troubled by the wrinkled hand on her behind, she hid the fact well.

Turlang waited while the human finished his song, then rustled his branches. "Forgive the intrusion, tree-friends."

At the sound of the treant's voice, Galaeron's mother smiled broadly and turned to look, the delight in her eyes bespeaking the regard all elves held for the forest master.

"Turlang?"

"I have need of words, Lady Morgwais."

"Of course," Morgwais called. She jumped off the human's lap, then spread her arms wide and started forward. "Welcome."

The treant dipped his leafy crown. "Always a joy."

"What brings you to Rheitheillaethor, my friend?" As she slipped past the other elves, she finally seemed to notice Aris kneeling beside the stormlodge. "And who is your tall friend?"

"Aris is neither friend nor foe to me—yet." Turlang lowered a limb toward Galaeron. "He is companion to one claiming to be your son."

"Galaeron?" Morgwais's gaze shifted to where Galaeron stood beneath Turlang's shadowy boughs, and she slipped past the treant to embrace him. "I didn't feel you enter the wood!"

"No?" The comment caused Galaeron to feel strangely resentful, as though she were accusing him of trying to surprise her. He cast a bitter glance toward the white-bearded human, now trailing his mother forward like a hart after his hind. "Perhaps you were distracted by your man-friend."

Morgwais retreated to arm's length and cocked a chastening eyebrow. "Did Aubric send you to look in on my virtue? Because I am certain your father has more important things to worry about."

This drew a chorus of titters from the Wood elves, who considered jealousy perverse. Galaeron felt the heat rise to his cheeks and started to grow angry with his mother for embarrassing him, then realized he had brought the ridicule on himself. To Sy'*Tel'Quess,* flirtation was as much a part of a good life as savory food and abundant drink, and even his father would not have been upset to find Morgwais sitting on someone else's lap. The cause of Galaeron's indignation was not her behavior; it was something much deeper and darker.

"I apologize," said Galaeron. "I doubt Father even knows I'm here. I was just so astonished to find you keeping a human's company I didn't know what to think."

The smile that returned to Morgwais's lips was only half doubtful. She took Galaeron's hand and motioned the white-bearded man forward. "Elminster is no ordinary human."

"Elminster?" It was Melegaunt who gasped this. "Of Shadowdale?"

"The very." As the old man stepped to Morgwais's side, the twinkle in his eye turned fiery. "And ye be Melegaunt Tanthul, I believe."

Melegaunt's eyes narrowed, and his expression changed from one of concern to something between awe and terror. "I am he—but you know that already."

Elminster puffed his pipe. "Thy efforts have not gone unnoticed, lad. There is talk of all ye've done for Evereska."

"And that's why you are here?" Galaeron was as dazed by the idea that anyone would call Melegaunt "lad" as he was excited to hear that Elminster himself had taken notice of his home's plight. "To help us?"

Elminster continued to look at Melegaunt. "That depends on what ye seek in Karse."

Melegaunt arched his brow. "What makes you think . . . ?" He seemed to suddenly realize the answer, then said, "The stone giants, of course—and Lord Imesfor thinks I'm Netherese."

"And I am not convinced he is wrong."

"Believe what you wish, but if you spoke to the stone giants, you must also know the phaerimm are desperate to stop us. That alone should convince you we serve the same goal."

Elminster's tone grew sharp. "I'd be more convinced, had there not been an illithid after Lord Imesfor's brain when he arrived at Khelben's. He said ye set a whole band on him."

"Then he is well." Though Melegaunt's reply was a statement, his audacity did not prevent him from cringing in the face of Elminster's ire. "Sometimes right and wrong are not so clear. Imesfor had to suffer that Evereska might live."

"Is that so?" Elminster's tone suggested it was not. "Had he arrived with no holes in his skull, methinks Khelben would have been on his way that much sooner."

"Khelben is going to Evereska?" Galaeron asked. "Khelben *Arunsun*?"

"Of course, lad. Did ye think he'd let the phaerimm take it?" The wizard pointed his pipe southward. "As we stand here talking, he's leading a company across the western plains to raise a translocational gate."

"What kind of company?" There was alarm and sorrow in Melegaunt's voice. "You are only sending live men after dead."

Elminster's irritation showed in his eyes. "Ye should not underestimate Khelben Arunsun."

"Never, but he is no more a match for the phaerimm than the Evereskans." Melegaunt gestured to Galaeron. "And young Nihmedu will tell you what became of them."

Galaeron met Elminster's eye and nodded. "The tomb guard, the border guard, the spell-guard—"

"Yes, yes—and half the high mages as well." Elminster dismissed Galaeron's account with a wave of his pipe. "Imesfor told us all about it, but Khelben has certain, ah, resources unavailable even to thy high mages."

Galaeron did not ask the old wizard to elaborate. At least in Evereska, it was well known that like Elminster himself, Khelben was one of Mystra's "Chosen." Nobody knew exactly what being Chosen meant, but it seemed fairly well accepted that these individuals were invested with some of the goddess of magic's divine power. According to rumor, they were nearly immortal and could call upon the power they carried to perform fantastic feats of magic. Certainly, it was good to have the Chosen taking Evereska's side—but still Galaeron did not think one would be enough.

"Good mage, you'd do well to listen to Melegaunt in this," said Galaeron. "If it's not too late to contact Lord Kh—"

"There be few men as stubborn as Khelben Arunsun." Elminster cocked his brow and fixed a questioning eye on Galaeron. "But it could be that I can call him off—if the reason be good enough."

"I can only tell you that without Melegaunt Tanthul, Lord Imesfor would be hatching an egg for the phaerimm right now," said Galaeron. "Melegaunt is the only one who seems able to engage our enemies on an equal footing."

Elminster shook his head. "Khelben is a proud man, I fear. Perhaps if ye could tell me what ye seek in Karse."

"Something to defeat the phaerimm." Galaeron looked to Melegaunt to elaborate, but the shadowmage kept his gaze fixed on Elminster and pretended not to notice. "That's all he's told me."

"Ye are a trusting spirit, lad," said Elminster. "It speaks well of thy own honesty—if not thy cunning wit."

"The phaerimm have been close on our trail the entire time," explained Melegaunt. "I thought it best to keep the plan to myself, lest bad come to worse."

"A wise precaution." Elminster stepped closer to Melegaunt and offered his ear. "But ye can tell me."

Melegaunt retreated, and Vala interposed herself between her master and his interrogator. Elminster might have missed the subtle tension that came to her body, but Galaeron did not.

"I can handle matters here," said Melegaunt. "If you truly want to do some good, you'll join Khelben in the south. A second hand flinging Mystra's silver fire would go far toward saving his company."

This drew a wry smile from Elminster. "Ye know more about me than I about thee . . . and I can see ye mean to keep it so."

"Your deeds have made a great name for you," said Melegaunt. "I have lived a quieter life, but Galaeron can tell you my intentions are good."

Elminster's voice turned hard. "I keep my own counsel about such things."

"That is your privilege," said Melegaunt. "Just as it is mine."

Elminster waited for him to elaborate, then finally sighed and shook his head. "Ah, well, I had hoped to do this a simpler way."

He slipped a hand into his pocket. Vala was instantly moving, one hand chopping for his throat and the other reaching for the offending arm.

A few hairs shy of his body, a blue aura flashed beneath her hands. She cried out in shock and pulled her arms back, then took one glance at her smoking fingertips and plunged them into the snow. Elminster gave her a bemused look, then pulled a small wad of fireweed out of his pocket and refilled his pipe.

"What'd ye think, girl? That I meant to enchant his secrets from him?" Elminster snapped his fingers, then held a small flame over the bowl of his pipe. "I've better ways than that."

The wizard puffed on his fireweed and glowered at Melegaunt through the awful-smelling smoke. The gaze Melegaunt returned was too nervous to be called a glare, but neither did he look away. Galaeron and the others watched in tense silence, reassured by Turlang's presence—and the great boughs he stretched over the pair's heads—that the matter would not come to a duel of spells, yet worried enough that they hardly dared breathe for fear of touching off a fight. Even Aris tore himself away from the stormlodge to come loom over the standoff.

Galaeron did not know what to make of the situation. Elminster was, by all accounts, a loyal elf-friend and a man of character, yet he seemed to presume a great deal in the demands he made of Melegaunt. On the other hand, Melegaunt had used Lord Imesfor to lure the illithids away—an act destined to be viewed in a dim light by anyone who did not understand how important their escape had been. Even knowing that Imesfor had survived, the thought still sent a guilty shudder down Galaeron's spine. How could Elminster, who had never seen Melegaunt risk his own life for others, react to the shadowmage's furtive nature with anything *but* suspicion?

Galaeron interposed himself between the mages. "It pains me to see you two off to such a bad start." He turned first to Elminster. "Given what happened to Lord Imesfor, your suspicions are reasonable, but Melegaunt did nothing wrong. Imesfor's life was Melegaunt's to do with as he pleased."

Elminster's were not the only human eyes to grow wide, but the mage was almost as quick as Lady Morgwais to take Galaeron's meaning.

"The Rule of Saving?" Elminster said. "I haven't heard that invoked in five hundred years!"

"Handsome as you are, you are not an elf," said Morgwais. She sidled up to Elminster and gave his beard a meaningful tug. "If Melegaunt saved Imesfor's life. . . ."

"And he did." Galaeron deliberately left out mention of his own part in the rescue. "I saw that much with my own eyes."

"You see? Melegaunt did nothing wrong!" Morgwais flashed Elminster a brilliant smile, then took him by the hand and started toward the river bank. "Let's go back to the party and drink this misunderstanding under."

Elminster flashed Melegaunt a scowl that said their meeting was far from over, but he was too well-mannered to refuse such a request from the Lady of the Wood. He allowed himself to be passed off to a young elf maiden and led back toward the Honor Chair. Morgwais turned to the treant.

"My thanks for bringing my son to Rheitheillaethor, Turlang. Do join us."

Turlang shook his leafy crown. "That cannot be. A magicgrub followed your son and these others into the forest, and I must return to watch it." He lowered a bough toward Galaeron. "I want only to be certain this one is who he claims. There is a darkness in him I do not trust, and I would know if you will vouchsafe his conduct, and that of his friends."

The light faded from Morgwais's face. "A darkness, you say?"

She took Galaeron's hand, then looked past his shoulder. Her gaze grew unfocused, as it would during the Reverie, and a single furrow appeared in her unblemished brow. She remained that way for several moments, then finally opened her eyes and nodded.

"It's true. You seem lost to me, child. It is as though you are . . ." She started to look away as though embarrassed, then hesitated and forced herself to look back. "It feels as though you are *asleep.*"

The comment struck Galaeron like a blow, and he realized with a start that he did not feel the other elves either. The absence had seemed normal enough during his travels with the humans—especially given his trouble falling into the Reverie—but he should have sensed other elves as they traveled deeper into the High Forest. Instead, there had been nothing—no sense of welcome, no warmth, no safety. He had felt nothing—nothing but the anger and jealousy he had experienced upon seeing his mother on Elminster's lap.

Galaeron forced himself to meet his mother's gaze. "I have been through some trying times, and it may be that even I shouldn't trust myself." He gestured to Melegaunt and Vala and added, "But I do know I can trust these humans."

Morgwais studied the humans for several moments, her gaze lingering on Vala longer than on Melegaunt, then she finally cracked a melancholy smile and stepped toward Vala.

"Vala," said Vala, extending her hand. "Vala Thorsdotter."

Unfamiliar with human customs, Morgwais stared in confusion at the out-thrust arm. "You will watch after Galaeron?"

Vala glanced briefly at Melegaunt, then gave a solemn nod. "That promise I have already made."

Morgwais shrugged and turned to Turlang. "I am Galaeron's mother." She glanced at Vala, then her smile broadened, and she said, "Of course, I will vouchsafe their conduct!"

She took Vala's hand and thrust it into Galaeron's, and that was when a svelte Wood elf in a brown Tomb Guard cloak pushed through the crowd. She had a familiar cupid's bow smile and a pair of doe brown eyes Galaeron would have recognized through a keyhole. The instant she stepped to Morgwais's side, her gaze dropped to the hands clasped between Galaeron and Vala.

"T-Takari!" Galaeron gasped.

Takari's gaze rose, the light already fading from her eyes. Her face remained hollow-cheeked and sallow from her wound, and her cloak hung more loosely than usual on her bony shoulders.

"I really shouldn't be surprised," said Takari, looking Vala up and down. She sighed dramatically, then reached past the human to pull Galaeron to her lips. "But she'll have to share!"

CHAPTER FOURTEEN

28 Nightal, the Year of the Unstrung Harp

Khelben had barely crested the slope before the first crack of war thunder rumbled across the frozen tussocks. Less than a mile distant, a rank of figures became visible along the moor's edge, their invisibility spells fading as they hurled sling stones and magic bolts down on Lord Ryence's elves. Khelben used his thumb and forefinger to make a circle over his eye and uttered a spell. The figures resolved themselves into a couple of hundred bugbears, perhaps twenty beholders, and a dozen mind flayers. A pair of phaerimm hovered together near the center.

"As you predicted, milord," said the scout Shantar, landing his invisible hippogriff beside Khelben. "We'll ambush the ambushers and be done with it."

"Our enemies would not make things so easy," observed Naneatha Suaril, cresting the slope beside Khelben. A blonde beauty whose pearly smile and shining eyes belied her fifty winters, Naneatha was Priestess of the High Moonlight of the House of the Moon in Waterdeep—and the unofficial commander of the small band of priests accompanying Khelben. "They are creatures of darkness, full of treachery and deception."

Khelben nodded and glanced over his shoulder. The rest of the company was scrambling up the slope, wands and bows at the ready. He directed the Sword Captain to form a combat line and the Wand master to scatter the battle mages behind it, then turned back to Naneatha and Shantar.

"The other scouts will be returning to the sound of battle?"

Shantar nodded. "They'll be here any minute."

"And your mounts can carry extra riders?" Khelben asked.

"For a short while." Shantar's eyes showed curiosity. "And lance work will be out of the question."

"Spells will serve you better," said Khelben. "Have the scouts assemble behind the battle line and take up Naneatha's priests. They are to circle high, half a mile behind us. That will keep even phaerimm from seeing through your invisibility."

Naneatha frowned. "A priest's place is in battle."

"And so it shall be." Khelben pointed his staff toward a scraggly pine hummock, then toward a cluster of moss-covered boulders. "Watch there for their rear guard. You and the scouts must strike them from behind—and strike hard."

Naneatha's scowl remained. "And if there is no rear guard?"

"There will be." Khelben turned to Shantar. "Do your *sending*, then wait until Lady Suaril is free to join you."

"As you command."

Shantar flicked his thumb over his scout's ring to activate its sending magic, and Khelben turned to find his small force ready. The archmage laid his staff aside, then he and Naneatha began to cast combat guards over the company. The spells required several minutes to complete, but Khelben did not even consider advancing until they were finished. Without spell shields, sending men against phaerimm would be murder.

Once the last spell was completed, Khelben sent Naneatha off with Shantar, then took up his staff and led the way forward at a run. The company followed in silence, the normal clamor muted by his war magic. Despite the frozen tussocks and wind whistling into their faces, they covered the ground swiftly, invigorated as much by approaching battle as by the prayers Naneatha had said over them.

Even Khelben, who had fought too many battles to enjoy the prospect of another, felt his pulse pounding wildly. This was the rousing part of war, the anticipation of the victory, the fear of a violent end, the reckless joy of a mortal gamble. Later came the hundred stenches of death, the grieving, the maimed bodies. The company passed the scraggly pine hummock Khelben had pointed out to Naneatha, closing to within three hundred paces of the enemy. The archmage slowed to a walk and raised his staff, signaling his archers to nock their arrows.

A pair of thunderclaps erupted from the pine hummock, and two lightning bolts exploded into the company spell shield and filled the sky with silver light. Next came a chorus of bugbear grunts, followed by a stone rain.

The sling stones struck the missile guard and bounced away, but a dozen of Khelben's archers shot arrows into the ground.

Not bothering to look back, Khelben brought his company to a halt and lowered his staff. The archers loosed a cloud of dark shafts into the air. Half the arrows fell short and the others came to a sudden halt, hanging motionless twenty feet above their targets. The phaerimm tipped their toothy maws toward Khelben, but seemed the only ones who noticed the attack. The bugbears and beholders with them continued to hurl death down from the moor's edge, paying no attention as the reciprocating barrage of elven magic burst harmlessly against their spell shields.

Another flurry of sling stones and lightning bolts struck Khelben's own missile guard from the rear, then Naneatha's priests sent a cacophony of crackles and booms rolling across the frozen moor as they unleashed their wrath. The answering chorus of anguished bellows left no doubt about the fate of the rear guard. Khelben leveled his staff at the phaerimm and advanced at a deliberate walk, assailing them with a stream of fiery missiles and magic blasts. The attacks exploded into fire storms and starbursts against the enemy spell shields, causing no damage, but blinding the phaerimm to Naneatha and the other hippogriff riders.

The phaerimm used their own fireballs and lightning bolts to disorient the humans, and a small band of beholders and bugbears turned to face Khelben's advance. He felt almost insulted. He had destroyed the phaerimm's rear guard and arrived behind their line uncontested, and still the creatures believed they could destroy his company with a handful of spells.

The beholders floated forward behind a screen of bugbears, using the hairy giants like shields until they closed to two hundred and forty paces—close enough to use their magic-disrupting beams on Khelben's spell-guards. He brought his company to a halt, then planted his staff at his side and pulled a piece of amber from his pocket. After rubbing this against his beard, he began to stroke a handful of silver pins over the amber one by one.

By the time he finished, the leading bugbears had closed to within a hundred and seventy paces, well outside the phaerimm spell-guards. He tossed the pins into the air and uttered a mystic syllable, then groaned as a bolt of lightning exploded from his chest and arced to the closest bugbear. The huge creature exploded into red haze and scorched fur, as did the beholder behind him and the next two bugbears, then the bolt continued down the line in a blinding flash that seemed to last forever. A second beholder and two more bugbears burst into flames, then another half dozen creatures spawned smoking holes in the centers of their bodies.

Had any other wizard cast the spell, the bolt's rampage would have fizzled there, but Khelben was no ordinary mage. He was Chosen of the goddess of magic herself, imbued with the power of the Weave and—at over nine hundred years old—nearly immortal himself, capable of withstanding energies that would incinerate any common man. The lightning continued, blasting through another dozen victims before the first dozen hit the ground. With each strike, the smoking holes shrank from the size of melons to fists to acorns. Finally, there were no more holes. One bugbear and two beholders died of nothing but shock. The last bugbear escaped altogether, stumbling three steps back and grabbing for his chest.

After the spell sputtered out, all that remained to carry on were half a dozen bugbears and two wide-eyed beholders. The bugbears turned to flee and perished instantly in a curtain of fire—phaerimm did not tolerate cowardice in their thralls. The two beholders focused their big central eyes on one another, encasing each other in a purple cone of magic-dispelling radiance.

"Arrows at the beholders!" Khelben commanded.

A flight of shafts leaped toward the beholders. The creatures had no choice but to deactivate their magic-dispelling rays and bring their other eyestalks around to defend themselves. Khelben's battle mages unleashed a veritable shower of magic, and the eye tyrants vanished into a roiling storm of fire.

"Forward walk!" Khelben called.

As the company started forward, the phaerimm assailed Khelben's spell shield with a tempest of fire and magic. Though the accompanying dazzle made it impossible to see what was happening ahead, Khelben was glad to have his foes finally showing him some respect. A little caution would do much to ease the attacks against the elves.

Had he wished, Khelben could probably have frightened the pair into a full withdrawal. As one of Mystra's Chosen, he carried within him a small part of the goddess's power—a power which manifested itself as silver fire. He could call upon silver fire to protect himself from most sorts of harm—hence his nine hundred years—and to assail his enemies with a blast of white, pure Weave magic. Even the mightiest magic-users quavered at its sight, for they usually recognized its true nature and knew what it meant for their survival, but Khelben was not ready to reveal all his secrets. The two phaerimm would teleport away the instant the battle turned against them, and he did not want them telling their friends back at Evereska what they were facing.

Khelben and his battle mages returned the phaerimm assault in kind, filling the area between them with a blinding wall of starburst radiance. Eventually, they would draw close enough to assail each other's spell-guards with dispelling magic, and the killing would begin.

Khelben flicked his thumb over his signet ring, activating its sending magic. He pictured Shantar's face in his mind, then spoke to the scout with thoughts. *Can't see. What's happening?*

Elves regrouping slowly. Shantar's reply came to Khelben in his mind's voice. *A hundred and fifty paces to hand-to-hand. Half their company is turning to face you.*

Khelben sighed in relief, then boomed an order, "Ready arrows—and it will be to the swords."

A hundred warriors nocked a hundred shafts and continued to advance. A black fog appeared over their spell shield. Khelben blew it aside with a magical wind.

"Mages halt—let the warriors screen you!"

The mages stopped in their tracks, adjusting their wands to arc fireballs and ice storms over the heads of their advancing comrades. Khelben himself slipped in behind a pair of archers and continued forward. He judged he would be close enough to dispel the enemy spell shields in thirty steps.

"Steady now," he called.

Half a dozen beholders zipped out of the enemy ranks, forsaking the safety of the phaerimm spell shields for a field of lightning and fire. Amidst all the flashing and streaking, they looked like mere cloud shadows, but that did not prevent Khelben's followers from peppering them with fiery bolts and hissing shafts. Three creatures erupted into flames the instant they left their spell-guards, and two more fell to arrows.

The sixth eye tyrant dodged and weaved its way forward by flashing its magic-dispelling gaze on and off so its other eyestalks could spray the sky ahead with their various magics. It destroyed several arrows with its disintegration beam and deflected a whole cloud with its telekinesis rays, but even that was not enough. It sprouted a dozen shafts and plummeted to the ground, then rolled forward three paces and came up facing Khelben.

A cone of blue light shot from the creature's huge central eye and touched the front wall of Khelben's spell-guards, creating an oval of shimmering radiance. The circle flickered, then swept over the rest of the shield in a flash of magic-dispelling brilliance. The enemy spells changed from dissipating starbursts to crackling bolts and sulfur-stinking ribbons. Men began to scream, flesh to sizzle, the frozen ground to rumble. Suddenly, the moor stank of charred flesh and opened entrails, sling stones hailed from the sky, and warriors fell by the dozen.

"Charge!" Khelben boomed, using a cantrip to make himself heard. *"Charge or die!"*

Khelben had barely given the order before the air turned silver and fresh-smelling around him. The man beside him erupted into a spray of boiling blood, then a lightning bolt blasted through the archmage and struck the next man in line. Khelben was hit in the head by a disembodied shoulder and knocked to the ground. By the time he could raise his head, the lightning bolt was already sputtering to a stop ten men away.

Before rolling to his feet, Khelben screened himself behind his charging warriors. He was protected from lightning strikes and magic bolts by Mystra's silver fire, but every second the phaerimm delayed him cost a dozen human lives. He scrambled forward on hands and feet, then laid his staff aside and stood. Though the phaerimm spell-guards still blazed with the dazzling starbursts of dissipating magic, a dark line of bugbear silhouettes stood just inside the barrier, axes raised and ready to meet the charge. The last few beholders—Khelben counted four—hovered along the line at even intervals, their eyestalks whipping this way and that as they sprayed the charging line with death rays of a dozen varieties. Only the mind flayers were nowhere to be seen. Khelben raised his hands toward the enemy spell-guard and spoke three mystic syllables.

The barrier flickered once, then faded. Khelben's battle mages rushed forward, using their war wands to assail the bugbears and beholders with lightning bolts and fireballs. The two phaerimm responded with a horrifying array of flame geysers and needle showers, black fogs and acid clouds, steaming pits and strangling tentacles. Half a dozen wizards fell in as many steps.

Khelben wrapped a pinch of coal in a swatch of gingham and flicked it in the general direction of the phaerimm. When the nugget landed, he raised a hand to point and began his incantation. As he rattled off the mystic syllables, he was careful to keep his finger aimed at the ground instead of at the creatures themselves. Centuries earlier, Khelben had learned that phaerimm were beings of magic and naturally resistant to its power. Any spell striking their bodies had a good chance of ricocheting back at the caster or being used to heal their wounds, so he was careful to use magic that affected the area around the phaerimm instead of the creatures themselves. He finished his spell, and a sphere of black gauze billowed up around the pair, encasing them in a cocoon of inky fibers. Though their spell flurry continued unabated, it was to far less effect.

The swiftest of Khelben's swordsmen were within fifty paces of their foes, where the bugbears seemed content to wait in rank. It was a mistake they would regret. Khelben retrieved his staff.

"Mages, redcloud!"

The battle mages exchanged their war wands for red candlewicks and began their incantations. As they spoke, they used simple cantrips to ignite the wicks, then held the burning strands at arm's length.

Determined to keep the phaerimm from interfering with the redcloud, Khelben rolled a parchment spell scroll into a cone and held it to his mouth. When he began to boom out the syllables of another spell, his voice sounded much closer to, and on the other side of, the black cocoon.

The phaerimm did not respond, even when the spell he had uttered turned the cocoon into a block of solid stone. Either they were not fooled, or they had decided it was time to flee. Khelben hoped it was the latter.

The first of the battle mages' candlewicks burned out. Above the heads of the bugbears appeared a single wisp of red haze, crackling so softly that only a handful of the creatures looked up. As more wicks burned themselves out, the red wisp became a ropy bank of crimson fog, and the crackling grew louder. Whole bands of bugbears glanced upward, and the eyestalks of the few remaining beholders swiveled overhead. By then, the last candlewicks were expiring, and the fog had coalesced into a roaring cloud of flame.

"Now!" Khelben boomed.

The battle mages crumpled the candlewicks' sooty remains, and a curtain of flame rolled down from the red cloud.

A single beholder managed to whirl itself backward and bring its magic-dispelling eye to bear, opening a small gap in the long wall of fire. Khelben leveled his staff at the creature's exposed underside and blasted it with a fireball. The resulting eruption engulfed not only the eye tyrant itself, but the handful of bugbears whose lives it had spared.

With nothing ahead but a swirling curtain of flame, the charging swordsmen drew up short. There were far too many gaps in their line to please Khelben, for the phaerimm had taken a terrible toll. Fully a third of his warriors had fallen, and perhaps a quarter of his battle mages. Another "victory" like that one, and he would not have enough men left to defend the gate—even if Ryence had managed to keep his high mages alive to establish it.

Khelben raised his arms to dispel the fire curtain so he could take the survivors of his company and save Ryence's elves—then he saw a bushy-bearded warrior kneeling behind a frozen tussock. The man cried out and lifted the corpse of a dead comrade to his armored breast. When the archmage saw that nothing remained of the body beneath the shoulders, he lowered his arms and reached into his cloak for a feather instead. His men had done enough for the elves that day.

Khelben! Come quick! This time, Shantar's message came in the form of a soft whisper. The scout could use the sending magic in his ring only once per day, but, as one of Mystra's Chosen, Khelben could hear the next sentence or so when someone spoke his name anywhere on Toril. *They're after the high mages!*

Khelben did not ask who "they" were. Unlike a sending spell, his eavesdropping gift did not allow a reply. Besides, he had a sinking feeling he knew who the scout meant. He brushed the feather over his arms and legs, then spoke an incantation and launched himself into the air.

After flying over the wall of fire, he found himself above a slope of peat that fell sharply away to the sheer banks at the confluence of the Serpent's Tail and Winding Water. Judging by the number of pointy-eared corpses strewn along the lower half of the pitch, Ryence had tried to screen his crossing by sending part of his force to attack uphill. That the final line of bodies lay near the top of the slope spoke well of the elves' courage—if not of their commander's wisdom.

An enemy charge had caught the main body of the company preparing to cross the stream. The elves had felled most of the mind flayers and easily half of the bugbears on the way down, leaving the lower half of the slope strewn with almost as many foes as elves. The survivors had slammed into the rest of the company atop the gravelly bank of the Serpent's Tail, where a terrific melee continued to rage, with the bugbears trying to shield their last two mind flayers from an onslaught of gleaming elven steel. Nearly two dozen of Evermeet's swordmages lay writhing on the ground, their palms pressed to their ears in a futile attempt to shut out illithid mind blasts, but Khelben did not pause to hurl any spells into that quarter of combat. Even as he swooped down toward the battle, a pair of bugbears fell with elven steel through their hearts, and a trio of golden bolts shot through the resulting gap to blast the nearest mind flayer.

The scene in the middle of the Serpent's Tail was far less encouraging. Ryence sat astride his horse, tumbling ever so slowly to the water. Just ahead of him, Bladuid and two other Gold elves—presumably the rest of Ryence's high mages—were also slipping from their horses, one bent almost in two by the torpidly rising water column of a spell blast. They were followed by several dozen slow-motion bodyguards, all caught in midtwist as they turned in their saddles to fling bolts and blasts at two phaerimm hovering behind them.

One of the phaerimm was moving as slowly as the elves, as much a victim of its companion's powerful reality-altering magic as Ryence and the high mages. The caster of the spell was floating forward through the contingent of bodyguards, its four arms lashing out to rip open their throats as it bumped its way forward toward Ryence. Had Khelben believed the target to be Ryence alone, he would have tried mightily to save the elf, to blast the phaerimm with a death spell or banish it to the depths of the Ninth Hell.

But Ryence was not alone. He was with the high mages, and Khelben could not take the chance that his spell would be reflected or absorbed by the phaerimm. He needed something powerful and direct, something that would burn through even a phaerimm's natural magic resistance.

He needed his silver fire.

Not for the first time, Khelben cursed the name of Laerm Ryence. The phaerimm cleared the last of the guards, reaching for Ryence's throat with one arm and for Bladuid with the other three. Khelben swooped down behind the creature, plummeting headfirst down from the sky, pointing one hand at the thing's open mouth and summoning his silver fire. A blissful pain hissed through his body, gathered for an instant in the pit of his stomach, then left his arm in a long streak of roaring fire. The phaerimm spun toward the sound on its tail, and the silver flame shot straight down its gullet. The creature came apart in a halo of white flame.

The reality-altering spell ended with the thing's death. Ryence and his high mages completed their falls, hitting the water with a loud series of splashes. Khelben wheeled toward the remaining phaerimm, frantically searching his mind for the safest way to destroy the thing quickly. It would take an hour for his body to reabsorb enough of Mystra's raw magic to use his silver fire again, so he would have to chance a spell.

A thunderous chugging filled the air, and elves began to wail. A scintillating tornado of gem-colored light appeared below him and began to dance across the river, raking the bodyguards of the high mages with spinning tentacles of death-dealing radiance. Each color brought an end more terrible than the previous. Those struck by red erupted into flames. The flesh of anyone touched by green sizzled away in a cloud of emerald gas. Blue brought death by choking, yellow by the foulest of stinking diseases, orange by spontaneous bleeding from every pore. Those touched by a black tentacle oozed away putrid part by putrid part, while those caught by white froze solid and floated away in the cold current.

Khelben had never before seen such a war spell. Nearly half the bodyguards already lay dead or dying, and the other half were scattering in every direction. The phaerimm itself did not seem to be aware of him, high in the air above it. Leaving the tornado to wander on its own, the creature glided toward the splashing forms of the high mages.

It was too late to be safe. Khelben stopped to hover and summoned to mind his most deadly spell. The phaerimm paused above a tangle of elf corpses, then reached down beside an ice-capped boulder to retrieve its companion's shredded tail. Khelben turned his palm toward the creature and barked out a syllable.

The phaerimm did not wave its arms or try to swing itself upright, nor even to make a last, desperate counterattack. At the sound of Khelben's voice, it simply teleported away, leaving his spell to splash harmlessly into the icy stream.

Damn, but they were fast.

CHAPTER FIFTEEN

28 Nightal, the Year of the Unstrung Harp

The celebration was an uneasy one, and not only because Elminster spent the evening glowering at Melegaunt. Galaeron kept glimpsing a dark shape just beyond the glowcircle, a stout little figure that vanished into the shadows the instant he turned to look upon it. Were it not for the agitation of the sentries, he would have dismissed the apparition as the product of a weary mind, but the night watchers kept flitting about up under the stars, swinging from tree to tree or rushing silently along barren limbs to scrutinize something on the ground. Still, they never gave the owl call, so perhaps it was no more than the playmagic of mischievous Wood elf children, and Galaeron was content to take his cue from his mother's people.

The moon rose silver and bright, filling the wood with a milky snowlight, and out came the starlutes. The melodies were airy and cheerful, as always among Wood elves. Takari made a show of dragging Galaeron away from his mother—and coincidentally also Melegaunt and Vala—and being the first to dance. Though the song would have been more suited to a feather step, she pressed herself into Galaeron's arms and began a matched gambol.

"Don't overdo it," Galaeron said, struggling to stay in step as they skipped through the moonlit snow. "You still look weak."

"I'm well enough." Takari pursed her lips into a playful pout. "The only wound that troubles me is the one in my heart—the one you put there tonight."

"I'm sorry." Galaeron's apology was sincere, for he had been so absorbed with Elminster, Turlang, and the rest that he had not even thought of inquiring as to whether Takari had arrived. "I should have stopped by your nesting as we came in."

"My nesting?" Takari raked her heel down his shin. "I'm talking about Vala, orc nose! What's wrong with you, taking a human for your mate . . . over me?"

"Vala?" Galaeron's foot nearly slipped from beneath him. "I haven't taken her!"

Takari gave him a doubtful look. "Not even once?"

Now Galaeron did slip, stumbling over a half-buried log and bringing them both down in the snow. The fall drew a chorus of laughter, and the musicians embarrassed them further by slipping into a slow meter.

"Not even once," Galaeron whispered, lying in the snow. "Though it's not really your business who I take."

Takari gave him a frisky smile. "But it could be." With that, she leaped to her feet and took a good-natured bow, then stretched a hand toward Vala. "Come help me, human. This one is such a hoof-foot it will take two to keep him in step."

Before Vala could object, Morgwais pushed her out to join Takari and Galaeron, and soon the three of them were whirling around the glowcircle arm in arm. Vala could keep even the quickest meter, but her steps were heavy and conspicuous by elf standards. Nevertheless, their antics proved inspirational, and soon the rest of the Wood elves were gliding about the glowcircle in whirling trios, stomping the beat and pumping their knees like centaurs on parade. Even Lady Morgwais joined the merriment, slipping one arm around Elminster's waist and the other around Melegaunt's—no easy task, given the girth of the pair.

Sometime during the festivities, Aris dropped a six-foot boulder next to the Honor Chair and set to work, hammering and clinking to the music. The boulder quickly assumed the rough shape of three whirling bodies, and it was not long before dancers began to spin past to check his progress. The figures emerged as if by magic, the giant not so much giving them form as finding it within the stone, and it soon grew apparent Aris would be leaving his hosts with a treasure worthy of Rheitheillaethor's greatest masters.

Half a night later, the eyes of the humans began to droop, as did Galaeron's. Not wishing to admit publicly that he now felt the need to sleep, he excused himself on the pretext of showing his companions to someplace they could rest—Takari was quick to volunteer her nesting—and they fell asleep to the sound of Aris's clinking and elven star lutes.

Galaeron awoke to darkness and silence, no snoring from Melegaunt's corner, no more of Vala murmuring her son's name in her sleep, no star lutes in the distance, none of Aris's hammering. There was only the breeze rustling against the walls and the creaking trees, and, farther off, the Heartblood gurgling down its channel. A hand touched his shoulder and gave it a tentative shake. Galaeron opened his eyes, then found his dark sight blurred by a thin film of mucus and wiped his eyes. That was one of the many hard things for him to accept about sleeping, the half second of thinking he was going blind whenever he woke.

When his sight cleared, he found Takari kneeling beside him, the corners of her cupid's bow mouth turned up in a slight sneer. There was no one else in the nesting.

"The others are outside," she explained, following his gaze. "They needed time to get down quietly, and I wanted to watch you sleep."

Galaeron grimaced. He had seen drool running from the corner of human mouths often enough to know what sleep looked like. "Not a pretty sight."

"Awful," Takari agreed, twisting her nose up. "Why do you do it?"

Why indeed? Galaeron wondered. "A bad habit I picked up from Melegaunt, I think." He sat up and shrugged, then found himself running his palms over his face the way humans sometimes did. He tore his hands down. "What's going on?"

"There are beholders coming."

Galaeron was on his feet and instantly awake. "But the owl calls—"

"The night watchers don't know yet." Though Takari wore her tomb guard's cloak, she made no move to rise as he shrugged into his chain mail. "Your frog-eyed friend warned me."

"Frog-eyed friend?"

"I think his name was Malik," Takari said. "Why didn't you bring him to the celebration?"

"I didn't know he was still with us," Galaeron confessed, struggling to make sense of what he was hearing. "Did he mention phaerimm?"

"He said there was one. Melegaunt thought it best to leave quietly and draw them into the Dire Wood."

Galaeron nodded, then pulled his cloak over his shoulders and reached for his sword belt. Having seen what the creatures had done to Thousand Faces, Galaeron was not eager to have a battle fought in Rheitheillaethor—not even with the great Elminster there to help.

Takari caught his hand. "Melegaunt said he can go without you. The rest would do you good."

"That doesn't sound like Melegaunt. Are you sure?"

"Look at yourself," said Takari, not answering. "You're turning into a human, sleeping half the night and struggling with something inside.

Lady Morgwais isn't far wrong, you know. Maybe you are falling in love with Vala."

"Hardly." Galaeron's voice was sharper than he meant. He freed his belt from her grasp and started for the door. "But I do need to see this through with the humans. I'm the one who breached the Sharn Wall."

"You were doing your duty."

Galaeron slipped through the door without answering.

Takari followed him out onto the branch. "And you weren't the only one there."

In the creamy moonlight, Galaeron could see the edge of her leather scout's armor showing above the collar of her cloak. "You're still not strong enough. And if Melegaunt doesn't need me, he doesn't need you."

"He certainly does." Takari sprang off the limb and caught a rope, then slid toward the snowy ground. "Unless you think you can find the Dire Wood?"

Galaeron knew by how she had asked the question that he could not. As an elf, he felt reasonably at home in most forests, but he also knew how maddening it could be to navigate through an endless expanse of trees—especially if one's goal happened to be concealed by protective magic. Offering no further argument, he caught hold of the rope, then started down after Takari.

They touched ground not far from the glowcircle, where Melegaunt, Vala, and Malik stood waiting beside Aris and his sculpture. The statue depicted Galaeron dancing with Vala and Takari, and it was every bit the masterpiece he had expected—if a little embarrassing. Vala's body was pressed close against his, her scabbard and legs almost horizontal as she whirled on his hip. Her chin was raised slightly, as though they were about to kiss, and the smile on her face seemed both beguiling and tender. On Galaeron's other side, Takari was wrapped into his arm, their bodies not quite touching, her head thrown back in wild abandon. Though her mouth was open in laughter, there was a wistfulness to her expression that Galaeron had seen on a Wood elf's face only once, when his mother called the family together to tell how her heart ached to return to Rheitheillaethor.

Galaeron's own smile seemed lost and lonely, his gaze fixed a short distance away. Though caught physically between the two women, he was separated from them in mood by a lowered brow and narrowed eyes. The expression made him look sullen and hinted at a darker struggle within, but it was impossible to say whether Aris had actually captured this or whether Galaeron was reading it into the work on his own.

Takari circled the statue for a long time, then finally stopped at Vala's side and took her hand. Vala cocked her brow and looked down at their intertwined fingers, but did not try to free herself.

"It's remarkable!" Takari gasped. She turned to Aris and, finding herself staring at his knee, tipped her head back. "That is the most beautiful stone I have ever seen!"

This drew a meager smile from the stone giant. "The beauty was in the dance." Though he did not speak loudly, his deep voice rolled through the trees like thunder. "It is only a small matter to capture what one sees."

Melegaunt held his finger to his lips. "Quiet, or we will be what is captured." He turned to Takari. "Unless Elminster left?"

"Have no fear of him," said Malik. "Elminster will not be waking soon."

Melegaunt's face grew alarmed. "What? You didn't do anything—"

"Me? An assassin?" scoffed Malik. "I cannot even tell a decent lie! I mean only that he is asleep in the stormlodge."

"Asleep?" Melegaunt frowned at this. "You're sure it was Elminster?"

"Of course I am sure," said Malik. "I saw him myself, tucked under his furs with two women."

"Triplewild will do that to a man," chuckled Takari.

Galaeron was not quite so amused. *"Elf* women?" A cold anger was welling up inside him. *"Which* women?"

The jealousy in his voice drew a frown from Takari. "Not your mother. I saw Lady Morgwais leave for her nesting alone."

"That means nothing." The words slipped from Galaeron's mouth almost before he realized he was speaking. "She might have sneaked back."

Takari's scowl changed from disapproval to shock, but it was Melegaunt who spoke.

"Careful of that shadow, my friend." He nodded to Takari. "Perhaps we should go, if we want to lay another trail for the beholders."

"Fine by me." Takari continued to look at Galaeron. "I think Galaeron has had his fill of Rheitheillaethor."

She led them away from the river, passing close enough to the stormlodge that Galaeron could hear wet human snoring. He veered over to look inside, but felt a hand on his shoulder.

"You are doing yourself harm," said Melegaunt. "Suspicion is the food of wrath."

"If Lady Morgwais is not there, my suspicions will be allayed."

"They won't." Melegaunt released Galaeron's shoulder, leaving him free to do as he chose. "You'll doubt what you saw, or you will think that even if she wasn't there when you looked, she could have been there the night before. Doubt is the way of the shadow, and it is a powerful way indeed. Only trust can defeat it."

Melegaunt walked after the others, leaving Galaeron to his decision.

"Go ahead and look," said Malik, coming up behind Galaeron. "In my experience, you cannot watch a woman too closely. They are all faithless harlots who will betray their husbands every chance they have."

"And you know this how?" asked Galaeron.

"As I told you, by my experience," said Malik. "My own wife I always kept safely locked in my house in Calimshan, and still she betrayed me at the first opportunity."

"Truly?" Shaking his head at the strangeness of human customs, Galaeron started after the others. "Then I shall take a lesson from you."

Malik looked puzzled, but fell in at Galaeron's side. "I suppose there are things a man does not want to know about his mother."

"Fortunately, I am an elf." Though Galaeron resented the human's witless slighting of his mother, he held his tongue for fear of giving his shadow another foothold. "My mother's decisions are her own to make. She and my father have not shared a house for thirty years."

Malik nodded knowingly. "I'm sorry to hear that. It must be hard for your father to see your name besmirched in such low fashion."

"Besmirched?" Galaeron felt himself growing angry over the disgrace—and knew instantly that the ire was not his own. No elf would consider it dishonorable for a woman to follow her heart. "It is not the same with elves as humans. There was no dishonor in her decision."

"Truly? I was not aware that elves were so free with their women." Malik looked into the dark forest, muttering something about there being no honor among fools.

They passed the village boundary, where the night watchers were observing from their perches in the trees. Takari offered no explanation for their furtive departure. Inhabitants and guests of Rheitheillaethor were free to come and go as they wished, so long as they did nothing to betray the village. Nor did she or Galaeron return the waves of farewell that came their way. With humans present, it would have been unthinkable to betray the positions of the sentries.

A hundred paces beyond the village, Galaeron asked, "Didn't you have a horse, Malik?"

"Her name is Kelda."

Malik opened his hand to display a set of reins, and suddenly the mare was behind him, her breath shooting white plumes over her master's shoulder. Galaeron looked back at the silvery snow and was astonished to see a long line of hoof prints alongside their own.

"I am beginning to see how you sneaked into Rheitheillaethor," said Galaeron. "Very impressive."

Malik shrugged. "It is a gift of the One."

"The One?"

Malik pretended not to hear the question, which only raised Galaeron's curiosity to the height of suspicion. He began to imagine the little man being the agent of some powerful archwizard or merciless tyrant—or even of the phaerimm themselves—but of course that was ridiculous. Malik hardly seemed able to attend to himself and his horse, much the less the business of some powerful and nefarious master. Such suspicions could only be the work of Galaeron's shadow.

They continued in silence for some distance, then Galaeron said, "Thank you for coming back to warn us about the beholders. If we can spare Rheitheillaethor their depredations, you will have the gratitude of every elf in the High Forest."

"You must think nothing of it," said Malik. "It was no great trouble. Because you cannot see a man does not mean he is not there."

Galaeron spent a few moments sorting through the statement, then asked, "You were with us the whole time?"

"A little distance behind," said Malik. "Talking trees have always made Kelda nervous."

Galaeron frowned. "If you were with us, then how could you know the beholders escaped Turlang?"

"I don't know they have," answered Malik, "only that they will be here soon."

Galaeron grew irritated. "How do you know?"

"Because Turlang's followers did not misdirect all of our pursuers," explained Malik. "One of the beholders was a very beautiful and cunning one. It lagged behind the rest and entered the wood a little north of the others and found, er—" He seemed to struggle with the words, then said, "Truly, the thing was a genius! I did not see it until it was on me, staring at me with all those wonderful eyes."

Galaeron had a sinking feeling. "How did you escape?"

"I, uh . . . Kelda is very . . ." Malik struggled to recall, then finally gave up and shrugged. "Why is that important? All that matters is I am here to warn you."

The qualmish feeling in Galaeron's stomach changed to fear, and he felt his hands curl into fists. "And what happened to the beholder? The one with the wonderful eyes?"

"It went after the others, I think. It wouldn't have been safe for it to go after you alone."

The grinding of his own teeth filled Galaeron's ears. "And how did you mark our trail?"

"What?" Malik's hand slipped inside his cloak, no doubt reaching for a hidden dagger. "You accuse me of betraying you?"

"Of course not." Certain that the anger he felt was as much his shadow's as his own, Galaeron reminded himself of how the beholder had beguiled Aris in Thousand Faces. Even if Malik had laid a trail, he was not to blame for his actions. "But why do you think the beholder let you go?"

"I see what you are thinking." Malik slipped a hand under his turban to scratch at something on his brow. "I am not that big a fool. Beholders are certainly cunning and handsome creatures, but I am a man of great will and stronger mind. I could never be tricked by one."

"Oh, never."

As Galaeron spoke, he waved his hand across Malik's face, and taking care not to use Melegaunt's coldmagic, started the incantation of a magic-dismissing spell.

"Murdering sorcerer!" Malik's hand dropped from his turban into his cloak and came out with a curved dagger. "Hold your tongue!"

Galaeron finished his incantation in time to jump back and avoid being sliced open. A torrent of fear and excitement raced through him, and with it came his shadow self, welling up from the darkness deep inside him. He saw his foot lash out and catch Malik behind the knee, dropping him to his back. Then Galaeron was over him, standing nose to snout with an angry-looking Kelda, using one foot to pin the little man's dagger hand in the snow.

"Stay your hand, I beg you!" Malik raised his free arm to shield his head. "I swear on my life, I never meant to betray you or your friends!"

Vala caught hold of Galaeron's arm. "What in the name of the Red Gauntlet are you doing?"

Galaeron pushed Kelda's snout aside, then stepped off Malik's trapped wrist. "One of the beholders beguiled him. I had to dispel its magic."

Vala glanced down at the arm she held. "So why do you need that?"

Galaeron looked down and was astonished to find his hand holding a half-drawn sword.

"By the Moon Harp!" Galaeron swore. He was so shaken he could only stare at the weapon. He had no memory of reaching for the weapon, even less of what he intended to do with it. He let the blade slide back into its scabbard, then began to fumble at his weapon belt, his hands trembling so hard he could not undo the clasp. "I could have killed him!"

"Yes, and you would have been lost." Melegaunt slipped past Vala and stood beside Galaeron. "Did I not warn you about using magic?"

"I didn't use coldmagic, only my own."

"No magic is your own," Melegaunt said. Despite the sternness of his words, his voice was soft. "All magic is power borrowed, and ever has unearned power opened the door to ruin."

Galaeron's hands finally stopped trembling long enough to undo his belt.

"Leave it," Melegaunt said. "Better to reach for a sword than a spell."

"That is easy for you to say." Malik pushed himself upright. "You are not the one he attacked."

"At least his sword is still in its scabbard," said Vala, eyeing Malik's dagger. "I would say neither of you had his wits about him."

Malik seemed as surprised as Galaeron to find a weapon in his hand. He shrugged. "A man must defend himself."

Aris and Takari arrived, Aris kneeling down behind Vala and still looming over the group, Takari stopping at Vala's side and raising her brow at the sight of Malik's horse. Before standing, Malik gathered a fold in his robe and drew his dagger through it to dry the blade. As it emerged, Galaeron noticed a resinous smear on the face of the blade.

"Malik, did you mark our trail with a blaze?"

"A blaze?" Malik asked. "What is that?"

He opened his robe to put the dagger away, but Takari snatched it from his hand. She ran her finger over the sticky resin several times, then held it to her nose.

"This blade has sap on it." Takari looked as though she might sheathe it in Malik's chest. "You've been cutting bark."

Malik's eyes bugged out like a pair of bird eggs. "By the Black Sun—the beholders! I marked our trail for them!"

"The Black Sun?" demanded Vala, who looked like she might kill Malik before Takari had the chance. "You worship Cyric?"

Malik winced, then closed his eyes and nodded. "But I beg you, do me no harm! It is not on his account I betrayed you."

"No one will harm you," said Aris. The giant stood the little man on his feet. "I myself have felt the beguiling magic of beholders."

Malik dared to look up. "You will protect me?"

"The blame is not yours," said Aris. "Their magic is powerful."

"But he *did* cut Turlang's trees—and we brought him into the forest," said Vala. She looked to Galaeron. "What will that mean for your mother?"

It was Takari who answered. "Turlang will never trust Lady Morgwais's word again, but if the village attends to the wounded trees and doesn't let them die, I think he will permit us to stay."

"Permit you to stay?" Galaeron drew a calming breath, then turned to Malik. "When was the last time you saw the beholder?"

Malik thought for a moment, then shuddered. "After the dancing ended. They are waiting up . . ." He paused and looked ahead, searching the forest for a familiar landmark, then gestured vaguely ahead. "Up where the trail turns toward the village. I, uh, 'blazed' that trail, too."

Takari glanced at Galaeron with a question in her eye, but he gave a quick shake of his head and looked away. Both knew exactly where Malik meant, but Galaeron did not want to tell the humans about the trailmaze—not when he had already done so much to endanger Rheitheillaethor.

"There's nothing to be done about the blazes now," said Galaeron. "And every minute we hesitate only makes it more likely they'll try to find the village itself. We have to leave another way and draw them after us."

Takari pointed at Malik. "What about that one? You are responsible for him by the pledge that Lady Morgwais vouchsafed to Turlang."

Vala set a hand on the pommel of her darksword. "I can think of a solution."

"That would not be fair," rumbled Aris. "I do not know about this Black Sun he worships, but he has been a true friend to me."

"Then I suppose we have no choice except to take him along," said Melegaunt. "We certainly can't leave him running lose in Turlang's forest."

"No?" The smile that creased Malik's face was suspiciously broad—or so it seemed to Galaeron. "May the One rain a thousand blessings down on you all!"

"I'd leave well enough alone, were I you," growled Vala. "Aris only owes you one life, as best I can figure."

Galaeron fell in at the end of the line behind Vala, then suggested to Melegaunt that he and Aris follow a few dozen paces behind Takari. As they angled off to the north, Galaeron looked behind them and saw the trail Malik had blazed. Within a few hours, someone from the village would discover the atrocity and dress the wounds with special salves to aid the healing bark, but the damage would never fade. For as long as the trees remained standing, the long line of blazes would point straight toward the Heartblood River, where Rheitheillaethor stood hidden on the bent shore. Not for the first time, he wondered just how high a price he would be forced to pay to save Evereska.

A few minutes later, they crossed into a region of impenetrable thorn hedges and hidden precipices where the only safe footing was down the center of the snowy path. A bewildering array of forks and branches split off the main trail, winding along the rims of hedge-capped abysses and down bramble-walled tunnels, but the humans failed to notice any of the alternatives. The labyrinth's magic worked counter to intuition. Instead of presenting the intruder with a bewildering array of choices, the trailmaze allowed intruders to see only the path they happened to be following at the time. All of these trails twined back on each other in a tangled snarl of endless loops, slyly feeding the interloper from one circle to another without his knowledge. Though Rheitheillaethor suffered few invaders, those who did assault the village were usually found in the maze, either dead of starvation or trapped in the bottom of a hidden pit.

At last, they emerged from the trailmaze, the humans none the wiser. The gray light of a winter dawn was brightening the sky behind the eastern treetops, filling the forest with shadows so faint they almost did not exist. They traveled a little more than a mile, then Galaeron called to Takari with the *wit wit wit* of a cardinal. She responded with a buzzing chick-a-dee call, and Galaeron knew she had located their foes. He studied the wood to the south and saw nothing except an endless tangle of snow-caked branches. Along the Desert Border, he might have hoped to match Takari's sharp eye—but here in her home, he would have to leave matters in her hands. He told her as much by repeating the cardinal's call twice more, and she led the way onward.

They traveled in single file, stepping only in Takari's tracks to avoid snapping an unseen stick or rustling a jumble of twigs. Aris's footfalls were as silent as Galaeron's, but Malik and his mount were by far the quietest in the group, Kelda placing her hooves more like those of a unicorn than a horse. There was more to Malik than being a simple Cyric worshiper, Galaeron felt certain—but he did not dwell on his suspicions, lest he invite a badly timed attack from his shadow self.

The morning shadows were just growing darker when Takari began to move more rapidly, leading them just fast enough so that it became difficult to travel without making noise. Melegaunt sent a shiver up their spines by stepping on a stick and filling the air with a low crunch. Vala slipped on a slope and fell to her knees with a soft thud and muffled curse. As they crossed a broad creek, Aris broke through the ice, and a loud splash purled through the trees. Galaeron did not need to look to know their foes were following somewhere behind. Takari had increased the pace to attract their attention, and now she was leading them closer to the Dire Wood.

The sun finally made a full appearance, an orange disk hanging low in the trees, shining down into the forest and striping the snow with trunk shadows as long as some roads. Takari began to vary the pace, slowing for a time and wandering an erratic course, then plowing ahead in a sudden, steady surge. Galaeron knew without looking that their enemies were preparing to attack, trying to slip unseen along their flanks to cut the party off. Takari was using the same trick that a band of Darkhold Zhentarim had once used against Galaeron's patrol, feigning fatigue and poor discipline so the pursuers would hold their attack in hopes of catching the quarry at rest. Galaeron tried to help by acting the part, gulping down handfuls of snow and quietly instructing the others to do likewise. Once or twice, he even lagged behind, trying to convince the beholders that with enough patience, they might pick off a straggler and make their job that much easier.

At last, the forest seemed to thin ahead, the barren trunks of the sugar maples and shadowtops giving way to a broad, blurry expanse of white. At first, Galaeron thought they might be coming to a meadow or snow-covered lake, but as they drew closer, the pale blur resolved itself into a wall of albino oak trees. Amazingly, they were still in full leaf, and they were completely white, from the bases of their alabaster trunks to the height of their blonde crowns. Galaeron could even see a few ivory acorns hanging from their white stalks.

Takari gave a series of sharp siskin *shicks,* and Galaeron realized he was looking at the Dire Wood. He had expected it to be darker, more ominous—twisted, somehow, and tangibly evil. Instead, it looked like something out of an elven myth, beautiful and illusory and ancient beyond the ages. Galaeron answered with his cardinal's *wit wit wit,* and Takari stopped, nocking an arrow and spinning to fire in the same quick motion.

"Run for the white trees!" Galaeron shoved Vala forward. "Melegaunt can use his magic there."

Takari's arrow hissed past Galaeron's head and thudded into something soft. He pulled his bow from his back and dived over a log, then came up with his own arrow nocked and pointed in the same direction.

A shrieking beholder hovered seventy paces distant, its eyestalks spraying colored rays in every direction, the fletching of Takari's arrow protruding from its big central eye. Galaeron leveled his shaft at the same target—then, twenty paces ahead of the creature, glimpsed a plume of snow rising from the ground as some invisible foe raced for the Dire Wood. In a breath, Galaeron adjusted his aim and loosed the arrow.

The shaft flashed across the plume at about rib height, then drew a startled cry before it ricocheted away and sank into the snow. Galaeron uttered a curse on all phaerimm, then leaped up on the log behind which he was hiding and pointed in the direction he had fired.

"Watch over there!" he yelled. "The phaerimm's invisible, with an arrow shield!"

He was rewarded for his bravery by a black flash from one of the beholder's eyes, but he was already diving for cover behind a snowy boulder. The log he had been standing on shriveled into a mass of rotten pulp, then the eye tyrant screeched again as another of Takari's arrows sank into its body. Galaeron nocked another arrow and hurled himself from his hiding place, aiming as he rolled. A cone of golden light flashed from one of the beholder's eyestalks, and the boulder dissolved into dust. Galaeron loosed his arrow at the creature's big eye and saw it sink out of sight.

This time, the beholder did not cry out. It simply dropped into the snow, its eyestalks drooping over its body like so many withered vines. Galaeron and Takari each planted a guarantee arrow into the lifeless orb and darted to new hiding places, and only then did they raise their heads to take stock.

Malik and his horse were nowhere to be seen, of course. Aris was charging in the direction Galaeron had pointed, swinging a ten-foot deadfall log back and forth in a noble, if somewhat misguided, effort to smash their invisible foe through sheer chance. Vala and Melegaunt were running in the wrong direction, charging through the snow toward Galaeron and Takari.

He waved them back, only to have them stop and gesture him in their direction. He tried again, this time more urgently. Once Melegaunt reached the Dire Wood, he would be free to use his shadow magic—and if they stood any chance at all of escaping the phaerimm and its minions, it was the archwizard's magic.

Vala ignored him, instead pointing her darksword at the fallen beholder. "It was only the scout," she yelled. "Now, will you two stop clowning around and get your pointy ears over here?"

When no rays of any color leaped out to silence her, Galaeron dared to look behind him. Much to his relief, the rest of the beholders were a hundred paces distant, coming up fast, but still fist-sized spheres weaving through the trees. Behind them hovered the tornado-shaped figure of a phaerimm, no larger than Galaeron's thumb, yet terrifying enough even at that distance.

A dull thump echoed through the wood as Aris connected with their invisible foe. To Galaeron's amazement, the stone giant did not instantly erupt into a pillar of flame or drop dead with a gaping hole through his torso. Instead, he gave a deep groan of satisfaction and started forward again, shaking the snow from the trees around him as he beat the ground with his makeshift club.

"Aris!" thundered Melegaunt. "Stop that at once!"

A series of colored flashes filled the air in front of Galaeron as the approaching beholders began to test the range of their eye rays. They were not close enough to strike yet, but it would not be long before the beams began to hit. Seeing that the foolish humans were determined to enter the Dire Wood together or not at all, he whistled to Takari and turned toward them. Even at their best pace, he doubted they would be fast enough to outrun the beholders' eye rays, but with a little dodging and weaving, they stood a reasonable—well, acceptable—chance of reaching the wood alive.

As Galaeron and Takari approached, Vala grabbed their hands and pulled them behind a tree. The beholder rays were starting to blast through the forest around them now, boring holes through massive shadowtop trunks and withering whole maples. Turlang would not be happy about the damage done to his forest, but as long as Melegaunt did not use his shadow magic within the wood, the treant would not hold them—or Lady Morgwais—responsible.

As Aris approached, a golden ray caught him square in the leg. The beam would have taken the torso off a normal man, but it merely drilled a melon-sized hole through the stone giant's thigh. He let out a great bellow and collapsed, shaking the ground beneath their feet as he crashed down behind Melegaunt.

"That will do!" yelled Melegaunt, directing himself to Vala.

Vala grabbed Galaeron's hand and pressed it into Takari's, then looped her own arm through his and grabbed hold of Melegaunt's with the other. The archwizard locked her hand in the crook of his elbow, then pressed his other palm to the giant's biceps and began the incantation to a shadow spell.

Galaeron jerked free of Vala's grasp. "What are you doing? If he breaks his word to Turlang—"

"Look to the shadow, elf!" Vala grabbed hold of Galaeron again, then used her chin to gesture along the length of the trunk shadow in which they all stood. "He's drawing his magic through the Dire Wood."

Galaeron looked in the direction she indicated and saw that the tree's shadow extended clear through the ring of white oaks. Though he wasn't sure Melegaunt was living up to the letter of his pledge to Turlang, there was no time to debate the matter. A half dozen beholders appeared to either side of them, lacing the air with gleaming beams of destruction.

The rays shot past without touching anyone in the party, and only then did Galaeron notice how dim and hazy the eye tyrants appeared. Several of the creatures passed by within an arm's reach of the party and did not seem to notice them.

"Don't lose touch with me," warned Melegaunt. "At the moment, we are only shadows to them . . . and that is all that protects us."

"Then let's get out of here," said Takari. "The Dire Wood is not a hundred paces away."

"And may as well be a hundred miles," said Aris. "Look ahead."

An ankle-high curtain of black fire had arisen at the edge of the white forest. Though Galaeron guessed the flames would be invisible to anyone outside the Fringe, he saw no reason it could not be dispersed by a wizard of Melegaunt's power.

"We cannot hide in the shadows forever," he said. "Dispel it and let us be on our way."

"Gladly—were that not what Elminster expects," said Melegaunt.

"Elminster?" demanded Aris. "But he was sleeping—"

"Mystra's Chosen do not sleep," interrupted Melegaunt. He pointed in the general direction of the giant's feet and ran his fingers through the motions of a detection spell. "And they most certainly do not snore."

A ghostly figure in a floppy hat appeared twenty paces beyond Aris's feet. He was slowly creeping toward the Dire Wood, peering over his shoulder at the main body of beholders, then farther back at the hovering phaerimm, and finally at the eye tyrant scouts still passing back and forth through the shadow where Galaeron and his companions stood hiding in Melegaunt's spell.

A knowing twinkle came to Elminster's eye, and he started toward their hiding place. Melegaunt finished his spell, directing a finger in the archmage's direction. Almost at once, the beholders swung their eyestalks toward Elminster and began to assail him with rays both black and golden. Without exception, the attacks exploded into harmless starbursts against the archmage's spell shields, but the flurry was enough to stop the old man in his tracks. He lowered his bushy eyebrows, and Melegaunt uttered another spell. Instead of stopping a foot short, as had all the other attacks, the next beam—a golden one—struck the ancient wizard broadside and sent him cartwheeling across the snow.

"What are you doing?" Galaeron came near to releasing Takari to grab Melegaunt's arm. "You'll get him killed!"

"Hardly."

Elminster tumbled to a stop and came up glaring in Melegaunt's direction. He raised a shaming finger—and the phaerimm came floating up, waving all four arms in his direction.

Elminster vanished in a cloud of crimson flame, and Melegaunt immediately uttered the reverse of a teleport spell.

In the next instant, Elminster's ancient figure appeared fifty yards to the east, cloaked in fire and shaking a long finger of flame. Though the gesture was directed roughly in Melegaunt's direction, it was easily ten degrees to the left, leaving no doubt in Galaeron's mind, at least, that the greatest mage in all Faerûn could not see through the simplest of the shadow wizard's spells.

The phaerimm streaked off toward the archmage, whistling something angry in its breezy language that drew the beholders after it. Elminster turned and fled, covering his retreat with a wall of scintillating colors. The phaerimm and beholders paused long enough to dispel the wall, then flew after the archwizard.

Melegaunt smiled. "*Now* we are ready for the Dire Wood."

CHAPTER SIXTEEN

29 Nightal, the Year of the Unstrung Harp

The Dire Wood was much darker and ominous than it appeared outside. Within a dozen paces, the pristine snow turned to soggy peat, and the albino oaks gave way to the shadowy depths of a petrified forest. The trees were as black as coal, with ebony limbs that ended in jagged stumps and twisted trunks propped against each other at every odd angle. The ground beneath the trees was as red as blood, full of scum and rot and the smell of decay. Galaeron could not imagine how they would ever wade through such a morass—much less find and reach Karse.

He looked to Takari and asked, "Which way?"

She shrugged. "I've never been beyond the Pale Ring, but no need to worry. Jhingleshod will find *us.*"

"Jhingleshod?"

Takari gave him an enigmatic smile. "Wulgreth's servant."

"His *servant?*" exclaimed Malik. Once the phaerimm and beholders had gone off chasing Elminster, the little man had appeared alongside their hiding place, whispering after them until Takari jerked him into the shadow. He still had not forgiven her for the indignity his fright caused him to visit upon his pants. "It might be easier to attract Wulgreth's attention by finding some trumpets to blow."

"Not every servant loves his master," replied Takari.

"While that is certainly true, it does not mean he will love us."

"We'll worry about Jhingleshod later," said Galaeron, looking back toward Turlang's forest. "But we can't wait here. Sooner or later, either

Elminster or the phaerimm will be back—maybe both. We'll leave as soon as Aris is ready."

Kelda eyed the bog and snorted, prompting Malik to pat her neck. "There is nothing to worry about, girl. Aris will be happy to carry you."

Galaeron was not so sure the giant would be able to carry himself, much less Malik's horse. Aris was seated along the inner edge of the Pale Ring, madly chipping at a small rock into a granite cylinder just small enough to fill the hole the beholder's disintegration ray had left through his thigh. He blew the dust off, held the stone over the wound for a moment, tapped a couple of flakes off one side, then passed it down to Vala, who carefully lowered the rock into the wound.

The giant winced in pain, then laid his hammer over the wound and rumbled an incomprehensible prayer to the dour god of his race. A plume of crimson steam shot from the hole on both sides of his leg, then Aris pressed his back against an oak and held the hammer in place as the wound filled with stone-colored flesh. Though his clenched jaw betrayed how much the healing hurt, he remained stoic and silent.

When the rising vapor paled to pink, Aris returned his hammer to his pouch. The wound was still a puckered mess, but there was nothing tentative about his movements when he pushed himself to his feet and reached down for Kelda. The mare nickered, and dragging Malik along, backed toward the Pale Ring.

"You won't need to carry her," said Melegaunt. He turned to Takari and held out a palm. "If you will lend me your sword."

Takari glanced at Galaeron, then reluctantly passed her weapon over. Melegaunt tipped it toward the sun and uttered a conjuration spell, all the while passing his palm over the underside of the blade. The side facing his hand grew black and hazy, while the steel facing the sun gleamed with silver sunlight. Takari scowled and started to reach for her weapon, but Galaeron waved her off. Though he had never seen anything quite like this spell, he recognized the general form as a Making, and he doubted it would harm Takari's weapon.

By the time Melegaunt finished, the dark side of the blade was as black and deep as a fissure in a cavern floor, while the light side shone too brilliantly to look at. He turned the dark face toward the bog, and a black stripe appeared on the surface of the water. When he adjusted the angle, the stripe broadened to a width of two feet and stretched to thirty paces.

Melegaunt returned the sword to Takari. "Lay the shadow where you wish. It will keep our feet dry."

Takari accepted the weapon with a gaping mouth, then stepped gingerly onto the shadow. When her foot did not pass through into water, she started forward.

Melegaunt motioned the others onto the black band. "Quickly. The path lasts only a few moments."

Vala drew her sword and started along the trail without hesitation, followed by Malik and Kelda, who was persuaded to step onto the shadowy trail only by the threat of being picked up again. Aris took two precarious steps before announcing it was like walking on thread and stepped off to wade alongside. Melegaunt went next, and Galaeron brought up the rear.

The bog was more of a mess than it looked, with a muddy bottom that sucked at Aris's boots and filled the petrified forest with a steady cadence of slurping. Takari's trail was by necessity crooked and irregular, detouring around blockades of tangled trees, occasionally narrowing to mere inches as it passed beneath a half-fallen trunk. The air was damp and biting, numbing their faces and stiffening their fingers with cold. They were all shivering within a hundred steps, and the anemic rays of the rising sun were too thin to warm them.

"I have been in howling blizzards warmer than this swamp!" complained Malik. "How can the water not be ice?"

"It is not cold you are feeling, it is death," said Melegaunt. "Death ancient and mad and mighty, death sorrowful and ashamed."

"Then what are we doing here?" demanded Malik. "If this Wulgreth is mighty enough to drain the heat from an entire swamp, we have no chance at all."

"Not Wulgreth," said Melegaunt. "I am speaking of Karsus. It is his magic that makes the Dire Wood, and his mad regret that twists everything within it."

Karsus was a name that Galaeron, at least, recognized from his years at the Academy of Magic. Karsus was the foolish Netherese wizard who had tried to steal the Weave from the goddess of magic and brought the floating cities of Netheril crashing to the ground.

Daring to hope he was finally beginning to understand Melegaunt's plan, Galaeron asked, "So it is Karsus's magic you mean to use against the phaerimm?"

"In a manner of speaking, yes." Melegaunt ducked under a tree trunk and came face-to-flank with Malik's horse, which had slowed as the little man paused to eavesdrop. The wizard slapped the horse on the rump, urging her forward and nearly knocking Malik off the trail, then said quietly, "You will see."

Galaeron silently cursed the Cyricist, then found himself debating the merits of killing him and being done with it. Takari would not think much of the idea, but Melegaunt clearly had his suspicions about the fellow, and the wizard had proven on more than one occasion that he would not balk at doing whatever was necessary to save Evereska. Vala would agree to whatever Melegaunt decided, so the only problem was Aris, and if it came to that, even Galaeron's magic was powerful enough to . . . the thought brought him to a stunned halt, scarcely able to believe how easily his shadow had crept up on him. The dark thoughts had seemed so normal.

So shocked was Galaeron that he barely noticed Melegaunt disappearing around the next tangle of stony trees, but he did notice when the path vanished beneath his feet and plunged him to his waist in icy water.

His breath left him in a shriek, and his feet turned instantly to blocks of numb flesh. His knees began to ache with cold, his thighs felt like slabs of ice, and his body drained into the swamp. He staggered a single step and nearly fell when the mud refused to release his boot. Something large and soft bumped his leg and stayed. He cried out again and pulled his dagger, but could not bring himself to reach into the icy water to find out what it was.

Galaeron heard another splash and looked forward to see Melegaunt dropping into the water as the shadow trail vanished beneath him. The wizard let out a surprised roar, then spread his hands and levitated himself out of the water. The path was fast disappearing behind Malik and his horse, but with Vala and Takari spinning around to look toward Galaeron, they were helpless to continue forward.

Galaeron waved them on. "K-k-k-keep m-m-moving!"

The trail vanished beneath Kelda's rear hooves, and that was all the impetus the mare needed to nose Malik forward. He gave Vala an urgent shove, and they were moving again, staying a few bare steps ahead of the vanishing shadow trail. Takari started to lay a crooked course back toward Galaeron, but Aris gestured them forward again.

"Go." The giant plucked Melegaunt from the air, then sloshed back to Galaeron. "I'll get them."

The soft thing on Galaeron's leg slithered around his thigh, a tiny set of scales or barbs or whatever ticking against his elven chain mail. He took a deep breath, then reached into the water with both hands and felt something huge and fleshy around his leg. He jabbed his dagger into its body, then pulled it from the water and immediately wished he had not.

The thing was as long as his arm, with a slimy black body tapering from a round head to a narrow tail. He could not imagine what it was until he turned it over and saw a ring of sharp little teeth surrounded by a fleshy-lipped sucker.

"By the Fey Wand!" He held the thing at arm's length. "It's a leech."

"More my size, I'd say." Aris stooped down and crushed the creature between two fingers, then plucked Galaeron up in his free hand. "And you should see the dragonflies up here."

Galaeron saw a lacy blur nearly four feet across dart past the giant's head, then said, "As l-long as there aren't any s-spiders." Though the swamp was no longer draining his body heat, he could not seem to stop shivering, and even Melegaunt looked a little blue around the lips. "Can you c-cast a warming spell?"

Melegaunt gave a wry smile. "Unfortunately, sh-shadow magic does not create heat." He shivered, then added, "From normal cold I can protect us, but from this life-draining chill . . ." He only shook his head.

Galaeron hesitated, already knowing Melegaunt's response, then said anyway, "I can use the Weave—"

"How often must I warn you?" Melegaunt glared at Galaeron a moment, then looked up at Aris. "You do not seem troubled."

"Nor do I seem troubled by the leeches—but seeming does not make a thing so." He raised a foot out of the water to display the bloated black forms dangling to his ankle. "If we can find a stone, I can ask Skoreaus Stonebones to make it warm for us."

Galaeron eyed the petrified trees they were passing, but decided not to suggest using one of them. The magic that had stolen their lives seemed as corrupt as the shadow trying to steal his.

Aris weaved through the petrified tangle until he caught the others, then placed Galaeron behind Takari and Melegaunt behind Vala, leaving Malik and his horse to bring up the rear. Recalling that Cyric was the human god of strife and murder, Galaeron was not so certain he liked the idea of having Malik behind everyone else—but a few stumbling steps convinced him he was too weak to assume the post himself.

Conscious that the phaerimm and beholders—or perhaps even Elminster—would soon be coming up behind them, they continued westward at their best pace, Aris now assuming the duty of watching for foes behind. The strength continued to drain from Galaeron's body, and he began to shiver uncontrollably. Vala sheathed her sword and carried him in her arms long enough to strip him out of his wet clothes, then volunteered her own cloak to keep him warm instead. When that did not work, Takari volunteered hers, and even Malik produced a heavy woolen cape. The extra weight only seemed to tire Galaeron all the more. He began to feel queasy and lethargic, and it became a regular duty for Vala to catch him by the arm.

Melegaunt and Aris fared better, though the swamp had clearly taken its toll on them as well. The archwizard stumbled along mumbling to himself about hearts and heavy magic, and even became muddled enough to explain a little of his shadow magic to Malik. Aris simply started to slow, pausing now and again to brace himself against a petrified tree and check back for enemies.

The sun was high overhead when the trees finally vanished and the bog became a broad river that seemed to flow one direction on the near side and the opposite way along the other side. The far bank sloped up from the water in a gentle slope covered with gnarled black oaks—no doubt as petrified as the bog trees—but at least standing on dry ground.

Takari laid the shadow path perhaps halfway across the river and started across, only to watch the swirl of a dark eddy catch it near the end and sucked it beneath the surface. She saved them all by flipping the sword around and severing the trail with a flash from the bright side of the blade, then quickly laid another path and tried again. This time, the eddy caught the trail only a dozen paces ahead, barely giving her time to flip the blade.

The horse whinnied from the back of the line, and Malik called, "Keep going! There is an eel behind us large enough to eat Kelda!"

Takari laid a trail along the edge of the river and, when the shadowy ribbon did not swirl away in a new eddy, raced forward to give the others room.

"Given what the bog did to Galaeron, I don't fancy taking a swim in the river," she called over her shoulder. "I don't suppose you've another way to cross, Melegaunt?"

"Cer . . . tainly."

Melegaunt's voice was so weak and thick-tongued that Galaeron hazarded a glance over his shoulder—prompting Vala to extend a guiding hand as the trail rounded a bend in the river.

"Why don't we use that bridge?"

"Bridge?" Galaeron asked, confused.

"There's always a bridge," said Vala, pointing past Galaeron's nose.

Galaeron looked forward again and saw the river purling over a stretch of dark, submerged stone. At each end of the stretch stood ruined bridge towers, their crowns jagged and broken, their windows black and unbarred. In front of the near tower stood a hazy figure in plate armor, his hands wrapped around the hilt of a huge two-handed sword resting tip-down in front of him.

"And a knight," called Malik. "There is always a knight."

Galaeron drew his sword and heard the others doing the same, but Takari waved their weapons down. As they drew closer to the knight, it grew apparent he stood ankle deep in the river, water gurgling around his feet and mist swirling around him. His armor was coated in rust, while the face peering out from his raised visor seemed nothing but moldering bone and watchful, coal-dark eyes.

As they approached, he unsheathed his great sword and held it before him, the tip pointed at Takari. She stopped in her tracks and lowered her own sword.

"Well met, old Jhingleshod," she said. "Oft have I watched your wanderings from the Pale Ring."

"And there you should have stayed, elf. You have no business in the land of death."

"Not I, but my friends." Takari stepped aside and gestured to Galaeron. "They come in need of your aid."

"My aid?" Jhingleshod's black eyes shifted to Galaeron. "What aid can I give thee but a quick death?"

From the end of the line came a pair of splashes, then a startled whinny and hissed curse as the shadow vanished beneath Malik and his horse. Jhingleshod lifted his chin at the sound, but kept his attention—and his great sword—fixed on Galaeron.

"We have need of Karsus's magic," Galaeron said. "If you can show us—"

"Not we." Jhingleshod jabbed his sword at Galaeron's chest. "You. What come you seeking?"

"I come to save—"

"Think well, elf," Jhingleshod warned. "To answer wrong is worse than death."

Galaeron paused to consider the question. He had been about to say he came to save Evereska, but Jhingleshod's reaction left little doubt that the answer would not have been the one the dead knight wished to hear. Another splash came from the end of the line, and this time it was Melegaunt's voice that cried out.

Jhingleshod paid the noise no attention and kept his dead gaze fixed on Galaeron. "Your answer? You have come far, elf—you must know what you are seeking."

"I do." Galaeron glanced at Takari, then over his shoulder to Vala. "Absolution. I seek pardon for my mistake."

A black light flared in Jhingleshod's eyes, and his skeleton's jaw opened as though smiling. "There is a boon I would ask for my help, elf. Will you give it?"

Galaeron started to ask what the boon was, then thought better of it. Jhingleshod would not react well to pointless barter. He demanded unflinching honesty of those who sought his help, and the truth was that Galaeron would pay anything to absolve his mistake. He simply nodded.

Jhingleshod's eyes shifted to Takari as though to ask something, but seemed to find the answer they were seeking in her frightened expression and looked back to Galaeron.

"Go," the knight said. He pointed through the rusted-out remains of a portcullis to the submerged bridge. "If you have the strength to reach the other side, I will do what can be done to help you."

Galaeron left the shadow trail and stepped through the portcullis without hesitation, but stopped on the other side. "My friends—"

Jhingleshod whirled on him, bringing his great sword around so swiftly that Galaeron could not have blocked the rusty weapon had he tried. The flat of the blade caught him full in the shoulder and slammed him into the musty tower wall.

"Go!" Jhingleshod motioned again toward the bridge. "My bargain with you is done."

Galaeron felt an angry darkness well up inside him and gathered himself to spring, but Takari desperately shook her head and flicked her eyes toward the bridge. Galaeron remained crouched, trying to fight down the black fury within. Together, he and his companions might be able to destroy Jhingleshod, but what then? Takari had said he could guide them to Karse, and Galaeron had seen enough of the Dire Wood to know how valuable such assistance would be. He gathered himself, and letting his aching arm dangle at his side, staggered through the cold water.

Jhingleshod turned to Aris next, and as Galaeron passed through the shadowed archway asked, "What seek you?"

Galaeron stepped out of the tower onto the mossy surface of a submerged bridge. Though no more than three inches of water ran over the surface, the river's purling drowned out Aris's answer. Reluctant to anger Jhingleshod by tarrying, Galaeron continued forward.

The stone was as slick as ice, so that even the shallow flow threatened to sweep his feet from beneath him. He sheathed his sword and dropped to a low crouch, carefully sliding one foot ahead of the other and twisting it into the mossy surface. He could feel the heat of his body rushing down through his feet into the water. A light fog rose around him, veiling the far shore behind a pale haze, and he grew dizzy from the cold.

As Galaeron crossed the midpoint of the bridge, the river changed direction and began to flow across from the other side. The effect was more than a little disorienting, making him feel he had somehow gotten himself turned around and was now approaching the wrong tower. He closed his eyes and continued blind until the current's new direction felt right.

Galaeron was nearly across when the purling changed pitch, and the water began to surge over his feet erratically. A flicker of dark motion next to the bridge caught his attention, then he saw the bloated body of a drowned human floating on the surface, bobbing in place as the current pitched him repeatedly against the bridge.

Dressed in knee high boots and black leather armor, the man was bearded and large, with a crooked nose and skin as blue as his open eyes. There were no signs of any wounds or broken bones, though the absence of a helm and weapons belt suggested there had been time to shed both before drowning. Galaeron shuddered, wondering if the fellow had fallen victim to the river's life-stealing waters and simply fell in. The man's eyes rolled toward Galaeron, then a blue hand rose out of the water, stretching out as though reaching for help.

Galaeron cried out and sprang back, landing on his seat when his feet slipped out from beneath him. The current immediately threatened to sweep him into the riffle on the other side of the mossy bridge. He rolled to his stomach and flung his arms out, catching hold of the bridge on the upstream side. The current whirled him around, spinning him so that his feet hung over the downstream edge. The river poured over his head and down his throat, chilling him to the bone and threatening to fill his lungs. He clamped his jaw shut and felt the water bubbling into his nose, a mad, animate killer determined to have his life. Already his body was growing weary and stiff, the life draining out of him everywhere the river touched. He blew the air from his lungs, forcing the water out through his mouth and nose, then drew a stiff leg up so he could stand—and felt the dead man's hand clamp his wrist.

Screaming, Galaeron shook the water from his head and found himself staring into the man's undead eyes. The fellow's lips drew back in a gruesome grin, displaying a mouthful of broken fangs and a black wagging tongue. A dozen spells leaped at once to Galaeron's mind. As a tomb guard recruit, he had been well-drilled in the weaknesses of the undead—almost as well-drilled as he had been in horrors awaiting those who fell to them. He thrust a hand into the creature's face and opened himself to the Weave—then felt the icy ache of shadow magic rushing into him instead. Galaeron let the spell drop, and holding onto the bridge only with his free hand, rolled his wrist around against the creature's thumb.

A living man would have released Galaeron's arm and pulled his hand away in pain. The ghoul continued to hold, trying to use strength against leverage. So weak was Galaeron that the tactic nearly succeeded. The first time he tried, the strength simply left his arm, and his hand stopped halfway through the motion, hanging palm up between him and his blue-faced attacker.

Galaeron shoved the arm forward, jabbing a fingertip into the creature's eye. Even a dead man had to flinch, and Galaeron finished his motion, bringing his hand over and down behind the ghoul's. The thing's thumb snapped with a sharp crack, folding over backward to expose a jagged spear of coal black bone.

Galaeron shot his hand up behind its neck and caught it by the back of the skull. He slammed its head into the side of the bridge, at the same time pulling himself back onto the walkway and swinging his feet up beneath him.

The ghoul lashed out madly with both arms,.catching Galaeron behind the ankles and trying to sweep his feet from under him. The elf drew his knees straight up, and reaching across his body for his sword, came down kicking. One heel caught the ghoul in the back of the head. The other landed on the mossy bridge and slipped free, dropping Galaeron to a knee directly in front of the beast. His sword cleared his scabbard and struck the ghoul's face in the same motion, its gleaming elven steel slicing through the head just above the jawline.

Galaeron followed through gracefully, his head turning to follow the sweep of his blade tip, and saw a second creature springing out of the water in front of him. This one was smaller than the first, with a female's rounder curves, long black claws, and the yellow eyes of a wight. She was also much faster, stomping Galaeron's sword arm down on the bridge and pinning it there as she snapped her other foot around in a vicious kick.

Thinking to trap her foot with a hook block, Galaeron caught the blow on his forearm—but he was simply too tired and weak. The impact knocked him to his back, then the current spun his feet downstream again, leaving him affixed to the bridge only by his pinned sword arm.

The wight crouched down above his head and grabbed his throat, her icy claws piercing his flesh in so many places he was surprised not to see warm blood spurting up before his eyes. She bared two long rows of sharp teeth and pulled him toward her, twisting her head around to bite.

Galaeron tried to break free and roll away. He was too weak even to push his free hand into the crook of the wight's arm. He tried to kick his feet up to wrap her head in a leg lock, but his legs felt as numb and heavy as gold. His life was seeping out by the second, being sucked out by the spirit-stealing touch of the undead, being robbed from him by the vigor-draining waters of the shadowed river.

The wight pressed her teeth to Galaeron's throat. He spun toward her with the little strength remaining to him, thrusting his free hand into her face and summoning the incantation to a spell of light. A surge of icy power flooded Galaeron's body as it filled with coldmagic, but he had more pressing worries than his shadow at the moment. He called out the mystic syllable, and a brilliant beam of silver light shot from his palm.

The wight screeched madly and spun away, leaving Galaeron to float across the bridge. He rolled after the wight, digging the numb fingers of his free hand into the cold moss and whipping his sword across the back of the creature's feet with the other. The thing stumbled two steps forward before crashing into the water with a pair of severed heels. Galaeron pulled himself to his knees and brought his sword down across the wight's back. The blow was clean and, had there been any strength to it, he would have cleaved the thing in half. As it was, his elven steel bit deep enough to maim even a beast of the undead.

The wight stiffened and tried to roll toward her foe, but succeeded only in twisting her torso open along the wound. As she looked down in bewilderment, Galaeron raised a hand and spoke a single mystic syllable. This time, he barely noticed as the coldmagic flooded his body, nor did he care that the bolts shooting from his hand were as black and frigid as shadow. It only mattered to him that the undead thing before him had finally gone limp and lost her hold on the bridge, and that the murky current was at last carrying her away over the riffle.

The gate tower stood only a dozen paces away, the dry ground beyond its shadowed archway offering warmth and refuge, or at least an escape from the cold battle on the bridge. Galaeron staggered to his feet and discovered he did not feel nearly as weak as he had several minutes before. To the contrary, while he felt tired and cold, his strength seemed to be returning. There was a peculiar ardor burning inside him, not so much anger as resolve, not so much brutality as ruthlessness.

When no more undead appeared to attack him, he started toward the gate tower, no longer concerned about the slick moss underfoot, thinking only of the battles to come and the magic he would find in Karse—then he recalled Melegaunt following behind, and the others he was traveling with, all following in his footsteps, all trying to cross the dark bridge behind him.

Galaeron spun on his heel and saw Takari slipping and sliding toward him, pushing her sword into its scabbard. Twenty paces behind her, Vala was spinning and whirling across the bridge, her black blade weaving a dark mesh around her and Melegaunt as she slashed at the translucent figures of two withered, shrewish-looking ghosts trying to dart past her flashing defenses. Beyond them, a pair of inky silhouettes were flitting around Aris's steam-shrouded head, darting in to slash at his eyes and ears with black talons. Malik and his horse were nowhere to be seen, of course, but Jhingleshod was not far behind the others, a hazy glimmer of orange that appeared briefly every time the stone giant took a step.

Galaeron pointed his sword over Takari's shoulder. "The others!" He staggered a few steps back across the bridge, his numb legs and weary body stirring themselves for another fight. "They need help!"

"Are you mad?" Takari intercepted him and pressed her hand to where the wight had clasped his throat. Her palm was as hot as fire against his skin. "The humans can take care of themselves. We need to get you to shore."

"Shore? What do you take me for?" Galaeron jerked her hand down. "A coward?"

Takari's eyes flashed. "Only a fool." She thrust her palm into his face, displaying a coating of blood so dark it was almost black. "Half your throat is ripped away, your face is as pale as glass, and all you can think about is a human minx with wild eyes and milkbags the size of a thkaerth's!"

Too stunned to reply, Galaeron raised a hand to his throat and felt a gash four fingers wide. How the wound had missed his veins he could not imagine, any more than he could understand how he had the strength to continue standing. There was no pain, no dizziness, no sign of the injury except an overwhelming sense of cold, and even that seemed to be fading.

Takari drew her sword and, grasping Melegaunt's arm, turned back to help the others. "Let's go, then—but I'll never forgive you if you get yourself killed over a human."

They had barely taken two steps before Vala's darksword found one of the ghosts, cleaving it down the center. The creature came apart with a horrid screech, the two halves of its gossamer form paling into wisps of fading light. Melegaunt reached over her shoulder, spraying a string of shadowy darts through the second ghost. The black bolts vanished inside the creature with no visible effect.

Seeing what had become of its fellow, the ghost darted away from Vala and hovered alongside the bridge, well out of her reach. It stretched a hand toward her sword, then flowed into the dark glass and vanished from sight. Galaeron stretched out his arm, trying to slap the weapon from her grasp with the flat of his own blade. His reach fell just short.

"Vala, drop your sword!"

Even as Galaeron called out, Vala's eyes went glassy and white. She whirled on Melegaunt, her movements now fitful and rigid as she raised her arm for an overhand chop. Jaw dropping, the wizard pivoted into the clumsy attack, throwing his arms out in a desperate block and catching Vala square in the chest. He bellowed two syllables and sent her body blasting past. She landed two paces away on the downstream side of the bridge, flat on her back and dazed from the explosion.

Vala's hand began to open, and the darksword dipped into the water.

"Grab her sword!" As Galaeron tried to spring past Melegaunt, he slipped on the mossy stone and fell to a knee. "It has her soul!"

Melegaunt stooped down and reached for the weapon, then her white eyes flicked in his direction, and he abruptly drew back. "She'll kill me!"

Vala slipped over the riffle and started a lazy spin downstream, quickly starting to sink as her scale armor pulled her beneath the surface. Ignoring the fact that even elven chain mail was not light, Galaeron dropped his own sword on the bridge and sprang over Melegaunt after her.

He entered the icy river headfirst and pulled himself down through the riffle with two quick strokes, then caught a handful of hair and continued to kick deeper. It would do no good to save Vala if he allowed the darksword to sink with her soul. He drew himself down by her hair, stretching his free hand toward the glass sword—then suddenly found the point driving up through the water toward his heart.

Still holding onto her hair, Galaeron rolled behind her and changed hands, then reached around her shoulder to grab her sword arm from behind. Vala whirled and kicked, trying to spin free, but managing only to drive them a few feet upward before they began to sink again. Galaeron released her hair and slipped his arm around her throat, using the crook of his elbow to clamp down on the vulnerable veins in her neck.

Vala went limp almost instantly. Her head tipped to one side and her eyes rolled back in their sockets, and the hand holding the darksword came open even before Galaeron could twist the weapon free. He caught it by the hilt and kicked for the surface, already so cold he barely noticed its freezing touch.

Had he been fresh, or had Vala's scale armor been as light as elven chain, he might have pulled them both to the surface. As it was, he barely had the strength to keep from sinking deeper—and that strength was fading fast. Slipping her darksword back into her scabbard, he drew his dagger and began to cut the buckles on her heavy breast plate.

Galaeron had just finished one side when he saw Malik's chubby silhouette drift past above. He thought for a moment that he was merely imagining things, or that the cold water had finally taken him. The little human did not strike him as the heroic type, but there had been that time in Thousand Faces, and now here he was again, his turban unwinding behind him as he dived for them from above. Not taking the time to sheathe his dagger, Galaeron let it fall and raised his hand.

Malik ignored it and circled around behind them, trailing a thin rope. Galaeron felt the human pushing something under his arm and took the line from his grasp, then passed it around Vala and back to his rescuer. Malik tied a quick knot, then the current began to pull at them as the cord caught. Wrapping his legs around Vala for extra security, Galaeron grabbed the rope with both hands and pulled.

He had barely begun before the rope jerked them to the surface, and his breath returned in a series of cold coughs. He felt Malik clinging to his belt, crying out in terror and all but dragging him back beneath the surface as he struggled to reach the rope. Galaeron caught hold of the little man's collar and pulled him up.

"Malik! Our thanks!" Galaeron guided his hand to the rope. "That was a brave thing you did."

"Think nothing of it," coughed the little man. "I have a bad habit of doing brave things in bad causes."

Unsure of just how to take this, Galaeron rolled Vala onto her back, then finally looked upstream, to where the other end of the rope was attached to Kelda's saddle. The mare was just trotting into the archway beneath the bridge tower, pulling them diagonally across the current as she moved. Takari and Melegaunt were slipping and sliding along the bridge as they scrambled after her, while Aris, having somehow freed himself of the two shades, was kneeling at the edge of the bridge, stretching a long arm out to grab the line.

He finally succeeded, then pulled them to the side of the bridge and hoisted them to safety. Malik whistled Kelda to a stop, and Galaeron set to work on Vala. Her armor was scorched and dented from the spell that had launched her into the river, but any injuries the blast had caused her appeared less important than her near drowning. He turned her on her side and, bracing her between his knees, pushed on her back to force out the water. She began to cough, spewing cold river water from her lungs, and started to breathe on her own.

"She'll live," pronounced Aris.

"But not recover." This from Jhingleshod, who was stepping around Aris's far side. "Not until she is free of this river."

Galaeron glared up at the ghostly knight, barely able to restrain his dark anger. "You might have warned us."

"And what would you have learned by that?" Jhingleshod looked away and continued forward, following Melegaunt and Takari into the shadows beneath the next bridge tower. "Were you not strong enough to defeat the servants, I do not think you would have been strong enough to defeat the master."

Galaeron glared after the rusty knight for a moment, then scooped Vala up and started after him. As they passed into the shadows beneath the bridge tower, she began to stir, her arm slipping around his neck, her eyes fluttering open.

"G-Galaeron?" She seemed barely conscious, hardly able to utter his name. "You . . . came after me?"

"Did you think I would let you drown?"

"Then we're alive?"

"At the moment, yes."

He smiled, and, as they stepped out onto the dry road, Vala's lips were suddenly pressed to his, her warm tongue dancing softly against his. Surprised as he was, he would not have minded, were it not for the guilty shame in Melegaunt's eyes—or the hurt in Takari's.

CHAPTER SEVENTEEN

30 Nightal, the Year of the Unstrung Harp

A bevy of meadow quail broke from the grass some miles distant, two dozen plump flecks scattering into the air. The sight of so many juicy birds brought the water to Aubric Nihmedu's mouth—as it did to the mouths of all the Noble Blades and Lordly Wands tucked into their spider holes across the sun-baked hillside. For nearly a tenday now, the Swords of Evereska had subsisted on crisped lizard and spell-baked mouse, forsaking even cacti and wolfroot for fear that the phaerimm would notice any plant-gathering. It was hardly the ordeal proud aristocrats envisioned when they joined the Swords of Evereska, but no one complained. Since forsaking open combat for ambushes and surprise attacks, they had cut their losses from staggering to merely heavy, and they had killed more than twenty phaerimm. By Aubric's estimate, the Swords would need only ten lives apiece to eradicate the remaining phaerimm from the Shaeradim.

Two hundred paces ahead of the quail, a pair of moon foxes darted across a stream, herding four young kits along between them. There was something out there, slinking into the eastern end of the Blazevale—the broad, sand-scoured valley that separated the Shaeradim from the Greycloak Hills to the north. Though curious, Aubric resisted the temptation to augment his keen elf sight with magic. Not two hours before, sentries had sent the Swords scrambling for cover with news of an approaching company. Aubric had to settle for staring out across the plain with his naked eye, waiting patiently for the next hint of the creature's presence.

Soon enough, he noticed a narrow riffle in the grass. The disturbance was advancing steadily toward a high, bowl-shaped outcrop known as Rocnest, a natural citadel that had housed elf garrisons for nearly a thousand years during the Crown Wars. Though the fortress had been abandoned after the fall of Aryvandaar, its location between Evereska and the Greycloak Hills had lately prompted talk of reclaiming it as a watch post.

Aubric's heart began to pound faster. The riffle was easily half a mile front to back, too long to be caused by an animal and far too straight. It advanced steadily toward the natural fortress, pausing neither to search for prey or check for predators. There was only one creature that traveled so efficiently, so confidently in the open plain. Aubric flipped the top off his spider hole and turned up the hill, flashing the signal to prepare for battle.

Rhydwych Bourmays, the company artmaster, poked her sable-tressed head out of the next hole. "You cannot be thinking to attack!" she hissed. "Ten thornbacks is too many—especially with illithids and beholders to back them up."

"Tell your Wands to prepare themselves," Aubric said, sidestepping the argument. "There is help for Evereska out there, and I won't stand idle while the phaerimm ambush it."

Rhydwych arched her thin eyebrows and looked across the plain. "Invisible is good." She studied the line a few seconds longer, then said, "And fast, I'll give them that. But help is an exaggeration. There can't be two hundred riders in the column."

"We don't know who those two hundred are, Artmaster—or what they intend." His tone was sharper than he intended, perhaps because of the disappointment Rhydwych's question had engendered in his own heart. By the Swords' best estimate—an estimate they had been unable to communicate to Evereska or anyone else—there were two hundred *phaerimm* in the Shaeradim. "Will you signal your wands, or must I?"

"No need to get nasty, Lord Nihmedu," snipped Rhydwych. "I know the ladder of authority—though you may be sure the House of Swords will review it if matters go badly."

"If matters go badly, they will have no need."

He shooed Rhydwych off with a wave, then turned to find a watchman bounding down the shoulder of the hill. Aubric signaled his Noble Blades to hold steady, then began to tighten his armor. By the time he finished, the sentry was beside him, and a hundred Swords stood scattered across the hill.

"The phaerimm weren't hunting *us*, Aubric." As a superior noble, it would have been beneath the Gold elf to address Aubric by his title. "They're on the move."

"Down the Blazevale, Lord Dureth?"

Dureth nodded. "How—"

"Someone is trying to reach Rocnest." Aubric pointed toward the grass riffle. "It may be help."

The elf looked in the direction indicated. "If it is, it's not much." Dureth narrowed his eyes, then said, "Unless . . ."

"Your thoughts do me no good unless you speak them."

"I'm wondering about the Rocnest," explained Dureth. "Why trap yourself there—"

"Unless you'll be able to fight your way out—"

"But you need to defend yourself until you can," finished Dureth. "Could they be erecting a gate?"

Aubric nodded. "It's all that makes sense."

Dureth pointed toward the hill's western shoulder, which descended gently to the plain near the mouth of the Blazevale. "We'd better hurry. They'll be closing on the Deadwall."

Aubric signaled the Swords to follow Dureth. "Lead the way—and quickly."

The Noble Blade started forward at a steady jog, and Aubric hurried after him. The Deadwall was the intangible barrier the phaerimm had erected around the Shaeradim and Greycloak Hills. It had earned its name not because it killed everything that tried to walk or fly through it—though it did—but because it blocked all magical communication and travel with the outside world. Rhydwych and her mages spent every spare hour trying to defeat the barrier, but had yet to succeed.

The Swords bounded up the slope in utter silence. At the top of the ridge, Dureth, Aubric, and Rhydwych crawled to the crest and peered into the Blazevale.

They found themselves a few hundred paces above the phaerimm, who were advancing toward Rocnest. In addition to the ten thornbacks, there were a dozen illithids, a like number of beholders, and two hundred mindslaves. The slaves were a mixed bunch, mostly humans and bugbears, but with an alarming number of elves as well. A fair number of elves wore the elaborate, beast-head helmets favored by Evereskan nobles. It filled Aubric with despair to recognize a gilt hawk and two stylish lions as the helms of Noble Blades.

Leaving Dureth to skulk along behind the crest and watch the enemy, Aubric and Rhydwych slipped down the slope and led the Swords along a parallel course. Soon enough, the ridge fell to a bare seven feet, and the enemy company streamed out beyond the shoulder to the line of decomposing birds and rabbits that marked the Deadwall. Aubric signaled his company to wait.

On the plain, the ruffle had closed to within four hundred paces of Rocnest. Though it was impossible to tell whether the invisible newcomers had seen the enemy, the phaerimm were making no secret of their presence. They stopped at the Deadwall only long enough for one of their number to run his four hands through a spell, creating a shimmering half-disk of greenish light.

"Four hands! No wonder we couldn't find the spell!" whispered Rhydwych.

The first two phaerimm pressed themselves to the shimmering doorway and melted through it, their bodies spreading across one side, then oozing out the other. Aubric grimaced. The slow process precluded a mad dash to take the enemy from behind. They would have to fight for the doorway and hold it, like an army claiming a crucial bridge.

The other phaerimm floated through the portal one after the other, leaving the illithids and beholders to herd the mindslaves through. Arrogant as always in their power within the Shaeradim, they were not even worried about being attacked from behind—an unfortunate testament, Aubric realized, to how little damage the Swords had truly inflicted on their enemies.

By the time the last phaerimm had crossed the barrier, the fast-moving newcomers had reached the base of Rocnest—or at least their riffle had. In front of the tor, a steady progression of birds began to take wing as invisible warriors fanned out to set up an advanced defense line.

The phaerimm huddled together arguing, filling the air with strange whistles and angry gestures. After a few wasted moments, they returned to the Deadwall and created nine more shimmering portals. The beholders and illithids began to shove mindslaves through en masse, while the thornbacks worked frantically to arrange them into battle ranks. Aubric could not help smiling. It was the first time he had seen anyone disrupt a phaerimm plan.

The newcomers seemed eager to press. A dozen golden meteors arced away from Rocnest, landing short of the phaerimm lines, but exploding into huge curtains of amber fire.

"That's Vhoorflame!" hissed Rhydwych.

Aubric raised a finger to his lips, drawing an irritated—but silent—scowl. He did not take offense, for he understood the excitement that had led to her exclamation. Vhoorflame was a specialty of Evermeet's fleet mages, invented for the rare occasions when the island nation found it necessary to defend itself at sea.

A stiff wind—no doubt magical—rose behind the flames and drove it toward the Blazevale. The mindslaves grew agitated and more difficult to arrange, angering the phaerimm enough that they killed a handful as an example. That only sent the others into a panic, and several dozen turned to flee through the portals back into the Shaeradim.

A pair of the smaller phaerimm left the group and called up an opposing wind that stopped the Vhoorflames three hundred paces from the Deadwall. When the blaze continued to burn, they called rain down from a clear sky. The water merely turned to steam. They used a ground-moving spell to flip a huge wall of dirt back onto the fire. The Vhoorflames continued to burn, consuming the dirt as though it were coal. The fire began to advance again.

Finally, one phaerimm tried to dispel the magic that had created the fire curtain. Normally, dismissing the spell of a fleet mage was no easy task, but the phaerimm were far more than normal magic-users. The creature had barely stopped waving its arms before a section of flame faded, leaving a thirty-foot breach in the blazing curtain.

A blinding bolt of silver fire came streaking through the gap to catch the phaerimm in the torso. The thing erupted in a dazzling flash, hurling thorns and arms thirty feet into the air.

"In the name of Angharradh!" hissed Aubric, turning to Rhydwych. "What manner of spell was that?"

Rhydwych only gestured to the plain, where a robed man stood with a black staff in one hand. Aubric was just starting to make out the shadow of a thick beard when another ball of Vhoorflame streaked down to seal the gap in the fire curtain.

"It appears our help may not be needed," whispered Rhydwych.

"I pray we will be so lucky," said Aubric, "but we must be ready. Prepare the eye shield."

"There is no harm in being prepared." Rhydwych turned away to join her small cluster of Lordly Wands.

If the newcomers thought the destruction of one phaerimm would discourage the others, they were badly mistaken. The creatures merely spread out and floated forward in a line, then dispelled the entire wall of Vhoorflame at once.

This time, there were no streams of silver fire, only a flurry of lightning and golden bolts. The phaerimm vanished inside nine columns of roaring magic, each one pelted by such a tempest of spells that the ground split and the sky shook. One creature spun madly around and dropped in a heap of gashed flesh, but the others floated firm where they were, returning the attacks in kind.

A long rank of wizards—some looked human, others elf—was approaching through the fading smoke, all visible now that they had attacked.

They fell in twos and threes, or sometimes just vanished into blood and smoke. Fearing his allies were not as well-prepared as he'd thought, Aubric longed to call out to them to change tactics, for he and his Swords had discovered the hard way that spells hurled at phaerimm had a nasty habit of ricocheting back at the caster. On the other hand, there was value in keeping the thornbacks busy, and perhaps that was all the newcomers intended. Clearly, they had come with a plan—and at least a few surprises.

Aubric tried to find the bearded figure again, but quickly realized it was hopeless. Deciding the time had come for Evereska to unveil a surprise of her own, he stood and drew his sword.

"Arrows and spells!" he yelled. "Loose at will, slow advance!"

Bowstrings thrummed the air, sending a wall of hissing death down into the mindslaves trapped against the Deadwall. The first volley and most of the second dropped the illithids before they had a chance to whirl and use their mind blasts against the company's spellcasters. The Lordly Wands hurled a few fireballs and ice storms to keep the enemy off balance, but eight of the dozen remained quiet and assumed positions in the first rank of advance.

When the beholders finally recovered and turned their death-dealing eyes toward the invaders, Rhydwych called, "Eye shield!"

Together, the Wands uttered an incantation and poured a handful of powdered silver to the ground. The air in front of them shimmered with mirrorlike brilliance, and the beholders' rays ricocheted off in all directions. Aubric's archers took aim at the eye tyrants and waited, then, when the creatures spun their big magic-dispelling eyes around to dispel the eye shield, they loosed their arrows. Most of the beholders dropped to the first volley. The handful that survived perished in the second.

The confused mindslaves, now on their own, turned to meet the attack in a jumble.

"Spare them if you can, but be quick!" Aubric cried. "We must show our friends at the Rocnest how to kill phaerimm!"

Rhydwych and her Wands unleashed a flurry of spells, dropping a full third of the mindslaves into a deep slumber. Another twenty fell into helpless fits of laughter, and dozens more dropped their weapons and simply wandered off. A handful went blind and fell to their knees screaming. Unfortunately, a full two-dozen warriors remained to block the Swords' advance.

Aubric led the crash into them, using his elven sword to parry the wild axe of a vacant-eyed human, then slipping inside to knock the man unconscious with a mailed fist to the jaw. As he spun away, he snatched the fellow's axe and hurled it into a charging bugbear, dived under the monster's legs, and came up flinging sand into the eyes of three elves standing in front of the portal.

"Rest well," he said, adding the arcane syllable that gave his command its magical force.

The knees of two elves buckled, but the third danced forward in the practiced steps of a bladesinger—a pattern that Aubric Nihmedu had often taught his most promising students at the College of Arms. He should have backed away and called to one of Rhydwych's Wands for a killing spell, but he could not do that to one of his own pupils. Knowing what would come next, and trusting his own skill to defeat it, he blocked the low attack, slipped the lunge, parried the returning backhand, and knocked the fellow unconscious with an elbow to the jaw—then felt something hot and sharp pushing through his chain mail.

Aubric looked down to find a silver dagger protruding from his flank. "Oh, very good." He pressed himself into the shimmering Deadwall portal. "Very sneaky."

The world grew hot and flat looking. He experienced a strange instant of infinite expansiveness and intoxicating energy, then his side erupted in pain, and he fell.

The pain, Aubric promptly shunted to one side of his consciousness, to a place where he would be aware of what it told him, but not dominated by it. The falling, he threw himself into, flinging himself over his shoulders and rolling to his feet, his own blade and the dislodged dagger weaving a defensive pattern around him. He felt his sword slice across a body behind him and knew a human was trying to rush up on his left, which meant someone else was coming from the right. He flipped the dagger under his sword arm, aiming high for the throat and a quick kill. A strangled gurgle betokened an intuition still as sharp as two centuries before, but Aubric barely noticed. He had fallen into the grasp of the blood dance now, his mind and his body becoming one, an instrument being played by a will indistinguishable from the mad whirl of combat around him. His foot lashed out in a blind back kick, drawing a pained howl from the man he had wounded an instant earlier.

Aubric spun, blade flashing, blood coursing. It would have been wrong to say he became a bladesinger again—such a thing was impossible for an elf of so many responsibilities and so little time—but a gift hard won and long nourished returned. He became stronger, quicker, more supple—if not quite the dancing sword with whom Morgwais had fallen in love those few centuries ago, then at least once more a whirling blade. The old battle song tolled in his ears, and he began to feel in the Weave everything happening on the field of combat. He saw the wall of glassy-eyed mindslaves rushing up to attack, felt Lady Bourmays and Lord Dureth pushing through the Deadwall behind him, heard the voices of Lordly Wands calling out incantations to both sides of him. In the plain ahead, he saw the phaerimm streaking forward through a tempest of blades and bolts, heard one of the creatures fife its pain as an iron spear impaled it, felt the crackling energy as a blue force-dome rose up to cover all of Rocnest.

A strand of silk appeared in Aubric's hand of its own accord. He flung it at a dozen charging mindslaves and called three arcane syllables. A golden web engulfed their legs and brought their charge to a halt. Pounding feet sounded to his left. He dropped to a whirling crouch and swept his attacker's legs with an extended foot, then knocked the woman senseless with a heel kick to the head. The smell of musk saturated the air, and he launched himself backward, somersaulting into the legs of an astonished bugbear, thrusting his blade up through its guts, rolling free before the gore came showering down. He sprang up and heard a pair of light feet approaching from his wounded side.

Aubric lowered his sword, then seeing no more mindslaves to attack, stooped down to clean the blade on a human's tunic.

"Impressive," said Rhydwych. She thrust a healing potion into his hands. "But you might want to leave the bladesinging to younger nobles."

"Old habits die hard." Aubric allowed himself a wince, then drank the potion down. Its healing warmth coursed through his weary body, but there remained a chill deep in his wounded side. "Damn, that's one youngblade I wish I hadn't taught so well."

Rhydwych cocked her brow. "If you are too badly hurt—"

"When I am in too much pain to defend Evereska, you will know it by the pieces on the ground."

Aubric glanced over his shoulder and found the rest of the company assembling. They had lost perhaps twenty Noble Blades, but still had all twelve Wands. He waved his sword toward Rocnest and started after the phaerimm.

"For Evereska!"

"For Evereska!"

If the reply was weaker and softer than Aubric would have liked, so was his own voice. The pain was spreading, filling his abdomen with cramping fire. The blade had pierced something vital, but there was nothing to do about it. Both of the company's healers had long since been killed, so he could either fight through to Evereska's allies and hope they had a good healer, or he could sit down and die.

Aubric closed off all awareness of the pain, calling on his old bladesinger talents to draw strength from the Weave and lead the charge across the charred plain. As they drew closer to Rocnest, he was astonished at the newcomers' losses. Elves and humans alike lay scattered by the dozens, most motionless and quiet, some writhing and groaning. He saw at least seventy or eighty casualties himself, and guessed the total could easily be twice that number. He assigned half a dozen of his own walking wounded to do what they could for the injured, though everyone knew that would be all too little.

Seventy paces from the enemy, a tremendous crack echoed across the plain. The newcomers' blue dome flickered and dimmed, then flashed out of existence. The phaerimm started forward again, only to be met by a volley of arrows and spears from Rocnest. The dark shafts struck in a clattering cloud, many ricocheting harmlessly off the thornbacks' scales, but a few finding soft seams. One monster dropped to the ground with the butt of an elven spear in its mouth, and two more trilled in anguish, but most showed no reaction at all to the sticks bristling in their bodies.

A hundred warriors appeared atop Rocnest, visible now that they had attacked and turning to scramble down behind the jagged lip. They made it only a step before the rim erupted into curtains of golden fire and showers of fuming black rain. There was a cacophony of crackling flame and anguished screaming, then another sound—four roaring voices booming out the same intricate spell, complementing each other, working jointly to twine together separate strands of the Weave in one creation.

"It's a Circle!" Rhydwych said, coming to Aubric's side. "The high mages are trying to open the gate!"

"How long?" Aubric asked.

"Too long." Rhydwych pointed at the surviving phaerimm, who were plucking the last of the arrows from their bodies and rising toward Rocnest. "Ten minutes, at least."

Aubric's heart sank. The whole battle so far had taken only fifteen minutes, and the newcomers had done well to delay the phaerimm that long. He thrust his arm into the air, extending his thumb and smallest finger in the "bow" signal.

"Arrows!" He turned to Rhydwych. "How many of us can you magic up there?"

"None, if you expect us to put up a fight," she said. "There's a moment of confusion after any translocational spell—and a moment would be all the phaerimm need."

Aubric nodded, then closed his fist and lowered his arm, calling the Swords to a halt. "Dying that way would do no good, but we must buy them time. Take your Lordly Wands and do whatever you can. The Blades will follow as we can."

Rhydwych's face paled, but she nodded. "For Evereska."

"For Evereska—and all the elves remaining to Faerûn." Aubric's stomach turned hollow and queasy. It was one thing to lead the charge into peril, quite another to order a dozen brave elves to their certain deaths. "May the Harp Archer watch over you."

"And you as well, Lord Nihmedu." Rhydwych gave him a weak smile, then kissed his cheek. "Don't let them make a mindslave of me."

"Nor you of me," answered Aubric.

Rhydwych drew a pair of battle wands, then closed her eyes and used her magic to mindspeak with her fellow wizards.

Aubric looked toward Rocnest again, where five healthy phaerimm were already halfway to the rim. The other two remained closer to the ground, wobbling about on their tails as they tried to recover their wits.

"Loose and advance!" Aubric yelled.

A volley of arrows darkened the sky, a dozen flying toward each phaerimm. Perhaps a quarter of the shafts directed against the injured creatures struck home, lodging themselves deep between their scales or in the pulpy rim of the mouth. One thornback dropped writhing and flopped like a trout out of water. The second vanished in the glimmer of teleport magic. The other flights streaked to within a few inches of their targets, then struck some invisible shield and bounced harmlessly away.

By the time the arrows tumbled to the ground, Rhydwych and her Wands were in the air, streaking after the phaerimm like sparrows after hawks. Aubric started to raise a hand to call a ground charge, then saw a dark-bearded human step onto a jagged spur atop Rocnest. He held a black mage's staff and wore heavy winter robes, and Aubric felt certain he was the same man whose silver flames had destroyed the first phaerimm.

Hit them again, my friend, and this time your arrows will strike home. On my signal.

Aubric did not question how the voice came to his head, nor hesitate to implement its command. He raised his thumb and little finger in the "bow" signal and called a halt.

"Nock and aim!" he yelled. "Choose your targets well."

Even as he yelled this, the phaerimm unleashed a tempest of magic at the figure atop the rock. There were fireballs and ice storms, swirling clouds of vapor and black bolts of death, lightning forks and even a great disembodied hand. The human stood through it all, his arms spread wide, his black staff raised high above his head, its body surrounded by a purple aura as it drew attack after attack down into its shaft.

The figure could only be Khelben Arunsun. Aubric's spirits rose at once, for with one of the Chosen fighting in Evereska's defense, surely it could only be a matter of time before the phaerimm were driven from the Shaeradim.

He waited patiently for the promised signal, all the while watching his Wands draw closer to the phaerimm, and the phaerimm closer to Rocnest, until he began to worry about distance and accuracy, and to fear that his archer's shafts might strike the Swords' own wizards.

Finally, the bearded figure lowered his staff. Though it was impossible to hear the archmage's voice over the booming chant of the high mages and the general battle roar, Aubric saw the human's fingers flashing through the familiar gestures of a magic dispelling spell. He lowered his arm.

"Loose!"

The thrum of eighty bowstrings sounded as one, and a cloud of arrows hissed through the sky. As they neared the phaerimm, the shafts bunched into swarms, almost like wasps streaking out to sting the fools who dared disturb their nests.

The flights struck with an almost audible thud, driving the phaerimm closer to Rocnest's basalt cliffs and a little downward. Fully half the arrows snapped against the creatures' scaly armor, but the others sank deep, adding their feathery tails to the forest of spines already rising on the backs of the phaerimm.

The Lordly Wands adjusted their course and swooped to engage, but were brought up short when a handful of battered human mages appeared alongside Khelben to hurl a fusillade of bolts and flashes at the phaerimm. Several blasts ricocheted off their intended targets and streaked back to the caster, and a full half dozen merely vanished without causing visible harm. The other spells hit on mark, spraying cracked scales and broken thorns in every direction.

One phaerimm lost an arm and went tumbling groundward, only to vanish in a silver flash. The other four fought back in kind, swinging out to spray Rocnest's scorched rim with every color of hissing bolt. There were lightning blasts and fire streams and storms of exploding hail, but the most destructive attack was a surge of invisible force that slammed into the cliff itself, creating a boom so loud it hit Aubric like a punch. A web of fissures shot across the rocky face, bringing the rim down in a crashing mass of stone and black dust.

Rhydwych and her Wands swooped into the roiling cloud somewhere beneath the phaerimm. Aubric raised his arm to signal the blade charge and was startled to realize he was already half a dozen steps behind everyone else. Determined not to dishonor his position by being the last into battle, he reached out to the Weave and felt its strength surge into him—but he found also that his legs would not rise faster, nor his lungs draw deeper, nor [illegible] pump harder. He could not understand what was wrong—until he noticed the dull burning in his abdomen and felt the wet warmth pouring down his leg. The pain he had shunted aside, but one could demand only so much from a body, and he had long ago passed that threshold.

As the landslide settled, brilliant flashes and deep rumblings filled the dust cloud. A Lordly Wand tumbled out of the roiling mass in a dozen pieces and rained to ground amidst the Noble Blades. They paid no attention and vanished, screaming, into the swirling murk.

Aubric raced after them, lungs aching and muscles burning. The plain turned into a hazy field of jumbled stone and ghostly silhouettes, and the air grew thick with choking dust, filling his throat with racking coughs. It occurred to him he might not survive to thank Evereska's new allies, and his thoughts turned briefly to Morgwais—the Red Lady, with skin so bronze it was scarlet—and he was sorry he had not gone with her into the High Forest, not because he feared what was about to befall him, nor even because he knew he would never see her again, but because he had let her think that his duty meant more to him than she did.

Aubric came to the base of the landslide and saw his ghostly Blades scrambling up the boulders, chasing after handfuls of long gray cords dragging across the stones. One elf sprang off a stone, and letting his sword fall free, caught hold of the rope. He began to climb, and the line dragged across the ground more slowly. Another warrior caught hold and dropped to his seat, bracing himself between two boulders to hold it in place.

Coughing and hacking so hard he could hardly hold himself straight, Aubric ran his gaze fifty feet up the line to the amorphous blob above. In the swirling dust, it looked like some sort of jellyfish, with a shapeless body and a string of long tentacles dangling below. It took the blademajor a moment to recognize what he was seeing, to identify the tangled knot of limbs as the grotesquely broken arms and legs of three Lordly Wands, wrapped tight to their foe by the sticky white strands of a magic web.

A rolling ball of flame engulfed the phaerimm, drawing an anguished shriek from a lone elf voice. Aubric thought for a moment that Khelben or a human wizard had hurled the spell down from above. When the creature did not come crashing to the ground, he realized that the fireball had been no more than a desperate attempt to free itself—but elven ropes did not burn. A half dozen Noble Blades grabbed hold with the other two warriors and hauled their foe down toward its death. The thornback had other ideas and vanished in a twinkling of silver spell light.

A second phaerimm, still reeling from the fury of earlier attacks, was not so lucky. A trio of elves caught its ropes, then drew it down while their fellows poured arrows into it. By the time the dazed creature finally thought to raise a shield, they had it on the ground, dragging it past a teetering boulder. When their fellows pushed the monolith over, the spray of green blood left no doubt about its fate.

Aubric clambered over the rocks toward Rocnest, searching the sky for the last two creatures. The booming voices of the high mages continued unabated, as did the cries of the wounded and the rumble of shifting stone, but an ominous pause had descended over the battle itself. By the time he reached the base of the cliff, the dust cloud had thinned to a mere haze.

Dureth came up beside him. "Aubric, you look in a bad way."

Aubric nodded and searched the landslide below. "Did you see what became of the last two phaerimm?"

A worried look came to Dureth's eye. "No."

"Then tell those who can to hurry." Aubric turned toward the cliff. There was perhaps fifty feet of vertical face, then another hundred of steep bowl where the avalanche had caved away. He sheathed his sword and looped a coil of rope over his shoulder. "I'll see you above."

Dureth caught his arm. "You can't do this, my friend," he said. "Not alone."

"How can I not?" Climbing as nimbly as a spider despite his wound, Aubric started up the cliff. "I doubt there is anyone left who can keep up."

"Aubric, no one expects the blademajor to—"

But Aubric was already twenty feet up, his fingers and toes moving quickly from one hold to another. Dureth began to yell at the others to regroup, asking if anyone had a spell of flight. By the time the high lord had everyone gathered, Aubric was pulling himself off the vertical face onto the treacherous slope left by the landslide. He yelled for the others to stand clear and scrambled up through the loose stone, twice falling and nearly sliding to his death.

The high mages continued their spellcasting, their voices rising to a fevered pitch as they neared completion. When the top of the slide basin came into view, Aubric began to think Rhydwych had killed the other two phaerimm herself—and that, of course, was when the crackle of a war spell rumbled over the crest of the slope. He tied the rope off to a spar of rock and tossed the free end to the others, then drew his sword and scrambled into the saddle.

At the top, Aubric dropped to his belly and peered into Rocnest. All that remained of the ancient fortress were a few sections of elf-raised wall along the jagged rim. But down in the basin stood a rectangle of lustrous black stone, still shining with the magic that had drawn it from the ground. In front of the block stood a gossamer-robed Gold elf female, her voice ringing heavenward as she plucked strands of Weave from the air and plaited them into the dark monolith. She was fashioning an elegant keel arch, its purple depths growing ever darker and richer. With every fiber she laid, the mage herself seemed to grow wispy, translucent, as though she were braiding herself into her work. Aubric thought it so, for though the high mages kept their art to themselves, he had heard that their magic often involved the binding of their own spirits.

Arrayed around the elf woman were three male mages, their bodies as black and opaque as the female's was translucent. They held their arms spread skyward, spraying shimmering arcs of magic into the circle. Their voices were booming to a crescendo, each calling out a separate spell of support, yet weaving their incantations together in music-like harmony.

The slope directly below Aubric was more dirt than rock, strewn with bodies both human and elf—many writhing in agony, none able to stand. Halfway down hovered the two phaerimm, still swaddled in Rhydwych's magic webs and flinging spells at a scintillating dome of colors. Though Aubric recognized the dome as one of the most powerful defenses taught by Evereska's Academy of Magic, he could not understand why the phaerimm were wasting their time destroying it when the high mages were so close to completing the gate.

Khelben Arunsun stepped out of the dome, hurled a spell at one of the creatures, and dived back into his sphere. The stricken phaerimm froze and began to sink into the ground. Whistling in alarm, the other floated around the sphere and dispelled the magic drawing its fellow down into the stone.

In the basin below, the voices of the high mages rose to a thunderous roar. The archway glowed deep purple, and the female elf faded to a shimmer.

Khelben popped out of the dome again and cast a ray of black death at the second phaerimm, only to have the magic reflected back at him. He tried to bring his black staff down to intercept the spell, but even Mystra's Chosen could not catch their own spells. The bolt took him in the chest, hurling him a dozen paces up the slope. He landed in a heap, brown vapor rising from the puckered hole in his chest.

Aubric was already bounding down the rocks, his knees quivering with weakness, his breath coming in hot, wet wheezes. As he passed Khelben, he was relieved to see the edges of the hole already closing, but it seemed clear the archmage would be of no further use in this battle. The closest phaerimm spun to meet Aubric's charge, its barbed tail tangling in its skirt of elven ropes. The second creature extracted itself from the ground and started down the slope toward the high mages.

Aubric sprang six feet to the right, then right again, as though trying to work his way around the first creature. When he gathered himself for a third leap, his foe took the bait, spraying his path with sizzling black acid. Aubric jumped left, drawing on the Weave's magic to launch himself into a glorious flying somersault, his sword whirling about him as his panicked target filled the air with flashing magic.

In the basin below, the voices of the high mages fell silent. The female vanished in a brilliant burst of purple radiance, and the gateway glowed with a magic so deeply violet it was black.

A magic bolt caught Aubric in the shoulder, but he twisted around, launched himself off the phaerimm's fleshy lip—one of the few areas not covered with magic web—and dived over the scintillating dome. The startled creature whistled an alarm, and its fellow spun on its tail, splicing the air with a sheet of scything magic.

Aubric was already on the ground, rolling to his feet and dancing toward the phaerimm in a tornado of flashing steel. The creature called to its fellow and moved to block the elf's path across the hill. Aubric feigned an attempt to circle above it, then saw the weary mages below lower their arms and knew the gate was complete. He changed directions, barely escaping as a nest of tentacles sprang from the ground to snatch at his legs. The second phaerimm streaked by, trilling in anger as it swept down into the basin.

"Watch yourselves!" Weak and croaking as it was, the call sent Aubric into a spasm of coughing. Bright blood sprayed from his mouth, taking with it what little remained of his strength. He dropped to his knees, then tried again to warn the high mages.

"Behind you!"

Whether or not they heard the cry was impossible to say, for the elves turned almost sedately to look up the slope. Their golden faces had gone sallow and gaunt with exhaustion, and when they raised their arms, it almost seemed they were trying to ward off a blow instead of preparing to cast a spell.

The phaerimm was faster. Still wrapped in its amorphous cocoon of magic web, it stopped at the bottom of the slope and struck the ground with its tail. A deafening crash shook the entire Rocnest, then a network of magma-belching fissures shot across the basin floor toward the black gate.

The high mages crossed their arms in front of them and calmly awaited the assault. The fissures shot to within a dozen feet of the trio, then turned aside and scribed a fiery loop around the floor of the basin. The phaerimm warbled its frustration and struck the ground again, causing a blinding ring of magma to roar dozens of feet into the air.

The archway's black silhouette remained visible through it all, but when the fiery curtain sank back into its crevices, all that remained of the three mages were fuming black robes, lying rumpled and empty along the edge of their circle.

Though it seemed minutes had passed, Aubric knew by his labored breathing and trembling muscles it could only have been seconds. He looked away from the receding fires more disheartened than awed. The gate had been raised—but to what purpose? Even if others wanted to help, Evereska remained as alone as ever. Any forces sent by Evermeet or Waterdeep would be destroyed the instant they left the gate—or, worse, added to the ranks of the phaerimm mindslaves.

A shadow fell across the ground before Aubric, then he heard something wispy and sibilant inside his mind. *Come along quietly, and you will live.*

It was all Aubric could do to find the strength to look at the dusty, web-swaddled mass before him. "I doubt it."

Do not. I have a fondness for you brave ones. You hatch strong larvae.

Aubric heard a soft rustle and brought his sword up beside him, catching the phaerimm's tail just above the barb as it came whipping in at his flank. There was a wet slashing sound, then the feel of hot blood as the severed tail sprayed his face.

Leaving his pain to come flooding into him, Aubric called upon his last tiny reserve of strength to launch himself into a mad, cartwheeling attack.

He did not make it, of course. The phaerimm floated aside and let him tumble down the slope, and the searing spray of green vapor came sizzling down on him from above.

Aubric hardly noticed, for the strength had fled from his body. He felt the sword slip from his grasp, and the last thing he saw was the luminous face of the female mage watching him from the mouth of the black gate, and he was struck by how much her smile looked like that of his beloved Morgwais.

CHAPTER EIGHTEEN

30 Nightal, the Year of the Unstrung Harp

To Galaeron's eye, Malik looked a touch ill at the prospect of letting Melegaunt cast any spell on him, much less a spell involving a darkdagger and rope. His gaze kept darting from the bridge into the black wood beside them, where the others were breaking camp after a dry night's rest around a magic-heated boulder.

"Have no fear, my friend," said Galaeron, knotting his elven rope around Malik's wrists. "You may trust Melegaunt."

Malik looked over his shoulder. *"You* may, but I heard what he said to Jhingleshod before crossing the bridge."

Galaeron wanted to ask for an explanation, but saw Melegaunt approaching with his darkdagger and knew there was no time. He leaned closer to Malik's ear. "Then you may trust me, human. I do not allow those who save my life to be murdered—even if they are Cyric worshipers."

"That is little enough reassurance," said Malik, "considering who is the student and who is the master."

Melegaunt stopped before them and glowered down at the little man. "I could not find you in the dawn shadows." He paused, allowing Malik to consider the implications. "If you don't wish to continue—"

"Oh no, you are not leaving me!" Malik glanced at the darkdagger, then raised his chin. "Do what you must."

Melegaunt cast an inquiring look in Galaeron's direction, and receiving a curt nod, kneeled at Malik's feet. Beginning a long incantation, he laid a small pair of braided shadow-silk manacles in the little man's shadow. The shadow instantly grew broad of chest and slender of waist, with a strange pair of what looked like antlers on its head and a blurry area of white in the center of its chest. Malik's teeth ground together loudly, but he did not try to flee as the shadowmage had warned he might.

Melegaunt cocked a bushy brow. Still chanting his spell, he drew his dagger along the edge of Malik's feet. The shadow came free, peeling itself off the stones to stand looming over them all, brown sky showing through the hazy-edged hole in its chest.

Malik gasped and would have collapsed, had Galaeron not been there to slip his hands under the little man's arms.

A pair of crimson eyes appeared in the shadow's head and peered at Melegaunt. "I am bound to your will." Its voice was as resonant as Malik's was nasal. "Though you do me a grave disservice. I know your purpose and would aid it gladly."

"All the same, we will keep matters as they are." Melegaunt pointed across the bridge. "I wish you to keep watch. You know our enemies?"

"The phaerimm—or Elminster?" the shadow asked.

"Both, and their servants as well," replied Melegaunt. "When you see any of them, return to Malik and give us warning."

The shadow inclined its head. "As you command."

Melegaunt studied the silhouette for a moment, then turned back toward camp. Galaeron started after him, pulling an awestricken Malik along beside him. The little man glanced at his feet and back to the shadow, then turned to Galaeron.

"That demon cannot be anything of mine!"

"Exactly." Doubtful he could explain the shadowself as well as Melegaunt, Galaeron did not even try. "You don't seem very disturbed. The first time I saw my shadow, I was terrified."

"Oh, I have seen things worse than my own shadow," scoffed Malik. "After all, I am much favored of the One."

They joined the others in camp, where Vala and Takari stood over a half-sized relief Aris had sculpted into an expanse of bedrock. Depicting Malik's rescue of Galaeron and Vala, the work was amazingly fluid and detailed. Malik's character looked more confused than resolute, and perhaps a little angry at himself for being foolish enough to jump into the river. Vala was unconscious in the crook of Galaeron's arm, more dead than alive. Galaeron was holding the rope and glancing down at Vala, his expression leaving no doubt that the terrible fear in his eyes was for her alone.

Takari and Vala were huddled together on the opposite side of the work, talking quietly and studying the relief so intently they did not see the others approach.

". . . don't want either of you hurt," Takari was saying. "You've seen yourself why it can never be."

"I have?" Despite her curtness, Vala's voice was surprisingly mild. "When was that?"

"You met his father," Takari explained. "You saw what became of Aubric when Morgwais returned to the forest."

"We're getting ahead of matters here, but I'm no Wood elf," Vala said. "Were I to make a life pledge, I would honor it as my mother and father honored theirs."

"And how long would that be?"

Vala raised her chin. "My parents have been sharing the fur for forty years and three."

"A blessing for them both, but forty years and three is not the same to an elf." Takari laid a hand on Vala's arm. "Forty years from now, Galaeron will still be young, with four centuries before him."

When Vala did not answer, Galaeron said, "There's no need to poison her against me, Takari." He waited for the pair to turn, then gestured at Aris's relief. "It's only art—and what business is it of yours? I'm your prince, not your nestmate."

The flash that came to Takari's eyes was more sorrowful than angry. "And no fun as either." She turned and slipped through the black tree trunks. "Sorry to forget my place."

Vala shot a scowl at Galaeron. "I only kissed you," she growled, starting after Takari. "I have done more with half the men in my clan!"

This drew a crooked smile from Melegaunt, but he made no comment and turned to Jhingleshod, who stood studying the work with the enigmatic gaze of the dead.

"It appears we are ready to go," Melegaunt said.

"You are ready," said the knight. "But there is still the matter of my payment."

Galaeron cast an anxious glance after the departing women. "If the bridge is any example, you are not worth much of a price," the elf said.

"You learned what you needed to learn," replied Jhingleshod. "If you recall what happened there, you may survive to claim what you seek."

"I have no fondness for these games of yours," said Galaeron. "If you would have something from us, then you must tell us what we need—"

Melegaunt stepped in front of Galaeron. "We have already agreed to your price, Sir Knight. If you wish to tell us what it is, we are listening."

"I ask little," said Jhingleshod. "Only your word that you will do what already you must."

"Yes?" asked Melegaunt.

"Destroy Wulgreth, my master, as I once attempted."

"As you once attempted?" Galaeron asked, more wary than before. "If you betrayed your master, how are we to know you won't betray us?"

"I have no care for what you know or do not know, elf," said Jhingleshod. "But I tell you this: I bear no small part of the blame for the evil here, and I am damned to wander the Dire Wood until what I should have done then is done at last."

"How is Wulgreth's crime your doing?" asked Melegaunt. "I sense no great evil in you."

"But I relished the bounty of his shadow," said Jhingleshod, "and so I stood by. After Wulgreth summoned the demons to Ascalhorn, for six decades I watched their evil and did not raise my voice against them. When the demons turned on him at last, I followed Wulgreth into the wilderness and sat in his shadow feasting on stolen bread and drinking the wine of murdered wayfarers. And after he came here to Karse, I was waiting outside the black crypt when he returned with its dark power."

Jhingleshod let his chin fall.

"And yet, you found the strength to slay him," prompted Melegaunt.

"It was despair, nothing more," said Jhingleshod. "The power was twisted and evil, and it corrupted all it touched. First, the forest died and turned to black stone, then the ruins became a city of the dead. When I begged Wulgreth to send the monsters away and build a city for the living, he struck me blows, saying he would never be avenged on the demons with a living army. Seeing that my dream was not to be, I felt betrayed and vowed he would never again bring ruin to any city. I killed him in his sleep that night."

"Which proved unwise," surmised Melegaunt.

Jhingleshod nodded. "He caught me as I fled the city, a cackling dead thing of heinous power. He chased me through the forest, using his magic to flay me an inch at time, until I ran myself to death. I awoke as I am now, condemned to wander the Dire Wood until the vow I made is kept." He turned to Galaeron. "And that is why I won't betray you."

"And if we fail you as Wulgreth did?" asked Galaeron. "Will you turn against us, too?"

Before Jhingleshod could answer, Melegaunt said, "What you say can't be right. Wulgreth was a Netherese arcanist, killed much earlier when a magical experiment went awry and Karsus had to push an orb of heavy magic off his enclave."

"Heavy magic?" Galaeron asked. He knew "enclaves" to be the legendary floating cities of ancient Netheril, and Karsus was the deranged archwizard who had caused the empire's fall by trying to steal Mystryl's godhead, but Galaeron had never heard of "heavy magic."

"A powerful sort of magic discovered by Karsus—and nothing I want you playing with until you bring that shadow under control." Melegaunt fixed Galaeron with a disapproving eye. "It's appallingly dangerous, a force made tangible that Netherese archwizards once used to heighten their other magic."

"Once used?" asked Malik. "Then you do not have any of this 'heavy magic'?"

Melegaunt glowered at the little man. "No. It vanished with the Netherese." He turned back to Jhingleshod. "But it was Karsus's heavy magic that turned Wulgreth into a lich, not your attack."

"Netheril fell a thousand years before I lived," said Jhingleshod. "And Wulgreth was much alive when I served him. One does not turn from a lich into a man and back to a lich again."

"There is no record of such a thing in the Tomb Guard chronicles," said Galaeron. Recalling Malik's cryptic comment about what Melegaunt had told Jhingleshod before crossing the bridge, he studied the wizard with narrowed eyes. "The Tomb Guard *would* have a record."

Melegaunt's eyes grew stormy. "You accuse me of lying?"

"I ask for an explanation."

"You—or your shadow?" Melegaunt countered.

"I have my shadow in hand," said Galaeron. "It has not troubled me since the sunken bridge."

"Why should it?" Melegaunt turned back to Jhingleshod. "I am not mistaken about my dates. Wulgreth never forgave Karsus for the accident, and there are records of him plaguing Netherese enclaves for decades afterward. It's the reason Wulgreth haunts the Dire Wood at all."

"Wulgreth haunts this wood because I killed him here," Jhingleshod insisted. "The Dire Wood did not exist before that."

"But Karse did," countered Melegaunt. "The city was founded over sixteen centuries ago, a little after Karsus brought Netheril down. A refugee group was drawn to his corpse by dream visions and began to worship his dead body—and *that* really angered Wulgreth. He destroyed the entire city and moved into the ruins so it would never be rebuilt."

Jhingleshod fixed his dead eyes on the sorcerer. "I know nothing about heavy magic and worshiping dead bodies. I killed Wulgreth, and he became a lich."

"If I may, the answer is plain enough," said Malik. "In a thousand years, there were certainly many wizards named Wulgreth. Does it seem so unlikely that two ended up here?"

Melegaunt raised his brow, then nodded thoughtfully, but Jhingleshod did not seem to hear the suggestion. In fact, Galaeron realized, though Jhingleshod's gaze was fixed on the same point as Melegaunt's—Malik's face—the knight's eyes were focused on the ground behind the little man, and the slight tilt of his helmet suggested he might be wondering what the wizard was looking at.

"I think we can trust Jhingleshod's account of events." Galaeron chose his words carefully. "But we'd better be off before Takari and Vala get too far ahead of us."

Jhingleshod's dead gaze shifted to Galaeron. "Then you give your word?"

Galaeron nodded. "I will destroy Wulgreth, if we can find him."

"He will find you," said Jhingleshod.

The ghoulish knight walked across Aris's sculpture, leaving the river stained with rusty footprints, into the trees. The forest here was dark, tangled, and dead—much the same as the bog, save that it stood on dry ground and did not drain their strength. The group soon caught up to Takari and Vala, and Jhingleshod took the lead, clinking and squeaking his way deeper into the tangled wood.

Huge webs of yellow-green filaments began to appear in the branches. Galaeron kept watch for ball-shaped silhouettes and sticklike legs. Instead of spiders, he started to see slender leaves and moldy pods clinging to the tendrils. As they climbed away from the river, the vines grew longer and the vegetation thicker, until it became difficult to see more than a few paces. It was impossible to walk without brushing against the vines, and soon after their hands and faces erupted into white boils. Aris used his prayer magic to powder a stone and create an ointment that reduced the sores to an itchy rash, though Malik refused the salve out of fear of offending his god. To the amazement of all, he continued at as strong a pace as anyone, even when the blisters began weeping and he had to cut his eyelids to keep them from swelling shut.

The vines began to grow in broken squares and straight meshwork, taking the shape of the ruins beneath. Jhingleshod walked more quietly and carefully now, prompting Galaeron to send Takari ahead to scout and take a position beside Vala. Malik and Melegaunt remained in the center, with Aris in the rear. As they advanced deeper into the city, the patterns grew more regular and even, arranging themselves into crooked streets and sunlit meadows that had once been plazas.

Vala kept her hand on her sword, her eyes following Takari's stealthy figure with remarkable ease for a human. After a time, she said to Galaeron, "You shouldn't have said that to Takari. She's only trying to protect you—and me."

"That's not what it sounded like to me."

"Maybe not," said Vala. "But then, you didn't hear what she told Jhingleshod about why she wanted to cross the bridge."

"Whatever she said, it is not her place to protect me from our relationship." Galaeron glanced over at Vala. "Not that there *is* a relationship."

"No?" Vala glanced at him sidelong, her mouth cocked in a crooked smile. "Then why should you care what she says about it?"

"I prefer to make those choices myself," said Galaeron. "As I'm sure you do."

"We have a saying in Vaasa," she said. "In love and death, only the gods choose."

"It sounds a handy excuse," said Galaeron.

Vala gave him a roguish smile. "One that makes life interesting." She watched Takari poking her sword into a tangled mass of vine, then asked Galaeron, "When you told Jhingleshod you were seeking pardon for your mistake, was that the truth?"

"More than I knew," Galaeron said. "It had to be, or I doubt Jhingleshod would have let me pass."

"I thought so." Vala remained quiet for a moment, then said, "I had to think carefully, but Takari didn't hesitate."

"I take it the answer concerned me?"

Vala nodded. "Takari said she had to cross because you're her spirit-deep mate . . . and you refused to see it."

"She . . ." Galaeron closed his eyes. "She knows I don't return her affections."

"Because of your father's pain," Vala said carefully. "Or so she says."

"That's part of it," said Galaeron. "Moon and Wood elves live different lives. When they join, sooner or later there will always be sadness."

"Of course." Vala sounded almost irritated with him. "Sooner or later, every joy comes to an end—but that is a poor reason to turn your back on the gifts the gods *do* send your way."

"I'm just being prudent," said Galaeron. "I'm not turning my back on any gift from the gods."

"Oh, I think you are." Vala's voice turned teasing. "And you will be sorry. There is no fury worse than Sune's when she has been rejected!"

"Fortunately, I am an elf," laughed Galaeron. "I doubt our Hanali Celanil is so vengeful as your Sune."

"Maybe, but Takari isn't the only woman I've been talking about, you know."

An owl hoot rang out ahead, bringing their conversation to an abrupt end. Galaeron drew his sword and saw a vine web fluttering as Takari vanished into the trees. Jhingleshod was continuing up the street, paying no heed to whatever had alarmed Takari. Galaeron suspected their guide of betraying them—until a half-rotten corpse dashed out of a side lane and hurled itself headlong into the iron knight's flank.

Jhingleshod rocked up as though he might fall, then brought his axe down and split the ghoul through the side. He turned to Galaeron and pointed down the lane.

"Beware those dead, elf." There was a hint of mockery in the knight's bleak voice. "They have a hatred of the living."

Vala at his side, Galaeron started forward to block the attack, but heard a warning chirp from Takari's tree and turned in the opposite direction. He found himself staring at an alley full of monks, their eyes sunken and their robes in tatters, but looking as alive as Galaeron. Behind him, Vala's sword hissed through the air on the opposite side of the street. There was a wet slash, the thud of a falling body, another slash, another thud.

Galaeron pointed his sword at the first monk, now less than a dozen paces away. "Stand and name yourselves!"

The entire company of monks stretched their arms out, turning their hands palm up as though begging alms. When they continued forward without speaking, Galaeron whistled the clear *tee-yeer* of a meadowlark. He was answered by the hum of a bowstring, and a warning arrow appeared in the dirt in front of the leading monk.

The monks stopped, their gazes following the angle of the arrow into the nest of vines from which it had come, but Galaeron knew without looking that Takari was already gone. He quietly pulled a ball of sulfur wax from his pocket.

"Name yourselves or go."

The first monk responded to the challenge with an incomprehensible moan. Behind Galaeron, Vala's sword continued its gruesome work, and now he heard Aris's mighty club and Melegaunt's bellowing voice as well. Malik remained as silent as usual during battle, but the elf had no doubt the little man would appear when needed most.

The lead monk cautiously stepped around the arrow and continued forward, his cupped hands still stretched before him. Finally convinced he was looking at undead impostors, Galaeron tossed his sulfur ball into the group and spoke his incantation. The cold magic filled him for an instant, and the alley erupted into black fire. Galaeron backed away from a long tongue of dark flame, then beheaded a pair of blazing monks as they staggered from the alley.

A powerful hand clamped Galaeron's shoulder. Surprised, he jammed his elbow back and drove his attacker off a step, then spun with sword flying. By the time he realized it was Melegaunt, his edge was an inch from the wizard's head. Galaeron tried to pull the attack, but to no avail. The blade caught Melegaunt square in the temple.

There was a black flash and dull ping as the edge stopped. Pain sizzled up Galaeron's arm, then his hand opened and let the sword fall to the ground.

Melegaunt touched three fingertips to his head and came away with a thin smear of blood. "Is this how you repay my gift? By defying me at every turn?"

"I can hardly be blamed for your stupidity." Still trembling, Galaeron stooped down to retrieve his sword. "Grabbing a warrior in the middle of a fight—what's wrong with you?"

Melegaunt stepped on Galaeron's sword. "That's not what I'm talking about."

"I used the magic, yes. It was necessary."

Behind Melegaunt, a ghoul slipped past Vala. One of Takari's arrows took it square in the forehead and knocked it off its feet, but the creature merely rolled to its knees and snapped off the shaft.

Galaeron tried to jerk his sword free, but found the wizard's foot impossible to move. "The magic hasn't hurt me. I'm more in control than before."

"Yes, I have seen how well you are mastering your shadow." Melegaunt touched his head again, then flung a hand in the ghoul's direction and blasted it into a dozen pieces. "Leave the magic to me."

The wizard started up the street after Jhingleshod, calmly directing Vala and Aris against individual ghouls and wights while he blasted larger concentrations with shadow magic. Galaeron gathered his sword and followed behind, quietly venting his anger on any creatures foolish enough to come his way. The undead continued to assault them in erratic fits, occasionally stopping a short distance away to attack with a spell, screech, or gaze. Sneaking along through the treetops, Takari prevented such attacks from succeeding, usually by distracting the creature with an arrow until Melegaunt could blast it. Twice, Malik saved the company by appearing out of nowhere to harry a lurking wight or ghoul until someone more adept could destroy it.

Eventually, the attacks grew less frequent, then, when an enormous butte of red stone began to loom over the treetops, ceased altogether. Jhingleshod guided them to a barren plaza near the head of the butte. There was no sign of the black pyramid he had described Wulgreth entering.

"I believe that is what you seek."

"It is," said Melegaunt. "The fallen body of Karsus."

The butte did resemble a body—albeit a broken and twisted one. The small knoll closest to them looked like a head resting on its side, with a round oversized forehead, hooked nose, and thin-lipped mouth over a weak chin. There was a bent and crooked arm coiled at an unnatural angle, a sunken chest and the round swell of a pot belly—at nearly a hundred feet above the surrounding ground, easily the butte's highest point. From the side of the chest, at about heart level, gushed the source of the Heartblood River, a frothy red spring that flowed away in a meandering stream.

"I see why the refugees took it for a dead god," said Vala. "It certainly looks like a god's body."

"It is a god's body—though Karsus was a god for only an instant," said Melegaunt.

"And this dead god will save Evereska *how?"* asked Galaeron, seeing no sign of the help Melegaunt had promised. "You can't mean to resurrect him."

"In a manner of speaking, yes," said Melegaunt. "But first we must find the black pyramid."

"First, you must find Wulgreth," said Jhingleshod. "You cannot enter the pyramid until you keep your promise."

"As you wish." Despite Melegaunt's words, his tone was impatient. "Tell us where to look."

Jhingleshod ran his gaze over the plaza. "He should have made his presence known by now."

Melegaunt turned to Galaeron. "You're the tomb guard. What's Wulgreth planning?"

"Maybe nothing." Galaeron turned to Jhingleshod and asked, "How long has it been since you last saw him?"

Jhingleshod looked at the sky. "Time is difficult to judge, but several winters. It might have been eight or nine—or a dozen. It is hard to know."

"But it *has* been some time?" asked Takari.

Jhingleshod nodded. "Since before Tianna Skyflower and her ilk began to roam the Dire Wood."

"That makes it nearly a decade," said Takari. She looked to Galaeron. "What do you think?"

Galaeron shrugged, knowing without asking what she was thinking. Often, liches evolved into beings of pure spirit, forsaking their bodies to wander other worlds beyond Toril. When that happened, their corpses began to decay, until all that remained was a skull and some dust to which the lich had only the most tenuous attachment. It was often easier to destroy such creatures than younger liches, but Galaeron knew better than to think they would be that lucky—especially if Wulgreth had only been gone a decade.

Galaeron shook his head. "We'll keep it in mind, but there's too much that doesn't make sense here. The Netherese Wulgreth is certainly old enough, but not the one Jhingleshod served—and there's that time gap to consider."

"So what do we do?" asked Malik.

"The only thing we can do," said Galaeron. "Draw it out."

CHAPTER NINETEEN

30 Nightal, the Year of the Unstrung Harp

From atop the Karsus Butte, the ruins of Karse seemed one huge mold blossom, sickly yellow and reeking of decay, studded with shadowtop snags and crisscrossed by dragonflies the size of eagles. There was a tornado of crimson mist whirling down the Heartblood River and a curtain of smoking hail sweeping across the ruins, but Galaeron had been assured by Jhingleshod that such "wizard weather" had nothing to do with the lich. Strange storms had plagued the area since long before Wulgreth's death.

Galaeron and the others were standing on Karsus's "chest," outside a two-story pyramid of black marble. Though the building's darkness and gloss were a stark contrast to the butte's coarse sandstone, the pyramid seemed melded to the rock, almost as though it had been grown instead of built. Aris was studying the workmanship, but everyone else was keeping watch for Wulgreth.

"Anything?" Galaeron asked.

"Flaming rain and green lightning," reported Vala.

"Silver snow by the steaming lake," said Takari. "It can't be more than a couple of miles. Maybe a bath—"

"No!"

Melegaunt and Jhingleshod spoke over each other, the wizard declaring they had important business at hand and Jhingleshod claiming that distances within the Dire Wood were deceiving.

Takari pouted. "We've already wasted an hour."

"An hour you do not have," said a wispy voice.

Galaeron and everyone else spun toward the sound and found themselves looking at a pale, quivering Malik.

"On my life, I said nothing!"

Galaeron frowned—since the sunken bridge, it seemed people were always giving him reason to be suspicious—then he noticed a powerful-looking silhouette at Malik's feet. Galaeron gestured with his sword.

"Malik, your shadow has returned."

Malik looked down. "What a joy to have you back!"

"You must know I cannot say the same." As the shadow spoke, its antlers grew thinner, and the fuzzy hole in its chest began to close. "It is bad enough to follow a man about like a slave one's whole life, but when that man is the inept Seraph of a—"

"Enough!" growled Melegaunt. "You have something to report, shadow?"

"I do." The antlers grew as thin as twigs, and the crimson eyes turned pale. "There was a fight in the swamp, but only one creature survived."

"Which one?"

"A human." The shadow's voice was soft and wispy, almost inaudible. "With the pipe and . . ."

"Elminster?"

The silhouette's eyes closed, then it melded into Malik's pearlike figure and was just a shadow once more.

"We must go inside." Melegaunt started around the pyramid.

Jhingleshod clanged after him. "This Elminster is not my concern. You must destroy Wulgreth first."

"And we will." Galaeron scrambled after the pair. "But Melegaunt's right. It's time to go inside."

Jhingleshod turned his lidless eyes on Galaeron. "You are not lying?" Though he asked it as a question, to Galaeron the words felt more like a command. "You will keep your word?"

"If this is Wulgreth's lair, we'll find him inside," said Galaeron. "If he's not there already, he'll come when we enter."

Jhingleshod studied Galaeron with his vacant eyes for a moment, then followed Melegaunt and Vala into the crooked entrance corridor. Galaeron had Aris call upon his god to bless a full skin of water, then took Takari and Malik after the others. Too large to enter with them, the giant waited outside.

The darkness and close confines reminded Galaeron of the cairns in the Shaeradim, though the passageway smelled more like blood than dust, with just a hint of sulfur and steam. Within a few steps, the corridor opened into a vestibule lit by silver spell light. In the moment it took Galaeron's eyes to adjust to the harsh light, he heard Melegaunt saying, "Jhingleshod, here is your Wulgreth. Nothing but dust and bones."

Galaeron glimpsed the wizard's burly shape stooping to pick something up, then heard Takari hissing a spell and knew she had realized the same thing he had.

"Don't touch—"

Takari's spell erupted in a terrible ringing, causing Melegaunt and Vala to cover their ears and spin toward the clamor. Galaeron pushed his way past the pair and found a cloud of dust whirling in the corner, a gray skull rising into the air atop it. He motioned the others away, then breathed a silent sigh of relief when Takari canceled her spell.

"What spell was that?" he asked, keeping a wary eye on the dust pillar. "You nearly broke my eardrums."

"It was supposed to be a silence spell," Takari answered. "Something went wrong."

"Wild magic," explained Jhingleshod. "The Dire Wood is full of it, and the closer to the pyramid, the worse it grows."

"Then let me be the first to suggest we are in terrible trouble," said Malik. Hanging the skin of blessed water over his shoulder, he drew his curved dagger and waved it at the spinning dust, which was now taking a vaguely human shape. "I fear we have found Wulgreth."

"There is nothing to fear." Melegaunt took out a sliver of obsidian and pinched it between his thumb and forefinger. "My spells are not affected by wild magic."

"No!" Galaeron and Takari yelled, then Galaeron added, "Whatever it does, do nothing in return."

"Nothing?" Malik gasped.

"It's a demilich," Galaeron explained. "It will absorb your attacks and use the energy to return to this world."

"A *demi*lich?" echoed Malik. "Then it will be easier to destroy?"

"Trickier," Takari said. "If we strike too early, we bring it back. If we strike too late . . ."

"Yes?" Malik raised his brow. "If we strike too late?"

Galaeron answered, "The Tomb Guard has accounts of demiliches killing an entire company with a single screech."

"Accounts?" Malik said. "I thought you had fought many of these things!"

Galaeron and Takari exchanged looks, then he said, "There was one lich."

Malik's face was not the only one that went pale, and even Jhingleshod's lidless eyes seemed to bulge. The dust coalesced into a skeletal figure clothed in rotting silks.

"That is not Wulgreth," Jhingleshod said. "Wulgreth wore no such robes."

Jhingleshod stepped toward Galaeron, but stopped when the demilich cut him off. The creature flailed at the knight's skeletal face, prompting him to step away and heft his axe.

"Don't!" Galaeron yelled.

Jhingleshod checked his swing, and the demilich's claws burst into harmless clouds of dust as they struck. Fiery points of light began to burn in its empty eye sockets, then it held the stumps of its arms before its face, let out a powdery snort, and whirled on Galaeron. He lowered his sword, and the creature stepped to within a hand's breadth of him, a handful of brown-crusted gems glimmering dully in the place of several teeth. It smelled of musty dirt and stale air, and the hiss of alien winds whispered on its breath. Though Galaeron's whole body went cold and clammy, he forced himself to meet its burning gaze and show no fear.

The demilich raised an arm, where a dusty hand was forming anew, and pressed a fingertip to Galaeron's face. Though the claw did not cut, the otherworldly cold of its touch traced a line of numbness down his cheek. The elf willed himself to stand fast, and though he knew it would anger Melegaunt, readied the necessary spell. The thing opened its mouth and spewed a plume of dust into his face. Caught by surprise, he began to cough and choke, stumbling back as he tried to spit the powdery stuff from his mouth.

"Poison!" Malik started for the exit.

Vala dropped an arm to block his way. "We may have need of that holy water you're carrying."

Galaeron snorted the dust from his nose, then felt his gorge rise as the reek of decay filled the room. A fringe of red, straw-coarse hair sprouted from the lich's head, then a mask of shriveled skin began to creep over its face. The open nasal cavities did nothing to improve the thing's appearance, but with a rounded forehead, overhanging brows, and hideously skewed jaw, it would have been grotesque even with a nose.

A terrible aura of cold filled the room, and Galaeron knew the demilich's spirit had finally returned to its body. He stepped forward and circled his palm before its face.

"Forget." He spoke in the ancient language of magic, calling upon Melegaunt's coldmagic to empower the spell. *"Return to your rest."*

The demilich lashed out, catching Galaeron by his chain mail and ripping a handful of magic-forged loops from over his breast. Vala leaped forward to attack, but the links were already falling through the creature's hand. Galaeron raised a hand to check her attack, then watched as the thing's body dissolved back into dust. When the skull sank to the floor, he motioned her forward.

"Now, Vala—before the spirit flees. Cleave it in one blow."

Vala's sword descended in a black flash, splitting the skull lengthwise and dividing both sides again before they toppled to the floor. A crimson flamelight shot from the bones and streaked through Vala's body, then circled the room with a blood-curdling keen. Her jaw dropped and she looked as though she might collapse of shock, then a cold wind ripped through the room and the whirling flamelight faded from view.

Galaeron glanced around the room. "Where's Malik?"

The little man stepped out of a shadowy corner, dagger clutched in his trembling hand. "Have no fear on my account."

Galaeron motioned at the skull fragments. "Douse them well—and hold your breath."

Malik did as he was asked, and the blessed water began to eat through the skull fragments, filling the room with an evil-smelling fume that troubled the little man not in the least. Everyone else withdrew to the tunnel and took turns gulping down fresh air. The bone fragments dissolved, mixing with the dust in a single muddy heap. Malik continued to pour, but no matter how much he stirred, the whole mess adhered together like bread dough. Finally, when no chips of the skull remained visible, Galaeron returned and prepared another spell.

Melegaunt caught his arm. "Allow me."

"If you're not too weary, old man." Galaeron was surprised to feel his lip curl into a disparaging sneer. "All you need do is dispel the magic."

Melegaunt glowered at him. "I can manage. And I could have handled the forgetting magic as well."

The archwizard muttered a few syllables and waved his hand. A purple shadow fell over the doughy mass, then the mud lost its cohesiveness and spread across the floor. Malik dropped the waterskin, and on the pretext of stooping to pick it up, deftly swept up the six brown-crusted gems that had been in the demilich's mouth. Having no interest in the stones himself, Galaeron pretended not to notice.

Jhingleshod came to their side, then propped his axe on the floor and looked at his iron palm. When the gauntlet showed no sign of flaking or disintegrating, he turned to Galaeron.

"What next?"

"I don't know." Galaeron glanced around the chamber, searching in vain for some hint of a forgotten step. "The lich is gone."

"What of its phylactery?" Malik quietly pocketed the gems. "I have heard it said that liches hide their life-forces in repositories—usually an item of great worth?"

"They do," said Galaeron. "But not so with a demilich. They have abandoned their repositories for worlds beyond, and remain connected to Toril only through their remains."

"Liar! Do you think your excuses can fool me?" There was a note of desperation in Jhingleshod's voice. "Had you destroyed the lich, I would not be here now."

"Unless we destroyed the wrong one," said Galaeron, recalling the argument between Melegaunt and Jhingleshod over the lich's true identity. "Malik, let me see those gems you took."

"Gems?" asked the little man. "What gems are those?"

"These."

Vala slipped an arm around Malik's throat and used the other to pluck the brown nuggets from his pocket. Galaeron took them and carefully scraped the brown crust from their faces. He was down to the sixth, a deep ruby, before he found the inner light for which he had been searching. Returning the others to Malik, he displayed this one to his companions.

"The chronicles suggest that this will be an imprisoned spirit," he said. "If we free it, perhaps it can help us."

Melegaunt cast an impatient eye toward the tunnel. "How long?"

"Not as long as trying to defend yourself from my axe," warned Jhingleshod.

"It will need a body," said Galaeron. "Perhaps one of the undead?"

"I can make a body for it," said Melegaunt. "One that will be safer for it—and us."

The archwizard took a piece of shadowsilk from his cloak and laid it on Vala's shoulder. Repeating a long incantation over and over, he began to knead the stuff with his fingers, spreading the dark substance over her, carefully covering her flanks, limbs, even her head and face. When he finally finished, Vala resembled a living, breathing sculpture of the blackest basalt.

Melegaunt took her hand and pulled. She emerged from the shadow as though from a dark corner, leaving a dark likeness as perfectly shaped as one of Aris's sculptures.

"If the spirit is troublesome, we can dismiss it with a little light."

Galaeron laid the gem next to the figure, then waved Jhingleshod over. "If you would smash it."

"If this is one of your tricks. . . ."

"By the shadow deep!" Melegaunt cursed. "We haven't time for trickery."

Melegaunt brought his heel down and ground the gem to powder. A crimson radiance flowed out from beneath his heel and began to climb his leg.

"Oh no, my friend!"

The archwizard plunged his foot into the body he had created, then sighed in relief as the luminescence melded into the shadow. A glossy sheen spread over the figure's black flesh, then the eyes opened and stared at the ceiling. It raised a leg, and twisting it around at an impossible angle, studied its heel. Then, seemingly unaware of the arms hanging motionless at its side, did the same with the other leg—and crashed to the floor.

Galaeron rushed to its side. "We didn't know what kind of creature you were." He waved at the body. "We made this in our own fashion."

The shadow sprouted a pair of eyes on the side of its head. "You did well. The color is right."

Galaeron glanced at Melegaunt and found the wizard staring at the dark figure with a dropped jaw. When the elf looked back to the creature, it had wrapped its arms around its legs, and all four limbs were melding into the body.

"We were wondering if you could tell us . . ." Galaeron looked away. He could not quite keep from asking, "What are you?"

"A sharn." It was Melegaunt who said this. "At least that is what I think."

A smiling mouth appeared in the flank of the drop shaped body. "You think right, wizard." Another mouth appeared on Galaeron's side. "What is it you want to know? I am obviously in your debt."

Galaeron was too stunned to answer, as was everyone except Jhingleshod.

"We would know who captured you, and whether he has been entirely destroyed."

The sharn rose off the floor and floated toward the door. "That was the lich Wulgreth, who took my soul when I came thinking to end his depredations against the empire."

"Wulgreth?" echoed Jhingleshod. "*Which* Wulgreth?"

"The only Wulgreth that is a lich," replied the sharn. "How many do you think there can be?"

Iron shoulders slumping, Jhingleshod whirled on Galaeron. "You have not destroyed him, not completely."

"Wulgreth is completely destroyed," said the sharn, now struggling to squeeze itself into the exit tunnel. "Were that not so, I would not be free."

Jhingleshod whirled on the sharn. "Liar! If Wulgreth were destroyed—"

"Jhingleshod, wait," Galaeron said, stepping in front of the iron knight. "You asked the wrong question."

"Then ask the right one—and quickly." The sharn paused in the tunnel mouth, peering out from a bulbous extrusion that might or might not have been a head. "Grateful as I am, I hunger for better company than yours."

"Which empire were you trying to protect?" Galaeron asked.

"Which *empire?*" The sharn withdrew completely into the tunnel. "Why, the *only* empire of course—unless you mean to include your quaint elven confederacies."

"The Netherese Empire?" Galaeron pressed.

"The very one." The sharn's voice faded as it retreated up the passageway. "And now, if you'll excuse me, I shall return later to repay the favor you have done me."

"Wait!" Melegaunt stepped forward, speaking in a language of strange syllables. When the sharn did not reply, he turned back to the others, shaking his head sadly. "He doesn't know. It's all gone, and he doesn't know."

"The sharn were Netherese?" Galaeron gasped.

The question jolted Melegaunt out of his despair. "I don't know." He shrugged. "No one does, I suspect. There are some who claim they were Netherese arcanists who transformed themselves in order to battle the phaerimm. Others claim they came from another world. What is clear is that they had a hatred of phaerimm, or they would not have erected the Sharn Wall."

At the mention of the Sharn Wall, Galaeron cast a hopeful look up the tunnel, but Melegaunt shook his head. "He's gone, my friend—and even were he not, I doubt he could help us. Before we can patch the hole, we must fight our way through the phaerimm who have already escaped."

Though it angered Galaeron to concede the argument, he nodded and turned toward the back of the chamber. "Then let's find the help we need and get to it."

✡✡✡✡✡

Keya Nihmedu stood atop the Livery Gate watchtower, slightly self-conscious in her form-fitted chain mail and painfully aware that the magic pike in her hand was no defense at all against phaerimm. Her eyes were as sharp as any in Evereska, and she had seen enough of the battle in the High

Vale to know that fifty years of half-hearted blade drill—suffered daily at her father's insistence, Hanali bless him—would stand her in poor stead against the thornbacks. The unsightly monsters had already turned the high slopes into a forest of bare-limbed scarecrows, and now they were working their way onto the upper terraces of the Vine Vale, using their hideous magic to turn the vineyards into dead tangles of thorn hedges.

Most of the Long Watch felt their duties were of little real importance to the war, that they were only standing a post to free the real soldiers to fight, but Keya was not so sure. She had it from Manynests—if she understood his scattered peeptalk correctly—that the Cloudtop Magi Circle had divined the phaerimm's plan. They intended to capture Evereska much the same way they had destroyed the Netherese Empire, by using their life-draining magic to devitalize Evereska Vale. Without the surrounding lands to sustain it, the city's mythal would slowly lose its magic, and eventually it would grow too weak to keep out the thornbacks.

At first, Lord Duirsar had not been overly worried. The groves and lands within the mythal were large enough to sustain its power for a year or two, by which time help would surely arrive. Then the high mages of the Bellcrest Spire had reminded him that plants need light and water, and the Moondark Circle had named a dozen spells that could shut off both. According to Manynests, Lord Duirsar had decided on the spot to create the Long Watch, and that was how Keya knew her duty to be as important as whatever her father and Galaeron were off doing—wherever they were off doing it.

Keya selected a wand from her belt and dutifully swept it across the four quarters of the sky, studying its wake of blue radiance for any telltale glimmers of invisibility magic. The wand was one of a trio quietly supplied to each member of the Long Watch by the three towers of high mages. Keya had not known there were that many circles in Evereska until Manynests had "slipped" during a rather curious visit to inform her that Lord Duirsar had not heard from her father and the Swords—a fact well known to all of Evereska.

After a day's reflection, Keya had dutifully let it slip in gossip that she had heard from a reliable source that Evereska still had three full towers of high mages. This had done much to reassure her friends, who had promptly spread the secret so efficiently that it was repeated to her twice over the next two days—exactly as Lord Duirsar had intended, she was sure. What she had not passed along was the high mages' concern about the mythal, since she felt certain the bird had, in fact, not meant to reveal that bit of bad news.

When Keya found no invisible phaerimm lurking above the mythal, she returned the wand to her belt and started a slow, top-to-bottom scan of the encircling cliffs with her naked eye. She was about halfway around when she noticed a crag hawk circling its nest, claws extended as though it would like to attack but could not. As she had been taught, Keya did not dwell on the spot or immediately reach for a wand, but marked the place in her mind and continued her routine to fool any watching phaerimm. Then, feigning boredom—also a part of Long Watch's meticulously rehearsed routine—she yawned and shook her head, studied her nails for a moment, and glanced back to the spot.

The bird was still circling.

Keya retreated casually down the stairs and found a window from which she could see the hawk. Standing in the shadows, she pulled the first wand from her belt and swept it over the area. She was rewarded with a row of telltale sparkles. For the first time, her heart began to pound with excitement. Though she descended the stairs a dozen times every watch to check on something, this was the first time she had ever found anything suspicious. She pulled her second wand and waved it at the street-side window.

The image of a beautiful Gold elf appeared in the window. "What is it, Keya? If you are thirsty, I can send a boy with some wine."

"No wine, Zharilee." Keya could not keep the excitement from her voice. "I've something to report."

The Gold elf arched her brow. "You're sure?"

"Crawling down the face of Snagglefang," she said, trying to remember the elements of a good report: what doing what, where, when, how many. "A group of invisibles. Maybe a dozen, side-by-side. Just passing the crag hawk's nest."

"Crawling, you say? Why would they crawl?"

Keya looked back to the cliff, where the invisibles continued to descend in a crooked row. "It might be a battle line."

Zharilee frowned doubtfully. "Phaerimm don't need to crawl. Why wouldn't they just float . . ." She let the sentence trail off and grew more serious. "I'll send word to Cloudtop. Keep watching."

The image faded, leaving Keya to her invisibles. They were descending rapidly, three of the twelve bunched together. She waved a different wand. The cliff drew close enough to see individual crags and crevices, but the wands would not work together and the twinkles were no longer visible. She went back to the first.

The invisibles reached the base of the cliff and started down the jumbled talus boulders beneath. Several of the other twinkles gathered around the close-bunched trio, helping them over the rough terrain. Was the trio carrying something? No—more likely, they were two carrying a third. A pair of warriors carrying a wounded comrade.

Any lingering doubts about their identity vanished. Even had it been phaerimm crawling down the cliff, they would not be carrying wounded. From what she had seen of the thornbacks, they did not carry their wounded anywhere—least of all *into* an attack. The invisibles had to be elves—or elf-friends—trying to reach Evereska.

Keya reported her observations to Zharilee, then switched wands and examined the surrounding mountainside. As she had feared, there were five phaerimm and a dozen times that many beholders and illithids scurrying through the denuded forest to intercept the band. She reported that as well.

Zharilee said she was passing the information to Cloudtop Tower, and that she was sorry, but Keya would have to watch what followed. Keya replied that watching was the least she could do. Seeing that there was no longer a danger of giving the party away, she returned to the roof for a better view. Though she would appear only a speck to the invisibles even if they knew where to look for her, she pointed toward the ambush.

The warning proved unnecessary. The invisibles paused at the bottom of the talus, then one sprayed the wood ahead with a stream of silver fire so brilliant it spotted Keya's vision from more than a thousand paces away. The five phaerimm reeled away, pouring columns of smoke into the air and slapping at their burning bodies with all four hands, and the invisibles followed the assault with a volley of enchanted arrows. As each of the shafts struck their targets, they exploded in golden flashes of magic and filled the wood with blazing red smoke.

When Keya used her wand to report this development, the too-gaunt face of Kiinyon Colbathin appeared next to Zharilee.

"This silver fire—who cast it?" he demanded. "Was it a human?"

After losing the entire tomb guard in the initial battles with the phaerimm, Kiinyon had apologized to all of Evereska and tried to resign. Lord Duirsar had refused the resignation and placed him in charge of the vale's defenses, saying that Evereska had need both of his experience and the wisdom he had earned by it.

"I can't see," Keya reported. "The smoke is too thick."

"Well look, damn it!"

Keya looked, but, as she said, the smoke was impervious to sight and magic—at least any magic she had been given. All she could see was the curtain of smoke billowing across the hill, a handful of illithids scrambling up into the talus—and it occurred to her what she did *not* see. The invisibles had attacked, so now they should be visible—but she still couldn't see them, not with any of her wands. Realizing how well the small band had planned its attack, Keya swept her gaze down the mountainside.

She found them halfway down the Vine Vale, staggering out of a small black door in the middle of an arbor-covered terrace. The first was a bearded human in scorched robes, the hair on his bare chest singed away around a grotesque brown scar. The second was a Gold elf in the elaborate armor of an Evereskan noble, as were the third, fourth, and all the others that followed.

"It's the Swords!" Keya cried. "They're back!"

"The Swords?" gasped Kiinyon. "Of Evereska?"

"Well, some—a few." No sooner had Keya said this than she thought of her father and began to search the faces in the party. "I see Lord Dureth, and Janispar Orthorion, and a black-bearded human."

"That human, could it be Khelben Arunsun?" This time it was Lord Duirsar himself asking. "And tell us how you can see them, damn it! The tower mages can't find them in that wretched smoke."

"I'm sorry, milord—they're down in the Vine Vale, in the ThistleHoney Vineyard," said Keya. "And I don't know Khelben Arunsun, but the human is carrying a black . . . by the golden rose, no!"

"What?" demanded Lord Duirsar. " 'No,' what?"

Keya did not answer, for the last two elves emerging from the black door held a litter bearing the shrouded figure of a dead body. She could not see who lay beneath the shroud, but there was no mistaking the acid-pitted helmet lashed across the figure's chest. A simple basinet of silvery mithral steel, it was by far the plainest of any worn by the Noble Blades. It belonged to Aubric Nihmedu.

"Watcher!" roared Kiinyon. "Answer Lord Duirsar!"

"I—I apologize, milords," said Keya. "The human has a black beard and black staff, and he shows sign of a grave injury. More than that, I cannot tell you of him."

"And why did you cry out?" prompted Zharilee. "Lord Duirsar asked about that as well."

"I saw . . ." Keya paused to clear the catch in her throat and saw a patrol of elves rushing past the Swords to meet two phaerimm that had teleported in to attack the battered company from behind. "Excuse me, but if you want to see Khelben Arunsun alive, you must send some war mages to help."

Before she had finished the sentence, a circle of high mages appeared between the fleeing elves and their would-be attackers. With a sweep of her hand, the center erected a wall of golden radiance and sent it rolling toward the enemy. The phaerimm countered by sending a cone of cold blasting through the wall to strike down one of the mages, then it teleported away. The surviving Swords were swept up by the patrol and hurried toward the protection of the mythal. So went the battles for Evereska, swift and deadly and neverending.

"We'll see to the Swords, Keya." Now that things appeared to be under control, Lord Duirsar's voice was gentler. "Tell us what you saw."

"Lord Nihmedu . . ." She stopped to choke back a sob, then realized that her brother was now Lord Nihmedu and began to wonder what had become of him, and she could not stop the tears. "I'm sorry to report the Swords' blademajor has fallen."

"Your father?" Zharilee gasped.

Keya nodded and looked away from the wand-window.

"I'm sorry, Keya. He was a good friend and a loyal Evereskan," said Lord Duirsar. His voice grew softer, and he spoke to Kiinyon Colbathin. "Under the circumstances, Vale Marshall, I wonder if the Long Watcher might be excused."

"Of course," said Kiinyon. "Feel free to retire, Watcher."

"Thank you, milord." Keya wiped the tears from her eyes and turned to the wand-window. "Do you have someone to relieve me, Zharilee?"

The Gold elf hesitated. "We're well-covered in other posts."

"But none of the other posts reported the Swords' return?" Keya asked.

Zharilee shook her head. "There are a couple that should have seen it, but no."

"Then I'll stay." Keya turned back toward the High Vale. "The Long Watch has its duty, too."

CHAPTER TWENTY

30 Nightal, the Year of the Unstrung Harp

Wulgreth number two."

"Definitely two." Peering around the chamber, Galaeron nodded his agreement with Takari's conclusion. "This has to be Jhingleshod's Wulgreth."

The pyramid's second room was as dusty as the first, but packed with implements required by any practicing wizard. There were mortars and kettles and vials, balances, braziers, and bottles, tablets, scrolls, and librams—many librams, all lined up on shelves and safely protected behind glass doors. There was also a thick tome of spells, resting on a stand beneath a hovering glowball, open to a spell near the back and not at all covered in dust.

A loud grating sound came from the far corner. Galaeron turned to see Takari springing away from a small crawlway, sword in hand and the first syllable of a fire spell gliding off her tongue. When nothing sprang out to attack, she gestured at a depressed trigger stone in the floor.

"That was easy."

"Too easy." Galaeron kicked a loose stone into the crawlway, then winced as a wall of green magic descended behind it. "This lich is a tricky one."

"Something he learned from the demons of Ascalhorn," agreed Jhingleshod, stepping into the room. "Easier to lead a victim to his doom than to push him into it."

"A lesson Galaeron would do well to remember," Melegaunt said. He followed the others into the room, and seeing the open spellbook, shook his head in scorn. "A little too inviting, I would say." He flicked a hand at the stand, and a pall of shadow fell over the pages. "To guard against a straying glance."

Though Galaeron suspected the comment was directed at him, he did not object. The open book was too obvious an invitation. Sooner or later, someone would glance over to see what Wulgreth had been studying and would find himself compelled to continue reading, activating some spell of possession or imprisonment. He was beginning to understand this lich. Unlike the first, which had wanted to drive them off, this one wanted to control them.

The glowball brightened of its own accord, filling the chamber with harsh light and deep shadows. Along the back wall stood a small collection of gilt armor and bejeweled weapons, all enchanted so heavily that an aura of magic showed through the thick coating of dust. Next to the weaponry stood a rack of wands and staves, and next to that sat a row of treasure chests. In front of one chest kneeled Malik, his hands plunged to his wrists in a bed of jewels, his gaze blank and empty.

Galaeron pulled the little man from the chest, spraying jewels across the floor, and slammed the coffer shut. "Don't!"

Malik blinked several times, then reached for his dagger. "No need to be greedy, elf. There are gems enough here to make rich men of us all!"

"To make us Wulgreth's slaves." Galaeron looked to the others. "Don't touch it. This is bait."

"Bait?" Vala was eyeing a suit of gleaming chain mail.

Galaeron stepped in front of her. "It's how he recruits his undead servants, I think. You saw Malik's eyes."

She nodded.

"A clever scheme." Takari eyed the treasure as though it were offal. "If we can't touch anything without becoming slaves, we can't sort through it to find his phylactery."

"Unless we dispel the magic first," said Melegaunt.

"Then dispel it," Jhingleshod said.

"My magic is not unlimited." Melegaunt eyed the wall of magic items. "It will take someone more powerful than I to dispel all this."

"I am no fool," said Jhingleshod. "You cannot have what you want until I have what I want."

"It's not possible," said Melegaunt. "I've already used that spell once today. I can cast it one more time, but after that I must spend the night imprinting the magic on my mind many times over. By the time I finish, Elminster will be here."

"Perhaps Elminster could dispel it," suggested Jhingleshod.

"You don't have a bargain with Elminster," said Galaeron, "and I doubt he'll be inclined to rescue the one who helped Wulgreth bring demons to Ascalhorn. You can only trust Melegaunt."

"Trust *him?*" The veins in Jhingleshod's eyes grew red and thick. "I am not so naive as you."

"Naive?" Galaeron's gaze flashed to Melegaunt, then back to Jhingleshod. "What do you mean by that?"

"Galaeron, a man can intend two things at once." Melegaunt tried to interpose himself between Galaeron and Jhingleshod. "I am still Evereska's only hope."

Galaeron continued to look at Jhingleshod. "Tell me."

"There is no need to tell you what you already know," said Jhingleshod. "You saw him betray Vala on the bridge. You should not be surprised to learn he has been lying to you."

Galaeron whirled on the archwizard and found Vala blocking his path, one hand on her sword. "No, Galaeron." She pushed him back gently. "You know I can't let you."

Galaeron felt something in his hand and realized he was holding his own sword. He released it, turned to Jhingleshod, and asked, "What did Melegaunt tell you?"

"After Wulgreth is destroyed," the knight promised.

Galaeron turned next to Malik and said, "You heard it."

"I told Jhingleshod I came to save my people," said Melegaunt. "You, of all people, should understand that."

Galaeron continued to look at Malik. The little man sighed and nodded. "First he claimed he came to save Evereska, and for that lie he received the same blow you did. Then he said he came to save his people, that he needed the Karsestone to return shade to his home."

"Not *my* home, *its* home." Melegaunt shook his head in frustration, then sighed and said, "Shade was a Netherese city. Our shadow masters read the empire's fall in the dawn shadows and took us to safety in the Demiplane of Shadow. We've been trying to return to our home—you call it Anauroch—ever since."

"Seventeen centuries is a long time trying," Takari said.

"Time is not the same in the Demiplane of Shadow," Melegaunt said. "Nor the task of returning a simple one."

"Not with the phaerimm in your way," said Galaeron. The anger in his voice prompted Vala to draw her sword. "First, you had to move them someplace else!"

"It was not meant to be Evereska," said Melegaunt, now growing as angry as Galaeron. "But what if it had been? For seventeen of your centuries, we have been trapped in a dark hell, unable to return because of the phaerimm. For the first millennium, we kept our freedom by paying tribute in lives to the demon lords who thought to make us their own, and for the last seven hundred we have fought the Malaugrym for our very survival. Would it be too much to ask of Evereska—and the rest of the world—that they help us destroy the phaerimm so we could return in peace?"

"You didn't ask," said Galaeron.

"Not Evereska." Melegaunt shouldered Vala aside and drew himself to his full height, reminding everyone present—including Galaeron—that he had little to fear from an angry elf. "But what would the answer have been, had a Netherese city asked your Hill Elders for help?"

The question sent a cold bolt through Galaeron, for the answer was as obvious to him as to Melegaunt. The ancient elves had disapproved of Netheril's careless magic, and as he knew from ancient writings in the Academy of Magic, taken a secret delight in the fall of the ancient empire.

"You can be sure I am doing more for Evereska than Evereska would for Shade," said Melegaunt. "Whether you believe that is up to you—and your shadowself."

Without awaiting Galaeron's reply, the wizard spun on Jhingleshod. "I presume the Karsestone to be beneath this pyramid. If there is an easier way to reach it, do not make me waste precious time and magic opening a shadow tunnel."

Jhingleshod's eyes flared angrily. "Your promise—"

"Whether you value Melegaunt's promise or not, you may trust mine." Galaeron did not know whether the all-too-human fury in his heart was his own or that of his shadowself, but he did know that much of the criticism Melegaunt had leveled at Evereska was true. He turned to the wizard and said, "Were the circumstances of our cities reversed, perhaps I would do as much to save Evereska. But know this, wizard, I will hold you to your promise. If Evereska falls, I will see to it that Shade suffers a fate many times worse."

Melegaunt gave him a dark smile. "It already has, elf. It was never our intention to loose the phaerimm on your city—and they remain more our enemy than yours. There is no need to worry on that account."

Galaeron turned to Jhingleshod. "My promise stands as before."

Jhingleshod studied Galaeron for a moment, then nodded. "Do not fail me, I warn you."

He went to the crawlway Takari had discovered and swung through feet first, his body erupting into a cloud of dust as it passed through the green barrier. Galaeron and the others looked at each other with dropped jaws.

Finally, Takari said, "An illusion. This lich is a very clever one, indeed."

She stepped over to the passage and swung her legs through the opening, then vanished in a cloud of dust. Galaeron went next and found himself plummeting into a high, silver-lit cavern. He glimpsed a colonnade of curved pillars arcing up to a central support, then splashed into a pool of foul-smelling liquid the color and consistency of quicksilver. A small hand caught him by the hair and dragged him to one side just as Vala hit beside him. Next came Melegaunt, fluttering down on the magic of a slow-fall spell, and Malik plummeted into the pool screaming.

A moment later, the group found itself standing waist-deep in a silvery pond, staring across a mirror-bright surface at a luminous white boulder the size of Malik's horse. From a jagged crack in the center poured a steady stream of the shimmering fluid, filling the pool and slowly disappearing down a whirlpool at the far end. As the liquid swirled down the hole, it assumed a crimson tinge and began to steam, almost like blood.

"It's touching," said Takari, ever the romantic. "Karsus's heart bleeds for what he did."

"You might say that, though Karsus was too mad for true remorse," said Melegaunt. "The Weave filled him to bursting when he tried to steal Mystryl's godhead. What you see pouring from the Karsestone is all that remains of that ancient whole magic."

"Whole magic?" It was Malik who asked this. "Since when has magic been less than whole?"

"Since the Fall of Netheril," Galaeron surmised, thinking back to the tiresome texts he had studied at the Academy of Magic. After the fall, Mystryl had saved the Weave by reincarnating herself as Mystra, but the surviving archwizards had quickly discovered that without the goddess's direct intervention—a very rare occurrence indeed—they could no longer cast their most powerful spells. Most sages conjectured that Mystra was simply limiting magic to protect the Weave from another disaster, but Galaeron saw that another explanation made more sense—and explained the source of Melegaunt's cold magic. "It split," he said.

Melegaunt was too busy pressing strands of shadowsilk onto the Karsestone to answer, but Malik was hanging on every word.

"What split?" the little man asked. "Do you mean the Weave?"

Galaeron started to answer, then recalled Malik's previous interest in shadow magic and thought better of it. "You ask too many questions, human." He started toward the little man. "You're no wizard. What is it to you if the Weave split?"

Malik's eyes grew wide, and he began to retreat. "Remember your shadow, my friend. You are placing yourself in grave danger with these questions!"

"But I'm not," said Vala, approaching from the other side. "And I've been wondering myself. It wasn't any coincidence that we found you camped outside Thousand Faces, was it?"

"You would threaten *me*?" Malik gasped. "After I risked my own life to save yours?"

"I'd like to know why." Vala rested a hand on her sword. "In my experience, Cyricists are rarely so selfless."

"Don't kill him—I'm going to need him," said Melegaunt, still working his way around the Karsestone. "His presence is no mystery. He's investigating my magic for Cyric."

Malik's jaw dropped. "You knew?"

Melegaunt peered out from behind the Karsestone. "Do I strike you as an idiot?" The archwizard pointed his chin at Malik's turban. "Pull that off, and you'll find his antlers. Our companion is no ordinary thief—he's the Seraph of Lies."

Galaeron did as Melegaunt instructed and found a pair of small antlers—they looked more like cuckold's horns—then asked, "You knew, and you let him stay?"

"Better the spy you know than the one you don't—and he has proven useful, wouldn't you say?" Melegaunt began to point to spots in a circle about six feet from the Karsestone. "Now spread yourselves out, and we'll call the power we need to save Evereska."

The companions did as Melegaunt requested, leaving a sixth spot open for him. The archwizard grabbed two handfuls of silvery magic from the pool, then floated into the air above the Karsestone. He hung the globes about six feet apart and touched a plain copper ring that he wore on his left hand to each. A magical light spread upon the orbs, which began to glow with the blinding radiance of the sun. Galaeron turned away with spots in his eyes.

As his vision cleared, he saw a pair of shadows lying on the silvery surface of the pool, both so black and deep they looked at once like solid bodies and empty wells. Galaeron reached to find out which was his, and his fingers vanished in the darkness without creating a ripple on the pool's surface. When he pulled them back, all four digits were missing above the middle knuckle. There was no pain, no impression of heat or cold, no sensation at all. The fingers simply weren't there.

Gasping in alarm, Galaeron spun to berate Melegaunt for not warning him—then saw the translucent shape of his fingers outlined against the brilliant glow of the lights and realized he had been assuming the worst again. Atop the Karsestone, Melegaunt completed a spell he had been casting and noticed Galaeron watching him.

"Only a moment now," the wizard said. "All is ready."

Melegaunt stepped off the Karsestone and floated to his place in the circle. He asked the group to join hands, then spoke a few words in a strange language Galaeron assumed to be Netherese. Next to him, Vala hissed in surprise as a tingling stream of energy passed from her hand into Galaeron's, then Malik gasped aloud as the stream passed into him. Galaeron began to feel lightheaded, and growing suspicious, opened his hand.

"Don't break the circle!" Melegaunt commanded. "Let no one break it, or we will all be pulled into Shadow."

Vala clamped down on Galaeron's hand with astonishing strength. "Trust us, not your shadow!"

Galaeron's two shadows began to grow longer and broader, taking on a shape completely unlike his own. One assumed the form of an armored human with immense shoulders and a narrow waist. A pair of curved horns sprouted from his blocky head, then a pair of yellow eyes appeared in his dark face. The second silhouette was as large as the first, though squarer of body and clothed in swirling robes of darkness. Though it sprouted no horns, its profile revealed a grotesquely square chin and a crescent-shaped mouth full of sharp teeth.

Both shadows sank beneath the silvery surface and disappeared, only to reappear a moment later as huge, murk-swaddled figures. When Galaeron glanced around the circle, he found a pair of similar figures standing in front of each of his trembling companions. He could not quite decide whether he was looking at men or demons.

Melegaunt opened his hands and bowed so deeply that his brow touched the silvery pond. "My Princes, welcome back to Faerûn."

"Stand, young brother." The largest, a copper-eyed brute nearly three heads taller than Vala, motioned Melegaunt upright. "That is the heavy magic?"

"It is," said Melegaunt.

Paying no mind to the others in the chamber, the rest of the princes waded to Melegaunt's side. Galaeron and the others followed, but stopped a respectful distance away.

"All has gone according to plan?" asked the copper-eyed figure. "We are ready to proceed?"

Melegaunt's face betrayed the barest hesitation. "All has gone well, my lord Escanor, but one matter may trouble us."

The horn-helmeted prince cast an admonishing glance at Galaeron's hip. Galaeron looked down, but did not realize what the dark warrior was staring at until he felt Takari pull his hand away from his sword.

"I think that would be foolish, my prince," she whispered.

The murky warrior looked back to Melegaunt without comment.

The one called Escanor said, "Yes, young brother?"

"I have spoken of one called Elminster," said Melegaunt.

"The gray-bearded Chosen," said the horned warrior. "We have observed him. A powerful ally—or an inconvenient enemy. Which?"

"That is yet to be decided, my lord Rivalen, but I fear unexpected events have turned him a little against us. As you know, his parents were slain by a shadow mage, and that has made him suspicious of us. Only two days ago, he tried to stop us from entering the Dire Wood, and I have been informed by a darksentry that even now he comes after us. I fear he would think to interfere with the Return—and he has the power to do it."

Rivalen and Escanor glanced at each other.

"We will need to set matters straight with him before proceeding, that is all," said Escanor. "And these unexpected events?"

Melegaunt motioned Galaeron into the circle. "Galaeron Nihmedu is in a shadow crisis and losing badly." Several princes cast knowing looks at each, and Melegaunt continued, "He has done much to aid our cause. Through no fault of his, he and I opened the Sharn Wall in Evereska instead of Hartsvale."

"The phaerimm are out already?" gasped Rivalen.

Melegaunt hung his head. "My fault entirely. I chose a poor place to meet my darkswords, and Galaeron's patrol took us for tomb robbers. They were not to blame."

"There is no blame here," said Escanor. "We will adjust our plan, that is all." He looked to Galaeron. "We cannot undo the anguish your people have already suffered, but your home will be saved—have no fear of that."

"The war will be farther south," Rivalen said. "Unfortunate, but no great disaster."

"Evereska has a mythal," warned Melegaunt.

Rivalen shrugged. "And it will take a little longer than planned." He clasped Galaeron's shoulder. "But it will be won. On that, you have the word of the Twelve Princes of Shade."

Galaeron's first thought was of what the prince left unsaid. "At what cost to Evereska? It is well and good to slay the phaerimm, but not if you mean to fight the war on elf lands."

Rivalen exchanged a concerned look with the others, then a third prince, the square-chinned one who had arisen in front of Galaeron, stepped forward.

"I know it is difficult during your shadow-struggle, but you must trust us. Evereska will suffer—it has already suffered, as you must know—and we will do what we can to help. But it is the phaerimm who attack your land, not us. We did not set them to it any more than you did."

"But *I* did," Galaeron said, nearly collapsing beneath the weight of his mistake. "I ordered the wrong spell."

"You did your duty," said the prince. "You would have been remiss not to attack to your best judgement. Any blame you feel comes from your shadow, no one else. You must ignore it, or you are lost."

The prince's words lifted the burden from Galaeron's heart a little—but not as much as when Takari slipped her arm through his.

"Listen to the murky one, my prince. He is telling you what everyone who was there already knows."

Galaeron nodded. "I'll try."

"Good," said Melegaunt. "And we'll be there to help—so long as you stop casting spells."

"And I will see to that," said Vala, coming to take Galaeron's other arm.

Rivalen smiled, baring a pair of fangs that would not have looked out of place on a vampire. "Good. Now, we must be off."

"What of Wulgreth?" Jhingleshod shoved his way into the circle and glared at Melegaunt. "Do not think—"

"I would not think of it," said the archwizard. He turned to Escanor. "There is the matter of a small promise I made to this spirit. Can you dispel all the magic in the room above?"

Escanor eyed the iron knight, then motioned the other princes toward the ceiling exit. "As you wish." He started to rise after the others. "We'll do it on our way out."

"On your way out?" Melegaunt waved a hand at the Karsestone.

"We must deal with these little problems," said Rivalen. "And from the sound of it, the sooner the better."

"But what of the Return?"

Escanor smiled broadly, baring a mouthful of needle-thin fangs. "That honor is for you, young brother. Levitate the boulder into the sky, then use your magic to call our people home."

"Me?" Melegaunt gasped. "I am the lowest of us all!"

"But the most worthy," said Escanor. "You cannot have forgotten the words."

"Never." Now it was Melegaunt who smiled. "Hear me now, people of Shade. Follow me now, for the Return is at hand!"

CHAPTER
TWENTY-ONE

30 Nightal, the Year of the Unstrung Harp

A hoarse phaerimm whistle rasped through the stone trees above Elminster, prompting him to hurl his ample bulk through a tangle of the Dire Wood's poison vines. He rolled out the other side with astonishing grace for a man of his considerable age, then spun around to find a cascade of harmless gray spiders fluttering to the ground before him. The archmage spied a pair of fiery lich-eyes peering over a vine-shrouded wall opposite him and countered with a swarm of meteors that turned into a colony of bees, then the phaerimm—there were two of them, floating through the treetops above the street—unleashed their own flurry of magic. Three silver rays disintegrated into scintillating rainbows, two black death beams became winged snakes and flew off, and one spell actually worked, a lightning bolt that dissipated against Elminster's spell-guardin a silver flash.

Such was any battle in a wild magic area, nine parts futility and one part danger. Seeing Wulgreth starting to rise into view—with a fringe of coarse hair, noseless rotting face, and lipless skeleton's mouth, the lich looked much the same as the hundreds Elminster had disposed of during his long lifetime—the archmage spun around and crashed down a vine-choked ally. At the corner, he turned toward the center of the city, hoping to circle back to the main road and follow the trail of mangled corpses to Melegaunt and the others.

That the shadow wizard had destroyed so many undead in the middle of the largest wild magic area on Faerûn spoke volumes to Elminster. It also raised some disturbing questions—many, many disturbing questions. He had faced enough shadow mages to know they drew their magic from some dark power that slowly corrupted them, inexorably twisting them into monstrous mockeries of themselves. He had long suspected that the dark power was not part of the Weave, a suspicion now confirmed by the fact that Melegaunt's magic worked well in an area where the lingering effects of Karsus's madness had twisted the Weave into an unpredictable snarl.

What Elminster did not know and hoped to learn before this day ended was the exact nature of that other source of magic—and which god controlled it. He had his suspicions, of course. As Mystra's enemy, Cyric would go to great lengths to create a source of magic other than the Weave, and Talos the Destroyer had long been attempting to wrest a part of the Weave from her control. The now certain knowledge that someone had succeeded was enough to make even Elminster's silver fire-warmed blood run cold. There was already more than enough evil in the world to keep the Balance—even without its own special source of magic.

Elminster darted down a vine-choked lane back to the main street, and stepping over the cleaved body of a wight, renewed his pursuit. After his fight against the phaerimm outside the Dire Wood and the running battle he had been waging against Wulgreth since crossing the bridge, there was nothing he would have enjoyed more than a nice spell of flying—he just didn't want to turn into a butterfly. He continued down the road in a heavy-footed jog, keeping one hand close to his wand belt and hazarding a glance over his shoulder every ten paces.

The silhouette of Karse Butte was just beginning to loom above the treetops when a chirrupy voice sounded inside his mind. *Elminster, haven't . . . Khelben . . . days . . . should . . . try Rocnest . . . twenty . . . wizards.*

Garbled as the sending was by wild magic, Elminster understood enough that he forgot to watch his feet and tripped. He landed sprawled on his hands and knees, huffing for breath and shaking with fatigue. *Only twenty, Laeral?*

If Laeral answered, it was lost in the cacophony of clanging and banging that erupted around him. Elminster rolled and found himself being buried under an avalanche of cake steel. Heavy as the ingots were, they merely bounced off his body shield and piled around him, but he was more concerned to find Wulgreth standing outside the shower, ready to attack the instant it was safe. The touch of a lich could paralyze even one of the Chosen, which would instantly trigger his evasion magic and—under normal circumstances—whisk him to his Safehold to recover. Given the wild magic in the area, however, he doubted even Mystra herself could say where he would find himself.

Better to try something over which he might have more control. Elminster envisioned the vine-tangle he had left a few moments earlier, then uttered a single mystic word.

There was a brief moment of black timeless falling, then he found himself staring at an overgrown street through a tangle of thin-leaved vines. He was familiar enough with the afterdaze of teleporting to recognize the effects instantly and trust that he would remember where he was and why he was there in a moment, but something seemed especially strange about this time. He felt both hugely large and unable to move, and for some reason he seemed to be holding his arms spread wide.

He saw a pair of phaerimm come floating past about a dozen feet below his nose and remembered if not *what* he was, at least where he was—in a wild magic area in the Dire Wood, fighting a running battle against Wulgreth and trying to escape an army of pursuing phaerimm—and something had gone wrong.

The phaerimm were about a quarter the size they should have been, and the overgrown street was no wider than a foot path, and the petrified trees looked no larger than a man. One of the huge dragonflies buzzed past, snatching a small black finch that looked no larger than a mosquito, and Elminster had a sinking feeling in his . . . no, it wasn't his stomach. It was more like his trunk. He tried to turn his head and discovered he could not.

The dragonfly buzzed back by and landed on an outspread branch, its mandibles popping as it consumed the black finch. Elminster let out a sigh too deep to be heard by any creature that was not a tree, then saw the phaerimm zip past in the wrong direction and vanish into the tangled wood.

Elminster stood motionless and quiet for a moment—it was about all he could do—trying to imagine what kind of magic a mere lich could possibly have summoned that would frighten two phaerimm so. Then he heard a murky voice call his name and realized Wulgreth had not frightened the creatures at all. Another voice called for him, then yet a third. He recognized a little of Melegaunt's accent and timbre in both, but they were deeper and more powerful, and more assured of themselves—far more assured.

Too wise to reveal himself in his present condition, Elminster did not even try to speak. He could escape with a mere thought, so the tree seemed a safe enough place to hide for now. The deep voices continued to call out, drawing closer each time, and twelve murk-swaddled figures soon marched into view.

They looked vaguely human, but with the grotesque features he had long ago learned to associate with shadow magic, and they were by far the largest, most powerful looking men he had ever seen. Most wore the dress of warriors, several the cloaks of wizards, and two were shrouded in clerical robes. They all had the brightly colored eyes of creatures from the lower planes, and an aura of darkness seemed to swirl around them like fog.

The largest, a copper-eyed brute as tall as an ogre, stopped and turned to the others. "If he is here, he is hidden well. I see nothing in the shadows."

A figure in a horned helm spread his palms in resignation. "Then we must make him find us."

"How so, Rivalen?" asked the first. "He is not one to be so easily manipulated, and we have other problems to attend to."

"Let three of us go to Evereska, and three to Hidden Lake," said Rivalen. "That will leave six for Shadowdale. I am sure Elminster will find us then."

✡✡✡✡✡

It had to be the loneliest camp in Faerûn, a single tent in the heart of a barren salt pan, a young father staring across the horizon at the white winter sun, a haggard mother dripping water into her children's mouths one sip at a time, a bony camel so sick and weary it did not even groan. Earlier in the day, the camel had collapsed on the waterskin, and the children had pressed their faces to the salt and made themselves sick trying to lap up the last drops of water. The mother had wailed and beat her husband's chest, and the husband had struck her and turned away to hide his tears. That much the princes had read in the twilight shadows, and they could guess what would come tomorrow. Even in winter, no one crossed the Shoal of Thirst without water.

The irony was not lost on the three princes. To the east, a mantle of shadowy clouds was already coalescing out of the empty twilight. They were bringing water—enough to mire the camel, enough to sweep away the tent and all it contained—but water would not save the family. Quite the opposite. Even if these desert nomads knew how to swim, they could not swim for miles.

The princes rolled to their sides, peeling themselves out of the tent's shadow, then rose to their feet in a silent motion. There was a deep bristling as their bodies returned to shape, followed by the cold nausea that always accompanied a flight through the shadow deep.

It took only an instant for the feelings to pass, but by then the camel had raised its nose to test the air, and that was the only alarm the family required. The mother called her children and disappeared into the tent, and the husband leaped to his feet, his scimitar clearing its scabbard.

Brennus spread his palms to show they were empty. "By the Little Gods, friend, we mean no harm."

The nomad looked past the three princes across the darkening salt pan, then peered around the other side of the tent to make certain no accomplices lurked there. Only then, when he was sure they were alone, did he speak.

"What would you have of me, *djinn*? As you can see, I have nothing worth stealing—save my daughter, and I will slay her myself before I let you make her a slave."

"That won't be necessary." Brennus bent at his waist. "We beg your forgiveness, but a small party cannot be too careful in a place such as this."

The nomad eyed the trio warily. "You do not have the look of those who need worry."

Brennus avoided the temptation to smile, knowing his ceremonial fangs would alarm the nomad. "It is often a mistake to judge men by their appearance. We are not djinn."

"I have no desire to argue the point," the nomad replied. "Name your business or be gone."

"You would do well to curb that tongue," said Brennus's brother Lamorak. With night almost upon them, Lamorak's swarthy face had assumed an almost spectral murkiness. "It makes no difference to us whether you live or die."

The knuckles on the nomad's sword hand whitened, and Brennus realized the threat angered the man more than frightened him.

"We are not here to hurt you, only to warn you," Brennus said. "Pack your things quickly. This place will soon be a mire."

"The Shoal of Thirst? A mire?" The nomad looked at the first stars twinkling in the west. "I do not think so. The heavens themselves do not hold that much water."

"The heavens hold more water than you know." Brennus pointed east, where a wall of purple clouds was already sweeping in from the dusky mountains. "Enough to fill the Shoal of Thirst and sweep away your tent. Enough to drown your camel and your children, too."

"There is no reason to believe it will all fall here," the nomad said stubbornly. "Only a djinn would claim to know otherwise."

"Call us what you will," growled Lamorak. "We know."

"Surely you noticed the casting," said the third prince, Yder. "You could hardly have missed it."

"That was your doing?" The nomad's swarthy face grew sallow and yellow. "That ground-shaking thunder, and the black bolt that tore the sky?"

"We didn't know you were camped in Hidden Lake." As Brennus spoke, whirling clouds of salt-laden air began to skip through the camp, drawing an alarmed groan from the camel and gasps of surprise from inside the tent. "You must hurry. The rain will soon be falling in sheets."

"Sheets of rain?" The nomad looked east and saw the black wall of rain. "By the light of Elah!"

The wife pushed her head out of the tent, her face veiled by a purple scarf, her eyes rimmed in kohl. "Shall I pack, my husband?"

"What good would it do?" the nomad gasped. "We cannot outrun the wind! Better to wait in the *khreima* while it passes."

"If you wait in your khreima, you will drown in your khreima," said Brennus.

The nomad narrowed his eyes. "Surely, those who can summon the rains can send them back?"

"Do you think such magic is easy to work?" demanded Lamorak. "A matter of a few syllables and a handful of powdered silver?" He turned to the woman, pointing a talonlike finger at her veiled face. "If you wish to live, pack your things."

The woman's eyes grew round, and she looked to her husband for instruction. He glared at Lamorak. "What would you have us do? Fly to the Sister of Rains?"

Brennus interposed himself between the man and his brother. "And if you could?"

"Men do not have wings, *berrani*."

"They do not need them." Brennus took a strand of shadowsilk from his pocket and shaped it into a small ring, then tossed it on the ground and spoke a single mystic word. The circle swelled to the size of small wagon, then darkened and floated off the ground. "There are other ways."

"Not for the Bedine." The nomad brought his scimitar down on the flying disk, slicing it down the center. "The Bedine do not abide the magic of devils!"

The two halves dropped to the ground and melted into the twilight darkness. Brennus watched the pieces disappear, then looked back to the nomad.

"As you wish."

The winds arrived in a whistling flurry of salt and mist, and Brennus signaled his brothers. They backed away from the camp, fading into the darkness with silent acts of will.

"We Princes of Shade are hardly devils," Brennus said. "Not even close."

✡✡✡✡✡

Elminster returned to find Shadowdale blanketed in war smoke. Exhausted as he was by his long fight against Wulgreth, the archmage circled the village, reconnoitering the battle before joining himself. The clang and crackle of hard-fought combat rose from a dozen places along a great circle scribed by Toad Knoll, Castle Krag, and Harper's Hill. Golden bolts of magic flashed back and forth along the length of Shadow Ridge, silver lightning limned the walls of Castle Krag, swarms of meteors flew over the Ashaba down by Mirrorman's Mill.

Much as he longed to swoop to the defense of each embattled townsman, Elminster bided his time. His battle against Wulgreth had left him exhausted physically and magically. He had used half his spells before becoming trapped in the tree, and most of the rest—including his emergency evasion spell, the last of his teleports, and both worldwalking spells—escaping Wulgreth (again) in the wild magic area. He left the Dire Wood with only three magic-dispelling spells, a single set of golden bolts, three speed enchantments, and the ability to fly.

These last four spells he had expended on a triple-hasted flight across Anauroch—with a long detour around the Shoal of Thirst, where the most furious storm he had ever seen was pouring water into the ancient lake bed—and a breakneck descent into the Dales . . . where nothing made sense. Elminster had expected to find Rivalen and five other princes attacking Shadowdale, yet he could see a dozen separate battles raging in the woods. Moreover, he saw no sign of shadow magic, only the standard bolts and blasts, with a little bit of arrow- and axe-work for good measure. If Rivalen and his brothers were here, they were disguising themselves well.

Finally, Elminster spied the blinding swarm of bolts for which he had been searching and dropped through the trees onto Mistledale Mount, where a small line of warriors were working their way through the undergrowth toward a charred phaerimm. In their midst ran the tall, smoky, as-always-stunning figure of Storm Silverhand.

Too weary to run, Elminster called, "Storm, lass! Wait for me."

Storm whirled, eyes flashing and ready to fling fire. "Elminster, there you are!" Her voice was not exactly joyful, and she was slow to lower her spell-ready hand. "Would you please tell me what in the Nine Hells you're doing?"

"Me?" Elminster gasped. "I've been in the Dire Wood chasing a shadow mage—or twelve, as it happens—too long a story to tell now." He waved at the phaerimm's crisped form. "What's this? Have the phaerimm decided Evereska is not enough to chew in a bite?"

"I doubt they care what is happening in Evereska." Storm was looking as puzzled as Elminster felt. "These phaerimm came from Myth Drannor, demanding that you stop your assassinations."

"What?" Elminster jammed his pipe into his mouth. "These killings, do they continue?"

"I assume so, since the phaerimm continue to attack." Storm sounded less angry than intrigued. "There've been seven so far."

Elminster cocked a brow. "Been doing well, have I not?"

"I *thought* so," Storm answered cautiously.

Elminster lit his pipe with the flick of a finger. "How are matters here?"

"Not bad," she said. "Between Sylune, Mourngrym, and myself, we have killed nearly a dozen, and I don't think the phaerimm want this any more than we do."

"I imagine not." Elminster took a long puff, then extinguished his pipe with a word. "Well, let's put a stop to it then. Stay out of sight and follow me."

"Follow you where?" Storm asked.

But Elminster was already in the air, streaking toward his tower to collect a few necessaries for the upcoming battle. The princes were clearly trying to lure him to Myth Drannor, no doubt reasoning it would be wiser to attack him away from his home territory. With a little luck, their ambush would be set up along the Ashaba somewhere near Shadowdale, and he and Storm would be gone only a short time.

Given his luck over the past couple of days, Elminster should have known better. As he approached his tower, a half dozen murky figures stepped out of the shadows and arrayed themselves before the entrances. There was the horn-helmed one called Rivalen, a square-chinned one in wizard robes, a cleric with a face as round as a dark moon, and three more swaddled in dark tabards that might have been covering armor or mere flesh.

Like all good assassins, they wasted no time with preliminaries. The square-chinned wizard took the lead, launching himself straight at Elminster, his dark fingers already flashing through a spell to dismiss his foe's magic shields. Elminster countered with his own dispelling enchantment, and Storm sent a ball of silver fire over his shoulder toward the wizard.

Elminster had a bare moment to wonder if that was a good idea, then the sphere of blazing raw magic struck the shadow mage's spell shield. Instead of blasting through the barrier, as it would have any normal protection, the silver fire spread over the wizard's shadowy shield, silhouetting his body in white radiance. The shadow mage howled and covered his eyes, then the silver fire imploded, crushing the fellow in its iron grip and shrinking to a brilliant orb barely the size of an eyeball.

The remaining shadow princes countered with a volley of dark bolts and black flame. For the first time in a century—perhaps twice that—Elminster actually cringed at the thought of what might happen next. The attacks came roaring and thundering at him—then suddenly curved toward the silvery sphere and vanished from sight.

A deafening rip filled the air, and the silvery orb stretched into a jagged line. Elminster pulled his thumb away from the ring it had been rubbing and pointed at the ground.

Too late. The blue ray extended only feet from his hand, then curved upward and vanished into the crooked streak of brilliance—as did the lightning bolt Storm sent dancing over his shoulder. There was another zipping sound, so powerful Elminster felt it in his guts. The jagged line expanded into a rift—a deep, silver-sided crevasse with crimson flames at its bottom—and continued to expand.

"By all the holy gods, it's—it's ripping!"

It took Elminster a moment to realize he was the one yelling—and even he was not sure exactly *what* was ripping. He knew only that he had seen those fuming swirls once before, when, searching for a lover as cherished as she was flawed, he had dared look where no man should.

And now those same flames were licking at Shadowdale, boiling out of the Nine Hells to lap at his beloved home. The raw magic of his silver fire had fused with the shadow mage's dark magic and imploded, tearing a hole in the world fabric itself. It was, he realized, exactly what had happened when Galaeron's magic bolt struck Melegaunt's shadow magic at the Sharn Wall—but the things that might flee this breach would make the phaerimm look like mere cantrip-tossing goblins.

When the rift continued to open, the shadow princes drew their dark weapons and began to circle warily. Though hardly concerned about Shadowdale's safety, they were as surprised by the breach as Elminster—and hardly eager to get themselves knocked inside. Storm took advantage of their hesitation to unsheathe her own sword and start forward.

Elminster raised an arm to stop her. "No."

"But these shadow princes—"

"Are welcome to follow me, if they dare." Elminster glared at the circling princes. Seeing no sign that any of them intended to accept his invitation, he shooed Storm away. "See ye to the phaerimm. I'll tend to this other trouble from the inside."

"From the *inside?*" Storm stopped outside the circle of shadow princes and cast a wary eye toward the widening rift. "Elminster, tell me you're not—"

"But I must, dear Storm." Elminster started forward. "I can't have the Nine Hells erupting beneath my own tower, can I?"

The flames leaped up, a lot like a lover's arms reaching for an old friend, and Elminster flew into Hell.

CHAPTER TWENTY-TWO

30 Nightal, the Year of the Unstrung Harp

Galaeron spread the last coffer of gems across the table. Melegaunt passed first one hand, then the other over the stones. Finding nothing, he worked his way around the table, repeating the process from all sides to be certain his hand passed over every stone. Finally, he shook his head.

"No magic, no evil. If Wulgreth's life-force is here, it's undetectable by my best magic."

Unable to control his frustration, Galaeron swept the gems onto the pile of scintillating wealth already heaped on the floor. Malik, kneeling half-buried in the heap, winced as they struck him, then began to sort with a expert eye, pitching the most valuable stones into the second of two large coffers he intended his beloved horse to carry back. Vala, who had grown more distrustful since learning he was the Seraph of Lies, eyed him suspiciously.

"Have you taken anything that wasn't checked?"

"I have touched nothing that did not come from the table," Malik replied. "Do you think I am eager to keep a lich in the treasury of my new manor?"

"If you're lying—"

"How many times must I tell you?" Malik demanded. "I was crippled by that harlot Mystra's truth magic and cannot lie! You may inspect everything I have taken."

Vala reached for a coffer, but Galaeron put out a hand.

"He hasn't lied to us yet, which is more than we can say for Melegaunt," he said. "The phylactery's not here, or Wulgreth would be on us like a spider on flies."

Takari turned to Jhingleshod. "Is there another place he lairs?" When the knight did not seem to register the question, she gingerly pushed his arm. "Are you still with us?"

The iron knight disappointed them all by meeting her gaze. "There is no other place. He stays near the butte."

"Then he would store the phylactery somewhere visible from here." Galaeron glanced toward the door. "As overgrown as the ruins are, it will take time to find."

Melegaunt stepped in front of Jhingleshod. "I have done everything possible to keep my word, but there is more at issue here than Wulgreth. We *will* find the phylactery, I promise you, but Aris should be finished with his passage by now. Would it not be possible to take the Karsestone outside and summon Shade? There are thousands in the city, and they will help us search."

Jhingleshod looked to Galaeron.

"It would be best," Galaeron said. "Otherwise, it could take months."

"Months?" The disappointment in Jhingleshod's eyes was as easy to read as Galaeron had prayed it would be. The promise of the end to any ordeal could make days seem like tendays, and this looked to be as true for Jhingleshod as for an elf.

Glancing at his weary companions, Galaeron added, "I don't know that we could survive that long."

Jhingleshod waved Melegaunt toward the crawlway in the corner and said, "Summon your city."

"A wise choice." Though Melegaunt tried to sound restrained, the joy in his voice was unmistakable. "You won't regret it."

Giving Jhingleshod no time to change his mind, the wizard led the way through the green barrier. Vala, Takari, and Malik followed, with the iron knight next and Galaeron last.

As the elf dropped through the door, a booming crash shook the cavern below. He looked down to see Melegaunt skittering across the silver pool on his back, limbs flaying and forks of magic dissipating against his spell-guard. Leaping off the Karsestone after him was a skeletal form with a rotting, noseless face and lipless mouth. The filth-stained claws and fiery pinpoints in its empty eye sockets left no doubt that they had finally found Wulgreth.

Hurling himself into an oblique somersault, Galaeron grabbed his sword and had it half drawn by the time he splashed into the pool. He swam half a dozen strokes toward the rear of the cavern, then surfaced behind Jhingleshod.

The iron knight was splashing toward the battle behind Vala and Takari, his big axe raised to strike. At first Galaeron thought their guide was rushing to attack Wulgreth, but something inside much wiser and darker suggested otherwise. Jhingleshod had been trying to exterminate them since the sunken bridge. Had he not forced them to cross separately, so it would be easier for the undead to attack? After they survived that, he had led them through a savage gauntlet of wights and wraiths. When even that failed, he had found excuse after excuse to stall until Wulgreth returned. Probably, it had even been Jhingleshod who alerted the lich to their presence in the first place—after all, they had only his word that he had ever killed Wulgreth at all.

Galaeron swung at Jhingleshod's neck. Even sharp elven steel did not bite deep into the iron flesh, but it did catch the knight's attention. He whirled around, his gruesome jaw hanging almost as low as his guard. Galaeron sprang for the opening, driving his sword at the knight's exposed throat.

Jhingleshod's arm flashed up, deflecting the attack almost before the elf saw it move. "Are you mad?"

"Hardly!" Galaeron slipped his free hand into his sleeve. "I see how you have been playing us."

"Playing you?" A long crackle sounded from the melee behind Jhingleshod, prompting the knight to glance over his shoulder. "I am not one to play at anything."

Galaeron pulled his hand from his sleeve, cupping a small glass rod, but Malik's chubby arm knocked it away before the elf could cast the spell.

"Matters are bad enough without this shadow folly!" Malik pointed to the artistic trefoil passage Aris had cut into the side of the butte. "The giant told me there are phaerimm coming!"

Galaeron realized he should have been disappointed in himself, but he was not. After learning of Melegaunt's lies, the line between his shadow and himself had blurred. Suspicions that might have seemed groundless before were suddenly reasonable. He peered past Jhingleshod and saw that matters were, indeed, bad enough. Melegaunt was kneeling in the pool, beard scorched away and eyes glazed with pain. Only the constant attacks of Vala and Takari, harrying the lich from opposite sides, kept Wulgreth from finishing the wizard in a blow.

Jhingleshod let out an eerie wail and hefted his axe. Trusting more to Malik's word than his own instincts, Galaeron pointed at Wulgreth's head and summoned a spell. Vala lunged in, blocking Galaeron's lightning bolt, and Takari attacked from the opposite side.

The lich flicked a finger and sent Takari stumbling away, wailing and shaking her head, eyes red with blood and fixed blindly ahead. Vala's darksword took some small vengeance, slashing off a moldering arm, then whipping around to open Wulgreth's side from spine to navel. Hissing and spitting in anger, the lich grabbed her by the throat with its good arm.

Vala went instantly rigid, mouth gaping, eyes rolling back. Jhingleshod buried his axe deep into Wulgreth's back, driving both the lich and the woman down beneath the pool's silvery skin. The iron knight hefted his axe again, lidless eyes bulging as he tried to see beneath the surface. He began to shuffle through the basin, trying to locate his quarry with a series of savage kicks.

"Jhingleshod, you'll break her ribs!"

"Galaeron?" This from Takari, who stood with her back to the wall and her sword weaving a blind-fighting pattern before her. "I can't see."

"You're fine," Galaeron said, realizing Vala was in the most danger. Even if the lich released her, its touch would leave her paralyzed and unable to return to the surface. "Stay there."

"But Galaeron—"

She was interrupted by a startled cry from Melegaunt. The archwizard pointed his hand into the basin and started a spell, then vanished beneath the surface. Galaeron rushed forward, sweeping his sword back and forth across the bottom, trying to think of some spell that would allow him to find Vala before she drowned. Jhingleshod opted for a more direct method and dived under the surface.

A muffled crack rumbled out of the pool, then Melegaunt's body floated to the surface, the smell of charred flesh rising from a hole in his back.

"Galaeron?" Takari called.

"Stand still," Galaeron ordered, starting after the wizard. "Stab anything near you."

His sword touched a body on the bottom of the pool. When it did not attack, he ducked down and grabbed hold of an armored elbow, then pulled Vala to the surface. She began coughing, spewing liquid magic from her nostrils and mouth. Dragging her along beside him, Galaeron went to Melegaunt's side and rolled the archwizard over.

The spell had blown open Melegaunt's whole chest. Incredibly, the archwizard's heart continued to beat. Galaeron could see it.

"Meleg-ghaunt!" coughed Vala, more or less recovered from her near drowning. "He needs help!" She spun her head around the room. "Malik!"

Malik appeared in the mouth of Aris's tunnel. "Quiet!" he hissed. "The phaerimm are already coming out of the forest."

"We need to get him to Aris." Vala motioned to Melegaunt.

"Waste . . . of . . . time." It was Melegaunt who gasped this. He grabbed Galaeron and pulled him close. "Promise me—"

A flurry of splashing near Takari interrupted the archwizard. She cried out and began to hack blindly at the pool.

"Where is it, Galaeron?" she yelled. "Which way?"

"To your—"

"Elf!" Melegaunt boomed, jerking Galaeron to him with a strength born of his dying magic.

"Don't worry, Melegaunt," Galaeron said, trying to rise. "I remember: 'Hear me now, People of Shade—' "

"No!" Melegaunt gasped, now loosing his strength. "You must leave it . . . to the princes, or you'll be . . . lost."

Galaeron started to promise, but stopped when the sour clang of a breaking sword sounded from the far wall. Takari cried out—no longer calling for him, just shrieking—and he turned to find her slashing at the pool with a broken sword, Jhingleshod and Wulgreth rolling across the surface in front of her.

Vala started across the pool. "Move left, Takari!" she yelled. "And don't panic. I'm coming."

"Malik!" Galaeron started toward the battle. "Hold Melegaunt."

"Galaeron!" Melegaunt demanded. "No more spells."

"Yes, I promise."

Seeing Malik approach, Galaeron started to push Melegaunt over—until the archwizard's fingers dug deep into his arm, drawing blood and pouring a dark river of anguish into him. Galaeron's knees buckled, and he slipped beneath the surface, swallowing a mouthful of silvery liquid. Swirling shadows filled his mind, then he began to feel weightless and weak, and his last conscious thought was that Melegaunt had finally betrayed him, that the archwizard had used his shadow magic to switch bodies.

Then Malik was pounding him on the back, yelling in his ear. "Cough it out, stupid elf!"

A heavy blow landed on Galaeron's back, then he opened his eyes to find Melegaunt floating in front of him, lifeless eyes staring at the ceiling. He had no memory after his mind began to fill with swirling shadows, no idea how long he had been beneath the surface with Melegaunt—or of what had happened there. His mind felt heavy and clouded with darkness, his head ached as though it would split, and his lungs were burning for air. He had to have been under for a good long while.

Another blow landed on Galaeron's back, and he realized the little man was holding him up by the collar, trying to hide behind the Karsestone while Jhingleshod continued to wrestle with Wulgreth. Vala stood pressed against the wall, one hand ineptly flailing at the lich with her sword, the other holding Takari's broken and bloodied body above the surface.

"What happened?" Galaeron gasped. He could not help wondering just what Melegaunt had done to him—but now was hardly the time to puzzle it out, not with Takari wounded and the phaerimm on the way. The last time he saw Takari, she was blind but still healthy. "What happened to my scout?"

"What do you think happened?" Malik released him. "Wulgreth struck her while you were doing your pool dance with Melegaunt's corpse."

"Pool dance?" Galaeron gasped. "Never mind! Keep a watch on the phaerimm."

Galaeron shoved Malik toward the tunnel, then pushed off the Karsestone—and that was when he understood why they had not been able to find Wulgreth's phylactery. Liches always stored their life-forces in something of great worth, something hard to destroy and harder to find.

Jhingleshod went limp and vanished beneath the surface. Wulgreth spun toward Galaeron, tiny forks of green lightning dancing on the fingertips of his one remaining arm. For an instant—for more than an instant—Galaeron thought the lich had finally destroyed its ancient servant. The elf thought he would be next.

Then Jhingleshod came up beneath Wulgreth, lifting him out of the pool. The lich twisted his one arm around behind his back, fingers spraying his life-stealing magic into Jhingleshod's iron breastplate. A loud, watery knelling echoed off the cavern walls, and Jhingleshod wailed in unearthly pain. Had the magic been powerful enough to destroy him, Galaeron knew, the lifeless knight would gladly have endured the suffering. As it was, it only melted a hole in his armor and filled the air with a forgelike stench. Galaeron sloshed forward and plunged his magic sword into the lich's fiery eye socket.

Wulgreth howled in rage, and the elven steel began to melt and sag. Galaeron started to blast the lich with his magic bolts, then remembered his promise to Melegaunt and drew his dagger, flinging it into the other eye in one smooth motion.

The blade sank deep—then vanished in a flash of blue flame.

"Galaeron!"

Galaeron glanced toward the voice and saw Vala's black sword spinning toward him. The pool swirled around his legs as Wulgreth kicked at him. He dodged sideways, caught the black hilt and winced in pain—it was still as cold as a night hag's kiss—then brought the dark blade across the lich's neck.

Wulgreth's head toppled into the pool, then bobbed to the surface and spun toward Galaeron, eyes still burning with hatred. It shrieked, "You won't destroy—"

And Galaeron brought the darksword down again, cleaving the head in two, then forced himself to hold the flesh-freezing hilt and hack at the lich's body until all of the pieces sank out of sight. Then, when no counterattack came and he began to believe none would, something bumped his back. He turned to find the two halves of the skull still surging toward him. He cried out and backed away, raising the darksword to strike yet again.

"What are you doing?" Jhingleshod snatched the halves of the skull out of the pool. "We'll need those!"

Galaeron stared at the iron knight in uncomprehending shock, then slowly began to understand that it was over, that Wulgreth had been hacked and blasted into so many pieces that it would take him the better part of a tenday to draw himself together again.

Galaeron lowered the sword. "That's right," he said, realizing that Jhingleshod believed they would destroy this Wulgreth in the same way they had the demilich. "Hold onto those pieces until we find the phylactery."

Even had he the heart, Galaeron knew better than to tell the iron knight what he had surmised about the Karsestone. His heart feeling almost as cold and numb as the hand that held the darksword, he waded over to the wall and returned Vala's blade, then laid his icy hand on Takari's mangled shoulder.

"This will slow the bleeding," he said. "And don't worry. We'll be back in Rheitheillaethor before you know it."

Takari opened her eyes and pushed his hand away. "No, Galaeron. You made your choice."

✡✡✡✡✡

Another death scream rolled across the brown water, muted by the gossamer curtain of steam, yet still accusatory in its anguish. Laeral ducked beneath the surface and swam toward the voice, using her magic to move almost as fast underwater as she could have through the cold dawn air.

After her garbled sending to Elminster (she still had no idea if he had understood her), she had taken an escort of ten warriors and ten war mages through the new gate to Rocnest—and promptly been ambushed by a half dozen phaerimm. Though they were prepared for that possibility—even expected it—all of their magic protections were dispelled before they cast a single spell.

At that point, Laeral should probably have ordered her small company to teleport back to Waterdeep. Instead, desperate to discover what had become of Khelben and hoping to recapture the gate, she moved her group to the rim of the basin. Four of the phaerimm rushed to press the attack, driving her company into the Marsh of Chelimber before they had time to regroup.

In the confusion that followed, the small force became separated, and the phaerimm began to pick them off one at a time. She managed to slay two of the creatures during the long night, but those losses had been more than replaced by reinforcements from Evereska.

The thornbacks were using their magic to heat the marsh. Having raised the temperature to a simmer already, they no doubt intended to either force their prey out of hiding or boil it alive. Neither possibility frightened Laeral, for she could easily teleport back to Waterdeep before either grew necessary—but she was loathe to abandon those who could not.

Laeral pushed her head up to confirm her bearings. The voice was weaker now, having faded to a whimper, but it was also closer—just beyond a willow brake. Fearful of making any noise that would betray her approach, she ducked beneath the surface to circumvent the thicket underwater.

As she rounded the corner, three concussions pulsed down through the water, nearly rupturing her eardrums and jolting her so hard that the last air left her lungs. She pushed off the mucky bottom and launched herself into the air with a flying spell, her fingertips crackling with a silvery ball of her most potent magic.

On the other side of the willows stood a trio of murk-swaddled men, one cradling the mangled figure of a Waterdhavian warrior, the other two using black glaives to pin down the writhing remains of a spell-blasted phaerimm. The men were all the size of bugbears, with brilliant gem-colored eyes and flesh as dark as shadow. While their weapons were familiar in form and function, the ebony blades looked more like black glass than steel, and the shafts might have been wood, metal, or neither.

The tallest, a copper-eyed figure in a flowing tabard as dark as night, glanced at the silvery ball on her fingertips.

"If you are who I think you are, it really wouldn't do to throw that at us. We mean you no harm." He used his glaive to raise the phaerimm's twitching tail. "Two more remain, but we have found ten of your men, recovered six more bodies, and have reports of four teleporting away too wounded to fight. Would that be all?"

"So it would seem." Laeral let the magic die on her fingers. "And you are?"

"Escanor Tanthul." The shadowy figure flourished his cape and bowed. "These are my brothers, Aglarel and Clariburnus."

The other two figures bowed and said in unison, "At your service, milady."

Laeral closed her open jaw and returned the gesture with a curtsy. "Laeral, Lady of Blackstaff Tower."

"Yes, we know," said Escanor. "Perhaps we should be gone from here. If you will excuse me for saying so, you seem to have bitten off a bit much even for one of Mystra's Chosen."

Laeral raised her brow. "You seem very well informed . . . for a Netherese."

Escanor flashed a fang-filled smile. "As do you, Milady Blackstaff. I can see that it will be a pleasure to fight at your side in the war to come."

"War?" Laeral began to grow cold at the thought of an alliance with these dark Netherese. "Let's not get ahead of ourselves."

"We are hardly ahead of anything," said Clariburnus. He severed the phaerimm's tail with a flick of his glaive, then tucked the barb into his belt as a trophy. "The war has begun already. Surely you do not expect the phaerimm to surrender without a fight."

"I know they will fight," said Laeral. "They have proven that already, but that does not mean—"

"Our army is already on its way, I am sure," interrupted Escanor. As he spoke, he passed a hand over the face of the wounded Waterdhavian, cloaking the man's eyes in shadow and putting him into a restful sleep. "We will try to limit the destruction to the Shaeradim, but even the Chosen must see that if we hope to defeat the phaerimm, we will need to fight—and fight together."

CHAPTER TWENTY-THREE

1 Hammer, the Year of Wild Magic (1372 DR)

They had spent the night inside the pyramid. Galaeron had not realized that until they crawled through Aris's artistic trefoil tunnel and saw the rectangular shadows stretching across the overgrown city. He wished he had Melegaunt to look into them and read the coming day, or perhaps not. With two distant phaerimm drifting toward them across the ruins, he could see for himself what the day would bring—at least the short part they were likely to survive.

There were no signs of mind flayers or eye tyrants, nor of Aris and Malik's horse. The illithids and beholders had probably fallen to Elminster or the undead at the sunken bridge. Galaeron could only hope that Aris had recognized how badly events had turned and had managed to sneak quietly away, but he rather doubted it.

"Sooner or later, they'll notice the tunnel," said Vala. She was crouched on her haunches beside Galaeron, with Jhingleshod staring over their shoulders. "We could take the Karsestone out through the river opening."

"What good would that do?" Galaeron looked along the flank of the butte, to where the waterfall poured out of the sandstone and plunged fifty feet into a pool of scarlet water. "They'd only catch us out in the open."

Vala watched him carefully. "It might give you time to summon help."

"You mean Shade," said Galaeron. "I promised Melegaunt I'd wait for the princes."

"Do you think that will be possible?" asked Vala. She turned to Jhingleshod. "Would the Karsestone fit through the river passage?"

"It would be easier to go without it." The knight looked toward the interior mouth of the tunnel, where the scorched cinders of Wulgreth's corpse were already trying to coalesce into a body again. He pushed his axe back to stir the ashes, then said, "And the phaerimm might not care that you escaped."

"They'd care," said Vala, rolling her eyes.

Galaeron suspected that she also understood what Jhingleshod was really saying—that without the Karsestone, they might live long enough to destroy Wulgreth's phylactery. But Galaeron did not know whether Vala also realized that they had the phylactery—that the lich had stored his life-force in the Karsestone.

Galaeron was struggling desperately with what to do after it finally dawned on Jhingleshod that the phylactery and the Karsestone were one in the same. The knight would, undoubtedly, want the stone destroyed, but Galaeron was not even sure such an artifact *could* be destroyed—and that was quite aside from what such a thing would mean for Evereska and Melegaunt's people. It might be possible to extract the lich's life-force from the stone, but that would take time.

When Jhingleshod did not answer her question, Vala said, "The phaerimm have been hunting us since Evereska, Jhingleshod. They aren't going to let us go now, even if we don't have the Karsestone. Can we get it out through the river passage or not?"

"If you can hold your breath so long," said Jhingleshod. "But how will that help you keep your promise to me?"

"By bringing help," said Galaeron. Realizing he had to get Jhingleshod's mind off the Karsestone or lose any chance of saving Evereska, he slipped past the iron knight and started down the tunnel. "You heard what Melegaunt said, and you saw the Twelve Princes. Don't you think a thousand citizens of Shade have a better chance of finding the phylactery than we do?"

"Perhaps so, were Melegaunt here to make them honor his word." Jhingleshod grabbed a handful of Wulgreth cinder and followed Galaeron into the silvery pool. "As it is, I have only your promise."

"Then perhaps I may be of some small use," said Malik. He sat atop of the Karsestone attending to a groaning, half-conscious Takari. "I would be happy to see to the stone's safety—"

"No." Galaeron and Vala spoke simultaneously.

Malik continued unflustered. "I understand your hesitation—namely that I will give the stone to Cyric—but it *would* give you a chance to escape with your friend's life." He lifted Takari's head, but lowered it again when she managed a weak shake. "And a chance to keep your word to Jhingleshod and look for Wulgreth's phylactery."

"Cyric is trouble enough without a toy like this." Galaeron was beginning to believe the Seraph's strange claim about being unable to lie. He pulled Takari off the stone and passed her to Vala, then motioned Malik down. "You don't want to be there."

Malik slid into the water. "You have a plan?"

"Perhaps." Galaeron took a piece of shadowsilk from his pocket and pressed it to the side of the stone opposite Aris's tunnel, then went across the pool to the cavern wall. "It occurs to me Aris might not be the only one who can bore a tunnel."

"You're going to use the stone's magic?" gasped Malik. "An excellent plan!"

Galaeron shrugged. "The best I can think of, but it might be better than waiting for the phaerimm to find us here."

"And if it fails?" asked Jhingleshod. A whirling cloud of ash cloaked the hand holding Wulgreth's cinders. "The phaerimm will kill *you*."

Galaeron nodded grimly, then glanced out Aris's tunnel and saw one of the distant cones coming straight toward them. He arranged a circle of shadowsilk on the face of the cavern wall. "Anything you can do to slow them would certainly help."

"Help *you*," said Jhingleshod. "If the phaerimm are as powerful as you say, perhaps *they* could find Wulgreth's phylactery."

The shadowsilk slipped from Galaeron's fingers, then vanished into the silvery pool. He turned, slowly, and said, "It seems to me that such selfishness is how you became undead in the first place."

"I do not think promise breakers have any right to rebuke others."

Jhingleshod turned toward Aris's tunnel, but found his way blocked by Malik.

"Selfishness is not always a bad thing," said the little man. "Especially when everyone can be made to see that their own ends are best accomplished by working together. I am sure that if we all put our heads together, we will find the solution lying right in front of us."

Galaeron shook his head urgently, but found the line to Malik's sight blocked by the iron knight's huge form. Forcing himself to move calmly so he did not alarm Jhingleshod, he stepped sideways.

Malik continued, "Wulgreth is certainly a trickster, and I have been in the counting rooms of enough tricksters to know that they enjoy hiding their treasures in plain sight."

Galaeron shook his head desperately, and when Malik did not see him, he called out, "Malik!"

Jhingleshod raised his hand to silence Galaeron. "This one is making some sense. Perhaps we will can help each other yet."

"If I were Wulgreth, I would have hidden my life-force in the most obvious place," said Malik. "Perhaps in the pyramid itself."

"Would Melegaunt not have detected that from inside?" interrupted Jhingleshod, growing more excited.

Galaeron caught Vala's eye and nodded toward the tunnel. She turned to look; and seeing the phaerimm still approaching slowly, gave him a reassuring nod.

"Maybe in the butte itself," said Malik.

"That's possible," said Jhingleshod.

Letting slip a silent sigh of relief, Galaeron turned to the wall and pressed a fresh circle of shadowsilk to the stone.

"What about Jhingleshod himself?" asked Vala. "That might explain why *he* can't die."

"What an excellent thought! Or it might even be that . . ."

Galaeron's stomach sank as the Seraph let his sentence trail off. He turned around and found Malik staring at the Karsestone.

"Be what?" demanded Jhingleshod.

Malik's mouth snapped shut, and for a moment Galaeron thought the little man might actually cover his mistake.

Then Jhingleshod demanded again, "Or *what?*"

"Nothing," Malik said, but he seemed unable to stop there. His mouth twisted into a lopsided grimace, and more words began to spill out. "Only that it occurred to me that the thing Wulgreth valued most is right here."

Jhingleshod fell quiet, then turned toward Galaeron. "You were going to take it. You knew, and you were still going to take it."

"I don't *know* anything." Galaeron finished his circle and stepped away from the wall. "And I don't really see what difference—"

"Liar!"

Jhingleshod's axe shot up so quickly Galaeron barely had time to fling himself into the pool before the rusty blade came tumbling past, spraying magic links of elven chain mail in every direction, and the weapon clanged off the wall.

Jhingleshod was already following his weapon across the chamber, hurling himself toward Galaeron. A black sword caught the iron knight from behind, slashing through his armor and cleaving his yellowed shoulder down to his armpit. Roaring in fury, he spun, slamming an iron elbow into Vala's head and bouncing her off the Karsestone. Her eyes rolled back, and she would have fallen, had Jhingleshod's hand not clamped her throat. His fingers started to close, and a wet rasp gurgled from Vala's mouth.

"No!"

Galaeron leveled a hand at the knight's iron back and uttered a mystic syllable. A familiar surge of cold power rushed up through his body, then the silky, liquid fire of the Karsestone's whole magic flooded into him from the silver pool. He gasped in surprise, and Jhingleshod started toward Galaeron, dragging Vala after him. The elf's arm swelled visibly, the muscles convulsing so hard he thought his elbow would snap.

The spell erupted from his hand in a blinding flash of gold light, blasting the nails off his fingers and scorching the tips, then streaking across the cavern into the knight's stomach. There was a deafening clang and the mordant smell of molten iron. Jhingleshod's legs flew in one direction and his torso in the other, eyes bulging and locked on Galaeron's face. The upper half came down a dozen paces away and skipped across the pool's surface, then rolled to its stomach and sank beneath the surface.

Galaeron started toward Vala, who was stooped over holding her throat, gasping down breath between harsh coughs.

"Galae . . . ron!" Takari's voice was so weak he barely heard it above Vala's wheezing. "Phae-r-rim!"

Placing a hand under Vala's elbow as he passed, he looked across the chamber to Aris's tunnel. Takari was draped across the entrance, pointing down the passage. Outside, two cone-shaped blurs were streaking toward the butte. Galaeron pushed Vala toward the crimson whirlpool in the cavern's far corner.

"Time for your plan, I think," Galaeron said.

He turned to ask Malik to take Takari and found the Seraph already wading toward her. To Galaeron's surprise, the little man reached for his treasure coffers instead. Galaeron blasted the coffers with a lightning bolt, blackening his fingertips some more and strewing the tunnel with gems.

Malik whirled with fire in his eyes.

Galaeron merely pointed at Takari and said, "If she dies, so do you."

"As you wish." Malik grabbed her and started toward the whirlpool. "But I will have my fortune from you!"

Galaeron paid him no attention, for the phaerimm were so close now he could make out the sticklike arms surrounding their mouths. He considered staying to ambush them inside, but suspected that even with the power of the Karsestone, he would be little more than a gnat to a pair of wasps. He turned back into the cavern, nearly falling as he tripped over Jhingleshod's disembodied legs, then pointed at the shadowsilk on the far wall and spoke an incantation.

Again, he was filled with the silky fire of the Karsestone's magic, the power of the magic turning the skin on his hand black and leathery. The rock wall drew away from the dark circle, fashioning a long tunnel that was, if not as elegant as Aris's, nearly as straight. Turning away even before it broke into the light, Galaeron touched a hand to the Karsestone and uttered a levitation spell. He was beginning to enjoy the feel of the boulder's magic, the power of it flowing through his arm, even the searing tingle it left in his hand.

In response to his summons, the Karsestone rose from the pool. He glanced out Aris's tunnel and saw the phaerimm still coming, so close now he could make out the barbs on their tails. Galaeron started toward the corner, where Vala was already vanishing down the whirlpool. Malik and Takari were close behind, swinging around the rim as the current drew them in.

Galaeron and the Karsestone were a dozen paces behind when an iron hand grasped his ankle. He cried out, then saw Takari glance in his direction before she and Malik vanished down the whirlpool. Galaeron tried to kick free, then stomped down on the unseen wrist.

A second hand snatched at the attacking leg. He jerked away and lunged toward the whirlpool, dragging Jhingleshod's top half along with him. His captured foot twisted, then Galaeron felt—almost heard—a bone snap. His ankle erupted in pain and buckled.

Barely catching himself on his good leg, Galaeron heaved the floating Karsestone ahead of him, then held on tight as the current drew it forward.

Jhingleshod caught him by the second ankle. Galaeron kicked madly, but could not free himself. The ceiling began to spin as the whirlpool caught them. He took a deep breath and glanced toward Aris's tunnel, expecting to find the phaerimm streaking into the chamber, but seeing only Wulgreth's ghostly form coalescing out of his untended ashes.

Galaeron's second ankle snapped, and he nearly passed out from pain. He waited until the ceiling vanished from sight, then released the Karsestone and reached for his buckle. Having lost his sword and dagger against Wulgreth, he had no blades left with which to fight, nor could he use another spell. Most required at least a word of spoken magic, and the only thing speaking would get him now was drowned.

They swirled down into darkness, bumping and scraping along the slick walls of the passage. Galaeron pulled his belt off and stretched it between both hands. Jhingleshod clawed his way up the elf's legs, his fingers digging through the magic chain mail as though it were silk.

They slammed into the Karsestone, which had become lodged in a choke point, and Jhingleshod's truncated waist swung up, smashing Galaeron in the face. The elf thought for a moment his attacker might swirl away, but the iron knight held fast. Galaeron tried to kick free—then nearly drowned when his mouth opened to scream.

The Karsestone twisted in the choke point, and the iron torso drifted away from Galaeron's face. Jhingleshod pulled himself around, lining himself to continue climbing the elf, and Galaeron saw his chance. He stretched the belt across the top of his attacker's arms, then pulled one end underneath the wrists and encircled them in the thick belt. With the deft finger work of any spellcaster, he drew the tail through the buckle and jerked it tight, then circled the knight's iron wrists again and clasped the belt.

The Karsestone slipped past the choke point, freeing the pent-up river to churn down the passage. Jhingleshod's hands came loose, and the undead knight tumbled away, gurgling in outrage. Galaeron caught hold of the boulder and jammed his arm into the crack in its center, then swirled along behind it like a wagging tail. The world turned bright, then the bottom fell out as the river plunged from the butte into the crimson pool below.

Galaeron plummeted after the Karsestone, then slammed into it headlong. His initial thought was that his plan had not worked so well, that the cunning phaerimm had foreseen such an attempt and left someone outside to intercept the artifact—then, when his world did not explode into magic oblivion, he began to slip down the stone's face and recalled the levitation spell he had used to move it in the first place. He wedged his other arm into the crack, and fighting the steady stream of silver liquid that continued to pour out of the stone, dangled beneath the boulder.

As it sank toward the river, Galaeron searched the area for signs of the phaerimm. Vala and the others were bobbing in the crimson pool beneath him, struggling to move away from the expanding ring of ripples that marked the entry of Jhingleshod's torso into the river. An instant later, the knight's legs came tumbling out of the butte and plunged, still kicking, into the water. When a pair of spell flashes brightened the mouth of Aris's tunnel—no doubt the phaerimm's response to Wulgreth's coalescing form—Galaeron finally dared to believe Vala's plan would work.

He settled onto the surface not far from his friends, and continuing to hold onto the Karsestone with both hands, began to drift after them.

"Watch your feet!" he yelled. "Jhingleshod caught me from beneath and—"

Galaeron was interrupted by a tremendous crash from the other side of the butte. He glanced up in time to see a silver bolt of lightning striking down from the heavens, then Aris's deep voice bellowed in rage. The loud crash of a shattering boulder shook the butte, and the golden flare of two more war spells flashed against the sky. The stone giant's bellow changed to a cry of anguish.

Malik swam alongside the Karsestone and pushed Takari's hand toward Galaeron. "My Kelda is over there!"

Galaeron pulled Takari onto the boulder. She looked weak but alert, and the wounds in her shoulder were no longer bleeding. Aris's cries continued to reverberate over the butte, growing more intense. Vala surfaced beside them and pulled herself onto the Karsestone.

"What are they doing to him?" Galaeron asked, unable to look away from the butte.

"Torturing him," said Vala. "They probably think he was covering our escape."

"In that case, I suggest we put his sacrifice to good use," said Malik, struggling to pull himself onto the crowded stone. "My Kelda will find her own way back to the bridge, if she is not there already. We can float down the river to the swamp and pick her up there."

"You would . . . abandon him?" Takari gasped.

A scream of anguish came from the other side of the butte. Galaeron looked to Vala, hoping to see some glimmer of an idea in her green eyes.

She met his gaze steadily. "It's what Melegaunt would do."

Galaeron's heart sank. "I'm not Melegaunt."

"Then you must . . . try," said Takari. "I would not want to live . . . knowing I had deserted one so . . . noble."

Galaeron nodded. "All right, but how?"

"You know how." Vala sheathed her sword and took Takari in her arms, then slipped off the Karsestone. *"We* don't stand a chance against the phaerimm. There's only one way."

Malik's eyes bugged out. "What are you talking about?"

"You know." Galaeron slipped into the river beside Vala and Takari, then turned toward the Karsestone. "Up."

The boulder left the water, Malik still clinging to its side. "Wait!" the Seraph called. "There must be another—"

"Up!" Galaeron said again. The boulder rose faster, and Malik let go, dropping into the river beside them. "Up!"

Now the Karsestone fairly shot skyward, the ribbon of silver magic trailing it like a glittering comet tail. The screams from the other side of the butte softened, and the two phaerimm rose into sight, flying skyward after the stone.

"Up!" Galaeron cried again.

The Karsestone pulled away, shrinking to a tiny speck visible only because of the horsetail cascade falling behind it.

"Now," said Takari. "Hear me now . . ."

She let the sentence trail off, too weak to finish.

Vala turned to Galaeron. "Say it. You're the one who sent the stone up. You must be the one who calls them home."

"No doubt," Galaeron said. "Just remember the promise you made to Melegaunt—and to me."

"I do," she said. "And I also remember the one I made to your father. I'll be there to take care of you."

Galaeron nodded, then looked skyward. "Hear me now, people of Shade. Follow me now, for the Return is at hand!"

The silver horse tail vanished, and nothing else happened. Aris's cries faded to muffled groans. The companions swam to the riverbank and dragged themselves to shore. Vala and Malik set Galaeron's broken ankles. Then, with Vala cradling him in her arms and Malik carrying Takari, they started around the head of the butte to see what could be done for Aris.

They were just passing the waterfall when Malik pointed across the pool, to where Jhingleshod was dragging himself to shore. The knight had finally snapped Galaeron's sword belt and recovered his legs. As they watched, he pulled his two halves together and slowly began to work his flesh like clay, kneading it and pushing it together, filling in the gaping hole opened by the elf's spell. He glanced across the pool and glared at Galaeron, then looked skyward, to where a shadowy ribbon of darkness was beginning to swirl down out of the heavens. Tiny flashes of silver and black began to streak back and forth between the end of the ribbon and a pair of specks streaking southward across the sky.

As the companions watched, the specks resolved themselves into tiny cone-shaped figures, the dark ribbon into a long line of bat-winged mounts, each carrying a murky rider armed with a long death-spewing lance.

At last, the phaerimm had their fill of running. They spun on their pursuers, and in a flurry of spellcasting, set the sky alight with flame and magic. A dozen riders vanished into the maelstrom and came tumbling out the bottom, their mounts reduced to charred husks of wing and talon. Still, the riders behind never faltered. One raised his hands, and with a quick gesture, opened a hole in the fiery barrier before them. The rest whirled through the breach on their dark-winged mounts, pelting their quarry with black bolts from their lances.

One of the phaerimm started to writhe about madly and began to drop—then vanished in a mote of spell light. Taking its lesson from its companion, the second creature also teleported away, leaving the bat riders to wheel through the air in swirling pinwheels of darkness.

A shadow fell over the butte, then Malik gasped, "By the One! A mountain is falling from the heavens!"

Galaeron looked up to see the summit of a craggy black peak hanging upside down above them, just low enough that its jagged tip divided the rising sun. On top of the overturned mountain sat a murk-swaddled city of shimmering black walls and ebony towers, trailing wisps of shadow and layered in bands of hazy black cloud. It was swarming with hundreds—if not thousands—of bat riders, all circling the city in a mad wheeling stream, trailing pennants of royal blue and amethyst and black-red ruby, tipping their lances and performing wild acrobatics for hordes of cheering, gem-eyed citizens gathered along the dark ramparts.

"There is the help Evereska needs," Vala said. When Galaeron did not respond, she looked into his eyes, her brow furrowed in concern. "Galaeron, you should be happy. What's wrong?"

Galaeron did not know how to answer. After breaking his word twice in one day, he had expected to feel disgraced, even corrupt or evil. Instead, he merely felt hollow—hollow and a little cold.

Vala's expression grew hard. "Galaeron?"

He just looked away.

THE SIEGE
RETURN OF THE ARCHWIZARDS

CHAPTER ONE

26 Tarsakh, the Year of Wild Magic (1372 DR)

Twenty Lords of Shade stood chest-deep in a lake that had never before known the color of light, pulling strands of shadow up from the milky bottom and splicing them into a curtain of umbral darkness that hung down from the cavern's thousand-needled ceiling. Save for the ripples of grime rinsing out of their travel-worn cloaks, the water was as clear as air, and thousands of limestone cave pearls could be seen gleaming in the inch-deep shallows along the shore. Farther out in the heart of the pool, a garden of white faerie stalks rose out of the limpid depths and blossomed across the surface in a carpet of alabaster mineral pads. Of the hundred natural wonders Vala Thorsdotter had witnessed since departing her home in Vaasa, this one was by far the loneliest and the eeriest, the one that felt most forbidden to human eyes.

"This will be the ruin of it, you know."

Galaeron Nihmedu was sitting on his haunches beside Vala, watching the shadow lords work. Tall and solidly built for a moon elf, he had the pale skin and regal features common to his race, but two decades of Tomb Guard postings along the Desert Border South had left his face rugged and weather-beaten enough to be considered handsome even by Vaasan standards.

"The ruin of what?" she asked.

"The lake," Galaeron explained. "The dirt washing out of their clothes will settle on the cave pearls and stop them from growing. The oil from their bodies will work its way into the mineral pads and break them up. A hundred years from now, this will be just another mud hole."

Vala shrugged. "It's for a good cause."

"Spoken like a human." Galaeron's tone was more remorseful than unkind. "And I find myself in agreement. How sad is that?"

"Not as sad as feeling sorry for yourself," Vala answered sharply. Elves worshiped beauty like a god, but there were more important concerns at stake than a lake no one ever saw, and she couldn't let its destruction sink Galaeron into one of his dejections. "If we could ask Duirsar what he wanted, I'm sure he'd tell us to go ahead."

"He would tell us to find another place to complete the Splicing—or not to finish at all. Elves do not destroy nature's treasures to save their own."

Vala rolled her eyes. "Galaeron, you *know* this is the only way. If the phaerimm aren't contained, they'll destroy more than this one lake. Far more."

"Being the only way seldom makes something the right way."

Galaeron looked back to the lake, watching the shadow lords weave their dark curtain, then laid a hand on Vala's arm.

"But what's done is done," he said. "You can stop worrying about me."

"Sure I can," Vala said. "Someday."

Her gaze followed Galaeron's out across the lake. The cavern was lit by three magic glowballs hovering among the stalactites. The shadow lords working most directly beneath the brilliant light looked most human, with swarthy complexions, dark hair, and gem-colored eyes. Others, laboring in the dim boundaries or shadowed areas, looked more like silhouettes, their lithe bodies bending and stretching in ghostlike whorls as they stooped down to pluck dark filaments out of the water. They would braid three strands together and give the resulting ribbon a single half twist, then splice it into the curtain fringe. After half a dozen splices, they would weave a few strands of shadowsilk into the fibers and speak an arcane word, and a dark fog would fill the empty spaces and solidify into a translucent veil of murk.

Galaeron and Vala watched in silence for another quarter hour, then Galaeron said, "They're sly, these Shadovar."

"That surprises you?"

"They always surprise me." Galaeron pointed at the shadowy curtain. "You see the way they're turning the fibers back on themselves?"

Vala gave a tentative nod. "I see, but I don't understand magic."

"Dimensional twisting," Galaeron explained, "to make the shadowshell one-sided."

Vala gave him a blank look.

"So nothing can leave," he said. "Anything that passes into the shadow goes all the way around the shell and comes out where it entered. It would be like stepping through a gate and always returning to the same garden."

"Not much gardening in Vaasa," Vala commented, trying to wrap her mind around the idea of twisting a dimension. "You can tell that just by watching?"

Galaeron looked at her askance. "The magic isn't difficult." His expression grew distant and dark, and he peered through a section of uncompleted curtain into the black depths beyond. "If I can understand it, so can they."

" 'They,' Galaeron?" Vala asked. She didn't like the emphasis Galaeron had placed on the word *they*—or the look that had come to his eyes. "The Shadovar?"

"No." Galaeron touched two buckles, and his Evereskan chain mail loosened its form-fitting embrace. "*Them*. You know." He continued to speak as he pulled off his armor. "They're out there, somewhere there in the dark."

"*Who*, Galaeron?" Vala asked, more concerned about what had come over Galaeron than what was lurking in the dark. "The phaerimm?"

Galaeron nodded. "Giant scaly slugs that've been down here in the dark for a long time, since before I felt the cave breathe, since before I followed that little crack down here to this place no one has ever left."

He let his chain mail breeches clink to the ground, then waded out into the water, kicking cave pearls loose with every step.

"They were out there then," he said, "and they're out there now, lurking in the dark, their tails just aching to stick someone with an egg."

"Galaeron, you know that can't be." Vala was fumbling at her own buckles, struggling to remove her heavy scale mail. "Wait!"

She was furious with herself for being caught off guard; she had seen him slipping toward dejection but had allowed herself to be taken in by his reassurances.

"Galaeron, you're imagining things."

He half turned, a wild look in his eyes, and spoke over his shoulder. "You know how they like that, Vala, putting an egg in some wretch's gut and watching it grow until it's as big as his arm and squirming up his throat. They love that. It's the only thing they love at all."

Vala let her armor clank to the stone and splashed in after him, her shins still covered by her greaves. The Change had never been this deranged before.

"There aren't any phaerimm," she called, loudly enough to draw the attention of the Shadovar. "Prince Escanor checked."

"No, he didn't. Not well enough." Galaeron sank to his chin as the bottom dropped away beneath him, then floated back to the surface and began to swim toward the curtain. "They're out there. It makes sense. They *have* to be there."

Vala reached the drop-off and swam after him, half breaststroking and half treading water because the weight of her greaves prevented her from floating her legs to the surface.

"Maybe they don't know where we are," she suggested. "Or maybe they couldn't get here. Not everyone can just turn into a shadow and slip down a crack, you know."

Galaeron rolled into an easy backstroke. "How long did they take to capture the Shaeradim? Five days—five days to take what Evereska has held for fifteen centuries." A hand came down on the edge of a mineral pad, shattering the whole thing and sending it fluttering to the lake's milky bottom. He appeared not to notice. "If I can find this place, *they* can find this place."

"There is a difference between *can* and *have,* elf." It took a moment to recognize the raspy voice. While Prince Escanor was ten places away splicing strands into the shadow curtain, his magic made him sound as though he were in the water beside them. "If the phaerimm were here, they would have attacked by now."

"The phaerimm *are* here—they must be—and have they attacked?" Galaeron asked, facing the prince. "No, they haven't. So, you're wrong. Absolutely wrong."

Escanor's copper-glowing eyes flared. "How am I wrong, elf?" He began to wade toward them, a bugbear-sized silhouette limned in silver spell-light. "Explain."

Galaeron looked as though he were about to answer, then he cocked his head and, passing within a lance-length of an astonished shadow lord, vanished through a breach in the curtain. Vala followed as quickly as she was able, but the steel greaves on her shins made her slow. Escanor, swimming as well, beat her through the gap. She cringed at what was likely to follow. One did not ignore a prince of Shade Enclave.

Vala passed through the gap and found them standing close together in the shallows, Galaeron's lean form submerged to the waist and Escanor's to the knees. Like all the shadow lords, the prince was swarthy and powerful, with a mouthful of ceremonial fangs and a long, rawboned face that lent a demonic aura to an already otherworldly mystique. They were standing close together, speaking intensely but quietly.

" . . . are spell collectors," Galaeron was saying. He sounded less irrational but just as intense. "They haven't attacked because they want to watch the Splicing."

"You suggest they're spying on us?" Escanor asked.

"If I can learn to use shadow magic, why can't the phaerimm?" Galaeron replied. "If they understand it, they control it."

"What you say stands to reason, as far as it goes." Escanor glanced over as Vala touched bottom beside them, then looked back to Galaeron. "But if the phaerimm were here, we would have detected their magic. They cannot hide that from us."

"Only phaerimm know what the phaerimm can do," Galaeron said. He was looking past the prince into the darkness, studying it as though he could find the enemy by sheer force of will. "And only a fool would believe otherwise."

Escanor's eyes brightened to a fiery red. "Watch that tongue, elf. A shadow crisis excuses only so much."

Vala slipped between the two, placing her back to Escanor and raising a hand to silence the elf before he could make a retort. "Galaeron, you know better. The Shadovar have killed more phaerimm than all of Evereska's High Mages together, and Prince Escanor has slain three personally. If there is a fool here, it is the one who speaks to him as though he were some Waterdhavian pikesman on his first march beyond the city gate."

The rebuke shocked Galaeron into silence, for Vala was the one person in the world whose loyalties he could never question, the one person in the world who could break through the Change to tell him such things. Together, they had traveled the dark pathways of the shadow fringe, fought beholders, liches, and illithids, seen their friends and comrades die in ways horrible beyond imagining. Vala had stood fast through everything and had nursed him back to health when all was done, and that had connected her to his true nature in a way no shadow crisis could obstruct.

Galaeron continued to stare past Vala and Escanor into the darkness for a long time, then finally shifted his gaze back to Vala and said, "I didn't mean to imply that the Shadovar are anything but the finest warriors." He looked to Escanor, but his eyes remained distant and dark. "The prince is right. If the phaerimm were using magic to conceal themselves, I'm sure your divination spells would reveal where they're hiding."

Galaeron held Escanor's gaze a moment, then glanced toward the cave ceiling.

The prince seemed oblivious. "Good." His eyes did not stray from Galaeron's face. "We're almost done with the Splicing. Evereska need hold only a few months longer, elf. The phaerimm are doomed."

"My city is grateful for the aid of Shade Enclave, Prince, but it would not do to underestimate our enemies." Galaeron furrowed his arched brows and again rolled his eyes toward the ceiling. "I recall one of our high mages saying the same thing shortly before a phaerimm larva tore its way from his throat."

This drew only a condescending smirk from the prince. "When will you learn, elf? We are not your high mages." He reached over Vala to clap a huge hand on Galaeron's shoulder. "The Shadovar have been preparing for this war for centuries."

Vala barely heard this last part, for Galaeron's efforts had drawn her attention to the mass of limestone fangs hanging down overhead, each with a single drop of water clinging to its stony tip. With broad roots narrowing down to sharp points, the stalactites were shaped more or less like phaerimm, save that they lacked spiny hides and four thin arms. There were hundreds in the lit area alone. At only three to six feet, most were too short to be phaerimm, a few were so long their flattened tips actually touched the lake surface, but a handful hung down in the ten-foot range. It didn't take Vala long to locate three with suspiciously dry tips and odd dark lines where their bases pressed against the ceiling.

" . . . that right, Vala?" Escanor asked.

"Is what right?" Hoping that all the blood had not drained from her face, Vala tore her gaze from the ceiling and tried to look calm. "Sorry."

Escanor cocked a disapproving brow but said, "I was just assuring Galaeron that we Shadovar were hardly likely to make the same mistake as the elves and Waterdhavians."

"I'm sure you won't," Galaeron said, still trying to draw the prince's gaze to the ceiling. "But new mistakes will prove—"

"Rare, I'm sure," Vala said, taking Galaeron's arm.

The prince should have recognized the elf's signal, and they didn't dare push things too far. Once the phaerimm realized they were discovered, they would attack instantly—and there were few mistakes more grave than letting a phaerimm have the first blow.

"If you will excuse us, Prince," Vala said, "it's time we let you return to your work."

Escanor dismissed them with an easy wave. "Of course."

Vala drew Galaeron away, her iron grasp permitting no argument. Once they were a few steps away, with their backs facing the suspicious stalactites, she released his arm and began to twist her hands through the gestures of Evereskan finger talk.

You're never going to get Escanor to look up. As Vala made the statement, she was careful to remain alert to any alien presences in her mind. The phaerimm were not so adept at telepathy that they could eavesdrop on a person's thoughts without revealing their own presence, but it never hurt to be careful—not around these enemies. *Are you sure they were phaerimm?*

No, Galaeron admitted, *but it's better to be sure they aren't. You saw what I was looking at?*

Disguised as stalactites, Vala said. Her tempo was slow and awkward, for it was a complicated language, and she had only taken up its study as a way to pass the time while Galaeron lay immobile with a pair of broken ankles. *Dry tips and a dark line where they're pressing their bases to the ceiling.*

Galaeron raised his brow. *I missed the lines,* he said. *We can't run the risk of alerting them. We have to take them ourselves.*

Ourselves? Vala shook a fist downward to show emphasis. *How?*

You take the closest one, Galaeron instructed. *Throw your sword. I'll blast the other with a shadow bolt.*

Vala's fingers turned slow and clumsy. *I thought you were done casting spells.*

You have another way? Galaeron's gestures came so fast and sharp, Vala could barely follow his meaning. *Maybe you can convince Escanor he's wrong—without alerting the phaerimm?*

The question required no answer. Vala knew as well as Galaeron that the prince could not be persuaded that he had made a mistake. They had no choice except to launch the attack on their own, and that meant Galaeron would have to use shadow magic to have any effect at all on the phaerimm, and using his shadow magic meant giving a little more of himself over to the darkness that was slowly devouring him from within.

Resigning herself to the heartache of watching the Galaeron she knew slip even deeper into shadows, Vala gave a curt nod, then asked, *What about the third one?*

You're joking, Galaeron replied.

I could be wrong, but I'm not joking. One above Escanor, one over the mineral pads—

That one I missed. Galaeron's fingers fell motionless for a moment, then he said, *I'll have to try a shadow door.*

Bad idea, Vala said, even more concerned. Shadow magic was far more dangerous for the wielder than normal Weave magic. If a magic-user overreached his limits, he invited in just the sort of darkness already consuming Galaeron. *You're barely holding on as it is.*

Then it's good you are watching over me. I am grateful—very grateful.

Vala looked away, then spoke aloud. "Galaeron, it isn't fair to hold me to that promise . . . not now."

"Nevertheless, I do hold you to it." Galaeron's voice was firm. "When the time comes, you must not hesitate."

"*If,* Galaeron." They reached the shore, and Vala sat down to remove her greaves. "If the time comes."

Galaeron turned away without answering and started down the shore, moving far enough away that they both could not be struck down by the same spell. Vala looked back across the lake to where the shadow lords were just closing the last few breaches in the shadow curtain. Though the shadow lords had left their armor on shore, all were armed with glassy black weapons similar to Vala's darksword—one reason, no doubt, that the enemy was being so careful to remain concealed.

The two phaerimm Galaeron had noticed hung about fifty feet apart in a rough line on the interior side of the curtain. On the flanks of their conical bodies, Vala could see a regular pattern of bumps where their body thorns lay concealed beneath the hardened lime-mud they had used to disguise their scaly hides. The third phaerimm, the one Galaeron had missed, hung over the mineral pads about forty paces away, barely noticeable in the gloomy boundary between dark and light. Though Vala had no way of guessing whether the creatures had seen enough to defeat the shadow curtain, the simple fact that they were making no attempt to stop the final Splicing made clear what they believed.

Finding no signs of any enemies beyond the three already located, Vala stood and waded back into the lake, angling toward Prince Escanor to avoid alerting the phaerimm. She had no idea how Galaeron had sensed the enemy's presence—or why that had brought on a Change—but she felt confident in his conclusions. Every good warrior knew the value of camouflage, and the thornbacks were nothing if not good warriors.

When Vala drew within throwing range of the nearest phaerimm, she stopped and looked back. Galaeron was just setting a loop of shadowsilk on a stone beside him. He peeled another strand off the mat of dull fabric he was holding, then soaked it in a drop of armor oil and glanced in Vala's direction. She nodded. He pressed the filament to the limestone wall, his lips already moving as he spoke his spell incantation.

A film of oily shadow spread across the ceiling, filling the cavern with a soft, rainlike patter as thousands of drops of water lost their tenuous hold and plummeted into the lake. Vala drew her darksword and in a single smooth motion sent it whirling up at the nearest phaerimm. The glassy black blade tore a three-foot gash across the thornback's body and became lodged with little more than the hilt showing.

The stain on the ceiling swept past overhead. The astonished phaerimm came loose one after the other, the hardened lime-mud camouflage falling in cakes from their squirming bodies, and their strange language of winds stirring the air into whistling vortexes. The phaerimm hit the water almost as one and sank beneath the surface.

Escanor and his shadow lords stopped working and whirled toward the splash rings, shouting to each other in their own language and trying to make sense of what was happening.

"Phaerimm!" Vala stretched her hand toward the one she had attacked and thought of her darksword, and the blade rose out of the water and flew back into her grasp. "Three of them!"

She heard Galaeron intoning his second spell and looked over to see him flipping the ring of shadowsilk toward the place the third phaerimm had entered the water. A disk of black shadow appeared two inches above the surface. Vala was distracted as the startled phaerimm activated their floating magic and began rising out of the water. The two nearest the curtain came up in the midst of the astonished shadow lords, who quickly proved the truth of Escanor's boasts by assailing them with shadow webs and darkswords.

Even caught off guard, the phaerimm reacted like the terrors they were, unleashing a flurry of fire strikes and lightning bolts that left a dozen Shadovar bobbing dead in the darkening waters. A pair of scorched shadow lords popped up beside Vala, their arms and legs blasted off by the force of the strike that had killed them. Vala threw her sword again, only to see her target scythed down the middle by a falling wall of black glass as Escanor unleashed his own magic.

Vala glanced over to see the third phaerimm's tail vanishing into the circle of shadow Galaeron had placed over its splash ring. The elf himself was pointing across the lake roughly in her direction. Knowing the creature would be disoriented for a moment when it emerged from Galaeron's shadow door, Vala nodded and reached out to summon her sword back.

Galaeron's finger shifted in Prince Escanor's direction.

"No, Galaeron!" Vala cried. "Here!"

Too late. The third phaerimm had already reappeared, stunned and disoriented by its dizzying journey through the shadow plane. But Escanor happened to be turning to attack their other surviving foe, and so this thornback appeared behind him instead of in front. Vala's stomach turned to ice. With the prince at least twenty paces away and in a direct line beyond the dazed phaerimm, she did not dare throw her sword again.

She started toward him, yelling, "Escanor, behind you!"

The prince cocked his head in response but only stretched a hand toward the second phaerimm, who was assailing five of his lords with a roaring storm of meteors. A sphere of spinning darkness shot from his hand and streaked through the thing's torso, leaving a basket-sized hole in the heart of its body. The creature splashed into the lake and slowly sank out of sight.

The third phaerimm was already bringing its tail out of the water, ten steps away.

"Watch your back!" she cried.

A murky aura of darkness—more of Galaeron's magic, Vala guessed—enveloped the phaerimm, but the spell did not prevent the creature's tail from catching Escanor in the pit of the stomach as he spun to meet the attack. The barb sank to its root, doubling the prince over and drawing an eerie gurgle of anguish.

Vala hurled her darksword. The blade tumbled three times, then sank hilt-deep in the phaerimm's torso. The creature began to flicker between material and immaterial, and Vala was astonished to realize that Galaeron had not cast his spell to protect the prince but to trap the phaerimm beside him.

Had Galaeron finally been taken by his shadow self?

Escanor wailed in pain and slipped off the barb, then rolled to his back and floated, groaning. Vala called her darksword back to her grasp and began to angle in the prince's direction.

"Vala, no!" Galaeron splashed into the water. "The phaerimm! It knows too much!"

Vala glanced at the prince, who, unlike most of his wounded lords, was at least floating faceup. She decided to place her trust in Galaeron a little longer. She sprang at the phaerimm, her black sword blocking the tail as it arced toward her throat, lopping the dangerous barb off at the root. On the backswing, she removed two of the thing's four arms, then reversed her grip, jammed the blade into the creature's enormous mouth, and split it down the side.

The dark aura vanished from around the phaerimm—only to reappear an instant later as Galaeron recast his snare spell. The phaerimm flickered between materiality and immateriality again as it tried once more to teleport away, and again Vala sank her sword deep into its body. It pummeled her with one of its remaining arms, and the other clamped onto her throat, trying to crush her windpipe. She kneed it in the flank and felt sharp pain as one of its body thorns impaled her thigh. The phaerimm began to overpower her, pulling her face toward the fang-filled mouth atop its shoulders. She croaked in Galaeron's direction.

He was already pointing a sliver of obsidian at the creature and yelling a string of mystic syllables. A finger-thin ray of darkness left his hand, catching the phaerimm in one of its remaining arms and severing it at the elbow. Vala snapped the other arm with a palm strike, then kicked free and brought her darksword around in three eviscerating swings.

The thing's heart slipped out of the second gash, still beating. Vala sent it flying off with a flick of her blade, and the phaerimm dropped, motionless, into the water. She struck again and again, not stopping until she had opened it from tail to lip and left it floating in the water like a dressed eel.

Galaeron waded up. "Are you hurt?"

"I'm alive." She shook her head clear and gave herself a cursory glance, then looked over and found herself staring into a pair of black, empty eyes. "G-Galaeron? How many spells did you cast?"

Instead of answering, Galaeron pushed her toward Escanor's floating form. "See to the prince and the others," he said as he turned and started toward the shadow curtain. "I'll finish the Splicing."

CHAPTER TWO

28 Tarsakh, the Year of Wild Magic

The city appeared just before dusk, hovering low over a rosy desert butte, a distant diamond of umbral murk silhouetted against the purple twilight of the eastern sky. As usual, the city was surrounded by wisps of black fog, giving it the appearance of a storm cloud, a mirage, or an angry djinn. The V-shaped specks of a hundred or so vultures wheeled in lazy circles beneath the city, chasing the constant rain of garbage that dropped from its refuse chutes.

"There," Galaeron said.

Though it had been two days since he'd completed the Splicing, the icy tingle of shadow magic still permeated his body—and he hungered for more, longed to cast spells until he was numb and cold from head to foot, until he was filled with the power of shadow and beyond mortal frailty.

Instead, he pointed at the floating city and said, "See it?"

"So far?" Malik complained.

A pudgy little man with a moon-shaped face and bug-eyes, Malik el Sami yn Nasser was the Seraph of Lies, a favored servant of the evil god Cyric and an oddly stalwart traveling companion, who had saved Galaeron's life more than once.

"I apologize for my accursed luck," the little man said. "It has always been its nature that just when I think matters could seem no worse, a turn of bad fortune comes along to prove me wrong."

"In this desert, things look farther than they are," Vala said. Limping a little from her wounded thigh, she started down the dry wash at their backs. "We'd better get moving, or we'll lose sight of it when dark really falls."

Nodding, Galaeron turned to follow. As a precaution against attack, Shade Enclave appeared only briefly each evening and always in a different place. Given that Escanor's company had failed to finish the Splicing and raise the shadowshell at the appointed time, it made sense to put some distance between the floating city and the Shaeradim battlefields. Assuming they were lucky enough to reach the city before it vanished again, Galaeron only hoped they would not fall victim to any new defenses intended for the phaerimm.

In the bottom of the wash, they found the Shadovar survivors preparing the company's mounts for departure. Though most of the shadow lords had already recovered from the cavern battle, Escanor had taken an egg when he was impaled and remained incoherent with fever. The longer the egg stayed inside him, the harder it would be to remove, but his chances were far better than those of most humans would have been. Shadovar were fast healers. Most of their wounds had closed within an hour after the battle, so it seemed likely that the prince would survive even a difficult extraction.

Galaeron followed Vala over to the nominal leader of the group in Escanor's incapacity, a ruby-eyed lord so swarthy that he looked more like an obsidian statue than a live man.

"Lord Rapha," Vala said, "we've located the enclave."

"That is well." Rapha did not look up. He was looping a length of shadow strand around the hands of a dead comrade, using it to secure the man in his saddle. "We'll soon be ready."

Galaeron and his companions waited for Rapha to ask where or how far off the enclave was, or to give some indication that he was concerned about getting Escanor to the city quickly.

Rapha ignored them.

Finally, Galaeron said, "The enclave is a long way off. You might want to send Escanor ahead."

The Shadovar fixed his ruby eyes on Galaeron. "Concerned for the prince, are we?"

"Of course," Vala said.

"Most concerned," Malik agreed. He hesitated for a moment, then was unable to keep from adding, "But we are even more concerned for ourselves. We know who will be blamed if he dies."

This drew a sour smile from the shadow lord. Like everyone in the company, Rapha knew that Malik had been cursed by the goddess Mystra to speak only the truth or not all. It was an irony in which Shadovar seemed to take special delight.

Rapha clapped a hand on the little man's shoulder. "You have nothing to fear, my stubby friend. You were not even at the Splicing."

"But *you* were," Galaeron said, wondering what Rapha was playing at. "You know I meant no harm to the prince."

"I know what I saw," Rapha said. "You used a shadow snare to keep the thornback trapped beside the prince."

"Had I let the thing teleport away, the shadowshell would be no prison at all," Galaeron retorted. "Those phaerimm were there to learn its secret, and what they discovered was important, or they would have attacked us long before I found them."

Rapha considered this, then his voice grew quiet and menacing. "How is it you know so much about the phaerimm, elf? Why could you find them when twenty shadow lords could not?"

Galaeron glanced away. "I can't say why," he admitted. "It just seemed right that they would be there."

"It just seemed right," Rapha echoed dubiously.

"I think his shadow knew," Vala said. "He didn't say anything about them until his shadow self asserted itself."

Rapha shook his head impatiently. "The shadow self is only an absence of what a person is, a darker image of himself that he creates simply by being what he is. It cannot know more than its creator, any more than its creator can know more than it."

Galaeron shrugged. "Then I can't explain it," he said. "I just had a feeling they would be there—and I was right."

"And risking Prince Escanor's life?" Rapha asked. "You just had a feeling about that?"

"I had to do it to save the shell," Galaeron said. "I knew that, just like I knew the phaerimm would try to teleport away."

Rapha shook his head. "You can't be sure," he insisted. "Your shadow self has you in its grasp. Your thinking could have been subverted—"

"But I *can* be sure that he needs a healer—and soon," Galaeron interrupted. This Rapha was a sly one, accusing Galaeron of trying to harm the prince—and wasting valuable time. "Unless you have some reason for delaying? Perhaps you'd like to see Escanor hatch a thornback egg?"

Rapha's eyes flared from ruby to white-orange. "I have nothing but love for all the princes of Shade, elf."

"Then wouldn't it be wise to have someone return him to the enclave at once?"

"It would, had Prince Escanor been lucid enough to tell us today's word of passing," Rapha said. "As it is, anyone who tries to enter through the shadows will find himself plummeting through to the Barrens of Doom and Despair."

"So we must return the slow way," Vala said, placing herself between Galaeron and Rapha to cut off further argument. "Can Escanor ride?"

"It would be better if he didn't," Rapha said. "Perhaps your friend would be kind enough to take a passenger."

The shadow lord motioned across the wash to where a grim-faced stone giant with sad, gray eyes was kneeling over a ten-foot block of quartzite. He was clinking away with his sculptor's tools, fashioning a life-sized model of the struggle between Escanor and the phaerimm that had wounded the prince. Though the work was still rough, it was obvious by the snaking forms and undulating hollows that he had captured not only the details, but the spirit and swiftness of the battle—and from little more than a description of the events.

"I am confident Aris would be pleased to be of some small service to the prince," Malik said. "While we were watching the camp, he said many times—if once can be considered many—that he wished he were small enough to accompany the rest of the company into the Underdark and do his part to seal the fate of the phaerimm."

"Good. Will you be kind enough to ask him for me? I'll have the prince brought over directly." Rapha waved Malik toward Aris, then turned to Galaeron and Vala. "You can tell which mounts are yours? We'll be leaving shortly."

"We'll be fine," Vala said. "I banded a leg on each of ours."

The precaution was not a frivolous one. The Shadovar's flying mounts—veserabs—were odd, furless creatures that had no faces and uniform midnight-blue skin. With four spindly legs, fan-shaped ears, and a pair of gargoyle-like wings folded alongside their tubular bodies, they looked like an unfortunate cross between bats and earthworms. Once they impressed on a rider, their devotion was absolute—to the point that they would spit noxious fumes into the face of anyone else who tried to mount them.

Galaeron followed her down the draw until they found a trio of veserabs wearing copper bands on their legs. Vala pointed to one with a band on its right foreleg. Galaeron gave the wing joint a tentative squeeze and slipped a foot into the stirrup. The creature did not react until he lowered his full weight into the saddle, when—much to Galaeron's relief—an undulation of pleasure ran down its long body.

A few moments later, Malik returned and climbed into his saddle, and Rapha signaled the departure. The veserabs charged down the wash until they gathered enough speed, then spread their wings and rose into the air in flawless formation. Many of the shadow lords were tied across their saddles, but only Escanor's mount was riderless. The company had recovered all of its casualties and carried them through fifty twining Underdark miles back to the surface.

As they climbed out of the wash, a huge dome of darkness rose into view over their shoulders at Anauroch's western edge. Even from a dozen miles into the desert, the barrier was immense, curving away high into the sky and stretching north and south as far as the eye could see. Through its black translucency, Galaeron could just make out the stacked crests of the foothills of the Desert Border South and, looming behind, the familiar crags of High Shaeradim itself. He could not help thinking of what lay beyond those peaks, the vale and city of Evereska—and his sister, Keya, safe within the city's protective mythal. He knew better than to think that his warrior father had been lucky enough to survive his duties to return to her side, but Lord Aubric Nihmedu was as resourceful as he was brave, and there was no harm in praying it so.

Once the veserabs had ascended high enough to avoid being surprised by an attack from the ground, Aris rose into the air on an ancient Netherese flying disk. Though the bronze saucer was neither as swift nor as maneuverable as a veserab, it was capable of carrying not only the giant's weight but also that of the wounded prince, his campaign tent, and Aris's half-completed statue. Its one drawback was that Aris could not defend himself in an air battle. The disks had been designed as battle platforms for Netherese archwizards, not stone giant clerics.

As the company leveled off and fixed their course on the murky silhouette of Shade Enclave, the formation began to loosen, giving the veserabs room to relax and stretch their wings. The creatures did not fly so much as swim through the atmosphere, reaching forward to grab a piece of air, then pulling themselves past. The turbulence and slipstreams created by tight formations made it more difficult to stay aloft with this strange motion, so they usually divided into smaller groups and flew side by side when traveling long distances. Vala and Malik drew up on opposite sides of Galaeron, spacing themselves about thirty feet apart.

Even had they been close enough to speak comfortably, the pounding veserab wings would have made it impossible to hear. They continued toward the dusk with only their own thoughts for company, leaving it to their mounts to steer a course toward the enclave while they watched their assigned slice of sky. Though most of the phaerimm were trapped inside the shadowshell, their hosts of servants and slaves remained free and apt to attack at any time. Twice, Rapha dispatched fliers to chase down and slay asabi lizardmen lest they were scouting for a larger company, and once they themselves had to swing into the shadows beneath a long line of cliffs when Vala spied the flea-sized spheres of a distant beholder troop bobbing across the moon's face.

Galaeron spent most of the trip brooding over the bitter words that had passed between him and Rapha. When they reached Shade Enclave, the lord clearly intended to blame him for what had befallen Escanor, and part of Galaeron even wondered if that could be justified. His shadow self was as insidious as it was dark, always working to make him see dishonorable motives in the actions of everyone around him, and for some time he had been growing angry about the hungry look in Escanor's eyes whenever he addressed Vala. Was it possible that Galaeron had sent the phaerimm to Escanor not because he wanted to be certain of killing it, but because his shadow self wanted to see the prince harmed instead?

The thought sent a shiver down Galaeron's spine, for it meant that the darkness had begun to invade his actions as well as his perceptions. The idea was driven from his mind as quickly as it had arrived, though. The prince had already killed one phaerimm and was about to slay the second, so it just seemed wisest to send him the third as well. Besides, if he really thought about it, Escanor deserved what had happened. Had he listened to Galaeron in the first place, the company would have been ready for the attack, and—

"No."

Galaeron spoke the word aloud and, alarmed at how powerful his shadow was growing, shook his head clear. The rationalization had come so smoothly, felt so natural that he had almost accepted the reasoning as his own. He would have to speak with his friends about this as soon as they landed. Aris had suggested that the best way to combat the influence of his shadow self was to be completely open about what he was thinking and feeling and let the opinions of his friends guide him. So far—as long as he didn't listen to Malik—the stone giant's strategy had not only worked, it had kept Galaeron more or less in control of himself. It had also brought him closer to Vala than was probably wise, considering the fleeting and intense nature of human lives.

Galaeron's thoughts came to an end when the veserabs let out a single, high-pitched screech and abruptly started to climb. Night had fallen, and it was so dark that he could see clearly no more than sixty feet in front of his face, but the light of the stars above was being blocked by Shade Enclave's looming form. It was not long before a few bats from the growing colony on the enclave's underside began to flit about their heads. Rapha called the company back into a tight formation, and the shadowy crags of a capsized mountaintop appeared over their heads. They circled the funnel-shaped peak in an ever-growing spiral, exchanging silent salutes with the jewel-eyed sentries watching from hidden nooks and crannies. Finally, they came to the Cave Gate, hidden in the deep shadows beneath a massive overhang and all but invisible even to Galaeron's dark sight.

The veserabs climbed so close to the roof that the riders had to lean forward and press tight against the creatures' fleshy backs. Then, one after the other, the veserabs gave short screeches, folded their wings tight against their bodies, and dived through a square of nothingness so dark that Galaeron could not tell it from the black gates themselves. He felt his sleeve brush against one edge of the wicket gate, then the air grew muggy and warm and he knew they had entered the vast Wing Court.

His mount spiraled downward into a dimly lit mezzanine area and landed in formation, six places behind Rapha and between Vala and Malik. Galaeron was astonished to see the Princes Rivalen, Brennus, and Lamorak standing at the head of the landing yard with a full company of shadow warriors.

Following the lead of Rapha and the rest of the Shadovar, Galaeron slipped off his veserab and kneeled on the floor, pressing his forehead to the cold stone. He cast an apprehensive glance in Vala's direction and saw her looking at him just as nervously, but neither dared to speak the question on their minds.

When the rest of the riders had dismounted and assumed similar positions, Galaeron sensed the princes and their guards coming across the floor. There was no sound—no tramping feet or clinking armor, nor even the whisper of boots scuffing cold stone—only a growing sense of stillness and apprehension.

Finally, Prince Rivalen's deep voice sounded not ten paces ahead. "Who is in command here?"

"I am," answered Rapha's quavering voice.

He stood and gasped softly, then described what had occurred at the underground lake, making clear what he had observed with his own eyes and what had been reported to him by others. When Rapha came to the attack on Prince Escanor, he took care to relay only the facts, though his acid tone made clear—at least to Galaeron—where he was trying to lay the blame. The shadow lord finished by reporting the successful completion of the Splicing and venturing the opinion that the phaerimm trapped within the Shaeradim would perish within a few months.

"And what of Escanor?" The voice that asked this was sibilant and pervasive, like a whisper echoing into the chamber from some distant passage. "Where is he now?"

"On the flying disk with the native giant," Rapha reported.

Like Aris himself, the flying disk was too large for the wicket door that opened into the passage leading down to the Wing Court. The stone giant would have to wait outside the Cave Gate until it was opened, then land on the great Marshaling Plaza itself.

"Most High," Prince Brennus said, "I'll summon a healer and see to our brother."

If there was a response, Galaeron did not hear it. The air grew chill and motionless, and he sensed someone standing above him.

"You are the one who held the phaerimm beside Escanor?" asked the same wispy voice that had spoken before.

Galaeron started to lift his head, then—after a hissed, "Are you mad?" from Malik—thought better of it and pressed his brow back to the floor.

"I am, Most High."

"And you did this why?" The voice seemed more interested than angry.

"To prevent it from escaping with the secret of the shell." Galaeron did not enjoy speaking to the floor, and he could not keep his irritation from creeping into his voice. "That was why the phaerimm were there, to learn how to defeat the shell so they could take Shade Enclave unawares later."

"Truly? And how do you know this?"

"The same way I knew they were there in the first place," Galaeron replied. "To tell the truth, I don't understand it myself. All I can say is that I knew."

The voice remained silent.

"It just made sense," Galaeron said, as confident that the voice desired further explanation as he was of his fate if he failed to provide it. "They had to know what we were doing, and they couldn't allow that. They had to be planning something."

"That explains why you held the phaerimm beside Escanor?" the voice asked.

Galaeron started to agree, then realized that was not what the voice wanted. There was still a question to be answered.

"The prince had just killed one phaerimm," Galaeron explained. "I thought it would be easy for him to kill another one, especially when it was teleport dazed."

Again, the silence.

"The only other place to send it was at Vala," Galaeron said. "I thought if it *did* kill someone, better Escanor than her."

"Stupid elf!" Malik shrieked, forgetting himself and raising his head. "Think what you are saying, before you get—"

The objection ended with the dull thump of a halberd butt striking Malik's cloth-swaddled head. Galaeron glanced over and found the little man sprawled unconscious but still breathing.

The voice asked, "You are struggling with your shadow, are you not, elf?"

"Losing, I think," Galaeron said. This time, he needed only the hint of a silence before realizing that he was to continue. "Prince Escanor has been looking at Vala. I didn't like it."

"Ah."

Galaeron felt the weight of Vala's stare and tried to keep his eyes fixed on the floor, but the voice remained silent, and eventually he felt compelled to peer in her direction. He found her returning his gaze as best as she was able, a look of surprise and triumph in her emerald eyes.

"It is nothing to be concerned about." The voice sounded amused. "Shadows are by nature unconquerable and unknowable. You can defeat them only by defeating yourself."

More silence, but this time Galaeron did not feel compelled to speak. The air grew muggy and less still, and Galaeron felt as though he could dare breathe again.

When the voice spoke this time, it was farther away. "Hadhrune will see to it that you and your companions are lodged near the palace. If I am to avoid losing any more of my princes, it seems I must teach you how to live with your shadow."

Uncertain of whether that was a good thing, but hoping it was, Galaeron started to raise his head—and felt the butt of a halberd on the back of his neck. He touched his head to the floor again.

The voice asked, "That will meet with your approval, will it not, elf?"

"Of course," Galaeron said. His heart was pounding—whether with joy or fear remained to be seen, but definitely with excitement. "Thank you."

Silence, heavy and expectant.

"And, of course, I'll repay you any way I can."

"Good, Galaeron," said the voice. "Now we understand each other."

✡✡✡✡✡

Though the month of Tarsakh had nearly passed and the Greengrass festival was fast approaching in Waterdeep, a fierce blizzard was roaring in from the east, battering the window panes with its angry winds and dropping more snow on a city already buried to the doorknockers. Nor was this the wet slosh that blew in from the sea early every Greening. This was needle-snow, tiny spears of ice crystals formed over the High Ice and swept across the continent in howling walls of frostbite.

There was no prospect of it melting any time soon. Melting required warm breezes and bright sun, and the closest thing to either that Waterdeep had seen in three months was the steady flow of pearl-colored storm clouds sweeping across the sky. Matters had grown so bad that the city guard had covered the frozen harbor in mountains of excess snow, the woodcutters were finding it impossible to keep smoke in the city's chimneys, and the area farmers had yet to till their frozen fields. In short, Waterdeep was facing a natural disaster of the worst proportions, which was what made the news Prince Aglarel brought so fortuitous—suspiciously so, at least to anyone who knew how such things worked.

The Shadovar stood before Piergeiron Paladinson and seven of the Masked Lords of Waterdeep, his eyes glowing silver and his ceremonial fangs flashing white as he addressed the imposing assembly in the marble-walled majesty of the palace's Court Hall. In addition to Piergeiron and the Masked Lords, the gathering included the Silverhand sisters Storm and Laeral, Lord Tereal Dyndaryl from the isle of Evermeet, Lord Gervas Imesfor of Evereska, and the inevitable host of gawkers that could be expected whenever such a group of dignitaries came together.

If Aglarel was aware of the power and influence of those whom he addressed, his easy manner and confident voice betrayed no sign of the knowledge. Huge and dark, with a blocky face and long ebony hair, he wore a flowing black cape and purple tabard that almost gave him the appearance of floating as he strode back and forth behind the podium, now and again emphasizing a point by stabbing the air with a black talon that looked more like a shard of obsidian than a human fingernail.

"The Shaeradim has become the prison of the phaerimm," the prince was saying. "Now that my people have completed the shadowshell, the wisest thing to do is to wait and let it do its work."

"Wisest for you humans, perhaps," said Lord Imesfor. Though a powerful, well-respected lord in Evereska, he was a withered and disheartened husk of an elf whose fingers had been so badly mangled by a group of phaerimm captors that he could barely dress himself, much less cast a spell. "What of the elves still trapped in Evereska? What of our lands?"

"The enemy has already ravaged your lands. The shell will do nothing to change that," Aglarel answered. "As for your elves besieged in Evereska, we can only hope we reach them before the phaerimm do."

"We will reach no one hiding behind this shadowshell of yours," Tereal Dyndaryl said. Relatively tall for even a Gold elf, he had a gaunt face that made his already sour countenance seem absolutely bitter. "We don't have time to starve the phaerimm out. We must carry the fight to them!"

"You know how to do that, Lord Dyndaryl?" Aglarel asked. Considering the accusatory tone Dyndaryl had employed, the prince's voice remained surprisingly cordial. "If the elves have a faster way to defeat the phaerimm, the Shadovar are eager to help."

Dyndaryl's flaxen cheeks darkened to amber. "We are working on a few ideas, but nothing I can share at the moment."

"When the time comes, then," Aglarel said, without a trace of disbelief. "For now, the shell remains our best choice. Please advise your commanders to give it a wide berth. Those coming into contact with it will lose whatever touches it, and anyone using Mystra's magic on it will accomplish nothing and may well regret the results."

"And why would that be?" demanded Storm Silverhand.

A striking, silver-tressed woman who stood more than six feet tall, Storm was garbed in form-fitting leather armor and armed for battle. Though she lived half a continent away and had arrived at the meeting uninvited, Piergeiron had nevertheless welcomed her attendance. When dealing with one of Mystra's Chosen, it was usually the wise thing to do.

"No one here cares for your Shadovar threats," added Storm.

"You misunderstand, Lady Silverhand," Aglarel said. He probably meant his smile to seem forbearing, but the line of fang tips hanging down behind his black lip made it look rather more sinister. "The Shadovar are not threatening anyone. I am merely informing Lords Piergeiron and Dyndaryl of the shell's dangers."

What are those dangers? whispered Deliah the White, one of the Masked Lords of Waterdeep. Like the other masked lords, her identity was concealed beneath a magic cloak, helm, and mask, and her words could be heard only by Piergeiron and her fellows on the council. *Knowing of these dangers does us little good unless we also know what they are.*

"What, exactly, is the nature of these dangers?" Piergeiron asked. As the Open Lord, it was his duty to serve as the council's common face and speak for the others in public. "It does us little good to know of them without knowing what they are."

Aglarel cast a meaningful glance over his shoulder at the gawkers in the public gallery. "It wouldn't be wise to reveal the shadowshell's nature at present," he said. "Suffice it to say that we all know what happened when a mere Tomb Guard's magic hit a shadow spell."

Along with Deliah the White and several others, Piergeiron found himself nodding. This whole mess had started when a patrol of Evereskan Tomb Guards interrupted a rendezvous between a powerful Shadovar wizard and what the elves took to be a company of human tomb robbers. A phaerimm had been drawn to the sound of the resulting turmoil, and during the terrible battle that followed, the patrol leader's Weave-based magic had clashed with the Shadovar's shadow-based magic. Nobody really understood what had happened next, except that the result had torn a hole in the mystic barrier that had kept the phaerimm imprisoned beneath Anauroch for over fifteen hundred years.

After allowing his audience a moment to contemplate his words, Aglarel continued, "Can you imagine the consequences if that spell had been loosed by one of Waterdeep's battle wizards?" He glanced at Gervas Imesfor. "Or perhaps a high mage from Evereska?"

"There is no need to imagine," Storm said darkly. "We all know what happened at Shadowdale—which is why I am finding your concern for our welfare so difficult to believe now."

"What happened at Shadowdale was a misunderstanding," Aglarel countered, "and it was *your* attack that opened the Hell breach. We lost one of our own to it as well."

"A small price to be rid of Elminster," Storm spat.

"That was never our intention," Aglarel said. "Rivalen and the others were there to talk—"

"Perhaps you forget that I was there, Prince," Storm warned. "I saw what your brothers did."

Before the lightning that flashed in her eyes became bolts flying from her fingers, Piergeiron raised a hand and said, "As concerned as we all are about Elminster's fate, that is not the matter before this council."

He could not allow Storm to turn this discussion into a quarrel over who had caused Elminster's disappearance. The argument was a sore one, and growing more so since the Simbul had turned up missing as well. There were some who suggested she had already recovered Elminster and spirited him off to some other dimension to recuperate. But Storm insisted on holding the Shadovar responsible for Elminster's continued absence, and she never missed an opportunity to rebuke them over the matter.

Piergeiron did not know what to believe—he had heard convincing evidence that supported both sides—and it really didn't matter to him. His only goal was to keep the matter from erupting into a full-blown magic duel anywhere within a hundred leagues of Waterdeep—much less within the walls of his own palace.

He locked gazes with Storm and said, "Whatever happened that day in Shadowdale, the last thing Evereska—or Faerûn itself—needs is war with the Shadovar, too."

"Whatever happened?" Storm fumed. "I have told you what happened! The Shadovar are as bad as the—"

"Come now, Sister," Laeral said. Almost as tall as Storm, she had the same silver hair but emerald eyes instead of blue. "Exaggeration serves no one, and I have seen for myself what the Shadovar can do against the phaerimm. We need all the help they can provide."

"Help from a nest of vipers will prove poison in the end," Storm retorted.

"We are asking for no more than was Netheril's in the days of our fathers," Aglarel said. "Leave us to Anauroch, and no one on Faerûn need fear Shade Enclave."

"Anauroch is not Waterdeep's to grant or deny," Piergeiron said, trying to guide the conversation back to the matter at hand. "Just as Evereska is not the Shadovar's to quarantine."

"I could not agree with you more, Lord Piergeiron," Aglarel replied. "Which is only one of the reasons we should establish a coordinating council. I'm sure we can all agree that it would be in Evereska's best interest if our nations shared in the responsibility of making these sorts of decisions."

"A magnanimous gesture, Prince Aglarel, considering that the Shadovar have dealt the phaerimm the few losses they have suffered in this war," Laeral said warmly. She knew whereof she spoke; her beloved Khelben "Blackstaff" Arunsun had vanished during a battle early in the war, and she was spending much of her time at the front trying to determine what had become of him. "I am certain Lord Imesfor would welcome such a council."

Before the elf could voice his approval or disapproval, Storm asked, "Who would lead this council? The Shadovar?"

Aglarel nodded without hesitation. "For now," he said, "it appears we are best equipped to assume that duty."

When dragons kneel before halflings! scoffed Brian the Swordmaster. As one of the Masked Lords of Waterdeep, his words came to Piergeiron as a barely audible whisper. *They're trying to take control of the war zone.*

Aglarel cast a brief glance in Brian's direction, then looked back to Piergeiron and said, "If the Lords of Waterdeep find our leadership uncomfortable, we would not be adverse to naming Lord Imesfor master of the council. It is, after all, his home that is in peril."

Piergeiron was almost too astonished to reply. The discussions between the masked lords were shielded by the same magic that protected their identities, yet Aglarel had plainly heard what Brian had said.

"The lords will discuss the council you propose later—in private," Piergeiron said, "but we do appreciate your suggestion."

Many of the spectators in the hall would be mystified as to why he did not immediately agree to name Lord Imesfor the council leader, but they had not seen how the elf trembled at the slightest sound or heard the screams that echoed through the palace halls whenever he retired to his room to attempt the Reverie. Gervas Imesfor was in no condition to lead a horse, much less a political and military alliance of this magnitude. Piergeiron felt quite certain that Aglarel had known that when he proposed it.

I'm sure our deliberations would be more meaningful if we knew more about the nature of the shadowshell, Deliah said, still pressing for details. Like nearly every respectable wizard on Faerûn, she seemed more alarmed by the Shadovar's mysterious magic than by the evil of the phaerimm. *If the prince is concerned about spies, perhaps we could meet later—*

"I am at liberty to reveal the nature of the shell only to our declared allies," Aglarel said, drawing an audible gasp from three of the lords who had not previously realized he was listening in on their private conversations. "However, it is difficult to predict how the phaerimm will respond. It really would be better to establish the coordinating council at once."

"You have doubts that the shell will hold?" Lord Dyndaryl asked.

"Not at all. The shell will hold." Aglarel deliberately looked at Imesfor and said, "It is Evereska we are concerned about. We do not understand the mythal well enough to know how long it can withstand a sustained assault."

"It's still up?" The relief in Imesfor's voice was obvious. "You know that?"

The phaerimm had enclosed the entire Shaeradim within a magic deadwall that prevented any sort of travel to or communication with Evereska, and he was not the only one in the room who had been wondering if the city was still in elf hands.

Aglarel hesitated a moment, then gave a nod so slight it was barely perceptible.

"Thank Corellon!" Imesfor gasped.

"Then you are in contact with the city?" It was Laeral Silverhand who asked this. "Do you know if Khelben is there?"

Aglarel looked away. "Unfortunately, I am not at liberty to answer your questions, Lady Silverhand." He managed to sound genuinely apologetic. "That information would be available only to our allies."

"To your *allies!*" Laeral fumed. "Who do you think has been fighting at your side—"

"Were the choice mine, Lady Silverhand, I would tell you," he said. "Your contributions have not gone unnoticed by our Most High, but your allegiance is obviously to Waterdeep, and Waterdeep has not declared itself our ally."

Nor are we like to, said Brian. *Waterdeep won't yield to strong-arm tactics. Never!*

Aglarel looked directly at Brian. "This isn't strong-arming. How many of its secrets would Waterdeep reveal to a city that refuses to call itself an ally?"

"We are not asking for any of your secrets," Laeral said, straining to sound patient. "Only the simple courtesy of—"

"The Shadovar are showing you *every* courtesy, Lady Silverhand," Aglarel said. "That is what I'm doing here. It is Waterdeep that is being discourteous, that receives information given in good faith with suspicion, that rebukes our offer of friendship with high-handed accusations of coercion, that allows a visitor under its palace roof to call Shade Enclave a den of liars and vipers."

Aglarel allowed his gaze to linger on Storm Silverhand for a moment, then looked back to Piergeiron. "You have been advised of the shadowshell's danger. It is not our intent to interfere with any of your own missions. Should any of your forces wish to pass through, we will be happy to send an escort along to make that possible."

The arrogant devils! Brian ranted, either forgetting or ignoring the fact that the prince could obviously hear every word. *They're claiming control of the war zone whether we like it or not!*

Aglarel shot a glance in Brian's direction but chose to ignore the outburst. "While we regret that it will not be possible to coordinate our efforts, Shade Enclave does thank you for this audience."

The Shadovar bowed deeply, then turned toward the door to leave. Though Piergeiron could feel the gazes of the elves and the Silverhand sisters burning into his brow, it was what he knew his fellow lords were leaving unsaid that weighed most heavily on his mind. As usual, Brian the Swordmaster had cut straight to the heart of the matter. Whether Waterdeep and the elves liked it or not, the Shadovar had taken control of the war zone. What Piergeiron didn't understand was why they had bothered to send an envoy to announce an already obvious fact. Were they really hoping to establish an alliance, or was there something more, something broader and more nefarious?

There was only one way to find out. Piergeiron drew himself up to his full height, then called, "Prince Aglarel!"

To his credit, Aglarel looked properly shocked as he stopped and turned. "Yes, Lord Paladinson?"

"I did not dismiss you."

The prince looked as though he were biting a smile back. "Of course." He inclined his head. "I apologize."

Piergeiron resisted the temptation to let the Shadovar remain in the deferential position. The point had been made.

"Prince Aglarel, Waterdeep has not rejected your offer."

This seemed to catch the prince by surprise. "Then you have accepted it?"

"As I said earlier, the lords will discuss the matter later."

"That is the same as rejecting it," Aglarel said. "As *I* said earlier, the council needs to be established at once."

"Then you must be expecting something to happen soon," Piergeiron said. "Perhaps Waterdeep and Evereska should withdraw our armies."

Finally, Aglarel's silver eyes flashed in surprise. "Withdraw?"

"At once," Piergeiron confirmed. "We certainly wouldn't want to interfere with your city's plans."

Aglarel considered this for a moment, then lowered his gaze. "It is not our intention to drive you from the field," he said. "Let me consult with the enclave."

Piergeiron smiled. "Of course." He dismissed the prince with a gracious wave. "Take all the time you need. We will."

"Yes," Aglarel said, "I am quite sure you will."

The prince returned the Open Lord's smile, then bowed again and, with a courteous flourish of his dark cape, turned to leave.

CHAPTER THREE

9 Mirtul, the Year of Wild Magic

As with so much of Shade Enclave, Villa Dusari struck Galaeron as a monument to the allure of darkness and beauty half-glimpsed. The gates opened into a round courtyard paved in gray pearl—not stone exactly, but not quite glass either. In the center, a small fountain stood bubbling water into a black pool. The colonnade ringing the enclosure was deep and shadowed, with nine arched doorways opening like cave mouths into the house interior. In front of each pillar lay one of the precious urns wealthy Shadovar used for decoration, a hole knocked in one side to let the magic shadow spray gurgle out in a formless knob.

"A pity," rumbled Aris. The gate had no lintel, so the stone giant had no need to stoop as he stepped into the court. He kneeled and gingerly pinched one of the urns between his thumb and forefinger. "Who would do such a thing?"

"A sign of mourning," explained their guide, Hadhrune. A slender man dressed in a flowing black robe, he was swaddled in so much shadow magic that at times he seemed to vanish into his own umbral aura. He used the black staff in his hand to point at the half-completed statue beneath Aris's arm and said, "Your work is of suitable quality that no one would object if you replaced them with your own sculptures."

The giant nodded. "It would be my privilege."

"Indeed, it is always a guest's privilege to increase the wealth of his host with treasures of art," Malik said. He sat on the rim of the central basin and drew a disapproving frown from Hadhrune by using his hands to scoop water into his mouth. "May it please you to stay at my house sometime . . . when the One allows me the funds to purchase one."

"Until then, it is the hope of the Most High that you will find this one adequate," Hadhrune said. He took the dipper from its hook and pointedly offered it to Malik. "Consider it your home."

"Indeed?" Ignoring the dipper, Malik wiped his hands on his tunic and studied the courtyard with an appraising eye. "This is a little cramped for Kelda, but—"

"I am afraid your horse must remain in the stables," Hadhrune sniffed. He turned to Aris and waved his staff around the courtyard. "This is to be Aris's quarters. Will it do? We can have a roof erected, but space so near the palace is at a premium. Outside of the Grand Hall itself, no building in the area is large enough for you."

"I have no need for a roof, thank you." Aris studied the area with a growing look of discomfort, then tried to hide his disappointment and said, "There is room enough for me to sleep."

"Do not fear, my large friend," Hadhrune said. "Sleep is all you need do here. The Most High has declared that you may keep your workshop in the goodshouse where you have been staying. He was quite taken with your depiction of Escanor's fight."

This actually drew a smile from the grim giant. "Then he shall have it when I finish."

"Aris will fill the city with his work, if you let him," Galaeron said, stepping to Hadhrune's side. "When am I to begin my lessons with the Most High?"

Hadhrune ran a black thumbnail along a deeply-worn groove near the head of his staff. "I thought you would first wish to make yourself comfortable in your new home."

"It took you a tenday to find this place," Galaeron said. "I have no time to waste."

"The Most High has been occupied with the war." Hadhrune's amber eyes were burning. "I'm sure you understand."

"What I understand is that he said he would teach me to control my shadow," Galaeron said, "and that *you* turn me away every time I present myself."

Hadhrune's staff rose as though he might strike Galaeron, who felt Vala's hand clamped around his forearm.

"Galaeron, get a hold of yourself!" She dug her fingers into the underside of his wrist and twisted, forcing him to open his hand and release the hilt he had not realized he was grasping. "If he doesn't want you seeing the

Most High, drawing your sword would be just the excuse he needs to see you never do."

Hadhrune gave Vala a thin smile. "I do want him to learn from the Most High," he said. "We all do."

Moving more slowly, he waved his staff over their heads and aimed the tip at the gate, where a dark-haired woman dressed in the robe and veil of the Bedine desert people was attempting to sneak into the courtyard. Judging by her kohl-rimmed eyes—all Galaeron could see of her—she was a little older than Vala and not quite as swarthy as the Shadovar.

"You there," Hadhrune said. "Do you know what we do with thieves in this city?"

The hint of a cringe flashed across the woman's eyes, then she drew herself up straight. "From all I can tell, you harbor them." She spoke Common without a trace of Bedine accent. She locked gazes with Hadhrune and crossed the courtyard, a silver harp-and-moon pinned to her collar growing visible as she drew near. "I am searching for one rumored to keep company with these people."

She regarded Galaeron and Vala as though they did not deserve the honor of her gaze, then glanced past Aris's kneecap and into the shadowy depths of the colonnade. Galaeron was not all that surprised to realize Malik had vanished. The little man had an astonishing capacity for stealth, and he had mentioned his troubles with a certain Harper often enough for Galaeron to guess who this was. Vala caught his eye and barely raised her brow. He flattened his fingers in a signal to wait, and the Bedine Harper looked away, pretending not to see.

If Hadhrune noticed the woman's discretion, he hid it well. "How did you enter Shade Enclave?"

Her dark brows arched. "In the usual way," she said. "I have been serving Princes Clariburnus and Brennus as a desert guide, a position arranged in Waterdeep through Laeral Silverhand and Prince Aglarel. If there are closed districts, they did not inform me when they brought me into the city."

"The district is not closed," Hadhrune clarified, "but it is well guarded."

"And you would know everyone who enters?"

"Yes," Hadhrune answered.

A twinkle came to the woman's eyes, and she said, "I think not."

Galaeron liked her instantly.

"Ruha," he said, "it is a waste of your time to look for Malik with us. He is hardly the sort a wise company welcomes for long."

The witch turned her mocking gaze on Galaeron and said, "If you know who I am, then you must also know I am not so easily fooled. I found his horse in the stables." A small chain of gold dropped out of her sleeve into her cupped hand, though it was done so deftly that Galaeron doubted anyone else had noticed. "A pity—she was such a fine mount."

"Harper shrew!" Malik screamed. "What have you done to my Kelda?"

The little man came charging out of the shadows at her back, a stone loaded in his sling and his arm rising to attack. Ruha spun around deftly, holding the golden chain up before him and uttering a common imprisonment spell.

Galaeron was already halfway through the reversal. He timed his incantation to finish in the same instant as Ruha's, and a bolt of shadow magic rushed up through his body, cold and jolting, raw enough to sting his bones. A cord of brown magic spiraled up Ruha's body, binding her knees to each other and her arms to her sides, then the golden chain vanished from her hands and appeared in Galaeron's.

Malik loosed the stone in his sling. Galaeron gave the chain a quick tug and jerked Ruha out of the way. The rock sailed past, striking Hadhrune square in the chest. The seneschal barely flinched, but Malik's eyes bugged out so far they looked like they might fall from their sockets.

"Your Darkness, a thousand pardons!" he cried. "But surely a man has a right to defend—"

"Enough!" Hadhrune lowered his staff at Malik.

Galaeron cursed under his breath and raised a hand to cast another spell—only to have Vala slap it down.

"Are you mad?"

Hadhrune spoke a word, and a tiny sphere of shadow shot from the tip of his staff and struck the ground at Malik's feet. Malik cried out and tried to leap away, but the dark circle expanded beneath him. When he came down, he fell in as though it was a hole. The shadow circle drew in on itself and vanished from sight.

Aris, who had been watching all this from far above, groaned and dropped to a knee, his big hand already reaching for Hadhrune. The seneschal raised his staff overhead and caught the middle of the giant's hand on its tip.

"There is nothing to be angry about, Aris. Your friend will return shortly."

"He better." Aris removed some of his hand's weight from the staff, but tried to sound threatening. "I owe him my life."

"There is no need to pay today, my large friend," Hadhrune said, lowering his staff. "I just wanted time to sort matters out."

He went to stand in the place where Malik had vanished then motioned Galaeron to bring Ruha over. "Since you all seem to know of each other, perhaps you would be so kind as to enlighten me?"

Ruha glared daggers at Galaeron, then, with her hands still bound by the brown cord of magic, said, "I have no business with the elf or his harlot—"

"Harlot?" Vala stormed. "I've never taken a copper!"

She reached for her darksword and started forward, but stopped at a warning dip of Hadhrune's black staff.

"Let's finish this without bloodshed, shall we?" He turned back to Ruha and asked, "What do you want with Malik?"

"To take him to Twilight Hall to answer for his crimes."

"Which are?"

"More murders than I can count, but including that of Rinda and Gwydion, guardians of the evil *Cyrinishad*, and the theft of that same foul book," Ruha said. "If the Shadovar truly wish to be the good allies to the nations of Faerûn that they claim, you will release me and turn over this miscreant."

"I assure you, our desire is sincere," Hadhrune said, "but I was not aware that the Harpers controlled so many nations."

"We control none," Ruha admitted, "and influence many."

"A distinction we Shadovar understand as well," Hadhrune said, smiling politely. Unlike the grins of the princes and most shadow lords, his did not reveal a mouthful of ceremonial fangs. "We also know there are two sides to every argument. Galaeron, what say you? How would you advise the Most High in this matter?"

Galaeron considered Hadhrune, recalling his distaste for the little man, then said, "I know what you'd like to hear."

"Is that so?" Hadhrune cocked his brow. "Tell me."

"Do you think I'm that far into my shadow?"

Vala grabbed his arm. "Galaeron . . ."

"I know what's right," he said, shaking her off. "I won't betray a loyal companion for access to the palace."

"Galaeron, Hadhrune's not asking you to betray anyone," Vala said.

"I am only asking for the truth," Hadhrune said. "If you cannot see that, you *are* in the grasp of your shadow." Leaving Galaeron to fume, Hadhrune turned and craned his neck up at Aris. "What would you tell the Most High, my friend?"

Kneeling beside the fountain, the giant still loomed over the Shadovar by half again his height. "It's true that Malik serves an evil god," Aris said, "but I am life-debted to him and honor bound to stand with him against any foe."

Hadhrune looked to Vala. "And you?"

"I wouldn't be here, were it not for him."

Galaeron still found it difficult to believe that Hadhrune was truly interested in his opinion, but he had no choice except to trust Vala's judgment over his own. He did not feel as though he was in the grasp of his shadow, but neither had he at the Splicing—and he had just cast a spell.

"Nor would I," Galaeron agreed. "He's saved us all."

"For his own reasons," Ruha interjected. "He's been playing you for fools—just as the Shadovar are now."

Hadhrune's eyes flashed. "You will not help your case by trying to poison the opinions of our guests against us, Harper."

"The truth is not poison." Though Ruha spoke to Hadhrune, she was looking at Galaeron. "You're from Evereska, are you not, Galaeron?"

"What if he is?" Vala demanded.

Ruha's eyes narrowed. "How long has it been since you have been outside this city's murk?"

Galaeron frowned, wondering what the witch was trying to accomplish. "Not that it's any business of yours, but more than a tenday."

Even Ruha's heavy veil could not hide her smirk.

"What?" Galaeron demanded.

The witch looked at Hadhrune.

He glared amber flames at her, then turned to Galaeron and said, "The enclave is moving."

"Moving?" Galaeron echoed. "It's always moving."

"Deeper into the desert," Hadhrune clarified. "Away from Evereska. That's why—"

"Traitors!" Galaeron lunged for the seneschal but went down heavily, Vala on his back. "You promised!"

"And we will keep our promise," Hadhrune said. "The shadowshell has cut the phaerimm off from the Weave. Eventually, they will deplete the magic remaining to them—but it will take time, Galaeron, many months. You know better than anyone that we dare not attack until they have depleted their powers and begun to starve, until they grow too feeble to defend themselves."

"So, you are only abandoning Evereska for a little while?" Ruha asked, her voice surprisingly cynical. "Oh yes, that makes a great deal of sense."

Hadhrune kneeled in front of Galaeron, who was not struggling only because he knew how easily Vala could choke him unconscious with the arm already around his throat.

"We are not abandoning Evereska," Hadhrune said, "but the situation is stable now, and we must think of our own needs as well."

"When were you going to tell me?" Galaeron demanded.

Hadhrune hesitated and looked away.

"It's a fair question," Vala said.

Hadhrune let out a weary sigh. "As you wish," he said. "The Most High thought—"

That was when Malik appeared behind the seneschal, clambering out of a circle of shadow like a cat out of a well. He let out a bloodcurdling scream and dashed half a dozen steps across the courtyard before running into Aris's palm and stopping to see where he was.

Turban half undone, Malik whirled on Hadhrune and said, "If you knew what I had for a heart, you would not think that funny—not at all." Seeming to forget all about Ruha, Malik started toward the seneschal, wagging his finger. "It is a good thing for you that I did not die of fright in there, or the One would surely visit on you a hell a thousand times worse—or else laugh so hard at my miserable fate that he split his rotten sides."

This last admission, forced by Mystra's truth curse, seemed to take the fire out of him. Malik spent a moment taking in the scene in the courtyard, then slipped to Ruha's helpless form and raked his foot down her shin.

"Hag! What did you do to my Kelda?"

Ruha's eyes flared, but she showed no other sign of pain. "Why is it you care more for your horse than for your friends?"

"Because my horse is more loyal," Malik answered. He reached under his robes and pulled out his curved dagger. "Now answer, or your death will be even more painful."

"No!"

Vala and Galaeron were not the only ones to yell this, but it was Hadhrune's staff that came down across the little man's wrists and knocked the dagger from his hands.

"Not here," the Shadovar said. "Murder is as forbidden in Shade Enclave as it is in Waterdeep or Shadowdale." He cast a meaningful glance at Malik. "And our justice is swifter."

"Then you have no choice," Malik complained. "The witch will never leave here until I am dead!"

"Or my prisoner," Ruha clarified.

"That, we will never permit," Aris warned.

Hadhrune considered this for a moment, then shook his head wearily. "You place Shade Enclave in a difficult position, Harper. Either we harbor this miscreant against you, or we allow you to violate our guest guard."

"There is no reason to concern yourself with that," Galaeron said, glaring up at Hadhrune. "We'll be leaving within the hour."

Hadhrune studied Galaeron for a moment, then nodded. "That is your privilege, of course, but as long as you or any of your friends remain in Shade Enclave, Malik is protected as our guest and may not be killed or taken captive."

"You would truly harbor a murderer?" Ruha demanded.

"He has not murdered anyone here," Hadhrune said. He touched his staff to her binding, and the magic cord dissolved. "Nor have you. The same law that guards him guards you—and if something unfortunate should befall either of you, we will know whom to execute."

Again, Hadhrune cast a warning glance at Malik.

"I'm free to stay?" Ruha asked.

"In this very house." Hadhrune seemed unable to avoid smirking. "Shade Enclave would never want it said that we made it difficult for a murderer to be brought to justice."

"Justice?" Malik scoffed. "You have no idea what you're condemning me to!"

"Not for long," Galaeron said. He scowled up at Vala. "If you'll get off of me, that is."

Vala studied him doubtfully. "You're not going to attack?"

"I'm going to *leave*," Galaeron said. "I'm going to go back to Evereska."

Hadhrune motioned Vala off, then offered a hand. "If that is what you wish, but the Most High will be very disappointed tomorrow."

Galaeron ignored the hand and stood on his own.

"He will," Hadhrune insisted. "He wanted to explain himself why the city was moving. That's why I didn't tell you."

"Sure it is." Despite his words, Galaeron took no steps toward the gate. "Tomorrow?"

Hadhrune nodded. "He would like to break fast with you. All will be explained."

Galaeron turned to Vala.

"One more day?" She looked around the villa and shrugged. "What could it hurt?"

✡✡✡✡✡

The humans were at it again, clambering around on Malygris's mountain, kneeling and standing and kneeling again outside his cave, chanting, singing, groveling, begging his favor. That was a snort. He had told Namirrha he didn't want the cult members dallying about outside his lair, but did the mammal listen? What Malygris ought to do was clatter up there and bolt the whole lot, but then he would have to go out and devour something, and he just didn't feel like eating. Dracoliches needed food only to recharge their breath weapons, and Malygris hadn't discharged his (hadn't even left his lair) in over a year—or so Namirrha had told him the last time the necromancer deigned to visit.

Something alive—something human—appeared in the shadows over by his number three platinum heap. A bitter sense of outrage rising to fill his empty ribcage, Malygris swung his big horned skull toward the intrusion. Could the warmbloods leave him not even his seclusion? A pair of dark silhouettes rose, not emerging from the darkness so much as peeling themselves out of it, and turned in his direction.

How the mammals had bypassed his teleport traps, Malygris did not know, or how they had avoided activating his alarm magic. What he *did* know was that he could bear only so much and that this entering of his lair was the final insult. He opened his jaws and loosed a mouthful of lightning. In the crackling flash that filled the cavern, he glimpsed a pair of swarthy humans in dark robes cartwheeling across his hoard and smashing headlong into his wall. They collapsed among his diamonds and lay there scorched, smoking, and—amazingly—more or less alive.

Malygris continued to look in their direction. When Namirrha had made him a dracolich, he had grown acutely aware of everything alive within a wingspread of himself, and he knew the two humans were badly injured. Mammals were fragile, so they seemed likely to die within a few hours anyway, and he was not about to waste another breath attack on them. If he conserved, he still had two good lightning blasts left before he would have to leave his lair and eat.

But the pair did not expire. Instead, over the next hour, they grew steadily stronger, first crawling behind a pile of gold coins fused into a solid lump by the heat of his lightning, then hiding there and recovering by the minute, speaking to each other in some ancient human tongue even Malygris had never before heard. It was the ultimate warmblood insult—not being frightened enough to flee or at least to cower in silence. Malygris would have torn them limb from limb, save that over the last year, his hideless skeleton had sunk to his spine in his nest of sapphires, and he simply did not want to abandon such a comfortable bed.

A voice, deep and booming, at least by human standards, called out in Common, "Most Mighty Malygris, there is no need to attack. We come in peace."

Malygris considered this, then said, "If you come in peace, why do you cower behind my hoard piles like dragon hunters and treasure thieves?"

A soft clinking echoed off the walls as the pair rose from their hiding places. They stepped into view, revealing themselves to be a warrior and a priest, both dressed in the melted remains of some glassy, gleaming black armor.

Malygris blasted them again.

This time, his electric fury pinned them to the wall and held them there, stiff-limbed and smoking, the warrior's steel-colored eyes and the priest's bronze-colored eyes glowing like mage-light. Their glossy armor ran off their bodies in runnels and gathered at their feet in black puddles. Their swarthy flesh melted and burned away from their chests, revealing the black organs and dusky bones beneath. Their heels and fists hammered themselves into pulp against the stone wall.

Still they were alive when Malygris ran out of breath—limp as scarecrows and reeking of charred flesh and in places naked to the bone, but alive. They dropped to the floor and lay there groaning for half an hour, then finally grew strong enough to pull themselves behind treasure piles as they had before.

Interesting.

It was the first thing that had interested Malygris since Namirrha had gotten his mate, Verianthraxa, killed in the senseless attack upon the keepists—an assault forced upon them by Namirrha's profane magic. Malygris searched out his legs beneath his nest of sapphires and bade them serve. He lifted himself out of the gems and clacked his fleshless bones across the cavern to where the two humans lay cowering.

No, not cowering.

The two were sitting, propped against the wall, staring up at him with their little molten eyes, not even trembling. The charred chest bones that had been exposed just moments before were already covered with dark flesh, and the scars were vanishing from even that. Malygris snatched up one in each claw, then watched in amazement as their shattered hands and feet returned to their normal shapes.

"What manner of human are you that heal like trolls?" he demanded.

"We are princes of Shade Enclave," said the bronze-eyed one. "I am Clariburnus. My brother is Brennus."

"Do you think your names matter to me? Your arrogance is insufferable!" Malygris squeezed the one that had called itself Clariburnus and was pleased to hear the crackle of breaking bones. He felt the body go limp in his hand, but that was the only way he knew the mammal was in pain. He swung his bony muzzle toward the one with the eyes of steel. "I asked *what* you are, not who."

"We call ourselves Shadovar," this one said. "In our tongue it means 'of the shade.' "

"Ah, then you are shades." Malygris said. Shades were two-legged mammals who traded their souls for shadow essence. In the light of day, they seemed normal men, but as the light grew dim, they grew strong. "I understand now. I have met a few shades in my centuries."

Curiosity satisfied, he tightened his grasp to crush them—and felt his claws close on air. He sensed them emerging behind him and whirled around to find the steel-eyed one stepping from the shadows in front of his nest. The other, the one with the crushed body, lay in a hollow on top.

They were between him and his phylactery.

"Clariburnus and I are shades," the one with steel eyes said. "But not all Shadovar are shades, and not all shades are Shadovar. A Shadovar is a citizen of Shade Enclave."

"I see your game." Malygris started forward, his great tail launching whole mountains of coins into the dark air as it flailed back and forth. "Try, then. One way or the other, I will take pleasure in the end."

The steel-eyed one—Brennus—raised his hand and said, "Stop. We're not here to attack you, but you are done attacking us."

Malygris stopped, not because the human had commanded it—he hadn't—but because he found himself snorting in laughter. "You threaten me?" Tiny forks of lightning began to dance around his nasal cavities. "Truly?"

"We are not threatening." This from the crushed one, who had already healed enough to sit upright. "We came to talk."

"Talk?" Malygris settled onto his haunches and waved a claw at the floor before him. "Very well, you may present your gifts."

The two humans—Shadovar—glanced at each other, then Brennus said, "We bring you no gifts."

"No gifts?" Malygris gasped. Even more interesting—insulting, but interesting. "How can you beg without gifts? How can you grovel with nothing to offer?"

"We're not here to beg," Clariburnus said. He stood—so soon after being crushed—and limped down to stand beside his companion. "But Shade Enclave does have something to offer."

Malygris sensed Namirrha's arrival within the lair and whirled toward the entrance. The necromancer, a balding and wrinkled figure even by mammal standards, was already well inside, striding down the golden aisle between Malygris's carefully stacked chalices.

"You warmbloods!" he hissed. "Do you all think my lair yours for the entering?"

Namirrha made a show of appearing frightened, stopping to steeple his fingertips together and bow deeply. "A thousand pardons, Sacred One. I was informed that you have been hurling lightning about and thought you might be in need of assistance."

The necromancer cast a meaningful eye at the Shadovar.

"You think I need the assistance of a human?" Malygris sneered. "When that is so, you will scatter my bones across the Blight."

"As you command, Sacred One," Namirrha replied.

As Malygris had known he would, the necromancer stroked his amulet, and all of Malygris's anger drained away.

Malygris hated that, really *hated* it, but there was nothing to be done about it. He could no sooner attack Namirrha than he could regrow his long-rotted hide and scales. He was the necromancer's creature from nosebone to tailbone, and the fact that the sly old warmblood took pains to make it seem otherwise only added insult to injury.

Still, Malygris found himself saying, "Perhaps you can serve me, however. These shade things—" He flicked a claw in the Shadovars' direction. "—have come with an offer."

Namirrha's white brows rose. "Have they?" He advanced along Malygris's flank—a somewhat long journey that took the better part of a minute—and stopped across from the Shadovar. "And what is it that Shade Enclave wishes to offer Mighty Malygris, Suzerain of the Blight and all its wyrms?"

The two Shadovar glanced at each other, then Clariburnus shrugged and said, "We would be happy to remove the Zhentarim from Anauroch."

"Remove them?" Malygris growled. "What will my followers eat? I would sooner remove you—"

"What harm will it do to hear them out, Sacred One?" Again, Namirrha stroked his amulet, and again a numb calmness descended over Malygris. A smirk came to the necromancer's face, and he asked, "And in return for this small service, what do the Shadovar wish?"

"The service is more than a small one," Brennus said, addressing himself directly to Namirrha, "and so is what we expect in return: peace with the dragons, and their aid in the war against the phaerimm."

Malygris craned his neck to look down at Namirrha. "There is a war against the phaerimm?"

"Have I not suggested that you get out more, Sacred One?" Namirrha replied. "They have escaped their prison and captured the Shaeradim."

"Evereska's Shaeradim?" Malygris snorted in amusement. "The LastHaven of the elves? Well done, I say. Let them have it!"

Again Namirrha reached for his amulet. Malygris tried to flick a claw out to stop him, but found his foot too heavy, his toe too stiff.

"The matter is not as simple as that, Mighty One," Namirrha said. "The phaerimm pose a danger to us all. Even your shipments have been forced to detour far north or south."

"Ah, the shipments." Though Malygris had no idea what shipments the necromancer meant—and would not have cared if he did—he found himself nodding sagely. "We mustn't let them interfere with my shipments."

Namirrha smiled at the Shadovar. "If Malygris commits, the host he will bring to this war is without rival. Surely, his aid is worth more than simply driving the Zhentarim from Anauroch."

"How much more?" Clariburnus asked.

Namirrha grew serious. "Malygris would like to see them gone—wiped from the face of Faerûn."

"Then let Malygris do it himself, if his host is so mighty," Brennus said. "The Shadovar will not."

"Will not?" Namirrha demanded. "Or can not?"

The eyes of both Shadovar flared. "It is the same to you," Brennus growled. "We did not return to Faerûn to fight the Cult of the Dragon's battles for them. If you will not strike a bargain, you may be certain the Zhentarim will."

Namirrha stepped forward, perhaps trusting more than was wise to Malygris's imposing presence to back him up. "Then why aren't you speaking with the Zhentarim instead of me?"

Clariburnus craned his neck to look up. "Because the Zhentarim don't have Malygris."

"If it is my help you seek, then you should have brought gifts," Malygris rumbled, angered at being so obviously cut out of the negotiations. He knew as well as anyone who was in control of him, but he insisted on appearances. He still had that much pride. "You should be begging me."

"There is no need for that, Malygris." Namirrha stroked his accursed amulet. "This is something I should negotiate for you."

"Fine," Malygris said, and he meant it.

The Shadovar said nothing and stared at Namirrha.

Namirrha remained silent for several moments, then nodded and said, "Done." He offered his hand to Brennus. "We have a bargain."

The Shadovar stared at the appendage as though he wasn't quite sure what should be done with it, then glanced over the necromancer's shoulder at Malygris. "The Mighty One will honor the deal?"

Namirrha nodded and stroked his amulet. "Of course."

"Good." Brennus smiled broadly, baring a mouthful of needle-tip fangs that even Malygris had to envy. "Done."

The Shadovar clasped Namirrha's hand then, in a move so swift even Malygris hardly saw it, pulled him forward onto the blade of a glassy black dagger. Namirrha screamed in surprise and tried to call on his servant for help, but the Shadovar's hand was over his mouth in a black blur, and Malygris felt no urge at all to defend the necromancer. Brennus finished the attack by first pushing his black blade down to Namirrha's crotch, then splitting him up the center and letting the two halves of the body fall separately.

When he was done, the accursed amulet was hanging from the back side of his dark blade. This he dropped at Malygris's feet.

"There is your gift, Malygris."

Malygris eyed the amulet warily, as he did the bloody mess in which the Shadovar stood. "If you think to ingratiate yourself with your warmblood treachery—"

"We think to avenge the insult he paid us by implying that Shade was not the equal of a piteous bunch of wretches like the Zhentarim," Clariburnus said, "and the insult he paid you as well, in treating the Blue Suzerain like a trained attack dog."

Had Malygris still had lips, he would have smiled. "For that I thank you—but why should I honor the bargain he made? My dragons need Zhents to eat."

"They will have plenty to eat in the war," Brennus said. "That I promise you."

"If you think on it, you will find yourself still bound by Namirrha's promise," Clariburnus said. "You sold yourself to the Cult of the Dragon, and even we princes of Shade cannot free you now."

CHAPTER FOUR

9 Mirtul, the Year of Wild Magic

Night in Shade Enclave came as a deepening of the general murk, when the air grew heavy and tepid and drew in on itself in inky mist. Galaeron sat on the balcony outside Villa Dusari's master bedchamber, not keeping watch, but watching. Despite the hour, the steady murmur and clatter of passing traffic growled up out of the ebony gloom, just loud enough to keep a company of restless householders from their pillows. Aris was down in the lower warrens of the city, plinking away in his workshop. Ruha was skulking about the house searching for Malik, who was obviously somewhere other than his chamber. Only Vala was in bed, on the other side of the door from where Galaeron sat. She was not sleeping, just staring into the blade of her black sword, a wistful smile on her full lips and a softness in her eyes alien to them during the day.

She was, Galaeron knew, looking in on her son in Vaasa. At night, her darksword often lulled her into a trance and showed her what was happening in the bedchambers of the Granite Tower—'dream walking' she called it, though it was more akin to spying. During their months together, he had learned to read her expression and tell when she was visiting Sheldon. That the sword seemed to be looking in on the boy more often these days was one of few things that made Galaeron think the weapon might not be entirely sinister.

Though he did not begrudge Vala these glimpses of her son, Galaeron did envy them. His own father and sister were lost to the fog of war—dead or beyond reach, he did not know which. The Swords of Evereska's desperate attempt to save the gate at the Rocnest had already become the stuff of legend. By all accounts, Aubric Nihmedu had been leading the charge, and Galaeron was not fool enough to believe a mere bladesinger likely to survive any combat in which Khelben Arunsun—one of Mystra's Chosen—had vanished without a trace.

His sister, Keya, remained trapped in Evereska—though Galaeron could not be certain of even that much, as the phaerimm had long ago stopped all communication with the LastHaven by raising a magic deadwall around the Shaeradim. He could hardly bear to think of his little sister—at eighty, barely an adult—sitting alone in Treetop, sad and frightened, probably hungry and perhaps even in despair, while outside the phaerimm circled the city waiting for a chance to enter. Yet, the alternative—that the mythal had already collapsed and Evereska fallen—was too horrible to contemplate.

And it was Galaeron's doing—the escape of the phaerimm, the besieging of Evereska, the whole war. He had caused it in one of those terrible moments a person replayed in his mind a thousand times, telling himself that if he had done this or said that or just left it all alone, everything would have been fine. Instead, Galaeron and his Tomb Guards had followed a band of crypt-breakers down into the long-forgotten workings of a dwarven mine and found Vala and her Vaasan warriors preparing to rendezvous with their shadow mage master, Melegaunt Tanthul. In the confusion that followed, Galaeron had given the order that breached the Sharn Wall, nearly two dozen men and elves had died, and the phaerimm had escaped to begin their assault on Evereska.

Vala and the Shadovar had told him a hundred times that he had only been performing his duty and wasn't to blame, but their words could not change what had happened—or how he felt about it. Eager to undo his mistake, Galaeron had joined forces with Vala and her shadow mage master and set out to summon the only help that seemed capable of defeating the evil he had unleashed. Along the way, he had learned to use shadow magic and had overreached his limits, opening himself to the corrupting influences of the Shadow Weave and beginning a desperate battle against his own shadow for the possession of his spirit. At every step of the way, it seemed, he had made the wrong decision, and now that he could not be certain whether the thoughts running through his mind belonged to him or his shadow self, he was almost afraid to decide anything at all.

But there was one thing he knew for certain, one decision he knew to be his own. He would do anything to save Evereska, make any sacrifice to amend his terrible mistake.

Galaeron settled back and tried to clear his mind, but found himself too agitated. His thoughts kept returning to the morning, wondering whether

Hadhrune would arrange the promised audience or find yet another excuse to put it off—and whether the Most High's help would be the solution to his shadow problems, or just one more mistake. Certainly, it did not bode well that the Shadovar had concealed the fact that Shade Enclave was moving away from Evereska. But even Galaeron could see how his shadow would have used that information to feed his suspicions and make him distrust the one most able to help him win his spirit back.

While there was a time when he could have stilled his thoughts by retreating into the Reverie, Galaeron had lost touch with that facet of elf nature when he allowed his shadow to invade. Instead of slipping into a semilucid trance of memories and the shared emotions of other elves, he sank into the same insensible, nightmare-filled slumber as humans.

But this night, even sleep would not come. He passed the black hours staring out into the darkness, listening to the city clatter past beneath his balcony, replaying the same thoughts and doubts over and over again until the gloom paled from night-ebony to dawn-gray and Aris came striding out of the murk carrying his statue of Escanor's battle against the phaerimm.

Already completed, the piece was Aris's finest yet, so flowing it seemed in danger of writhing from the giant's hands. The prince's figure was noble and majestic, one hand still stretched toward the phaerimm he had just killed as he twisted around to face his new attacker. The creature itself was connected to him by the tail piercing his abdomen, and also by two hands wrapped around his throat, an artistic license taken to impart the impression that the beast was hovering beside him unsupported.

"Aris, it's magnificent!" Vala said, joining Galaeron on the balcony as the stone giant stepped into the courtyard. "You did that in one night?"

"I could not have finished without Malik," Aris said. The statue was at balcony level, and the giant was speaking down from above. He half-turned toward the empty gate. "He did most of the polishing."

"And what has this favor cost you?" demanded Ruha, stepping out of the colonnade to meet them. "An arm or a soul?"

"That is no business of yours, shrew," Malik said. "You cannot be expected to understand what one friend does for another, since you have none of your own." He craned his neck up toward the balcony. "You would do well to make yourselves decent. The prince is on his way here."

"The prince?" Galaeron asked. "Which one?"

"Escanor, of course," Malik said. "If you are wise, you will benefit by my experience and do nothing to encourage him to return. There is no thief worse than a royal."

Galaeron glanced at Vala, who merely shrugged and turned to don her armor—by Vaasan standards, a far superior mode of dress to any of the dusky gowns Hadhrune's servants had delivered. Galaeron opted for his scout's cloak, as even the coarsest Evereskan cloth was considered extravagant by non-elves.

By the time they had changed and joined the others in the courtyard, Escanor's entourage was pouring through the gate. Tall even by Shadovar standards, the prince was visible in the middle of the group, his coppery eyes glaring out over the heads of his escorts. Galaeron and the others dropped to a knee and waited while the guards took their stations around the perimeter of the courtyard.

Escanor went directly to Aris's statue and circled it slowly, running his fingers over its smooth stone. When he came to where the tail barb punctured his stomach, he winced visibly and turned away, craning his neck to address the kneeling giant.

"Very lifelike," he said. Though Escanor had spent three days in bed recovering from the removal of the phaerimm egg, he showed no sign of weakness. "I could swear it's moving."

"Thank you," Aris said. "That means much, coming from you."

"In truth, I am so fond of it I would like it for my villa," Escanor said. He motioned an unarmored servant forward. "Mees will pay whatever you think fair."

"Pay?" Aris seemed to puzzle over this for a moment, then said, "Unfortunately, I have already promised this piece to Hadhrune."

A collective gasp went up from the entourage, then Escanor snapped, "To Hadhrune?"

"For the Most High, Esteemed Prince," Malik said quickly. "Though I am sure Aris can make another in no time at all, especially considering that price is of little concern."

"Another?" Aris echoed. "Why should there be two?"

"There are many good reasons," Malik said, daring to rise and start toward Escanor's entourage without permission. "I'll tell them all to you later, but first let me speak with the prince's steward."

Escanor motioned his guards to stand down and glared at the little man as he crossed the courtyard. When Malik had nearly reached the steward, the prince said, "Malik, would you really want to affront the Most High by copying a palace treasure?"

Malik's face went pale. He began to stammer an apology, but Escanor waved him silent and started across the courtyard, motioning for the others to rise.

"Seeing the statue was only one of the reasons I asked to show you the way to the palace." He stopped in front of Vala and took her hands in his own. "I wanted to thank you for saving my life. Rapha tells me you were really quite the trazt fiend."

Vala actually blushed, and Galaeron instantly resented the way her green eyes held the prince's gaze.

"It was nothing," she said, leaving her hands in Escanor's. "Your attacker was distracted."

Galaeron edged closer to Vala. "You turned away at the wrong time, Prince, or you could have killed it yourself while it was teleport-dazed."

"Yes, a pity I could not read your mind," Escanor said, fixing his coppery gaze on Galaeron and releasing Vala's hands. "You were right to hold the phaerimm in the cavern. It would have been dangerous to let them escape with the secret of the Splicing."

Leaving Galaeron to fume, Escanor turned to face Ruha. "You are the Harper pursuing Malik?"

"I am."

Escanor regarded the little man as though he found this difficult to believe. "Is he really such a terrible criminal?"

"It would not do to underestimate him, Prince," Ruha said. "Those who do often pay for the mistake with their lives."

This drew a fang-filled smirk from Escanor. "Then I am glad you are here to watch him, Harper, but mark well Hadhrune's warning—Malik has committed no crime in this city, and if he does, it will be our justice that settles the matter."

Ruha inclined her head. "My only desire is to see that he does no more harm than he already has."

"Good." Escanor turned to Vala and gestured toward the gate. "If you and your friends care to accompany Galaeron, it would please the Most High for you to see the palace this morning."

Vala nodded and started forward. Galaeron stepped to her side, making sure to place himself between her and Escanor as the others closed around them. Whether the prince noticed the maneuver was impossible to say, but Vala's frown was unmistakable.

As the entourage left the gate, she leaned in close and whispered, "Your shadow is showing, Galaeron. What do you think is going to happen?"

"Nothing I can help."

A twinkle came to Vala's green eyes, and she surprised him by smiling. "So you *are* jealous."

"Elves don't feel jealousy—and even if we did, there's nothing to be jealous about," he said. Though the feelings they shared for each other had grown too strong to hide over the last few months, Galaeron remained reluctant to act on them. Not only was Vala a human who would grow old before his eyes, she had promised to stay with him only until his shadow crisis ended—or she was forced to end it for him. After that, she would be returning to her son in Vaasa, and Galaeron did not think a few months of love worth the heartbreak of watching her leave—that was going to be hard enough already. "I don't want you to forget your promise."

"Why would I?" Vala asked.

Galaeron shrugged. "Because the prince is powerful and wealthy, and you humans have such a weakness for fleeting pleasures."

"Galaeron," she said, shaking her head wearily, "fleeting pleasures are not weaknesses! They're the stuff of life."

Vala looked away, and the entourage continued up the street. Paved in a duller version of the same black stone that lay in Villa Dusari's courtyard, the avenue was narrow and winding, meandering through a canyon-like labyrinth of dusky buildings so tall that even Aris had to crane his neck to look up at many of the residents who called greetings and fond wishes to Escanor as the procession passed. There were not many side streets, and those that they did intersect always ran uphill to the left and downhill to the right. It slowly grew apparent to Galaeron that they were spiraling up a gentle mound, though one so encrusted in looming structures that its terrain was all but impossible to discern. As they ascended, the villas grew ever larger and more magnificent, eventually becoming so enormous that it took the entourage close to a minute to pass by.

As they passed one of the largest, a many-spired mansion with flying buttresses and a line of long barrel vaults leading into the shadowed interior, Prince Escanor stopped long enough to wave in its direction.

"My abode," he said. "I hope you will attend me here soon, when we are not quite so occupied with our war duties."

Though Escanor took pains to address himself to all his guests, Galaeron—or his shadow—knew that the invitation was meant primarily for Vala. Biting back the urge to suggest that the invitation would come the first time only Vala was free to answer, he merely looked up the street and inquired how much farther it was to the Palace of the Most High.

Escanor waved him on. "Not far."

Indeed it was not. Just past the prince's home, the street opened into a broad hilltop piazza surrounded by similar mansions, all with their grandest entrances facing center. In a ring around the plaza stood a forest of gloom sculptures, all rooted in urns of polished obsidian with a single ribbon of shadow rising in the ever-shifting figure of a Shadovar warrior or wizard.

Not far from Escanor's mansion stood the only likeness Galaeron recognized, that of the Shadovar who had helped cause the release of the phaerimm, Melegaunt Tanthul.

"The Ring of Heroes," Escanor said, waving his hand at the wall of figures. "Everyone represented here died accomplishing some great service to Shade Enclave."

"There must thousands!" Vala gasped.

"Tens of thousands," Escanor said. "Shade Enclave is an ancient city with ancient enemies, and much of our time in the shadow plane was spent defending ourselves from the assaults of the malaugrym."

"The malaugrym!" Ruha gasped. "Then the phaerimm must seem weak enemies to you, indeed."

"Different, but not weak. The first rule in the shadow plane is never to underestimate an enemy," Escanor said. He turned to Aris. "If you wish, I will have someone teach you to read the stories of the gloom sculptures in their changing shapes."

This drew a rare smile from the giant. "No gift would please me more."

The prince had only to glance in his steward's direction, and Mees said, "It shall be done this day."

Escanor nodded and turned to Galaeron. "You are wondering what Melegaunt's story says about you?"

Galaeron shook his head. "Only if it'll say he's honored for drawing Evereska and Waterdeep into the war against the phaerimm."

Vala started to hiss a reproach, but Escanor stopped her with a raised hand. "We must expect him to be suspicious." Despite the prince's patient words, the color of his eyes had deepened to angry red. "I think we should hurry to the Most High. Galaeron's shadow is making him foolish as well as distrustful, and that is a bad sign."

Escanor led them through a hundred paces of gloom sculptures and emerged on the far side of the Ring of Heroes. Directly ahead stood the dusky grandeur of the Palace Most High, its seamless walls fashioned of polished obsidian, and its shadowed spires vanishing into the umbral haze above. Like so much in Shade Enclave, it seemed all sinuous curves and exaggerated proportions, with a shape that could not be named, nor even held in mind for more than a passing impression. Paying no noticeable attention as a company of Shadovar spell-guards snapped to attention, Escanor steered his entourage into a keel-arched portal so high that Aris barely had to duck his head.

After passing through a short vaultway, the entryway opened into a vast hall of glassy curves and dusky translucence where every buttress soared into darkness and each corridor vanished into shadow. A hundred or more highborn Shadovar drifted in and out of the doorways, or stood rasping in tight knots of conversation, or sat patiently on the benches along the walls, their gem-colored eyes glowing bright against the murk at their backs. Ignoring the bustle of murmured greetings and inquisitive stares shot the entourage's way as it passed, Escanor marched his group down the center of the floor to a crowded seating area outside an enormous pair of guarded doors.

The detachment commander kneeled and informed Escanor that he had already sent word of the prince's arrival. A few moments later, one the doors opened and Hadhrune slipped out to inform them that the Most High was engaged and would see them as soon as he was able.

Escanor's eyes looked as though they might burn holes through the chamberlain. "You informed him that I am here with the elf?"

Hadhrune met the prince's angry gaze without flinching. "He is with—"

"Did I ask who he was with?" Escanor growled, stepping toward the door.

Hadhrune turned to cut him off. "I'll announce you now."

"We'll be right behind you," Escanor said, catching the door as the chamberlain tried to close it. "The elf should begin his studies at once."

"Of course."

Hadhrune waved Galaeron and his companions through, but Mees, Rapha, and the rest of the prince's entourage remained behind. Galaeron and company found themselves in a room even murkier than the great reception hall, where the gloom fell on their skin like ash and wisps of shadowstuff floated past in long smoky ribbons. As Hadhrune and Escanor marched the group forward, the voices of unseen whisperers rose and fell in the surrounding darkness, and cold chilblains rose to prickle Galaeron's skin.

Finally, they approached a set of whispers that did not fade and, as they continued walking, eventually hardened into the fuller tones of normal speech. Galaeron recognized one speaker as a female and the other as the voice that had addressed him in the Wing Court. Before they drew near enough to understand what was being said, Hadhrune had them kneel and press their brows to the floor.

The two voices ceased murmuring, then the air grew chill and motionless.

"I know how busy the war is keeping you, Escanor," the Most High said. His voice was as sibilant and forceful as before. "My thanks for bringing these to me."

If the prince replied, Galaeron did not hear it.

Instead, Hadhrune said, "I have arranged an offering from the giant, Mighty One."

"An offering? Let us see."

The air grew less chill as the Most High moved away, then Escanor's feet appeared beside Galaeron's head.

"Have you power enough over your shadow to keep a civil tongue, elf?"

"If he doesn't, I can hold it for him," Vala said.

Escanor considered this, then said, "Good. Rise."

Galaeron and the others stood and found themselves facing a set of stairs at the base of a murk-swaddled dais. Escanor pointed toward the rear of the party.

"It is customary to face the Most High when in his presence."

Galaeron turned and saw a gloom-shrouded figure standing next to Aris's ankle, cowled head turned toward the statue. He began to circle it slowly, nodding in approval as he took it in. Galaeron glimpsed a pair of platinum eyes shining out from beneath the Most High's hood, but that was all of his face that could be seen.

After completing a full circuit, he stopped at Aris's ankle again. The murk in front of his body swirled and there was a clapping noise, then he tipped his head back to address the giant—and Galaeron still could not see his face.

"Truly, you are the equal of any gloom-shaper in the enclave," the Most High said. "I shall be proud to display this in the Gallery of Treasures with the city's finest works."

"You honor me beyond my skill," Aris rumbled. "If you could have seen the story galleries at Thousand Faces before they were destroyed, you would know how feeble my talents truly are."

"The phaerimm have taken much from us all," said the Most High. "I am sure their destruction cannot replace what you lost, but know that they will pay for it with more than their lives."

"So Melegaunt promised, and so am I here," Aris said. "Thank you."

Malik astonished Galaeron and—judging by the gasps of surprise—everyone else by appearing out of the gloom behind Aris's legs. "I also come bearing gifts," he said, reaching beneath his robes. "The One has charged me—"

"Stop!" Ruha was instantly rushing toward him, tossing sand at his hidden hand and uttering some kind of Bedine nature magic.

Before she made it far enough for Galaeron to infer what spell she meant to cast, the Most High gestured in her direction, and she was entwined in half a dozen murky tendrils. Her veil continued to flutter as she spoke her incantation, but the only thing that came out from beneath it were clouds of dark vapor.

"Did Hadhrune not warn you, Harper?" the Most High asked. "What Malik does here is no concern of yours."

Malik smirked in the witch's direction, then, still holding his hand beneath his robe, turned back to the Most High. "As I was saying, the One—"

"Your gift will have to wait until later." The Most High moved away from the little man. "Hadhrune will arrange a time. Now, I really must start with Galaeron. If you others will excuse us, Rapha and Mees are waiting to tour the palace with you."

So saying, he turned and vanished into the murk.

Escanor motioned Vala toward the others. "Feel free to enjoy the tour with the others. Galaeron will be fine with us."

Vala stepped closer to Galaeron's side. "That's not going to happen."

"It is." As polite as was Escanor's smile, it was also filled with fangs. "You have no need to worry while he is in the company of the Most High. The shadow has not been cast that Telamont Tanthul cannot tame."

"Tanthul?" Galaeron gasped. "The same as Melegaunt Tanthul?"

The prince nodded. "And Escanor Tanthul," he said. "All the Princes of Shade are Tanthuls."

Telamont's sibilant voice filled the murk around them. "Escanor!"

Escanor bowed briefly to Vala, then took Galaeron's arm and led him away.

"Galaeron?" Vala called.

"I'll be . . . fine," Galaeron said, choking on the last word. Whether he was excited or frightened even he could not tell, but his heart had risen so far into his throat that he could barely draw breath around it. "We'll meet back at the villa."

"When?"

"When he is finished," Escanor said. "I will bring him myself."

They passed the statue and vanished into the darkness, then emerged a dozen steps later on what felt like the mezzanine of a very high, very large atrium. Through the hole in the center, he saw what looked like half the continent of Faerûn lying spread out beneath him, from the Sword Coast in the west as far east as the great Shoal of Thirst in the desert Anauroch, from the ruins of Arabel in the south to the High Ice in the north. At the moment, most of the land west of Anauroch lay hidden beneath storm clouds, while all to the east was brown and parched with an uncharacteristic drought.

"I have brought you to our war room to show why Shade Enclave is moving away from Evereska," said Telamont Tanthul's wispy voice. "You wish to know."

"I do," Galaeron said.

"You suspect us of betraying my son's promise," Telamont continued.

Galaeron bit his tongue, fighting the urge to say that he *knew* they were.

"Speak freely," Telamont urged. "In the war room, no opinion is dismissed lightly."

"Very well." Galaeron's throat was so dry that the words stuck at the bottom. "As Netherese, you lost Anauroch to the phaerimm once."

He paused there, trying to sort out what he believed from what his shadow believed—but Telamont was in no mood to wait.

"And you believe Melegaunt intentionally loosed the phaerimm on Evereska so that Waterdeep and the rest of Faerûn would be drawn into our war," the Most High continued. "Say what you mean, elf. The only way to live with your shadow is to give it a voice."

"Did you?" Galaeron asked, anger rising.

Telamont remained silent for a time, and Galaeron began to hear other voices around the rim of the war room—whispering quietly or discussing heatedly, sometimes even laughing or shouting—but when he looked toward the voices, he never saw more than a few pairs of glowing eyes, usually gem-colored, but sometimes the metallic of a royal prince.

A few moments later, Telamont Tanthul finally responded. "Drawing the elves into the war would certainly have been a useful thing to do, but *you* were the one who breached the Sharn Wall. How could we have foreseen that?"

How, indeed? Galaeron wondered—then, "By breaking a crypt. Melegaunt may not have known I would come, but he knew someone would."

"That is certainly a possibility," Telamont admitted, "but could even we Shadovar be clever enough to be sure that you would cast the proper spell at the proper time?"

"And if we are, wouldn't you rather have us as allies than enemies?" Escanor asked.

"If you are allies," Galaeron said, struggling to focus on the question at hand. "So far, I have seen little enough proof of that."

"Have you?" Telamont asked. "Look again."

Galaeron returned his gaze to the continent below and was surprised to find himself looking at nothing but storm clouds. As he watched, the clouds grew larger and darker, with flashes of lightning stabbing through their roiling heads. Then he was through, diving into a vast, rain-soaked swamp where hundreds of lizardmen were swarming a much smaller company of Shadovar.

"The Marsh of Chelimber, on the far side of the Greycloaks," Telamont said, just a trace of pride in his voice. "You see, Shade Enclave does not need to be near to project its strength. Our warriors are shades who can walk the shadows and cross the breadth of Faerûn at will. Evereska will not suffer for our absence."

Armed as the Shadovar were with shadow magic and shadow weapons, the shade warriors were holding their own against the primitive lizardmen. Galaeron would even have gone so far as to say it looked like they would carry the day—but it was not like lizardmen to march so steadfastly to their deaths, and never in the even ranks of a disciplined army. There was something forcing them to attack, something that made them hate the Shadovar beyond all reason—or something they feared more.

"Can you call them out?" Galaeron asked, not bothering to conceal the panic in his voice.

"That will not be necessary," said the gravely voice of Prince Rivalen. "We are not afraid to lose a life or two in defense of our allies, and the scaly ones will lose an army."

Galaeron looked up and saw Rivalen's horn-helmed figure coming down the balcony, then found himself shaking his head. "There's more to this battle than we're seeing," he said. "You're the ones who lose—and to the warrior, unless you act quickly."

Escanor asked, "You know this?"

Galaeron nodded. "I do."

"How?" demanded Rivalen.

Galaeron could only shrug. "I don't know how I know, only that I do."

Escanor and Rivalen exchanged glances, and Escanor asked, "As you did at the Splicing?"

Galaeron considered this, then reluctantly shook his head. "It's a feeling, but not as strong. It just makes sense—lizardmen don't fight like that. Something must be driving them."

"Phaerimm?" asked Rivalen. "We always expected a few would be outside the shell when Escanor raised it."

"I am the one who raised it," Galaeron said, angry that the Shadovar kept slighting the role he had played in the Splicing. "And it's not the phaerimm. This is too direct for them." The words seemed to be spilling from his mouth of their own accord. "They prefer to remain hidden and work through intermediaries. It must be a beholder, or maybe a squad of illithids."

Both princes turned toward the Most High. Astonished at having won the argument so easily, Galaeron did likewise—and found Telamont Tanthul standing only a few paces away, his platinum eyes glaring down out of the depths of his cowl. Galaeron still could not make out the shape of his face, or even whether the Most High was bearded like Melegaunt or clean shaven like most of the other princes.

Telamont looked over Galaeron's head to the princes and said, "Our question has been answered."

No sooner had he spoken than the Shadovar company began to bleed into the flashing shadows of the lightning storm, leaving the astonished lizardmen free to overrun the position—and the beholder that suddenly grew visible behind their lines so angry that it began to spray its disintegration ray around at random. Galaeron glared at the scene for a moment, then turned to find Telamont Tanthul still staring down at him with those platinum eyes.

"You were with Melegaunt when he died," Telamont said. "Something passed between you."

"I blanked out," Galaeron gasped, recalling the confused battle in which Melegaunt perished. "When I came to, he was gone."

"Not gone." Telamont drifted closer, until he was near enough to raise a murky sleeve and lay something dark and cold on Galaeron's shoulder. "Through you, he still serves."

"That's why you brought me here?" The air was so cold and still that Galaeron was finding it difficult to breathe. "Because Melegaunt passed his knowledge of the phaerimm to me?"

"That is not a bad thing," Escanor said. "Partners in need forge the strongest alliances."

CHAPTER FIVE

14 Mirtul, the Year of Wild Magic

In the dark sky, the sun was but an ashen disk peering over Eastpeak's craggy shoulder, too weak to burn through the dusky mantle Evereska's enemies had drawn over the Shaeradim, too pale to feed the few light-starved buds dauntless enough to emerge on the scorched and withered stalks of the Vine Vale. Murky as the morning was, it was bright enough for Keya Nihmedu's elf eyes to make out the faint swirl of ash and dust drifting down the other side of the Meadow Wall. A couple of lance-lengths from her hiding tree, it was moving slowly, quietly, and carefully, bouncing along Evereska's protective mythal, trying again and again to cross the boundary into the untouched fields beyond.

Every instinct screamed at Keya to throw off her camouflage and flee for the cliff gates. She stayed. The mythal would protect her, and she had promised to be there when Khelben and the Vaasans returned. *If* they returned. Keya looked at the pale disk in the sky and wondered if even the Chosen of Mystra could be that good. A full night among the phaerimm.

The swirl halted in front of Keya's tree, so faint she began to doubt she was seeing it. Perhaps the whorl had been just a breeze stirring up ash as it rolled down the Meadow Wall. Not every dust devil dancing down a scorched terrace was an invisible phaerimm—but a lot of them were. Had she been at her post inside one of the city towers, Keya could have waved a wand and known at once what she was looking at, but the thornbacks could see mystic energy the way dwarves saw body heat, and so the Long Watch did not use any magic—did not even carry it—this close to the boundary.

The swirl vanished, but Keya could still hear dead vine stalks stirring in the breeze and the distinct sibilation of air moving over the stones of the Meadow Wall, and she *knew*. The phaerimm were surrounded by an aura of moving air, which they used to communicate among themselves in a strange language of whistles and roars. There was not just one invisible thornback pausing on his circuit of the mythal—there were two, whispering quietly, lurking directly in front of Keya's tree—the same tree she had told Khelben Arunsun and the Vaasans to mark as their rendezvous point when they returned to the city.

Keya remained in her hollow in the linden's thick trunk, standing behind her screen of bark, hardly daring to breathe. She spent the next few minutes wondering why the phaerimm had picked this particular place on this particular morning to hold a conversation and what she was going to do if—when—Khelben and the Vaasans returned. She could not speak the word of passing with two thornbacks lurking outside—not even for one of the Chosen, not for her Vaasan friends, not even if her own brother, Galaeron, were to suddenly appear outside Meadow Wall. When an elf opened a gate in the mythal, she could not control who used it. Once the phaerimm were inside, it would take only a moment to cast the same life-draining magic that had already withered the vineyards of the Vine Vale and denuded the once-majestic spruce stands of the Upper Vale, and that was something Keya could not permit—not when the mythal was already growing weak.

It took Keya a moment to realize it when the phaerimm fell silent, for the difference between stillness and the sibilation of their whispering voices was no more than the flutter of a moth's wings. She thought for a moment the phaerimm had moved on, but when she looked along the Meadow Wall, she saw no swirling ash or any other sign of their departure. The thornbacks had fallen quiet for the same reason they were invisible, because they wanted to keep their presence secret, and their prey was close enough to hear them.

It had to be Khelben and the Vaasans, as invisible as the phaerimm, but walking into a trap. Keya knew Khelben would have his detection magic up and—assuming he was still with the group—would see the enemy as soon as he came into range. The thornbacks would know that as well. The war around Evereska had become one of stealth and magic, with the combatants sneaking through the barren landscape, silent and invisible, searching for foes who were just as silent and just as invisible. More often than not, the victor was the one who detected his enemy first—and the phaerimm had obviously already detected Khelben and the Vaasans.

Keya knew she could warn Khelben simply by speaking his name, for he had told her that the Chosen heard a few words whenever their names were spoken anywhere on Faerûn, but that was really not much different from a magic sending. She had to assume that the phaerimm would detect it just as easily. No, she needed to startle the thornbacks, to confuse them for just the half-second it would take Khelben and the others to discern the trap and react.

Assuming they were really out there.

Keya wished she had her wand of seeing—really wished she had it. Instead, she fixed her eye on the Meadow Wall and grabbed the shaft of her spear. It was a plain spear with an oak shaft and a head of mithral steel, and it weighed almost a third of what she did. She whispered a prayer to Corellon Larethian, then kicked her screen of bark aside and burst from her hiding place.

Two swirls of ash and dust went up behind the Meadow Wall as the startled phaerimm reacted. She angled toward the one on the right for no other reason than it was half a step closer than the other. The thing reacted by instinct, spraying bolts of golden magic in Keya's direction and growing instantly visible. The bolts blossomed harmlessly against the mythal, then Keya was at the Meadow Wall, shoving her spear through the magic barrier to strike at the creature's scaly midsection.

The phaerimm's magic defenses turned her spear as easily as the mythal had turned its golden bolts. A ball of Khelben's silver spellfire exploded into the thing from behind, pinning it against the mythal and holding it there as it was incinerated by the special magic of the Chosen.

Shielding her eyes from the silver brilliance, Keya stumbled away and turned to see the other phaerimm coming apart beneath the Vaasans' darkswords. One of the black blades was emitting a sort of musical purr—a brisk tune that sounded almost like someone humming. The song sent a shiver down Keya's spine. She had heard Dexon's sword talking while he slept and seen Kuhl's grow pallid because he had neglected to plunge it into a vat of mead that day, but this was the eeriest oddity of all. The melody was joyful and light, as though the weapon enjoyed its bloody work.

The three Vaasans finished the phaerimm quickly, then cut off its tail barb and fell to arguing as only Vaasans could about who deserved the trophy. Khelben appeared behind the trio and silenced them with a sharp word before turning to Keya with a grateful bow.

"Quick wit and brave deeds, Keya Nihmedu," he said. Tall and dark-bearded, Khelben had a grim manner that lent a sullen dignity to even his simplest acts. "You have our gratitude."

"It was nothing." Keya spoke the word of passing, then motioned the wizard and the others over the Meadow Wall. "I was never in danger."

"But we were," said Dexon, the darkest of the dark and burly Vaasans. "They would surely have taken us by surprise. I could kiss you."

This caused Keya to cock her brow. "Really?"

Weighing somewhat less than a rothé and possessed of a flashing white smile, Dexon was the handsomest of the Vaasans. She whispered the word of closing to seal the mythal behind them, then smiled up at the human. "Well, why don't you then?"

Dexon's jaw dropped, and he began to leer at her with that hungry look that seemed to come to the Vaasan eye at the slightest flash of skin. Though Keya knew her friends on the Long Watch were revolted by humans in general and by being ogled by them in particular, she did not withdraw her smile. The truth was that once a person got to know them, humans were really rather fun. She had even come to enjoy the glances that they cast her way—at least those Dexon cast her way—whenever they went to bathe in Dawnsglory Pond.

When the Vaasan seemed too shocked to do more than stare at Keya, Burlen stepped forward to take his place. "What's wrong with you, Dex? You can't keep our hostess waiting."

Burlen spread his burly arms wide and closed his eyes . . . and suddenly found himself holding a glowering Khelben.

"Keya is the one who deserves the reward, Burlen, not you."

Keya giggled at this, causing the archmage to turn his glower on her.

"And you, young lady, should be careful of baiting bears. I'm sure Lord Nihmedu would take a dim view of you kissing something with more wool on his face than a thkaerth."

Keya raised her chin. "I'm sure he would, Sir Blackstaff, but Galaeron is neither here nor my keeper." She sneaked a glance at Dexon, then added, "Now, pray tell how your scouting mission went?"

Something like humor may have flashed in Khelben's dark eyes, but it was gone before Keya could be certain. Speaking over his shoulder, he turned and started across the meadow toward the cliff gates.

"Lord Duirsar has reason to be concerned about the shadow sky," he said. "The Vale is dying outside the mythal even faster than it is inside."

Keya stumbled and, were it not for the speed with which Dexon's hand leaped out to catch her, would have fallen. The life of the Vale, both inside the Meadow Wall and beyond it, was what sustained the mythal.

"We must find a way to tear that shadow from the sky, and quickly," Khelben continued, "or we will soon be fighting phaerimm in the streets of Evereska."

✡✡✡✡✡

Galaeron stood in the cold stillness at the Most High's side, peering down into the world-window, watching a miles-long column of mixed volunteers trudge along the knee-deep mud trough that had once been the Trade Way. There were folk from all over the northwest—Evermeetian elves, Adbarrim dwarves, Waterdhavian men—but only the Uthgardt barbarians seemed untroubled by the blizzards and constant downpours that had been plaguing western Faerûn all spring. The rest of the volunteers were coughing and staggering, so weakened by fever and fatigue that the army could barely slog three miles a day, much less join battle at the end of the march.

Yet fight they must. Telamont's cowled head looked toward the High Moor, and the scene in the world-window shifted to a horde of bugbears being herded through a waterfall of rain by a troop of beholder officers. Supporting them were two companies of illithids and another of Zhentilar battle mages—though why the enemy would need human spell-flingers with five phaerimm overseeing their attack was beyond Galaeron.

Telamont's gaze shifted again, this time to a rocky ridge of ground that stood along the Trade Way opposite the High Moor. Laeral Silverhand and her sister Storm already stood atop the ridge, their long tresses streaming in the gale wind as they laid magic traps. Though it was far from certain that their army would cover the mile and a half remaining to it before the phaerimm's bugbears covered the eight remaining to them, the ridge meant everything. The army that controlled it would have the advantages of both height and solid ground, while the one that did not would be forced to wade into battle through a muddy morass.

Withdrawal was not an option for either force, not with the kind of magic that five phaerimm or two Chosen of Mystra could call down on an army mired in the mud. There would be a battle that evening, perhaps the fiercest of the war, one that would annihilate both sides no matter who remained alive to claim the field—and why?

Telamont's attention turned to the phaerimm themselves, and the scene shifted yet again. Accustomed to the Most High's rapid changes of focus, Galaeron turned his own attention to the thornbacks and began to let his thoughts wander over the question of why so many had gathered in one place. He had been coming to the palace every day since their initial meeting, spending most of that time peering into the world-window and trying to get in touch with whatever Melegaunt had passed on to him during those last few moments of life. Sometimes it worked, and he was able to divine the enemy's intentions in time to save a few dozen—or even a few hundred—lives. More often, he had no more to offer than anyone else.

Regardless, Telamont Tanthul spent part of each day—sometimes most of it—with Galaeron, never teaching him directly, but always approaching the subject obliquely, as if concentrating too bright a light on his shadow self would only send it into hiding. No matter how long these sessions lasted, Galaeron always returned to Villa Dusari exhausted, numb, and irritable—so much so that Vala was beginning to question whether Telamont was helping him control his shadow or the other way around. Though she was not allowed into the war room—even Escanor had not been able to prevail on the Most High to allow her inside—she insisted on coming to the palace each day and waiting out in the throne room's whispering murk. Given how peevish that was making her, Galaeron was beginning to think she was the one struggling with a shadow crisis.

Telamont stepped away from the rim of the world-window and fixed his platinum eyes on Galaeron, and—as always—Galaeron felt the question on the Most High's mind.

"I can't see the sense in forcing this battle," he admitted. "When we raised the shadowshell, there were only ten phaerimm outside—"

"The figure is now twelve," Hadhrune corrected from the other side of Telamont. "Our agents located one in Baldur's Gate, and another in . . . that little kingdom south of the Goblin Marches—"

"Cormyr?" Galaeron asked.

Hadhrune nodded, his thumbnail digging into the deeply worn groove atop his ever-present staff. "In what was once the city of Arabel."

"Still, that is nearly half of their number outside the shell," Galaeron said. "Why risk so much to stop an army that may well die of the ague before it ever reaches the Shaeradim?"

"To slay a pair of Chosen?" Hadhrune asked.

Galaeron shook his head. "The phaerimm know better than that," he said. "The Chosen can be defeated but not slain—at least not by Mystra's magic."

Eyes sparkling at this last correction, Telamont said, "Whatever their purpose, this is a battle we cannot permit." He turned to where Escanor and Rivalen had appeared without any apparent summons, then raised a murk-filled sleeve toward the world-window. "You will take your brothers and your best legions and save those sick fools if you can. Leave the phaerimm until we understand their game."

"It shall be done."

Both princes placed their palms to their breasts, then turned and were gone.

Galaeron felt the weight of Telamont's unspoken question and knew that something was being demanded of him that had, until now, only been asked. He turned to the world-window and focused his attention on the High Moor, then on the horde of tiny figures swarming over it, then on the five figures drifting along behind it between the two companies of illithids. Each time, the window responded to his will, the image shifting and growing larger to show him what he wished to see.

When Galaeron was finally looking at only the thornbacks themselves, he shifted from one to the other, studying each one in turn, looking for scars or scale patterns or anything that might trigger one of Melegaunt's memories. Had the world-window been capable of carrying sound, he would have cast the spell that Melegaunt had taught him to understand their languages, but even the Shadovar could not eavesdrop without sending a spy. The Most High had already made clear to Galaeron that until he grew adept enough with shadow magic to find and pass on the knowledge that Melegaunt had entrusted to him, he would not be allowed to risk his life in any manner. For a Tomb Guard prince accustomed to chasing cutthroat crypt breakers down narrow passages strewn with magic death traps, the restriction was not an easy one to observe.

After several minutes of allowing his thoughts to wander over the phaerimm, Galaeron finally looked away from the world-window.

"I'm sorry," he said. "I can't summon anything."

Telamont accepted the failure with a patience uncharacteristic toward anyone except Galaeron.

"Do not let it concern you," he said. "I'm sure it is just your shadow interfering. The harder you try to control it, the stronger it becomes."

"I'm not trying to control it," Galaeron said. "I'm just letting my mind wander."

Telamont's eyes twinkled beneath his cowl, and there was a flash of what might have been a white-fanged grin. "You are always trying to control your shadow, elf. You are the kind who must control what he fears."

"What I fear is becoming a monster," Galaeron insisted. "Of course I want to control my shadow."

"As I said," Telamont replied. His sleeve rose, then a cold weight settled on Galaeron's shoulder. "It is no matter. The princes have their orders."

The world-window filled with a foggy expanse, which gradually grew less hazy as the Most High brought into focus what he wanted to see. Even after the scene stopped shifting, it took Galaeron a moment to notice a series of faint bluish lines that he recognized as crevasses in the High Ice.

The crevasses broadened into the dagger-shaped ribbons of deep, icy canyons, and Galaeron began to notice an odd patchwork of vapor columns rising off some sections of the massive glacier. One of these columns expanded to fill the world-window, and a square plot of snow gradually darkened from white to gray to ebony as the column continued to grow larger. Finally, Galaeron found himself looking at something that appeared to be a huge, black carpet being unrolled by a company of ant-sized Shadovar.

"A shadow blanket," Telamont explained, answering Galaeron's question sooner than he could voice it. "A square mile of pure shadowsilk."

Galaeron frowned, as puzzled by what the Shadovar were doing as why Telamont was showing it to him. At the end of the blanket already laid out, a thickening vapor haze was beginning to rise into the air, while tiny rivulets of crystal water were flowing out from beneath the edge, braiding themselves into sparkling streams that merged into broad creeks and vanished down the blue crevasses in silver horsetails of falling water.

"You're melting it!" Galaeron gasped.

"Yes." If Telamont noticed the alarm in Galaeron's voice, his tone did not betray it. "The shadow blankets absorb all of the light that falls on them, then trap it below in the form of heat. We have already laid hundreds along the edge of the High Ice."

"Hundreds?"

Galaeron concentrated on a larger area of the High Ice. Sensing his change of focus, Telamont yielded control of the world-window, and the scene drew back to show the hundreds of vapor columns rising off the ice.

"You're changing Faerûn's weather!"

"We are rejuvenating what the phaerimm destroyed," Telamont corrected.

The scene changed again, this time to the southern edge of the High Ice, where dozens of huge rivers were gushing out of blue-tinged caves in the base of a mountainous wall of snow and ice. The water was pouring into enormous basins that had been dry for a thousand years, re-creating the lakes that had once lain along the northern fringes of Netheril.

"Cold air is rolling down from the High Ice and picking up moisture as it sweeps across the lakes and grows warm," Telamont explained. "As the effect grows stronger, the winds will carry rain and fog farther south into Anauroch, forcing the hot desert air to rise and draw more winds down from the High Ice. The system feeds on itself. We are already seeing showers as far south as the Columns of the Sky."

Though Galaeron had no idea where the Columns of the Sky were—the name had a Netherese ring—he needed no explanation of what the shadow blankets meant for western Faerûn. He had already seen it in the blizzards plaguing Waterdeep and the deluges that had turned most of the farms south of the Ardeep Forest into hip-deep marshes.

"That is well and good for Shade," he said, "but what about the rest of Faerûn?"

Telamont's gloom-cloaked shoulders rose and fell. "Every good thing has a bad side. For Shade to reclaim its birthright, others must suffer."

"This is too much," Galaeron said.

He looked toward the west, and the scene shifted to Daggerford, where the River Delimbyr's frigid waters had risen into the streets, and residents kept boats tied outside their second-story windows.

"Surely, you could pursue a more gradual approach, one that would not force so many into homelessness and hunger."

Telamont seized control of the world-window from Galaeron, bringing the shadowy dome over the Shaeradim into view. "I thought your concern was for Evereska."

"The two are hardly related," Galaeron said.

"Aren't they?" Telamont asked. "Shade must be strong if it is to prevail. So whose people do you want to save, elf? Yours or theirs?"

"That isn't the choice," Galaeron said. "Even at the rate you're melting the High Ice, Anauroch will take decades to restore. Evereska will be saved or lost in a year."

Telamont's murk-filled cowl tipped down toward Galaeron. "It is the choice I have given you, elf. Which will perish—Evereska or the West?"

"I—I can't believe you would ask me such a thing!" Galaeron stammered.

He thought he had to be misinterpreting what he was hearing, missing some important nuance that would make clear what the Most High was really asking of him.

Something cold and angry rose inside him, and he understood. The Shadovar were trying to trap him, trying to corrupt him, perhaps, or test him, or move the burden of all those deaths from their heads to his.

Galaeron shook his head. "I see your game, and it won't work on me."

"You think this is a game?" Telamont lifted a sleeve toward the world-window. "Look and think again."

The scene had returned to the High Moor, where the princes of Shade and their legions were just rising from the dusky ground, thousands upon thousands of silhouettes peeling themselves out of the shadows and growing whole as they charged, flinging spells of umbral death and waving weapons of indestructible black glass.

Caught from the rear and the flank, the bugbears were roaring in confusion and fighting their beholder masters with far more ferocity than they were the Shadovar. One company of illithids was already under the black sword, while the other was rushing to fan out behind their battle lines and find the most powerful spell-flingers to target with their mind blasts. The search was proving a difficult one, for most warriors of Shade Enclave fought with both spell and blade, often slipping from one to the other with a grace that even an elf bladesinger would envy.

No more eager to engage the princes than the princes were to engage them, the five phaerimm hung back, assailing their enemy's ranks with fireballs, lightning bolts, and sheets of burning light that felled whole ranks of Shadovar. Though this last spell was one that Galaeron had never seen before, it bore a semblance to certain elements of a prismatic wall, and he felt sure it was little more than a simple modification the thornbacks had developed especially for combat against shades.

That was when it hit him. "This battle is a diversion."

"An army that large may be many things, but a diversion is not one of them," said Hadhrune. "A force that size requires resources that our agents assure us the phaerimm dare not waste lightly."

"Your agents don't know the phaerimm well enough to make that judgment," Galaeron replied, somewhat surprised to discover he felt he did. He pointed at a flickering fan of azure light. "That spell is a new one, designed for battle against Shadovar."

"Even if you could know that," Hadhrune began, "I fail to see—"

"I can know it, and you do fail to see," Galaeron interrupted, confident of his judgment. "If the phaerimm were expecting to do combat with the Chosen, they would not clutter their minds with spells designed for Shadovar—and they would not announce their presence by floating into battle fully visible."

All of Anauroch and western Faerûn appeared in the world-window, clouds stripped away to reveal the swollen rivers beneath.

"What are they trying to hide?" Telamont asked.

Galaeron studied the divination for several minutes, focusing on the area around the shadowshell, Rocnest, and the Greycloaks for the longest period. Finally, he shook his head.

"I can't see it."

"Perhaps because there is nothing to see," Hadhrune said. "With these five in plain view, we know the locations of all twelve phaerimm who escaped the shadowshell."

"Your knowledge is current?" Telamont asked.

Hadhrune's amber eyes vanished behind their dark lids for a moment, then he nodded. "The shadow-watchers have seen them all within the quarter hour. Five are visible at this moment."

Galaeron nodded. "Of course. They would know we're watching."

"Our watchers would know if they were simulacrums or magic images," Telamont said. "Perhaps this is no diversion, after all."

"We cannot know what the phaerimm make of the shadowshell," Hadhrune said, smirking down at Galaeron. "It may be that they fear it is the Chosen's doing, and this army is part of their plan."

"Or it may be that the Myth Drannor phaerimm have a part to play in this," said Lord Terxa, whom Galaeron had not even realized was listening from the shadows. "What remains of the mythal there interferes with the shadow-watchers, and they are not even certain they have found them all."

Galaeron recalled how Melegaunt's shadow magic had failed inside Evereska's mythal but frowned and shook his head. "A good thought, but phaerimm are not social. They work together only when each one benefits personally, and there's no reason for the Myth Drannor phaerimm to think that helping the others would be worth their trouble."

Terxa's expression grew uncomfortable, and he peered into the darkness under Telamont's cowl. "Perhaps he should know, Most High?"

"Know what?" Galaeron was instantly resentful. "Now you are keeping secrets from me?"

Telamont's eyes twinkled as though he was amused—or satisfied. "Have you told us all *your* secrets, elf?"

He raised a sleeve, and a sleepy forest hamlet appeared in the world-window. Not too long past, a battle—or several—had been fought around it, for several new meadows had been burned into the woods around its boundaries. In front of a high tower not far from the heart of the village, a strange seam of distortion hovered in the air, emitting wisps of flame and dark fume.

"Many things are better kept secret," Telamont said. "Among them, deeds of shame done in moments of necessity."

Hadhrune moved to interpose himself in front of Galaeron and asked, "Most High, is this something—"

Galaeron stepped forward to block Hadhrune. "It is, unless you wish to let the phaerimm have their way with your legions."

"He needs to know," said Terxa.

Telamont spread his sleeves. Flames and smoke sprang up in the charred clearings, and Galaeron began to see familiar cone-shaped bodies drifting through the trees. A moment later, Elminster's familiar figure appeared over the village and began to circle.

"After Melegaunt summoned his brothers to the Karsestone," Telamont began, "Elminster was proving most difficult to locate. In order to find him, the princes found it necessary to slay a few of the Myth Drannor phaerimm—"

"And leave the smell of Elminster's stinkweed in the air," Galaeron finished.

"As I understand, it was not necessary to leave anything," Telamont said, almost chuckling. "The thornbacks could not imagine anyone else capable, and went to take their vengeance on Elminster."

"And when he returned to see what was happening, the princes ambushed him and sent him to the Nine Hells?" Galaeron demanded. "How could you—"

"It was an accident," Hadhrune said firmly.

"In any case, its not relevant to the question at hand," Telamont said. "What is relevant is that the Myth Drannor phaerimm may have learned who was actually responsible—"

"And made a pact with their fellows to be rid of you," Galaeron finished.

He was growing angrier by the moment, and not just because of what they had done to Elminster. He saw how Telamont had manipulated him as well, deliberately drawing his shadow out by showing him the shadow blankets and telling him he must choose between saving Evereska or the whole West. Though Telamont remained silent, the force of his unspoken question pressed down like a boulder. So infuriated was Galaeron that he wanted not to answer, to deny what he saw so clearly, or lie about it, or do something to make the Shadovar pay—but he could not hold the knowledge inside. The pressure of the Most High's will was insufferable, as though he had somehow brought the entire weight of Shade Enclave to bear on that one pressure point.

At last, Galaeron had to ask, "You have a mythal?"

The air grew even more still and cold than usual next to Telamont. "Of a sort. There is a mythallar here, as were found on all the enclaves of Netheril."

"That's what they'll attack."

"Impossible," Hadhrune said. "They'd never make it through the shadow moats."

Galaeron shrugged. "Then you have nothing to worry about."

Hadhrune looked to Telamont.

The Most High turned to Galaeron and said, "You know our defenses. Can the phaerimm breach them?"

"They already have, or your sentries would be sounding the alarms by now." Then, in answer to what the Most High wanted to know next, Galaeron said, "It's likely a small company of infiltrators. If it was only one or two, they would have relied on stealth instead of trying to lure your strength away."

"An entire company?" Hadhrune shook his gaunt head. "Impossible."

"It would not hurt to be certain," Telamont said.

Hadhrune's amber eyes vanished beneath their lids, but Telamont was not waiting. He started for the throne room, motioning Galaeron to follow—and many others as well, judging by the cold swirl of darkness that accompanied them.

Hadhrune appeared at Telamont's side, his eyes opened again. "A veserab patrol did return unexpectedly, Most High. The officer cannot be found, and the mounts have burns where they were harnessed with Weave magic."

"Not impossible," Telamont said. "Recall the princes."

They were in the throne room, striding through the whispering shadows toward the reception hall, surrounded by a throng of increasingly substantial figures. Several of the silhouettes drifted apart long enough for Vala to emerge and step to Galaeron's side.

"What happened?"

"Phaerimm infiltrators," Galaeron explained. "They're after the mythallar."

Vala raised her brow, but said, "That's not what I was asking about."

"No?"

"You, Galaeron," Telamont said, speaking from a dozen paces ahead. "She wants to know what happened to you."

Galaeron frowned. "My shadow?" He glanced over at her. "You can tell just by looking?"

Vala nodded. "Galaeron, I don't even have to look anymore," she said, "and I don't much like that."

"Ready weapons!" Hadhrune called.

Vala reached for her darksword and asked, "They're coming here?"

They were somewhere else, dropping out of the shadows into a huge obsidian basin, sliding down the glassy slopes with purple sheets of light burning all around them, voices screaming, bolts cracking, air reeking of charred flesh. It took Galaeron a moment to recall where he was and why, a moment longer to realize the pain in his arm was Vala's free hand digging into his biceps, then he finally began to make sense of what he was seeing.

At the bottom of the basin sat a huge ball of obsidian, easily a hundred and fifty feet in diameter, with pale, ghostly shapes gliding about inside and a halo of deepening darkness radiating from its surface. A flight of phaerimm were descending out of the gloom above, flinging spells of fire and light as they came, trying to fight their way through the swarm of teleport-dazed Shadovar tumbling and sliding down the slopes of the glassy basin along with Galaeron and Vala.

An orb of darkness streaked up out of the basin and drilled a fist-sized hole through a creature close over their heads. It dropped onto the slope above and started to slide down toward them, roaring its pain in a swirling tempest of winds and lashing out with a wild flurry of lightning and burning light. Galaeron took a white fork of energy in the shoulder and went rigid, biting down on his tongue so hard that his teeth met through the flesh.

Vala hurled her sword, slicing off one of the phaerimm's arms and a good portion of its sinewy shoulder. The creature rolled away, then whistled something in the phaerimm wind language and vanished.

Galaeron felt Vala catch him by the collar, then their descent began to slow as they reached the bottom of the basin and the slope lost its steepness. She called her darksword back to her hand, and only after it had returned did she turn her attention to the smoking hole in his shoulder.

"How bad?"

Galaeron managed to unclench his jaw and, with a mouthful of blood, said, "Stiff, but all right."

He tried to rise, making it as far as his knees before discovering his muscles would not obey. Vala moved his leg into a stable kneeling position, then they both scanned the area. The battle appeared to have ended as quickly as it had started. Shadovar warriors and pieces of Shadovar warriors were sliding down the slope toward them, accumulating in groaning, knee-deep piles. Half a dozen phaerimm—or rather sections of half a dozen phaerimm—lay interspersed among the smoking bodies.

Telamont Tanthul stood a quarter of the way around the basin, Hadhrune at his side as always, calling for his princes and ordering the survivors to arrange search parties. There were no thornbacks in sight; once a battle started to turn against them, it was phaerimm instinct to teleport away. Galaeron knew the enclave defenses would prevent them from leaving the city via translocational magic—but he also knew the phaerimm would have anticipated that and picked a safe rallying point.

Galaeron grabbed Vala's arm and pulled himself up.

"Take it easy," she said. "You're not looking so good."

Though he was still angry with Telamont for drawing out his shadow and at that moment truly *wanted* to see the Shadovar mythallar destroyed—considering the number of deaths that would mean, he hoped that particular desire was his shadow's instead of his own—Galaeron also knew that Evereska's fate depended on Shade Enclave's continued survival.

"It's not done," Galaeron said. "They're still in the city."

Vala wrapped him in a supporting arm and started toward the Most High. "Telamont isn't going to like this. Didn't he order you to stay out of fights until you're able to pass on Melegaunt's knowledge?"

Galaeron nodded at the huge sphere of obsidian they were circling past. "He seems to have made an exception for the mythallar."

Vala glanced at the orb and raised her brow. "That's the mythallar? I was sort of expecting it to be the Karsestone."

"Me, too," Galaeron said.

After unleashing the phaerimm, they had journeyed into the Dire Wood, fighting liches and other undead guardians in order to help Melegaunt recover the famed Karsestone and use its "heavy" magic—from a time before the Weave and Shadow Weave split—to return Shade Enclave to Faerûn.

"I guess they only needed the stone to open a large enough gate between the dimensions," he said. "Apparently, the Shadow Weave can still support spells powerful enough to levitate a city."

"The Weave can't?" Vala asked.

"It hasn't," Galaeron answered, shrugging. "Not since the fall of Netheril."

If Vala saw the danger in that, her expression didn't show it. "That is good news for Evereska, if it means the Shadovar are more powerful than the phaerimm."

Galaeron nodded, but didn't say what it might also mean. If the Shadovar were more powerful than the phaerimm, then they were also more powerful than most of the great wizards of the realms. Only the Chosen themselves, or perhaps an entire circle of high mages, could rival their power.

They were almost to Telamont and Hadhrune when the first of the princes, with half a dozen Shadovar lords at his back, stepped out of the murk at the rim of the basin and began to descend the slick wall. Galaeron recognized Brennus by his large, crescent-shaped mouth and the orange tinge of his iron-colored eyes. Not slipping on the steep obsidian slope, he and the others began to angle more or less in Telamont's direction, their faces showing no reaction at all to the carnage around them. When they reached the body piles at the bottom, they began to clamber across without drawing so much as a moan or disturbing even one arm.

"Vala, do you see that?" Galaeron asked.

"What?" she asked.

Like almost everyone else in the basin, Vala was focusing her attention on the murk near the rim, blithely awaiting the arrival of the rest of the princes.

"Lower. Look at Brennus's feet."

Vala looked, then frowned at the way no one seemed bothered that Brennus was stepping on them. "That's just wrong."

"So I thought," Galaeron said.

He and Vala were still thirty paces from Telamont, perhaps half that from Brennus and his companions. He stopped and pulled a small flake of obsidian from his robe pocket.

"Galaeron, no." Vala grabbed his arm. "You're—"

"Let go!" Galaeron ripped his arm free, then began to scrape the flake over his palm. "If that's really Brennus, he'll never know."

Galaeron began the incantation of a shadow divination—a more powerful one than he should have been using but necessary if he was to dispel a phaerimm's disguise magic. A surge of cold shadow magic rushed into his body, chilling him down to the marrow in his bones and filling him with a cold, bitter resentment at . . . well, everyone: Melegaunt and the other princes, Telamont, Hadhrune—even Vala.

The spell ended as the "prince" and his escorts were stepping over the last of the casualties onto the basin floor. The shadow drained from their bodies like water, revealing six phaerimm and a strange, three-eyed, three-tentacled orb with a huge, finchlike beak.

"*Impos—*"

That was as far as Vala's warning got before the basin erupted into flying shadow balls and sizzling fans of light. Two of the phaerimm and fifty Shadovar fell in the battle's first breath, and the three-eyed creature spun toward Galaeron, its tentacles whirling like the scimitars of a drow blademaster. Vala intercepted it, her darksword rising to meet the spinning tentacles—and fell back as the thing beat down her guard, slashing her up the cheek, above the eye, and then across the neck.

Galaeron pulled her back and drew his own sword, his elven steel severing one hooked tentacle as it struck at the hollow of her throat, then falling to his back as the thing's wicked beak clacked at his head. Another hook came whipping down toward Galaeron's unarmored heart—and was intercepted by Vala's darksword. She twined her black blade into the tentacle and pulled the creature toward her, bringing her iron dagger up to meet it. The blade sank a finger's depth, and the third tentacle came around, burying its hook in the back of her knee and trying to jerk her off her feet. Vala was too nimble. She gave it a dead leg, letting her foot rise while she pushed and twisted the dagger. The blade sank perhaps another knuckle.

Galaeron pulled a strand of shadowsilk from his pocket and wadded it into a ball, beginning the incantation for a shadow ball.

"Galaeron!" Vala yelled, hopping on one foot as the thing whipped her impaled leg to and fro. Somehow, during all this, she still managed to knock the shadow-silk from his hand. "No more—"

"Shut the hell up and fight!"

Galaeron kicked the thing's beak off of him and rammed his sword up through its body. Leaving it buried there, he pulled a small cylinder of glass from his pocket and rolled through the incantation for a normal lightning bolt and felt nothing.

Well, not nothing, exactly. There was a cold prickling as the shadow magic tried to rise into him where his body was touching the ground, but he pushed this down and opened himself to the Weave so he could cast a normal, bright, searing lightning bolt—and there was nothing. He had lost the Weave.

Vala exchanged her dagger for his sword's hilt, pushed, twisted, slashed, then cried out in alarm as the thing wrapped its dehooked tentacle around her ankle. Instead of allowing it to pull her foot out from under her, Vala dropped to her back, pulling Galaeron's sword from the creature's body and bringing a cascade of entrails with it.

The thing screeched in anguish and exploded into a bloody cloud as a huge shadow ball burst through its center. What remained plopped down between Galaeron and Vala, its slimy tentacles still twined around Vala and her darksword. She quickly used Galaeron's sword to cut herself free, then flipped it around and shoved the hilt at him.

"Don't ever—I don't care how darkly shadowed you are—don't *ever* tell me to shut up."

"And don't you ever—*ever*—interrupt a spellcasting," Galaeron snapped back. "Or the next time, I'll let it snap your head off."

"Better a . . ." She looked at the three-eyed thing and curled her lip in disgust, then continued, " . . . a monster I don't know than one I do."

She dropped his sword in the mess, then rolled to her feet and limped off through the carnage, leaving Galaeron to face Telamont and Hadhrune as the pair came up behind the monster's disemboweled body. The Most High nudged it with a dark boot.

"Our enemies from the shadow plane attack us even here," he said. "The 'monster' is called a malaugrym. You did well to unmask it. One might even say that we all owe you our lives."

"One might," Galaeron said, struggling to his feet, "but it seems a simple 'thank you' is too much to ask."

Telamont's eyes sparkled. "If that is what your shadow needs to hear."

"My shadow?" Galaeron growled. "It's just common courtesy."

Then, remembering how Vala had saved his life when his lightning bolt failed, he realized Telamont was right. Vala had been, too. His shadow had been completely in control—perhaps it still was.

Telamont motioned to Hadhrune, and both kneeled before Galaeron—causing every shadow lord who happened to be looking in the direction to do likewise.

"Galaeron Nihmedu, on behalf of Shade Enclave," Telamont began, just a hint of mockery in his voice, "please accept our most sincere—"

"Not necessary," Galaeron said, realizing how ignoble he was to be demanding thanks when so many had died. "Forgive me for asking."

Telamont did not rise. "You see, you *can* live with your shadow."

"Sure I can," Galaeron scoffed, looking past the Most High's shoulder. He owed someone an apology. "Where'd Vala go?"

Telamont rose and turned, then said, "There are some things even I do not know."

"Have no fear for her comfort," Hadhrune said, looking in the same direction as Galaeron. "Vala saved Prince Escanor's life. She will always be welcome in his villa."

CHAPTER SIX

15 Mirtul, the Year of Wild Magic

With Boareskyr Bridge hidden somewhere beneath the brown lake that had once been the plains north of the Trollclaws, Laeral's relief army was crossing the Winding Water on a fleet of rain-soaked log rafts. Laeral herself had flown three magic guidelines across two miles of muddy water, and along with her hippogriff-mounted scouts and several dozen of her best battle mages, she was standing guard on the western shore, expecting a phaerimm attack at any moment.

This was the last river they would cross before reaching Evereska, and if the enemy meant to stop them, it would be there, and Laeral knew there was a good chance that they would.

In addition to slowing the progress of the relief army to a crawl, the horrid weather was taking a terrible toll on the health and spirit of the army. There was not a fighter among them who doubted that they owed their lives to the forces of Shade. Had the Shadovar not appeared when they did at the High Moor, the enemy horde would have beaten them to the high ground and obliterated the army to a warrior.

Many officers were beginning to question the wisdom of continuing the march at all. While the priests and healers were keeping deaths from illness to a bare minimum, most soldiers were feverish and—with the constant rainfall spoiling rations—weak from hunger. Even if they reached Evereska in time, it seemed likely that their poor condition would only be a burden on those already in place.

Laeral refused to hear these arguments. Sooner or later, the weather would break—it had to—and a few days of sunshine would do wonders to rejuvenate the army. More importantly, she felt certain the phaerimm would eventually find a way to defeat the shadowshell. When that happened, the thornbacks would learn from their mistake and scatter across Faerûn, and the only thing capable of stopping them would be the sheer numbers of Laeral's relief army.

Most of all, there was her beloved Khelben to think about. He had vanished at the Battle of Rocnest, defending a trio of Evermeet's high mages as they attempted to open a translocational gate that would have allowed Waterdeep to send relief forces in a matter of moments instead of months, and Laeral was determined to find out what had become of him. She would have known if he had died—as a Chosen herself, she would have felt his loss in the Weave—so he had either been sucked into another plane when the phaerimm captured the gate, or trapped inside Evereska with the elves. She was gambling on Evereska, if for no other reason than she had already done what little was possible to contact him in the planes beyond.

The first rafts appeared out of the rain, the deep voices of two hundred Uthgardt barbarians chanting a somber hauling song as they pulled themselves along the guide rope. Laeral began to think her army would actually make the crossing successfully. The rafts were spaced about thirty paces apart, just far enough to avoid being caught if a magic fireball, meteor storm, or some other area attack struck the raft in front, yet close enough that the warriors on any one raft could help the others if they did come under attack.

A distant thunder began to roll over the horizon from the direction of the Forest of Wyrms. Laeral assigned her battle mages to ground defense, then took her hippogriff riders into the air to establish a protective screen fifty paces ahead of the shoreline. The thunder grew into the unmistakable roar of pounding boots and growling voices, but the rain clouds were so thick that Laeral couldn't see their enemies even from a hundred feet above the ground.

The roar grew steadily louder and passed underneath her. Laeral dropped down until she saw first the hazy darkness of land, then thousands of oblong bootprints simply appearing in the mud. Someone had turned the entire army invisible, and that meant phaerimm—probably several of them.

She aimed her palm at the front rank and spoke a few syllables of dispelling magic, and a ten-yard circle of charging bugbears appeared no more than thirty paces from the shoreline.

Several of the battle mages raised their hands in spellcasting, and a mile-long wall of flame rose up to devour the first rank of bugbears. Most fell where they stood, but hundreds of the beasts stumbled forward, roaring in pain and raising huge double-headed axes as they staggered toward the thin line of mages. The first Uthgardts were already splashing ashore to meet the beasts, but the mud was deep, they were few, and time was short.

Laeral pulled a nugget of coal from her spell pocket and flew low in front of the burning bugbears, crumbling the coal into powder and uttering a complicated incantation. The ground turned black and viscous beneath the charging beasts, miring them to their knees, then to their waists and, as they continued to struggle, their chests. Wherever their flaming bodies came into contact with the black sludge, it began to burn as well, and the band was soon filled with roaring scarecrows of orange flame.

At the end of her attack run, Laeral rose into a storm of sling stones and hand axes. None of the attacks penetrated her shielding magic, but the sheer volume was enough to slow her ascent. She turned and found herself staring out over a sea of bugbears and gnolls, all visible the moment some had begun to attack. Pushing through the horde were small bands of beholders and tentacle-faced illithids, coming forward to punch holes in the magic defenses holding their masses at bay.

Of the phaerimm who controlled the army, Laeral saw no sign at all. It was even possible that the illithids and beholders themselves did not know where the creatures were or even that they were there. The phaerimm delighted in using their magic to make other beings do their will, and often the victims were not even aware they were being controlled.

A chorus of shouts drew Laeral's attention back to the flood-swollen river, where two flights of beholders were bobbing in from the flanks to attack the raft line. She flicked a finger over her thumb ring to activate its sending magic. She pictured the craggy face of the leader of her hippogriff scouts and thought, *Aelburn, they're trying to take the rafts from the flanks.*

As you predicted, Milady, came Aelburn's reply. *We'll turn that against 'em.*

Aelburn's mount voiced a series of sharp screeches that caused the scouts to divide into two groups and wheel around to dive on the two flights of beholders from behind. Laeral watched the gray sky to be certain that no phaerimm emerged from the clouds behind her scouts. A tempest of crackling and booming exploded over the river as the mages and clerics on the rafts began to fling spells at the attacking beholders. An instant later, the sound was joined by the screams and shrieks of drowning warriors as the creatures responded with disintegration rays and death beams. Hippogriffs started shrieking and crossbows clacking, and bodies from both sides began to splash into the water.

When Laeral turned back to the main battle, the first beholder was already at the wall of fire, spraying a green ray from its huge central eye and slowly dispelling the magic that had kept it burning. She pointed her fingers down at the creature and tore it apart with ten golden bolts of magic. The battle mages filled the gap with a new curtain of fire even as the first bugbears pushed forward to exploit the opening, but a dozen beholders more were already floating up to spray the flames with their magic-killing rays.

Laeral pulled a pair of wands from her belt and flew down the line, flinging bolts of magic with one hand and forks of lightning with the other. The nearest beholders died before they could open a breach, but those at the far end extinguished huge swaths of flame, and bugbears and gnolls poured through by the dozens. They were met by storms of fiery meteors and dancing chains of lightning, but the battle mages could not stop them all. The meager bands of Uthgardts were forced to meet them at Laeral's tar trench, and all too often it was the barbarians who fell. More warriors were rushing up from the second and third waves of rafts, but with the raft convoy still under attack from the beholders, the flow would soon stop.

Laeral finished her run and took out the last of the beholders—then turned and found another two dozen assailing the fire wall behind her. She started down the line again and felt a mental jolt as an illithid tried to blast her with its mind-numbing powers. Her thought shield held firm against the assault, but she knew it would only be a matter of time before the creature had one of its beholder companions turn its magic-dispelling ray on her and tried again, and *that* would work.

She would have to call her sister . . . again.

"Storm." Laeral did not bother to use magic. Like all the Chosen of Mystra, when Storm's name was spoken anywhere on Faerûn, she always heard it, and the next few words. "Need help. I'm in—"

Laeral was still speaking when Storm appeared, reeling from teleport afterdaze and plummeting toward the ground. Laeral barely caught hold of her wrist in time to keep her from falling into the morass of bugbears and gnolls clamoring to get past the fiery wall below.

"If you'd have let me finish," Laeral said, rising above the range of the bugbears' slings, "I would have said 'in the air.' "

"By the bleeding stars, where do they find so many brutes?" Storm asked, getting her bearings and staring down on the horde below. Having been warned about the crossing, she was fully armed and armored. "No help from Shade this time, I see."

"The Shadovar may have better things to do than look after me," Laeral said. "That doesn't mean they're betraying us."

"Doesn't it?" Storm activated her own flying magic, then drew a pair of wands and cocked her brow. "Heard from Khelben yet?"

"The Shadovar didn't have anything to do with his disappearance." Laeral pointed her sister toward the opposite end of the battle line, then added, "They weren't even here, yet."

"One of them was," Storm replied. "Do you think we ought to call some more sisters?"

"Absolutely not," Laeral answered, diving toward her own end of the battle. "You're bad enough."

They spent the next quarter hour flying back and forth over the battle lines, blasting beholders and illithids with magic from on high, occasionally resorting to more powerful magic like sunburst spells and incendiary clouds when they fell behind and the enemy creatures broke through in numbers larger than the battle mages could stop. Once, Storm was caught in a beholder's antimagic ray when an illithid mind-blasted her, and Laeral had to use time-stopping magic to rescue her. After being restored to capacity by one of Tempus's war clerics, Storm returned the favor twice, once enclosing Laeral in a protective sphere of scintillating colors and the other time creating a magic hand that beat would-be attackers away until she arrived to carry her sister to safety.

Eventually, they simply ran out of beholders and illithids to kill. Laeral's plan for defeating the flank attacks against the raft convoys also worked, and the bugbears and gnolls were forced to stand idle while the relief army hauled itself to shore behind its protective wall of fire. The sisters knew by the simple fact that their monstrous foes remained to fight that there were still phaerimm somewhere in the horde, but they also knew that the creatures would be careful not to reveal themselves in the presence of Mystra's Chosen. The special weapon of the Chosen, silver fire, was one of the few forms of magic that was sure to harm thornbacks, and the creatures were nothing if not cautious.

Once the last of the rafts was across, Laeral and Storm descended to join the commanders of each of the different companies in a war council. It was raining harder than ever, their warriors were exhausted from the crossing, and their foes were both fresher and stronger. On the other hand, they had a slight advantage in numbers and a large advantage in magic, and Laeral felt confident they could carry the day.

Though the wall of flame was a good twenty paces behind her, Laeral could feel its heat chasing the dampness from her rain-soaked clothes.

"What do you think, gentlemen?" she asked. "Attack now or rest the night behind our wall of fire and take the battle to them in the morning?"

"We elves will be no fresher in the morning," said Lord Yoraedia, who commanded Evermeet's five hundred warriors and mages. He glanced at Laeral with an unmistakable expression of scorn, then turned to the black-haired leader of the Black Lion Uthgardts, Chief Claw, and said, "I cannot imagine that even your tribesmen would sleep well this night."

Claw shrugged. "Sleep or not, it is nothing to us," he said, "but night favors the yellow hides and the walking dogs. We will take more to the death fires with us by attacking before dark."

Uncertain whether she was more surprised or alarmed by the fatalism in their voices, Laeral scowled and started to rebuke the commanders—then caught herself and forced a smile.

"You gentlemen are letting the weather cloud your judgment," she said. "There are two of Mystra's Chosen here. Do you really think we can be defeated by a few thousand gnolls and bugbears?"

"You? No," Chief Claw replied, waving his hand vaguely in the direction of the army, "but the rest of us are not Chosen. The rest of us will die."

Laeral heard a nervous murmur building in the ranks but ignored it and kept her attention focused on the commanders.

"Even Chosen die," she said, "but this army is not going to die—not today."

"Forgive me if I find your judgment somewhat clouded," Lord Yoraedia said.

"Clouded?" Laeral was growing angry—and the rising murmur in the ranks was not helping matters. "In what way is my judgment clouded?"

"You fear for your man." Chief Claw glanced over his shoulder, then looked back to Laeral just as she found herself clenching her fists to keep from doing something she would regret. "Your devotion does him honor, but it blinds you to our danger."

Laeral felt as if she had been struck. Yoraedia, Claw, all of the commanders were looking at her as though they truly believed she had led them all to their deaths for Khelben's sake alone.

"I am not the blind one here," she said. "If you can't see—"

"Laeral, wait," said Storm.

She pointed upriver to where a flight of dozens of huge, scaly wings was just appearing out of the rain. They were as large as sails and blue enough to show their color in the gray light, and even had the sisters never before seen a Rage of Dragons, they would have known what was coming by the sight of so many fang-filled mouths.

Storm said, "Maybe they have a point."

✡✡✡✡✡

Through the world-window in Telamont Tanthul's palace in Shade Enclave, the dragons looked like an expanse of blue sea shining up through a hole in the clouds, their great wings undulating like waves, their blue scales flashing like light on water—all but the leader. The leader was naked bone, with blue embers gleaming in the empty eye sockets of its skull and claws large enough to grasp the heads of even its biggest followers.

It could only be Malygris, the foolish blue who had traded his soul to the Cult of the Dragon in order to slay his hated ruler, Sussethilasis, and claim for himself the title of the Blue Suzerain of Anauroch. Though Galaeron had never met the dracolich himself, the younger blues who came to the edge of the desert to feed on tomb thieves and their horses often made a show of defiance by speaking of their suzerain's folly. They were not too rebellious, though—several of the smallest wyrms in the Rage were the very ones who had taken such delight in deriding their ruler to Galaeron.

A tilted plain of brown appeared before the dragons, with an orange half-circle of fire lighting the top edge and thousands of tiny flecks blackening the surrounding ground. Galaeron recognized the specks as warriors, but he didn't identify the brown plain as a river in flood until a few moments later, when the diving dragons drew near enough for him to see the current pouring over a barn's roof.

Galaeron focused his attention on the fire wall, and the specks resolved themselves into two armies. The greater one, composed of larger figures as well as superior numbers, was being held at bay by the crackling wall of fire. The smaller army was trapped against the river, with a flotilla of log rafts beached on the muddy shore behind them and the much larger army in front of them. They were, by all appearances, aware of the dragons swooping down behind them, for their orderly ranks were dissolving into chaos, bleeding into the river or bunching against the wall of fire.

The image in the world-window began to grow blurry and coarse, with wisps of shadow closing in around the edges. Galaeron focused his attention in the center of the panicking army, where a small knot of figures stood looking up toward the dragons in relative calm. The world-window struggled to obey his will, but whatever was interfering with it was too powerful. He glimpsed a pair of women with familiar faces and long silver tresses, a frightened Gold elf, and a black-bearded, blue-eyed Uthgardt barbarian. Then the image became an unrecognizable blur, the shadows rolled in, and there was nothing but darkness.

A cold and familiar stillness settled over Galaeron. He turned and found the platinum eyes of Telamont Tanthul shining out at him from beneath his shadowy cowl.

"That's the relief army from Waterdeep!" Galaeron said. "What are you trying to hide?"

Telamont's sleeve rose, and Galaeron sensed a wispy finger wagging in front of his nose. "You mustn't allow your shadow self to draw your conclusions for you, elf."

Telamont waited, and as usual Galaeron felt the weight of the question without hearing it. "I apologize, Most High. When the world-window closed, I naturally assumed you had taken control."

"Because I wished to hide something from you."

Galaeron nodded.

Galaeron's skin prickled beneath Telamont's sigh. "Not everything is my doing, elf. The fear of the Chosen's army is to blame. The fools are sending thoughts to their loved ones, and the magic they use to carry them is interfering with that of the world-window. The image will clear in a few minutes."

And show us what, Galaeron wondered. He felt the weight of another question but could not quite sense what the Most High wished to know.

"Your attention is elsewhere today, Galaeron," Telamont said. "It is dangerous to let it wander. Your shadow will take advantage."

Galaeron nodded. "We have been watching them prepare for the crossing for some time now," he said. "I was wondering why you have still failed to send aid."

"You were wondering what I hope to gain by failing to send aid," Telamont corrected. "You must know your own thoughts, Galaeron, or you will never live at peace with your shadow."

Galaeron nodded. "Very well—what do you hope to gain by not sending help?"

Telamont's eyes brightened with approval. "Better, elf. The answer is nothing. I sent help."

Galaeron glanced at the world-window. The picture remained a black fog, but he knew better than to insult the Most High by questioning the veracity of his words.

"The relief army's losses will be small. They may even reach Evereska someday—though I can't see what good they can do there. It's you we must be concerned about, Galaeron. I do not like this preoccupation I sense. It's dangerous." Telamont lifted a sleeve to wave Galaeron toward his private sitting room, and together they went into the gloom. "What is it that troubles you?"

Galaeron was so astonished to hear the question asked aloud that the answer began to spill out before he was conscious of formulating it.

"You know that Escanor has asked Vala to accompany him on the assault against the Myth Drannor phaerimm."

"She is a fine warrior, and her darksword has power," Telamont said. "It is a good choice."

"I want you to keep her here."

"Vala is not the kind to hide from death," Telamont said. "Even were such a thing possible, she would think less of herself for it."

"That's not what I'm worried about," Galaeron said. "She can take care of herself, even in a cave full of phaerimm, but I need her here."

"Ah, the promise."

They reached an archway and passed through into a small corner chamber with windows of thin-sliced obsidian on two walls. Beyond the windows, the customary murk that swaddled the enclave appeared to be almost nonexistent, allowing a spectacular—if rather darkened—view of Anauroch's sands rolling past below.

Telamont motioned Galaeron to a chair next to one of the windows and took the one opposite, then said, "The promise she made was to kill you if your shadow self takes over."

Galaeron nodded. "I need to know she's there to keep it."

"No, you don't."

Hadhrune appeared unbidden at the Most High's side, again running his thumbnail along the deep groove in his staff. Telamont ordered wine for himself and Galaeron, and the seneschal dug into the groove so deeply that the tip of his thumb paled to light gray.

Telamont continued, "Vala will never need to keep that promise, not while you are in my company."

Galaeron inclined his head. "You are capable of many things, Most High, but even you cannot solve my shadow crisis for me, as you have said—"

"Many times myself." Telamont raised a sleeve to silence him, and Galaeron saw the translucent form of a withered claw silhouetted in gray against the faint light of the obsidian windows. "But if you are going to lie, lie to me, not yourself."

Galaeron frowned. "What are you saying?"

"You know what I am saying," Telamont said. "At least your shadow does."

"That I don't want Vala to go because I'm jealous?"

Telamont remained silent.

Galaeron rose and strode across the room, nearly bumping into a small writing table before he noticed it floating in the murk. "Elves don't get jealous."

"Nor do they fall asleep," Telamont replied, "or dream like humans."

Galaeron swallowed his rising anger, then turned to face the Most High. "What if I am jealous? I still want you to keep her here."

Telamont looked out over the passing desert. "And who wants this?"

Galaeron considered a moment and realized he was thinking only of his own needs and not Vala's. She would feel diminished to think that he didn't trust her—and he still didn't want her to go.

"Does it matter?" Galaeron asked.

Telamont's cowled head bobbed in approval. "You are beginning to understand, but I will not interfere with Escanor's mission." He turned away from the window and fixed Galaeron with his platinum glare. "Forget this woman. Your shadow will use your love against you, and such emotional attachments can only interfere with your studies."

Galaeron's head was swirling. He had, of course, been aware of his growing attraction to Vala but had never called it love, even in his mind. Elves had to know each other for years—sometimes decades—before they felt anything close to what humans described as love, and he had only known Vala for a few months. To say that he loved her . . . well, most elves didn't sleep or dream, either. Galaeron felt the weight of a question and looked up to find Telamont's gaze still fixed on him.

"Studies?" he asked, hoping to cover what was really going through his mind.

Telamont's eyes twinkled. "Your magic studies," he said. "You are quite a gifted *innatoth*. Once you are at peace with your shadow, I will begin to teach you in earnest."

"Truly?" Even to Galaeron, the response sounded less than enthusiastic, but he kept seeing Vala in Escanor's arms, and that was an image he never wanted to feel comfortable with. "This comes as something of a surprise. Melegaunt warned me to stop using magic altogether."

"Melegaunt was ever the cautious one," Telamont returned. "A fine attribute for spies . . . but limiting."

Hadhrune emerged from the gloom with the wine. He served Telamont first, then crossed the room to offer Galaeron a glass of some vinegary black swill that would not have been used to pickle thracks in Evereska. Galaeron raised his hand to decline and bowed to Telamont.

"You have given me much to think about," he said. "If I may, I should return to Villa Dusari to meditate."

Telamont's eyes dimmed, but he raised a sleeve and dismissed Galaeron with a wave. "If you think that best. Perhaps Hadhrune will join me in your place."

"I would be honored, Most High." Hadhrune glared fire at Galaeron, then spun toward the window so fast that the goblet flew off the tray and spilled. "What a pity—I'll have to fetch another."

Galaeron left the sitting room with the hair prickling on his neck and his thoughts roaring like one of the sandstorms that occasionally forced the city to rise into the cold air miles above the desert. Like Melegaunt before him, the Most High clearly had plans to help Galaeron realize his full potential as a magic-user—and no hesitation about what it might cost Galaeron or those around him. Given the price he had paid merely for learning how to draw on the Shadow Weave, he was not at all eager to increase the depth of his knowledge—especially considering what Telamont had just said it would cost him. He was still enough of an elf to balk at the idea of giving up his emotions, but losing Vala was unthinkable—especially losing her to Escanor.

Galaeron arrived at Villa Dusari angry and determined. He found his companions gathered in the courtyard, sitting on cushions on the ground so they could share the evening meal with Aris, who was reclining along one side of the courtyard with his head propped on a palm as large as a saddle.

"Galaeron, what a surprise," Vala said.

There was no real enthusiasm in her voice. She had yet to forget the sharp words he had spoken to her after the battle at the mythallar, and every time Galaeron thought to apologize, the shadow in him seemed to turn the moment into something awkward or bitter.

"Fetch yourself a plate and mug," she said. "There's plenty to eat."

Instead of stepping into the shadowed colonnade to do as Vala suggested, Galaeron crossed straight to the group. Ruha glanced from him to Vala, then back again, and rose with ghostlike grace. Malik kept his seat, watching the witch with narrow eyes. Aris nodded a welcome to the elf.

"You sit," the witch said. "I'll go."

She vanished into the building. Vala reluctantly moved over to make a place for Galaeron, but he stopped at her side and remained standing, ignoring Malik and the giant altogether.

"Vala, you can't go with Escanor tonight."

She looked up at him with an expression of disbelief. "Who are you to tell me what I can't do?"

An angry heat rose to Galaeron's face. "I . . . I . . ."

Surprised to find it was a question he could not answer, he let his reply trail off. What right could he claim over her decision? He had never spoken the words of love to her, had in fact denied even to himself that he felt such a thing—until Escanor had begun to take an interest in her. Only one oath had ever passed between them.

"You made a promise to me," he said.

"Were I you, that is not something I'd be eager to remind me of."

Realizing he would get nowhere butting heads with a Vaasan, Galaeron took a moment to calm himself—and to quell his shadow, which was whispering dark warnings about the sincerity of the threat implied in her words.

When he finally felt under control, he said, "Vala, I need you to stay."

"You've a funny way of showing it—and I'm not just talking about what you said at the mythallar," she said. "You've been treating me like some two-copper wench and everyone else like house servants. I don't much care for it."

The outrage Galaeron felt from his shadow quickly gave way to a colder kind of anger, something more subtle and cunning. He found himself nodding and looking at the ground.

"You're right," he heard himself say. "I owe you an apology."

Vala cocked an eyebrow and said nothing.

"And I'm going to give it to you at the proper time," Galaeron said. His shadow would not let him say he was sorry. He actually wanted to, but those were not the words that rose to his lips. "And in the proper place."

Vala frowned. "Now is fine."

Galaeron shook his head. "No, when we're out of this cursed city."

Vala's jaw dropped. "You want to leave?"

"As soon as possible."

Galaeron sat beside her. He felt a little sick inside because the words were only what his shadow knew Vala wanted to hear, but what was the harm, really? If Telamont would not do a small favor like keep Vala in the enclave, then Galaeron *was* ready to leave.

"We'll start planning after dinner and be gone as soon as we can collect everything we need," he said.

Malik rose so fast he spilled his plate. "Leave? What of your training?"

"As far as I can tell," Vala said, "Telamont is less interested in teaching Galaeron to control his shadow self than in turning him into a tool of Shade Enclave. He's getting worse, not better—we all see that."

"*I* have not seen that!" Malik tried to stop there, but his face contorted, and he continued, "Except, of course, that what I mean by 'better' is much influenced by the current needs of the One."

"There can be no doubt of what Vala says," Aris said. "Galaeron is turning evil."

"And so what if he does?" Malik demanded. He turned to address Galaeron directly. "Have you forgotten Evereska? Telamont needs the knowledge inside your head to defeat the phaerimm."

"The need cannot be that great," Vala countered, "or he would not have moved the enclave so far from the battlefront."

"You can't know that . . . though there is much to be said for your argument." Malik grimaced at the curse that forced him to add this last part, then tried another tack. "Even if the need is not great, there is an implied bargain. If you desert the Shadovar, why should they defend Evereska?"

"I don't think anything Galaeron does will influence the Shadovar one way or the other," Aris said. He sat upright and spoke even more thoughtfully than usual. "The Shadovar serve the Shadovar in all things. They will defend Evereska because that is the best way to destroy their enemies."

"Can no one here let a man make his arguments without spoiling them with logic and common sense?" Malik demanded. Fuming, he began to shake a leg of roasted fowl at Galaeron. "And who is this 'we'? I am going nowhere."

"You *are*," Galaeron insisted, feeling vaguely betrayed. "Do you think Hadhrune will let you stay in this comfortable house after we're gone? You are here only because I am."

Malik drew himself up to his full height, which was only a little taller than a dwarf. "I have means of my own," he said. "And even if they fail me, I have lived in gutters before, when service to the One demanded it . . . or when I could afford no better."

"And you prefer that to our company?" Aris asked. "My friend, I do not understand."

Malik sighed. "I do not prefer that at all. You are the best friends I have ever known . . . at least without paying." Face darkening, his beady eyes caught Ruha as she returned to the courtyard with a mug and plate for Galaeron. "It is what is safest. The minute we are gone from this city, the hellwitch will plant a *jambiya* in my back."

"Only if you are fleeing the Harp's justice," Ruha said from behind her veil. "But why be fearful? You are safe in Shade Enclave . . . unless you are planning to leave?"

"That is no affair of yours," Malik said, face contorting as his curse compelled him to continue speaking. "Except that my friends are the ones leaving, not I. The One demands my presence in this city so that its denizens may bathe in the light of the Black Sun."

"Ah." Aris nodded as though this made perfect sense. "My behorned friend, I know too much of your god to wish you success, but duty I understand. Your assistance will be missed at the shapings."

Galaeron continued to feel betrayed but knew better than to think he could argue the Seraph of Lies out of obeying his god's will.

"Do as you must, Malik. Can we trust you to keep our secret?"

"Of course," Malik answered. "I am sure I could profit handsomely by running to Hadhrune the moment you are gone and announcing your escape, but in truth Aris's talent has already made me a wealthy man, and I have learned enough of his art to continue the business until his departure is discovered. You may be sure that I will be as loyal to you as I am to my own god and for the sake of my own profit will remain silent on the subject of your departure . . . at least until someone tricks me into revealing it against my will."

"We can ask no more," Aris said. "With luck, we will be far out in the desert by then."

"Desert?" Ruha asked. "You will try to cross Anauroch . . . on foot?"

"I do not think Galaeron has the magic to carry us across any other way," Aris replied, looking to Galaeron for confirmation.

Galaeron shook his head. "That is beyond me."

"And it would be unwise for him to push his limits," Vala added.

"Wiser than trying to walk across Anauroch," Ruha said. "You know nothing of the desert."

"No matter—they must leave, and the sooner the better." Vala took his hand. "You have been scaring me, Galaeron. I was beginning to think you meant to hold me to my promise."

Galaeron barely heard this last part. The word "they" was still reverberating through his head. "They?" he demanded.

"I can't go with you," Vala said. "I'm due to leave with Escanor at midnight. If I don't show, he'll know something is wrong—and we all know they'll never let you leave willingly, not with Melegaunt's knowledge still locked inside your head."

"Then we'll wait until you return," Galaeron said. It was all he could do not to accuse her of *wanting* to leave with Escanor. "That's simple enough."

Vala shook her head. "It's not. I may hate what Telamont is doing to you, but the Granite Tower's debt to Melegaunt is not yet discharged."

"Melegaunt is dead," Galaeron objected.

"So his duty becomes my duty," Vala said. "And there is the matter of my men trapped in Evereska. I can't return to Vaasa until I know what has become of them."

"A convenient excuse," Galaeron said.

Vala's face clouded with anger. "Convenient?"

"So you can spend time with the prince," Galaeron said. He didn't really believe this, but the words were spilling from his mouth anyway. "If I were gone—"

"Galaeron, don't do this." Vala's expression turned from angry to sad. "You have to go."

"And leave you to Escanor?"

"Galaeron," Aris began, "she would never—"

Vala raised a hand. "Yes, I would, Aris." She turned to Galaeron. "You're right, Galaeron—I haven't felt anything for you since the mythallar."

"That doesn't matter," Galaeron said. Who was this speaking, he wondered, because it *did* matter. "You made a promise."

Vala's eyes narrowed. "And now I'm breaking it." She turned away from him and started for the interior of the villa. "I'm going with Escanor. Do us both a favor, Galaeron, and don't be here when I get back."

CHAPTER SEVEN

15 Mirtul, the Year of Wild Magic

Piergeiron arrived in Castle Waterdeep's unadorned Chamber of Common Command to find the captain of the City Watch and his senior armsmaster and wizards-commander already in conference with their counterparts from the City Guard. Brian the Swordmaster was also present, hidden behind his Lord's cloak and helm. Even the Master of the Watchful Order of Magists and Protectors was there. Strictly speaking, the order was a civilian guild and not subject to military edict, but these were extraordinary times, and Piergeiron had often called private citizens to service when the security of the city was threatened. The question was, when the threat lay five hundred miles distant at Boareskyr Bridge, would they answer?

Piergeiron stepped over to a free seat—there was no head at the circular table—but did not sit. "You heard?"

Rulathon, the wiry, gray-haired captain of the watch, nodded grimly, waved a hand vaguely in the direction of his armsmaster, and said, "Helve received a sending himself."

Piergeiron turned to the scarred veteran. "Lassree?" he asked.

Helve nodded. "She wanted to fight at Laeral's side."

Piergeiron's heart rose into his throat. Lassree was Helve's daughter, a watch-wizard who often fought at her father's side during major disturbances.

"I'm sorry," he said, turning to the others. "What can we do?"

"Against a Rage of Dragons?" asked Thyriellentha Snome. The commander of the watch-wizard forces, she was a dusky woman of proud bearing and uncertain age who had been Mage Civilar since long before Piergeiron assumed office. "Not much, I am sorry to say."

Though Helve's eyes were watering, he nodded. "Lassree said they were trapped against a wall of bugbears and gnolls, with all the blues of Anauroch dropping out of the clouds behind them. It's ending as we speak, I'm sure."

"Be that as it may," the Open Lord said, "we must do what we can."

Piergeiron ran his gaze around the table, pausing at each of the commanders to search for any hint of disagreement. They were brave soldiers all, but their duty was to Waterdeep, and if it was necessary to spell out how saving a relief army bound for Evereska contributed to the security of the city, he needed to know that.

With Waterdeep still buried under a constant wave of blizzards, and ships in the harbor capsizing under the weight of their ice-crusted masts, no one present needed any reminder of the danger posed to their city since the phaerimm had escaped their prison in Anauroch. He found no questions in the eyes of the gathered commanders.

"Good," Piergeiron said. "As we speak, Maliantor is calling Force Grey to my palace. She will begin a scrying to determine what she can about the course of the battle. What I would like from you is to send a force of volunteers—a hundred battle mages and two hundred swordsmen—to meet her at the palace within the quarter hour. I have a store of teleport scrolls—"

"That won't be necessary," rasped a voice in the corner.

Piergeiron turned to find Prince Aglarel's swarthy form stepping out of the shadows beside the fireplace, his black cape and purple tabard almost seeming to solidify out of the darkness.

"How dare you!" Piergeiron demanded. What he really wanted to know was just plain "how." The room was supposed to be shielded against magic intrusions of any kind, though this obviously did not seem to apply to Shadovar shadow magic. "This is a private council."

"Forgive me," Aglarel said, stopping to bow, "but I wanted to save you the trouble of teleporting a company to rescue your relief army."

"I want to know how you can know our intentions," said Brian the Swordmaster. While it was customary for Piergeiron to speak for the other lords in the Court Hall, they usually spoke for themselves in less formal gatherings. The helm's magic transformed his voice into a hollow, anonymous baritone that even Brian's oldest friends would not recognize. "We have barely formed them ourselves."

Aglarel fixed a silver-eyed glare on the lord. "A short time ago, many of your citizens received farewell sendings from their relatives accompanying the

Chosen." The prince did not bother to explain how he knew this. "Knowing the kind of men you Waterdhavians are, it only stood to reason that you would want to do something to help. I called at the palace and was told that Lord Paladinson had left to attend to an urgent matter of state."

"Which raises the questions of how you slipped past the invader wards that guard the castle," said Thyriellentha, "or knew to look for Lord Paladinson in this chamber."

"I will be happy to demonstrate later," Aglarel said, dismissing the questions with a flip of his hand. "For the moment, I suggest we concentrate on the matter at hand."

He stepped to the circular table and stretched forward to circle his hand over the surface. A shadow fell over the center, then opened like a hole in the clouds to reveal a battle raging far below. The scene expanded to fill the entire table, and Piergeiron soon recognized Laeral's relief army trapped against the shore of a muddy lake that could only be the Winding Water in high flood. Much to his surprise—and relief—they were standing in good formation behind a wall of guttering flame, shields raised and weapons drawn but engaged in no combat more serious than swatting the flies and mosquitoes swirling around their heads.

The scene on the other side of the burning wall was far different. Dozens of blue dragons were tearing into an army of bugbears and gnolls, swooping down to gather up great clawfuls of warriors, then wheel out over the flooding river and drop them into the muddy waters. Despite the gaps being ripped in their lines, the monsters were holding ranks, doing their best to fend off the attacks with axes and flails better suited to smashing human heads than piercing draconian scales.

"The dragons weren't sent by the phaerimm?" Piergeiron gasped, unable to tear his eyes from the tabletop.

"Even in Anauroch, there are some things the phaerimm do not control," Aglarel said.

The wings of one dragon went limp, and it plunged toward the ground, tumbling end over end and tangling itself into a knot of tail, neck, and wing. Piergeiron glimpsed a huge black hole in its chest and realized that it had been killed by some very powerful death magic.

In the next instant, the polished bones of a huge dracolich dived down out of the clouds, discharging a thunderstorm's worth of blue lightning at a tiny, cone-shaped figure near the back of the bugbear ranks. A salvo of crackling red meteors streamed up to blast the dracolich in the flank, dislodging two ribs the size of trees and sending the skeletal dragon rolling through the air in a crackling ball of flailing claws and forks of flashing blue energy. Thyriellentha gasped at the mighty magic being hurled about in the battle—the magic required to send a two-hundred-foot dracolich tumbling would have reduced any normal wizard to a smoking cinder—then the thorny shape of a second phaerimm appeared behind the gnolls.

The first dragon had barely crashed to the ground before four long-tressed women rose into the air above the relief army's ranks. They streaked toward the visible phaerimm, balls of the Chosen's silver fire streaking from their hands. The two thornbacks vanished in a blinding explosion of light.

"*Four* Sisters," Aglarel said, clearly awed. "That was unexpected. When last I looked, there were only Storm and Laeral."

"The Chosen stick together," Brian said from behind his helm. "You Shadovar would do well to remember that."

Aglarel smiled tolerantly. "You seem to think we would have reason to fear them."

The bugbears and gnolls finally lost their courage and turned to flee, drawing the dragons down after them. Piergeiron had to look away from what came next.

"I think we've seen enough, Prince," he said.

Aglarel waved his hand over the scene, and the table returned to its normal brown surface.

"You're welcome," Aglarel said, assuming the thanks Piergeiron had deliberately omitted. "I'm sure Waterdeep has many genuine problems with which to concern itself."

"No more than we can handle," Piergeiron said.

He did not like this Shadovar, and because of that he did not trust him. Still, even he had to admit that aside from its part in releasing the phaerimm in the first place, so far the city of Shade had done nothing but help Waterdeep, Evereska, and their allies.

"Are we to take it that the dragons were your city's doing?" Piergeiron asked.

Aglarel nodded, then, without being invited, took a seat at the council table. "Our riposte force is occupied with other problems, so we had to call upon our ally Malygris to watch over your relief army."

"Malygris?" Brian demanded. "You would ally with the Cult of the Dragon?"

Aglarel turned and craned his neck to look up at the helmed lord. "Our alliance is with Malygris. His relationship with the cult is none of our concern."

"But you have allied yourself with a dracolich?" Thyriellentha clarified.

Aglarel nodded. "We hope to reclaim our home in Anauroch. It seemed wiser to ally with the Blue Suzerain than to fight him." He waved his hand at the blank tabletop and added, "I am sure Laeral and her sisters will attest to the wisdom of that decision . . . just as I'm sure that Waterdeep and its allies would benefit from a similar arrangement. Shade Enclave has demonstrated the benefits of working with us twice already."

"You let the Chosen speak for themselves," Brian said. He turned his helm toward Piergeiron. "There may be more to this than is apparent . . . or less."

"What are you saying, Lord?" Piergeiron asked. "That the prince misled us?"

Brian shrugged. "I'm saying it's possible. He could have shown us an illusion as easily as a scrying." The helm turned briefly toward Thyriellentha, who could only shrug and spread her hands, then he demanded, "How do we know those dragons aren't tearing Laeral's army apart right now?"

"Because you must have half a wit somewhere inside that helmet," Aglarel said, growing exasperated. "Why would we save the army at the High Moor, only to summon a flight of dragons to destroy it later?"

"I don't pretend to know the ways of shadow," Brian said, "but I do know better than to trust those who bargain with dracoliches."

Aglarel rose, then—to Piergeiron's amazement—responded in a civil voice. "Your point would be better taken, Masked Lord, had Shade Enclave not proven more reliable than any of your other allies."

"Reliable?" Brian scoffed. "We have seen how reliable you were in your dealings with Elminster."

Aglarel's hand knotted into a fist, and Piergeiron realized that he was allowing his own dislike of the Shadovar to interfere with his judgment as a diplomat.

"My Lord," he began, "your caution is well placed, but in truth the Shadovar have done nothing but serve our mutual cause."

Brian would not be called off. "No?" he demanded. "And what of Blackstaff's disappearance? How do we know they didn't send him to the hells with Elminster?"

"Because we were not even here when Khelben vanished," Aglarel said, not unreasonably. He turned to Piergeiron. "Milord, this really is too much. I demand an apology."

Piergeiron almost let his chin drop. He had no authority to make a Masked Lord apologize, and—even were he sure that Brian was wrong—he knew what the brusque weaponsmith would tell him if he dared suggest such a thing openly.

"Prince Aglarel, there are those in this room who have relatives in the relief army," he began. "You can understand their concern. When our own mages have confirmed what you showed us, I'm sure the Masked Lord will reconsider his opinion."

Brian started to object, but Aglarel spoke over him, his raspy voice seeming to reverberate from all corners of the room at once.

"You will allow this insult to stand?"

"It is not my place to speak for another Lord," Piergeiron said, reminding himself not to look away. "Any more than it would be yours to speak for another prince."

"Were a Prince of Shade to insult a guest in that manner, he would be a prince no longer," Aglarel said. He turned to Brian and bowed stiffly. "I thank you for your candor. You have shown me that I am wasting my breath in Waterdeep."

"Think nothing of it," Brian said. Even the helm's magic was unable to conceal the smugness in his voice. "Though I wish you luck in your alliance with the dragons and scorpions."

Aglarel's eyes flashed, then he turned to Piergeiron. "With your permission, I will remain in the city long enough to purchase some things that have caught my eye."

"Of course," Piergeiron said. "All are welcome in Waterdeep. I'm sure this will blow over—"

"Please, Lord Paladinson, I think it is time to be honest with each other," Aglarel said, raising his hand. He stepped away from the table and crossed to the door, then turned and executed a formal bow. "In that spirit, it is only fair to warn you that the attention of Shade Enclave is required elsewhere. Your relief army will be receiving no more protection from us."

✡✡✡✡✡

With the soft footfalls of the Guards Most High rustling in his ears and his own hands thrust in his cloak pockets to hide how they were trembling, Galaeron followed Telamont down into the murky passages beneath the Palace Most High. As they descended staircase after staircase, Galaeron was sometimes almost able to recognize the strange tinklings and odd raspings that resonated from the dark sanctums of each level and was sometimes unsettled by eerie gurglings and ominous rumblings too macabre for an elf's ear to discern. Though he had no idea where they were going, or why the Most High had picked the last hour of darkness on the same night as Vala's departure to have him fetched to the palace, Galaeron refused to ask. If his plan to leave the enclave had been discovered, he refused to give Hadhrune—walking a bare two paces behind him—the pleasure of seeing him squirm. If the summons concerned something else, any questions he asked stood a risk of revealing his intentions to Telamont.

They were twenty levels deep when the leading guards finally left the stairwell, then led the group down a winding tunnel through a large archway into a vast chamber with a high, vaulted ceiling. At one end of the cavern lay a hundred-yard slit through which the purple light of the predawn morning could be glimpsed outside. Several dozen Shadovar were pulling a large, comblike device back toward the slit. Closer by, several dozen more were folding a huge section of shadow blanket into a compact bundle similar to several others stacked neatly along the near wall.

When the laborers saw Telamont Tanthul and his party in the room, they immediately dropped to the floor and pressed their brows to the floor. Though this hardly seemed the sort of place where the Shadovar confined their prisoners, Galaeron's heart beat no easier. Malik and Aris had left Villa Dusari before Hadhrune arrived with the Most High's summons. Once Aris had collected his supplies, Malik would stage a diversion to make it easier for Galaeron and the giant to slip away from the enclave unnoticed.

"One of our shadow looms," Telamont explained. He waved a sleeve toward the comblike device being drawn toward the slit at the opposite end of the room, then motioned his guards onward. "Not what I brought you to see."

They followed the guards around the edge of the room, then stepped through another archway into an even larger chamber where hundreds of Shadovar were busy sewing sections of blanket together with strands of shadowsilk. Again, the laborers stopped work to press their brows to the floor as Telamont entered. This time, the Most High turned to Hadhrune, his platinum eyes flaring with displeasure.

"We cannot have this," he said.

"I shall see to it." Hadhrune left the group and went over to the edge of the work floor. "Return to your work, lazy ralbs! Do not dishonor the Most High by shirking your duty in his presence."

The workers scrambled to return to their sewing, though all were careful to keep their gazes fixed on the areas directly in front of their noses. Telamont motioned Galaeron to his side then led the way along the edge of the work floor through a broad archway at the far end. In the room beyond, Prince Escanor stood on a bronze flying disk, holding a folded shadow blanket, while Vala, suspended by a new pair of magic wings, flew a line over the top.

"This is what I brought you to see, Galaeron," Telamont said, crossing to the disk. "I thought you might wish to say farewell."

"Is that so?" Galaeron asked, trying to sense whether there was a double meaning behind Telamont's words. Did the Most High know what had passed between he and Vala at Villa Dusari the previous night? Or was he only trying to gauge the depth of Galaeron's feelings for her? In either case, his answer had to be the same. "Why would I want to do that?"

Telamont's eyes brightened beneath his cowl, then a breeze brushed Galaeron's face as Vala swooped down to land. Escanor came to stand beside her, saying nothing but absentmindedly running his dark fingers along the feathers of one of her magic wings.

"We've said our good-byes, Most High." Her green eyes flashed, hard and cold, over Galaeron's face, then she directed her full attention to Telamont. "I'm sorry you put yourself to such trouble."

"No trouble, my dear." Telamont tipped his cowl in her direction, then turned and studied Galaeron for a moment. Finally, he said, "You surprise even me, elf. I had not expected you to release your emotions so easily."

"I doubt it was as difficult as you think, Most High," Vala said, with enough bitterness in her voice to bring a pain to Galaeron's heart. "As it happens, they ran shallower than any of us thought. I'm glad to be rid of him."

"Indeed?" The purple line of a smile appeared in the shadows beneath the Most High's eyes. He turned to Hadhrune, then said, "This one may someday rival even you, my servant."

"Yours to see, Most High—but we must remember that only one of us serves the enclave." Hadhrune allowed his glare to linger on Galaeron just a second too long, then turned to Telamont and said, "I am afraid I must beg my leave, Most High. There is a disturbance in the Trades Ward that requires my attention."

"Of course." Telamont had barely raised his hand to dismiss Hadhrune before the seneschal melted into the darkness and was gone. The Most High turned to Galaeron and said, "If you will allow me a few moments, the battle with the Myth Drannor phaerimm is going to be a difficult one. I would like a few words with Escanor before he departs."

"Take all the time you need, Most High." Though Galaeron's voice was calm, his heart was pounding. The disturbance in the Trades Ward was Malik's diversion. Aris would be expecting Galaeron at the Cave Gate within a quarter hour. "With your permission, I can find my own way home. The route was not complicated, and the company here is not to my liking."

He cast a meaningful glance at Vala, who smiled cruelly and brushed the edge of her new wing against Escanor.

Telamont took all of this in with his metallic eyes, then raised a sleeve in dismissal. "Perhaps that is wise," he said. "I shall need you at the world-window by midday tomorrow, rested and alert. When Escanor lays the shadow blanket over Myth Drannor, we will need all of Melegaunt's wisdom that you can summon."

"As you command, Most High."

Galaeron bowed, more to hide his smile than to show subservience, then turned and left. He did not say good-bye to Vala or even wish her well in combat. He could think of nothing but of how she had betrayed him for Escanor, how Escanor had stolen her from him, how Telamont had permitted it . . . and, most especially, how he was going to make them pay.

All of them.

✡✡✡✡✡

The greatest danger, Malik realized, was not that the witch's stolen *haik* would slip through his grasp—though it might—or even that the merciless winds would beat him unconscious against the enclave's stony underside—though they might. The greatest danger was the lazy vultures who spent their lives in search of easy meals from the city rubbish chutes. Already, one creature was perched atop his right shoulder, pecking at his fingers, and two more were circling above his head, fighting over the left shoulder, and a dozen more were circling beneath his dangling feet, ready to snatch up any bloody morsels the others let fall.

"You are sure this is a good idea?" Aris called down.

"Undoubtedly one of my best."

Malik craned his neck and ran his gaze up ten feet of camel-wool *haik* to the jagged breach they had punched through the exterior wall of the workshop. Aris had carefully sculpted the hole to look like the crater of a powerful blasting spell, ingeniously fashioning two cragged teeth into the edge to bind the upper end of the cloth.

"Who would believe I would dangle myself here on purpose?" Malik asked.

"I'm more concerned that you still be there for them to find," Aris said. "It is a long way to the ground."

Malik did not look down. He had already done that once and through a hole in the murky haze glimpsed Anauroch's sands drifting past a thousand feet below.

"I will be here," he called, taking one hand off the *haik* to swat at the vulture pecking at his fingers. "Just sprinkle the sand and be gone. By the time this is sorted out, you and Galaeron will be far away."

Aris did not withdraw. "You are certain Ruha will not suffer for this?"

"Did she not say she wished to help?"

Aris nodded. "Yes, but—"

"Then let her help. No harm will come to the witch—I am not that lucky—and you know I cannot lie." Malik struggled to hold his tongue but was compelled by Mystra's curse to add, "Except by my silence, and when have you ever known me to hold my tongue for more than two minutes?"

Aris considered this, then said, "Only when you are sleeping." He tested the *haik* to make certain it was securely wedged in place, then waved. "Fare you well, my friend . . . and thank you."

Before Malik could reply, the battling vultures obscured his view, and Aris was gone by the time he could beat them aside again. He spent the next few minutes fighting off birds and cursing all creatures with feathers as the wind slammed him into the enclave's rocky exterior time and again. Though his body ached from a hundred horrible bruises and his cramped muscles burned like someone had pushed hot pokers into them, Malik did not worry that his strength would fail him. As the Seraph of Lies, he had been gifted with the ability to suffer any amount of pain and still perform his duties to Cyric, and while helping Aris and Galaeron escape the city did not necessarily serve the One, the second part of his plan most assuredly did.

When he judged he had allowed the giant sufficient time to leave the trade warrens and be on his way to the Cave Gate, Malik began to scream for help.

"Save me! *Help!*"

After a few minutes of screaming, someone finally poked her head out of the hole. She had long sable hair, dark sultry eyes, and, above the veil that covered the lower part of her face, a dusky complexion. The face was the last one he had hoped to see.

"So there you are," Ruha said. She squatted above the teeth where her *haik* was caught, scared the vultures off, and reached down to grab the cloth. "And with my *haik*, no less."

"Meddling witch!" Malik said. "What are you doing here?"

"Looking for you, of course. And now that we are alone, I think the time has come for us to take our leave of this flying city."

Still holding onto the *haik*, she held her free palm in front of her face and blew on it lightly, then began the incantation of one of her Bedine nature spells.

"Stop!" Malik began to climb the *haik* hand over hand. "Shrew! Harpy!"

Ruha finished her spell, then wrapped her hand into the *haik* and looked down, a smile in her dark eyes. "Is that how you talk to the one who holds your life in her hand?"

"Who will feed my poor Kelda?" Malik cried. He was halfway up the *haik*, almost within striking range. "I am going nowhere with you!"

"You prefer to fall?" Ruha twisted around, reaching back to collect something behind her. "Because that is your only choice."

"Not my only choice." Malik wrapped a hand into the *haik*, then reached under his *aba* and grabbed the hilt of his *jambiya*. "I have another I like much better."

Pulling her *kuerabiche* shoulder bag around with her, Ruha spun around to face him, exposing her throat just as he had hoped, and started to reach for her own dagger—then she fell backward as a swarthy Shadovar hand caught the strap of her *kuerabiche* and jerked her away from the edge.

Malik shoved his *jambiya* back in its sheath and began to scream. "Help! I am down here!"

Hadhrune's amber eyes peered over the edge. "I know where you are, Malik."

The Shadovar whispered some barely audible shadow spell, then Malik floated up through the hole into the goodshouse that had been serving as Aris's workshop. The place was crowded with Shadovar warriors but still looked as though a troop of bugbears had crashed through it. Statues lay toppled on their sides, some—mostly half-finished pieces that had little value anyway—shattered or irretrievably broken. The walls were marked with streaks of soot and pocked with hollows the size of a giant's head, and a broad smear of Aris's blood ran along the wall, pointing out the huge hole through which Malik had just been retrieved.

After taking all this in, Hadhrune turned to Ruha. "Did I not warn you what would happen if you violated our guest guard?"

Eyes widening, Ruha looked around the workshop and shook her head. "This is not my doing."

"Do not lie to me, Harper. With my own ears, I heard you give Malik the choice between death and leaving in your custody. That is violation enough." Hadhrune looked to Malik. "Where is the giant?"

Biting his tongue lest he speak and give himself away, Malik simply turned and looked out the big hole where he had been dangling.

"I see." Hadhrune flicked a hand in Ruha's direction, and suddenly she was swaddled in black shadow web. "You will be executed as soon as the Most High pronounces your sentence. What do you wish done with your property?"

"Nothing. I killed no one, and he knows it." Ruha glared at Malik, and in her stare he felt the unspoken threat to reveal Galaeron's escape plans. "Ask him. He has no choice but to tell the truth."

Hadhrune considered this for a moment, then nodded. "A reasonable request." He turned to Malik. "Did she kill Aris?"

"I have no wish to see her executed," Malik said.

"You don't?" This from Ruha and Hadhrune both.

"Not at all. It will be enough to banish her from the city."

Hadhrune frowned. "I didn't know Cyric-worshipers were so merciful."

"Oh, we are not," Malik said, allowing a half-smile to crease his lips, "but I can think of no greater torture for Ruha than to know I am living like a king in Shade Enclave while she is sucking the dew out of sand down in Anauroch."

"That is not how justice works in Shade Enclave," Hadhrune said. "Tell me if she killed Aris or not."

Malik shook his head—truthfully.

"If I banish her, Aris's life will be your responsibility," Hadhrune warned. "Tell me now, or the weight of her crime will rest on your head."

"On *my* head?"

This was something Malik had not planned on. He glanced at Ruha and found her smirking at his predicament—that he had to either exonerate her or be executed for the crime he had accused her of. He shook his head in despair.

"Let me make certain I understand," he said. "If she killed the giant, then you will execute her, and I will remain in Shade Enclave living like a king?"

Hadhrune nodded. "Did she kill him?"

Malik raised his hand. "But if she did not, you will banish her and execute me?"

Hadhrune nodded. "Yes. When someone is murdered, someone must pay. That is the law."

"My miserable life is only one unfair circumstance after another," Malik complained. He took a deep breath, then said, "I have no wish to die, but the truth is this: No one killed Aris. He and I staged this whole thing so that he and Galaeron could escape into the desert."

"Malik!" Ruha gasped. "I should have known you would—"

"Silence!" Hadhrune raised his hand toward her. The shadow web rose to cover her mouth. The seneschal glared at Malik for a moment, then said, "As you wish, little man."

Still pointing at the Harper, Hadhrune swept his hand toward the jagged hole, and Ruha flew from the room and arced down toward the desert.

When her black cocoon finally tumbled out of sight, he pointed at Malik and whispered something arcane. Malik found himself swaddled in sticky black shadow.

"Now you will stand before the Most High and answer for the giant's death," Hadhrune said. "To think, I nearly believed Galaeron when he said you could not lie."

CHAPTER EIGHT

16 Mirtul, the Year of Wild Magic

Escanor's army cascaded from the Cave Gate in a long river of flapping wings and shadowy pennants that curved down toward the east and vanished into the umbral mists beneath the city. Galaeron waited until the last rank of riders was well past the Livery Most High, then walked his veserab out to join the rear of the great formation. When no one objected—or even seemed to notice—he waved to Aris, who drifted into the Marshaling Court kneeling on a flying disk so overloaded with waterskins that it wobbled under the giant's slightest gesture.

Aris leaned down toward Galaeron, tilting the dish so precariously that it would have spilled its cargo had he not lowered a massive arm to hold the waterskins in place.

"You're sure the guards won't notice?" asked the giant.

"They'll notice," Galaeron replied, wincing at the gusty volume of the giant's whisper, "but we've traveled with Escanor before. A pair of gate guards isn't going to question our presence now."

"That I know, but this they would question," Aris said. He pointed at his knees, which were resting on a section of shadow blanket Galaeron had stolen as he left the looms. "You are certain we must take it?"

"I'm certain—very certain," Galaeron said. "That's how I repay them."

"Repay who?" Aris asked.

"All of them," Galaeron hissed. "Telamont, Escanor, Vala . . . everyone who's betrayed me."

"This is your shadow speaking, Galaeron," Aris said. "No one has betrayed you—especially Vala."

"Then where is she?" Galaeron hissed. "Why is she not here to keep her promise?"

"Because not being here is the only hope she sees of not having to keep it," Aris answered calmly. "You must leave this place before you are lost, and that would be impossible if she deserted Escanor to come with us. I am sure she will track us down later—especially if it proves necessary for her to keep her promise."

Galaeron shook his head. "You are too trusting, my large friend. Once we're gone, she will have no way of knowing when it becomes necessary."

"But she will," Aris said. "I will tell her."

They came to the watch balconies, and Aris clamped his mouth shut and stared ahead so rigidly that he looked suspicious even to Galaeron. The guards' gem-colored eyes fixed on the giant and followed his advance until they had passed under the great portcullis and launched themselves out into the sky, then they were curving down under the enclave with the rest of Escanor's army. Once they had passed out of view of the Cave Gate, they began to lag behind the others, and Galaeron used his shadow magic to make them both invisible. He was not really surprised to find the familiar chill of the Shadow Weave quenching a thirst that had lain buried just beneath the surface of his subconscious.

They dropped out of the shadow haze to find themselves over a mazelike warren of deep ravines and sheer pinnacles that marked the transition between the rolling sea of sand dunes over which the city had been drifting for most of the past tenday and the jagged spine of desert mountains toward which it was floating. Escanor's army was flying more or less in the same direction as the enclave but angling just a little bit south straight into the rising sun. Whistling an elven tune to help Aris keep track of him, Galaeron turned in the opposite direction—west toward Evereska.

"Galaeron?" Aris called.

"Here. Can't you hear my song?"

"If one can call that lip-trilling music, yes," Aris replied, "but shouldn't we have a look down there? It looks like someone might be in trouble."

Galaeron searched the sands ahead and saw nothing. "Where?"

"South of our bearing," Aris said. "Lying in the hollow on the crest of that dune, perhaps a mile back."

Galaeron looked and saw nothing but golden sunlight shining on the eastern faces of an endless chain of sand walls. "Where?"

"Follow me," Aris said.

The sonorous purr of stone giant humming arose beside Galaeron. He reined his veserab back and fell in behind his invisible companion, then followed the sound down toward the desert at a gentle angle. After a few moments, he saw the tiny dimple toward which they were descending, a circle the size of his fingertip with a minuscule fleck of darkness in the center. The fleck gradually grew large enough so that Galaeron could see it was indeed wriggling about like a chrysalis struggling to escape its cocoon.

"He lied!" Aris boomed.

"Who lied?" Galaeron called.

"Malik!" the giant exclaimed. "He told me Ruha would come to no harm."

Galaeron eyed the dark cocoon. It was about as long as his hand, and he could see that it had a vaguely human shape, with a head-shaped lump on one end and a feet-shaped tail at the other.

"How do you know that's Ruha?" asked the elf.

"How could it not be?" Aris demanded. "How many dark-haired women in veils do you expect to find lying about in this desert?"

"More than you might think," Galaeron replied. The giant's description could fit any Bedine woman Galaeron had ever seen, though it would have been an unthinkable coincidence to find one lying about trussed up beneath Shade Enclave's path. "But if you say it is Ruha, I will trust to your eyesight. It is obviously better than an elf's."

"Oh yes, it is definitely the witch," Aris said. "I recognize her now."

To Galaeron, she was still an indistinguishable lump of darkness. They descended to the crater in silence, and a minute later, Galaeron recognized Ruha's dark eyes peering out above her customary purple veil. Judging by the size of the crater in which she lay, she had hit the dune with a fair amount of speed, but she either had magical protections or was exceptionally resilient even for a Bedine. Swaddled in a cocoon of shadow web that would have dissolved in another hour anyway, she was writhing about, rolling back and forth in an effort to work her hands free so she could dispel the magic that held her bound.

"Don't hurt yourself," Galaeron called. "We're here."

"It is about time!" Ruha rolled onto her back and looked more or less toward Galaeron's voice. "I was beginning to think you meant to leave me out here to die."

"Meant to?" Aris said, speaking from the side opposite Galaeron. "We did not mean to do anything. It is a lucky thing we saw you at all. How did you end up here?"

"Do not feign innocence with me, Gray Face. You are not much better at lying than Malik."

"Lying?" Aris gasped. "He said that you would not be harmed."

"And so I am not," Ruha said, "but your plan has miscarried."

"What plan would that be?" Galaeron dismounted and tried to dispel the shadow web. To his astonishment, the spell failed—and even that felt good. "Who cast this on you? One of the princes?"

"As if you didn't know!" Ruha scoffed.

Galaeron had a sinking feeling. "I don't know," he said. "What do you think our plan was?"

"To make it look like I had violated the Shadovar's guest guard, of course," Ruha said.

"Why would we do that?" Galaeron asked.

"To have me exiled, so I would have to serve as your guide." Ruha was beginning to look less angry and more perplexed. "But Malik could no more keep your secret than he could neglect an untended purse."

Galaeron glanced eastward and, finding Shade Enclave little more than a dark diamond barely visible against the shadowed slopes of the distant mountains, dispelled his invisibility spells. He found Aris looking more than a little chagrined.

"Aris, what happened?" Galaeron asked. "You were only to create a distraction."

"We *did* create a distraction," the giant said. "We made it look like Ruha had attacked Malik and knocked me out of the enclave."

"That much worked," Ruha said, "but Hadhrune isn't naive. He knew Malik was hiding something, and eventually Malik had to admit that you and Aris had left the city."

Galaeron and Aris immediately looked toward the city.

"You have a little time," Ruha said. "Hadhrune didn't believe him. But sooner or later, they're going to discover that you're gone—and when that happens, Malik will be in trouble."

"As will Vala," Aris said. "It won't take them long to realize we were all part of the plan."

"Unless we return to the city at once," Ruha said. "Hadhrune still believes that I killed Aris while trying to capture Malik. If we return to the enclave with Aris alive, matters will be confused, but there will be no crime. Things will be as before. You will be able to bide your time and escape when it is safe for Vala."

Galaeron shook his head. "Except for the shadow blanket." He pointed at Aris's bronze flying disk. "Once they realize that is gone, they're not going to believe anything we say."

"Shadow blanket?" Ruha asked.

Aris pulled a corner up from behind his waterskins. "Galaeron's vengeance," he said. "It will be the undoing of us all."

Ruha frowned. "What is that?"

Galaeron explained about how the Shadovar were using the blankets to melt the High Ice and upset the weather all along the Savage Frontier and Sword Coast.

"Once they realize I've taken this, I doubt they're going to trust us much further."

"I believe that time has come," Aris said. He pointed toward the floating city, where a single dark line could be seen descending beneath the enclave. "They seem to be turning in our direction."

"In the name of Kozah!" Ruha cursed. Still encased in her shadow web, she began to roll toward the shadowy side of the dune. "Quick, send your veserab and flying disk into the west. We will hide beneath the sands, then sneak away after they pass by."

Galaeron nodded and sent his veserab into the sky, then turned and rushed across the crater to where Aris was unloading his waterskins.

"Leave the water. There is no time!" he said, jumping onto the disk. "Get the blanket!"

"The blanket?" Aris gasped.

"The blanket!" Galaeron said, hurling the heavy shroud into the crater. "Water, we can find later."

✡✡✡✡✡

To the eye of Keya Nihmedu, the silver magicstar drifting past the window of the Livery Gate watchtower looked even brighter than the sun that once blazed down on Evereska from high above the craggy peaks of the Shaeradim. It hurt her eyes even to look under it to the yellowing meadow that surrounded the city cliffs, and its light flooded the cramped chamber with a white brilliance that brooked no shadows.

The magicstar was no sun. It hissed and sputtered like a guttering torch and drizzled a constant trail of cinders in its wake, filling the air with the acrid stench of brimstone and lamp oil. When Keya closed her eyes, she could not sense it at all, could not see its glow shining through her eyelids or feel its heat sinking into her skin. It was as though the magicstar cast only the illusion of light or that its radiance simply lacked the true substance of sunlight.

It lacked something. Though there were more than a hundred of the spheres floating in and around Evereska, the grass continued to yellow, the great bluetops and sycamores still dropped their leaves, and the liliap blossoms withered and grayed. Even Zharilee and the other sun elves were beginning to lose their color and turn sickly shades of saffron and ocher.

Something would have to be done to bring real sun to the Vale, and Keya was not the only one who thought so. Khelben Arunsun was standing at the next window with Kiinyon Colbathin and Lord Duirsar, staring out at dying lands within the mythal and quietly arguing for an assault on the enemy shadow mantle.

"We need only a company of spellblades, a dozen Long Watch sentries, and the Cloudtop Magi Circle," Khelben was saying behind her. He motioned at Dexon and the other Vaasans, who had become a more or less permanent escort—when they were not at Treetop, eating and drinking the Nihmedu larder into nothingness. "We just need to hold our position long enough to attach a magicstar—"

Lord Duirsar raised a finger to interrupt. "Did you not say the shadow mantle was *outside* the deadwall, my friend?"

"I did."

Keya turned just enough to see Khelben nodding as he spoke. While she was honored that Lord Duirsar and the others felt comfortable speaking of such matters in her presence, she was acutely conscious of the disparity in their ranks and tried to be as inconspicuous as possible in her eavesdropping.

"The shadow mantle's appearance suggested an interesting possibility," Khelben continued. "I'm beginning to think that the deadwall is actually three walls, a sphere of imprisoning magic sandwiched between two layers of dead magic."

Duirsar nodded eagerly. "That would explain why no spells can pass through it."

"Exactly," Khelben said. "So I may be able to burn through with my silver fire."

"Surely you've tried that before," Kiinyon Colbathin said, his too-gaunt face sneering in disapproval.

"I have," Khelben confirmed. "I've noticed a disturbance, but the imprisoning layer has always remained intact—the silver fire has no effect on normal magic—and the phaerimm have always come to chase me off before I had a chance to dispel it."

"Which is why you need assistance," Lord Duirsar surmised, "to hold the enemy at bay long enough for you to cast a second spell."

"A little longer than that," Khelben admitted. "The Cloudtop Circle would need enough time to cast a magicstar and attach it to the shadow mantle."

"I don't like it," Kiinyon said, shaking his sharp-featured head. "That will take easily a quarter hour. By then, my spellblades will be trying to hold off a hundred phaerimm. The circle would be doing well to finish its spell before they were all dead."

"The Vale is dying, Kiinyon," Lord Duirsar said. "We must do something, or the mythal will die with it. Keya, what do you think?"

Keya felt like her heart had leaped into her throat. "Milord?"

"About Khelben's mission!" Kiinyon snapped. "This is no time to play coy, Watcher. If we didn't want you to hear, we would have sent you to the rooftop."

Keya felt the heat rise to her cheeks. "Of course, Swordlord." She turned to address Khelben and found him looking at the ceiling with his head cocked and a vacant expression in his eyes. Eager to avoid another rebuke, she spoke anyway. "If Lord Blackstaff feels that our lives would be well-spent, I am sure I speak for Zharilee and the others in the Long Watch—"

Khelben raised a silencing palm, then spoke to the ceiling. "Laeral? Was that you?"

Lord Duirsar and Kiinyon exchanged astonished glances. They knew as well as Keya that while all Chosen heard the next few words when their name was spoken anywhwere on Faerûn, the deadwall had limited the range of Khelben's ability to the Shaeradim. If he was in contact with Laeral, either she had entered the Shaeradim or something had weakened the phaerimm's barrier.

"Laeral, of course I'm alive," Khelben said. "I'm in Evereska."

The excitement was too much for the others in the room. Lord Duirsar and Kiinyon began to call Laeral's name and bark requests for weapons and magic, while the Vaasans inquired about Vala and whether the phaerimm had attacked their homes. Even Keya could not restrain herself from asking for news of her brother.

Khelben turned a dark eye on them all. "Do you mind?"

The room fell as silent as a tomb, then Keya and the others spent the next few minutes listening to a strange, one-sided conversation punctated by the use of Laeral's name every few words.

After establishing that she was still well outside of the Shaeradim, struggling through the Forest of Wyrms, the two Chosen spent a few minutes filling each other in on events inside and outside of the Shaeradim. Once they each had a basic idea of what the other had been doing for the four months or so, they began to test the extent to which the deadwall had been weakened, trying various forms of communication magic. When all of their spells proved unable to penetrate the barrier, Khelben decided to try another tack and used a spell to send his dagger to Laeral's hand. The weapon vanished when he uttered the incantation.

"Laeral, it's on its way." Khelben was silent for a moment, then frowned. "It didn't—er, Laeral, it didn't?"

A loud thunk reverberated through the ceiling, then an astonished Watcher cried out, "Hey, who's dropping daggers?"

Khelben closed his eyes for a moment, then said, "Laeral, no good. We'll talk later."

Khelben continued to stare at the ceiling, then turned to Lord Duirsar. "How much were you able to glean from my end of the conversation?"

"It would be better for you to retell all," Lord Duirsar said. "I take it Lady Laeral has found a way to weaken the deadwall?"

"Not Laeral," Khelben said. "The Netherese."

"The Netherese?" Lord Duirsar gasped.

"Shade Enclave, to be more precise," Khelben said. "They are the ones who created the shadow mantle—to cut the phaerimm off from the Weave and weaken them for a final assault."

"Then there is no need to sacrifice a company of spellblades to affix a magicstar to it," Kiinyon said. "If Shade Enclave is on our side, we need only ask them to lower it before the mythal is weakened."

Khelben's expression grew darker. "Matters are not so clear, I'm afraid." He glanced at Keya and the Vaasans, then took Lord Duirsar's arm and started for the stairs. "Perhaps we should discuss this in Cloudtop. There are difficult decisions to make, and you may have need of the Hill Elders' advice."

Keya bit her lip and managed to remain silent, even when Khelben started down the stairs with Kiinyon and Lord Duirsar.

Once they were out of sight, Dexon came to her side and wrapped a burly arm around her shoulders. "I'm sure Galaeron's all right," he said. "We'll ask later, after they've sorted out their strategy."

Keya nodded and squeezed Dexon's hand. "Thank you." She closed her eyes and raised her face toward the heavens. "I pray to Hanali that, just this once, the Hill Elders will move with a speed more human than elf."

✡✡✡✡✡

After just three days beneath the blazing Anauroch sun, Galaeron's tongue was swollen to the size of a rothé's. His head throbbed and his vision blurred unpredictably. His heart beat in slow, listless thumps that barely seemed to pump the viscous blood through his veins, and he was close enough to water to smell damp sandstone. Sometimes, through the screen of emerald foliage growing along the base of the cliff ahead, he even glimpsed a flash of rippling silver. Had Ruha not insisted that they pause to study the oasis before entering, he and Aris would have been at the pool already, doing their best to drink it dry.

Two minutes later, though, Aris and Ruha would have been dead and Galaeron on his way back to Shade Enclave in a pair of scaly claws.

It had taken Ruha only a few minutes of watching to realize the oasis was too quiet, there were no birds flitting through the treetops or hares scurrying through the underbrush. A few minutes later, Aris had spotted the dragon, a young blue tucked onto a hidden ledge just above the treetops, little more than its eyes and horns visible at one end and a tip of dangling tail at the other.

Galaeron motioned to his companions, and they slipped down behind the crest of the dune and retreated into the trough nearly four hundred feet below. There was no shade, so Aris dropped to his seat on the stolen shadow blanket, which lay folded on the face of the opposite dune. His eyes were glassy and sunken with dehydration, his lips cracking and his nostrils inflamed.

The giant glanced up at the midday sun, then said, "I need that water." His voice was a raw croak. "Even if I have to fight a dragon for it."

"The dragon will only be the beginning," Galaeron said. "It looks too small to have many spells, but I'll wager the Shadovar have arranged a way for it to communicate with Malygris."

"Maybe it has nothing to do with them," Aris said. "It seems like oases would be good places for young dragons to hunt."

"But not to guard," Ruha said. Though she had drunk no more than a few swallows since their departure from Shade, her voice betrayed no sign of thirst. "Nothing will come while a dragon is here. When they are hunting, they must swoop in and take what they can. Otherwise, the silence of the birds betrays them."

Aris let his head drop. "I can't go another day," he said. "If I go in alone, maybe we can fool it."

"How many stone giants do you think there are wandering the desert?" Ruha asked. "If the dragon sees any of us, the Shadovar will realize we turned toward Cormyr instead of Evereska."

Aris glanced toward the crest of the dune, his eyes growing large and wild. "Then we have to kill it," he said. "We have to sneak up and kill it."

"You're sun sick, Aris," Galaeron said. "You can't sneak up on a dragon."

"There will be water in the Saiyaddar." Ruha stood and started south, walking on the trough's steep wall so the slope would collapse and slide down to cover her tracks. "We will be there soon. It is not far."

Aris groaned and buried his face in his arms.

"Come on," Galaeron said. "I'll take the shadow blanket."

Aris raised his head high enough to fix a single eye on Galaeron. "It is twice your size. How can you carry it?"

Galaeron pulled a strand of shadowsilk from his cloak and began to fashion it into a circle. "How do you think?"

"No!" Aris boomed the word sharply enough to loose a small avalanche on the slope behind Galaeron. "No shadow magic."

Ruha spun around. "Are you *trying* to call the dragon down on us?" She glared at the giant for a moment, then looked to Galaeron. "Leave the blanket. It is too heavy and hot for him to carry."

"It's proof," Galaeron said as he began to twist the ends of his shadowsilk together, "and I'm not leaving it."

"Then I'm carrying it." Aris stood and slung the huge blanket over his shoulder. "Because you're *not* casting another shadow spell."

With no place to hide from the sun and concerned about attracting vultures and giving away their position even if they did stop, the trio spent the rest of the day marching south. Every so often, Ruha would climb to the crest of a dune to study the terrain and search the sky for signs of pursuing dragons, then wave her companions up behind her and lead them eastward in a mad dash over one dune crest after another. The effort never seemed to tire the witch, but Galaeron and Aris would grow so weary after a dozen or so crossings that their legs gave out and left them crawling on their hands and knees.

Galaeron spent much of that time seething over Vala's desertion, relishing the prospect of the vengeance he would extract on Telamont for refusing to intervene with Escanor, and plotting how he would emphasize the prince's part in the melting of the High Ice.

The Shadovar had betrayed him, had stolen Vala away and made her turn a blind eye to the promise she had sworn to him, and for that they would pay. For that, he would expose their true nature to the world, reveal how they were melting the High Ice and upsetting the weather all along the Sword Coast. What that decision might mean for Evereska, Galaeron did not even consider. Shade Enclave had its own reasons for destroying the phaerimm, and his departure was unlikely to have any impact on their plans.

Finally, as the afternoon shadows began to extend their stretch toward evening, they crested a dune and found themselves looking over a vast prairie of pale green grasslands. In the distance, the brown blot of a gazelle herd was slowly drifting over the purple horizon, while the rest of the plain was speckled with the tiny flecks of foraging birds. Scattered here and there along the course of a dry riverbed were the puffy crowns of several dozen big cottonwood trees.

"Skoraeus strike me now!" Aris cursed. "The river is as dry as bones."

"Only on the surface." Ruha slipped over the crest of the dune and started down the other side. "There is water underneath."

"Underneath?" Aris cast a longing look north toward the cliffs where they had left the young dragon. "How far underneath?"

"Not far," Ruha said, waving the giant after her.

"You have said that before," Aris observed.

Despite his protests, the giant raced down the dune past the witch and started across the plain.

"Aris! Wait until dark!" Ruha called. "The birds!"

She was too late—and even had she not been, it was doubtful that the giant would have stopped. With the heavy shadow blanket still draped over his shoulders, he started for the riverbed in long, booming strides that sent a cloud of startled birds screeching and cackling into the sky.

Ruha looked to the north. "How close do you think—"

"Too close," Galaeron said. "I have heard blue dragons brag that they pick meals in the Shaeradim from a roost in the Greycloaks."

"You speak with dragons?" Ruha asked.

"On occasion," Galaeron said. "The Tomb Guard had an arrangement with several young blues."

Instead of asking about the arrangement, Ruha nodded and started across the plain after Aris. "Then we must hurry."

Galaeron caught her shoulder and pointed toward a fan of alluvial gravel spilling out of the foothills that separated the Saiyaddar from the parched slopes of the Scimitar Spires.

"We stand a better chance hiding," he said. "A young dragon will be arrogant in its approach, and we can take it by surprise."

"You would use your friend as bait?"

"He's the one who scared up the birds." Galaeron's tone was defensive. "I'm just trying to keep us all alive."

Ruha considered this, then started along the edge of the plain. "Your plan makes sense—though it would be better if he had been given the chance to volunteer."

"He volunteered when he let his thirst put us in danger," Galaeron said, joining her.

"Perhaps so," Ruha said, "but had you taken his waterskins from the flying disk instead of your shadow blanket, his thirst would not be so great."

Galaeron's only reply was an angry scowl. They were only about halfway to the gravel fan when the birds suddenly began to flee southward. Ruha pulled Galaeron into a bramble thicket and crouched on her haunches, pulling a clump of thorny stalks over their heads so they would be concealed from the air. Aris did not seem to realize anything was wrong for another dozen steps, when he noticed the fleeing birds and stopped to turn around. He spent several moments searching the plain behind him, calling out to Galaeron before finally raising his gaze skyward and looking north toward the oasis where they had seen the dragon.

Though Galaeron was hiding close to five hundred paces away, he was close enough to see the giant's jaw fall and his shoulders sag. Aris spent another moment searching the plain behind him, then, still carrying the heavy shadow blanket, turned and ran for the foothills, angling toward a narrow gully not far from where Galaeron and Ruha were hiding.

"Good," Galaeron whispered.

He began to fashion a tiny stick figure out of shadowsilk. Ruha looked to the sky. It was only a moment before she nudged Galaeron and the cross-shaped shadow of a small dragon began to sweep across the Saiyaddar. Galaeron finished his effigy, then pointed it at Aris and uttered an incantation. A circle of shadows appeared around the giant. One after the other, they peeled themselves off the ground and assumed Aris's form, then fanned out in a dozen different directions.

An angry cackle sounded from the sky, then the dragon swooped into view, its blue scales flashing like sapphires in the dusky light. It leveled off a dozen feet from the ground and, starting at one end of the fleeing replicas, opened its mouth and loosed a huge bolt of lightning that stretched in front of three of the fleeing shadow giants.

Lacking any wits of their own, the images continued straight into the bolt and vanished from sight.

"This is a smart one," Ruha whispered, pulling a small flint and steel from her *aba,* "and it wants us alive."

"It wants *me* alive," Galaeron corrected. "Don't overestimate your value—or Aris's—to the Shadovar."

The dragon breathed again, spraying another bolt of lightning in front of four more running giants. This time, they stopped and fled in the opposite direction. The dragon wheeled on a wing tip and extended its claws, slashing through two illusionary giants on its first pass. The dragon pulled up less than fifty paces from them, exposing its thin belly scales as it wheeled around to snatch up the fleeing giant. Ruha started to rise from their hiding place, pointing the flint and steel at the dragon's abdomen to cast what Galaeron knew would be a fire storm.

"Not yet!" Galaeron hissed.

He caught her arm and pulled her back down, then pointed his effigy at a figure he knew to be a false Aris. He whispered the same spell, and a circle of shadows appeared around each of the remaining giants on the plain. They began to rise by the dozen and flee in every direction. The dragon roared in frustration and blasted the nearest circle with its third and final lightning bolt.

By unlucky chance, his target proved to be the correct one. Aris bellowed in pain and went down on his face, then the dragon was on him, pinning him to the ground with a huge claw and hissing something angry that Galaeron could not quite hear from so far away.

"Coward!" Ruha hissed, throwing off the brambles. "You should have let me attack when we had a shot at his belly!"

She started across the plain at a run, pointing her fingers at the huge dragon. Blood boiling at her insult, Galaeron started after her—then stopped as she poured a volley of golden bolts into the wyrm's flank. The resulting blast sent a fountain of blue scales spraying into the air, along with a fair amount of draconian blood and flesh.

The dragon roared and brought its huge head around—only to receive another volley of the witch's golden bolts in the snout. This time, the eruption sent a nostril, two horns, and one slit-pupiled eye tumbling away over its shoulder. As surprised by Ruha's power as was Galaeron, the creature spread its great wings and launched itself into the air.

It was clutching Aris and the shadow blanket in its massive claws.

Ruha switched to her flint and steel, crying out a Bedine fire spell and striking sparks into the air. A long line of tiny meteors streaked into the air, taking the dragon in the right wing and burning several dozen melon-sized holes through the leathery skin. The creature pitched right and plummeted a hundred feet toward the foothills, then leveled off and began to fly for freedom—still clutching Aris and the shadow blanket.

Galaeron was not going to let it escape with his shadow blanket. He fashioned a strand of shadowsilk into a noose, then uttered a long string of magic syllables and flicked the loop after the fleeing dragon. The filament stretched to nearly half a mile in length, allowing Galaeron just enough time to slip his end of the line under his foot before the noose expanded to the size of a wagon wheel and flipped itself up to slip over the dragon's head.

A version of a Tomb Guard enchantment used to capture fleeing crypt breakers, the spell worked even better with shadowsilk than with elven thread. As soon as the dragon hit the end of the line, the noose closed and the filament contracted to a small fraction of its previous length, both cutting off the wyrm's air supply and jerking it around to crash down within a few dozen paces of Galaeron.

The stunned wyrm impacted face-first, then lay in a crumpled, convulsing heap as it clawed in vain at the magic line. Keeping his foot on his end of the line to keep the noose tight, Galaeron leveled his palm at its already mangled head and drilled a hole through the wyrm's skull with a single shadow bolt. His body was filled with so much shadow magic that it was almost numb, but he didn't mind at all. The cold felt good.

Ruha came to his side and paused as though to say something, then thought better of it and went to the dragon's head.

"Dead," she confirmed.

"Good."

Galaeron stepped off the magic line, which vanished as soon his foot lost contact with it, and started forward as Ruha crawled over the wyrm's neck to its underside.

"And my blanket?" he asked. "Still in one piece?"

Ruha snapped her head around to glare at him. "Yes, the blanket is still in one piece." She dropped out of sight behind the dragon, then added, "Which is more than I can say for your friend."

"Aris?" Galaeron broke into a run. "He's hurt?"

"Yes, and badly." Ruha peered over the wyrm's back, then said, "That is what happens when you use someone for dragon bait."

Galaeron reached the dragon's back and clambered over to find Aris trapped beneath the wyrm's body. There were four talon punctures in his chest and one arm was twisted around behind him at an impossible angle. The giant's gray eyes were barely open, and when they fell on Galaeron's face, they looked away.

CHAPTER NINE

19 Mirtul, the Year of Wild Magic

By dusk of the day of its arrival, the Shadovar army was drawing the last corner of its shadow blanket over legendary Myth Drannor. The cracked spires and vine-wrapped columns of the city, already half-hidden behind a wall of spring mist, vanished beneath an undulating mantle of darkness, and a silence that had been eerie and foreboding for most of the day grew perfect and still. As the edges were affixed to the ground, a few birds and other woodland animals rushed to escape in ones and twos. These creatures were allowed to flee, but companies of warriors were waiting to slay any monster that might return later to harass the veserabs. From her airborne vantage point at the western end of the city, Vala saw them strike down a beholder, two gargoyles, and even a malaugrym in its true three-tentacled form.

The blanket would prevent their quarry from teleporting away or using the translocational gates rumored to be still functional inside the city, but that only meant the phaerimm would be even more dangerous and ferocious than usual. According to the Shadovar scouts and diviners, there were still close to thirty thornbacks inhabiting the ruins' subterranean levels, and if the attack was to succeed, most would have to be slain in their own lairs. For the first time in her life, Vala wished she could write. She would have liked to set down some thoughts for her son before the bladework began.

Vala dipped a magic wing toward the rolling meadow at the western end of the city and landed in the trampled grass outside Escanor's pavilion tent. The prince was waiting in the entrance, his coppery eyes watching every move as she undid her breastplate so she could remove the wing harness. His retinue of aides and subcommanders was there as well, though most seemed more interested in watching him watch her.

Though Vala had never been particularly shy—and even less so after her time among the elves—Escanor's gaze made her uncomfortable in a way that even the hungry leers of her own Vaasans never had. Instead of turning away, however, she smiled and cocked a playful eyebrow as she raised her tunic to undo the chest buckles.

"Never seen a girl take off her wings?"

Something that resembled a grin crossed the prince's face. "It was not your wings that caught my eye." Escanor left the pavilion tent, not coming to her so much as emerging out of the shadows at her side. "You are growing more comfortable with them?"

"Not comfortable enough to sleep in." Vala turned her back to the prince, placing the wings more or less in his hands. She let the shadowsilk straps slide through the slots in the back of her tunic, then began to roll her weary shoulders. "We *are* going to sleep before the assault, aren't we?"

"That will be up to you." Escanor waited for Vala to put herself in order again. When she had, he said, "I have some news."

Vala's heart sank. Her thoughts flew at once to Galaeron and Aris, but when she turned, she asked, "Something has happened at the Granite Tower?"

It was impossible to say whether Escanor meant his fang-filled smile to be reassuring or mocking. "Not at all. I am speaking of Galaeron."

"Galaeron?" Vala said, feigning disappointment. She had been considering this moment since they departed the enclave and had come to the conclusion that there was only one way to play it. "He actually left?"

The prince's eyes flared red. "You knew of his plans?"

"Knew?" Vala shook her head. "I thought it was just shadow talk. He started it after you asked me to come along on this assault. You made him jealous, I think."

"And you didn't tell the Most High?"

"Why would I tell my personal business to the Most High?"

"It is not only your business," Escanor said. "The knowledge he carries belongs to Shade Enclave."

Vala smiled and patted him on the cheek. "I guess you should have thought of that before you invited me on this trip." She picked up her wings and started for her tent. "I've got to go wash. When's dinner?"

Escanor walked alongside her. "You're not worried about him?"

"Should I be?" Vala did not stop walking. In this, above all things, she had to appear indifferent. If Escanor knew how she really felt, he would conceal his knowledge and play on her emotions to make her reveal what she knew. "The Most High had turned him against me. You saw."

"Then you can't tell me where he is?"

Vala almost smiled. If the Shadovar didn't know where Galaeron was, he was still free. "I'd watch for him at Evereska, were I you."

"That is the obvious choice, of course," Escanor said, "but he knows we have an army there. We were thinking he might have intended to go to Waterdeep, instead."

"Might have," Vala said. From the little she had overheard after leaving the dinner, that had in fact been Galaeron's plan. "It's going to be hell finding him. Anauroch's a big desert."

"Particularly on foot. We found their veserab and flying disk, with all of their water—but no sign of them." Escanor took Vala's arm and stopped her. "If you know where they're going, you must tell me—for their own sakes. Without their waterskins, they won't last a tenday, even if they can find the oases."

"Then they won't last a tenday," Vala said.

Though Escanor was right about their chances of surviving Anauroch—at least about Aris's—the Shadovar had already guessed the little she knew, so there was nothing to be gained by admitting her own small involvement.

She glared at the dark hand grasping her arm expectantly and said, "At least it will save me the trouble of hunting Galaeron down after he is completely lost to his shadow."

Escanor released her arm. "You truly don't know where they are?"

"Isn't that what I said?"

"And you are not in love with Galaeron?"

"I have more self-respect than that." As she told this lie, Vala made a point of staring directly into the prince's eyes. "All I am to him is a promise."

Escanor surprised her with an obviously sincere smile. "Just as I told the Most High." He waved her toward his tent. "Please, you will stay here tonight. It will be more comfortable."

"Comfortable?" Though Vala was cringing inside, she forced a playful half-smirk. "Don't you think we need our sleep tonight?"

"When we are done, you will sleep like a lioness after her kill," Escanor replied, showing his fangs. "In truth, I had thought your flirtations no more than a low attempt to mask your betrayal behind a veneer of desire, but I see now that Melegaunt's reports about the women of Vaasa were not exaggerated."

"Reports?" Vala demanded.

"That you are always in season," Escanor said. He took her hand affectionately between his. "Bodvar's daughter was a favorite of his."

"Bodvar's daughter?" Vala pondered this for a moment, then gasped, "Granna?"

"Have no fear. Even if Melegaunt is your grandfather, we are many generations apart. Our blood is hardly the same at all." He pulled her toward his pavilion. "Clear my tent!"

Vala stopped cold. "Wait!"

Escanor's eyes flared red. "You are not sincere?"

"I'm always sincere," Vala said, grimacing inwardly at the distasteful looks the Shadovar cast her way as they streamed from the pavilion tent, "but we've been on the wing for four days and pulling shadow all day for a fifth. I've got to wash."

"I have water in my tent," Escanor said. "You can wash here."

" 'Wash' is a figure of speech," Vala said. While hardly above sharing a man's bed for her own reasons, she was not in the practice of allowing herself to be ordered into one. The prince was pushing too hard, too fast. He was up to something, and she had to buy time to puzzle out what. "What I really have to do is—"

"You can do that in the garderobe behind my tent," Escanor interrupted. "It opens into the Gray Wastes."

"All right," Vala said, feigning surrender, "but we've got to eat first. I'm famished, and with the day we have tomorrow—"

"That will be no concern to you," Escanor said, leading her into the empty pavilion. "A prince's consort is not expected to fight."

"What?" Finally seeing her opening, Vala stopped. "Consort?"

"Of course," Escanor said. "We Shadovar are not barbarians. We do not cast a woman aside after we have used her."

"And I have to stop fighting?"

Escanor shook his head. "Not at all. A consort may fight at her own pleasure—but it is not expected." He waved her toward depths at the back of the tent. "If you please. I will have food brought later."

Vala refused to cross the threshold. "What about Sheldon?"

"Your son?" Escanor asked. "He will be brought to the enclave and raised in my house as a High Lord. Will that not please you?"

Vala needed to consider this only a moment before she shook her head. "No, he is Vaasan."

"Very well, he will remain in Vaasa," Escanor replied. "Whatever you wish, Vala."

Vala turned to look at him. "Whatever I wish?"

"For a consort of the First Prince, anything," Escanor said. "You could even return to Vaasa yourself—with Bodvar's debt repaid in full."

It was nearly enough to make Vala step into the tent. She had been gone from the Granite Tower for more than a year and longed for nothing more than to return to raise her son and see her aging parents—and that was what made the prince's offer too good to be true. He wanted more from her than to share the fur. There were a thousand courtesans in the Palace Most High that he could have for a smile, and most were—though it stung her pride to admit it—far more desirable than she.

She stepped away from the tent and narrowed her eyes at Escanor. "What does all this generosity cost me? My life? My will?"

Escanor spread his hands. "Nothing, if your desire is true."

"Let's say it isn't."

"Then there is a much easier way to secure the same privileges," Escanor said, dodging the question. "Just tell me what you know about Galaeron's disappearance."

"I already have," Vala said. "Beyond that, I don't know anything that would help you."

"Allow me to be the judge of that," Escanor said. "You cannot know what might help us."

Vala was tempted. She was almost telling the truth anyway. If Galaeron wasn't going to Waterdeep—and apparently he wasn't, since the Shadovar couldn't find him—then she was at a loss. Escanor was right, though, in that she couldn't know what might help them find the fleeing elf—or implicate those who had stayed behind. However she looked at it, she would be betraying her companions at least in spirit, if not in fact.

"Let's try this," Vala said. "Tell me what you know, and I'll tell you if anything I know can help."

Escanor surprised her by laughing—not a cold, threatening chuckle, but a warm, almost respectful guffaw.

"You are a brave woman, Vala Thorsdotter," he said, clamping a big hand on the back of her neck. "I do not want to see what will become of you if the Most High learns you have refused to recant your betrayal."

Vala's legs grew icy, and she looked down to see herself melting into the shadows at her feet. "What are—"

That was as far as she made it before her consciousness vanished into cold darkness. Sometime later—it could have been a second or an hour, Vala had no way of telling—she felt the humid Myth Drannor air warming first her face, then her body, and finally her legs. She saw herself rising from a puddle of darkness, her body returning to its normal proportions. When she dared to raise her gaze again, she found herself standing atop the shadow blanket, surrounded by the murk-veiled towers and trees of Myth Drannor. Standing half-glimpsed at varying distances along the narrow street were dozens of companies of Shadovar warriors.

Still holding Vala by the neck, Escanor pulled her around the corner of a huge, castlelike ruin into a tree-choked courtyard that had once served as the building's main entrance. There was a single attached tower to the left and an L-shaped wing on the right, all cloaked in the same mantle of darkness as the trees and the ground itself. A dozen Shadovar warriors stood near the entrance of the courtyard with their weapons and wands in hand and a nervous officer watching Escanor approach.

Sensing that she would not like whatever the prince had in mind, Vala allowed her hand to drift toward her sword hilt—and felt Escanor's iron grasp tighten on her neck.

"You saved my life once," he hissed. "Do not make me return the favor by snapping your neck."

"It's dark," Vala said. "Just wanted to see what's going on."

"Truly," Escanor sneered. He stopped in front of the nervous-looking officer. "This is the Irithlium?"

The warrior inclined his head. "It is, Prince."

"Good." Escanor thrust Vala forward. "Tell her what we've been able to learn about this place."

The officer nodded and turned to Vala. "Not much, Lady Thorsdotter. It was once a magic school, which naturally attracted the phaerimm. The upper layers seem to have been stripped bare, but there are at least six phaerimm lairing somewhere beneath the foundations."

"Six phaerimm?" Vala gasped, understanding why the patrol looked so nervous. "In one building?"

The officer nodded. "Our assignment is to map their lairs."

"No," Escanor said, "now your mission is to slay them."

The officer's topaz eyes paled to citrine. "Slay them, Prince?"

"There is nothing to fear, my servant." Escanor thrust Vala toward him. "I brought you a new scout. You may contact me to request another if she falls."

The officer raised his brow at this, then nodded and said, "As you order, my prince."

Escanor turned to Vala. "You said you wished to fight," he said. "If you change your mind, you know what you must do."

"I won't change my mind," Vala said, glaring at him.

"Of course not," Escanor said. He dismissed a young Shadovar from the patrol, then took the warrior's horned helmet and passed it to Vala. "This will prevent the phaerimm from controlling you—and if you should happen to change your mind, all you need do is touch the flat of your blade to a horn."

Vala accepted the helmet and used it to replace her own. "And if I don't?"

"Then I will report your death in battle to the Most High," Escanor said. "The Granite Tower will be informed of your bravery and devotion to duty."

"That's not what I meant," Vala said. "What do I get if we kill all the phaerimm? The same deal I would've by going into your tent?"

"If you kill six phaerimm?" Escanor's grin showed the tips of his fangs. "If you kill six phaerimm, then I will be *your* consort."

✡✡✡✡✡

Laeral stepped out of the forest mud onto the damp sand at Anauroch's edge, nearly three hundred miles away. Though she had known in principle what to expect, so stunned was she by the size of the dark orb in front of her that, in her teleport afterdaze, she grew confused and thought she had somehow arrived outside the Plane of Shadow. Just translucent enough to make out the silhouettes of foothills rising ridge after ridge, the murky sphere was as wide as the horizon itself and so high that only a slim crescent of cloudy gray sky hung above it.

Laeral was jarred out of her awestruck muddle when Chief Claw stumbled into her from behind, nearly flipping his body over her shoulder and growling an Uthgardt curse. Recalling that there would soon be a whole stream of soldiers pouring out of the teleport circle, she quickly stepped aside and grabbed the barbarian's enormous wrist.

"It's the shadowshell," she said, trying in vain to pull him aside. "You're outside the Shaeradim, remember?"

"Charideem," Claw repeated absently, head rolling backward as he struggled to take in the enormous dome of darkness rising above him. "The Great Dark Mountain!"

Lord Yoraedia blinked into existence behind Chief Claw and slammed into the barbarian's back as he walked forward.

"Corellon's arrows!"

Yoraedia stepped back, reaching for his sword—and was promptly knocked forward again when Skarn Brassaxe crashed into him from behind.

"What? Who?" the dwarf cried. "Where in the Underdark—"

"The shadowshell, remember?" Laeral set her feet and jerked Chief Claw aside, then released him and grabbed both Brassaxe and Yoraedia. "Snap out of it, good sirs, or our army is going to start teleporting in on top of itself—and if you think the Trade Way was a mess, wait until you see what happens when an elf and a dwarf try to occupy the same space!"

"Don't want that!" Claw said, recovering his wits.

The chief turned and literally began to toss the other commanders out of the teleport circle as they arrived. Laeral spent another moment with Yoraedia and Brassaxe, helping them overcome their teleport afterdaze by reminding them where they were. When they finally seemed to recall what they were supposed to be doing, she assigned them each a sector to keep clear, then helped the next batch of arrivals through the transition. She had rehearsed the entire plan with her commanders before creating the teleportation circle in the Forest of Wyrms, but with only three hours to march the entire relief army through an area little more than five feet in diameter, there was no margin for error.

Finally growing confident that her commanders had the situation under control, Laeral turned to inspect the area. Though hardly pouring rain, the weather was still overcast and drizzly, and she could barely make out the main Shadovar camp, positioned for easy defense atop a low butte at Anauroch's edge. The murky silhouettes of several dozen sentries stood at the brink of the cliff, using their dark spears to point down at the arriving army while their astonished comrades rushed up behind them.

Laeral raised an arm and waved at the amazed sentries, then used a sending spell to address the closest one. *Give your prince the compliments of Laeral Silverhand and tell him the Army of the North has arrived.*

The warrior cocked his head in surprise, then raised his spear in acknowledgement and turned to go. *It shall be done.*

Laeral nodded and started across the damp sand toward the shadowshell. Though still more than a quarter of a mile away, the edifice's imposing size made it feel like something natural, more along the lines of the High Ice or the Spine of the World than something created by the magic of men. Stationed at its base every half mile or so were small patrols of Shadovar warriors mounted on their strange flying worms, paying more attention to Laeral and her relief army than to the rocky slopes inside the dark sphere. It was too murky to tell whether the drizzle was also falling inside the shell, but the few withered trees visible through the barrier suggested that *something* was turning the Shaeradim as lifeless as Anauroch.

As Laeral drew nearer the shadowshell, her faint shadow darkened and split into three identical silhouettes. A pair of gleaming metallic eyes appeared in the heads of the two outer shapes, then they slowly assumed the shapes of two Shadovar warriors. She stopped and addressed the broad-shouldered figure on the left.

"A pleasure to see you again, Prince Clariburnus."

The prince's bronze-colored eyes lit with pleasure, then his silhouette peeled itself off the ground and, still expanding into its normal form, bowed.

"Clariburnus, please." He gestured at the other prince, a gaunt figure with talonlike fingers and eyes the color of rusty iron. "My brother, Lamorak."

Also returning to shape, Lamorak bowed and said, "Your arrival is a welcome surprise." He cast a meaningful glance toward the growing horde of warriors spilling from Laeral's teleportation circle. "We were given to believe it would be some time yet before you arrived with your army."

Laeral returned his bow with one of her own. "Yes . . . well, I was beginning to think you Shadovar would never stop coming to our rescue."

Lamorak frowned in confusion, but Clariburnus's grin was broad and appreciative. "Your long march was a ruse?"

Laeral glanced over her shoulder at the weary warriors spilling out of the teleportation circle. "Don't tell them," she said in a low voice, "but after the debacle at Rocnest, we decided it would be best to draw the remaining phaerimm out of the way before trying to bring another army in. According to my scouts, the last three free phaerimm are rushing down out of the Trielta Hills with their hobgoblins and illithids as we speak."

"By the time they realize that you are no longer in the Forest of Wyrms, your warriors will be resting in dry tents behind a screen of Shadovar pickets," Clariburnus offered. "My compliments. A sly plan well-executed."

"I thank you for the compliment," Laeral said, "but I fear I must decline your offer of protection."

Lamorak's eyes flashed crimson. "Surely, you do not believe the slander spewed against us in Waterdeep?"

"Only half," Laeral said, making light. "Tempus knows, we need the rest, but Evereska's mythal is failing."

The two Shadovar glanced at each other, their eyes full of mistrust and suspicion.

"I heard from Khelben," Laeral explained. "He's in the city."

"Of course," Clariburnus said, nodding in comprehension. "The phaerimm deadwall has begun to fail—the shadowshell is working."

A terrible thought occurred to Laeral. "Are you sure? If the shadowshell is blocking their access to the Weave, it would be blocking Khelben's, too. I wouldn't have been able to hear him."

"We're sure," Lamorak said, addressing Laeral as though she were a several-hundred-year-old child. "There is still Weave magic inside the shell, and it takes far less energy to carry words than to maintain the deadwall."

Clariburnus's eyes grew distant. He fell quiet and turned toward the shadowshell. Not familiar enough with the Shadovar to recognize what was happening, Laeral remained silent herself and looked to Lamorak.

"My brother?" Lamorak asked. "What is it?"

Clariburnus turned back to Lamorak, then slid his eyes in Laeral's direction and shook his head ever so slightly.

Laeral frowned and said, "If something's troubling you, Prince, tell me. The last thing we need right now is to start mistrusting each other."

Clariburnus thought for a moment, then said, "Very well. Your story can't be true. The shadowshell would have turned Khelben's communication spell back on him."

Laeral nodded, recalling how all of the spells they had tried after establishing contact had failed. "As a matter of fact, it did," she said, "and not only the sending spells. We tried transferring items, opening dimensional doors, and about a dozen other things. Nothing worked."

"Then how could you hear him?" Lamorak asked.

"It wasn't a spell—it's a gift to the Chosen from Mystra." She waited until a look of acceptance came to the prince's faces, then said, "Now, I must ask you to allow my army into the Shaeradim. We are not going to let that mythal fall."

Clariburnus looked to his brother, who raised a hand and turned away to think.

"Prince Lamorak, your brother Aglarel assured Lord Piergeiron that we would be given access," Laeral said. "If you refuse to honor that promise . . ."

"Have no fear, we will honor the promise." Lamorak glanced back at the burgeoning relief army, then returned his gaze to Laeral and gave her an icy, fang-filled smile. "With your permission, we will do even more. We will help you destroy the phaerimm."

"Of course, I welcome the help of the Shadovar." Laeral returned his smile with one just as cold. "You might even say I've been counting on it."

✡✡✡✡✡

As secret passages went, the one leading into the subbasement of the Irithlium was a masterwork. Concealed beneath the only false column among the thousands of real ones supporting the floor above, the entrance was nearly undetectable, with the door seams concealed by the column's base stone and the hinges hidden in the capital twenty feet overhead. Had Vala not seen the two-foot centipede crawling out from beneath the base as she approached, it was doubtful that she would have noticed anything unusual about the pillar at all. It looked just like every other support column she had passed, complete with mildew and moss-filled cracks. The elf builders had even taken the precaution of concealing the latch in a crack on the opposite side of an adjacent column.

"Scout, why are you stopped?" The demand came from ten paces back, where Parth Gal—Vala refused to call the Shadovar a lord, even in her own mind—stood peering out from behind a column. "Have you found something?"

"A secret door," Vala said, motioning him forward.

Parth raised a hand to halt the rest of the patrol and remained where he was. "Open it."

"This place was built by elves," she said. "It'll be trapped, and I don't have the word of passing."

Parth shrugged and did not come out from behind his column. "That is what scouts are for." He paused, then said, "Unless you would rather contact Prince Escanor and tell him where your friends are?"

Vala glared daggers at him. "One of you must have a spell for disarming traps."

"Of course—we are a reconnaissance patrol," Parth said. "Which means we should be locating phaerimm, not assaulting them. If you will just contact the prince, I am sure we will *all* live longer. Until then, I am afraid I must insist that you perform your duties."

A muffled thump sounded in the darkness somewhere behind Parth, then a strangled voice cried out in alarm. There was the sharp crack of a dark blade slicing through a thick carapace, followed by a sort of buzzing snarl and a wet crunch. Vala glimpsed a handful of Shadovar slipping through the columns toward the struggle, but the sounds died away almost as quickly as they started, and the warriors arrived too late to help their comrade.

"Balpor," someone announced. "Gone, except for his head and one arm."

It was the patrol's fifth casualty, and they had not even seen a phaerimm. Vala felt a sudden chill. Though the sensation seemed likely to be her own reaction to another casualty, she took the precaution of glancing around the immediate area to make certain nothing was creeping up on her. She thought she glimpsed a gray figure slipping behind the pillar where the latch was hidden but found only empty darkness when she stepped around the other side.

"What is it?" Parth called.

"My imagination," Vala answered. "Still want me to open that door?"

"Unless you've changed your mind about telling the prince what he wishes to know," he replied.

"Sorry." Vala dropped to her haunches and slipped the tip of her dagger into the crack where the latch was hidden. "Listen, if this goes bad for me, send word to Sheldon that I died for my word."

"Sheldon?"

"My son," Vala said.

"Ah . . . that would not be necessary, if only you would—"

"Can't do it," Vala interrupted. She had to suppress a shiver. The chill she had experienced earlier just wouldn't go away. "One more thing—if this leads to a treasury instead of a phaerimm lair, don't touch anything. There's nothing elves hate more than artifact thieves."

"Thank you for the warning," Parth replied.

"I wasn't thinking of you," Vala said, "but you know how fond I am of elves."

She took a deep breath, then, stretching her arm as far as she could, crouched down around the side of the pillar and flicked the latch.

Eltargrim.

So softly came the word that Vala was not even sure she had heard it. She spun on her heels and saw nothing behind her, but the chill remained. If anything, the cold felt deeper than before, though perhaps only because of the icy sweat running down her chest and sides.

"Vala?" Parth sounded as frightened as she was.

"Still here," she said. "Watch yourselves."

Vala rose slowly and went to the column. Half-expecting the Shadovar to tell her to wait for him to send someone forward to check for traps, she took a deep breath, then gave the door the gentlest of pushes. The entire shaft swung aside, revealing a narrow staircase spiraling down into the darkness beneath its false base. When no clouds of poison gas came billowing out, she waved the tip of her darksword around the entrance to check for motion-activated traps, then pushed down on the first stair.

Nothing happened.

"Well?" Parth called.

"No traps so far," she reported, "and no cobwebs. Something comes down here, and it doesn't leave tracks."

The Shadovar stepped out from his hiding place and motioned her down the staircase. "We're right behind you."

"Sure you are," Vala muttered.

Deciding Parth and his comrades deserved no warning about the gray figure she might or might not have glimpsed and the whispered word she might or might not have heard, Vala crouched on her heels and dropped to the fifth step down.

The steps continued to spiral downward through another ten feet of solid stone, then opened up into a grand corridor running parallel to the base of the stairs. By crouching on her heels and craning her neck, Vala could look far enough up the passage to see a series of arched doorways opening off to either side at irregular intervals, but the magic of her darksword did not allow her to see all the way to the end of the hallway. When nothing came charging up the stairs to meet her, she descended the first ten feet in two quick bounds, braced her hand on the banister, and leaped into the corridor facing the opposite direction she had been descending.

Vala found herself facing a large round silhouette with a wriggling crown of bulbous-ended tentacles. She had just enough time to recognize the silhouette as that of a large beholder before several eyestalks began to swing in her direction. Leaping into a foot-first slide underneath the thing, she flipped her darksword toward its huge central eye and grabbed for her dagger.

Vala hit the floor at about the same time her darksword found its mark—though, without the weapon in her hand, she could no longer see in the dark and knew that she'd hit the beholder only by the bloodcurdling screech that echoed down the corridor. She was showered in warm gore as she slid under the still-floating eye tyrant. Knowing better than to think even a perfect slash to the central eye could kill a monster this big, she reached up and caught the bottom of the cut with her free hand, then jerked its wounded side to the floor and smashed it into the stone. At the same time, she was bringing her dagger up behind it, driving the steel blade through its thick skull once, twice, half a dozen times, until the trapped beholder finally collapsed in a limp heap atop the arm that had been holding it pinned to the floor.

Vala pushed the thing aside.

"Vala?" Parth called down the stairs, then more loudly, "Vala?"

"No such luck, Parth," she yelled back. "Still here."

A deep rumble reverberated through the ceiling as the secret pillar was pushed back over the stairwell.

"Coward," Vala muttered.

She extended her arm to call the sword back but felt its hilt under her knuckles already. Counting herself lucky she had not found the blade instead, she rolled to her knees and took the weapon in hand—and, once she could see in the darkness again, found herself looking into a huge, toothy mouth surrounded by four arms. Even at this unfortunate angle, she recognized it instantly as a large phaerimm.

"Tempus give me strength!" she gasped.

Why pray to Tempus, my dear? I am your god now. The raspy voice came to Vala inside her head, not like the single whispered *Eltargrim* she had thought she heard earlier but definitely inside her thoughts. *Set aside your sword, and we will talk.*

Vala gathered her legs beneath her and sprang to her feet—then found herself rolling head over heels down the dark corridor.

What don't you understand, human? the voice demanded. *Put down your weapon.*

Showing no fear of the darksword whatsoever, the phaerimm continued to come down the corridor, two of its four arms pointing at the mossy floor. Puzzled by the thing's strange behavior, Vala wavered between doing as it ordered and throwing her sword at it—though she felt sure it was ready with magic to bat the weapon out of the air the instant it left her hand.

She made no move to do either, and the phaerimm stopped just beyond her sword's reach.

Obey!

Parth's muffled voice began to reverberate down the stairwell, demanding explanations and shouting threats about what would happen if she didn't open the door—and suddenly Vala understood. The phaerimm did not want to kill her. It had trapped her alone, believing that it could turn her into one of its mind-slaves—but Vala's helmet protected her against that.

"Y-yes," she said. Moving very slowly, she dropped to her haunches and set the sword on the floor. "I want to talk."

As soon as her hand left the hilt, she was plunged into blindness again. Unaware of the phaerimm's presence, Parth and the others continued to yell for her to open the door. Silently cursing them for fools as well as cowards, Vala kicked her darksword away and backed down the corridor. She was so terrified that her whole body was shaking. Without the sword, she could no longer see what the phaerimm was doing.

A bony hand clamped her shoulder. *That is far enough, child.*

Vala stopped and prayed it would not remove the helmet Escanor had given her. Without it, she would become the thrall it believed she was. Unless she lulled it into a false sense of security, she had no chance of killing it anyway. The things could cast spells as fast as she could think—maybe faster.

You are not one of the Shadovar.

It was not a question. Did the phaerimm expect an answer?

What are you?

"V-Vaasan," Vala replied. "My people owe them service."

Vala? the phaerimm asked. *The one Escanor favors to carry his egg?*

Vala had to concentrate to keep from gasping and asking how the phaerimm knew such a thing; instead, she merely nodded.

What are you doing here?

"I refused him," Vala said, "and so he sent me to kill phaerimm."

At the top of the stairs, Parth had finally realized something was wrong and stopped pounding on the column.

And could you?

Vala shook her head. "No!" At the moment, it was an honest answer. "Never again."

Again? The phaerimm seemed astonished, then said, *But I forget who you are. How do you feel about him now?*

"I hate him." It was not far from the truth.

Can you betray him?

"Perhaps," Vala said. A low rumble shook the ceiling as the false column began to slide aside. "He is very powerful."

I will help you with that, the phaerimm said. *Hold out your hand.*

Vala extended both arms, palms up. She felt something small and round pressed into her palm.

You will allow him to mount you, then press this to his back, the phaerimm said. *It will rob him of his power. Do you understand?*

"Vala?" Parth called down the stairs. "Are you there?"

Vala did not dare shout a warning. "I understand," she said.

"What?" Parth called.

She ignored him. "Then what, my master?" As she asked this, she called to her darksword in her mind. "Do I kill him?"

No! You sneak him into the woods, the phaerimm said. *This will make it easy.*

"Vala, answer me, or we're coming down!"

The darksword arrived.

"Hurry!"

As Vala yelled this, she was already bringing the darksword across the phaerimm's midsection. Her dark vision returned and she saw a fang-filled mouth the size of a cavern yawning before her. Instead of trying to back away or strike again, she twirled along the phaerimm's thorny body and saw a fiery column scorch the stone where she had been standing. Reversing her grip as she moved, she drove her black blade through the thornback's midsection and rolled back in the opposite direction, using the edge of the wound as a fulcrum to pry the darksword through three feet of tough flesh and scaly thorn.

The corridor exploded into howling winds as the phaerimm bellowed its rage and brought its barbed tail around in a classic distraction maneuver. It was a fatal mistake. Vala was already vaulting onto its thorny back, lopping off first one, then two more flame-shooting hands. She brought the darksword down on the rim of its mouth, and the phaerimm dropped to the floor, its tail lashing ineffectually at the stone where it had expected her to be standing. She spun around and risked another blow from her same location, this time slicing the creature cleanly in two behind her.

The tail struck at the stone twice more, then fell limp and lay motionless. Vala took the precaution of slicing the thing into a few more pieces, then finally heard boots pounding down the stairs and turned to find the first pair of Shadovar legs descending into view.

"Parth, take your time. The hard work—"

A loud *thrum* sounded from the stairwell, and a chorus of Shadovar voices cried out in astonishment. The first pair of legs buckled, then Parth's limp body tumbled into view. It was followed by Carlig's, Elar's, and four more, all that remained of the reconnaissance patrol.

Vala slipped over to the wall beneath the stairwell and pressed her back to the stone, darksword ready to lop off the next foot that came within reach. When none did, she hazarded a glance at the bodies at the base of the stairs. All seven Shadovar were dead, their faces, necks, and other areas of unarmored flesh flecked with tiny, cone-shaped darts. She waited a moment longer, then peered up into the spiraling stairwell itself. The steps were littered with spent darts, and the walls were flecked with the tiny holes from which they had come.

A voice at the top of the stairs, a voice so wispy that it seemed barely a hiss, called, *"Eltargrim."*

Vala ducked back out of sight, her heart pounding so hard that she could barely hear the darts clattering down the stairs as the newcomer kicked them out of the way. She wanted nothing more than to flee down the corridor as fast as her legs would carry her, but that would have been the worst thing she could do. The stranger knew she was there—had in fact whispered the password that kept her from meeting the same fate as the Shadovar—and whoever it was, he obviously knew the Irithlium far better than did Vala.

A chill came over Vala again. She raised her sword toward her helmet, wondering if Escanor would arrive quickly enough to save her if she touched the blade to one of the horns. Probably not—but maybe he would avenge her death or die himself at the hands of whatever was coming. Either way was fine, as far as Vala was concerned.

A bare foot appeared on the stair above Vala's head. Small and fine boned, it reminded her of an elf's foot, except that the flesh was so thin and white she could see the bone beneath, as well as the tendons and ligaments that made it move. The foot's mate appeared, also small and pale, with long broken nails hanging off the ends of the toes. Above the ankles hung the ragged cuffs of a pair of long-rotted trousers.

Vala grew so cold her flesh broke into goosebumps. Whatever this was, it could not be good. She took a deep breath and spun away from the wall, then brought her darksword around to strike the feet off at the ankles—and barely stopped her blade in time to keep it from burying itself in the stone steps.

The feet were gone.

But the cold was not.

Vala stepped away from the wall and found a small figure with alabaster skin and a willowy build watching her from the base of the stairs. Clothed in the tattered remains of what had once been a fine cowled robe, the stranger's features were sunken and shriveled, his eyes glowing orbs of pure white.

He pointed at Vala's sword, then wagged a bony finger and said, "You do not seem very fond of elves."

CHAPTER TEN

19 Mirtul, the Year of Wild Magic

The white elf turned his back to Vala and the dead Shadovar and started down the murky corridor.

"Come."

Vala stood where she was and didn't move. She didn't even lower her sword.

"*Come?*" she gasped. "After you killed Parth and everyone else?"

"I did not kill them, woman. I saved *you*." The elf continued away, but his head turned to face her, his neck giving a mushy crackle as it traveled the last few inches to sit backward on his shoulders. "From what I saw, I will be of more use to you than they were."

"Doing what?" Vala asked, starting after him.

"Surviving."

The elf rotated his head forward again. Deciding there was truth in what he said, Vala lowered her guard and moved to within four paces of him, where his chill aura grew so uncomfortable she began to shiver. She had seen enough undead in the past six months to recognize him as some sort of lich, but his presence did not engender the same sense of fear and corruption she had experienced back in Karsus when she and Galaeron and their companions had fought the lich Wulgreth. What she wouldn't have given to have Galaeron at her side, with his Tomb Guard's knowledge of all things unliving—but the old Galaeron before he fell victim to the corrupting influence of the Shadow Weave. Gods, how she missed that one, the Galaeron who had been so steady and earnest and noble.

The lich-elf turned down a smaller side corridor—still so wide three Vaasans could have stood abreast—and sent a spider the size of a pony skittering along the wall. Hanging in its web overhead were several silk-wrapped packages, some with clawed feet or beastly snouts poking out. From one dangled a halfling-sized boot, the toe still twitching. As she passed beneath this cocoon, Vala slowed and raised her sword to cut the halfling free.

"Leave him."

Vala looked up to find the lich-elf's head turned backward on his shoulders again, watching her.

"He is a relic thief and has met a relic thief's end," the lich-elf said.

Vala lowered her sword. She knew firsthand how elves felt about treasure thieves, and the last thing she needed was an angry lich . . . of any sort. She mouthed a silent apology to the halfling and followed her guide a hundred paces down the corridor to an iron door, which he opened by means of an ancient bronze key and a word of passing. They descended a long iron staircase filled with dog-sized rats and knee-high centipedes, all of which fled before the chill aura of the white elf.

"I'll say this, you make this place a lot safer," Vala observed.

The elf didn't respond.

The staircase descended into a natural cavern filled with limestone formations. The place stank so foully of offal and mold that Vala had to cover her mouth and nose to keep from retching. When they stepped onto the floor of the chamber, she recognized a strange regularity to many of the largest formations, where the stalactites and stalagmites met to form a wall of cage-like columns. Peering out from between many sets of bars were glowing red eyes of various shapes and sizes, some the size of Vala's fist, some no larger than pinheads. One of the nearest cages had no eyes, only a mold-covered skull with six ebony fangs propped against the bars with the tip of one dark horn poking out to touch the ground.

A chorus of low groans and rasps arose from the nearest cages, gradually mounting toward a din of bestial growling and rumblings. Though Vala was holding the hilt of her darksword, she could see nothing beyond the stone bars but red eyes.

"Mind the prisoners," the lich-elf warned. "They'll be hungry."

Vala eased away from the cage she had been peering into, only to hear a wet plop as something struck her armored thigh. The lich-elf cursed in some ancient language she did not understand, then spun toward the source of the saliva and loosed a flight of golden energy darts. When the bolts passed through the bars and exploded into her attacker, Vala glimpsed a bristly muzzle with long curved tusks, a pair of fan-shaped ears, and a set of folded wings rising up behind its shoulders. The creature roared and tore at the inside of its cage with four huge claws. When the energy bolts faded, it vanished back into the darkness inside its prison.

The lich-elf pointed at a glob of green mucus bubbling on the surface of Vala's armor. "Wipe that off before it takes root," he said. "The last thing I want is you spreading devil spawn through my Irithlium."

"*Your* Irithlium?" Vala tore a strip from the hem of her undertunic and wrapped it over the back of her darksword, then scraped the stuff off and flung the cloth into the creature's cage. "Who were you?"

The lich-elf's eyes brightened. "*Were*?"

"No offense meant," Vala said. "It's just that I'm not friends with many undead."

Nor was she friends with this one, as the lich-elf made clear when he turned and continued through the chamber without speaking. Taking care to avoid the occasional glob of mucus that came flying her way, Vala followed as closely behind as her tolerance for cold allowed. They passed through the strange prison and wandered the dark caverns beneath the Irithlium until her legs grew weary with exhaustion. Periodically, she would try to learn more about her guide by engaging the lich-elf in conversation, but he only spoke to utter a word of passing or warn her about some deadly hazard into which she had nearly stumbled. Twice they were ambushed by spell-flinging dark nagas, one of which actually succeeded in wrapping the lich-elf in a web spell before Vala diced it into six three-yard pieces. Before continuing on, her guide was grateful enough to inform her that his name was Corineus Drannaeken.

Finally, they ascended a vertical shaft into the subbasement levels, emerging in what had once been the central fountain in an elaborate two-story complex of work chambers. Clambering past a giant constrictor snake that had been immobilized by Corineus's aura of cold, they slipped out of the basin and sneaked down a narrow service corridor. Near the back, the white elf stopped and pulled a loose wall stone out of place. A section of stone wall grated open and rumbled aside. He uttered a word of passing, then motioned Vala through the opening.

Ever the cautious one, she dropped to a knee and peered around the corner—and found herself looking underneath a floating beholder into a large room filled with wands, crowns, bracers, and other items even she recognized as magical. There was also a mind flayer, whirling toward Vala's door, and half a dozen confused bugbears scrambling for their weapons.

Cursing herself for a fool and Corineus for a faithless double crosser, Vala whipped her darksword at the mind flayer. Waiting only long enough to see that the spinning blade was flying toward its target, she launched herself forward and rose beneath the beholder, pinning it against the ceiling of the opening while she drew her dagger.

"Ressamon, you idiot!" the beholder screamed. "Stun it—stun it before—"

Vala drove her dagger into the monster's underside. The resulting shriek was more angry than pained, and the mordant smell of powdered stone filled the air as the beholder began to spray the rock above with its disintegration ray.

"Ressamon!"

But Ressamon, if that had been the mind flayer's name, was already lying on the floor beside its amputated head. Finally gathering their wits, the bugbears sprang over the illithid's body to charge Vala.

Driving her dagger into the beholder's underside again, she extended her free hand to summon her sword. It flashed between two of the charging bugbears, slashing open a furry knee and buckling the leg. The astonished brute collapsed in front of two companions and sent them sprawling, prompting the rest of the band to stop and whirl around to see who was attacking from behind.

The darksword arrived in Vala's hand, and the beholder's disintegration ray finally cut through the keystone of the hidden archway. With a thousand tons of stone settling on her shoulders, she had no choice except to leap into the chamber ahead and let the wounded eye tyrant escape behind her. She tucked into a diving somersault, taking a bugbear's legs off at the knees as she rolled past, then came to her feet and brought her dagger over her head, driving it to the hilt in the nearest furry back.

The roars of the wounded bugbears were lost to the sound of the collapsing doorway. Vala ducked a massive axe as the quickest of the bugbears whirled to attack, then removed the arm holding the weapon and opened the creature's chest on the backstroke. She glimpsed another axe coming and barely managed to pivot away, though not before the blade slashed along her chest, denting steel scales and hurling her into a pair of hairy arms as big around as her waist. With her arms pinned at her sides, Vala brought her feet up over her head and smashed her booted feet into her captor's face.

The blow was not sufficient to drop a bugbear, but it did startle it. The creature's grasp loosened enough for her to bring her sword around beneath her. So weak was the attack that not even the sharpest steel would have penetrated the bugbear's thick hide, much less the apron of leather armor it wore over its loins.

The darksword's glassy blade slashed through the leather like gossamer.

The bugbear bellowed in shock and started to squeeze, and Vala cocked her wrist, driving the tip of her weapon deep into its abdomen. The hairy arms went limp and dropped her on her shoulders, her captor's huge body doubling over above her face. Reaching up behind it, she grabbed a handful of fur and pulled herself through its legs and to her feet.

A huge hand axe came tumbling through the air and smashed into her helmet, breaking one of the horns off and knocking it from her head. Sure of only the direction the attack had come from, Vala spun around to the opposite side of the bugbear she'd just wounded and found another big axe swinging toward her throat. Barely flipping her darksword up in time, she caught the weapon near the top, using the attack's own momentum to cleave the shaft and send the head spinning off to lodge itself in one of the attacker's wounded companions.

Faster than the others, this bugbear followed its first attack by slamming a huge fist into Vala's armored ribs, launching her across the room into a shelf full of artifacts. She dropped to the ground in a limp heap, still holding her sword and struggling to get the wind back in her lungs.

Snorting in triumph, the bugbear snatched a weapon from a wounded companion and stomped toward Vala. Behind it, she saw a spherical form float out of the dust cloud rising from the collapsed doorway. Of Corineus, there was no sign.

Vala bounced to her feet and raised her darksword to throw. The bugbear pivoted away and brought its big axe around to block. Vala hurled the blade anyway. As the weapon sailed past the astonished brute to split the beholder down the center, she charged after it. Seeing its mistake too late, the bugbear swung back into the attack, but Vala was inside the arc of its weapon by then, her boot heels driving for its face in a flying side kick.

The bugbear leaned aside in an attempt to slip the blow. Vala kicked her feet apart and caught its head between her ankles. As she swung into its torso, she scissored her legs and rotated herself around to the side. Though the bugbear was easily three times her size, the weight of her body acted like a pendulum, pulling it down face-first. It slammed to the stone floor with a heavy thump and immediately began to push itself up again.

Vala's sword was already returning to her hand. She brought it down on the back of her attacker's neck, then leaped up and dispatched the wounded bugbears in a series of cautious, darting attacks from the rear. By the time she finished, the dust in the fallen doorway had cleared enough for her to see Corineus standing in the service corridor on the other side of the rubble.

"Well done, woman." he said, pointing past her toward an iron door on the adjacent wall. "Above the door, you will find a holy symbol painted in black blood. Break it."

Vala turned in the direction he pointed. When she'd had a chance to examine the room, she could see that it was divided into two sections. She had entered the front area, which the bugbears, beholder, and illithid all shared with the assortment of magical items she'd noticed earlier. In the back, opposite the door Corineus was pointing at, an assortment of gem-studded scepters, rods, rings, tomes, and other powerful artifacts of magic—even a diamond ball the size of a halfling's head—floated inside a field of green spell light. Vala's throat went dry, for she understood the phaerimm well enough to realize when she was standing in one of their lairs—and to know that had the creature been present, she would have been too busy fighting to take in all that she was seeing.

"What are you waiting for?" Corineus demanded. "Break the seal."

"Not so fast," Vala said, retrieving her helm. She had no idea whether it would still protect her from the phaerimm mind control with only one horn, but it was worth a try. "Not until you answer a few questions."

"The phaerimm who claims this laboratory lair will soon realize it has been broken into and return," Corineus replied. "That is the only question you need answered."

"Afraid not," Vala replied. "You surrendered your right to claim my trust when you sent me through that door without warning."

"You had to be tested."

Vala bit back the rage she felt rising inside and said, "I passed."

She turned toward the nearest shelf and picked up a pair of fabulously decorated silver bracers.

"Put that back!" Corineus started forward, only to encounter a field of flashing blue energy that hurled him back against the wall. "You've no right!"

"No?" Vala raised her brow and considered threatening the lich-elf, then recalled how touchy elves could be about their ancestral treasures and decided to try a different tactic. "Consider these a token of good faith."

She tossed the bracers through the door.

Corineus's eyes went wide, and he nearly let the bracers fall. "The symbol, woman! You've no idea what you just did."

Vala's mouth went dry, but she managed to meet the white elf's gaze without shaking. "Don't be too sure."

Corineus's white eyes glared at Vala for a moment, then drifted to the symbol over the door.

"Have you ever heard of a baelnorn?" the white elf asked.

Vala shook her head. "I take it I'm looking at one."

"Sworn to a duty more sacred than you can know."

A dull clunk sounded from the other side of the door.

"The time has come for you to choose," he said. "Without my help—"

"One moment," Vala interrupted, jerking the iron door open.

A teleport-dazed phaerimm tumbled into the room, its four spindly arms windmilling wildly. Vala brought her darksword down across the thick part of its body and clove it cleanly in two, then stepped back and opened both halves along their length. When she was certain the thing was dead, she cut off the wicked tail barb, then finally reached up with her sword and broke the holy symbol painted above the door.

Corineus rushed into the room, his white eyes shining bright with rage. "How dare you disobey—"

"How dare *I?*" Vala tossed the tail barb into the baelnorn's face, then touched the tip of her darksword to his throat. "Let's get something straight, White Eyes. I need you as much as you need me, but if you *ever* send me into a lair again without warning me, it'll be you I'm carving into little pieces. Clear?"

The baelnorn moved closer, enveloping her in his chill aura. "I do not think you understand who you are talking to."

Vala stepped even closer, so close that her face and hands began to ache with cold. She laid a bloody palm on his flesh-freezing face.

"Oh, I understand," she said, "but what you need to know is I mean to see my son again, and I'll gut anything that makes that less likely."

✡✡✡✡✡

A low groan rolled from beneath the roots of the smoke tree, where Aris lay hidden in an undercut carved out of the dry riverbank by some long-ago flood. Galaeron, standing watch outside, dropped to his haunches and peered inside, where Ruha kneeled beside the unconscious giant's head, using a wet rag to drip water onto his cracked lips. His broken arm was stretched out beside him, splinted to the straightest pair of branches Galaeron had been able to find in a mile of dry riverbed. A shield-sized circle of charred flesh on his chest marked where the dragon's lightning bolt had entered his body, and a blackened foot marked where it had left. Of the most concern to Galaeron, however, were the giant's black and sunken eyes, which Ruha said were signs of the head injury he had suffered.

Aris groaned again, and a gray tongue appeared between his lips. Ruha squeezed the cloth hard, dribbling water directly onto the tip of the tongue, then tilted her head at the pair of empty waterskins resting on the shadow blanket beside the giant.

"More water," she said.

"More?" Each skin held two gallons, and Galaeron had filled them twice already since the dragon attack. "That's a good sign, isn't it?"

Ruha shrugged. "How much would a healthy giant drink in a day? I don't know." She placed the rag in a small hollow she had lined with dragon skin and filled with water. "It takes water to heal, and I would say the matter remains uncertain."

The witch did not look at Galaeron as she spoke, and her voice remained cold. He reached into the undercut and pulled the waterskins off the shadow blanket, then left the scant shade of the smoke tree to creep along the edge of the dry riverbed. Ruha's manner had been much the same since she'd used her air magic to float Aris into the shelter of the undercut. She clearly held Galaeron responsible for the giant's injuries, and he was not so sure he disagreed.

The shock of seeing Aris pinned beneath the dragon had jolted his conscience into asserting itself again, driving his shadow self back down into the dark realm beneath his conscious mind, and he had instantly realized how his actions must have seemed to someone else. Even given the spell he had cast to confuse the dragon when it wheeled on Aris, preventing the witch from attacking the dragon's belly must have reeked of cowardice. If Galaeron doubted his own motivations in that first instance, he did not in the second, when he had used a shadow snare to drag the dragon back to the ground. At that point, his only concern had been for the shadow blanket, and it had not even occurred to him that Aris would be further injured when the wyrm crashed into the ground.

The dragon's corpse still lay out on the Saiyaddar, surrounded by a ring of glutted predators and blanketed beneath a mountain of flicking feathers. Galaeron longed to move beyond sight of it, and not only because looking at it reminded him of his terrible selfishness. If a Shadovar patrol or another of Malygris's dragons happened across the corpse, he and his companions were certain to be found. Ruha lacked the magic to move Aris a long distance, and Galaeron was determined never again to use his own. He could no longer touch the Weave at all, and he recognized he was far past the point where he could wield shadow magic without yielding control of himself to his shadow. The next time he cast a spell, he feared, even causing a friend's injury would not be enough to bring him back.

Galaeron reached a clump of giant featherwoods growing along the outer curve of a bend in the riverbed and kneeled beside a deep hole nestled down among the tree's roots. Though the bottom was concealed in shadow, there should have been enough light for an elf to see whether it contained any water.

Galaeron saw only murk.

He was not even all that surprised. Since touching the Shadow Weave, he had gradually become less and less of an elf. He had lost the ability to enter the Reverie and started to sleep just like a human, and even to dream. He was awakened by nightmares almost nightly and occasionally talked in his sleep, and he no longer felt any mystic connection in the presence of other elves. He could no longer see in dim conditions. It was, he had decided, a symptom of his shadow's growing hold over him. Elves were born with a special bond to the Weave, and his connection was being weakened by the Shadow Weave's power over him. The only thing that remained was for his senses to grow as dull as those of a human. He thought of himself running around with a three-day sweat, thinking he smelled as fine as a spring rain, and shuddered.

Galaeron dropped a pebble into the hole and heard only a wet thud. The hole had not yet refilled. He gathered himself up and wandered half a mile down the riverbed to the next well—also in the roots of a featherwood—and found water. Ruha had explained that it was only worth digging under a featherwood, and only when they grew on the exterior curve of a river bend.

Though even this short trip in the hot sun was enough to make Galaeron thirsty, he filled both waterskins first, and by then there was barely a handful of muddy liquid left for him. He quaffed it down gratefully, then shouldered the waterskins and climbed out of the well to find a tall, silver-haired woman in elven chain mail, elven boots, and an elven cloak standing before him, her hand resting on the hilt of a fine elven long sword. The woman, however, was definitely human—and one he recognized from an ancient portrait hanging in the halls of Evereska's Academy of Magic.

"Well met, Lady Silverhand," Galaeron said, holding out one of the waterskins. "If you're not my dying hallucination . . ."

"You should be that lucky, elf," Storm said, not taking the waterskin. "After the evil you brought into the Realms, I'll send you to the Nine Hells to look for Elminster before I let you die a peaceful death in Anauroch."

"The Mage Masters at the Academy always said you were the merriest of the Seven Sisters," Galaeron retorted, concealing the hurt the words caused him behind a facade of cynicism. He hefted the waterskins onto his shoulders and started for the undercut. "If you are about to open a hell-mouth beneath my feet, at least wait until I deliver this water. My friend Aris is in danger of dying."

"I didn't come here to punish you, elf," Storm said, ignoring Galaeron's attempt to elicit her concern for the stone giant. "That is not my place—even were you worth the trouble."

Galaeron glanced up at the blazing sun and licked his cracked lips, then asked, "Well then, if you didn't come to help and you didn't come to punish, what are you doing here?"

"Delivering a message on behalf of Khelben Arunsun," she said. "He asks that I inform you that your sister Keya is well."

Galaeron nearly dropped the precious waterskins. "Keya is safe?" he gasped. "The siege has been lifted?"

"Not exactly," Storm replied, "but the shadowshell has weakened the phaerimm deadwall. Khelben is in the city."

Galaeron was so astonished he couldn't quite think of what to say. The Chosen of Mystra seldom took an interest in the affairs of individual people—how could they, when they were so few and those who needed them so many?—yet here was Storm Silverhand, delivering a message from Khelben Arunsun about his younger sister, Keya. It was so far beyond likely that Galaeron grew convinced he was suffering heat hallucinations.

Resolving to waste no more of his energy on illusions, he clamped his jaw shut and fixed his attention on the undercut where Aris lay resting.

The hallucination walked along at his side. "That's all?" she asked. "Not even a 'thank you for your trouble'?"

Galaeron ignored her and continued toward the undercut.

"Well, you would at least be wise to thank Khelben," the illusion said. "He's going to a great deal of effort to undo the trouble you and that shadow wizard unleashed."

"That may be true," Galaeron said, speaking aloud in the hope that the sound of his own voice would lend impact to his logic, "but why would Khelben Arunsun trouble himself to deliver a message about my sister?"

The hallucination made a lifting gesture with her hands, and both waterskins rose off Galaeron's shoulders. Thinking he had dropped them and was simply imagining this to conceal the fact, he cried out and dropped to his knees and began to run his fingers through the sand. The *dry* sand.

The hallucination came over to stand in front of Galaeron, holding both waterskins.

"He feels obligated," she said. "Your father saved his life at the Battle of Rocnest."

"My father?" Galaeron asked. "Did he . . ."

The hallucination shook her head. "He died in the battle." For the first time, a soft look came to her eyes. "I'm sorry."

Galaeron let his shoulders slump and was relieved to feel himself crying. At least he was still that much of an elf.

"None of that, elf—from the looks of it, you don't have the water to spare," Storm said, starting down the riverbed with the waterskins in hand. "Why didn't you levitate these? That's what magic is for."

"Not for me, not any longer," Galaeron said, rising. "I've a friend lying in there injured because I couldn't control my shadow magic, and I'll not insult him by using it now."

Storm glanced over. "Really? Even to save his life?"

Galaeron shook his head. "He wouldn't want it."

"You sound awfully sure of that." She studied him for a moment, then added, "Or maybe awfully scared."

Leaving Galaeron to ponder the truth of her words, Storm stepped into the air and flew the rest of the way to the undercut. She poked her head through the smoke tree's root and began to speak with Ruha. By the time Galaeron arrived, Storm was already inside dribbling her third healing potion into Aris's half-open lips. Though the giant's eyes were open, he remained as pale as a pearl and looked too weak to lift his head, even had there been room.

Storm tossed the empty vial aside, opened a fourth, and began to dribble it into the giant's half-open mouth.

"This is the last one for now, my large friend. They said five would be too many, even for a giant."

"Even for a giant?" Galaeron echoed, starting to realize that there was more to Storm's appearance than she had told him. "Milady Silverhand, exactly how did you know where to find us?"

Instead of answering, Storm exchanged glances with Ruha, and Galaeron suddenly knew the answer to his own question.

He looked at the witch and asked, "Was it Malik you were watching, or me?"

"You have a very large opinion of your value, don't you, elf?" Storm asked, her eyes sparkling in amusement. "It was the Shadovar we sent her to watch. You, we know already."

Galaeron found himself smiling, then—to his own surprise—he began to do something he had not done in a very long time.

He began to laugh.

✡✡✡✡✡

Keya was in Treetop on her Reverie couch, reliving in her mind the last homeagain embrace she had shared with her brother, when a white snow finch appeared outside her room's theurglass window and politely fluttered its wings. Rousing herself from her daze, she uttered the command word to make the theurglass passable, then swung her feet to the floor and extended her finger to form a perch. On the way across the room, however, the bird noticed Dexon slumbering on the floor and circled the Vaasan's hairy mountain of a body, nearly coming to a bad end when his wingtip brushed the sleeping warrior's nose and a massive hand rose up to swat at the disturbance.

The finch dived to safety, then flew up and, chirping in indignation, landed on Keya's finger.

"That is no concern of yours, Manynests," Keya said sternly. "Besides, he has to sleep somewhere."

Manynests warbled a question.

"*That* is none of your business," Keya retorted, "and I don't want you spreading it about Evereska that we are."

He chirped an assurance.

"I'm serious about this," Keya warned. "I'm sure you wouldn't want your mate to learn the real reason Lord Duirsar calls you Manynests."

The finch ruffled his feathers, then repeated his promise in a lower tone that, from what Keya understood of peeptalk, indicated a solemn vow. Given what a compulsive gossip Manynests was, she suspected her secret had about even odds of remaining secret.

"Are you here just to spy on me, or does Lord Duirsar require something?"

Manynests ruffled his wings and asked about Khelben's whereabouts.

"Did you try the contemplation?" she asked.

The bird chirped his thanks and flew out the door—then circled back into the room and tweeted a suggestion that she fetch the other Vaasans and join them there. His speech was urgent and rapid, as though he had just recalled the importance of his errand.

"Very well," she said. "We'll be there in a minute."

She roused Dexon and told him to fetch the others, then pulled on a robe and went down to her father's old contemplation, which was serving Khelben as a study and magic laboratory. By the time she arrived, the archmage was interrogating Manynests in peeptalk too rapid for Keya to follow. His battle cloak was spread open on the table, and Khelben was furiously stuffing gem powders, balls of brimstone, glass cylinders, and other spell ingredients into its component pockets. The archmage did not even look up as Keya entered the room.

"Lord Duirsar is calling the city to arms," Khelben said. "The phaerimm are massing outside the mythal."

Manynests tipped his head in Keya's direction and chirped something too fast for her to follow.

"Slow down, bird!" she admonished. "Master Colbathin what?"

"Says you are free to fight in my company, if I have a place for you," Khelben translated. "Welcome."

Manynests added another series of peeps, this time slow enough that Keya understood that the Long Watch would be assembling for battle in the meadow outside the Livery Gate.

"So I am free to choose?" Keya asked.

Manynests chirped a confirmation and took wing, circling toward the window and warbling about all the other messages he had to deliver.

Keya uttered the command word to open the theurglass, then said, "I'll fetch my armor and weapons."

"Good," Khelben said. "We'll assemble in the foyer—I want to conserve my teleport magic for battle."

"Battle?" Dexon echoed, leading Kuhl and Burlen into the room. "What battle?"

"The phaerimm are massing—"

That was as much as Keya said before the Vaasans turned and pounded off to armor themselves. She returned and pulled on her own armor—a hauberk of fine Evereskan chain mail and her father's magic helmet—then gathered her weapons and rushed down to the foyer. Khelben and the three humans were already waiting, looking out the door at the great sheets of spell-light already flashing across the surface of the mythal. As they watched, golden meteors began to rain down into the Vine Vale as the mythal activated its most ferocious—and best-known—defense. The phaerimm assault only intensified.

"What're the Hill Elders thinking?" Dexon growled. "I'd wager my shield arm that shower of magic bolts is what the thornbacks *want*."

"The mythal is a living thing," Keya explained. "The Hill Elders know better than any of us that the phaerimm are trying to drain it, but no one can prevent it from defending itself—or Evereska."

"Which is all the more reason we should hurry." Khelben stepped through the door and, continuing to speak over his shoulder, led the way head-first down the exterior of the tower. "Their success is not certain, but it is very possible. The more we kill—and the faster—the better the mythal's chances of holding."

"We're *attacking?*" Dexon gasped from a few feet above and behind Keya.

"That's what I intend to recommend to Lord Duirsar, yes," Khelben said. He reached the bottom of the tower and dropped off the wall into the Starmeadow, then turned to face Dexon. "Unless you know of a better way to kill phaerimm."

Dexon frowned, then swung his feet around and dropped to the ground beside Khelben. Armed and armored elves were rushing past on all sides, descending toward the juncture of trails at Dawnsglory Pond and continuing from there toward their assigned mustering points.

"I was thinking of Keya," Dexon said. He spoke quietly—though not quietly enough for Keya's keen elf ears to miss. "There's no reason she has to go, is there?"

"Only that this is my home we are defending," Keya said, jumping to the ground beside him. "You wouldn't be trying to rid yourself of me, would you Dex?"

The big Vaasan blushed. "No, of course not."

"Then you must think me incapable of carrying my weight in such an elite band of phaerimm killers." She grabbed one of the barbed trophy tails tucked into his belt and gave it a flick. "Perhaps you think I am not brave enough."

"I know you are brave enough," Dexon said, looking to his fellows for help—and finding nothing but amused grins, "b-but you don't have a darksword."

"Neither does Khelben," Keya pointed out.

Dexon rolled his eyes. "Khelben is one of the Chosen."

"Dexon just couldn't stand to see you hurt." Kuhl grabbed them by the arms and led them after Khelben, who was already halfway down the trail to Dawnsglory Pond. He leaned closer to Keya, then added in a quiet voice, "If you ask me, I think all those moonlight swims have gone and made him sweet on you."

Keya blushed and, unsure whether Kuhl was joking or really had not noticed how close she and Dexon had become, disengaged herself and glanced over at her Vaasan lover. As large and hairy as a bear, his emotions were in many ways just as alien to her. She had no doubts about the depths of his feelings—she would have known that by the way Khelben frowned whenever he saw them together, if nothing else—but it had never occurred to her that his passion would manifest itself in such a protective streak. To an elf, such paternalism implied that he believed her incapable of making her own decisions, and elves were not in the habit of falling in love with those whom they held in such low regard.

But humans were different. She had seen the way Dexon glowered when the other Vaasans looked at her during their swims, and she had noticed how he often tried to keep them away from her when the water games began. His affection for her seemed to manifest itself as though she were a treasure he feared someone might steal—and, with a sudden rush of comprehension, she understood that was almost true.

Their love *was* a treasure—and humans viewed treasure not as beautiful artwork to be shared with others, but as coins and gems to be hidden safely away. They were like dragons that way—and they would fight just as ferociously to protect their hoard. If, on the battlefield, Keya were to be threatened, Dexon would forget all else—his own safety, his duty to help Khelben, even the many thousand Evereskans whose lives were at peril—and rush to defend her.

They reached Dawnsglory Pond, where Khelben turned uphill toward Cloudhome, Lord Duirsar's citadel. Burlen and Kuhl started after him at once, but Keya stopped and turned down the slope toward the Livery Gate.

Dexon caught her arm and motioned up the hill. "Lord Blackstaff went this way."

"I know," Keya said, pointing down the hill, "but I must go that way."

"Then you're not coming with us?" Dexon looked almost as confused as he did relieved.

Keya shook her head. "My place is with the Long Watch."

"The Long Watch?" Dexon gasped. "But they've no training!"

Keya frowned. "More than you know," she said, raising her chin. "Our hearts are brave. We'll give a good accounting of ourselves."

"For as long as it takes the phaerimm to cast one spell!" Dexon objected, trying to pull her up the hill. "The Long Watch is fodder. You're coming with us."

Keya twisted her arm free. "No, Dex, you were right. I don't belong in Khelben's company."

She grabbed his shoulders and pulled herself up to kiss him on the lips, then let go and dropped back to the ground a pace away.

"I'll see you after the battle," she said.

"*If* we win," Dexon said, shaking his head and starting after her. "I can't let you—"

"Yes, Dexon, you can, and you will." Khelben's strong hand caught him by the shoulder and pulled him back. "Say your farewells."

Dexon's eyes grew a little glassy, then he kissed his beefy fingers and turned them toward Keya. "Till swords part."

Keya smiled and returned the gesture. "Back soon for soft songs and bright wine."

Khelben pushed Dexon into the arms of his waiting companions. He made a shooing motion and mumbled something Keya did not quite catch.

"I'm sorry," she said. "What was that?"

"Just the usual," Khelben said, turning away. "Sweet water and light laughter."

To Keya, that didn't sound like what he'd mumbled. Not even close.

CHAPTER ELEVEN

20 Mirtul, the Year of Wild Magic

"Loose!"

Keya released her bowstring on command. Her arrow hissed skyward with a thousand others, passing through the mythal and arcing down toward the thin line of beholders and phaerimm floating out in the Vine Vale. Shimmering rays of disintegration magic swept back and forth across the volley, dissolving hundreds of shafts before they neared the blackened vineyards. One of the mythal's golden meteors came streaking down from the heavens and burned a twenty-foot swath through the sizzling cloud of sticks. Hundreds of missiles missed their targets and planted themselves in the soil like a crop of newly sprouted feather sticks. Of the few dozen arrows that found their marks, most were deflected by powerful shielding magic and clattered harmlessly to ground, but a few enchanted shafts penetrated the phaerimm defenses and lodged themselves deep in enemy bodies.

One phaerimm and two beholders went limp and began to sink toward the ground, then a fierce counterattack blossomed against the mythal and prevented Keya from seeing if they recovered. She nocked another arrow—the last in her quiver—and awaited the next command. Like the rest of the Long Watch, she was standing inside the Meadow Wall with nothing between her and the enemy but the battered mythal and seventy paces of open ground—close enough that when she was not trying to blink the magic-dazzle from her eyes, she could see the big central eyes of the attacking beholders.

What Keya could not see were any bugbears, illithids, captured elves, or any other phaerimm mind-slaves. There were only the thornbacks themselves—less than two hundred in the whole vale, according to rumor—and perhaps a thousand beholders. With a full ten thousand elves ringing the city, it definitely appeared that the odds favored Evereska, but where the phaerimm were concerned, appearances were always deceiving. The mind-slaves could be anywhere, lurking invisibly on the other side of the Meadow Wall or hiding in tunnels under the Vine Vale, ready to burrow under the elven defenses the instant their masters weakened the mythal.

"Loose!" came the command.

Keya set her aim on the eye of the closest beholder and released her bowstring. She lost sight of her arrow as it joined the dark cloud sailing into the Vine Vale, but she chose to believe that hers was the shaft that survived to plant itself between two of her target's writhing eyestalks. Another phaerimm spell-storm exploded against the mythal.

An arrow runner lifted Keya's empty quiver off her belt and replaced it with a full one. She grabbed the next shaft and was horrified to feel green, moist wood. To save Evereska, even the trees had to sacrifice—not that they would live long if the mythal fell. She slipped the nock onto her bowstring and raised the tip to the air.

The phaerimm began to retreat, fleeing so fast that one flew into a mythal-meteor and vanished in a golden flash. In the next instant, a cone of sparkling gray flame shot out from behind the Meadow Wall, engulfing a pair of phaerimm who had made the mistake of drifting into a single line. They erupted into screeching tornadoes of silver fire.

Khelben Arunsun appeared at the Meadow Wall where the cone had originated, his hand still pointing at the two burning phaerimm. In the next instant, the Vaasans and the rest of the archmage's escort appeared on both sides of him, all grunting with effort as they hurled a flight of golden javelins after the fleeing phaerimm. The beholders caught the first wave of spears in their disintegration rays, which only turned the weapons into pure magic and sent them streaking into their targets with the speed of lightning bolts. The second wave followed a little more slowly, but two dozen weapons found their marks. Three phaerimm dropped to the ground and disintegrated into piles of dust, and two more were injured so badly they teleported away.

The surviving thornbacks came streaking back, driving their beholder slaves ahead of them and hurling such a spell tempest at the mythal that Keya had to turn her face away from the heat of the dissipating magic. Khelben and his escort simply laughed and strolled calmly away from the Meadow Wall, their backs to the enemy. They passed through the Long Watch lines not twenty paces from where Keya stood awaiting the command to loose her next arrow. If Dexon—or any of the Vaasans—noticed her standing in line, they did not betray the fact by looking in her direction.

"Well done, Khelben!" chortled Kiinyon Colbathin. "Five this time!"

"Yes," Khelben answered. "If we had forty hours and a thousand Corellon's Bolts, we could kill them all—but we don't. We're not going to save the mythal by teleporting in to attack once every hour."

"What do you suggest, Lord Blackstaff?" asked a familiar voice.

Keya glanced over her shoulder and found Lord Duirsar standing a dozen yards behind her with Kiinyon Colbathin and what remained of Evereska's Hill Elders. They were surrounded by the Company of the Cold Hand, a hundred hand-picked Spellblades chosen to wield the sixteen darkswords borrowed from the Vaasans who had fallen when the phaerimm escaped their ancient prison. Because the weapons would freeze the hand of any wielder not of the owning family, the idea was that the first warrior would use the weapon until his hand grew too cold to hold it, then pass it to the next, and so forth.

Khelben stepped to Lord Duirsar's side. "We must carry the attack into the Vine Vale, and soon."

"Leave the mythal?" Colbathin gasped. "Do you know how many warriors we'll lose?"

"A fraction of what we'll lose if we let them wear it down and enter Evereska," Khelben countered. "The shadowshell has already weakened it, and this battle is draining it by the minute." He turned to Lord Duirsar. "Milord, even if Evereska had arrows and magic enough to squander in this way, the mythal won't last. We must reduce the enemy."

"You forget that we will be reduced ourselves, tenfold," Kiinyon objected. "Surely, it is better to take what kills we can from the safety of the mythal—"

"Do those pointed ears not hear, elf?" roared Khelben. "The mythal won't last!"

In spite of herself, Keya found her attention wandering from Khelben and the high lords to her cherished Dexon. To her dismay, the Vaasan had noticed her as he passed through the lines of the Long Watch—was, in fact, studying her with the dark look of an angry bear, holding his darksword across his breast and towering over not only the elves, but Khelben and even his fellow Vaasans. Even the night before, when she had spent so many hours climbing over that massive body, she had not realized just how large—how brutish—a man he really was.

When he noticed her watching him, Dexon gave a melancholy smile and extended an index finger in her direction. At first, Keya thought he was trying to use elven fingertalk, but then she sensed someone looking over her shoulder and realized he was pointing. She looked forward again to find Zharilee, the sun elf who commanded her company, standing in front of her impatiently tapping a long finger on her extravagant armor of gold scales.

"Truly, Keya, it is nothing to me if you are attracted to these hairy brutes, but I insist that you leave the flirting until after the battle." Zharilee turned away, then raised her magic command horn to her lips and shouted, "Loose!"

Keya drew her bowstring back and sent an arrow arcing over the Meadow Wall into the blinding storm of flame and lightning that was the Vine Vale. She reached for another of the green shafts in her quiver.

"Hold!"

The command came not from Zharilee, but from Kiinyon Colbathin himself—and he sounded none too happy.

"Split by ranks, swords the first, spears the second, bows the third."

Heart leaping into her throat, Keya slung her bow over her shoulder and pulled her spear out of the ground beside her. Khelben's argument had prevailed, and Lord Duirsar had given the order to leave the mythal to engage the phaerimm. A low, ground-shaking rumble rolled up from the rear as the elite companies trotted up to take attack positions behind the Long Watch.

Even had Keya not learned tactics on her father's knee, she would have known what was happening. As the most inexperienced element of Evereska's military, the Long Watch would lead the charge over the wall and absorb the brunt of the phaerimm attack. With any luck, the elite companies following behind would reach the enemy ranks intact and force the thornbacks to engage in their least favorite kind of combat—close.

Though Keya desperately wanted to steal a last glance over her shoulder at Dexon, she resisted the temptation. Looking at him would only make him worry about her when he should be thinking of killing their enemies. As the rightful wielder of a darksword, he was one of Evereska's most potent weapons against the phaerimm. His shadowy blade could cut through even their mightiest defenses, and he already had three of their tails tucked into his belt to prove he knew how to get close enough to use it.

"Long Watch, charge in three ranks!"

Keya counted a one second delay, then set her spear tip at a slight incline and started forward at a two-step-per-second run—swift enough to cover ground quickly, but not so fast that the charge would disorganize their formation. Instead of starting forward to meet the charge, the phaerimm and beholders hung back, content to hurl spells at the mythal and create a gauntlet of magic for their attackers to struggle through. It was a tactic that would serve them well against the Long Watch—but bring the elite companies behind into the middle of their ranks.

Keya was ten steps from the Meadow Wall when Khelben's voice came to her in her mind. *Nothing to fear, my dear.*

Who's afraid? she retorted. *Just kill the thornbacks—and tell Dex to keep his mind—*

That was as far as she made it before the first rank reached the Meadow Wall. With only their swords in hand and light Evereskan armor on their bodies, they leaped onto the wall in one stride and disappeared over its crest on the second. Keya and the rest of the second rank were slower. They had to brace a hand on top of the wall and swing their legs up beside them—and by then, the first rank was already stopped dead in its tracks, filling the air with eerie wails as their legs crumbled into ash.

Keya kept herself from going over by dropping to her seat and bracing her spear on the other side of the Meadow Wall. In front of her, Zharilee and half a dozen other elves seemed to be melting into the ground as first their legs, then their hips and torsos dissolved into a pile of gray cinders. She nearly fell when the shaft of her spear crumbled as well.

A young Gold elf from the third rank crashed into her from behind, and she grabbed the back of his helmet to prevent herself from going over.

"What's the holdup?" he demanded. "Get a move on!"

"Not wise." Keya pulled his head over the wall and forced him to look at the dissipating ash piles. "Those are our friends."

The young sun elf turned the color of a withered birch leaf, but many in the Long Watch were not so fortunate. Much of the third rank simply leaped onto the backs of the second rank, forcing them over the wall into the Vine Vale and beyond the protection of the mythal. As soon as their feet touched the blackened ground, their bodies crumbled into cinders and collapsed.

Without the constant rain of arrows from the Long Watch, the phaerimm and beholders finally began to float forward, coming closer to the mythal. Keya glanced back and, over the retching figure of the elf who had nearly pushed her to her death, saw the Company of the Cold Hand charging up to vault the wall behind them.

Still sitting astride the wall, Keya raised both hands. "Khelben, stop them! You made a mistake!"

"Mistake?" Khelben's voice boomed across the valley like a clap of thunder. "Impossible!"

"Khelben, it *is* possible—the Vale is a death trap!"

For a long and terrible moment, the Cold Hand continued to rush forward. A golden mythal meteor roared down behind her, cratering the blackened ground and spraying her with so much dirt and stone that she was knocked off the wall back into the meadow. Lord Duirsar's mages launched a volley of lightning bolts and black death rays that streaked overhead and—so far as Keya could tell from where she was cowering down behind the wall—had absolutely no effect on the enemy.

Then, much to her horror, an avalanche of stones shot across the wall above her and found the young Gold who had nearly pushed her into the Vine Vale. The pile took him square in the chest, reducing his torso to a spray of blood and bone, then crashed to the ground behind him and rolled off trailing a spray of crimson.

That was enough to halt the charge of the Cold Hand—and send what remained of the Long Watch scurrying back toward Evereska. The enemy had attacked into the meadow. The mythal was weakening, and fast. Keya suppressed a gasp and rolled into a crouch, then poked her head up to find a beholder hovering not a spear's length away, its great central eye projecting a powerful antimagic ray into the failing mythal. Behind it, a phaerimm was floating forward to exploit the resulting gap in the LastHaven's magic defenses.

Keya had just time enough to see that the scene was much the same in other places along the wall before the phaerimm pointed in her direction. A stream of stones rose off a vineyard wall and came streaking in her direction. She rolled away. The rocks slammed into the Meadow Wall behind her, smashing through and raining shards of broken granite into the meadow. Finding herself alone next to the breach, she took a deep breath and reached for her sword.

Keya, no! came Dexon's voice.

She started to tell him to mind his own business and let her do her duty, then hesitated when she realized that would be the last thing anyone ever heard from her.

In that moment Dexon added, *Here!*

Keya looked toward the Company of the Cold Hand and saw Dexon's darksword flying toward her hilt-first. Reaching up to catch it, she thought, *Thanks, Dex—love you.*

Deciding those were much better last words than what she had been thinking a moment before, she brought the darksword up before her and spun into the gap in a squat—and came nose-to-mouth with a crawling phaerimm. For an instant, she was almost too stunned to comprehend what she was seeing. Thornbacks did not crawl, they floated . . . and why was she still alive anyway? It had only to think a spell and she would be an elf-shaped cinder.

It opened its toothy mouth and stretched four spindly arms toward her, and suddenly none of that mattered. She brought Dexon's darksword down, splitting it open for two feet past its mouth, then brought the blade around and slashed it in the opposite direction. The phaerimm whistled and recoiled, grabbing Keya by the shoulders and rearing up on its tail. She kicked at its torso with both feet, hacking herself free of its arms and dropping on her shoulder.

Still using no magic, the thing lunged and snapped at Keya's feet. She kicked free and rolled over her shoulder—then glimpsed one of the beholders shining its antimagic ray over the phaerimm and understood. She drew her dagger with her free hand and flipped it at the eye tyrant in one swift motion.

Keya was no bladesinger. The dagger struck pommel first—hardly fatal, but enough. The beholder blinked, and in that instant, the mythal's magic returned to the gap. The phaerimm screeched and started to retreat into the Vine Vale, but not quickly enough to avoid the golden meteor that streaked down from the heavens and slammed it to ground—where it quickly dissolved into a pile of ash only a little larger than those left behind by the first wave of the Long Watch.

Before the stunned beholder could recover, Keya leaped onto the Meadow Wall rubble and brought the darksword across the middle of its spherical body. A cascade of dark gore spilled out of the wound, and it dropped to the ground without so much as a curse. Keya brought the darksword around and started down the wall toward the next beholder, then cried out in astonishment when she felt a magic hand pluck her off the crest and carry her back into the Company of the Cold Hand.

"Let's not get carried away, young lady," Kiinyon Colbathin said, stepping to her side. He gestured down the way, to where the survivors of the Long Watch were charging back to the Meadow Wall behind a storm of spears and arrows. "Let someone else have a go at them."

"Yes, you've done your part many times over," Khelben agreed, plucking the darksword from Keya's hand. He hissed at the cold and quickly returned the blade to Dexon, then raised his swarthy brow. "That didn't freeze your hand?"

"As a matter of fact, no." She displayed her hands. Aside from the calluses she had earned in weapons practice, they remained as healthy as her eighty-year-old cheeks. "They didn't even get cold."

Dexon's jaw dropped, and Burlen and Kuhl fell to chuckling.

Khelben frowned. "What are you two laughing about?"

The battle din built to a roar as the Long Watch reached the Meadow

Wall and began to assail the enemy at close range. Unable to use their own magic within the antimagic zones created by their beholder slaves, the phaerimm hung back.

Khelben's scowl only deepened. "This is important. If there's a way for the Company of the Cold Hand to wield your comrades' darkswords—"

"The Cold Hand wouldn't care for it much," said Kuhl.

"The Cold Hand will do what it must to defend Evereska," Kiinyon growled. "They are elf warriors."

"It won't work," Kuhl said. "Most of the warriors in the Cold Hand are male—and I doubt even elven magic can get a Vaasan baby on a male warrior."

"B-baby?" Keya stammered. "What are you talking about?"

Burlen grinned and nudged her arm. "Come on, Keya, you know how these things work," he said. "You and Dexon are family now."

✡✡✡✡✡

From the ruins of the Secret Gate, high in Evereska's Upper Vale, Laeral had watched in horror as the first rank of elves poured over the Meadow Wall and disintegrated into swirling piles of ash. When the phaerimm launched their counterattack, using their magic to hurl half the stones in the Vine Vale through the breaches the beholders had opened in the mythal, she had gasped out loud. As the young warriors of the Long Watch somehow rallied themselves and came charging back to drive off the beholders, she felt tears sliding down her cheeks.

"The stuff of legends, my friend," Laeral said, looking across the window to Lord Imesfor. "If those are raw recruits in Evereska, I shudder to think what will become of the phaerimm when the time comes to unleash your seasoned warriors."

"I just wish I could be there with them," Imesfor said. Though the magic of Waterdeep's clerics had regrown his fingers, they were still too clumsy and stiff to cast spells, or even hold a sword in combat. "It is good to watch, to remind myself that the *Tel'Quess* never lose hope."

Forcing their mind-slaves to hold at the mythal's edge, the phaerimm continued to hurl whole stretches of vineyard wall into the meadow. The Long Watch fell by the dozens and continued to attack, playing a deadly game of dodge as they tried to avoid breaches in the mythal while continuing to pour arrows into the beholders. One eye tyrant after another sprouted more spines than a hedgehog, then sank to the ground and disintegrated. Some, maddened by pain, finally broke free of their masters' hold and turned to leave, only to be struck down by the phaerimm themselves. Though it would have been a simple matter to send the elite companies forward to support the Long Watch and finish off the beholders, Khelben and the elf commanders wisely resisted the temptation. One way or another, Evereska would need its most experienced fighters later, when victory or death hung in the balance.

Laeral could just see Khelben in the heart of one of the elite companies, a swarthy figure in black robes, his namesake black staff cradled in the crook of one arm as he discussed strategy with the elf lords clustered around him. How good it was to see her beloved again, even if he was little more than a black speck in a square of gleaming gray mithral.

"Lord Blackstaff seems to have them quite distracted," said Prince Clariburnus, peering out the watch-loop adjacent to Laeral and Lord Imesfor. "What say you, Lady Laeral?"

"I would say we dare not wait—the mythal is growing weak," Laeral said, noting that the rain of golden meteors had tapered to a drizzle. "You've seen their trap. We can't dismount."

"That trap we will turn against them," said Lamorak, who was watching opposite Clariburnus, "but let us be alert for more phaerimm trickery. You Chosen are not the only ones who know the value of guile in war."

Laeral met the prince's orange eyes. "Always a good thing to remember," she said, starting downstairs. "I will hold it in mind."

When the phaerimm had made no attempt to stop them from entering the Shaeradim, it had been Laeral who realized the thornbacks would attempt to breach the mythal and take refuge inside Evereska—and who had developed the strategy to take advantage of their plan. After emerging from the shadowshell and using her silver fire to open a gate in the weakened deadwall, she had sent the relief army to attack the enemy rear guard, then summoned Lord Imesfor from Waterdeep to serve as a guide. He had led the Shadovar army through the shadow fringe into the Secret Gate and safely past hundreds of elven traps—a gauntlet so devious and powerful that it had claimed several of the phaerimm before they finally gave up on clearing the passage and simply sealed the entrances—at least those they could find.

Laeral reached the exit vestibule at the bottom of the stairs, where a company of Shadovar cavalry stood beside its mounts in a long line stretching back across a marble bridge into the murky recesses of the Passing. With little more than lances, darkswords, and black helms, the veserab riders were lightly armed and thinly armored. Behind the cavalry, Laeral knew, ran an even longer line of infantry equipped just as sparingly. Against the magic of the phaerimm, massive blades and heavy armor counted for less than the swiftness of the strike and the agility with which one dodged.

Lamorak came and gave his orders, then turned to Laeral and said, "This is your plan. Would you care to launch the attack?"

"By all means—thank you." As Laeral waited for the riders to mount their veserabs, she turned to Lord Imesfor. "I know you'd like nothing better than to see the outcome of the battle, but the Shadovar infantry will need someone to lead them back to the relief army."

Imesfor raised his hand, displaying a set of stubby white digits that did not yet look quite like fingers. "Say no more. It will be my pleasure to guide them through the Passing."

"Once the outcome is apparent, of course," Lamorak clarified.

Imesfor nodded. "Of course."

Since the infantry would not be able to step foot into the valley below without being disintegrated by phaerimm magic, the prince's plan called for them to return to the holding action in the mountains and catch the enemy from behind. Given the tremendous advantages of holding the high terrain, the tactic was certain to save a lot of lives in the relief army.

The cavalry commander reported his readiness, and the two Shadovar princes mounted their own veserabs. Laeral cast a flying spell on herself, then raised her arm and led the way out of the Secret Gate down a hanging gorge that opened into the High Vale itself. The life-draining magic of the phaerimm had reduced the slopes to barren pitches of rock and dirt, lacking even a rotted stump to hint at the forest of old-growth spruce that had once covered the valley.

As soon as Laeral cleared the shelter of the hanging vale, she turned and streaked for the Vine Vale as fast as she could fly. The cavalry came behind her, fanning out across the slopes in a great blanket of flapping black wings. Mistaking the Shadovar and their mounts for a legion of some new, hell-spawned horrors come to aid the phaerimm, the elite companies of Evereska raised their voices and weapons and started to press forward.

Khelben raised his arms and staff and called out something in a thunderous voice that brought the Evereskan companies up short, but the damage was done. First one, then a dozen, then half the phaerimm at the Meadow Wall drifted away from the mythal and swung their toothy jaws toward the descending Shadovar. Laeral reached the highest terrace of the Vine Vale.

A scintillating wall of colors rose in front of her. Foolish phaerimm—still didn't know who they were dealing with. Laeral dispelled it with a gesture, then did the same to the curtain of flame that appeared next. By then, the Shadovar were sweeping past to both sides, spraying dark bolts into the enemy. The valley ahead became a storm of shadow magic and black flapping wings. Laeral saw a dozen thornbacks drop out from beneath the tempest and disintegrate into long mounds of ash. An instant later, she was among them, flashing past scaly, wormlike bodies and deflecting barbed tails with her quarterstaff.

Climb! Lamorak's voice came to Laeral as a bare, faint whisper inside her head. *Cast the shadow zone!*

Laeral and the Shadovar ascended high into the sky. The phaerimm started after them, but their floating magic was no match for the swift-climbing wings of the veserabs. Even Laeral had to extend a hand and allow herself to be drawn along by a passing shadow lord. Blasts of silver lightning and golden magic chased the riders skyward, filling the air with black blossoms of blood, wing, and shadow armor.

Clariburnus, Lamorak, and several powerful Shadovar spread out over the Vine Vale, then released the reins of their mounts and began to drop wads of shadowsilk. They spread their hands palm downward and called out something in ancient Netherese she could not quite catch. The wads flattened into translucent disks of darkness and fell to the valley floor, forcing the phaerimm and beholders down beneath them. As the first creatures touched ground, they wailed in pain and crumbled to ash.

Perhaps two dozen thornbacks and twice that many beholders perished before the disintegration spell was nullified. The survivors writhed about under the disks for a moment, then finally broke the surface of the shadow like fish rising from a pond. The Shadovar were already diving on them, peppering them with shadow bolts as they emerged from the darkness, their mounts spraying them with streams of noxious black mist. Laeral released her escort to join the assault and curved back toward the Meadow Wall, concentrating her own attacks on the beholders. Unlike the Shadow Weave spells of her allies, the phaerimm were less likely to be injured by anything she hurled at them than they were to absorb it and heal themselves. Of course, a blast of her silver fire was sure to slay even the mightiest phaerimm, but she could use that only once an hour, and so it seemed wisest to hold that particular attack in reserve.

A flash of silver light lit the vale behind Laeral. Her entire body erupted into fiery nettling as a bolt of lightning caught her in the flank and sent her tumbling through the air head over heels. She bounced off the mythal and quickly brought herself back under control, then turned to find a pair of cinder clouds settling to the ground where the attack had blasted through two Shadovar warriors before exhausting itself on her.

About twenty yards away floated the phaerimm that had hurled the lightning, its toothy mouth turned in her direction and hanging agape. The bolt had been a powerful one. By all rights, it should have torn through her and continued on to another five or six targets, but Laeral was one of the Chosen. She could use the Weave to protect herself from many forms of magical attack, and this was one of the most obvious ones.

Laeral raised her hands and was about to blast her attacker with silver fire when a pair of Shadovar warriors swooped down on it from behind, their veserabs engulfing it in a cloud of noxious black fume that made Laeral's eyes sting even at a distance.

Guiding their mounts with their knees, they poured shadow bolts into it with one hand and raised their black swords with the other, hacking the phaerimm into three pieces as they flashed past. Laeral waved her thanks and, praying that Waterdeep's hippogriff riders never found themselves taking the sky against such a deadly air cavalry, she turned back to the mission she had assigned herself.

Not far ahead, a pair of beholders were using their antimagic beams to cover each other as they retreated from the Meadow Wall and laced the sky above with disintegration rays. Laeral cast a quick invisibility spell on herself and dropped to a few inches above the ground, then came up beneath the creatures, pouring golden streams of magic into them. Both beholders erupted into crimson starbursts, coating her head to toe in foul-smelling gore.

Laeral only hoped that Pluefan Trueshot still allowed humans into the Hall of the High Hunt. She had not seen Khelben in nearly four months, and she could see that she would need a long dip in the Singing Spring before their reunion could be a proper one.

✡✡✡✡✡

Khelben's first glimpse of Laeral in the battle came when she emerged from the starburst of viscera and entrails that, until a few moments earlier, had been two beholders holding Keya Nihmedu's company of the Long Watch at bay. Even smeared in crimson, she was a sight for weary eyes—and not only because she had broken the siege of Evereska. Never had he spent four months as long as the last four, when he had not known when he would see his beloved Laeral—or even whether he would survive to do so. The Chosen did die, and—as he had so nearly learned at the Rocnest—the job of killing them required far fewer than two hundred phaerimm.

Khelben watched Laeral vanish back into the magic storm, then stood staring into the flashing bolts and scintillating sprays for a few minutes longer. Though the sheets of fire and swirling clouds of veserab breath made it impossible to catch more than glimpses of the action, the battle roar was as ferocious as ever, and the number of Shadovar wheeling up into sight was steadily diminishing. The phaerimm were standing their ground, no doubt because they understood what was at stake in this battle as well as Khelben did.

"Lord Duirsar, the time has come to commit Evereska's army," he said, speaking to the Hill Elders as much as he was to Duirsar. "We must break the siege now, while the phaerimm are still reeling."

"What remains to us is hardly an army," Kiinyon objected, "and even less so, after we followed your advice the last time."

"The attack cost more than I had anticipated, but it was also a crucial diversion." Khelben pointed at the Shadovar swirling above the vale, then started toward the Meadow Wall. "Now, with the Shadovar and the rest of the North's forces operating inside the Shaeradim, this is the phaerimm's last chance to breach the mythal. If we can make them withdraw now, we can break the siege and hunt them down at our will."

Unconvinced, Kiinyon grabbed Khelben's arm and tried to hold him back. "If we fail—"

"If we fail, we lose everything," Lord Duirsar interrupted. "We have been failing for the last four months, it's time to take a chance." He nodded to Khelben. "Call the charge."

Khelben used a spell to carry his voice to every corner of the vale. "Ready the charge! Long Watch, stand down!"

At the Meadow Wall, the young elves of the Long Watch began to disengage and fall back, clustering around trees, granite monoliths, and deep ravines where they would not hinder the charge. The process took several long minutes, for they were as inexperienced as they were exhausted, with casualties that would have reduced even the most stalwart company of veterans to a disorganized horde. At Khelben's side, however, Keya Nihmedu was cinching her chin strap and checking her armor. He turned a disapproving eye on her and was rewarded with a glare that could have cracked stone.

"If you say one word about my condition—"

Khelben raised his hands. "Wouldn't dream of it," he lied.

In contrast to Dexon, who was hanging at her heels with a dazed look in his eyes, she seemed to be taking the news of her condition in stride. Khelben removed the magic bracers on his wrists and tossed them to her.

"I want you to wear these for me—and stay close," Khelben said. "I may need them."

"Of course." Keya's expression changed to dutiful, and she slipped the bracers onto her biceps. "What are they?"

"When the time comes," Khelben said. He raised his staff and waved it toward the Vine Vale. "To battle!"

Unlike every human charge he had ever led, this one started in near silence and seemed to grow quieter. There was no yelling, no banging of arms or clanging of armor, only the soft patter of thousands of graceful feet—and the much louder sound of the Vaasan boots pounding along behind.

They came to the Meadow Wall, and Khelben cast a spell of flying. He sprang into the air on the run, sweeping his black staff across a line of beholders floating out of the haze, their writhing eyestalks spraying all manner of rays and beams at the first rank of charging elves. Khelben held his staff across his body and caught half a dozen rays directed at him, then spread the fingers of his free hand and sent a stream of golden bolts pouring back at his attackers. Three of the eye tyrants sank to the ground with clusters of smoking holes drilled clear through their spherical bodies, but one of the creatures managed to sweep its antimagic beam up in time to block Khelben's counterattack.

A tumbling darksword split this one down the center, then the Company of the Cold Hand was streaming past into the Vine Vale, leaping the bodies of deflated beholders, wounded veserabs, and groaning Shadovar . . . even a few hacked and mutilated phaerimm.

Khelben sensed his bracers drifting off to the left and turned to see Keya Nihmedu leading Dexon and the other two Vaasans through the remains of the vineyard gate. Cursing her impetuousness, he circled around to meet her from the other direction—and found himself somersaulting backward through the air as a flurry of golden magic bolts caught him in the chest.

Sting though they might, the attacks harmed him no more than had the lightning bolt that had sent Laeral tumbling. He righted himself and returned more cautiously, weaving and bobbing, coming in fast and low, staff at the ready and silver fire crackling on his fingertips. He found Keya and the Vaasans battling a pair of phaerimm, the elf dodging and somersaulting as black death rays and tongues of fire erupted all around her. Dexon barely stood on a withered, smoking leg, Burlen had one arm hanging limp at his side, and Kuhl was still attempting to sneak up behind the nearest creature for a killing blow.

Khelben loosed a bolt of silver fire into the nearest phaerimm. That was all it took. As the first crumbled to cinders, the second creature attempted to teleport away—attempted, because Kuhl was already leaping on it from behind, driving his sword down into its mouth. The Vaasan landed face-first on the ground, his sword coated in foul-smelling gore.

Khelben circled the vineyard once to make certain there were no more unseen threats, then dropped to the ground beside Keya, who was examining Dexon's mangled leg and assuring him—or perhaps herself—that Pluefan Trueshot and Hanali's priestesses were perfectly capable of restoring the limb.

Dexon's face was pained, but he seemed more concerned about the possibility of another attack than his gruesome injury.

"I told you to stay *close*, young lady," Khelben said.

As he spoke, he noted that the battle roar had all but vanished. Shadovar veserab riders were flying toward the edges of the valley, swarming around the tentacled orbs of fleeing beholders—the phaerimm had abandoned their mind-slaves and teleported away.

Looking back to Keya, Khelben gestured at the bracers. "What if I had needed those?"

"If you had *needed* them, you wouldn't have given them to me." Keya pulled the bracers off and thrust them into his hands, then, slipping a supportive arm around Dexon's waist, stretched up to kiss Khelben on the lips. "But thank you."

"Y-you're welcome," Khelben stammered. He felt himself blushing and smiled to cover it. "Very welcome, my dear."

Keya's eyes shifted past his shoulder and suddenly widened in surprise, as did Dexon's, and Khelben heard a familiar "ahem" behind him. He turned to find Laeral standing there, tapping the tip of a smoking wand against her crimson-streaked armor.

She cocked her brow, then shifted her gaze to Keya. "Tell me, young lady—what does a girl need to kill to get a kiss around here?"

CHAPTER TWELVE

21 Mirtul, the Year of Wild Magic

Vala hung motionless in the ceiling spider webs, watching in silence as Corineus spun around the sanctum below, slashing eyestalks from beholder heads and cratering illithid chests with bolts of golden magic, somersaulting under bugbears and diving over kobolds. All the while, he somehow kept himself between his enemies and the four spellbooks resting on a dusty oak table in the corner, amidst a pile of crowns, scepters, rings, bracers, and other magic relics recovered from the lairs of the phaerimm they had slain so far. The monster bodies were beginning to pile up, slowing the baelnorn's bladedance to the point that he began to take hits. It hardly mattered. Steel weapons only bounced off his white flesh, and he absorbed disintegration rays and mind blasts the way leaves drank sunlight. Even antimagic beams had no effect. The beholders casting them never lived long enough for their blade-wielding comrades to take advantage.

Finally, there were just too many bodies for Corineus to continue his bladedance. He stumbled, spinning in for a kill, and two kobolds bounced across the carnage into the corner, each grabbing for one of the spellbooks on the desk. Though they were no more than twelve feet below Vala, close enough that she could smell their musky odor even over the charnel stench that filled the room, she continued to hang under the ceiling, her arms and legs aching from the strain of holding herself in such an unaccustomed position. This time, Corineus had told her to be a spider, to let the prey twist itself into their web before striking.

As Corineus struggled to regain his balance, a pair of bugbears leaped onto his back and bowled him over. He started to throw them off, and more started to squeeze through the doors one after the other, adding their weight to the heap. The pile continued to rise, but more slowly, then finally sank back toward the floor. The baelnorn's muffled voice called out an incantation, and a brilliant spark flashed somewhere under the tangle of hairy limbs.

A sheet of silver lightning fanned across the room, momentarily blinding Vala. There was a single communal death-growl, then the room fell silent. The reek of scorched flesh pervaded her nostrils, and her chill-numbed flesh began to prickle as the baelnorn's cold aura suddenly vanished. She blinked the dazzle from her eyes to find the sanctum piled three layers deep in scorched body halves, many pouring smoke into the air and some still twitching.

Corineus was encased in a shimmering sphere of force, his withered face twisted into a mask of agony as he struggled to his feet. He was moving only slowly and with great effort, with his eyes bulging out of their sockets and lines of black blood running from his ears and nostrils. The sphere was contracting visibly, crushing the baelnorn in its inexorable grasp.

Vala remained where she was, all too conscious of the shiny red diamonds starting to peer at her from the corners of the web-strewn ceiling. The giant spiders had vanished through their hidden bolt holes the instant Corineus entered the sanctum, but with his chill aura gone, they were eager to return and reclaim their webs. Her goosebumps rose again, though this time they had nothing to do with being cold.

Finally, the object of her ambush appeared, the largest phaerimm yet, with amber scales and a tail-barb as long as the blade of her darksword. The creature paused a moment in the door, then floated over to the sphere in which Corineus was imprisoned and stopped. The baelnorn turned his head in its direction. His eyes were bulging so badly they were about to pop their sockets, and the black stuff running from his nose and ears had fanned across his entire lower face. The undead elf began to fumble through the gestures of an enchantment.

So clumsy were his efforts that even Vala knew the spell would never go off. The phaerimm simply floated there before him, and eventually Corineus stopped trying. The pair simply stood beside each other and did nothing. Vala was confused for the first several moments, until the baelnorn's gaze shifted to the captured spellbooks, and she recalled that phaerimm communicated with their captives telepathically. The thing was interrogating him, no doubt trying to learn how he had been slipping past the wards designed to keep him at bay.

Vala prayed to Tempus to give Corineus strength—then remembered herself and asked Corellon Larethian, the elf god of war, for the same thing. They had taken care to leave behind no trace of her presence in the lairs they had broken so far. If the baelnorn betrayed the secret, she would not survive long enough to realize their plan had failed.

A tremble in the web drew Vala's gaze to the opposite corner of the ceiling, where a wolf-sized spider was creeping out of its bolt hole. She fixed it in place with a glare but did not dare do more. Corineus had warned her not to move until the instant she attacked. Her only camouflage was spidersilk and darkness; any magic that the baelnorn might have used to hide her would have drawn the phaerimm's attention as surely as a flame.

Emboldened by the first, a second spider crept out onto the web, this one only half a dozen yards from Vala's feet. She glanced toward the phaerimm, trying to gauge her chances of making the leap. Not good. The thornback was over by the main door with the baelnorn; she was in the opposite corner, above the spellbooks. Corineus had said the thing would not be able to resist such a treasure. So far, it seemed to be withstanding the temptation all too well.

A third spider crept onto the web, this one in the corner above Corineus, who was enduring long past the point when a living elf would have been crushed. His eyes were hanging out of their sockets, flattened against his cheeks, while his arms and legs were bent at impossible angles and pressed back against his body. Vala wanted to yell at the baelnorn to give up and let himself be destroyed already, but she didn't even know if that was possible. Besides, he had to make it look real. If he gave up too easily, his tormentor would grow suspicious—and few things were more dangerous than a suspicious phaerimm.

The web began to tremble violently as the first spider darted for Vala, fangs dripping venom and pedipalps reaching out. The second made a dash for her legs but stopped to face the other one when it changed its direction.

Vala started to throw her sword in desperation—then had a better idea and looked back to the spiders. She ran her blade through the spider web, cutting a huge crescent around the bottom of her feet. The web came free with a series of brittle pops, and she swung down from the ceiling, descending toward her target in a swift-moving arc. The phaerimm swung its huge mouth toward her.

Vala leaped straight at it, whipping the darksword around for a vicious, two-handed downstrike. She heard scales cracking and felt the blade splitting flesh. A pair of phaerimm hands caught her by the throat and began to squeeze. She turned the blade and began to drag it through the thing's body. The barbed tail arced up, clanked off her backplate, and drew back to try again.

Vala knocked a phaerimm hand from her throat—only to have it replaced by two more. Her vision began to fade, and her right leg erupted into fiery pain as the tail barb penetrated her armor and began to pump its poison into her body. She pried her darksword free, swinging the blade up through two feet of tendon and flesh. Her vision darkened to something darker than black, and Vala's stomach suddenly rose into her chest. A bitter chill stung her flesh, and there was an endless eternity of falling. She grew queasy and weak and heard nothing but the pounding of her own heart, slowing with each beat, then even that was gone.

Vala's first hint that she was not . . . well, *gone,* was the reek of battle gore. The second was pain. Something was lodged in her leg, holding up her whole body by the big thigh muscle and flicking across the bone. She thought for a moment that she was dead and in the Nine Hells with no memory of how she had come to be there. Then she saw a huge, amber-colored phaerimm lying flayed and motionless on the floor above her—no, *below*—and recalled the fight in the sanctum.

Vala was not in the sanctum. Instead of the four captured spellbooks and great heap of recovered magic she and Corineus had piled in the corner, there was a single open book floating in a green spell field and several shelves of neatly arranged relics. There were the mind-slaves' sleeping palettes lined up along the wall, and the ward symbol above the door that kept her baelnorn ally at bay. Most of all, there was the thornback itself, lying motionless and gutted on the floor beneath her, its long tail preventing her from floating to the ceiling by the painful barb lodged in her thigh.

After Vala's attack, the thing had attempted to teleport to the safety of its lair and arrived dead. At least she thought it was dead. She brought her arm down to cut herself free—or, rather, tried to bring her arm down. It didn't move in response to her will, nor did her legs or neck when she tested them—or even her tongue, when she attempted to curse.

Eventually, Vala knew, the crushing sphere would destroy Corineus's body and free his spirit to seek one of the spare bodies he had hidden in the Irithlium—but that was not going to help her. Until she broke the warding symbol above the door, the baelnorn could not enter the lair. There was nothing to do but hang there in pain until the poison wore off.

✡✡✡✡✡

The Shadovar were not conspicuous in Arabel—or rather in what had been Arabel before the ghazneths and their orc hordes reduced it to rubble—but they were there. On the dark side of a broken tower, a pair of swarthy masons were using a shadow saw to size blocks. Through the window of a bakery, a potter with gleaming amethyst eyes was fashioning an oven from darkclay. In an alley, a tall and gaunt carpenter was installing an ebon-wood door.

None of them more than glanced in Galaeron's direction as he passed by with Aris and Ruha, but that meant nothing. With an elf, a Bedine witch, and a stone giant traveling together, the Shadovar had to know who they were looking at.

Aris stooped down to within three feet of Galaeron and Ruha. Though the giant had spent much of the past two days sipping Storm Silverhand's healing potions, he remained unsteady enough that Galaeron would rather he wasn't leaning over them.

"This is going to be harder than we thought," Aris said quietly. "I keep seeing Shadovar."

Galaeron nodded. "Sent to watch for us."

"So many?" Ruha shook her head. "The Shadovar have easier ways of watching than rebuilding a whole city."

"What do you know?" Galaeron snapped. "With the information I have about the phaerimm, the Shadovar would do anything to get me back."

"I am sure they would," Ruha said patiently.

She pointed at the base of a nearly rebuilt tower, where the foundation had been patched with the same dark amalgam that served as mortar in Shade Enclave.

"They have been here for some time," the witch continued. "Their purpose here is to make an ally of Cormyr, not find us."

Galaeron considered first the foundation, then the rest of the broad street, and had to nod. While the city still looked like a rubble heap at first glance, the outlines of its former shape were beginning to re-emerge. Many of the larger buildings were already rising to the second or third story, and most showed signs of Shadovar work—if not in the mortar then in the precision fit of the stones and the dark wood of the balconies, or even in the depth of the shadowed window alcoves.

"You're right, of course," Galaeron said, transferring his ire from Ruha to Storm Silverhand. "Even the Shadovar couldn't do this overnight—and Storm had to know it when she teleported us here."

"Most likely," Ruha admitted.

"So why send *us?*" Galaeron demanded. "It would have made more sense to teleport us to Waterdeep and come to Cormyr herself."

"Perhaps you have answered your own question," Ruha said. "That is what the Shadovar would expect. Or matters in Waterdeep may be more complicated than we know. I am given to understand that Storm's sister Laeral is friendly with the Shadovar."

"Say no more," Galaeron grumbled.

Storm's reaction to him in Anauroch had convinced him how unlikely he was to persuade any of the Chosen of anything. For loosing the phaerimm on the world, they might have forgiven him eventually, but for bringing the Shadovar into the world after them, and getting Elminster banished to the Nine Hells—never.

"We're better off taking our chances with the Cormyreans," Galaeron admitted.

"Then you accept that Storm did the wisest thing?" Ruha asked.

Galaeron shrugged. "How can I know? But she has to have a better hope in Waterdeep than I do. Lord Piergeiron certainly isn't going to take my word over Laeral's."

An approving twinkle came to Ruha's eyes. "You may survive this yet. I think you are finally learning to control your shadow self." She glanced over at a pair of Shadovar stone cutters who had stopped work to watch them pass, then added, "But perhaps we would draw less attention if we disguised ourselves and found a safe place to leave Aris."

"At this point, speed is better than stealth," Galaeron said. "The sooner we present ourselves at the palace, the more difficult it will be for Telamont Tanthul to have a troop of his lords spirit us back to the enclave."

"Well said," Aris agreed, glancing out over the half-built city. "Besides, there isn't a place to hide a stone giant within twenty miles of here."

It was no exaggeration. Though Storm had teleported them into a field only a quarter mile outside Arabel, the walk to the gates had been plenty long enough to bear witness to the devastation wrought by the dragon Nalavarauthatoryl and her ghazneths and orcs. Even a year after the terrible war, nothing grew in the once-lush fields except a few black thistles and carpets of foul-smelling moss, while the great forest that had once flourished to the south and west of the city was still struggling to put the first spindly leaves in its canopy.

Despite their presence in Arabel, the Shadovar were not helping matters. With the melting of the High Ice carrying so much rain and cool air west toward Waterdeep, a steady wind had been blowing northward through

Cormyr, carrying with it the heat of the southlands and the mugginess of the Dragonmere.

Had the zephyr but dropped a fraction of its moisture on its way over the kingdom, the change of weather might actually have helped matters. Instead, the air remained miserly with its water until it crashed into the northern Stormhorns and abruptly cooled. As a result, the kingdom was enduring its worst, hottest, most miserable drought in a thousand years, while at the same time its two largest rivers, the Starwater and the Wyvernflow, were flooding their banks and washing away whole villages.

Galaeron was far from certain that he would be able to secure an audience with the rulers of the kingdom, much less persuade the Cormyreans that Shade Enclave was causing their problems. But, as Storm had said, they would be eager for an explanation and inclined to listen. All he had to do was get the shadow blanket into Vangerdahast's hands. After that, the royal wizard would convince himself.

They reached the city palace, which—to Galaeron's great disappointment—had been rebuilt from the second story in the same pearly stone as Villa Dusari. Atop the highest spires, dozens of Shadovar polishers were crawling over the turrets like spiders, putting the final touches on the magnificent building. Fortunately, the guards at the door still wore Cormyr's purple dragon, or Galaeron would have concluded that the Shadovar had claimed Arabel for their own and left immediately.

As the trio ascended the steps, two of the guards crossed their halberds in front of the entrance. The sergeant—no older than his comrades, but with a badly scarred face and an eye patch—stepped forward to address them.

"You have business with Lord Myrmeen?" he demanded.

Galaeron shook his head. "Our business is with Princess Alusair and her wizard," he said. "It concerns the abnormal weather Cormyr has been suffering of late."

The sergeant seemed not to hear the last part of his explanation. "This is the palace of Myrmeen Lhal," he said. "The Steel Regent keeps her home—and her wizard—in Suzail."

Alarm bells started clanging inside Galaeron's mind. "You are saying Arabel is no longer part of Cormyr?"

The sergeant's one eye narrowed. "What I'm saying is that unless you have business with Myrmeen Lhal—"

"We have it on good authority that Princess Alusair and Vangerdahast are inside," Ruha interrupted. She removed the Harper's pin from inside her robe and pressed it into his hand. "Please deliver that to her with the message that our lives may depend on a swift audience—and perhaps the fate of Cormyr's growing season, as well."

"Harpers?" The sergeant barely glanced at the pin. "Why didn't you say so?"

He turned and vanished into the palace, then returned a moment later with a gangly, horse-faced man in a scarlet cape and purple sash of office. The newcomer returned Ruha's pin and waved them into the palace's grandiose reception hall—so large that, after crawling through the entrance, even Aris could stand upright.

"Welcome. I am Dauneth Marliir, Her Majesty's High Warden," the man said. "I'm sorry for the delay, but we have learned to be cautious with information about Her Majesty."

"We understand," Ruha said, returning the pin to its place. "I am Ruha—"

"Yes, I know." Dauneth flashed a big smile.

Galaeron ignored him and looked down the long arcade of pillars, where he was disappointed to see more Shadovar than humans polishing and buffing.

Dauneth continued to speak with Ruha. "There are not many Bedine witches in the Harpers."

"Only one, I am certain," Ruha laughed. She waved a hand at Galaeron. "This is Galaeron Nihmedu."

Dauneth's brow rose in shock, but he managed to recover himself. "Well met, Galaeron. I have heard of your bravery." He extended a hand and clasped Galaeron's wrist in the human fashion. "Prince Rivalen tells me that his father has been most concerned since your disappearance."

"Yes, I'm sure he has," Galaeron replied, surprised by the coldness in his own voice. "He has good reason to be."

Dauneth's brow rose, prompting Ruha to say, "It is related to our visit." She half turned to wave at Aris. "And this is—"

"Aris of a Thousand Faces," Dauneth finished. He paused and bowed deeply. "When the palace is finished, Myrmeen intends to display one of your pieces, 'The Descent of the Shadow Army,' here in the lobby."

"She does?" The giant's jaw dropped. "How did she come by it?"

Dauneth smiled enthusiastically. "A gift from Prince Rivalen, of course."

The High Warden led the way down a stately side corridor toward a pair of well-guarded double doors, and Galaeron's heart fell. He could see already that Rivalen and his gifts had won the hearts of the Cormyreans, that he had no chance whatsoever of winning Alusair's confidence. Soon, he would either be dead or on his way back to the enclave, and after seeing how close his shadow self had come to getting Aris killed, he knew which he was going to choose. He wanted nothing more than to use his shadow magic to do a sending to Vala and apologize for how he had parted, to let her know that, in the end at least, he had come to his senses and died thinking of her.

And he would have liked to apologize to Takari Moonsnow, as well, for refusing what she had offered. He had always known on some deep level that they were spirit mates and, because of that, assumed she would always be with him. But when he had chosen to help Vala instead of her in the final battle against Wulgreth, he had wounded her more deeply than any lich could have. He knew there could be nothing between them but pain. For the rest of her life, whenever she thought of him, it would fill her with feelings of betrayal and loss.

How could he have been such a coward? Perhaps there had always been a shadow on his heart because of his fear of following it—because in trying to avoid his own pain, he had inflicted it on others. Certainly his father had never turned his back on his feelings. He had loved Morgwais completely from the moment he had met her, for all the years they had lived together in Evereska, and for all the years she had lived apart in the High Forest, and if her absence had caused him anguish, their love had given him the strength to endure it without bitterness or regret.

They reached the double doors and were admitted at once. Aris had to hunch his shoulders to squeeze through this entrance, but inside lay the palace's formal audience hall, with an arched ceiling high enough that the giant could still stand upright by walking down the center of the aisle.

On a raised throne at the far end sat a striking woman with oak-brown eyes and amber hair, one arm resting on her knee as she conversed with a huge Shadovar beside her. Even had Galaeron not glimpsed the man's golden eyes and ceremonial fangs, he would have recognized Prince Rivalen by his immense shoulders and narrow waist. Next to the throne and a little behind it stood an elderly, tired-looking man in a voluminous robe and long white beard who could only be Cormyr's royal wizard, Vangerdahast. Adjacent to him stood the final member of the little group, a statuesque woman with dark hair and eyes as blue as a mountain lake.

Dauneth stopped opposite the throne and presented Galaeron and his companions, introducing the woman on the throne as the Steel Regent of Cormyr, Princess Alusair Obarskyr, and the one on the floor as Myrmeen Lhal, the King's Lord of Arabel.

When she was introduced to Aris, Myrmeen's eyes sparkled, showing flecks of gold almost like an elf's.

"I'm a great enthusiast of your work, Master Aris." She gestured to Rivalen, who was studying the group with a forced smile and said, "The prince has gifted me with 'The Descent of the Shadow Army.' I intend to display it prominently in the lobby."

"It will be an honor," Aris said with a certain practiced ease. "I only hope it will do your palace justice."

"It will *make* my palace," she said. "The way you impart a sense of the army's whirling descent while using the veserab wings to support the enclave is pure magic. But I find a hint of menace in how the riders fan out at the bottom, as though you found the coming of the Shadovar just a little frightening."

"You are very perceptive, Milady." Aris glanced in Rivalen's direction, then added, "Were I to do the same sculpture today, there would be more than a hint of menace."

"Really?" Myrmeen furrowed her brow. "I was under the impression you were quite content in the city of Shade."

"So were we," Rivalen said smoothly, "but we understand how temperamental artists can be. If Aris was unhappy, we would have been glad to transport him to any place he wished. There was no need for him to brave the desert with these thieves."

"We are not the thieves in this room," Galaeron began. "The Shadovar—"

"Myrmeen did not ask you to speak," Princess Alusair said, raising a hand to cut him off. She moved to the edge of her seat and addressed Rivalen. "So what'd they steal?"

Vangerdahast laid a restraining hand on her shoulder. "Princess, this matter really has nothing to do with Cormyr."

Alusair scowled. "They're in Cormyr now, Vangey." Her glance strayed in Myrmeen Lhal's direction ever so briefly, then looked back to Prince Rivalen. "At least I think it's still Cormyr."

"Shade would not recognize any other claims to Arabel," Rivalen said, not rising to the bait, "and we would certainly be very grateful if you would return these thieves to Shade Enclave for judgment by the Most High."

Alusair continued to watch the prince, and Galaeron began to see that there was more going on in Arabel than the rebuilding of the city—or at least the Steel Regent feared there was.

"Must I ask again, Prince?" Alusair said. "What did they steal?"

Rivalen hesitated just a moment, then gestured at the shadow blanket draped over Aris's shoulder. "The umbral mantle, to begin with. Also a flying disk and a veserab . . . that I know of."

Alusair looked to Ruha. "Is that true?"

"In its essence," she said. "I was not—"

"In its fact," Rivalen insisted. "You were all part of the plan from the start. Malik confessed all."

"Malik?" Alusair asked. "Would this be Malik el Sami yn Nasser, the Seraph of Lies?"

Rivalen nodded. "A despicable little man, but it is well known that Mystra's curse prevents him from lying." He looked in Galaeron's direction and sneered. "He was with Galaeron when we rescued his party from the Dire Wood. We should have taken that as a suggestion of what to expect when we realized who he was."

"Indeed," Vangerdahast said. "I am surprised you didn't. Malik was captured in the escape?"

"It was not an escape," Rivalen clarified. "Until they began stealing, they were free to leave at any time."

"Princess Alusair," Ruha said, "if you will permit me—"

"I will not," Alusair said, raising a hand to silence the witch. "The prince is speaking."

Ruha's face fell, and Galaeron could tell that she was feeling as hopeless as he had earlier. He caught her eye and smiled in encouragement. It was impossible to see how she responded beneath her veil.

When Rivalen did not continue, Alusair asked, "Do you have anything to add, Prince? Perhaps they murdered someone in the escape?"

Rivalen considered this a moment, then shook his head, "There were some injuries—but only to Malik, and he survived. Their only crime in Shade Enclave was theft. The Most High will be grateful when they are returned to answer for it."

"Of course," Alusair said. She turned to Ruha. "Have you anything to say before I return you to the prince?"

"Only that it is a mistake to do so in such haste." Ruha looked to Myrmeen Lhal for support—then let her shoulders slump as the lady lord looked away. Turning her gaze back to Alusair, she began, "On my word as a Harper—"

"If I may," Galaeron interrupted. Even in Evereska, he had seen enough of politics to realize that truth was seldom the most valued currency in such discussions. Addressing himself directly to Alusair, he said, "The gifts of the Shadovar come with a price—"

"Every gift comes with a price," Alusair shot back. "If you mean to waste the crown's time on such tripe, I'll have your tongue before I return you to Rivalen."

Galaeron's confidence of a moment earlier vanished. He had read the situation correctly—he was more sure of that than ever—but he had failed to anticipate just how astute the Steel Regent really was and how quick to anger when she thought she was being manipulated. He swallowed and tried again.

"The price of this gift is higher than you think." Galaeron sneaked a glance at Rivalen, who caught him looking and made a derisive motion for him to continue. He did. "The droughts and floods Cormyr has been suffering, they are the Shadovar's doing."

Myrmeen and Dauneth sighed audibly, and Vangerdahast looked as though he were struggling not to laugh.

Alusair turned her gaze to Prince Rivalen. "Well, Prince, what say you to that?"

Rivalen rolled his golden eyes. "I wouldn't think it necessary to say anything."

"It is true," Galaeron insisted. "Surely, you've heard about the troubles on the Sword Coast? The Shadovar are melting the High Ice. It's affecting the weather all across Faerûn."

"Melting the High Ice?" Vangerdahast scoffed. "The fire spell that powerful hasn't been written, even in Azuth's spellbook."

"They're not using a spell—they're using that." Galaeron pointed to the shadow blanket hanging over Aris's shoulder. "They're spreading them over—"

"Princess Alusair," Rivalen interrupted. "It pains me to see this thief wasting the crown's time with this nonsense. If you will allow me to summon a few of my lords—"

"Only a minute longer," Alusair said, raising her brow at the note of concern that had crept into the prince's voice. "Cormyr's law requires that the accused be allowed to speak before I can turn them over to you."

The princess nodded Vangerdahast toward the blanket, and Galaeron breathed a quiet sigh of relief as the old man shuffled out from behind her. Aris spread the blanket obligingly and draped it down where Vangerdahast could reach it, turning the darkest side toward the window so that it would absorb the sun's heat. The wizard rubbed his hand first over one side of the surface, then the other, and the way his eyes widened made clear that he had noted how efficiently it trapped heat.

Galaeron glanced over at Rivalen and found the prince's golden eyes locked on his face. In that moment, he knew that he had succeeded—and the prince knew it, too. Were it not for the knowledge Melegaunt had secreted inside his head, Galaeron had no doubt that Rivalen would have killed him on the spot and fled into the shadows. As it was, however, the prince had no choice but to play the game a little longer.

After a time, Vangerdahast removed a wand from inside his robe and waved it over the shadow blanket, then put it back and repeated the process three more times. Finally, he stepped away, folded his hands behind his back, and said nothing.

A full minute passed before Alusair growled, "Well?"

Vangerdahast jumped as though she had startled him out of a dream, looking around with an alarming expression of confusion on his face.

"Well, what?" the royal magician asked.

Alusair nodded at the shadow blanket. "The umbral mantle," she prompted. "Can it do what the elf claims?"

Vangerdahast turned and studied the blanket as though seeing it for the first time, then shrugged and turned away. "How should I know? I don't understand shadow magic."

The only thing that fell farther than Alusair's expression was Galaeron's heart.

"What's there to understand?" Galaeron cried, stepping toward the throne. "Just put your hand—"

"That's far enough, elf," Dauneth Marliir said, catching Galaeron by the arm and pressing a dagger tip to his ribs. "You've had your say."

Rivalen flashed his fangs in Galaeron's direction, then turned to Alusair. "If they have had their say, Princess, I will summon my lords."

Alusair lifted her hand in consent—until Vangerdahast gave a short, "Ahem."

Finally unable to contain himself, Rivalen spun toward the wizard. "What now?"

Vangerdahast gave him a synthetic smile. "Nothing to upset yourself over—a mere formality, really," he said, turning to Alusair, "but the law requires due regard for anyone seeking judgment before the crown."

Alusair frowned in confusion. "And?"

"This is not due regard," the wizard explained. "For that, you must consider the matter overnight."

"She must?" Myrmeen asked, puzzled. "Where does it say that?"

"In the *Rule of Law*, of course," Alusair said, somehow at once smiling at Vangerdahast and frowning at Myrmeen. "Do you mean to tell me one of the King's Lords doesn't know her Iltharl?"

Myrmeen's face fell. "No, er, of course not," she stammered, frowning. "I, uh, just hadn't considered that the, uh, passage applied to this situation."

"Well, it does," Alusair said. She turned to Rivalen. "I'm sorry, Prince Rivalen, but you'll have to wait until morning. You understand—laws can be such pesky things."

"Yes, can't they?" Rivalen smiled thinly and inclined his head. "I trust you have secure facilities."

"Oh, *very* secure." Alusair looked to her High Warden and said, "Dauneth, see to it that these prisoners are lodged in the citadel—and put them in the deep dungeon. When Prince Rivalen comes for them in the morning, I want them to be there."

CHAPTER THIRTEEN

21 Mirtul, the Year of Wild Magic

Slapping the warding symbol off the wall as she left, Vala ducked out of the tiny lair and scuttled down the ancient sewer in a low crouch. A knot the size of a fist was throbbing atop her thigh, and the wound itself oozed a steady stream of hot fluid. Fortunately, the cause of Vala's injuries had died without depositing its egg. She found the thing in the phaerimm's tail when she cut off the barb to add to her collection. After the levitation magic had finally lapsed, she'd fallen onto the dead creature and had to wait for the paralyzation poison to wear off. If the egg had been implanted, she would still have been lying atop the dead phaerimm with her face buried in its entrails.

As it was, Vala was so feverish that catching up to her quarry was out of the question. It required all of her strength just to limp down the tunnel in such an awkward stoop and avoid splashing her bandage with the cloudy fluid standing stagnant in the bottom of the passage. Though the sewer had not been used for its intended purpose in six centuries, the filth that filled it had been spawned of constant death and decay and reeked even more horribly than the offal it had been intended to carry. She came to a T in the passage and, ten paces up the right branch, glimpsed a short length of thorny tail disappearing around another corner.

Vala stepped into the mouth of the opposite fork and brushed her shoulder and arm against the filthy wall, leaving a broad drag mark in the mildew, then retreated back to the intersection and pressed her back to the wall. Having predicted the little phaerimm would flee to the right, Corineus was waiting a hundred paces up the tunnel, ready to drive the thing back toward its lair. Vala would have preferred to force the thornback into the baelnorn's ambush, but his aura of cold made it impossible for him to surprise anything in the dungeon.

The crack and rumble of an approaching spell battle heralded the return of the phaerimm. Vala kissed the blade of her darksword and said a prayer for her son in case Tempus should decide to take her in this rank place, then held her weapon ready next to the intersection. A few moments later, a brilliant orange light erupted from the tunnel mouth, blinding Vala and scalding her skin. She turned away, raising her free hand to shield her face as a crackling ball of flame hissed past and vanished down the opposite passage.

Vala opened her eyes and saw only circles of popping orange. The phaerimm could have been three inches from her face preparing to sink its tail barb into her throat, or it could have been lurking ten feet up the passage, waiting to see what its spell flushed out. Guessing the phaerimm would be a little behind its spell, she counted three seconds, brought her sword down, and hit something solid.

A fierce wind gusted through the sewer and died almost instantly. When Vala's sword fell free and touched the floor and she found herself still alive, she deduced that she had at least hit the thing and began to slash about the intersection at random, weaving her blade through a blind figure-eight defense and trying to blink the orange spots from her eyes.

"You killed the phaerimm," Corineus said from up the passage. "Are you trying to kill its ghost as well, or do you have no further use for me now that we have destroyed the last phaerimm?"

"It's dead?" Vala stopped weaving but did not return her sword to its scabbard. Phaerimm were tricky creatures, and even if the Shadovar helmet protected her from its mind control, it would be an easy matter for it to use its magic to impersonate the baelnorn. "You're sure?"

"I am sure." An icy hand grabbed hers and guided the darksword back toward its scabbard. "Put that away. I have something I want to give you."

Vala sheathed the weapon, certain of the baelnorn's identity. She had grown so accustomed to his chill aura that she'd scarcely noticed it until he'd taken her hand.

"You'll have to tell me what it is," she said. "I'm afraid my eyes are still a bit dazzled from that fireball."

"It is a treasure from Myth Drannor."

Corineus slipped a ring onto her finger, and she could see him—not the withered baelnorn she had come to know during her trials in the Irithlium, but a tall sun elf with gold-flecked eyes and a long mane of silky red hair.

"When you wear it this way," the elf said, "you will see things as they truly are."

He turned the ring a quarter turn, and Vala's vision returned to normal—which was to say that she couldn't see a thing, since her hand was not on her darksword.

"When you wear it this way, no one will know you are wearing it." He turned it another quarter turn. "And when you wear it this way, no one will see you."

Corineus started to remove his icy hand, but Vala caught it between hers.

"You know I killed the phaerimm for my own reasons," she said. "It's not necessary to gift me."

"I think it is, Vala Thorsdotter." Corineus freed his hands from hers and stepped away. "I have seen a little of the future while we were together."

The chill aura began to fade rapidly. Vala turned the ring and saw the dead phaerimm floating in the water in two pieces, neither as long as her arm. She nudged them aside and peered down the tunnel from which it had come, where Corineus's noble figure was wading into the darkness.

"Thank you, Corineus," she called after him, "and not only for the ring."

Corineus turned his head around on his shoulders and gave her a broad grin that reminded her of Galaeron's joyful smile—back when he had one.

"Thank you, Vala Thorsdotter," he said, "and not only for killing the phaerimm."

✲✲✲✲✲

As dungeons went, the one beneath the Citadel at Arabel was kinder than most—certainly kinder than the cramped cells of the Evereskan Tomb Guard, where crypt breakers were forced to kneel with their arms locked in stocks and gags in their mouths. Here, Galaeron and Ruha sat in side-by-side cages, with Aris chained to a wall in the interrogation chamber outside. There were no rats and only the typical human infestations of fleas and lice. Save for the acrid stench of the impure oil used in the wall lamps, the place didn't even smell that bad.

But it was secure. Aris had been scratching at the mortar around his chain mountings for half the night and done nothing more than bloody his fingertips. Ruha had tried half a dozen spells, only to have the magic sputter away as soon as it left her hands. Galaeron had kicked at the latch of his door until an ominous rumble sounded from above and he looked up to realize that the cell ceiling was a set of interlocked drop-blocks, with the keystone supported by the same jamb he was kicking. Fearful that ill-considered attempts might cost his life, he had given up trying to escape the cell at all.

Galaeron pressed his face to the bars and strained to see if there was anyone in the guard station, which was positioned at the end of the row of cages where it was almost impossible to see from inside a cell. He could see flamelight dancing on the walls, but no shadows that suggested someone upright and moving.

"No one there," Aris hissed, his whisper as loud as wind in trees. "The last check was about an hour ago."

"Confident in their dungeoncraft, aren't these Cormyreans?" Galaeron said.

"They have every reason to be," Ruha said, speaking from the corner of her cell. "I don't hear you kicking any more, and the spell-guard has defeated everything I've tried."

"Then we really don't have any choice, do we?" Galaeron stepped back from the door and, hoping the guards had missed a few strands of shadowsilk when they searched him, began to fish through his cloak pockets. "I can get us out of here."

Aris's eyes grew round and alarmed. "How?"

"Their spell-guard won't stop shadow magic," he said, "and since it didn't occur to Rivalen to erect his own—"

"Galaeron, no," Ruha said. "It is too risky for you to cast another shadow spell."

"What's too risky is waiting here for Rivalen." He found a strand of shadowsilk and began to tie it into a closed loop. "I'll have us out of here with one spell."

"And then what?" Aris demanded. "Wait until we are counting on you again, then let your shadow get us all killed?"

Galaeron stopped tying and looked across the chamber. "I'm sorry about the Saiyaddar, Aris, I truly am. Had I let you drop the shadow blanket, you wouldn't have been so eager to reach water—"

"And you would have had nothing to show Storm," Aris interrupted. "It is not what you did, my friend, but *why*. When your shadow self takes control, you lose sight of what is right and think only of vengeance."

"I'm entitled," Galaeron said, growing irritated with the giant's lecturing. "Telamont was trying to bring out my shadow, and Escanor . . . well, never mind Escanor."

"You were going to say that Escanor stole Vala," Aris said, "but you know that isn't so. You know you drove her away."

"You're right," Galaeron replied, "but I can see that now. I'm in control."

Despite the admission, Galaeron began to knot the shadowsilk again. Aris exchanged concerned gazes with Ruha, and the witch pushed a hand through the bars to grab Galaeron's arm.

"You're not in control now, Galaeron," Ruha said. "Your shadow is trying to tempt you into another mistake."

She slipped her hand down to his and tried, gently, to pluck the shadowsilk from his fingers. He held tight.

"Storm will send help," Ruha said. "I have told her of our troubles."

Galaeron started to demand how she could get a message past the spellguard but answered his own question when he recalled that the guard was fashioned of Weave magic. Because Storm was one of the Chosen, Ruha merely had to speak her name, and the Weave would carry the next few words directly to her ear—no spells required. What it would *not* do, however, was carry a reply.

"You know she is coming?" Galaeron asked. "You know that for certain?"

Ruha's eyes remained locked with his. "No, but it is wiser to trust in her than to believe you can control your shadow when it is so plainly controlling you. At the moment, I would rather place my life in Malik's hands."

The witch's frank words were enough to remind Galaeron of his remorse after Aris was wounded and to make him see that he was only using their situation as an excuse to cast a spell and feel cool shadow magic rushing through his body. It was an almost physical sensation, like being thirsty and longing for water or being exhausted and yearning for sleep, and it was just as hard to deny. The Shadow Weave was always there, within easy reach, inviting him to reach out and touch it.

Galaeron released the strand of shadowsilk, then watched as Ruha rolled it into a tiny ball and flicked it toward a lamp flame. She missed, but the wad bounced off the wall, then landed in the murk and was lost.

"You know what will happen if Rivalen takes me back to Shade?" Galaeron asked, talking to both Ruha and Aris. "I won't be able to stop Telamont from bringing out my shadow. It would be better to get us out of here and let it happen now, where you two can still do something about it."

"Only a fool would think us capable," Aris said. "Your shadow is still tempting you, Galaeron. If you yield to it—even for a minute—we are lost."

"Trust in Storm," Ruha urged. "I do, and I will die first if we are returned to the enclave."

That much was true, Galaeron knew. Aris's talent would probably buy his life, at least if he could find it in himself to continue sculpting. Galaeron himself would be kept alive and corrupted and might eventually find a way to overcome his shadow, but Ruha had nothing to offer the Shadovar except trouble. The interrogation that followed the trio's return would reveal that she was an agent of the Chosen—if Telamont didn't know it already—and Galaeron didn't even want to contemplate the fate that awaited spies in Shade Enclave.

Galaeron nodded and said, "Very well." He stepped away from the bars, and sat on the stone bench that served as his cot. "If you are willing to trust in Storm to save us, then I ought to be, too."

"But are you?" demanded Aris. "You must promise not to use shadow magic again, even if it means our deaths."

Galaeron shook his head. "I can only promise to try."

"That is no promise at all," Ruha retorted. "Trying is easy. Doing is hard."

Galaeron looked away. He had already broken that promise once, so he knew how difficult it would be to keep—even harder than the last time, perhaps impossible—but Ruha was right. Trying was easy, and doing the easy thing had been leading him deeper into disaster from the beginning. He had breached the Sharn Wall and released the phaerimm when he ordered his patrol to attack with magic bolts instead of swords. He had allowed his shadow to sneak inside him when he ignored Melegaunt's warning and used more shadow magic than he had the strength to control. He had loosed the Shadovar on Faerûn when he brought their flying city into the world to save Evereska from the phaerimm. He had lost Vala when he had been foolish enough to believe that Telamont Tanthul would teach him to control his shadow self. And he had nearly lost his closest friend in pursuit of an easy vengeance. The time had come to start doing the hard thing.

Galaeron looked across the interrogation chamber and said, "You're right. On my word as a Tomb Guard, I promise never to use shadow magic again."

Aris gave a curt nod. "Good, then you have already defeated the Shadovar."

"The defeat is in the keeping," Ruha said, "but it is a start."

She returned to her own bench, and they fell into silence again. Aris went back to tugging at his chains and scratching at the mortar around the mountings. Ruha and Galaeron tried to think of some way to escape that didn't involve using shadow magic. A little later, two night sentries came in and sat down at the table at the guard station. Constant companions through this night and no doubt many others, they exchanged a few stale words in a half-hearted attempt to stay awake, then fell to snoring within a few moments of each other. Galaeron was not surprised. Boredom was ever the watchman's curse and one that would be especially potent in a dungeon where escape seemed such a remote possibility.

A quarter hour later, the snoring came to a gurgled end. A pair of armored bodies clanged to the floor, and Aris's eyes grew wide. Galaeron pressed himself to the bars and looked toward the guard station. The sentries lay with their feet in view, surrounded by a circle of murk that might have been blood or shadow—without darksight, it was impossible to tell which. Rivalen and half a dozen Shadovar lords were stepping out of the shadows behind them.

Galaeron's throat went dry. The moment had come sooner than expected, but he knew that his temptation would have been the same in the morning—or anytime. His body was fairly aching for him to cast a spell. He felt feverish and hollow and thirsty for the cool sensation of the Shadow Weave, but even aside from his promise, it was too late for that. He could never hope to best Rivalen in a duel of magic. Still, when their eyes met, Galaeron maintained a calm composure and gave a nonchalant tip of his head.

"Rather early, aren't we?" the elf said.

"I grew tired of waiting for you."

Rivalen motioned a trio of warriors toward Aris and two more toward Ruha, then had the last one accompany him to Galaeron's cell.

"As a matter of fact," the prince said, "I was beginning to fear you had found some way other than shadow magic to leave the dungeon."

Galaeron shook his head. "No, just stopped using shadow magic."

Rivalen gave him a disbelieving smirk. "Of course you have." He came to Galaeron's door and studied his cell for a moment, then motioned him toward the back. "If you don't mind kneeling."

Galaeron did as the prince requested, though he took care to tuck his toes under him so he could spring to his feet quickly. To avoid letting his gaze stray toward the keystone in the ceiling and give away his plan, he kept his eyes locked on Rivalen.

"Why the hurry?" he asked. "A few more hours, and you wouldn't have to kidnap us."

The prince drew a set of lockpicks from his cloak pocket and kneeled in front of the door. "In a few more hours, you would have escaped and been in another realm betraying the Most High to someone else."

"Not actually," Galaeron said, "but I see your point."

He fell silent and allowed the prince to work. On the other side of the interrogation chamber, Aris's escorts finished binding his wrists and ankles with shadow line and set to work on the chains securing him to the wall. The giant kept jerking his arms and legs away, complicating their task to the point that one of them was drawing his sword.

"Aris, don't get yourself hurt," Galaeron ordered. He was beginning to see how he might help Aris and Ruha escape, but he needed the giant free of the chains. "It isn't worth it."

"Yes, you must be careful with those hands," Rivalen called, still working on Galaeron's lock. "The Most High values them nearly as highly as he does the secrets Galaeron carries from Melegaunt."

Ruha's escorts succeeded in opening her cell and motioned the witch out. As she approached the door, she glanced over her shoulder and raised her brow.

"At least you'll be in the same city as Malik," Galaeron said, nodding her out into the interrogation chamber. "Assuming he's still alive."

"He is, indeed," Rivalen said. "After betraying your plan, he is a favorite of the Most High."

The tumblers in Galaeron's lock clicked open. The prince smiled and withdrew the picks.

Galaeron leaped to his feet and launched himself at the doorjamb with as much force as he could gather in two steps.

"Run!" he yelled. "Save your—"

The prince waved a dark hand at him, and Galaeron slammed into the back of the cell so hard his breath left him. He slid halfway down the wall, then found himself floating out the door still gasping for breath.

"Did you think I would fail to see the trap?" Rivalen asked. He held Galaeron suspended in front of him. "You are foolish as well as ungrateful. If you try something foolish again, Weluk will cut the witch's throat."

One of Ruha's escorts pressed a glassy dagger blade to her throat, and Rivalen's assistant began to bind Galaeron's wrists.

"You Shadovar have a strange sense of gratitude," Galaeron said. "If you think I'll help you destroy Faerûn to save Evereska, you are wrong."

"Your thinking will change," Rivalen assured him. "And we have no wish to destroy Faerûn."

"Then your wishes are different from your actions," Ruha said, ignoring the knife at her throat. "You have seen for yourself what the melting of the High Ice is doing to the Sword Coast and the Heartlands. You are starving whole nations out of existence."

"The Shadovar have spent seventeen centuries starving, and we endure," Rivalen shot back. "If the Faerûnian kingdoms are too weak to survive a few decades of hunger so the Netherese lands can grow fertile again, then they were not meant to last."

"I would take issue with that," said a familiar—and very angry—female voice. "As would Waterdeep, Silverymoon, the Dalelands, and even Thay, I'm sure."

A tremendous clanking filled the dungeon as an entire company of Purple Dragons literally stepped out of the opposite wall of the interrogation chamber, followed closely by Alusair Obarskyr, Vangerdahast, and Dauneth Marliir. Galaeron was almost embarrassed to realize that he had been staring at an illusion the entire night without realizing it.

Galaeron looked over to Ruha, and she shook her head. The issue remained in doubt. Her confidence in Storm had not been because she knew they were being watched.

Alusair turned to a wiry priest who followed her out of the wall and gestured toward the two sentries lying on the floor over at the guard station.

"Owden," she said, "would you mind. . . ."

"Of course, Princess."

The priest scurried away. Alusair, attired in a full suit of battered plate armor, clanked across the interrogation chamber to where Rivalen stood.

"You will be kind enough to return the prisoners to their cells, Prince," she said, pointing to Galaeron and Ruha. "It is not yet morning."

Rivalen looked around the room and, finding several dozen crossbows not quite trained in his direction, seemed confused. He bowed but did not give the order—apparently deciding that since he was not yet under attack, Alusair had either not heard everything he had said or did not find it indefensible.

"I beg your forgiveness, Majesty," he said. "I did not mean to be presumptuous, but fearing the elf would use his shadow magic to escape, I assigned certain of my lords to keep a watch on their prison."

Alusair said nothing and looked to the guard station, where the one she had addressed as Owden was kneeling over the fallen sentries. He looked up and shook his head.

Rivalen was quick to cover. "As it happened, my caution was well-warranted. We spied a shadow whorl outside and followed it down to this dungeon." He waved a hand at the fallen guards. "Alas, we were too late to save your men, but we did capture the elf and his accomplices as they were attempting to leave."

"That's a lie!" boomed Aris. "We were—"

Vangerdahast made a motion, and the giant's lips continued to move without sound. Aris scowled and shook his head in angry denial. If Alusair noticed, she paid him no attention and kept her attention focused on Rivalen.

"Cormyr is grateful for your vigilance," said the princess, "but the prisoners have not yet been returned to their cells."

Ruha's escorts started to return her to her cell. Rivalen snapped something at them in ancient Netherese that prompted them to stop in their tracks, then he turned to Alusair with a smile.

"It is nearing dawn, Princess. Given how close the prisoners have come to escaping already, surely we can steal a few hours from the night."

Vangerdahast scowled and tottered forward. "That is not how the law works in Cormyr, Prince Rivalen." He pointed an ancient and crooked finger through the bars behind Galaeron's back. "Remove your bindings and return the prisoners to their cells—or take their place."

Rivalen's golden eyes glowed almost white at the threat. He sneered at the old wizard a moment, then turned to Alusair. "If that is the crown's wish, then, of course, we will obey."

Vangerdahast pointed a serpentine finger at Ruha's guards and spoke a word of magic, and the two lords were hurled into the cell's back wall with enough force to shatter their black armor and leave them slumped on the floor.

"The crown has already stated its wish," Alusair said, motioning a squad of Purple Dragons forward to surround Rivalen and the others. "Will you unbind the prisoners, Prince?"

Rivalen hesitated, and Galaeron felt the cold magic of the Shadow Weave welling up as the prince prepared to carry him to the enclave.

"Go ahead, Rivalen," he said. "Abduct me now, and all Faerûn will know I am telling the truth."

The swell of cold magic faded, and Galaeron instantly regretted his words. Another second, and he would have been back in Shade Enclave, with no choice except to immerse himself in shadow. The restraints came free of Galaeron's hands of their own accord, and Rivalen shoved him through the door of the cell with enough force to bounce him off the far wall and drop him to the floor.

"You will give the prisoners to us at dawn." Though Rivalen attempted to phrase it as a command instead of a request, the mere fact that he said it made the question implicit. "The Most High would find it difficult to understand why a friend would harbor fugitives from his justice."

"Would he?"

Alusair nodded, and Vangerdahast made a motion with his crooked finger. The doors slammed shut, locking Galaeron in his cell and the two

Shadovar in the one adjacent. The Purple Dragons escorted Ruha away and placed themselves between Aris and the Shadovar who had been holding him prisoner.

Alusair watched Rivalen watch this, then said, "But he would understand allowing his friends to starve." She gave him a cold grin, then echoed his earlier words. "After all, if the Faerûnian kingdoms are too weak to survive a few decades of hunger, they are not meant to last."

Rivalen's face turned so dark it almost vanished. "Majesty, to understand any comment, you must know the context."

"I suppose that is true." Alusair stepped toward the prince, her attitude more that of a warrior challenging another than a potentate delivering a message. "So the Shadovar are not melting the High Ice?"

Rivalen cast a disparaging look in Galaeron's direction, then said, "The princess surely knows that every kingdom has its disaffected. A discontented elf saying a thing does not make it true."

"That is not an answer," Alusair pressed. "Are the Shadovar responsible for changing the weather of Faerûn or not?"

"Us, Majesty?" Rivalen gasped. "We are only one city."

"A Netherese city—and Netherese cities have done worse," Alusair said, no doubt referring to the hubris that had caused the fall of the goddess Mystryl and altered the Weave itself forever. She turned her head over her shoulder and called, "Myrmeen, have you seen enough?"

"I have, Majesty."

Myrmeen Lhal stepped through the illusionary wall, bringing with her half a dozen Arabellan nobles bearing the shadow blanket confiscated from Galaeron and his companions. She directed the nobles to drop the blanket at the prince's feet.

"There is Shade Enclave's stolen property," she said. "You and the rest of the Shadovar in Arabel may return it to your father with my compliments."

"I don't understand," Rivalen said, stalling for time to think. "You are ordering us out of the city?"

"I am ordering you out of Arabel—and the entirety of Cormyr, you and all Shadovar," Alusair clarified. "You won't be welcome here until you stop the melting of the High Ice."

"You would begrudge us our birthright?" Rivalen gasped, changing tactics the instant it grew apparent his lies had been discovered. "By what right do you dare?"

It was the wrong thing to say to Alusair Obarskyr. She stepped forward until she was standing nose to breastplate with the huge Shadovar.

"By the right of law—and of arms." She shoved him back into Galaeron's cage, then turned to Dauneth Marliir and waved at the two Shadovar locked in the cell that had been Ruha's. "Are those the ones who killed our guards?"

Dauneth shrugged. "Perhaps, Majesty. These Shadovar are difficult to tell apart."

"Well, it matters not," she said. "They were at least party to the deaths of two of our guards. Execute them."

"Of course, Majesty."

Rivalen opened his mouth to object, but Dauneth was already dropping his arm. Two dozen crossbows clacked, peppering the two Shadovar inside with iron bolts. Both warriors fell without a scream, their faces and throats studded with expertly placed quarrels.

Alusair turned to Rivalen. "I believe that makes our position clear, does it not?"

✡✡✡✡✡

Vala limped out of the Irithlium's shadowed entranceway to find Prince Escanor standing with a full company of Shadovar in the tree-choked courtyard. Their armor was fastened and their glassy swords held at battle ready. They were divided into squads of a dozen, each commanded by a fang-mouthed shadow lord. As Vala approached, an astonished—or perhaps relieved—murmur ran through their ranks, and the tips of their swords began to drift toward the ground. Raising her brow at the unexpected reception, she checked the ring Corineus had given her to make certain it was in the undetectable position, then removed the phaerimm tails from her belt and presented herself to Escanor.

"Come to keep your promise, Escanor?" she asked.

Escanor closed his gaping mouth. "My promise?"

"For killing the phaerimm beneath the Irithlium." Vala slapped the tails into his hand. "There are six tails there. Count them."

The prince glanced down at the tails and gave a wry smile. "Most impressive, but no. When I made that promise, I actually didn't think you would be returning."

"What you thought matters less than what you do about it," Vala said. "Are the Princes of Shade men who honor their words?"

"Unfortunately, that won't be possible," Escanor said, smile vanishing. He returned the phaerimm tails, then caught Vala by the wrist. "I was just on my way to fetch you for the Most High. It seems he has finally located Galaeron."

The prince turned away and dragging her after him, started to walk. Within two steps, his body had grown diaphanous and ghostly. Another two steps, and they were completely immersed in shadow, the ground beneath their feet as soft as water. Vala tried to pull away but stopped struggling when she experienced a strange sensation of falling and her captor's arm stretched into a writhing rope of darkness. She turned her magic ring so that it would show affairs as they truly were.

The swirling darkness around her became a pearly, motionless void, more colorless than it was gray. Escanor was a black heart beating inside a cage of black ribs, with no limbs or skull, but two coppery flames where there would have been eyes and a sheaf of finger wisps wrapped around Vala's arm.

The prince's fiery eyes swung in her direction. She quickly thumbed her ring back to its concealed position, and he became the shadowy figure of a moment before.

"Walk," he said.

The prince took a step and became solid again. Vala followed. The ground grew hard beneath her feet, and wisps of shadow started to coalesce in smoky ribbons. The voices of unseen whisperers rose and fell in the surrounding darkness. Gradually, a set of murmurs hardened into the fuller tones of normal speech, and Vala recognized the sibilant voice of Telamont Tanthul, Most High. He was speaking harshly to someone—shouting, in fact—and there was an angry murmur in the air around him.

The figures of several shadow lords appeared in the murk surrounding Telamont's throne. Standing closest to the dais were the princes Rivalen and Lamorak, with Hadhrune a quarter of the way up the stairs. To Vala's astonishment, Malik was on a step between the seneschal and the princes, his cuckold's horns no longer hidden by his customary turban. Galaeron was nowhere in sight. Escanor brushed past the lords and stopped at the base of the dais.

". . . allow her to dictate terms to me?" the Most High was raging. "After all I have done to rebuild that wreck of a kingdom?"

"Most High, had the harlot dared utter a word against you, I would have stricken her down myself," Rivalen said, cringing visibly in the heat of his father's anger. "As her outrages were merely directed at me, I thought it best to endure them and return to consult."

"Return without the elf?"

"It was impossible to bring him," Rivalen said.

The Most High waited in expectant silence.

"When it remained possible, I still had hopes of salvaging our relationship with Arabel," the prince continued. "I know the value you place on controlling the border cities."

The Most High remained quiet, though the sense of expectation that had hung in the air was gone. Vala folded her hands in front of her, covering the gift from Corineus, and thumbed her ring around. The murk paled to the color of fog, thin enough for her to see that the throne room was really a vast courtyard surrounded in the distance by dark bands she took to be walls. Beyond the dais in front of her rose the shapes of many other platforms, their silhouettes growing progressively more indistinct with distance, but each surrounded by a crowd of shadow lords similar to those ringing Vala and the princes.

The shadow lords themselves were wrinkled, ghoul-like figures with sunken, red-rimmed eyes and leathery black skin often pocked by white sores. Rivalen and Lamorak appeared much the same as had Escanor when Vala looked at him during the journey from Myth Drannor, varying only in how much of their skeleton remained attached to the black ribs that enclosed their black hearts. Surprisingly, Hadhrune appeared the same as before Vala had turned the ring—as did Malik, save that he held himself more erectly and seemed far more wiry than Vala had grown accustomed to thinking of him.

Finally, Telamont sent Vala's heart jumping into her throat by crying, "Betrayer!"

It was at first impossible to tell whom the Most High was addressing, for he was only two platinum eyes floating in a vaguely man-shaped pillar of darkness. The gray fog that filled the throne room seemed to be flowing through him, entering his "body" in the general area of the feet and leaving at the hands. In the area behind one of the eyes, in what should have been the temple area, there was something black and wrinkled, about half the size of Vala's fist, pulsing in beat to the Most High's words.

"This is your doing, ungrateful Vaasan!"

Vala spun the ring to its concealed position and found the Most High's murk-filled cowl turned in her direction, his empty sleeve raised and pointing down the stairs at her.

Praying that Telamont had not sensed her magic ring, Vala raised her chin and forced herself to meet his angry glare. "Mine, Most High? I have not been anywhere near Cormyr."

"You knew of his plans before he left, did you not?"

The last thing Vala wanted to do was admit her complicity in Galaeron's escape, but Malik had almost certainly revealed her role already, and she knew better than to think the Most High would be swayed by any lie she could tell.

"I did," she said.

The Most High remained silent, and she felt the weight of his next question as tangibly as that of a fallen comrade's body.

"I wanted him to leave," she said. "You were giving him over to his shadow, not teaching him to control it."

"Yet you went to Myth Drannor with Escanor."

"So you wouldn't grow suspicious and stop him from leaving," Vala said.

Again, the silence, heavy and demanding.

"He didn't want to leave without me," Vala admitted. "I had to convince him that he had vexed me and that I was enamored of Escanor. He left swearing vengeance on you, Escanor, and Shade in general."

Telamont finally looked away and, shaking his head in disbelief, descended the dais to stand in front of Escanor.

"The blame in this lies in part with me," the Most High said. "I had not thought his shadow so much in control, but you were blinded by a woman's cajolery and allowed her to use you against the enclave—and for that, you should be executed as well."

Vala's knees grew instantly weak at the pronouncement, but Escanor only inclined his head. "If that—"

"Execute?" Malik interrupted, stepping to the Most High's side. "You cannot execute Vala!"

Telamont's platinum eyes grew as cold as winter hail. "You object, cuckold?"

"Of course not . . . only Vala is my friend, and it would break my wretched heart—whatever the One may still let me have of it—to see her killed." Malik frowned at the curse that compelled him to keep speaking when it would have been so much wiser to let the matter drop after the first few words, then apparently saw that he had nothing to lose and plunged ahead. "And even more importantly, it would break Galaeron's heart."

"Why should the One care about that, little man?" asked Hadhrune, descending the dais to stare down over Telamont's shoulder. "The elf is an ingrate and a traitor to all the enclave has given."

"True," Malik said, "but he is an ingrate and a traitor that Shade Enclave needs. If you slay Vala, you will make him an implacable enemy who will no doubt die in some foolish manner seeking vengeance against you."

Telamont rolled an empty sleeve, gesturing for Malik to continue.

"On the other hand," the little man said. "If you keep Vala here, holding her in some terrible manner certain to cause her great pain, letting it be known that she truly does love Galaeron and only went to Myth Drannor so he would leave and save himself, Galaeron is certainly the type of noble fool to return and try to rescue her."

"The fault in your thinking is that his shadow has almost certainly taken him already," Hadhrune pointed out. "If that is so, he will see through your plan and avoid us all the more."

"He seemed well in control of himself in Arabel," Rivalen said. "In point of fact, he seemed to be avoiding shadow magic altogether, even when he might have used it to free himself and escape us."

"If that is so, then perhaps our plan will work," Hadhrune said, as much the idea thief as ever. He stepped around to bring himself in line with Telamont's gaze. "May I suggest the drop pits? Surely, no torture can be worse than keeping those clean and clear—at least no survivable torture."

Vala had an unpleasant feeling that she knew what the drop pits were, but it hardly mattered. Any torture that kept her alive to return to her son was one she could endure.

Telamont considered Hadhrune's proposal for a moment, then gave a thoughtful half-nod. "It would certainly give the elf cause to come for her quickly." He turned his platinum eyes upon Malik and added, "What do you think, my short friend?"

Malik's brow rose. "Me?"

"The plan is yours," Telamont said. "Do you think the drop pits the worst we can do?"

"Milord, I really do not know Shade Enclave well enough to name the worst torture it has to offer."

Malik fell silent for a moment, then his face twisted itself into a familiar expression of distress, and Vala had a sinking feeling.

"Only, it occurs to me that the torture most likely to draw Galaeron back in a rush is to make Vala a scullery maid in Escanor's palace and to let it be known that he is using her horribly at night."

Vala swallowed. As terrible as was Malik's suggestion, it was still something she could survive. To return to Sheldon, she could endure anything.

"And, of course, you must put her darksword away someplace where she cannot call it," Malik added. "For Vala, the worst torture of all will be not looking in on her son at night."

Until then, Vala had felt a debt of gratitude to the little man for saving her life. For telling them to take her visits, she could have killed him—in fact, she might have, had Escanor's powerful hand not closed around her wrist and prevented her from drawing her sword.

"If you please," Escanor said, "leave it in the scabbard when you pass it over."

Telamont's eyes sparkled with delight. "I think Malik is correct." He turned his gaze on the little man. "You are proving yourself a surprisingly capable advisor."

Malik beamed. "I am glad you are pleased with my humble services."

"Yes, I would never have thought one of Mystra's curses would be of such benefit to Shade Enclave." Telamont left the dais and started across the throne room. "Come to the world-window with me, my friend. We must make an example of Cormyr and show Faerûn what it is to betray the generosity of Shade Enclave—and you will tell me how we are going to do it."

CHAPTER FOURTEEN

25 Mirtul, the Year of Wild Magic

Through the magic of the scrying ball, Galaeron felt as though he were an eagle on high, circling the walled city of Tilverton in search of some garbage-loving raccoon to feed the nestlings in its aerie. He had a view of the entire town and the four roads leading into it, yet he could still make out details as fine as shield insignia carried by the growing number of warriors encamped among the mansions and temples of the Knoll District. There were plenty of Cormyr's Purple Dragons, of course, but also the Twisted Tower of Shadowdale, the White Horse of Mistledale, even the Raven and Silver of Sembia, and dozens of other symbols Galaeron did not recognize.

According to Vangerdahast, Cormyr's neighbors had sent more than a hundred companies to help persuade Shade Enclave to rethink its melting of the High Ice, some as small as twenty well-mounted riders, but several numbering in the thousands—and with a generous mix of clerics and battle mages. To Alusair's dismay, the most enthusiastic response had come from the merchant princes of Sembia, some of whom stood to lose their entire fortunes if the weather disturbances continued. Always suspicious of Sembian designs on Cormyrean lands, the Steel Regent had not even informed the merchant princes of the alliance she was forming. They had sent large forces anyway, threatening to form their own alliance if she failed to accept their troops.

What Galaeron did not see were any companies on the roads outside the city. Though warriors were pouring into the Knoll District by the hundreds, trampling the grounds of the great estates in search of bivouacs, they were not entering through Tilverton's gates. The companies seemed to be sprouting from the city itself, marching out of shadowy cul-de-sacs or emerging from some ancient tower or keep to form up in the street.

Galaeron raised his gaze and looked over the scrying ball to Vangerdahast's bushy-browed eyes.

"It won't work," the elf said. "If you can scry this, so can the Shadovar."

"Not so." Vangerdahast raised his head, revealing a confident smirk not quite hidden beneath his beard. "This is what they will see."

He waved his hand over the scrying ball. When Galaeron looked back, the soldiers were gone, and the residents seemed to be having some sort of festival in the Knoll District.

"You can annul shadow magic?" Galaeron gasped. The implications for Evereska were distressing. If Vangerdahast could find a way to negate the Shadovar's spells, so could the phaerimm. "How?"

"I *am* a wizard of some power, elf."

"It's not a question of power." Galaeron gestured at the ball. "May I?"

"If you don't think it will draw out your shadow." Vangerdahast's voice was mocking. He had been trying to persuade Galaeron to demonstrate his shadow spells since Rivalen's departure and could not seem to understand why Galaeron refused. "I wouldn't want to be responsible for unleashing such a demon."

"I'll be fine."

Galaeron envisioned the world-window in the Palace Most High and waved his hand over the scrying ball. The crystal filled with dark clouds, then a circle of light opened in the center and several murky Shadovar figures grew visible along the edges. The image in the middle was that of a great lake ringed by desert mountains.

"This is Telamont Tanthul's scrying window," Galaeron said, disappointed that he had not caught the Shadovar looking in on Tilverton. "If shadow magic and regular magic were capable of annulling each other, don't you think this room would be warded?"

Vangerdahast studied the image for a moment, then said, "Of course the room can't be warded. The Weave is mightier than the Shadow Weave."

"Mightier, perhaps," Galaeron said, "but also different. They can spy on you as easily as you spy on them."

Vangerdahast's face appeared inside the crystal ball. "I am experienced in such matters, you know."

Realizing he would never win this argument, Galaeron decided to try another approach. "Even if you're right, the Shadovar do use spies—thousands of them, I am sure."

"Not in Tilverton—or any other Cormyrean city." Vangerdahast displayed a tile with a magic ward etched onto the surface. "My war wizards have been busy."

Galaeron took the tile and ran his fingers over the symbol. It was a variation on an ancient Cormanthorian sigil he had studied in Evereska's academy of magic, used to keep spirits of darkness and cold at bay. The workmanship was exquisite and the magic so powerful that the presence of his shadow self caused it to burn his hand. When he returned the tile to Vangerdahast, he was surprised to discover the symbol burned into his palm. Finding that even this copy of the ward made his eyes burn, Galaeron closed his hand.

"Impressive, but useless," he said. "All a Shadovar need do is enter the fringe, and your ward will have almost no power over him."

Vangerdahast's eyes flickered with alarm. "Really?" He turned the ward toward Galaeron. "Show me."

Galaeron had to look away. "I can't. You know that."

"I certainly do," Vangerdahast snorted.

"I've explained how it can be defeated," Galaeron said, raising a hand to block his sight of the symbol. "There is no need for me to prove it. The cost of satisfying your curiosity is too dear."

"Very well." Vangerdahast lowered the tile and set it aside—facedown, thankfully. "By the way, the last time I spoke to Storm Silverhand, she asked me to pass along a message from Khelben."

"From Khelben?" Galaeron's heart was immediately beating faster. "About Keya?"

"I believe that was the name mentioned, yes."

Galaeron waited for the wizard to continue—then, when he did not, asked, "What is it?"

Vangerdahast's eyes slid toward the ward.

Galaeron rose in disgust. "You're no different than the Shadovar!"

"There you are mistaken, elf," Vangerdahast said, peering at Galaeron over the shadow ball. "I am very different. What I do, I do for the good of Cormyr."

"Then you would do well to stay clear of the Shadow Weave." Galaeron started for the door. "You are already half shade yourself."

"Probably." Vangerdahast's tone was thoughtful. He remained silent until Galaeron reached for the latch, then said, "You're going to be an uncle."

Galaeron stopped, then turned. "What?"

"According to Khelben." Vangerdahast shrugged. "Your sister is getting married."

"Married?" Galaeron gasped. "She's only eighty!"

"And fighting the phaerimm on the front lines of the siege, from what I hear." Vangerdahast steepled his gnarled fingers. "People mature quickly in the face of death."

Galaeron studied the old wizard, trying to figure out what the human hoped to gain by making up such an outrageous story.

Finally, he gave up and said simply, "It won't work, old man. It takes years for elves to fall in love. An engagement can last a decade."

"I have found that war tends to speed matters of the heart," Vangerdahast said, eyes twinkling. "And humans are not so reticent. Especially Vaasans."

"Vaasans?" Galaeron released the door latch and stumbled into a nearby chair. "One of the Vaasans did this?"

"Someone named Dexon, as I understand it."

"The ice-hatched bastard!" Galaeron hissed. "I'll slit him from groin to gullet!"

"Really?" Vangerdahast chuckled. "I thought you were trying to control your 'shadow self.' "

✡✡✡✡✡

A deep barbarian bellow, muffled by distance and the thick walls of the tent, sounded down in the camps. Always concerned about friction between the disparate companies of her motley army, Laeral cocked an ear toward the sound. The voice was angry and a little bit puzzled, as though demanding an explanation. Probably just one of Chief Claw's warriors still trying to figure out the magic latrines the clerics insisted on whenever the army was encamped.

Khelben, lying on the camp rug beside Laeral, took her chin in hand and gently turned her face back toward his so he could resume kissing her. Though it had been several days since they had trapped the phaerimm in the Vine Vale, they had been so busy securing Evereska's defenses and hunting down survivors that this was the first night they'd found for each other. Khelben, who had, after all, nearly died at the Rocnest and been the one trapped by the thornbacks for all those months, seemed to feel the need to shut out the war even more keenly than did Laeral. With the dexterous fingers of a magician, he used one hand to undo the knot holding her jerkin closed and began to unlace her.

A tremendous fluttering sound pulsed somewhere high above the tent. Laeral rose to her elbows and looked up through the smoke hole and saw nothing but the starless mantle of the shadowshell.

"Do you hear that, Khelben?" she asked.

Khelben pushed her back down and rolled astride her body. "I hear nothing but the fervid drumming of my heart, beating its joy in anticipation of our first night together—our first *undisturbed* night together—since all this began."

Laeral smiled. To everyone else, Khelben might be the stern and dour Blackstaff, Lord Mage of Waterdeep and founder of the Moonstars. To her, he was a hopeless romantic, given to outrageous professions of love and a touch so gentle it wouldn't break soap bubbles.

She whispered, "Come here, you."

Deciding the fluttering sound had probably just been a hippogriff patrol trying to duck a flight of veserabs—Aelburn's scouts had learned the hard way that the things had a taste for anything with feathers—Laeral pulled Khelben down on top of her.

"I want to feel that heart drumming," she said.

Khelben kissed her again, then slipped off to the side and set to work on her laces with his dexterous fingers. By the time the next sound came—this time the distinctive crackle-boom of a lightning bolt—he had Laeral out of her doublet and her trouser laces untied.

"*That*, I heard," he growled, rising.

Laeral jumped to her feet and, throwing her cloak around her shoulders, followed him out the door of the tent. Scattered across the plain at the foot of their rise were hundreds of campfires, by the light of which it was possible to see thousands of silhouettes milling about in confusion, pulling on armor and buckling sword belts. Though no one seemed to have any more idea what was happening than Laeral and Khelben, an increasing number of figures appeared to be looking toward the area of inky darkness that marked the Shadovar camp.

Laeral turned to call for a messenger and found two of Khelben's Vaasan escorts, Kuhl and Burlen, rushing up fully armored—as always. Vaasans, as far as Laeral could tell, slept in armor. The third of their number, Dexon, was back in Evereska with Keya Nihmedu, recovering from his wounds.

"They're gone!" Burlen exclaimed.

"Gone as in 'departed'?" Khelben asked, not even bothering to clarify that the Vaasan was talking about the Shadovar. "Or gone as in 'dead'? "

"Gone is in 'not there,' " Kuhl growled. "What's the difference? An Uthgardt lookout noticed that the Shadovar tents were empty, and when he went to check on the veserabs, they took a fright and flew off."

"Weren't they hobbled?" Laeral asked.

"Not even a piece of twine," Burlen confirmed. "At least not on the one Yoraedia's sentry bolted down."

Laeral exchanged a worried glance with Khelben. The sound of arguing voices drifted up from the middle of the dark camp, and dancing lines of torches began to stream in from all sides. Khelben extended a hand and summoned his staff, and Laeral did the same for her broadbelt. Then, while Khelben sent the Vaasans to check on the night pickets and call the companies to alert, she tied her trouser laces and belted her cloak closed.

Once she had her clothes tied, she extended a hand to Khelben and said, "Shall we, my dear?"

Khelben sighed and took her hand. "If we must."

Laeral eyed a spot near the center of the converging torch streams and used a spell to open a small translocational door. She and Khelben stepped through into a tumult of shouting voices and bobbing torches. So belligerent was the argument that, during the moment it took the afterdaze to clear, she grew convinced she had emerged into the middle of a tavern brawl. She drew a fighting wand from her belt.

Khelben was even more alarmed. He began to whirl his staff around them in a practiced defensive pattern that sent a pair of elves and a Waterdhavian sergeant tumbling to the ground.

A pair of the sergeant's subordinates came rushing up, "You there, wizard!" Instead of stopping to help their superior, they stepped over his groaning figure and split up to come at Khelben and Laeral from opposite sides. "Who do you think you're batting around with that thing?"

Laeral's assessment of the situation took a decided turn for the worse. She leveled her wand at the nearest figure and said, "Hare."

The man took one more step, then curled to the ground and began to sprout fur. She pointed the wand at the second fellow, who was still trying to dance past Khelben's whirling staff, and said, "Ass."

He dropped to all fours, his nose and ears already beginning to lengthen.

Laeral waved the wand past the others in the growing knot of warriors. "Has our arrival offended anyone else?"

When no one else stepped forward, Khelben said, "Good."

He lowered his staff and led the way past half a dozen empty Shadovar tents to the assembly square in front of the command pavilion, where Lord Yoraedia was standing nose to belly with Chief Claw, his face twisted into a very unelflike scowl.

"Will someone tell us what's going on here?" Khelben asked.

Both leaders turned their gazes on Khelben and Laeral and began to speak at once, gesturing wildly and pointing at the other.

"One at a time," Laeral ordered. "You first, Lord Yoraedia."

The elf cast a superior smirk at Claw, then said, "This oaf's sentries fell asleep and allowed the Shadovar to slip past them unseen."

"Liar!" Claw deliberately stepped into Yoraedia, bumping the elf with his stomach and sending him stumbling half a dozen steps back. "My lookouts only *found* that the camp was empty. Your watchers are the ones who fell asleep."

"Elves," Yoraedia sneered, "do not sleep."

"Then they are blind!" Claw bumped the elf with his belly again. "The Shadovar did not leave by our side."

Yoraedia caught himself after three paces and stepped toward the barbarian, his hand dropping toward his dagger. "One more time, walrus, and I'll slit that gu—"

"That's quite enough, Lord Yoraedia." Laeral stepped between the two. "The Shadovar were not prisoners. No one is to blame for their departure."

"You will both be to blame if this continues," Khelben said, stepping to Laeral's side and using the butt of his staff to push Yoraedia back. "What madness has taken hold of you two?"

The solemn glance he cast in Laeral's direction was hardly necessary. She had already guessed the reason behind the group's anger and was searching her cloak pockets for a spell component.

Khelben continued, "No one could have stopped the Shadovar from sneaking away. As soon as it was dark, the cowards probably melted into the shadows and walked off."

Skarn Brassaxe and his dwarves marched into the assembly square, shouldering past elves and barbarians alike.

"It's bright enough to blind Lathander!" Skarn complained. "Are you all this stupid, or are you fools trying to light yourselves up for enemy long-casters?"

"Be careful who you call stupid, Beltwatcher," said Aelburn, stepping into the light from the opposite side of the gathering. "Some of us need the light. Not everyone has goblin blood running in their veins."

"Goblin blood!" Skarn stormed, reaching for his axe. "I'll show you gob—"

Khelben's staff crashed down, knocking the dwarf to his seat and causing his arm to go limp. Claw and Yoraedia continued to trade insults, with most of their followers adding their own voices to the tumult, and the dwarves and hippogriff scouts were starting in as well. It would have been a simple matter for Laeral and Khelben to start dispelling whatever magic was causing this madness, but until she knew whether the casters were Shadovar or phaerimm, it was better to let them believe their tactic was working.

Laeral found what she was looking for and unobtrusively began to sprinkle diamond dust in each direction, at the same time mouthing an incantation and running her fingers through the gestures of her most powerful spell. As the magic took effect, she had to bite her tongue to keep from gasping.

On the western side of the square, Skarn's dwarves were stomping in from their own camp flanked by the silvery blurs of well over a dozen invisible phaerimm. The scene was much the same on the north side, save that it was Waterdhavian volunteers and Aelburn's scouts who were being marched in. The situation to the east and south was even worse. With most of the barbarians and elves already in the square, the thornbacks had already formed themselves into battle ranks.

"Uh, Khelben?"

"Yes?"

With more leaders marching their companies into the dusty square every minute, Khelben had given up on ending the argument between Yoraedia and Claw and was using his magic to intervene in actual outbreaks of violence.

Khelben pointed at a scowling dwarf in the gleaming armor of the Knights in Silver who was charging toward the center of the quarrel with a drawn hand axe and asked, "Would you mind?"

"Not at all."

Laeral pulled two beads of tar from her cloak pocket. Voicing a short spell, she flicked first one, then the other bead at the scowling dwarf, whose progress immediately slowed to a sluggish crawl.

"As I was saying," Laeral said, "do you remember those detection amulets we passed out so the sentries would be able to see invisible infiltrators?"

Khelben frowned and used his black staff to sweep the feet from beneath one of Claw's barbarians who was reaching for one of Yoraedia's elves.

"I remember," he said. "You brought twenty of them "

"Twenty-five," Laeral corrected. "They don't seem to be working."

Khelben grimaced, then asked, "How badly?"

"Fifteen," Laeral said. "On each side."

Khelben considered this for a moment, then growled, "The bastards! The slippery, shadowy, betraying bastards!"

"I wouldn't go so easy on them."

Laeral had already done the math. After the battle in the Vine Vale, they had estimated that there could only be a hundred phaerimm left inside the shadowshell. Over the past few days, they had hunted down and killed another twenty, which meant there were only about eighty thornbacks left in the entire Shaeradim.

Somehow, most had converged on the relief army's camp within a few hours of the departure of the Shadovar. Clariburnus and Lamorak had not only abandoned their allies, they had invited the enemy to destroy them.

"What now, Khelben?" Laeral asked. She saw an elf reaching for his sword and waved her wand, turning him into a sleek hart. "Start dispelling and hope for the best?"

Khelben shook his head. "This requires something more . . . wondrous. Can you distract the phaerimm while I raise a sphere?"

"Of course," Laeral said, pulling a second wand from her belt. One of Khelben's favorite spells, the sphere of wonder created an area in which only one type of magic—chosen by the caster—would function. "But that won't hold forever."

"I'll open a teleport circle from inside," Khelben said.

"Good," Laeral said. "We'll meet at the Halfway Inn."

"Meet?"

"Somebody has to bring the rest of the army."

Laeral started across the assembly square, using one wand to paralyze anyone shouting and the other to turn those holding weapons into rabbits and raccoons.

"Quiet!" she called. "I have heard quite enough of this bickering!"

No one obeyed, of course, and several people were actually foolish enough to guarantee a shake of a wand in their direction by turning to argue. The distraction seemed to work, holding the phaerimm's attention so Khelben could raise his arms in the necessary circles and voice what was really rather a long and drawn-out incantation—an incantation that most of the Chosen except him agreed could use some editing.

Laeral paralyzed and polymorphed so many warriors that they were actually beginning to take notice of her commands and fall into a grudging silence, which all but guaranteed that the thornbacks would have to attack openly instead of using mind-slaves to goad the others into doing it for them—and that Laeral would be their first target.

Finally, a dome of faintly shimmering golden light rose up in the middle of the assembly square, prompting the phaerimm to reveal themselves by vainly hurling magic bolts and flame strikes against its wall. The dazed warriors stopped arguing and looked around with stunned expressions and arched brows. Leaving it to Khelben to help them recover, Laeral turned toward her tent and opened another translocational gate.

There was the familiar instant of falling before she emerged adjacent to the worst battle din she had ever heard. Blades were clanging off armor in mad cacophony and anguished voices were shrieking their pain. The air reeked of blood and opened guts, and warriors were streaming past in a torrent of dark silhouettes. A few were doubled over and some were missing limbs or pieces of limbs, but none had weapons in their scabbards or hands.

Still struggling with afterdaze and unable to make sense of what she was seeing, Laeral nevertheless responded instantly. She pulled a vial of granite dust from her cloak pocket and sprinkled it over her head, speaking the words of an armoring spell. Her skin grew cold and numb and as hard as rock. She turned toward the furor and found herself looking across the body-strewn cloth of a collapsed camp tent and finally recalled where she was and what she had come to do.

She was too late.

A whirling tornado of blades was coming across the tent toward her, plucking the swords and daggers from the hands and scabbards of the soldiers fleeing before it. A handful of brave warriors stopped to fire crossbow bolts or hurl spears into the heart of the vortex, but these were plucked up with the rest of the weapons and came flying back around to slash the brave souls into a spray of blood and shredded armor. There had to be a thousand weapons in the storm already, with a dozen more flying into it every second, and the whirling cloud of steel was so thick that Laeral could not see to its heart.

The edge of the blade-storm reached her side of the tent. Swords and daggers began to shatter against her spell-hardened skin. The shards were sucked back into the tornado, more deadly than before. Laeral waded into the tempest, staggering under the constant hail of weapons slamming into her from the side. The tent cloth was slick with blood and strewn with bodies and pieces of bodies, some still animated enough to reach out and clutch her ankles. Several times, she stumbled and nearly fell, and once she had to kick herself free of a blood-soaked half-elf who managed to wrap both arms around her legs begging for her to save him.

Finally, Laeral began to glimpse the heart of the storm, where the cone-shaped silhouette of a phaerimm was floating toward her at an oblique angle. She raised her hand and loosed her silver fire. In the same instant, the terrain opened beneath her feet as the thornback tried to suck her into the ground. Quick as the counterattack came, the tactic was a tired one against which Laeral had long ago developed a magic immunity. The Weave simply kept her suspended over the hole until it closed.

In all likelihood, the phaerimm never knew its attack had failed. It was engulfed in silver fire and spent the next few seconds whirling around madly as it disintegrated into ashes. The blade-storm came to a sudden halt, covering Laeral's collapsed tent in a steel carpet as a thousand swords clanged to the ground.

By the light of the fires raging in every camp, Laeral could make out the broad swath of motionless silhouettes and writhing forms the phaerimm had cut through her army. It was a broad belt beginning over by Silverymoon's

Knights of Silver and curving steadily inward, razing the entire camp of the Bloodaxe mercenaries sent on behalf of Sundabar and tearing a broad tract through the tents of the Slugsmashers representing Citadel Adbar before spiraling through the Waterdhavian encampment and coming up the hill to Laeral and Khelben's tent.

Nor was this phaerimm the only one to attack the outlying camps while its companions prepared the main ambush. There were firestorms and lightning squalls everywhere, another blade-storm, and more mind-enslaved warriors fighting each other than the phaerimm. Heart sinking with sorrow and despair—and more than a little guilt at having failed to foresee the Shadovar betrayal—Laeral removed a silver thimble from her pocket, then uttered a spell and held the thimble to her lips like a miniature horn.

"The Shadovar have betrayed us. Take who you can save and flee." Though she spoke softly, Laeral's voice would be heard by every commander and wizard in her army, save those who had fallen under the mental sway of the enemy—she had designed the spell with the phaerimm in mind. "We'll form again at the Halfway Inn. May the gods speed you."

From behind her came the sound of chiming steel as someone approached across the carpet of fallen blades. She turned and glimpsed the hulking form of a Vaasan running in her direction—then cried out in confusion as his sword came tumbling at her. She twisted away and instinctively raised her arm, but trying to block a darksword was a bad idea even for one of the Chosen.

A wave of searing cold shot up her arm, and the limb went numb below the elbow. She cried out more in shock than pain and dropped to her knees and nearly fainted when she saw her hand and forearm lying on the carpet of swords in front of her. The black blade that had severed her arm lay a pace or so away, wet with her blood. The darksword rose into the air and started to float back in the direction from which it had come.

Laeral turned her head and saw Burlen's hulking form striding toward her, his hand stretched toward the floating sword. Too dazed to understand why he had attacked her, she nevertheless knew that she had to stop him before he did it again. She reached into her cloak for a spell component—then experienced a wave of excruciating pain and recalled she was reaching with a stump. She reached with her other hand, but the angle was awkward and the movement unfamiliar. Burlen was almost on her by the time she found what she was searching for.

The Vaasan raised his darksword and said, "Your fault."

Laeral pulled the iron bar from her pocket and pointed it in his direction. The steel carpet chimed again as another hulking form came rushing up behind the Vaasan. Burlen dropped to a crouch and started to spin, only to have his guard kicked aside by a big Vaasan boot.

"Kuhl?" Burlen gasped. "What are you—?"

The pommel of Kuhl's sword caught Burlen at the base of the jaw, lifting him off his feet and dropping him flat on his back in the carpet of swords. Kuhl took a moment to make sure his comrade was out cold, then turned to Laeral—who, still in shock and uncertain of what was happening—was pointing the iron bar at him.

"My apologies, Lady Arunsun. There are infiltrators everywhere." He tucked a pair of phaerimm tails into his belt, then picked up Burlen's sword and sheathed it in his own scabbard. "Can you stand?"

Laeral tried and nearly passed out. "No." She pocketed the iron bar, then extended her hand. "Set me over there with Burlen and hold us tight."

"Hold you, Milady?"

Laeral nodded. "For your life." She pointed at her amputated arm. "It could be a rough ride to the Halfway Inn."

✡✡✡✡✡

A raw potato in one hand and a drawn throwing dagger in the other, Galaeron stepped off Aris's upraised palm directly onto the sill of the third-story lodging chamber Vangerdahast was using as a council room. The half-dozen war wizards gathered around the table cried out in surprise and reached for spell components, and one actually stood, pointing at the window and opening his mouth to loose a spray of magic bolts. Galaeron bounced the potato off the fellow's head, shocking more than knocking the wizard back into his seat, then turned his attention toward a large blonde woman holding a finger-length cylinder of glass.

"You don't want to point that in my direction," he said, raising his throwing dagger. "This is my good hand."

Vangerdahast, sitting with his back to the window, sighed heavily. He motioned his war wizards to their seats, then braced his elbow on the armrest and turned to look at Galaeron.

"Surely, you can see we're in a conclave?"

Galaeron lowered the dagger. "So the door guards informed me, but the interruption will be a short one. I have only one question: is it true?"

A murmur of alarm rustled around the table, and Vangerdahast closed his eyes and nodded. "I fear so."

Galaeron's heart sank. He could not bear to think of Vala in that place, being abused in that manner. He stepped to Vangerdahast's side.

"Why wasn't I told?" he demanded. "Why did I have to find out through palace gossip? If this is another of your bids to inveigle me into using shadow magic—"

"That would be your fourth question, if a question it is," Vangerdahast interrupted. He pointed at the wall, and a chair walked over to place itself behind Galaeron. "Have a seat and explain what you mean by palace gossip. Surely, the whole palace can't know so soon?"

"The whole city knows, as far as I can tell. I heard it from a gate guard." Galaeron ignored the chair. "What I want to know is why wasn't I told? Were you afraid I'd go back to the enclave?"

Vangerdahast cocked his bushy brow. "Actually, that's the last thing I would have expected from you," he said, "but the fact of the matter is that we only found out ourselves a few minutes ago. I was about to send for you to see if you might have any thoughts on their departure."

"Departure?" Galaeron asked. "Whose departure?"

A twinkle of comprehension came to Vangerdahast's eyes. "Then you didn't know," he said. Several of the wizards sighed in relief. "The Shadovar have left the Shaeradim—sneaked out in the middle of the night. Laeral's relief army was decimated, and she was horribly wounded."

Galaeron sat—fell, actually—into the chair. "What?" he gasped. "Is Keya—?"

"The mythal wasn't breached," offered the woman Galaeron had threatened with the throwing dagger. "Your sister and everyone inside Evereska are no worse off than before—better, in fact, since they've been reinforced and resupplied—but with the relief army decimated and Laeral wounded, the phaerimm will be free to focus their attention on the city again."

Vangerdahast laid a wrinkled hand on Galaeron's arm. "I'm sure I don't have to tell you what the shadowshell is doing to the mythal. If you know of anything Storm and the other Chosen can do to breach it. . . ."

"The magic must be renewed," Galaeron said. "All they need do is keep the Shadovar away from the Splicing. The bonds will weaken over time, and Weave magic will start to flow into the Shaeradim again."

Vangerdahast sighed in relief. "Good. Then our only problem is the additional magic the extra troops will require when the Heartland Alliance attacks the flying city." He looked around the table. "I think we can take this redeployment as Telamont Tanthul's answer to our demand that he stop the melting of the High Ice."

"Actually, no," Galaeron said. "This is about me."

The looks that came to the faces of the war wizards made clear what they thought of the theory.

"It is," Galaeron insisted. "I came here because there are rumors about that Vala has been made Escanor's bed slave. They abandoned Evereska to punish me for leaving Shade."

"You have an awfully high opinion of your worth," said the wizard Galaeron had hit with the potato. "I don't suppose they could be consolidating their forces to defend against an attack from the Heartland Alliance?"

Vangerdahast cleared his throat and said, "The elf may have a point. There are certain, um, secrets in his possession that they may desire to recover."

Vangerdahast and Alusair had elected to hold close the fact that Melegaunt had imbued Galaeron with a vast knowledge of the phaerimm, lest the thornbacks have spies in the Arabel palace.

"The damage he caused them by revealing the shadow blankets was immeasurable," the royal magician continued. "They may very well be doing this to punish him—and to force him to return to Shade."

"Or to force you to turn me over," he said, "and to punish you for harboring me—and daring to threaten them."

Vangerdahast scowled. "Punish *us?* They couldn't possibly—"

"They *could,*" Galaeron insisted. "When was the last time you checked on matters in Tilverton?"

CHAPTER FIFTEEN

26 Mirtul, the Year of Wild Magic

Ruha had crossed the Shoal of Thirst once before. It had been a long, thirsty journey over a salt pan as flat as a mirror, rife with tragedy and hardship, and she had considered herself lucky to reach the other side. Such a journey would have been impossible, save by ship or wing. Where once she had feared death because a camel collapsed and burst a waterskin, there lay an entire lake, vast beyond the belief of most Bedine and blanketed beneath the shadows of an evening rain.

"It is a different desert than when you left, Ruha. Better," said Sheikh Sa'ar.

A powerfully-built man of fifty who wore a gray *keffiyeh* over his graying hair, the sheikh was lying on a ridge crest, looking out over the lake along with Ruha and a Cormyrean war wizard named Caladnei.

"The lake has already brought us good hunting," he added.

The sheikh pointed down the shore, to a broad sweep of desert blossoms with a few young date palms already pushing their crowns above the foliage. Ruha did not see what he was indicating until a herd of gazelle emerged from an expanse of tall grass and began to drink. Apparently, whatever magic had made a lake of the Shoal of Thirst had also removed its salinity, for gazelle did not drink brackish water.

"Easier, perhaps, but not better," Ruha said.

Though it had been many years since Ruha lived in Anauroch—much less crossed the Shoal of Thirst—she felt violated. Undeniable as was the lake's beauty, it was already changing the surrounding desert, bringing with it an abundance and leisure that would destroy the Bedine's nomadic way of life.

"Those waters," she said, "are poison to the Bedine."

The sheikh furrowed his brow. "How can that be? I have drunk from its waters many times myself, and you see for yourself that I am stronger than ever."

"So you are," Ruha said, "but how long has it been since your *khowwan* left the lake?"

Sa'ar's face grew stormy. "We are leaving soon." He looked in the direction opposite the gazelles, to where a flight of veserabs were frolicking in a small bay. "Upon the heels of our raid, in truth."

"Stealing mounts from the Shadovar is not very safe, Sheikh," said Caladnei. "Their magic is strong."

An unveiled woman with striking amber eyes and a tall, willowy build, she insisted on dressing in a deliberately male fashion, with long tresses of red hair spilling out from beneath her *keffiyeh* and a slender sword hanging from her belt.

"Then it is good I have you." Sa'ar looked away from the lake and locked gazes with the war wizard. "Your magic must be very strong as well, for you to dress as you dare."

Caladnei's eyes flared. "We did not come to Anauroch to help nomads steal—"

"Take only the young veserabs, Sheikh—those still too small to ride." As Ruha spoke, she looked past Sa'ar to scowl at Caladnei. "The others will only spit in your face, and their breath is worse than that of ten camels."

"That awful?" The sheikh's bushy brow rose. "Then they must be fine mounts, indeed."

"So it seems to me," Ruha said, "but Shadovar magic is different from that of the Zhentarim. You must not blame us if the raid goes awry."

Before the sheikh could answer, Caladnei said, "Ruha, did you not tell me that the Bedine don't use magic? If we help, the Shadovar may realize we're here."

"Anauroch is a large desert, wizardess," Sa'ar said, "and the city of Shade well hidden. By the time you find it on your own, the Shadovar will certainly know you are looking for them."

"Are you threatening to reveal us?" Caladnei demanded.

"Sheikh Sa'ar would never betray his guests," Ruha said.

She glanced down the hill, where the rest of the Cormyrean scouting party stood in dusty *abas*, holding the reins of their recently purchased camels stiffly at arm's length. The handful of women in the company followed

Caladnei's example and refused to wear veils, and there was a marked lack of children and saluki dogs.

"But he is right," the witch continued. "We do not make a very convincing tribe. The sooner we find the Shadovar city, the better our chances of surprising them."

In truth, Ruha thought it likely they had been discovered already. When Vangerdahast had asked her to lead a scouting party into Anauroch to locate the flying city so Cormyr could launch a surprise attack, Ruha had asked for a company of swarthy, brown-eyed volunteers whom she could disguise as Bedine. Instead, the wizard had provided her with Caladnei and her equally stubborn superior, Hhormun, two fools who seemed to believe that riding camels and wearing *abas* was all that was required to disguise a company of fair-skinned Cormyreans as a Bedine *khowwan*. Had she not known that Alusair was preparing to launch a surprise teleport-attack from a secret base in Tilverton, she would have sworn the wizards wanted the Shadovar to notice them.

After a few moments, Caladnei said, "Very well, Sheikh, but you will take us to Shade, no matter how the raid comes out."

She started to back down the dusty slope.

"If you keep your promise, I will keep mine." Sa'ar crawled down beside her, then spit in his palm and offered it to her. "It is a bargain."

Caladnei spit in her own hand.

"You are sure Hhormun will agree?" Ruha asked, sliding down to join the pair before they clasped hands. "The bargain is yours if you make it."

Caladnei clasped the sheikh's hand. "Hhormun will follow me in this."

Ruha was not so sure. Old and portly though he was, Hhormun had proven surprisingly energetic in directing the activities of the company, from picking campsites to dictating the pace of the daily marches. When they reached the bottom of the ridge, however, he surprised her by not protesting at all and even allowing Sa'ar to plan the raid.

A few minutes later, Ruha, Caladnei, the sheikh, and a dozen of his men were rubbing themselves and the Mahwa tribe's strongest camels in veserab dung, collected by the warriors a few days earlier for just that purpose.

"You're sure this is necessary?" Caladnei asked, wrinkling her nose at the awful stench of the stuff. "I'm sure someone in the company has a spell that could eliminate our smell."

"It is not enough to eliminate our own odor," Sa'ar said. "We must smell like what we want. It pleases the little gods."

"And puts our camels at ease," Ruha added, explaining in terms Caladnei would understand more readily. "If they think the smell is ours instead of the veserabs, they will cause less trouble as we approach."

"*Less* trouble?" Caladnei grumbled. "I suppose none would be too much to ask for."

They waited until a lookout signaled that the veserabs had come out of the water to rest for the evening, then Hhormun used his magic to render the entire raiding party invisible, while Ruha and Caladnei used their own magic to cast a pall of silence over the group. Though the Mahwa had been part of the coalition that relied on Ruha's magic to destroy the Zhentarim army at Orofin, that had been many years earlier, and even the sheikh's stern glower could not keep the men from grumbling and cringing as the spells were cast over them.

Finally, the raiding party circled around to the downwind side of the ridge and—with the aid of yet more magic—crept out onto the lakeshore. The nearest veserabs were only a few hundred paces away, mostly solitary bulls so cranky and strong that the Shadovar herders left them to stand guard at the edges of the flight, trusting that the creatures' instincts would make them follow when the rest were moved. Ruha, who was leading the raid by virtue of being the only person present with any experience at all handling veserabs, picked a serpentine course around the beasts, giving them as wide a berth as possible.

Once, when they entered an area of tall marsh grass, a nearby bull flared its wings and started over to investigate. Sa'ar released a sand grouse he had brought along as a diversion, and the bird burst skyward with such a riot of flapping wings and terrified screeching that it drew three veserabs into the air after it. Ruha made good use of the distraction, leading the party to within twenty paces of the three Shadovar herders camped on that side of the flight.

A tug on a guideline attached to her waist brought her to a stop. Several moments later, ten fist-sized sling stones appeared in the darkening sky and rained down on the sentries. Two fell unconscious. By the time the third made enough sense of the assault to turn and see the raiding party—rendered visible when they attacked—galloping toward him on their camels, two warriors were already clubbing him senseless. Bruised as the young herder might be when he awoke, Ruha took the fact that the warriors used the butts of their lances instead of the tips as a sign of Sa'ar's concern about angering the Shadovar. Bedine raiders usually killed the sentries, so there would be that many fewer warriors available for the counter raid.

The sheikh and his other warriors were already charging into the flight of resting veserabs, hurling loops of braided rope around the necks of the smallest beasts and securing the other ends to their saddles. Most of them were coughing and reeling, struggling to stay on their mounts as the veserabs filled the air with their noxious fumes. Ruha cleared the air with a powerful wind spell, then saw an angry veserab cow leap onto a camel's neck and rip the thing's head off with four sharp-taloned feet.

More veserabs began to rise all around, filling the dusk air with fluttering clouds of dark wings. Most were simply trying to escape, but a few, especially those with calves whistling for help, were beginning to wheel toward the Bedine warriors. A veserab dived low in front of Sa'ar, pulling a grizzled warrior off the camel ahead, then dropping him back to the ground in pieces. Ruha dismissed the silence spell and pointed toward the wadi they had chosen as their escape route.

"Enough, Sa'ar!" she yelled. "Flee!"

The sheikh did not need to be told twice. He sounded three notes on his *amarat*. His warriors—those who were not fleeing already—turned as one, each pulling two or three panicked veserab calves through the air behind them. Ruha hurled a flurry of magic bolts into the air and dusted half a dozen adults off the raiders' tails, then Caladnei raised a force barrier behind them. A dozen veserabs slammed into the invisible wall and dropped to the ground with broken necks and wings. The confused survivors circled away, whistling in frustration and sorrow.

Ruha and Caladnei followed. By the time they reached the mouth of the wadi, the veserabs were beginning to find their way over the force barrier. Ruha leaped off her camel and scraped up a handful of sand, then voiced an incantation and blew it toward the growing number of creatures streaming after them. A howling wind rose at her back and, scraping the canyon mouth clean of sand and dust, roared out toward the lake. The veserabs vanished into a cloud of swirling dust and did not emerge.

"Your magic has grown stronger, witch," Sa'ar observed behind her. "Remind me to be patient with you."

Ruha turned to find him holding the reins of her camel. The rest of his warriors were emerging from their hiding places in the mouth of the wadi, half of them covering the raiders' back trail with bows and arrows, the other half pulling the captured veserabs down out of the air and binding them with leather hoods and wing jackets. Though most Bedine were adept at handling falcons and other birds of prey, veserab calves were both larger and more ferocious. The battle was not all that one-sided, and the warriors were paying in blood for every lace they threaded.

Ruha commanded her camel to kneel, then, as she mounted, heard one roar a little way up the wadi. She pivoted toward the sound and saw a line of tethered mounts collapsing, their throats and bellies being opened by glassy black blades as a Shadovar patrol peeled itself out of the shadows along the gulch. She loosed a lightning bolt at a figure rising up behind Sa'ar's camel and saw the fellow's head come apart before he sank back into the murk. Caladnei cried out in shock behind her, and Ruha turned to find the Cormyrean on the ground, pinned beneath her wounded camel with a ruby-eyed Shadovar warrior leaping over the top. She flung a ball of spider silk at the figure and uttered a spell, and he hit the ground encased in a sticky cocoon.

Finally, there was time to scream, "Shadovar! Defend yourselves!"

Even Ruha could barely hear her voice over the battle din that had already risen in the wadi. Bedine were shouting to each other about demons and djinn and, finding attackers at their backs no matter which way they turned, falling fast. The Shadovar were rising from the shadows to hack off an arm or leg, then vanishing back into the murk before they could be counterattacked.

Ruha grabbed Caladnei under the arms and pulled her from under her camel.

"Are you hurt?"

"Stunned," the wizard replied, mouth gaping at the carnage. She lowered her hand and sent a golden bolt streaking through a Shadovar rising behind Ruha, then shook her head in astonishment. "Where did they come from?"

"Out of the shadows," Ruha said.

She slipped around to Caladnei's back and shot a long stream of fire at a Shadovar rising behind a Bedine camel boy, no doubt holding reins on his first raid. The fireball exploded without harming the shadow warrior, as Weave magic sometimes did, and the dark figure ran his sword through the young warrior, then melted back into the shadows.

"This is how it often is with them," Ruha said.

"Really?" Caladnei gasped. She was silent for an instant, and Ruha glanced over her shoulder to see the wizard rubbing the purple dragon on her signet ring. "Hhormun, come quick. You need to see this!"

"Come?" Ruha cried.

She glimpsed a Shadovar rising up from behind a boulder with a blowpipe in his hands and flung a pebble in his direction, then spoke a single word. The pebble became a bead of magma. When it hit the boulder, the boulder erupted into a thousand drops of molten stone as well, and the warrior vanished in a searing orange spray.

"We should be fleeing!" said Ruha.

"Flee?" Caladnei shook her head. "There can't be more than two dozen left."

"And more where they came from," warned Ruha.

She had no idea how close they were to the city, but she knew the Shadovar well enough to feel certain this was just the first wave of the attack. Even if they didn't realize there were Cormyreans involved in the raid, they would send a company of veserab riders to make an example of any tribe that dared steal from them.

"They're just trying to delay us," Ruha said.

"Yes, so I guessed when they attacked our camels first."

The Cormyrean loosed a silver ray at a pair of Shadovar charging Sa'ar, who was still struggling to slip a hood and wing jacket over the last veserab tied to his dead camel. When the attack succeeded only in stunning the shadow warriors back into the murk, Ruha left Caladnei's side and, dodging one black sword and reducing the owner of the second to a cinder even darker than his normally swarthy complexion, stopped at the sheikh's side.

"Are you mad, Sa'ar?" She swatted the creature's head aside as it swung around to bite at her knee, then continued, "Let it go! A few veserabs cannot be worth so many Mahwa lives."

The sheikh did not even look up from his work. "Mounts that can fly across the sky? The Mahwa will be the masters of the desert!"

He finally managed to pull the hood over the creature's faceless head, then was struck from behind by a bolt of shadow magic that pitched him face-first over the waist-high calf. His arm went limp and Ruha saw ground through a jagged hole in it. Before she could sweep a pebble off the ground to counterattack, the sheikh had pulled a throwing dagger with his good hand and pivoted around to whip it at his charging attacker.

The throw missed, of course, but it distracted the Shadovar long enough for Ruha to pull her own *jambiya*. She grabbed the laces of the calf's hood and held it beside her for the half second it took the shadow warrior to close. Ruha came up beneath his guard and opened him from groin to ribs. She was mildly surprised to see that the stuff spilling out of him looked much the same as that coming out of the Bedine.

"May Elah smile on you," Sa'ar gasped, his good arm thrown over the veserab's back, supporting him. "How many times have you saved my life, now?"

"Too many times for one sheikh," Ruha said, pulling him to his feet. She took his curved *amarat* and pressed it into his good hand. "Now blow your horn and scatter your warriors. Veserabs are no good to dead men."

Sa'ar thrust the horn away. "They are *my* veserabs now," he said, "and no man steals from Sa'ar, Sheikh of the Mahwa."

Ruha let her chin sink. "You are a fool, Sheikh."

"Almost certainly," Sa'ar said, pushing the calf's head toward her. "Now help me lace this up, before the battle turns against us again."

"Again?"

Ruha looked around and saw that while the battle was continuing to rage, the Shadovar were now being assailed by magic and iron whenever they drew near a Bedine. She glanced up the slopes of the wadi and saw Hhormun standing atop a boulder, his *aba* tossed aside somewhere to reveal the black battle cloak of a Cormyrean War Wizard. He was wielding two wands at once, hurling blazing nuggets of fire or crackling forks of lightning whenever a Shadovar dared emerge from the murk to attack. Flanking him were two full ranks of Purple Dragons, loading and firing their iron crossbows by turn, while a smaller ring of three wizards and two dozen dragoneers stood by staring into the murk, attacking any shadow that so much as flickered.

"The fool!" Ruha hissed. "Does he think no one will see him? Or that the Most High will think the iron bolts came from Bedine crossbows?"

"I do not know what he thinks," Sa'ar said, "only that he is a man of his word. Now, will you help me or not, witch?"

After a quick glance around to ensure they were under no imminent threat of attack, Ruha helped him lace the hood. By the time she finished, Caladnei was standing at the upper end of the battlefield, waving the Bedine survivors up the wadi.

"Come along, and quickly!" The Cormyrean's gaze was fixed on the sky above the lake, where Ruha's sandstorm was still raging. "Be quick about it."

Ruha pushed Sa'ar and the reins of his three veserab calves into the arms of a group of stunned-looking warriors, then turned in the direction Caladnei was facing and saw a large company of veserab riders approaching from the north, flying high above the sandstorm. They were still too distant for her to tell much more than that there were several hundred of them, but Ruha would have bet her veil that a force of that size was being led by a Prince of Shade.

Hhormun and his dragoneers began an orderly withdrawal toward Caladnei—and Ruha was not at all sorry to see the Shadovar survivors concentrating their efforts on the Cormyreans instead of Sa'ar and his Mahwa. The shadow lords were being more careful now, emerging from the murk just long enough to fling a shadow bolt through a warrior's knee or hamstring a wizard, clearly attempting to delay their retreat until the veserab company arrived.

Ruha ran up the wadi and joined Caladnei, who was busily spraying magic into the hillside shadows in an attempt to help her struggling companions.

With her attack magic all but exhausted, Ruha prepared a sand dragon spell, but held it in reserve in case Caladnei irritated the Shadovar enough to draw an attack.

Between the wizardess's attacks, Ruha said, "Had Hhormun been waiting here with the rest of Sa'ar's warriors, the Mahwa might have lost fewer lives."

"Or we all might have lost more," Caladnei said. "This way, it was the Shadovar who were surprised, not us."

"And you had a chance to watch them fight." Ruha did not bother to keep the bitterness out of her voice.

Caladnei sprayed a pair of Shadovar with some sort of green ray Ruha was not familiar with, reducing both warriors to smoky wisps and opening the way for Hhormun's battered company to join them in the bottom of the wadi.

She cocked her brow and glanced at Ruha. "We had a chance to watch them fight, but it was their idea to steal the veserabs."

"True—and you took advantage." Ruha was fighting to keep from yelling. The story was an old one, the *berrani* from outside Anauroch entering the desert and using the nomads for their own purposes. "Sa'ar would never have attempted such a thing without Cormyrean magic."

"It sounds to me like we took advantage of each other." Caladnei shrugged and pointed up the wadi, where Sa'ar and his warriors were leading their new veserabs into the teleport circle that would carry them to safety—at least temporarily. "I don't see the sheikh complaining."

Hhormun and the rest of the Cormyrean scouts arrived, with half a dozen Shadovar close on their heels. Caladnei took out two with one of her green rays, then Hhormun and another wizard killed three more. The last warrior glanced over his shoulder and, finding the veserab company still too distant to aid him, began to run for the nearest shadow. When no one else started a spell, Ruha scraped a handful of sand off the ground and started hers—only to be interrupted when Hhormun brought his arm down across her wrists.

"Let him go," he said. "He's not hurting anybody now."

"Hurting anybody?" Ruha gasped. "He's seen your wizard's cloak. He'll run straight to the Most High and confirm that we're a scouting party from Cormyr."

"Will he?" A faint smile came to Hhormun's bearded lips, and he turned up the wadi. "Then we had better hurry to our next campsite, hadn't we?"

Ruha's jaw fell behind her veil. She stood there staring after the old wizard until Caladnei took her arm.

"Come along," the Cormyrean woman said. "The point has been made. Vangerdahast wouldn't be happy if you stayed behind to confirm it . . . not happy at all."

✡✡✡✡✡

Rivalen had battled three phaerimm at once, toe to thorn and with no chance to call for help. He had dallied with twin succubae and awakened to find them—well, he didn't want to relive that again. He had fought demons—bare-handed, by Shadow—and been the one who flew away. And never, not in eight hundred years—not even when he gave his spirit over to the shadowstuff—not once had he been frightened. Not like this.

"How?" the Most High asked. His voice was calm, gentle—even reasonable—in that terrible tone it assumed just before he condemned someone to an eternity of wandering the Barrens of Doom and Despair. "Can someone please explain this?"

They were looking down at the camp of the Harper witch and her Cormyrean scouts. Not scrying it through the world-window, mind you, but looking straight down on it from the Most High's personal observation balcony in the Palace Most High. Staring down through the shadow mists at an imminently defensible camp, located in a maze of canyons so narrow a veserab's wings would touch both sides. A maze of canyons flooded by magic light with no particular source, where the few shadows that did exist were guarded by a squad of sentries armed with both magic and steel. A maze of canyons where the Shadovar would have to fight their way in like common orc footsoldiers, and a maze of canyons with plenty of room for more Cormyreans . . . and Sembians . . . and Dalesmen . . . and the Hidden One only knew who else, all determined to deny the lands of lost Netheril to the Shadovar.

The witch could not see them, of course. Certainly, her Bedine vassals had reported to her the stream of veserabs that constantly dropped into the lake there, and no doubt remarked on the dark storm cloud that never seemed to leave the area, but she could not *see* Shade Enclave. There were still the shadow mists and the thousands of feet above ground and, not least of all, the Most High's magic, but Rivalen was not so sure.

"Rivalen?"

Rivalen felt the weight of the Most High's gaze upon him. He did not bother to look up. There was nothing there to see anyway. He simply swallowed his fear, then addressed his father.

"There is a reason Ruha hides her face behind a veil, Most High," he said. "Of all the races on Toril, the Shadovar have more reason than any to know the power of the hidden."

"True, but that explains nothing."

Rivalen swallowed—hard. "Most High, who can explain the will of the Hidden One? The witch is down there; that is all that matters—save my own failure in stopping her in Cormyr."

It was this last that saved him. The weight of the Most High's scrutiny vanished at once, and the air grew still and cold as he came to Rivalen's side.

"You did as you thought best, my son," Telamont said, and Rivalen's shoulder grew numb with cold. "I am sure you will make it up to us."

"As am I," Rivalen said.

"Good." The Most High squeezed his shoulder until Rivalen thought it would break. "Now, we must concern ourselves with what to do next."

"The answer is clear, Most High," said Clariburnus. "We must kill the witch."

The Most High was silent.

Clariburnus continued, the words spilling out of him like breath. "The magic of the Weave is impure and weak, no match for the Shadow Weave. All we need do is drop a shadow blanket—"

"And that will help us how?" the Most High asked, his voice alarmingly reasonable and calm. "By disposing of your mistake?"

"*My* mistake, Most High?"

"Was she not your guide, brother?" Rivalen asked. "Yours and Brennus's?"

"She was," Brennus answered, "and *we* controlled her."

"Enough!" the Most High spat. "There is no use in blaming each other. I am disappointed in all of you."

The Most High fell silent.

Escanor was the first who dared to speak. "What does the witch matter? If she cannot enter the city, what does it matter if she camps below us for a century?"

"It only matters if you are wrong," the Most High responded.

The question hung in the air as heavy as lead. None of the brothers dared answer.

Finally, the Most High said, "You have all failed me. All of you princes." The shadow mists briefly obscured the tents of the Cormyrean camp, and when they cleared again, the princes were looking at a circle of white rocks. "Do you see that circle?"

"A teleportation circle," Rivalen said.

His knees nearly buckled under the weight of the Most High's question.

"For retreat, I believe," Rivalen said.

More silence.

"But I could be wrong," Rivalen admitted.

"If he is, there will be an army below us in hours," Clariburnus said. "Laeral required less than three hours to transport her entire relief army to the Shaeradim."

Rivalen glowered into Clariburnus's bronze-colored eyes. As the Eleventh Prince—and the youngest still surviving—he was an ambitious one, always eager to raise himself at his brothers' expense.

"Do not blame your brother for your failures, Rivalen," Clariburnus said. "In Cormyr, the Steel Regent bested you handily."

Escanor, always Rivalen's favorite brother, said, "We have all underestimated the enemy."

"You certainly have," Clariburnus said.

Escanor took a step toward the junior prince—only to find Hadhrune blocking his way.

"Dear princes, if we allow the enemy to divide us like this, we have lost already." The seneschal—more ambitious than any of the princes and, in his own way, more dangerous—turned toward the Most High. "Mighty Telamont, if I may—"

"If you must."

Hadhrune continued, nonplussed, "If I may suggest a more conservative strategy, perhaps we should call our armies home and defend the enclave."

Telamont remained silent.

"Yes, Most High, I *do* believe the witch might know a way into the enclave," the seneschal added, glancing in the direction of Clariburnus and Brennus. "We do not know what she learned when she was brought here. You are aware of where I found her."

The Most High whirled away from the rail and stabbed an empty sleeve at Hadhrune's face. "The Faerûnians are not being reasonable!" he stormed. "What do we want, but what was Netheril's to begin with? By what right do they deny us?"

Rivalen breathed easier and settled in for the rant. Having not been born for seven hundred years after Shade left Faerûn, he did not feel the same sense of entitlement as the Most High, but he recognized the power it held over his father. The dream of reclaiming Anauroch and driving out the phaerimm was really all there was of Telamont Tanthul. At times, it made Rivalen wish he had been alive to see the glory that was Netheril, if only so he could understand his own phantom nature.

"Netheril was the most beautiful, the highest and mightiest, the worthiest civilization that Faerûn ever spawned!" Telamont complained. "And the Heartlands balk at a few decades of starvation! I would not hesitate—not hesitate at all, I tell you—to wipe them all from the face of the world if it meant the return of the floating cities. And the elves—I would *give* Evereska and Evermeet both to the phaerimm, for just the century of peace we need to restore Anauroch to its glory."

Brennus stepped forward, head bowed and ceremonial fangs displayed. "If it pleases the Most High, I would be happy to go to the Shaeradim to open—"

"Negotiations?" The Most High cuffed him—actually struck him—and sent the prince sprawling. "*That* I ought to allow."

The Most High turned to Rivalen, platinum eyes burning with a question.

"The alliance could have their army here all too soon," Rivalen reported. "Our agents in Tilverton report that it is already many thousands strong, and growing by the hour."

The Most High turned to Clariburnus.

"Our army from the Shaeradim is passing south of the Shadow Sea as we speak," Clariburnus said. "It will reach Tilverton by tomorrow evening."

"How soon could it be here?" asked Hadhrune. As usual, the seneschal's impudence was beyond belief. It was as though he believed that because he was not plane-spawned he had nothing to fear from the Most High's wrath. "In time to stop the Cormyreans?"

Clariburnus inclined his head. "It is but an hour away."

Hadhrune turned to the Most High. "Perhaps we could split the army. Recall enough to ensure against an assault."

"That way lies defeat in both battles," Rivalen said. "There are more than ten thousand enemy soldiers in Tilverton, many of them war wizards and clerics. If I am to defeat them, I will need our entire army."

"Even the army in Myth Drannor?" Escanor asked.

In truth, Rivalen thought it would take that army as well, but he did not dare alienate his closest ally among the princes—and his only older brother.

He inclined his head to Escanor and said, "Any troops you were able to spare would certainly add to the victory."

"Unfortunately, I fear it will be impossible to spare any," Escanor said. "The Myth Drannor phaerimm are proving as obstinate—"

"I am sure you can spare half your troops," the Most High said. "Our victory in Tilverton must be quick. We must return our largest army to the

Shaeradim within the month, before the shadowshell fails. The phaerimm are our greatest threat."

Escanor glanced at Rivalen, his coppery eyes burning with anger. "But if our losses are heavy—"

"We will be surrounded on all sides," Hadhrune confirmed. "Surely, a conservative approach is wiser."

The Most High considered this for a moment, then said, "You are half right. I will send princes to treat with polities more sympathetic to our cause. Lamorak, you will go to see the Red Wizards of Thay. Yder, you will seek out the true leaders of the Cult of the Dragon . . ."

The Most High continued on, outlining a strategy that would envelop the forces currently surrounding the Shadovar.

When he finally finished, Hadhrune tried again to assert his influence. "You have taken every wise precaution that can be taken, Most High . . . but what of my suggestion? Certainly, it is wisest to defend Shade Enclave first."

"Wait." The Most High turned to the Seraph of Lies, Malik. To the great credit of the little man's willpower, he did not seem to feel the weight of any unspoken questions, and Telamont was forced to ask, "You know Ruha better than any of us. Do you think she knows a way into the city?"

Malik's eyes grew as round as coins, and Rivalen thought he would have thrown himself over the balcony rail, had the prospect of a painful landing not been so great.

"In my experience, that witch can get into anywhere," Malik said. "She has intruded upon me many times in many delicate moments—and sometimes when I could have sworn she was a thousand miles away."

The Most High considered this, then nodded. "I suppose it would be safer to assume that she knows a way into the enclave." His platinum eyes flared in Clariburnus's direction, then he looked back to Malik and asked, "So you would advise me to call Shade's armies home?"

"Indeed."

For a moment, Rivalen thought Malik would leave the matter at that, then the little man's face contorted into a mask of displeasure, and he said, "Only, I think it would be wiser to advise you to give all your troops to Rivalen and order him to attack."

The Most High's hood turned in the little man's direction.

"Because that is what you truly want to do, Most High," Malik blurted, "and a wise advisor always tells his master what his master is eager to hear."

"Is that so?"

Telamont's empty hood swung in Rivalen's direction, and Rivalen felt the weight of his father's question pressing down on his shoulders.

He inclined his head. "I will capture Tilverton and destroy the Alliance army," Rivalen said, "or I will die trying."

"Die if you must, but death does not excuse failure," the Most High said. He turned to Malik, and Rivalen could have sworn he saw a smile beneath the Most High's hood. "Thank you, little man. Not only are you my wisest advisor, you are the most honest."

CHAPTER SIXTEEN

27 Mirtul, the Year of Wild Magic

To the west lay the setting sun, its orange fury igniting a rusty blaze across the darkening sky and painting the jagged Stonelands in a fiery copper glow. Behind the lonely trees and distant monoliths, the shadows were lengthening, stretching their pointed tips across the parched pasturelands toward the city of Tilverton. To the north, purple darkness already cloaked the Desertsmouth Mountains. To the south, a lake of umbral murk was spreading outward from the foot of the Stormhorns. The attack could come from any direction or from all three, and with no more warning than the time a shadow needed to sweep across the plain. Or it might not come at all, though Galaeron knew better than to count on that.

Along with Vangerdahast, Alusair, Lady Regent Alasalynn Rowanmantle, and more aides than was safe, Galaeron was atop an unfinished wall tower in the Knoll District of Old Town, standing on a makeshift scaffolding that creaked every time someone shifted his weight, watching the darkness for the first hint of the enemy. Vangerdahast's attention was fixed on the south, as that was the only side of the city without a gate, and he was convinced the Shadovar would want time to form ranks before the battle began. Most of the aides were convinced they would come out of the Desertsmouth foothills, since that was both the shortest route to Anauroch and one of the most sheltered. Alusair was keeping her eye—and her archers' arrows—trained on the sky, for she was troubled by the descriptions of veserab riders and the fact of the Shadovar's alliance with Malygris and his blue dragons. Galaeron didn't know what to expect, but he felt sure that whatever the Shadovar did, it would be as unexpected as it was devastating.

A soft clatter sounded below as the bodyguard companies at the base of the tower ran through the procedure of admitting a runner. Finally, a herald called for permission to send up one of Vangerdahast's wizards, and a surprised murmur rose atop the keep as the aides nearest the ladder saw who it was. Galaeron looked down to see a willowy woman in a red cape ascending the long ladder. With red hair and golden eyes, even he recognized her as Vangerdahast's favorite aide—and, some said, lover—Caladnei.

The old wizard stepped over to the ladder and, as she neared the top, extended a hand. "About time, my dear," he said, pulling her onto the scaffolding. "What news?"

"Good news." She turned away and bowed to Alusair, then made her report directly to the regent. "Ruha has found the flying city, and it appears but lightly defended."

"Where is it?" Vangerdahast asked. "On the new lake?"

Caladnei nodded. "Floating above the north end. There is fresh water, and a defensible camp. Hhormun is preparing a translocational circle now."

Alusair considered the report for a moment, then said, "There's a reason the city is only lightly defended."

Vangerdahast nodded. "Either Galaeron is right, and they're readying an attack . . ."

"Or they're hoping to lure us into a trap," Alusair finished. She turned to Galaeron. "What do you think?"

"The Shadovar are cunning warmakers," he said, "but the phaerimm are their most ancient enemies. Telamont Tanthul would risk freeing them only if he's allowing his anger to guide him."

"And angry men don't lie in wait," Alusair agreed. "They attack."

"Unless that's what he wants us to think," Caladnei pointed out. "Perhaps Telamont is confident he can defeat us quickly and return his army to the Shaeradim in time to keep the phaerimm in check."

"In which case, he can't let us set the pace," Vangerdahast said. "Either way, he's attacking *us*. Everything points to it."

Caladnei inclined her head to the old wizard. "I'll send word to Hhormun to save his spell."

Alusair raised a restraining hand. "Hold a moment." She bit her lip in thought, then turned to Vangerdahast with a half smile. "What if we could beat them to the strike?"

Galaeron's brow rose. "Beat them? If you timed matters wrong, Tilverton would be lost."

"True," Alusair said without losing enthusiasm, "but Cormyr has many cities. The Shadovar have only one."

Alasalynn Rowanmantle gasped aloud. "You would sacrifice Tilverton?"

"No, but I'd surely wager it," Alusair said, not grinning. "You do have an evacuation plan?"

Alasalynn's already pale face grew even paler. "I'll activate it."

She thumbed a ring on her middle finger and vanished in a crackle of magic.

Vangerdahast cocked his bushy brow and started to say something, then caught Alusair's warning glance and cleared his throat instead.

Alusair smiled. "Vangey, can you. . . ."

"Of course, Princess." Too plump and rickety for the ladder, Vangerdahast simply stepped to the edge of the scaffolding and looked for a clear place to land. "I'll prepare the device for transport at once."

Galaeron frowned but bit his tongue and managed to avoid asking about the "device." Their departure from Arabel had been delayed nearly a day and a half to give Vangerdahast and the war wizards time to prepare. Galaeron had assumed that they were gathering magic items and memorizing spells, but he had realized this was not the case when the wizards emerged from their armory pulling a huge wagon covered with a tent of black canvas. The wizard had ignored Galaeron's repeated inquiries about the thing, saying only that it would prove once and for all that the Weave was mightier than the Shadow Weave.

When Galaeron made no move toward the ladder or Vangerdahast, the wizard grabbed him by the arm.

"Come along, young fellow." Vangerdahast pulled him off the scaffolding, and they floated down the hollow interior of the unfinished tower. "You'll want to see this."

At the bottom, they gathered Aris and Vangerdahast's troop of bodyguards and threaded their way down the knoll past company after company forming up for the short march to the translocational circle. The officers were engaging in no bluster or bravado and offered relatively few words of encouragement. Everyone knew the Shadovar were a strange and powerful enemy, and most wise commanders had prayed that the mere fact of the Heartlands Alliance would force the princes to reconsider the melting of the High Ice. That the Alliance was being marshaled for a night march put to rest any hope of ending the matter without a fight.

At the base of the hill, where the mansions of the Knoll District gave way to the exorbitant shops and inns that populated the rest of Old Town, Vangerdahast turned through the gate of the Windlord's Rest, which he had appropriated to serve as the headquarters of the war wizards. Instead of entering the cozy inn itself, he led the way past a mixed troop of war wizards and Purple Dragons into the livery.

Inside, the "device" sat covered in its wagon, fans of golden light spilling through the slats of the cargo bed to illuminate the stable floor. The light was incredibly bright, though it did not seem to burn the eyes of either Vangerdahast or the guards the way it did Galaeron's. He had to shield his face, and his palm began to nettle.

Vangerdahast smirked at Galaeron's reaction, then removed from his pocket a ring bearing a crude copy of the Purple Dragon of Cormyr.

"Sorry for the workmanship," the royal magician said, "there wasn't much time." He passed it over. "Put it on."

Galaeron slipped the ring onto his finger and immediately felt better. He also saw that the light was not nearly as bright as he had thought, barely showing through the slats at all.

"Interesting," he said. "How does it work?"

"I'll explain at the circle," Vangerdahast said. He turned toward the main doors, where Aris was crouched on hands and knees peering into the stable. "I would be indebted if you would draw the wagon for us. Translocational magic tends to make draught horses panic."

"My pleasure."

The giant stretched an arm through the doorway to grab the hitch—then a cry of alarm sounded from the courtyard behind him, and he stopped to look over his shoulder.

"Stonebones shield us!" Aris cried.

Galaeron stepped to the door and saw a company of dark forms peeling themselves out of the shadows, spraying the astonished guard companies outside with darts of black glass and bolts of shadow magic.

Aris cried out as a dark ray lanced out to pierce his forearm, then lashed out at his attacker with the same hand. Before the giant could close his fingers, the Shadovar changed back to shadow and drained away, then emerged behind him and pierced his thigh with another beam.

Aris screamed and whirled around. Galaeron saw a trio of Shadovar emerging adjacent to the door and could pay no more attention to the giant. He drew his sword and, waiting until the warriors began to assume a semblance of solidity, beheaded the nearest one. The body simply drained back into the shadow, but the dead man's companions whirled on Galaeron, their hands rising to unleash shadow spells.

Galaeron ducked back into the stable. "Warn the princess!" he yelled. "They've found me!"

"They've found my device," Vangerdahast corrected, peering past Aris's dancing legs into the courtyard. "But how? This city is warded!"

His bodyguards were beginning to counterattack with lightning bolts, crossbow quarrels, and—Galaeron was disappointed to see—bolts of raw magic. Even after hearing how the Sharn Wall had been breached, Vangerdahast had ignored Galaeron's suggestion that the war wizards strike all spells of raw magic from their battle lists.

"I told you those wards were useless," Galaeron said, "as the Shadovar are about to prove."

The shadows inside the building began to undulate as more shadow warriors arrived. Galaeron tapped Vangerdahast on the shoulder, and the wizard glanced into the thicket of silhouettes rising behind them.

"Vexatious beings, aren't they?" the royal magician said.

Vangerdahast pointed at his device and made a lifting motion. The canvas cover rose to reveal a globe of living light, its exterior etched with hundreds of black glyphs similar to the warding tile Galaeron had seen two days before. The glyphs were swimming over the surface like water striders on a pond and casting dark shadows of themselves across the interior of the stable. As the silhouettes fell on the Shadovar warriors, the corresponding glyph stopped moving and affixed its shadow firmly in the center of the target's chest.

The Shadovar wailed in agony and tried to dodge aside or drop back into the shadows. It was difficult to say what happened to those who retreated into the fringe, but the others screamed in agony as their glyphs moved across the orb to keep the dark emblem painted on their torso. A second later, the symbol burst into golden flames, and they dissolved into sooty black smoke.

Galaeron noticed that, despite the ring Vangerdahast had given him, he was growing uncomfortably warm himself. He took shelter behind the wizard's ample form.

"Impressive." He glanced around behind them, expecting the ones who had retreated into the Shadow Fringe to reemerge at their backs. When the shadows remained as still as shadows should, he said, "Using a shadow to project the symbol prevents them from escaping into the fringe."

Vangerdahast beamed. "Imagine what I could have learned, had you actually demonstrated shadow magic." The wizard went to the front of the wagon and picked up the hitch. "Help me get this out where it will do some good."

Galaeron went to the other side and began to push against the crossbar.

The wagon was incredibly heavy, as if the orb it carried were made of gold metal instead of gold light.

"Corellon's bolts!" he gasped. "Wouldn't it be faster to use magic?"

"It is folly to rely on magic for things your own strong back can do better," Vangerdahast said, frowning across the bar at him. "A wise woman taught me that."

"So you're saying you'll need your telekinesis spells later," Galaeron surmised.

"Exactly." Vangerdahast leaned into the hitch. "Now put your back into it."

Galaeron braced his feet and did as the wizard commanded. The effort was almost enough to make him break his promise not to use shadow magic. The floor was slick with dust and there was a slight incline at the threshold, and the battle raging in the courtyard had already become a desperate one. Purple Dragons lay two and three bodies deep, and Vangerdahast's war wizards were having to stand back to back to keep their Shadovar attackers from slipping through the shadows to attack from behind. Even then, the Shadovar were far more adept at using their defenses to stop Weave spells than the Cormyreans were at using their magic to stop shadow spells, and more than a dozen of the kingdom's battle mages already lay among the fallen dragoneers.

Aris was staggering around like a drunken fire dancer, bleeding from a dozen wounds, alternately trying to stomp enemy warriors flat or kick them out over the inn's roof.

"Aris!" Galaeron yelled. "Help us!"

The giant crossed the battle in a stride, scattering a trio of shadow warriors with a sweep of his large foot. He dropped to a knee and pulled the wagon across the threshold so quickly that Galaeron and Vangerdahast had to leap aside to keep from being crushed under the wheels. The silhouettes of the old wizard's glyphs danced over the surrounding walls for less than a second, then began to settle on their targets. The wispy screams of anguished Shadovar filled the air, then a thicket of golden flames flared to life across the courtyard, and their attackers vanished as quickly as they had appeared.

Galaeron rolled to his knees and found Vangerdahast lying against the opposite doorjamb, his chest heaving and his face contorted with pain. Galaeron's mind leaped immediately to the worst possible conclusion.

"Vangerdahast?" He scrambled across the doorway and pulled the portly wizard into his lap. It wasn't easy. "Are you hit?"

"No . . . just getting . . . old," the old wizard groaned. He rubbed a shoulder, then looked from Galaeron to one of his assistants who had come running and extended a hand. "How bad?"

"We lost thirteen war wizards and most of your dragoneers." The fellow used both hands to pull Vangerdahast to his feet—then grinned broadly. "But you were right about those ward tiles, milord. They lured the Shadovar in through the fringe just like you—"

"Yes, well, we've no time to waste congratulating ourselves," Vangerdahast growled, casting a sidelong glance in Galaeron's direction. "Let's finish this."

He rubbed his signet ring, then looked into the sky and said, "Alusair, the time has come. Are you in position?"

The wizard was silent for a moment, then nodded and looked back to his assistant. "The attack is citywide. Leave them no place to hide. Demolish any building they enter, if you must."

"I'll pass the word." The assistant acknowledged the order with a bow, then turned to cast a spell.

A weary look came to Vangerdahast's eyes. He motioned Galaeron to follow and shuffled toward Aris and the orb of light. Seeing that the battle had already taken more out of the wizard than the old fellow cared to admit, Galaeron offered a hand in support . . . and was not rebuffed.

"You planned this?" he asked. "You picked one of your own cities as the battlefield?"

"We certainly didn't let them take us by surprise, if that's what you were thinking," Vangerdahast snapped. "Cormyr *has* fought a few wars . . . and won them all."

"If I underestimated you, I apologize," Galaeron said, "but all that talk on the wall tower—"

"For the spies," Vangerdahast said. "The Shadovar do use spies, you know."

"I know," Galaeron said. "I thought you weren't listening to me."

Vangerdahast fixed Galaeron with a rheumy eye. "Who says I was?"

Galaeron was too stunned to laugh. Though Tilverton's evacuation was under way, he had seen for himself that there had still been hundreds of women and children in the city earlier that evening—and the Cormyrean plan risked them all. How hard, he wondered, had been the lessons they learned in their last war against the dragon Nalavarauthatoryl? Had they truly grown so cold that they would knowingly sacrifice so many to win a quick victory—and save how many more? Perhaps that was what it required to defeat the Shadovar, and, more importantly, the phaerimm.

They reached the wagon, and the wizard stopped beside Aris's knee. "Stay close," Vangerdahast said. "I may have need of your talents."

Without waiting for a response, Vangerdahast cast a quick spell and lifted his hand heavenward. The golden orb shot high into the air, its glyphs growing motionless as they found their first targets. The battle din beyond the courtyard continued unabated for a moment, then slowly changed pitch as the symbol silhouettes began to take their toll. The wizard cocked his head as if listening to a distant voice, then moved his hand a few inches. The golden sphere floated a hundred yards across the sky.

"Come along. We need a better vantage point."

Vangerdahast laid a hand on each of them, spoke a magic word, and pulled them through the dark square of a magic door. There was a timeless instant of falling, then Galaeron found himself standing in bright golden light, feeling very hot and dizzy, listening to the sounds of a battle far below.

"Don't worry about being seen," said a familiar voice. "I've cast a couple of spells that will keep us hidden."

Galaeron recovered from his afterdaze enough to recall that he was somewhere in the middle of the battle for Tilverton.

Vangerdahast was shaking him by the arm and pointing down at the ground. "What's that he's doing?"

Galaeron looked down—a *long* way down—and grew so dizzy that it took him a moment to find what the wizard was pointing at. It was a dark figure more than a hundred paces from the tower where they stood looking out over the raging battle. Barely visible beneath the canvas awning of a patio tavern, the figure was waving his outstretched arms in small circles, apparently summoning the black fog that was rising out of the cracks of the flagstones at his feet and spilling out into Old Town—much to the confusion and distress of the companies of Alliance warriors rushing about the streets flushing Shadovar from their hiding places.

"It's hard to tell without seeing how he cast the spell," Galaeron said, "but he seems to be summoning shadowstuff."

Vangerdahast raised his brow. "Shadowstuff? Would that be raw—"

"Don't tell me!" Galaeron had a sinking feeling. "The glyphs—"

"Not the glyphs, or their silhouettes," Vangerdahast said, "but the sphere itself is raw magic."

"And the light?" Galaeron asked.

Vangerdahast shrugged. "Not in itself, but born of raw magic."

"Close enough," Aris said. He was kneeling on the other side of Vangerdahast, his elbows resting on the tower's stone crenellations to take some of his weight off the roof. "There is a disruption already."

He pointed into a street around the corner from the Shadovar, where the black fog was rolling out of the shadow of the building into the orb-lit street—and swirling about the shins of a company of Sembian mercenaries who had been attempting to sneak up on the object of their attention. Though the general battle din was too loud to hear their screams, their writhing arms and contorted postures left no doubt about their pain.

As Galaeron and the others watched, the warriors plunged to mid-thigh in the fog, then fell prone and vanished entirely. A moment later, the light of Vangerdahast's orb turned the shadowstuff itself to ash. It sank to the ground, covering the street in an inky stain of darkness devoid of shape or texture—or even any apparent substance.

Vangerdahast pointed at the fog and cast what Galaeron recognized as a spell of magic dismissal. The shadowstuff continued to roll out of the Shadovar's hiding place, floating across the dark stain to brush against the orb-lit foundation of the mansion across the street. The stone disintegrated as had the legs of the Sembian mercenaries, and the building itself collapsed into the inky murk that had been, until a few moments earlier, a cobblestone street.

The building vanished without raising so much as a dust plume.

Another building on the other side of the Shadovar spellcaster collapsed, then a company of Purple Dragons came charging into view with a tide of the shadowstuff rolling down the street behind them. It appeared they would be fast enough to reach safety—until the rear rank threw up their arms and fell, bringing down those in front of them, and so on until the entire company was gone.

Trees and buildings began to vanish in a widening circle as the shadowstuff spread, first creating lacy paths of nothingness where the black fog worked its way into orb-lit areas, then gradually developing into a solid disk of murk as adjacent areas were exposed to the golden light. The battle at the edge of the circle grew wildly intense as Shadovar and Alliance warriors fought for control of the escape lanes, filling the dusk sky with flashing lightning bolts and hissing rays of darkness. Only the patio where the fog-summoner himself stood remained untouched, revealing a huge figure in a horned helm still waving his outstretched arms, calling more shadowstuff up into the streets.

Galaeron clasped Vangerdahast's arm. "You're destroying the city!" he said. "Annul your spell, or at least move it out over the plain."

"And let the Shadovar destroy our armies?" Vangerdahast scoffed. "Better to lose a city than a kingdom."

Galaeron stared out over the collapsing city and thought of all the dying warriors, of all the innocents who would perish if the shadow fog continued to spread. Vangerdahast had tried to dispel it and failed.

But Vangerdahast could not use the Shadow Weave, and Galaeron could. What kind of person would turn his back on the deaths of so many—even if it meant the return of his shadow self? Galaeron had recovered from it once, and with Aris and Vangerdahast, and the entire kingdom of Cormyr to stand with him this time, he could certainly do so again. Even if he could not, what was he sacrificing, really? Only his life, and hundreds had done that already.

Galaeron took a deep breath, then raised his hands and started to open himself to the Shadow Weave—and found Aris's big hand reaching over Vangerdahast to pluck him off the rooftop.

"Galaeron, you are forgetting your promise."

"Not forgetting," Galaeron said, "but I can't let thousands die while I do nothing."

"So your shadow would have you believe," the giant replied, "but you know better than to think you can dispel the magic of someone like Prince Rivalen."

"That's Rivalen?" Vangerdahast gasped.

Aris nodded. "I would recognize that face anywhere. Can you not see his golden eyes?"

Galaeron was undeterred. "I have to try," he said. "If there's any chance I can save Tilverton—"

"There is not, and you know it," Aris said, "but the choice must be yours, or your shadow has already won."

He placed Galaeron on the roof beside Vangerdahast. Galaeron watched another mansion tumble into nothingness, then the golden blaze of a dozen Shadovar warriors burning into ash beneath the light of the war wizards' artificial sun.

Vangerdahast glanced into the street below. "Fog's coming this way," he observed. "Our tower will go soon."

Galaeron started to lower his arms, then felt such a pang of guilt that he realized he would not be able to live with himself if he just let all those innocent people die.

"I have to try—"

"No, you don't." It was Vangerdahast who knocked Galaeron's arms down this time. "You're no match for Rivalen, and we both know it."

"But—"

"There are other ways," Vangerdahast said. There was an emotion unaccustomed to the wizard's face in his expression, something sad and contrite, almost kind. "If you're going to throw your life away, at least do it wisely."

He placed Galaeron's hand on his sword, then motioned him to wait and looked into the sky. "Caladnei, I need you. We're on the Tower of Wond—"

Vangerdahast had barely finished before the air hissed with her arrival.

"My dear, what took you so long?" Vangerdahast mocked. As the wizardess struggled to recover from her afterdaze, he guided her hand to Aris's knee. "Take the giant and go to Alusair. If that shadow fog does not stop expanding in the next few minutes, you are to sound the retreat, then teleport to safety with the princess and as many others as you can take."

Caladnei's eyes remained vacant. "Fog? Retreat—?"

"I understand," Aris said. He clapped a big hand over Galaeron's shoulder. "Till swords part, my friend. Good luck."

"Good luck?" Galaeron asked. "What am I doing?"

"We'll decide that later," Vangerdahast said, taking his arm. "Just have your sword ready and start cutting when we get there."

The wizard spoke a mystic word, and Galaeron felt again the timeless falling of translocational magic. He was growing almost accustomed to the feeling, but that did not make the afterdaze any less disorienting when his stomach finally settled back into its proper place. The ground beneath his feet felt unsteady and yielding, almost as though he were standing on a soft human bed instead of anything like a street or floor.

Cut!

Vangerdahast's voice came to Galaeron inside his head. He felt the ground bouncing under him as the old wizard hobbled away. He recalled, dimly, that they were in some sort of battle and that his last instruction before the teleport had been to start cutting, so he jammed his sword into the softness beneath his boots and began to—

A loud ripping noise sounded between his feet, and he found his stomach turning somersaults again, this time more normally as he plunged through a canvas awning. Something sharp punctured the chain mail on his leg and sank deep into his thigh, sending a bolt of fiery agony shooting up through his body. He hung for a moment high up beneath the awning, until whatever he had landed on toppled over and dropped, crashing, onto a wooden table.

A raspy voice screamed in agony. The sharp point pulled free of Galaeron's thigh. He fell off the table onto a hard stone floor, then rolled to his knees and found himself peering over the table at the figure of a hulking Shadovar holding a horned helm in his hands.

"Elf!" Rivalen said, tossing the helm aside. "I thought we would need to look for you in Suzail by now."

"Here I am." Galaeron rose from behind the table and, glancing at the broad swath of orb-light that separated them, tried to appear confident. "All you need do is come get me."

Rivalen peered up at the rip in the canopy. "Yes, I'm certain you would like that." He smiled, then glanced over Galaeron's shoulders. "I think I will have my guards do it. Seize him!"

Heart sinking at the sudden clamor that erupted from the patio edge behind him, Galaeron vaulted the table into the swath of orb light, landing so that he had the prince on one flank and the approaching bodyguards on the other. Of course there were guards.

There were always guards.

Wondering what was taking Vangerdahast so long, Galaeron glanced up at the ripped awning. He had a chance of leaping high enough to grab hold and climb to safety—but, with one wounded leg, not much of one.

"Don't let him get away!" Rivalen ordered, starting forward from his side—apparently unaware that Galaeron had come with company. At least that much of Vangerdahast's plan was working. "Take him now!"

The guards, already rushing across the patio, began to vault tables and kick chairs aside. Galaeron leaped as high as he could and slashed at the torn edge of the awning.

The canvas, already weakened by his first cut, split down its length. More Shadovar than Galaeron could count in a glance howled in anguish as the orb light poured through and fixed them with the silhouette of a death glyph. Those closest to the tavern walls turned and dived for shade, their bodies bursting into sprays of golden flame as they tumbled through the windows. The rest perished where they stood, setting the wooden chairs and tables alight as they died.

Galaeron pivoted into the sunlight and brought his sword around into a guarding position. Where the devil was Vangerdahast? Rivalen stopped a safe distance back beneath the remaining half of the awning, his golden eyes burning almost white with rage.

"Enough, traitor. You will drop your sword and come to me." He pointed his finger at the far edge of the patio behind Galaeron and spoke a word of command, then continued, "Or you will perish with your friends."

Galaeron glanced over his shoulder and saw a plume of shadowstuff rising from a corner of the patio still shaded by a dangling flap of torn awning. It was slowly spreading across the flagstones toward him, bringing its tide of oblivion steadily closer. He looked back to the prince.

"You wouldn't dare," Galaeron said, trying to sound confident. "The Most High—"

He was interrupted by the sudden eruption of Rivalen's chest. Galaeron danced quickly aside as the dregs of the purple death ray shot past, then looked back to see the prince's body crashing to the floor and Vangerdahast standing behind him with ten smoking fingertips. Galaeron stepped into the safety of the awning shadows.

"Took you long enough," he said.

"I'm old," Vangerdahast replied, and he sounded it. His gaze remained fixed on the far corner of the patio, where wisps of shadowstuff continued to pour from whatever fissure Rivalen had opened into the shadow plane. "I thought that would stop when he died."

Galaeron frowned, then looked down to discover that all that remained of Rivalen was a long black spine and an ebony heart beating in a broken cage of black ribs. To his horror, it was rolling onto its back and rising in Vangerdahast's direction.

"Vangerdahast, watch your—"

The prince's remains—if that was what they were—hurled themselves at the wizard. A deep gash appeared across Vangerdahast's collarbone, and blood began to spurt from the wound in great red arcs. Vangerdahast cried out in pain and stumbled back, one hand crackling with fire and the other with lightning. Galaeron leaped to the attack, slamming his sword into the ebony spine with enough force to fell a fair-sized sapling.

The bone did not even chip, though the ribs did pivot slightly as an unseen heel slammed into his stomach. He doubled over and flew backward, his sword flying away as the air left his lungs. He crashed down just beyond the awning's shadow, less than an arm's length from oblivion's advancing edge. Behind him, the far wall of the patio crashed down and vanished into darkness.

Vangerdahast thrust one hand forward and poured lightning into the dark heart. It stopped beating—but only for as long as the lightning continued. A red gash opened in the wizard's cloak, and a sword-shaped spray of blood came out the back.

Vangerdahast bellowed—more in rage than pain—and filled the cage of black ribs with magic fire.

The wizard's head snapped sideways. Vangerdahast's arms dropped to his side, and Galaeron, already leaping back into the fray with a drawn dagger, screamed. The ribs half turned toward him, and for a moment Rivalen's golden eyes appeared in the air above the writhing vertebrae of the neck.

Vangerdahast's weary arms came up, wrapping themselves around the skeletal body, and he uttered a familiar command word. They vanished in a sizzle of teleport magic—

—and Rivalen's raspy voice erupted in anguish on the orb-lit patio. Galaeron spun around to find the prince—or, rather, the prince's ribs and heart—erupting into golden flame as Vangerdahast tried to push the black thing into the inky darkness creeping toward them both.

Galaeron was there in a leap, arriving heels-first to kick Rivalen over the edge. The ribs and heart vanished, burning, into black nothingness—and Vangerdahast started after them, suddenly spinning around on his back, sleeve stretching over his head into darkness. Galaeron landed alongside him facing the wrong direction, but grabbed the wizard's belt and pulled himself around, then hacked the cuff free.

Vangerdahast let out a pained gasp and jerked his hand back. All that remained of it were the fingers, thumb, and a small piece of flesh connecting it to the wrist. The rest was simply not there, as though it had been rendered invisible or lost to the bite of some very strange creature.

The adjacent wall of the tavern crumbled into oblivion, leaving only the corner with the shadowstuff fountain standing upright. Galaeron pulled Vangerdahast back under the awning and began to go through the pockets of the wizard's cloak.

"Do you have any healing potions?" Galaeron asked, tossing aside feathers and satchels full of iron filings.

With sunken eyes and skin as gray as a snow cloud, the wizard looked like he had died already. Galaeron could see at least two life-threatening wounds and suspected there were other injuries he could not even guess at.

"Any way to get us to help?" asked Galaeron.

Vangerdahast's gaze grew vacant and slid away.

"Vangerdahast?" Galaeron placed his ear close to the wizard's mouth and was relieved to hear a soft, steady wheezing. "Vangerdahast?"

When the wizard still made no reply, Galaeron stanched the bleeding as best he could, then stood on a table to search for help. He was not surprised to discover that the fighting was already over—cataclysmic magic had a way of ending battles swiftly—but he was astonished at the extent of the destruction. Much of Tilverton—all of Old Town below him and the rest of the city out past the Moonsea Ride—already lay beneath a sea of shadowstuff, and the stain was continuing to spread. The great Council Tower in the center of town was sinking into oblivion even as he watched, and he could hear warriors from both sides calling to each other in the dark streets beyond, all more concerned with saving their own lives than taking anyone else's. Whether Lady Regent Rowanmantle had succeeded in evacuating the rest of her citizens, Galaeron could not say, but he took the lack of matronly voices and sobbing children to be a good sign—one of the few of the day.

Finding no possibility of help there, Galaeron hopped down and went to the uphill side of the patio. The scene there was much the same as below, save that most of the shadowstuff had rolled downhill into the lower city, sparing much of the Knoll District, the jagged ruins of Tilver's Palace, and a lengthy section of wall.

It was there, atop one of the as-yet-unfinished wall towers, that he found their salvation. Atop one of the spires, no more than two hundred paces distant, stood Aris's looming figure, illuminated in the yellow light of Vangerdahast's orb, one hand raised to his brow as he searched the city. Galaeron stepped as near the edge of the awning as he dared and waved. For a moment, there was no response, and he began to fear that even the stone giant's keen sight would not be able to see him beneath the canopy.

When Aris pointed in his direction, Galaeron knew they were saved. He waited a couple of moments for the giant to return his wave, then dropped off the table to return to Vangerdahast's side—and found Caladnei already kneeling there, pouring a healing potion down the wizard's throat one drop at a time.

As Galaeron limped over, she looked up with an angry scowl on her face. "When you need help, call for it." She pointed her chin at the ring Vangerdahast had given him. "That's what the purple dragon is for."

✡✡✡✡✡

"What in the name of all the drow gods," the Steel Regent demanded, pacing back and forth in front of Galaeron, "did you do to my Royal Magician?"

It was almost dawn, and they were encamped—hiding, really—with what remained of the armies of the Heartlands Alliance, a mile outside of what had once been Tilverton. The shadowstuff had consumed the city almost completely, spreading well beyond the walls to engulf even the outlying stock pens and caravan campsites. All that remained of the city was the wall atop the Knoll District and the jagged ruins of Tilver's Palace, now backlit by the sinking sphere of Vangerdahast's magic orb.

Alusair waved a hand at the golden ball. "He won't look at anything but that damnable globe, and he keeps asking if we won. What do I tell him? That we won because we had more survivors than the Shadovar? Or that we lost because we lost our entire army? How do I snap him out of this?"

"Tell him the truth," Galaeron suggested. "Tell him that no one won."

"That would not be the truth," Aris said.

Alusair whirled on the seated giant and, despite the fact that she had to crane her neck to see his face, somehow still seemed to be looking him straight in the eye.

"Are you saying Shade won?" she demanded. "Because I know *we* didn't. Not if we've lost Vangerdahast."

"I am saying that the phaerimm won," the giant answered. "They still control Evereska, and now they will soon be free."

Alusair's already stormy face turned absolutely tempestuous. "Thank you for making an insufferable loss seem even worse." She whirled on Galaeron. "This is your doing, elf. Had Vangerdahast had a better understanding of shadow magic—"

"He would have done exactly as he did, Majesty," said Caladnei, stepping to Galaeron's defense. "You can ask a warrior to lay down his life for you, but not his soul."

"Elves don't have souls," Alusair shot back, "but I see what you mean." She cast a sidelong glance in Galaeron's direction. "That's as much of an apology as you're going to get, elf."

"And more than is required," Galaeron replied. "All I ask is that you let me assist when you do attack."

"Still thinking of Vala, are we?" Alusair asked.

Galaeron nodded. "Always."

The truth was that since escaping Tilverton, he had been able to think of nothing but the thing Vangerdahast had killed, wondering if Escanor was something similar, and of what Vala must be suffering in service to such a thing. However great her pain, whatever her humiliation, he was to blame. He had allowed his shadow self to drive her away, and it was because of his weakness—*that* weakness—that she was imprisoned in Escanor's palace.

"I have much to answer for," Galaeron added.

Alusair's expression grew almost sisterly. "We all do, Galaeron." She reached out and squeezed his arm, then turned to face Tilverton, where Vangerdahast's orb was just sinking behind the Knoll District wall. "We all do."

As the globe vanished from sight, a terrible rumbling rolled across the plain, shaking the ground so hard that the wounded—what few they had been able to evacuate—began to groan. The glow over Tilverton darkened for a moment, then returned in an exploding fan of golden light.

With that Vangerdahast was up and standing tall, looking as regal and powerful and truly frightening as the mighty wizard Galaeron had come to know—and perhaps even love—in his short time in Cormyr.

"To arms!" Vangerdahast's voice boomed across the plain. "Summon my war wizards! Call out the Purple Dragons! Azoun calls, and we ride—for king and Cormyr!"

Alusair and Caladnei were at the wizard's side almost instantly, taking him by the arms and soothing him with gentle words. Galaeron did not hear exactly what they said, for his attention was fixed on Tilverton, where the entire Knoll District was rapidly sinking into the dark plain, taking with it the last bitter reminders of the Heartlands Alliance—and all of Faerûn's hopes for a season without starvation. Soon, all that remained of the city were the backlit ruins of Tilver's Palace, surrounded by smaller piles of dark rubble. The last rays of Vangerdahast's light paled to darkness, and eventually even they were lost.

THE SORCERER RETURN OF THE ARCHWIZARDS

CHAPTER ONE

7 Flamerule, the Year of Wild Magic (1372 DR)

It was the sound of despair, this strained silence that greeted the end of every report. With each account of yet another pact struck by the enemy, with every confession that a realm could raise no more troops, the envoys would drop their gazes to the polished surface of the conference table and study their reflections, and there would be no sound in the room but the sputtering of the oil lamps.

Only Princess Alusair Obarskyr, the Steel Regent of Cormyr, received the news with a raised chin, but it seemed to Galaeron Nihmedu that with each account of another cyclone spawned by the melting of the High Ice, with each description of a new city in flood or a nation's barley fields withering under a blazing sun, the furrows in the princess's brow deepened, the circles beneath her eyes grew larger, darker, and more menacing.

Alusair turned her attention to Galaeron and said, "And what news from Evereska, Sir Nihmedu? How go matters for the elves?"

The question was for the benefit of the others present. Alusair was the one who had told Galaeron much of what he would pass along, and she was doing him an honor by asking him to repeat it on behalf of his city. Galaeron stood.

"Evereska will stand, Your Highness." This good news caused several envoys to raise their heads, and Galaeron continued, "The elven armies are camped outside the Shaeradim, ready to meet the phaerimm the instant the shadowshell falls."

"You're certain it will fall?" asked Korian Hovanay, the ambassador from Sembia. A foppish man with fleshy jowls and an outlandish feathered hat resting on the table before him, Hovanay glared at Galaeron as he spoke. "I see no reason the Shadovar should let it fade. The phaerimm are Shade's archenemies—and the Shadovar have succeeded in all of their other undertakings."

"All of their *diplomatic* undertakings," Alusair corrected. She had aged a decade in the forty days since Tilverton's loss, and her once striking face had become sallow and haggard with worry. "Their army—what remains of it—has been quiet since the Battle of Tilverton."

"My point exactly," Hovanay said. "How do we know they have not been marshaling their strength to renew their attack on the phaerimm?"

"That is wishful thinking, Ambassador," said Piergeiron Paladinson, who had come by magic all the way from Waterdeep. "Sadly, the Shadovar are too cunning to turn their attention elsewhere so our alliance can mobilize against the Melting."

"And the elven armies are as ready to meet the Shadovar as the phaerimm," Galaeron said. "The shadowshell damages Evereska as much as it does the phaerimm, and our people will prevent the Shadovar from renewing it."

What Galaeron left unsaid was that with two of Mystra's Chosen—Laeral Silverhand and her consort Khelben Arunsun—still trapped in the Shaeradim, Storm Silverhand was just as determined as the elves to bring down the shadowshell. At the first hint of trouble, she would teleport straight to the mystical Splicing that held the dark sphere together and join six of Evermeet's last high mages in preventing the Shadovar from renewing it.

Galaeron felt certain of little else in this strange three-sided war, but he was sure that the shadowshell would fall, and soon. What happened afterward was anyone's guess. With the phaerimm loose in the world, the Shadovar thawing the High Ice, and the weather wreaking flood and famine across all Faerûn, the only thing anyone could predict for sure was calamity.

Hovanay studied Galaeron with a sneer, then finally said, "How wonderful for the elves. I'm sure you'll forgive the rest of us if we don't share your enthusiasm."

"You have reason to wish Evereska ill, Ambassador?" Galaeron asked. "Perhaps Sembia hopes to strike a bargain for our treasure?"

Hovanay's eyes flashed. "I trust you are not suggesting that Sembia would traffic with thieves, Sir Nihmedu."

Galaeron braced his hands on the table and started to rise, but the Harper witch Ruha, seated next to him in her customary veil and head scarf, laid a hand on his forearm.

"Remember your shadow," she said quietly. "You assume too much."

Galaeron felt a sudden surge of anger toward her and knew instantly that something dark and sinister had risen inside him. His shadow self was asserting itself again, trying to make him see dark motives and evil betrayals in those around him. He lowered himself into his seat and folded his hands, then looked across the table to Hovanay.

"My question was unwarranted, Ambassador," he said. It irked Galaeron to apologize, but it was wiser to trust Ruha in such matters than himself. "I hope you will forgive the implication."

Hovanay smirked back at him. "Of course. We are all aware of your affliction."

"Which is not to say that we understand your point, Ambassador," Alusair said. She did not bother to disguise her own suspicion of the man, for there had been no love lost between their two realms since Sembia's not-so-veiled attempt to carve off a piece of Cormyr during the Ghazneth Scourge. "Why shouldn't we want Evereska to survive?"

"It is not Evereska's survival that troubles us," Hovanay answered. "It is the fall of the shadowshell. Commerce has suffered enough as it is. The last thing we need now is a legion of phaerimm making slaves and egg-bags of the few caravanners still bold enough to meet their obligations."

Galaeron restrained the urge to berate the man for worrying about his purse while brave elves were dying—but Alusair did not. She studied Hovanay with a sneer usually reserved for something she scraped off her boot, then shook her head.

"There is more at stake here than gold," she said. "Our subjects cannot eat gold—though I'll be happy to feed you some if you'd like to experiment."

Ruha snickered beneath her veil, and several other envoys had to bite their lips and turn away.

Accepting Alusair's affront with the casual poise of one accustomed to such treatment, Hovanay merely smiled.

"Perhaps we cannot eat gold, but we *do* need it to feed our armies. Is there a realm among us whose treasuries are not barren already?"

When the table remained silent, the ambassador continued, "If our losses grow any worse, I dare say the alliance will lack the means to muster any army at all, much less one powerful enough to defeat the Shadovar and stop the Melting."

Again, a tense silence fell over the council room, and Alusair's face turned stormy with frustration. Already exhausted of both gold and men, the realms of the alliance were stretched to the breaking point, and—just as Hovanay said—any pressure brought by the phaerimm would be enough to crush them.

Even to Galaeron, the implications were clear. If Evereska were to survive, it would be at the cost of every other civilized land in Faerûn.

Galaeron began to feel that all eyes were turned on him. When he glanced around the table, it was to see the gazes of the other envoys quickly slipping away.

Lord Nasher Alagondar of Neverwinter, who had come by the same magic as Piergeiron Paladinson, coughed softly into his hand. The quiet thus broken, Alduvar Snowbrand—a Sword of Archendale and one of the three envoys shared by the Dalelands—wrapped his fingers around his chair arms and leaned forward as though he were about to pounce from his seat.

"We are looking at this wrong, I say." A tall, strong man with silky black hair, Alduvar had a spectral face and deep green eyes that seemed strangely distant and dull. "Our enemies are the Shadovar, not the phaerimm."

"That is an easy thing to say when it is someone else's home they have besieged," Galaeron said. "The phaerimm are enemies to the elves, I assure you."

"And who's fault is that?" Alduvar turned to glower at him, but there was no anger in his eyes, no ire or malice—no emotion at all. "Was it not you who freed them in the first place?"

"And who cursed us with the Shadovar?" added Irreph Mulmar, the ruddy-faced Constable of the High Dale. Like Alduvar, he was one of the three envoys from the Dales, and like Alduvar's, his eyes seemed oddly empty. "Were you not the one who brought them back from the Plane of Shadow?"

Somewhere inside, Galaeron realized that the vitriol of the Dalesmen was strangely at odds with their vacant eyes, but his shadow was already rising to the bait, bristling at the accusations and urging him to answer with blade or spell. He started to stand and found Ruha's hand clamped to his arm, her nails digging in hard to remind him that he had to be strong, that to indulge his anger was to yield to the darkness devouring him from the inside.

"What is done is done," she said, continuing to hold Galaeron down. "Is there anyone here who can say he would not have made the same mistake?"

"Mistakes have consequences," said Mourngrym Amcatha, the third and last of the Dalelands envoys. A huge, powerfully built man with a brown mustache and neatly trimmed hair, his eyes were as vacant as those of his fellow Dalesmen. "The elf is the one who made the mistake. It's his people who should suffer for it—not ours."

Mourngrym's comment drew a chorus of astonished murmurs, for he was as respected across much of Faerûn as he was in his own dale. For him to speak so openly against Evereska's interests was to condone the resentment harbored in secret by many of the alliance's lesser leaders, who gathered at night in quiet little groups to complain of the hardships visited upon them by the mistake of one elf.

Galaeron was filled with such a black fury that he forgot about the vacant eyes and no longer felt Ruha's hand on his arm. He was up and leaning across the table toward Mourngrym, his weight braced on his hands and his words tumbling from his mouth of their own accord.

"And who would you blame had the Shadovar unleashed the phaerimm on the Dalelands instead of Evereska?" Galaeron demanded. "Some saurial from Tarkhaldale?"

Mourngrym's lip rose in a sneer, but his eyes remained as blank as before.

"A saurial did not release the phaerimm," he said. "An elf did. You, to be exact."

Suddenly finding himself off balance, Galaeron looked down to find his hand a foot above the table, his fingers curled as though to call a shadow bolt. Ruha was using both hands to hold his arm so he could not cast the spell. Behind her, Piergeiron Paladinson was rising to help, watching the struggle with an expression that was half alarmed and half forbearing.

The sight was enough to shock Galaeron back to his senses. He let his arm go limp.

"Humans!"

Knowing he was still not fully in control of himself, Galaeron freed his arm and turned toward Alusair.

"If the princess will excuse me—"

"She will not, Sir Nihmedu." Motioning him into his seat, she nodded at a pair of Purple Dragons posted along the wall. As they stepped forward to stand guard behind Galaeron's chair, she said, "Actually, I have a keen interest in hearing Lord Mourngrym's answer."

Galaeron sat, and Mourngrym turned to face Alusair.

"What answer would that be, Your Highness?"

"To Galaeron's question, Lord Mourngrym." Alusair replied, her expression growing suspicious. "Who would you blame if the Shadovar had unleashed the phaerimm in the Dalelands instead of Evereska?"

"But they didn't, Princess."

"Lord Mourngrym," Alusair said, "I am asking what if they *had*."

"The question is meaningless, Your Highness. It was the elf who unleashed the phaerimm."

An astonished murmur filled the chamber. Paying no attention, Mourngrym turned to gesture at Galaeron, and at last Galaeron understood what he had been seeing—or rather, not seeing—in the eyes of the Dalesman.

Anger clouded Alusair's face.

"Lord Mourngrym," she said, "as a guest in my realm, you owe me the courtesy of an answer."

Mourngrym responded with an counterfeit smile.

"Of course, Your Highness. What I fail to understand . . ."

Galaeron did not hear the rest of the answer, for his own thoughts were whirling like one of the cyclones that had of late been laying waste to so many of Faerûn's farms and villages. The Dalesmen's attack on him had been carefully coordinated, with the envoys of lesser stature laying the groundwork for a final indictment by their most respected member. Given that the three came from the same area, it seemed entirely plausible they had come together before the council and settled on the strategy, but Galaeron suspected another explanation—a far more menacing one.

He leaned toward Ruha and felt a Purple Dragon's armored hand grasping his shoulder.

"Milord," the soldier whispered. "I think the princess meant for you to stay in your own chair."

"As I will." Though Galaeron answered in an amiable tone, it was all he could do to keep from cursing the man aloud. If he was right—and he was—the last thing he needed was the lout drawing attention to him. "I only wanted to thank Harper Ruha for her support."

Ruha raised her kohl-rimmed eyes to the guard and said, "Galaeron will do me no harm."

The soldier regarded her suspiciously for a moment, then nodded gruffly and released Galaeron's shoulder. Ruha looked to Galaeron, and as Alusair and Mourngrym continued their argument in more heated tones, waited.

"Uh, thank you," Galaeron said. It was all he dared say, at least with one of *them* lurking somewhere in the room, eavesdropping on the council and manipulating its mind-slaves. "I'm afraid I lost control of myself."

Ruha knitted her black eyebrows and replied, "Considering what was said, I thought you did well to keep your shadow in check."

Galaeron continued to look at her, trying to think of some other way to convey his suspicions without alerting the one spying upon them.

Irreph and Alduvar were lending their voices to Mourngrym's, protesting that Alusair was wasting the council's valuable time with a meaningless exercise of imagination.

"Galaeron," Ruha asked, "is there something else?"

"No," he said. If only she understood fingertalk; as it was, he was beginning to fear he would have to use his own magic to save the council. "That's all."

Ruha nodded—a bit uncertainly—and turned back to the council.

Galaeron sat fidgeting, lost in his own thoughts, trying to think of some other way to do what was needed. It was easily two months since he had last cast a spell. Surely, he could cast this one, not even a very difficult spell. It was just a simple abjuration to reveal the spy he knew to be lurking somewhere in the council chamber putting words in the mouths of the Dalesmen. Of course, he would need to use shadow magic; he was no longer sure that he even *could* use normal magic, but shadow magic was better against the phaerimm anyway. Normal spells had a tendency to ricochet off their magic-resistant scales, but shadow magic always worked.

The thought of touching the Shadow Weave again sent a shiver of anticipation up through Galaeron's body. He could almost feel the cold power rising through him, quenching a thirst that had been building for two months. One simple spell was not going to do any harm. It would hardly give his shadow self the strength to overpower him completely—not for long anyway—and he had to expose the spy, didn't he? He had to make the council see that the Dalesmen's words were those of the enemy, that the phaerimm were trying to split the alliance—

A day never passed when Galaeron did not find some reason just as compelling to break his vow and reach out to the Shadow Weave. The temptation was always there, always awaiting the weak moment, always inviting him down the dark path, but he had only to remember Vala to resist, to think of her enslaved in Escanor's palace in Shade and imagine the abuse being visited on her nightly in the prince's bed.

It had been Galaeron's shadow self that had persuaded him to abandon her there, that had filled his thoughts with so many bitter suspicions that he had finally surrendered to the darkness and vowed to have vengeance on a woman who had never shown him anything but love. It was a mistake he intended never to repeat, even if it meant his life.

And, with Ruha pledged to prevent him from slipping again, it very well might. She was watching him out of the corner of her eye, her thoughts hidden behind her Bedine veil, but her hand not far from the curved dagger stuck behind her sash.

For the second time in as many minutes, Galaeron wished that the witch understood fingertalk—then realized she didn't need to. He caught her eye then dropped his gaze to his lap, where he was running his fingers through the gestures of the magic he wanted her to cast. Though he was not trying to cast anything, the very act of going through motions filled him with a powerful yearning to open himself to the Shadow Weave.

Ruha's eyes widened, and she looked as though she might reach over to interfere. Galaeron stopped in what would have been mid-casting, then started over again. Ruha seemed to relax. He continued the gesture, being careful to make each element slow and precise so that she would have no trouble deciphering what he was doing. When the glimmer of recognition came to her eye, he stopped and looked down the table in the direction of the Dalesmen, who were now pretending that they did not understand the true nature of Alusair's question.

". . . suppose that *had* the Shadovar tried to free the phaerimm beneath Tarkhaldale, there would have been no problem at all," Mourngrym was saying. "The saurials are far too intelligent to breach the Sharn Wall."

Without using his own magic, Galaeron had no way to be certain the phaerimm spy was anywhere near his mind-slaves, but it seemed like a good place to start. He glanced back and found Ruha studying Mourngrym almost too intently, hands lying in her lap and her veil billowing ever-so-slightly as she whispered her incantation.

"Very well, Lord Mourngrym, you win," Alusair said from her end of the table. "You have made it abundantly clear that the Dalelands have no interest in placing the blame for our troubles anywhere but Evereska. Now, would you care to explain why? I fail to see what you hope to accomplish."

Mourngrym's smile was so wooden it was almost a grimace. "Your Highness, the Dalelands have no interest in blaming anyone. We merely wish to point out—"

He was interrupted by the last syllables of a Bedine incantation as Ruha stood. Using the elemental magic of her native Anauroch, she sprinkled a few drops of water in his direction. A sharp crackle blasted through the chamber, and there was a bright flash near the ceiling above and behind the Dalesmen. Galaeron glimpsed the familiar, thorn-covered shape of a phaerimm's conical body, and the thing was gone, vanished in almost the same instant it appeared.

The chamber broke into a wild tumult of shouting and clanging as guards rushed forward. Several of the envoys—most notably Sembia's Korian Hovanay—dived for cover under the table. Others followed the lead of Piergeiron Paladinson. Grabbing polearms from the guards, they leaped onto the table and began to chink the ceiling in an attempt to find the intruder.

The three Dalesmen remained standing in front of their seats. Their vacant gazes were fixed on the envoys and soldiers closest to them, and they held themselves ready to spring into action.

"Order!" Alusair called. She had produced a sword from somewhere beneath her robe of office and was banging the pommel down on the table's polished surface. "It's gone."

Though the princess's assumption was a natural one—phaerimm usually teleported to safety at the first sign of danger—Galaeron rose.

"Actually, Your Highness, I believe it isn't." He pointed over Mourngrym's shoulder. "I think it's probably somewhere there."

A dozen Purple Dragons immediately rushed to investigate. The three Dalesmen stepped away from the table and closed ranks around a spot not too far from where Galaeron had pointed. Caladnei—the slender, red-haired sorcerer who had replaced addled Vangerdahast as Cormyr's royal magician—stepped into view behind Alusair's chair and leveled her staff at the trio.

Before she could speak the word of command, the phaerimm appeared in the midst of the Dalesmen.

Hold! You have nothing to fear from me—unless you earn it.

Galaeron heard the words inside his mind, and he could tell by the startled reactions of those around him that they had as well. Caladnei held her attack, and the guards settled for surrounding the Dalesmen and leveling their poleaxes in the general direction of the phaerimm. Their restraint, Galaeron knew, probably saved their lives.

Better.

Galaeron saw a familiar blankness come to Ambassador Hovanay's eyes and knew the phaerimm was not repaying its enemies' restraint in kind.

Alusair laid her sword on the table and stared across its length at the intruder.

"This is a private council, worm, and you are our enemy." She glanced over her shoulder and motioned Caladnei toward the creature. "Give me a reason I should not have my guards peel the thorny hide from your viper's flesh."

Because they would fail, the phaerimm replied. *And because even enemies need to confer, if they are ever to be anything else.*

Nasher Alagondar's eyes went vacant.

Galaeron leveled a hand in the phaerimm's direction. "Speak through Mourngrym, or not at all." Then, without looking away, he said to Alusair, "Your Highness, this is how the phaerimm make their mind-slaves. Through their thoughtspeech."

Very perceptive. But you have nothing to fear from us, Galaeron. From what I understand, my people are indebted—

"If you know who I am," Galaeron interrupted, "you know that my magic will kill you as fast as a Shadovar's."

I also know you fear to use it.

"Not as much as I fear becoming your slave," Galaeron said. "Another word within my head, and I will use it."

"Another word in anyone's head, and I will command him to," Alusair added. "If you wish to treat with us, you will release your slaves and speak aloud."

"I cannot do both." This time, the phaerimm's words came from Mourngrym's mouth. "Though once we are finished, I am willing to grant your request."

Alusair's eyes flashed at the word "request," but she held her tongue and looked to Galaeron.

He was tempted to lie and claim that the phaerimm was deceiving her, for he already knew by the tenor of the Dalesmen's earlier arguments what the creature intended. But Alusair had treated him with nothing but courtesy and fairness since the day of his arrival, and—even for the sake of Evereska—he would not repay her with treachery.

"Phaerimm speak to each other through magic winds," Galaeron explained. "With other races, they must use thoughtspeech or an intermediary."

Alusair considered this, then nodded to the phaerimm.

"Very well," she said. "What is it you want?"

"Evereska."

Though the answer was exactly what Galaeron had expected, the impact of hearing it actually spoken aloud was more than he could handle. He started to twist his fingers into a spellcasting—then his arm was forced to his side by the mailed hand of one of the Purple Dragons at his back.

Alusair cast a warning scowl in his direction, then said, "When I give the order, Sir Nihmedu—not before."

"Thank you, Princess," the phaerimm said. Its four arms appeared over the heads of the Dalesmen, spreading outward in what seemed to be a gesture of appreciation. "As I was saying, we and our allies from Anauroch will be content with Evereska and its lands."

This elicited a collective gasp from the envoys—at least those who were not still under the phaerimm's mental control—and even Alusair cocked a brow.

"Evereska is not ours to give," she said.

The noncommittal answer caused a dark anger to rise in Galaeron, and he had to fight it down by closing his eyes and reminding himself of all that Alusair had done on his behalf.

"Nor is it yours to defend," the phaerimm answered through Mourngrym. "All we are suggesting is that you concern yourselves with the Shadovar and leave Evereska to our brothers."

"Then you are not from Anauroch?" Alusair asked. She was stalling, trying to buy time to consider all the ramifications of the phaerimm's proposal. "You are here on behalf of the Myth Drannor phaerimm?"

"The Shadovar have made this the fight of all phaerimm," Mourngrym's voice replied. "Much as they have made it the fight of all the human realms."

"And what do we receive in return?" asked Ambassador Hovanay. The selfish light in his eye made clear that he was free of the phaerimm's influence. That was not, at least for Evereska, necessarily a good thing. "How will you repay us for our help?"

The phaerimm pushed its many-fanged mouth over the shoulders of the Dalesmen and said, "A better question would be what will *you* receive for *our* help."

Hovanay waited expectantly, and the phaerimm swung its mouth in Alusair's direction.

"Your enemy is our enemy," the phaerimm said. "Should your alliance strike a bargain with us, it would be in our interest to stop the melting of the High Ice. Your realms would be able to rebuild their armies and feed their people. They would be strong again."

Though every sinew in Galaeron was screaming for him to leap to his feet and denounce the phaerimm as a fraud and a liar, he knew he would win nothing by such a display. The humans would believe—rightly enough—that he was only trying to protect Evereska's interests, that he would claim such a thing whether the phaerimm could be trusted or not. Instead, he had to speak reasonably and make the humans see the pitfalls for themselves, make them realize that by selling out the elves, they would be selling themselves out as well.

"You are promising a lot," Galaeron said, not quite able to keep the quaver out of his voice, "but I've seen the Shadovar magic, and it is not defeated easily. If you can do what you promise, why do you need the humans at all? Why are your cousins still trapped inside the shadowshell?"

Instead of answering Galaeron, the phaerimm had Mourngrym turn to address Korian Hovanay again.

"We would pledge to leave your caravans in peace, even to protect them when it is in our power."

This brought a grin to the Sembian's lips, if to no one else's.

Piergeiron Paladinson said, "You have not spoken to Galaeron's point. If the phaerimm can do what you claim, why does the shadowshell still stand?"

"Because, as you yourselves learned at Tilverton, the Shadovar are formidable enemies," the phaerimm said. "We who are free are too few to prevail, and those who are trapped in the Shaeradim are weak and starving. When the shadowshell falls, that will change."

"So you say," Piergeiron said.

"So we will prove," the phaerimm replied. "You are familiar with the peak Untrivvin, in the east of the High Ice?"

"Where the tomb tappers rise," said Borg Ohlmak, the woolly-headed chieftain sent by the barbarians of the Ride. "We know the place well."

Mourngrym's head nodded to Borg. "There are three shadow blankets at the base of the mount. When the shell falls, we will destroy all three as proof of our capabilities."

"And still we will not be able to come to terms," Alusair said. "Evereska is not ours to bargain away. Wouldn't some other place serve you as well? The Goblin Marches, for instance, are—"

"Worthless wastelands," the phaerimm said. "It must be Evereska. We have no interest in your castoff barrens."

"Then perhaps the Tun Valley," Alusair suggested. "The lands there are as fertile as any in Cormyr, and I'm certain the alliance would be willing to provide any assistance required to take Darkhold."

"Evereska."

Alusair frowned, clearly trying to think of some other place the phaerimm might desire. She was, Galaeron knew, trying to reach an unreachable compromise. The phaerimm wanted Evereska for the same reason they lived in Myth Drannor: its mythal. They needed magic the way other races needed air, and the mythals that surrounded both cities were living mantles of woven magic. Asking a phaerimm to choose another place to live was like asking a fish to make his home someplace other than in the water.

"Evereska is not ours to grant," Alusair continued, still trying. "Name another place."

"He's not going to name another place," Galaeron interjected, though he did not say why. The existence of the mythal was an elven secret, and he no longer felt any trust for the humans gathered there, not even Alusair. "When will you learn? You can't treat with phaerimm—only surrender to them like cowards, or stand and fight them like warriors."

Alusair's head snapped around to glare at him, her eyes furious and black.

"And when will you learn, elf, that it is not wise to call someone a coward when it is her people's blood that must be shed to save that of yours?"

Allowing no opportunity for a reply, Alusair glanced at the guards behind Galaeron's chair and said, "I have heard enough from him."

One Purple Dragon pinned Galaeron's arms to his chair, and the other covered his mouth with a waist sash. A sinister voice whispered to Galaeron that Alusair had betrayed him and would seal the bargain by turning him over to the phaerimm, but he was wise enough not to struggle. The Steel Regent was famous for her fiery temper, and though some part of him knew she would never do as his shadow's voice suggested, he did not think she would hesitate to have him thrown in a very deep, dark dungeon.

Alusair nodded her approval, then turned back to the phaerimm and said, "You were about to name a place it is in the alliance's power to grant."

"Evereska," Mourngrym's mouth said again. "There is no other place. The elf is right about that much."

Alusair sank back in exasperation.

Through its mind-slave, the phaerimm said, "You have until the third blanket vanishes."

The creature drifted out from behind its shield of Dalesmen, and ignoring the ring of guards around it, panicked Borg Ohlmak and Nasher Alagondar by floating to their end of the table.

"We expect your assent by then."

Alusair's eyes hardened. "And if we do not give it?"

The phaerimm braced two of its arms on the table.

You will.

Alusair sat bolt upright and started to order the guards forward, but the phaerimm had already vanished.

Mourngrym and his fellow Dalesmen cried out in bewildered voices, then stumbled toward the nearest chairs, their hands trembling and their mouths hanging agape. The Purple Dragons looked to Caladnei for orders while the royal magician busied herself casting detection magic. The envoys sat in their chairs looking alternately relieved and uncertain as they considered the wisdom of betraying Evereska.

After a moment, Alusair brought order back to the chamber by turning to her royal magician.

"Can you tell me how that spy came to be in here?" It was a deft maneuver, turning the envoys' thoughts from the phaerimm's proposal to the threat it had displayed in its arrogant use of its power. "It could have killed us all!"

Caladnei paled and shook her head.

"The chamber is warded against invisibility, teleportation, scrying—"

"Obviously, it was not," Alusair interrupted. Still determined to keep the envoys' thoughts on the how of the phaerimm's presence rather than the why—no doubt buying time to gather her own thoughts on the matter—she looked to Galaeron. "Perhaps Sir Nihmedu can explain how it was done?"

When the guard lowered the sash covering Galaeron's mouth, he glanced around the council table and saw—or at least his shadow saw—guilty expressions on every face.

"Galaeron?" Alusair prodded.

No longer able to ignore the outrage rising in his breast, Galaeron glowered at the princess.

"You truly expect an answer?" he asked.

"Why shouldn't I?"

"Because I am no traitor to my people," Galaeron said. "I would never aid allies to the phaerimm."

An indignant drone filled the chamber, but the expression that came to Alusair's face was less anger than surrender.

"Leave us," she said.

The envoys fell silent and began to look to one another, waiting for someone else to take the lead and either object or start the withdrawal.

"Now!" Alusair said. "We will discuss the phaerimm tomorrow, when we have all had a chance to see whether we can strike such a bargain and still sleep at night."

The envoys rose in a bustle of scraping chair legs and sharp remarks and departed, leaving only Caladnei, Ruha, and a dozen Purple Dragons in the room with Galaeron and Alusair. The princess motioned them all toward the door.

"You, too," she said, standing and starting down the table toward Galaeron. "I am in no danger here."

Though their faces clearly showed their displeasure, the others knew better than to question Alusair's ability to take care of herself. They followed the envoys into the anteroom.

When they were gone, Alusair sat down at Galaeron's side and clamped a well-callused hand on his slender knee. Though she was not squeezing, he could feel strength enough in her grasp that, had she wished, she could have broken his bones.

"Elf, what am I to do with you?" she asked. "You are your own worst enemy . . . and yet, I can't say things would have turned out any differently if you were not."

Galaeron's heart fell.

"Then you are going to betray Evereska?"

"No, not Cormyr. That I promise," Alusair said. "But I'm afraid we won't be helping, either."

"You're leaving us on our own?"

Alusair looked across the chamber and said, "I didn't really think it would be possible to negotiate Evereska's safety, but . . ." She let the sentence trail off, then shook her head and turned to look at Galaeron again. "Diplomacy is the art of the possible, Galaeron—and there's nothing we can do. You must know that."

A surge of dark anger started to rise in Galaeron, but it was not difficult to fight down. He did know. Alusair was telling him the truth, and that was what friends did in circumstances like these. He took her hands.

"I know. Thank you." He glanced toward the door, then added, "It was Alduvar Snowbrand."

Alusair frowned in confusion. "Alduvar?"

"Who dispelled Caladnei's wards," Galaeron said. "The Dalesmen were already mind-slaves when they arrived, and the phaerimm knew they were the last ones you'd expect treachery from. He came in first and dispelled the wards, and the phaerimm came in between the other two."

Alusair raised her brow.

Galaeron nodded, but did not bother to explain further. When it came to the phaerimm, he just . . . knew. It was a little gift from a Shadovar he had known once.

"Well, thanks," Alusair said with a smile, then leaned over and kissed him—hard, and on the lips. "You watch yourself. I'm going to miss you."

CHAPTER TWO

10 Flamerule, the Year of Wild Magic

Beyond the shadowshell, Takari Moonsnow saw only dark forms—nebulous disks and hazy pillars that could be monster or mineral, that could be beholders and bugbears or boulders and broken blocks of stone.

They never appeared to move, which favored the inanimate, but whenever she glanced away for a moment and looked back the shapes were in different places. That favored the animate—the sinister, even, and the dangerous. Providing, of course, that the change was not just her imagination playing tricks on her. Reconnoitering through the shadowshell was like peering through an obsidian window. She could tell that something lay on the other side, but what it might be was anyone's guess.

Takari cursed and started back toward camp, her flesh warming in the hot Anauroch sun as she moved away from the shell's icy darkness behind. According to the latest news from within the Shaeradim, a trio of phaerimm had been seen several days before herding an army of mind-slaves in Takari's direction. Unfortunately, that was all anyone knew. Spying on the phaerimm was invariably lethal, so every report from inside came at a steep price.

Nor could the high mages sent by Evermeet scry the information. While the phaerimm's deadwall had long since fallen victim to the Shadovar shadowshell, the shadowshell itself remained strong enough to turn any spell on itself. Fortunately, the Chosen's ability to hear their names spoken anywhere on Faerûn had returned with the fall of the deadwall—apparently because the Shadovar had not thought to weave their shell against the god-gifted abilities of the Chosen. Khelben Arunsun and Laeral Silverhand, who remained trapped with Evereska's besieged defenders, were able to relay messages out through Storm Silverhand or another of the Chosen.

Takari reached the field where her reconnaissance company was camped and found it in a bustle, with wood elves strapping on armor, stringing bows, and rushing to assemble at the gathering circle. Her second-in-command, a sloe-eyed male with a sinewy build and a shad-mouthed grin, rushed up to her with their helms and battle cloaks in hand.

"What is it, Wagg?" Takari asked, taking her cloak from him and swinging it around her shoulders. "Shadovar?"

Wagg—actually Wizzle Bendriver, but everyone called him Wagg because he shook his head whenever he smiled, frowned, or spoke—shook his head.

"Lord Ramealaerub has issued the call." He waved a helm over her shoulder, toward the shadowshell, and said, "He thinks it's coming down."

Takari closed the throat clasp of her cloak and turned to find that the black shadowshell had faded to gray-blue. Even from a hundred paces away, the barrier was unbelievably immense, a dark wall stretching beyond the horizon in both directions, the curve of its dome imperceptible as it climbed higher into the air than she could see. Before her eyes, the gray-blue shell faded to just gray. She began to see the terraced crests of the hills of the Desert Border South and looming beyond, the unmistakable crags of the High Shaeradim.

Just inside the fading shell, a broad ridge rose gently away from the desert, snaking its way deep into the foothills before ascending to a high mesa that would serve as the elven army's first staging ground inside the Shaeradim. Takari was relieved to see that the foot of the ridge lay directly in front of her company's campsite. When suggesting campsites to Lord Ramealaerub, she had been forced to recall the terrain inside the shadowshell from memory and guess at good staging points for each arm of the elven advance. That her own company was in proper position meant the others would be, too.

Takari took her war helm from Wagg and with a sigh put the thing on her head. It was one of those gaudy—some would say ornate—pieces of armor made by Gold elves. Gilded in silver and trimmed in gold, it was as heavy as a rock and about as comfortable. A circle of Evermeet's high mages had bestowed on it several useful enchantments, including their most powerful mind-guarding magic and the ability to stay in constant contact with her commander.

Wagg snickered. "You look like a bandit bird—only louder and uglier."

"That's not all bad. Maybe now you'll stop begging me to play night games."

"You're going to wear that awful thing at night?"

"And so are you." Takari pointed at Wagg's helm, then at his head. "The phaerimm don't care when they take their mind-slaves."

Wagg frowned. Shaking his head, he sneered at the adornments hammered into the metal.

"Ships," he grumbled. "It's always ships and sails with that bunch. What's wrong with a few trees?"

"Who knows?" Takari was as genuinely puzzled as her deputy. "Maybe they don't *have* trees on Evermeet."

"You think?"

Wagg's eyes widened at this frightening thought, and Takari shrugged.

The shadowshell had faded from gray to a transparent damson, and it had become more of a struggle to see the flickering barrier than the terrain behind it. Takari saw nothing but boulders, and scattered across the hillside, leafless smokethorn trees and the withered silhouettes of a few spiny soapleafs. The soapleafs she would have to watch. In the two decades she had spent patrolling the Desert Border South with Galaeron Nihmedu and his Tomb Guards, she had never seen one this close to Anauroch.

When Takari didn't see anything else of interest, she turned her thoughts inward and activated her helm's sending magic by picturing Lord Ramealaerub's stern face.

"Lord High Commander," she said.

The image in her mind grew more substantial, assuming the scowling visage of a sharp-featured Gold elf with a dagger-thin nose and eyebrows arched as sharply as ship keels.

Moonsnow, the Gold elf said, his words echoing in her mind. *I was beginning to think something had happened to you.*

"I was at the shadowshell, milord." Takari glanced at Wagg and rolled her eyes. Ramealaerub was a typical Gold, full of himself and the way things ought to be. "Looking for those mind-slaves Khelben warned us about."

Ramealaerub's expression grew impatient.

And?

"I couldn't see a thing, Milord." Annoyed by his attitude, Takari was not going to make anything easy on him. "That was before the shadowshell fell. Everything was too dark."

The shell is not dark now, Ramealaerub said.

"But now I'm back with my company." Takari's tone was innocent. "Didn't you call us to arms?"

A storm cloud came over Ramealaerub's face. Irritated, he said something to someone beside him then composed himself and turned back to Takari.

Moonsnow, the Lady of the Wood and I agreed that the wood elves would serve as the army's reconnaissance company. Though Ramealaerub's eyes looked as though they were about to pop free of their sockets, he spoke in a deliberately patient tone that suggested he did not realize how Takari was playing with him. *Would you be kind enough to take your elves and see if there is any sign of the enemy?*

"Of course—all you had to do was ask." Takari was beginning to worry that Ramealaerub truly did not understand that she was playing a game with him. If so, that did not bode well for the elven army. "But I can tell you already they know we're here."

You can see them?

He was worried.

"Not exactly," Takari said. "It's the trees."

The trees?

"A few shouldn't be here, this close to the sand," Takari explained.

At least Ramealaerub was enough of an elf to understand what that meant.

He grew thoughtful, then asked, *Which ones?*

"The soapleafs," Takari said. "They're the—"

I know what a soapleaf is, Moonsnow.

He looked away and spoke to someone else, then returned to her.

We have a few here, but not enough to slow us down. They're probably just sentries.

"Probably," Takari said, "but with the phaerimm, you can never—"

That's why you need to secure our flank, he said. *We'll be going in fast and hard, but once the shadowshell comes down there's no telling how long it will take the phaerimm to regain their strength. You must stay ahead of us—and let me know when you run into problems.*

"Oh, is *that* what a reconnaissance company does?"

I mean it, Moonsnow, Ramealaerub said. *Toy with me if you like, but not with your mission. You know better than any of us how quickly this can turn into a disaster.*

Maybe this Lord High Commander did have more sense than Evermeet's previous generals.

Takari gave him a coquettish smile and said, "Lord Ramealaerub, I can't imagine why you think I've been toying with you."

She glanced toward the shadowshell and, seeing that it had faded to transparent shimmer, she said, "We'll cross over as soon as we can. If you don't hear from me every quarter hour . . . consider *that* an alarm."

Very sensible, Ramealaerub answered. *And Moonsnow, do try to avoid getting yourself killed. You're the only scout who really knows this part of the Shaeradim.*

Ramealaerub's image vanished from her mind, and Takari turned to find her company waiting at the gathering circle. Though all of the rangers had fastened their battle cloaks and strung their bows, not one had donned the gaudy war helms sent by Evermeet. Most of the helms lay tossed on the ground, and some were being used as footrests or stools.

Takari tapped her own helm and said, "Put 'em on."

"But they're ugly," complained Jysela Whitebark.

"And heavy," added Grimble Oakorn.

Takari shrugged and said, "Suit yourselves, but tell me now what you want done when the phaerimm make mind-slaves of you. Would you rather be killed or let them stick you with an egg?"

There was a scramble for the helms. Takari waited for them to go on, then explained their mission and led the way along a well-beaten trail to what had been the shadowshell. No sign of the barrier remained. The path just ended, and few paces later the rocky slope of their ridge emerged from the sand and began to rise in a jumble of boulders and barren ground toward the distant peaks of the High Shaeradim.

Takari dug into the sand until she found a pebble. Half-expecting it to vanish in a flare of darkness as had the hundreds of others she had tossed through the shadowshell, she threw it as hard as she could.

The stone clattered to the ground thirty paces up the ridge.

She studied the pebble for a moment, not quite able to believe that it had actually landed in the Shaeradim, then turned to her company. They were standing together looking nervous and a little frightened.

"After all this waiting, I guess expected something more somehow."

"I'm just happy it didn't melt or something," Wagg said.

As Wagg spoke, Takari began to speak in fingertalk, her hands issuing silent instructions that were being studied much more attentively than her deputy's ramblings.

"From what you've said about these Shadovar," Wagg continued, "I didn't think it would just disappear. I was sure it was going to explode or something and kill us all."

"Then I thank Rillifane Rallathil you were wrong," Takari said. Her fingers continued to weave commands, warning her warriors to be wary of other things aside from soapleafs. "This job is harder than I bargained for as it is."

Now! she signaled.

Nocking arrows as they moved, the company scattered and loosed. The shafts flew over Takari's head with a low droning whistle, and the slope behind her erupted into pained squeals and strange gurgling howls. She turned.

Where the soapleafs had been a moment earlier, she found half a dozen illithids collapsing to the ground, their bodies peppered with arrows and their mouth tentacles writhing in anguish.

The rest of the slope remained as still as before.

Nocking an arrow in her own bow, Takari dropped into a crouch and rushed forward. Taking cover behind the first boulder she came to, she scratched the surface with the tip of her arrow to make certain it really was a boulder, then looked left and right down the foot of the ridge. Camouflaged as they were by the magic of their battle cloaks, it took a few moments to find the nearest members of her company hiding behind boulders similar to hers. She did not attempt a head count. With the company spread across the width of the entire ridge, she would have been hard-pressed to find them all even had they been standing on tiptoe and waving their arms.

She envisioned her company waiting in the gathering circle a few moments earlier, then whispered, "Reconnaissance company, anything to report?"

When no reply came, she breathed a sigh of relief, then reported their progress to Lord Ramealaerub. He congratulated her on her success, informing her that the moon elves protecting the other flank were advancing as well, then reminded her that the main body of the army would start its advance in five minutes and urged her to keep moving. Takari bit back a sour reply and gave the order to ascend the ridge in two waves, each covering the other as it advanced.

Grimble Oakorn—her partner in this tactic—emerged from behind a boulder thirty paces to her right and raced another thirty paces ahead before ducking back into cover. Takari quickly left her own hiding pace, and weaving erratically to make herself a difficult target, ran sixty paces before finally kneeling behind the big trunk of a dead smokethorn. It was hard work, especially with the hot Anauroch sun beating down on the heavy helm she wore. Sweat began to trickle over her brow.

There was a three-second pause before Grimble and the others in the first wave emerged from new hiding places. Only fools left cover in the same place they entered it, and wood elf scouts were not fools. They raced sixty paces uphill and dropped back into cover. Takari and the second wave crawled to new starting points and rushed up the slope.

The depredations of the strange war had reduced this desert wonderland to a dismal ghost of its former self, leaving hundreds of smokethorns strewn across the hillside, their trunks snapped off at the base or their root-fan ripped whole from the rocky ground. The trees that remained standing were naked and bare, their dagger-shaped leaves scattered around their bases like withered gray skirts. Even the tough thorn-brambles, which seemed to flourish best in ground that was more rock than dirt and blossomed only in the worst of droughts, were withered and drooping, their tiny leaves brittle and brown.

The sight filled Takari with a cold anger, and not only because it pained her to see the Shaeradim defiled by war. The two decades she had spent patrolling the area with Galaeron Nihmedu had been the happiest of her life—even if he had spent the entire time refusing to acknowledge their spirit-bond—and the sight of the land withering away reminded her that her memories were also fading, that eventually she would be left only with the dry fact of the matter: that she had been a Tomb Guard on the Desert Border South and she had been in love with her prince. But the love itself—the simple joy of being always near him, the flutter that had stirred in her heart with his every smile—that would be gone, carried off by war and as lost to her as Galaeron himself.

Takari lost count of the times she and Grimble took turns rushing up the slope, but her breath began to come in ragged gasps, and her hair grew so sweaty it made squishing sounds under the helm. She kneeled behind a broken boulder and wiped her eyes on the shoulder of her cloak, then watched the slope above as Grimble raced ahead and kneeled behind a fallen smokethorn. His battle cloak turned the same pearly gray as the bark, a pair of streaks across his shoulders matching a band of furrows in the trunk. Half wishing she had picked a slower partner, Takari scrambled across the broken ground on all fours, emerged from behind a square boulder, and began her dash.

Takari had taken no more than three steps before her eye was drawn back to Grimble's hiding place. His cloak had turned dark and dappled, and so had his hair, ears, and boot soles—all she could see from behind. As she drew nearer, she could see that both he and his cloak seemed oddly rigid and were covered with tiny flecks of black and red.

Takari dropped behind a knee-high outcropping ten paces below Grimble, then used her helm to call the company to a halt. Without looking out from behind her cover, she pictured Grimble's handsome face.

"Grimble?" she whispered.

There was no reply.

Takari's pulse began to pound in her ears—just when she really needed to hear. She closed her eyes, set her weapons aside, and took a few calming breaths. When the noise finally died away, she picked up a good-sized rock, and rising from behind her outcropping, threw it at Grimble's back.

It struck with a stony clink.

Takari dropped back into her hiding place and activated her helm's sending magic.

"Reconnaissance company, watch yourselves. We're under attack—something turned Grimble into a statue."

Wyeka, too, Wagg whispered. *Didn't see what happened.*

"Me either," Takari answered. "Anybody?"

No one reported anything. Takari was not all that surprised. The phaerimm cast their spells entirely with their thoughts—no gestures or words required—and the eye-magic of their beholder servants was just as silent.

"We need to figure out where this is coming from," Takari said. She lifted her head just high enough to peer over the outcropping. "I'm just below Grimble, and I can see half a dozen good places to hide, starting with a clump of daggerhedge off to the left and ending with a three-boulder pile on the right."

I'm even with Wyeka, Wagg said through her helm. *I can't see the daggerhedge on the left, only the roots of the overturned smokethorn.*

"Then it's somewhere between the roots and the boulder pile," Takari said. "Everyone who can't see that keep advancing and circle a—"

Wait. An image of Alaya Thistledew's rosy-nosed face came to Takari's mind along with her voice. *Something's hissing. Maybe it's nothing, but I'll take—*

Her image vanished from Takari's mind.

"Alaya?"

Turned to rock, said Alaya's partner, Rosl Harp.

Though the two were lovers, Rosl didn't sound overly frantic. With a hundred battle wizards and three circles of high mages in the elven army, there were worse things that could happen to a warrior than being turned to stone.

It got her when she looked around the boulder, he continued. *She couldn't have seen any of the cover you were talking about.*

It's moving around, then, Wagg said.

You mean walking *around,* Rosl said, his voice coming to Takari's mind as a barely audible whisper.

"You're sure?" Takari asked. "Phaerimm float. Beholders, too."

I hear it, Rosl said. *Moving away.*

"A lot of feet?" Takari asked. She was beginning to think she knew what they were facing. "Maybe a tail dragging?"

Sounds like it, Rosl said. *I can't see anything, though.*

Takari rolled her eyes and replied, "You might have to risk a look, Rosl."

I am looking, Rosl spat. *I can't see anything but rocks and . . .*

"It's invisible!" Takari and Rosl reached this conclusion at the same time, then Takari asked, "You're sure you're behind it?"

I'm sure, Rosl said. *What do you think I am, a human? Be ready to cover, everyone. I'll do a cast-and-run.*

Rosl's voice vanished as he prepared his spell. Takari looked to her right. Fifty paces away, Wagg was turning in Rosl's direction, his bow slung across his back so his hands would be free to use his own magic. Though Takari could see none of the other scouts, she knew that everyone within two hundred paces of Rosl's position would be doing the same.

She was just beginning to wonder what was taking so long when a spark of silver cracked down the slope from somewhere above and flashed out of existence. An instant later, a low boom rumbled across the ridge.

"Rosl?" Takari asked.

He's down, Jysela Whitebark, appearing in Takari's mind, said. Her copper-colored eyes were opened wide in shock and horror. *Lightning bolt, I think. It wasn't that powerful. He's still smoking, and alive enough to be thrashing around.*

"Did you see where it came from?" Takari asked.

Jysela shook her head. Though she was undoubtedly the closest elf to Rosl, she did not volunteer—and Takari did not suggest—going to his aid. Their unseen attacker was waiting for just that, and Jysela would only have ended up lying on the ground beside him.

Moonsnow? Lord Ramealaerub's sharp features appeared in Takari's mind. *We heard a bang.*

"We've run into trouble," Takari reported. "An invisible basilisk, I think, and something protecting it."

Just one protector?

"Possibly."

Probably. Gwynanael Tahtrel and her rangers are having trouble with a phaerimm on the other flank. It keeps falling back, fighting to delay the advance. We think they're trying to buy time to recover their magic. You can't let that happen.

"Easily said, milord," Takari replied. "Not so easily done. We don't even know where it's at."

Find out, Ramealaerub ordered. *We're moving into the valley now, and we need you to stay ahead of us.*

"We're taking casualties. . . ."

And you'll continue to take them until you eliminate the problem! Ramealaerub's voice softened when he added, *You're a reconnaissance company, Moonsnow. You're supposed to take casualties. Move up.*

The Lord High Commander's face vanished, leaving Takari's curses to fall on no ears but her own. She peered over her outcropping and studied the slope above but could find no hint of where their attacker might be lurking. Were she the one up there, she would be hiding in the dark cavities within the boulder pile, but she was not. She was not even of the same race. She was an elf, and they were . . . she had no idea what they were facing. It was rare that beholders used lightning bolts, but the attacker could easily be a mind-slave from Evereska or Laeral Silverhand's relief army. Or it might be a phaerimm, as Gwynanael and her moon elves were facing.

Takari found no hints on the slope above.

She pictured Jysela in her mind and said, "Jysela, can you . . . ?"

When her memory of the face did not coalesce into a solid image, Takari realized there was no one there and let the sentence drop. She felt bile burning her throat and tried to swallow it back down. It returned two breaths later.

Hoping her voice did not sound too shaky, she had the entire company report by name. Only Jysela was missing, but as she took the roll call, the basilisk—or whatever it was—turned another scout to stone. Ramealaerub was right about one thing, at least. Hiding in the rocks was not going to spare them any casualties.

"I'm afraid we have to do this like the Golds would," Takari announced.

You mean a charge? Wagg asked.

More accustomed to hunting than fighting, wood elves preferred stealth and ambush to speed and ferocity—especially when speed and ferocity meant charging into the teeth of the enemy's defense.

"Advance in two waves," Takari clarified, "and keep a careful watch up that slope. There isn't much point in this if we don't see where the enemy's hiding. First line, go!"

The first wave had barely left their hiding places before another bolt of lightning crackled down the slope. This one was a little stronger than the first, loud enough that Takari actually felt the crack in the pit of her stomach. It struck about a hundred paces away, just close enough that she saw it blast one of her scouts off his feet. The injured elf's partner left her hiding place to help and was instantly struck by a flight of golden bolts of magic.

Both attacks came from somewhere far to the right of the ridge. Takari focused her attention in that direction but did not bother bringing her arrow to her cheek. Even if the angle were good—and it was not—she still had only a vague idea of where to aim.

The rest of the wave advanced only ten paces before the enemy struck again, this time with a lightning bolt powerful enough that the tip blasted through the victim's body and came out the other side. To Takari, it seemed that the flash had danced down the jagged ridge crest on the far right side, but she still failed to catch exactly where it had come from.

The elves managed another dozen paces before Takari finally saw a ball of red flame appear in the middle of a small cliff's jagged silhouette and streak over the ridge crest to strike a target somewhere beyond. She started to call the location out over her helm, but then a steady stream of dark shafts started to fly back toward the cliff, and she knew the target had been found.

Not that it did them a lot of good. By the time the first wave finished its leg of the advance and began dropping behind cover, an elf in the second wave had been turned to stone by the basilisk, and the hidden attacker had slain yet another in the first.

Each attack seemed just a little more powerful than the last, and Takari didn't think it was only because the victims kept moving closer. The lightning cracked more loudly, the magic bolts grew more numerous, the balls of fire grew larger and burned more brightly. The Weave was repairing itself in the Shaeradim, and as it did so, the enemy was growing stronger.

Their attacker had to be a phaerimm.

Takari's turn to advance came. She crawled a few paces on her hands and knees, then started up the slope at a run. As with the first wave, a lightning bolt lashed down the slope the instant they rose and blasted Yaveen Greeneedle—Takari's closest friend from Rheitheillaethor—into scorched pieces. Takari screamed, not only for Yaveen, but for all of the company's lost elves. These were more than the scouts she had trained to fight phaerimm. These were her childhood friends, her dancing partners and would-be lovers, the sons and daughters of parents who had begged her to bring their children home safe. Each time one died, a little of her died with them, but there was nothing to be done about it except kill the phaerimm and lose more friends doing it.

By the time Takari's wave was ready to find cover, she had lost three more friends. She was also close enough to their attacker to see that it had hidden itself in a rift in the cliff face. Her company's arrows were ricocheting off the opening one after the other, no doubt because the occupant had sealed the crevice with a missile guard and spell shield so it could watch over its invisible pet from safety. A crooked line of elven statues was angling up the slope toward the left side of the ridge, where the attacker's view would soon be blocked by the lip of its own hiding place.

The phaerimm was sending the basilisk to guard its flank. Like Ramealaerub, it was worried about what it could not see.

Again, the first wave of elves rose to renew their charge, and again the phaerimm took one of their number the instant he left cover, sending a ball of fire smoking and hissing into a big smokethorn tree. Young Harla Elmworm came staggering out of the conflagration, engulfed in flames and screaming in agony.

The spells were coming faster, a sure sign that the enemy was recovering all too quickly.

The attack on Harla was also a sign, Takari realized, that her company's camouflage was of little use against this foe. Phaerimm could literally see magic, and given all the magic her scouts were wearing they had to be about as obvious to the enemy as a lantern in the Underdark.

Takari activated her helm's sending magic and said, "Company halt! Find good cover and take it. Here's what I want you to do . . ."

As she explained her plan, Takari was unclasping her cloak and removing her boots, slipping off her rings and bracers, and shedding everything else that carried the faintest dweomer of magic. By the time she was finished, she was stripped down to her leather armor and not much more.

"I'll try to be fast," she finished. "Just keep the enemy's attention focused on you until you see me on top of the cliff, and in the name of the Leaflord, if you hear that basilisk creeping up behind you, don't look! Just fling a magic bolt at the sound and run the other way. I'm sure our good Lord High Commander thinks he has better uses for his battle wizards than turning us all back into people."

The last thing Takari removed was her helm. She bundled it with her cloak and other magic. Wagg and a dozen others began to pelt the phaerimm's hiding place with blasting spells, and the rest of the company began to crawl—very slowly and very cautiously—toward the rift.

The phaerimm countered by targeting its own spells at those advancing on its hiding place. Though scouts took care to stay behind solid cover as much as possible, their enemy was a deadly one, and all too many of its spells struck home.

When Takari judged the assault to be blinding enough, she stood and raced up the hill in her bare feet, carrying no magic at all and little else aside from her weapons. Twenty steps later, a solemn-faced wood elf startled Takari by suddenly falling in at her side. He was a century or two older than Takari, and like her he was stripped down to armor and weapons.

Takari cocked a brow and said, "This is a job for one, Yurne. Two only doubles the risk of being noticed."

"You hear me coming?"

"No," Takari admitted.

"Well, then."

Yurne took the lead, and that was the end of the matter. One of the hermit elves who lived alone in the depths of High Forest, Yurne had wandered into Rheitheillaethor after the reconnaissance company had completed its training and announced he would be coming along. Lord Ramealaerub's officer had made the mistake of suggesting it was too late then promptly found his sleeve pinned to a tree by one of Yurne's throwing daggers. The hermit had stepped over very close and began to quote the officer's lessons word by word, then asked the sputtering Gold what business he had leading a company of wood elf scouts when he could not even tell when he was training one.

After that, no one ever dared tell Yurne what he could or could not do, and a steady chorus of Green elf snickers had driven the affronted Gold elf back to the main army where he belonged. Lord Ramealaerub had transferred command of the company to Takari—who, as a ranger in Galaeron Nihmedu's Tomb Guard patrol, was the only one in the group with any experience that could be considered remotely military.

The conflagration outside the phaerimm's hiding place continued at no small cost in elf lives as Takari and Yurne ascended the slope. As soon as they were higher than the phaerimm's hiding place, Takari dropped to her haunches and, determined to put an end to the costly spell battle as quickly as possible, began to creep toward the little cliff.

Yurne continued up the hill, and Takari flashed an order for him to follow, but he did not see her fingertalk—or chose to ignore it—and proceeded as before. She cursed the hermit's stubbornness and resumed her advance, until she recalled the ease with which he had spied on the reconnaissance company during their training.

Takari cursed the hermit again, this time for his reticence, and followed him up the slope.

Several minutes later, they dropped to all fours and crept across the slope to a fallen smokethorn about twenty paces above the little cliff. They spent a few moments studying the rift from above, though Takari could see nothing in its depths except the constant flash of battle magic.

Yurne closed his eyes and began to sniff the air, and she finally understood why the hermit had insisted on approaching from above. There was not much of a breeze, but what there was came up the slope from Anauroch's hot sands.

Takari could smell nothing but the stench of brimstone and charred flesh, but Yurne's nose was more discerning. Eyes widening, he dropped behind the smokethorn and began to fingertalk in the clumsy gestures of one who seldom practiced the art.

Mime flamer guard!

Mind flayer? Takari asked. *An illithid?*

Yes! The gesture was sharp. *That's wham I seed!*

Where?

How should I nose? I smelled it, not seam it.

Takari peered over the log and saw only rock and dead scrub brush, though that meant nothing. The illithid could be in hiding or simply invisible, and using a spell to find it would be like shouting their presence to the phaerimm. On the other hand, the spell battle was continuing unabated and had diverted the attention of the sentry as well as that of the master. Takari dropped back behind the log.

Anything else down there we can't see? she signed.

A hare, paralyzed by fear, Yurne answered. *Nodding else.*

Really? Takari raised her brow. *That's some nose you have.*

Why do you thing I lib alone?

Recalling what a hundred wood elves could smell like after three days of drinking and dancing, Takari made a face and nodded her understanding, then turned to the matter at hand.

I don't think the illithid has noticed us. We need to keep it that way, or the phaerimm will just teleport up the hill and keep attacking.

You have a plant?

Takari nodded and explained her idea.

I lick it, Yurne said. *Except the captain shouldn't go first.*

With that, he slipped over the smokethorn's trunk and crawled down the slope, moving so quickly and gracefully that Takari barely had time to ready her bow before he was at the rift. He dropped to his belly and peered over the edge, doing a convincing job of pretending not to know there was an illithid lurking somewhere nearby. When nothing happened, he rose to a knee and took his bow from his shoulder.

Still lying behind the smokethorn, Takari nocked two arrows on her bow and began to regret she had not tried a more direct plan. Had they just rushed the rift, they would have been attacking by then. The phaerimm might even be dead. Apparently, the illithid's attention remained focused on the battle, and it was unaware—

Yurne gurgled in pain, then let the bow slip from his hands and reached for his head. Takari remained utterly motionless, quietly searching for the source of the attack. She found no hint. The illithid remained as invisible as before, with no telltale footsteps or shuddering bramble twigs to give away his location. Yurne's eyes went blank, and he began to crawl around on his knees, holding his temples and groaning incoherently.

There was a one-sided lull as the phaerimm ceased spellcasting long enough to consult with its minion telepathically, then the conflagration resumed even more fiercely than before. Takari bit her lip and tried to avoid thinking about how many of her friends were dying while she lay there hiding. If the phaerimm was worried enough about its own safety to use invisibility magic so powerful it would keep an attacker hidden, it was worried enough to pick a guard who would not make foolish mistakes.

A seeming eternity later, Yurne lowered his hands and began to shake his head clear. The illithid remained hidden, at least until the hermit stumbled upon his discarded bow. Apparently forgetting he still had a full quiver hanging from his shoulder, he began to search the ground for an arrow he had never drawn. A bramble twig fluttered ten paces behind him, and Yurne's head snapped back as an invisible hand grabbed his hair and jerked him over backward.

That was all the target Takari needed. Rolling to her knees in one swift motion, she set her aim just behind Yurne's head and let fly.

The arrows were still in the air as she leaped over the smokethorn and charged down the hill. The shafts thumped to a stop behind Yurne, in what appeared to be empty air. A cascade of dark blood erupted around the heads of the arrows and poured down on the scout's head. He screamed and rolled away as Takari jumped over him, her bow discarded ten steps up the hill and her sword and dagger already in hand.

A huge mouth filled with fangs and ringed by four thin arms was just rising out of the rift and turning toward the fallen illithid.

Takari knew better than to hesitate. She simply lowered her head and dived past the fangs, slashing and hacking as the thing's dark mouth rose around her. Her sword slashed through something sinuous and tough, then her dagger sank into a mound of ooze as large as her head. The jaws started to close, and she brought her legs to her chest just in time to avoid having them bitten off.

A sour-smelling liquid burbled up from the depths ahead and coated her face in hot, caustic slime. Gagging, Takari pushed off against the back of its teeth, driving herself and her sword deeper into the thing's gullet and dragging her dagger beside her, stabbing and chopping at anything that seemed like it could be cut.

The fleshy passage, now slick and warm with blood and other precious fluids, clamped down and began to push her back toward the mouth. Realizing she was about to be regurgitated, Takari spread her knees to wedge herself in place, then planted her dagger to the hilt and held on.

The muscles began to convulse, squeezing her so tightly she thought she would be crushed. Takari pushed her sword as far as she could reach, twisting the blade to and fro, circling the tip in awkward crescents that sometimes found nothing and sometimes cut through fleshy masses that could only be organs.

When her sword sliced through something soft and gauzy, the phaerimm stopped trying to expel her. A flood of warm blood rose up to fill the dark passage. Everything went limp, and Takari's stomach rose into her chest. She thought they were falling, but the feeling seemed to last forever—a timeless eternity—and a strange chill burned her flesh. She grew queasy and weak, her pulse hammered in her ears, and her mind began to reel.

Then she was simply somewhere else, someplace dark and foul, someplace filled with hot caustic slime. Her flesh was stinging, her eyes were burning. The stuff was in her nose and throat and lungs, suffocating her, choking her, drowning her. She coughed and felt hot flesh all around—not squeezing, merely touching and holding—and she recalled where she was.

Or rather, where she had been when the phaerimm teleported to safety.

Heart hammering, Takari pushed back up the dark passage. The flesh remained limp and motionless around her, but heavy and suffocating. She found herself fighting not to breathe and succeeding—fighting not to cough and failing. More of the phaerimm's foul bile gushed down her throat and made her want to vomit, but she managed to fight back the impulse by reminding herself that she would only end up swallowing more of the awful stuff. She came to the thing's teeth and, finding them clamped shut behind her, pressed her back against the roof of its mouth.

The teeth came apart. A shaft of brilliant sunlight came pouring in from outside, bringing with it a much needed draft of cool mountain air. Inhaling through her fingers to avoid swallowing any more blood or bile, Takari sucked it in, coughed out a flagon full of red mucous that might have been hers or the phaerimm's, then filled her lungs again. Only then, after she had gained control of her reflexes, did she turn and peer out from between the creature's pebbly lips.

Below her lay a vast staircase of dead and barren vineyards, descending toward Evereska's embattled walls in a series of smoke-shrouded terraces, with no living thing in sight except the cone-shaped forms of fifty floating phaerimm.

CHAPTER THREE

12 Flamerule, the Year of Wild Magic

Mount Untrivvin's east wall stood a mile away, a looming face of rock and ice hidden behind a curtain of milk-white steam, its form discernible only as a dim gray wedge against a bright gray sky. A blurry fleck of darkness could be seen in front of the mountain, flying a lazy oval about a third of the way up. When the speck reached the end of its loop and banked around to go in the other direction, it assumed a vaguely crosslike shape with a long, thin body and swept-back wings. Even without the clear-seeing spell she had cast, Arr would have recognized the figure as one of the Shadovar's worm-bat mounts, a veserab.

So we are seen, Tuuh whistled beside her. They were standing on the High Ice, staring at the sentry across the sunken vastness of a Shadovar shadow blanket. *We will not have long to wait.*

Arr turned to Tuuh. With a receding hairline, black beard, and dark eyes, he was an exact double of the famous—and very troublesome—Khelben Arunsun.

"Use your mouth and speak Common," Arr instructed. "The scout may have ears as well as eyes."

If that is so, you are more likely to betray us with your words, Tuuh replied, continuing to speak in Winds, using magic to stir the icy air into the whistling language of the phaerimm. *Even if he is listening, humans have trouble recognizing our voices.*

"The Shadovar are not human."

They are close enough.

"Perhaps, but this is my plan—one endorsed by the entire WarGather. If it fails, do you really wish to give them an excuse to blame you?"

The WarGather does not frighten me. Despite the boast, Tuuh said in Common, "And, if something does go wrong, you are the only one they will blame. I'll see to that."

Tuuh turned, and remembering to use his legs as would a human, he stormed off across the ice. Though she was burning inside to demand a gift of contrition—or at least remind him that the WarGather had placed her in charge—Arr had no choice but to let him go. This was the great shortcoming of the phaerimm, their inability to work toward a common cause.

They all knew it, of course—were they not all geniuses, the wisest race ever to inhabit Toril?—but that did not mean they could overcome their one weakness. Beings of such intelligence were too impatient with the folly of others and too easily bored by any company but their own. Sooner or later, every phaerimm compact was doomed to disintegrate in a tempest of clashing winds and bitter magic. That was the nature of her people, and it was only their fear and hatred of the Shadovar that had kept them working together at all through the dark months of their imprisonment in the Shaeradim.

But if Arr's plan worked, if she could trick the Shadovar and the other two-leg realms into making war on each other, then maybe—just maybe—she could keep her people united long enough to capture Evereska. Once they had claimed its magic-nourishing mythal for their own and the phaerimm saw what they could accomplish together, who knew how long their patience might be extended? Perhaps Arr could find even greater goals to unite them. If she planned carefully and always kept the meat dangled before the teeth of her fellows, it would not surprise her to see them take their natural place as the masters of the world—and she would be the master of masters. Why not? Was she not the wisest and most cunning of the phaerimm?

"Arr!" This from Beze, who had assumed the silver-haired form of Khelben Arunsun's paramour, Laeral Silverhand—right down to the tiny limb sprouting from the stump of the arm Laeral had lost in the Shaeradim. "Your feet!"

Arr looked down to find her feet dangling beneath her, the toes not quite touching the glacier. She felt something warm rush to the cheeks of her human face, then lowered herself through a conscious act of will and started to walk to her place in line.

"Watch your tone, sister," Arr said. Save that she stood a little taller than Beze and wore her silver hair somewhat longer, her appearance was much the same. She and Beze had assumed the shape of the Silverhand sisters, Storm and Laeral. "Remember who is leading this mission."

"How could I forget?" Beze nodded in both directions along the steep bank that led down to the shadow blanket and said, "Your humble followers await."

Arr glared just long enough to make it clear that the sarcasm would not be forgotten, then glanced in both directions Beze had indicated. The shadow blanket had melted a deep basin into the ice, and the rest of their number were carefully spacing themselves along its rim, each about a thousand feet apart.

Like Tuuh, Beze, and Arr herself, the last two phaerimm had assumed the likenesses of Mystra's Chosen: Alustriel Silverhand and Dove Falconhand. Arr would have liked to have a larger force, but given that Syluné was a ghost who never left Shadowdale, Qilué Veladorn seldom involved herself in the affairs of humans, and Elminster was still missing with the Simbul, five was largest number of Chosen they could reasonably impersonate.

Arr waited until Beze and Ryry signaled that everyone was in position—the fog was too thick for her to see Tuuh and Xayn at the far ends—then raised her arms and began to chant. The others joined in at once, gesturing and intoning odd-sounding syllables in a carefully choreographed imitation of a human casting. The process was, of course, absurdly slow and primitive—at least compared to how the phaerimm cast magic—but it seemed a necessary step for humans. Arr and her fellows wasted most of the next minute on this nonsense, then lowered their arms and simply thought the spell.

A long, crescent-shaped blade of magic light appeared before them, the lower lip teetering on the rim of the steep slope at their feet. Arr glanced through the steam bank and saw the dark fleck of the sentry still holding his position in front of Mount Untrivvin. She raised her arm and pointed forward, and as one the five "Chosen" pushed their creation over the bank.

The blanket peeler slid fifty feet to the bottom of the basin, where its lower lip slipped under the shadow blanket's edge and quietly rolled it one yard back.

That was all the sentry needed to see. When Arr next looked, the veserab was vanishing southward through the steam. She allowed herself a moment to savor the genius of her plan, then waved to the others and slid down the icy bank to the shadow blanket.

At the bottom of the pit, they found themselves standing in six inches of icy water. The discomfort was not something phaerimm were accustomed to, but it was a simple matter to fix with a little resistance magic. They soon started to push, and the magic peeler worked just as Arr had planned, cutting the blanket free of the ice and rolling it back on itself. The more material there was, the tighter the tool rolled it.

The only problem came when they encountered stones hidden beneath the ice, a surprisingly frequent occurrence since rocks often fell from the mountain, then were carried forward by the glacier and slowly buried by more snow. Still, the phaerimm quickly learned to push these obstacles out of the way with simple telekinesis magic. Two hours later, they had made so much progress that Mount Untrivvin blocked their entire view of the western horizon, and they could hear the faint ringing that gave the peak its name—in the native tongue, *untrivvin* meant "singing rock."

Arr was beginning to fear that her plan had failed when a jagged line of shadows began to appear in the steam ahead. She continued forward until the line resolved itself into a rank of Shadovar warriors, all fully armored and carrying their deadly black swords. Arr's companions were instantly at her back, arriving by teleport magic even as the enemy began to advance.

Instead of breaking into a charge as Arr had anticipated, the Shadovar line stopped thirty paces from the rolled shadow blanket. A huge warrior with braided hair tails and bright coppery eyes stepped forward and raised his dark blade in salute. He was the one they called Escanor.

"With the phaerimm loose in the world again, I should think the Chosen of Mystra would have better things to do than rob Shade Enclave of its water."

"If Shade kept its water to itself, we would," Arr replied.

She had not expected the Shadovar to be more interested in talking than fighting, but she had to respond in kind. While phaerimm never hesitated to use force, she and her fellows had to behave as the Chosen would, and the Chosen were reluctant to start a fight until they knew they had no other choice.

"Your shadow blankets are flooding half of Faerûn," she continued, "and robbing the rest of rain. Since you refuse to remove them, we will do it for you."

Escanor took one step forward and said, "Faerûn's suffering is the price for restoring Shade to its birthright."

"Then let *Shade* pay the price," Arr said, trying to put herself in Storm's place. "Your birthright is no concern of Faerûn's."

"It is. You abandoned us to the Plane of Shadow for seventeen centuries. You cannot imagine how we suffered."

"We abandoned no one." Arr wondered if she had conversed enough to seem like one of the Chosen, then decided probably not. They talked a lot. "Leaving was your city's choice."

"Choice?" Escanor scoffed. "It was leave or die."

"Then it is a pity Shade did not choose the latter," she said. The Shadovar's talkativeness puzzled Arr. Surely, he knew as well as Arr did that there was going to be a fight—so why was he stalling? "It would have saved everyone a lot of trouble."

"Rude, as well as ungrateful." Escanor looked from Arr to Ryry and said, "You are known to be the reasonable sister, Lady Alustriel. Surely, you can see that opposing us will only lead to more Tilvertons. Wouldn't your energies be better spent helping Faerûn's people adjust to the new climate than adding to their troubles by starting a war you cannot hope to win?"

"No one ever *wins* a war, Prince Escanor," Ryry said, sounding like Alustriel in voice as well as meaning. "They only lose less than the enemy. Given what Shade lost at Tilverton, I should think you would understand that."

"Our city is still here."

"And so are a hundred of ours," Arr countered. "Who do you think can stand to lose more?"

Escanor's eyes flashed orange.

"The question is not how many cities you can lose, Lady Storm." His voice was sharp and seething, yet he seemed as content as before to stand there talking instead of fighting. "The question is how many you can destroy. We have already proven what we can do."

"And if you lose an army with each city, we will not have to destroy your city at all," Arr said. As she spoke, Arr was running her gaze down the Shadovar line, searching for the other princes. "By the third or fourth city, it will be ours for the claiming."

"We have learned from our mistake." Escanor glanced at the shadow blanket rolled up between them and said, "You, apparently, have not. You will remove your tool and allow us to replace the shadow blanket. I will ask this only once."

Arr completed her search of the Shadovar line and finding no more princes placed a hand on her hip in the stubborn way Storm often did.

"And if we refuse?"

"The battle will not be fought here," Escanor said. "It will be Faerûn's cities that pay—"

"Liar."

Nothing would have made Arr happier than to think the prince was telling the truth, but the Shadovar were too cunning to announce their plan in advance. She raised her arm and with a thought unleashed the spell she had spent most of her imprisonment in the Shaeradim developing. A steady stream of silver-white flame boiled out of her fingertips toward the prince. His spell-guard flashed black as the fire struck. The shadow magic in this defense triggered a secondary spell, sending an antimagic beam shooting from the head of the flame stream.

A gapping hole appeared in Escanor's spell-guard, allowing the white stream behind to pour through. The effect was a reasonable imitation of the silver fire of the Chosen, and Escanor fell, screaming and engulfed in flames.

Arr started to whistle a command to her fellows, then caught herself and yelled, "Watch our backs! The other princes—"

She was interrupted by the hissing crash of a dark bolt striking home behind her. Beze went tumbling over the rolled shadow blanket and landed a dozen yards away, wisps of shadow rising from a gaping hole in her chest. She began to thrash about and whistle in pain, then rose into the air, too weak and dazed to hold herself on the ground.

"Laeral, no!" Arr yelled. "Get down and be—"

The word "quiet" was lost to a horrific roar as battle magic—both phaerimm and Shadovar—started to crack and sizzle behind her. Escanor's company answered with a thunderous war cry, then lifted their arms and began to gesture. Arr countered by raising a wall of scintillating color in front of them—Shadovar hated prismatic magic—then she realized she had forgotten herself and neglected to gesture and incant. She covered by waving her arm and booming out a dozen syllables of mystic nonsense, then toppled the wall over on the enemy.

A cacophony of crackling magic and anguished screaming filled the basin for a single instant then came echoing back off Untrivvin's stony face and faded to an low murmur. It was a sound Arr loved well, the sound of astonished survivors struggling to gather their wits and reorganize.

She glanced back to find her companions standing behind their spell-guards hurling magic at half a dozen retreating princes. The bars of a half-completed shadow cage lay at their feet, slowly melting into the slushy water as its unbound energies dispersed.

The sound of sharp commands drew Arr's attention forward again, where the Shadovar survivors had already regrouped. Half a dozen were gathered around their burning prince, attempting to smother Arr's silver flames with their own bodies. The rest, perhaps two dozen in all, were following a tall warrior forward, their swords drawn and their gem-colored eyes glowing with rage.

This time remembering to cast the spell as a human would, Arr called up a wall of flame.

By the time she finished the necessary gesturing and chanting, the Shadovar were almost even with Beze's writhing form. Arr would not normally have hesitated to engulf one of her own in the conflagration, but Beze's defenses had obviously been overpowered by the enemy attack. If the flames killed her, she would revert to true form and reveal the truth about who the Shadovar were fighting.

Arr raised the wall behind the charging warriors, then reached behind her and grabbed Tuuh by the collar.

"Come along, Khelben," she said.

She clambered across the rolled shadow blanket, Tuuh half-stumbling and half-floating over it as she pulled him along. When he turned and saw two dozen angry Shadovar only ten paces away, he forget himself and raised a barrier of thrashing blades without remembering to gesture.

"*Allak thur doog!*" Arr called, improvising.

The incantation was lost to the wet thud of the barrier's blades chopping through Shadovar armor.

Pulling Tuuh after her, Arr started around the far end, shouting, "Remember yourself, Khelben."

"A split second of warning might help next time," Tuuh answered. "Where are we going."

"To help Bez—er, Laeral."

"To *help* her?" Tuuh stopped. "What for?"

"Because she's supposed to be your mate!" Arr hissed. "And because my plan will be ruined if she dies and they see her revert."

They reached the end of the barrier. Arr peered around the corner to find that Beze had fallen unconscious and now lay floating in the air, her arms stretched over her head and her legs twined together in a distinctly tail-like braid. The eight Shadovar—all that had escaped Tuuh's spell—remained trapped between the blade barrier and Arr's wall of fire.

The tall Shadovar saw her looking and raised his hand to cast a spell. Arr pulled back in time to avoid the dark bolt that came streaking past the end of the barrier, then dropped to a knee and sent a fork of lightning crackling back in her attacker's direction. It caught him in the chest and knocked him off his feet, then dissipated harmlessly against his spell-guard. The warrior pointed at Beze and sent his followers rushing in her direction.

A stream of silver-white flame streaked over Arr's head, blasting through the Shadovar's spell-guard and engulfing him in flame. The sight made Arr wince inside. The spell was one of her finest, and though she had willingly shared it for the sake of her plan, it still pained her to see another phaerimm using it.

Arr glanced up and behind her at Tuuh's bearded face and said, "I hope that's the first time you've used my spell here." Because the Chosen could unleash the real silver fire just once every hour, she had instructed her companions to use her spell only one time. "My plan won't work if they realize—"

"It is the first time these Shadovar have seen me use it," Tuuh said. "That is all that counts."

He raised a hand and uttering a single syllable, wagged his fingers. Beze rose above the heads of the Shadovar and started to float in their direction. Several warriors cocked their arms to hurl their swords. Throwing up her hands and crying out something that might have sounded vaguely spell-like, Arr brought a swarm of fiery stars crashing into existence and sent it sweeping across the shadow blanket.

It roared into the Shadovar before they could turn their heads to see what was making the sound. Those who had no spell-guards simply vanished in an eruption of smoke and flame. The others were hurled across the shadow blanket, back through the wall of fire Arr had raised earlier. Judging by the screams and the greasy smoke rising from the other side, it seemed unlikely their protection magic had withstood the trip.

"A little quick for a human, don't you think?" Tuuh brought Beze to their side. "But you saved Beze."

"Well, send her somewhere," Arr ordered, "before she dies and ruins my plan."

Behind them Ryry, speaking in Winds, said, *The fate of your plan has already been decided. The Shadovar are gone.*

Arr turned to find Ryry and Yao standing behind the rolled blanket, staring out across the empty melt basin. In the frigid cold of the High Ice, the cloud of rising steam had already turned to ice and dropped back to the ground, and the slushy water through which they had been wading just a few minutes earlier had frozen into a jagged blue plain. The only sign of the Shadovar princes who had attempted to surprise them from the rear where the soot-smeared craters where they had been hurled into the basin walls by phaerimm spells.

"I am a genius," Arr said. "When we work together, none can challenge us!"

"That will be a great comfort to Beze's ghost," Tuuh said.

Arr looked back and found Beze reverted to true form. She was sinking to the ground, her tail and four arms hanging limp, her mouth open and pouring blood.

"Tuuh, did I not tell you to send her somewhere?" Arr asked. "There still may be spies."

Tuuh touched Beze, and a small tear opened in the air and sucked the corpse out of sight. Judging by the drone of insects and the stench of offal that lingered behind, Arr guessed that he had sent the body to the second or third of the Nine Hells.

Once the portal closed, Arr dismissed the magic walls she had created and was pleased to see the shadow blanket littered with dead Shadovar. There was no sign of Escanor, or of those who had used their own bodies to put out the flames engulfing him.

"I see no wounded," Ryry sounded disappointed. "Where are the wounded?"

"In Shade, by now," Arr said. "The Shadovar took them, I'm sure."

"Truly?" Ryry looked at Arr as though she had hidden the wounded and was keeping them all for herself. "Why?"

Tuuh shrugged and said, "What does it matter? Many two-legs do it, when they can."

Ryry studied him doubtfully, then finally seemed to accept what she was seeing.

"If you say so." She turned back to Arr and asked, "What now?"

"Finish the job," Arr said as she returned to the blanket roll and clambered over it. "That is what the Chosen would do."

CHAPTER FOUR

15 Flamerule, the Year of Wild Magic

Galaeron and the others had been waiting all morning when the muted crackle of a translocational spell finally sounded out in the heart of the courtyard, and their guest appeared in swirl of silver hair, a faint stench of gore and brimstone trailing after her. She was tall even for a human—and especially for a human woman—with a slender build and striking figure. Though her face was a bit rough-featured by elven standards, she was nevertheless a stunning beauty, with twinkling eyes, high cheeks, and a full-lipped mouth.

Ruha poured a goblet of Cormyrean wine—the finest available, though that was not saying much after the ravages of the Goblin War—and went out to meet her. Unsure of the greeting he would receive, Galaeron trailed a pace behind. Aris remained hidden in his sleeping arcade, lest he startle her before she recovered from her teleport afterdaze.

Ruha stopped at the woman's side and said, "Welcome to Arabel, Storm." She pressed the goblet into the woman's hands. "Thank you for coming."

The sound of a familiar voice seemed to bring Storm out of her daze. She quaffed the wine in one long gulp, then made a sour face.

"That's the sourest swill I've had in years." She pressed the goblet back into Ruha's hands. "But I'll have another. I've been trading spells with thornbacks and eyeheads all morning, and the thirst I have could drain the Moonsea."

"Perhaps you'd care to sit?" Galaeron suggested, waving at the table they'd set in the shade of the house—a house they'd bought with the proceeds of the sale of one of Aris's statues. "We can bring out some food, if you're hungry."

Storm eyed him warily, but followed him toward the table. "Sitting is good, but I won't have any food. The battle's not done, and fighting on a full stomach doesn't agree with me."

As they took their seats, Aris emerged from beneath his arcade and came to join them. His grim face looked even more somber than usual. When he sat down beside them, he let his body drop so heavily that the mugs rattled on the table.

Storm craned her neck and looked up into the giant's plate-sized eyes.

"It's good to see you, Aris. You're looking better than the last time we met."

Aris forced a smile and said, "I've been waiting for a chance to thank you properly for saving my life, lady."

The giant reached inside his tabard and brought out a three-foot sculpture of Storm kneeling on the ground. The likeness was perfect, of course, with an expression that was at once angelic and fiercely protective. It struck Galaeron that she looked very much like a human version of Angharradh, the elf goddess of birth, protection, and wisdom.

"Please accept this as a small sign of my gratitude."

Storm took the piece with a gasp.

"It's . . . it's . . . Aris, it's beautiful!" She set it on the table, then rose and studied it from all angles. "Too beautiful to be me . . . or any mortal woman."

"Not at all. That is the face seen by those you help." Aris glanced in Ruha's direction, then added, "Ruha helped me track down some of them, so I know."

Storm tore her eyes—glistening with unshed tears—from the statue and went over to him. Even sitting on the ground, the giant towered over her, and she ended up embracing the side of his arm.

"I'll treasure it always, Aris." She tipped her head back and blew him a kiss, which floated visibly up to his face and planted itself on his cheek like a silver tattoo. "Thank you."

Galaeron was glad to see that Storm treasured Aris's gift so highly—he had expected nothing else, really, for the giant's art never failed to move those who viewed it—but her reaction also dampened his own spirits. The giant did not approve of what Galaeron was about to suggest, and—given that Storm held him responsible for much of Faerûn's trouble—his idea was going to be hard enough to sell without adding any extra weight to Aris's opposition.

Leaving Aris with a foolish smile, Storm returned to her seat and turned to Ruha.

"Suppose we come to the point." Though her manner was brisk, her mood had been much improved by Aris's gift, and the concern behind her words seemed more a matter of time than displeasure. "I doubt you summoned me from the war in the Shaeradim so Aris could present his gift."

Galaeron winced. One did not "summon" a Chosen of Mystra anywhere, and the fact that she had used that word to describe their request for an audience was not a good sign.

If Ruha noticed the word choice, her eyes did not show it.

"Galaeron has an idea. I think it could work." Ruha's gaze rose toward Aris's gray face and she added, "Aris does not."

"And you asked me here to break the tie?"

Noting the sarcasm in Storm's voice, Galaeron said, "I want to bring down Shade."

Storm cocked a brow. "Bring it down?"

"Like the old cities of Netheril," Galaeron explained. "Crash it into the desert."

"If you're asking permission, feel free."

"Actually, I can't do it alone." So far, so good—at least she liked the idea. "To tell the truth, I need you and the other Chosen to do it for me."

Storm rolled her eyes as though she had been expecting something of this sort.

"At the moment, we're rather busy trying to save the Shaeradim. I thought you might have heard."

"And I am telling you how!" Galaeron snapped.

He caught the flash of concern in Aris's eyes, then paused a moment to calm his rising ire.

Finally, he asked, "Are you winning?"

Storm's eyes slid away. "No. Lord Ramealaerub's advance has stalled at the Vyshaen Barrows."

"The Vyshaen Barrows?" Galaeron gasped. "What's he doing there?"

"It's not a good base?"

Galaeron shook his head. "It looks like it from below, but he can't reach Evereska from there," he said. "If the phaerimm come up the Copper Canyon, he'll be trapped against the High Shaeradim."

Storm raised her brow and said, "I'll pass that along. Unfortunately, he's advancing blind."

She let the statement hang, leaving it to Galaeron to ask if he wanted to hear the details. He didn't, but he had to know.

"Blind?" he echoed. "I thought Takari Moonsnow was with him."

"Lost the day the shadowshell fell." Storm's manner grew soft, and for the first time since Galaeron had known her he saw some of the softness portrayed in Aris's sculpture. "She eliminated a phaerimm that was delaying Lord Ramealaerub's advance."

Galaeron fell back in his chair, his heart aching as though someone had punched him in it. He had not seen Takari since shortly after their journey into Karse, when he had returned her, battered and bloody, to Rheitheillaethor and left her there to recover. They had never been lovers, but he had finally come to accept—too late, after leaving her behind—that they were spirit-deep mates, linked on a level more profound than love. The choice to leave with Vala—another woman whom circumstances had forced him to abandon to a cruel fate—had been his own, but one made infinitely less complicated by Takari's harshness as she told him she hoped never to see him again. The thought that those words should be the last he ever heard from her filled him with a raw anguish—and with a bitter fury he knew to be not entirely his own that whispered to him that Storm was lying and demanded that he strike out at her.

Instead, Galaeron lowered his chin and whispered a prayer, asking Takari to forgive his folly and begging the Leaflord to watch over her spirit.

Storm laid a hand on Galaeron's arm—then took it away when his shadow recoiled from her touch and made him flinch.

"You know, Galaeron, you could be very useful to Lord Ramealaerub," she said. "I doubt anyone in the elven army would be foolish enough to turn away your help."

But there was always the question, Galaeron—or perhaps it was his shadow—thought. He was the one who had breached the Sharn Wall in the first place, then invited the Shadovar into the world to undo the damage. He was the cause of all this trouble, and even if they were wise enough not to say it to his face, he knew what his fellow elves would be whispering every time he turned his back.

"Now *that* is a plan that makes sense," Aris said. "Why not return to the Shaeradim, where we can do some good fighting phaerimm?"

Galaeron raised his chin and said, "Because we can't win the war by fighting phaerimm. Nor can we save Evereska that way."

"This is the part that makes no sense," Aris said. "The phaerimm *want* the Shadovar killed, and the Shadovar want the phaerimm killed. Destroying Shade—even if you could—does not help Evereska."

"But it *does*, Aris," Storm said. "The elves have little hope—I would say none—of defeating the phaerimm alone. The rest of Faerûn has been too weakened by the Melting to send help, and the few troops they do have must stay home to defend against the Shadovar. The Shadovar are in the same situation—they dare not engage the phaerimm for fear that the rest of the world will attack them and stop the Melting."

It was a great relief to Galaeron that Storm was the one explaining this. Perhaps one of the Chosen could change the stubborn giant's mind.

Aris burst that dream with a firm shake of his head.

"It won't work."

"Perhaps not at once," Ruha said, "but as the realms recover, they will be able to send troops to join the elves. Not even the phaerimm can stand against the combined might of all Faerûn."

Aris crossed his arms in front of his chest.

To Galaeron's surprise, Storm ignored the giant and turned to face him and Ruha.

"Your plan works only if Shade's destruction is a swift one," she said.

"Without its mythallar, the city will fall," Galaeron said. "The destruction will be instantaneous."

Storm nodded.

"That's what I thought you had planned for us. But how are we to enter the city? Shade's magic is proof against even us."

Galaeron smiled and told her his plan.

When he finished, Storm poured herself more wine, sat back, and thought it over. It took only a few moments before she drank the contents of the goblet and nodded.

"It could work."

"Wonderful!" Galaeron filled goblets for himself and Ruha. "We can be ready—"

"I said *could*." Storm raised her hand to stop him, then looked to Aris and said, "Before deciding, I want to hear Aris's argument."

The giant cast a guilty look in Galaeron's direction, then said, "Because Galaeron can't do it."

Storm furrowed her brow.

"What is there to do? All he need do is appear headstrong and careless." She glanced over at him, then added, "That is not out of character for him."

"Afterward," the giant clarified. "Once he's in the city, his shadow will grow too strong. We'll lose him . . . and this time, I fear it will be for good."

"That is a risk," Ruha agreed. "He's not strong enough to fight Telamont."

Galaeron shrugged and said, "There is cost to every plan. I can resist long enough to make this one work. After that . . . well, I doubt the Chosen will find it difficult to eliminate the problem before it can grow out of hand."

Storm studied him for a long time then said, "You would make that sacrifice?"

Galaeron answered without hesitation, "I have lost more already."

"And that is another wrong thing." Aris planted a big finger in the center of the table and nearly collapsed it. "When he is not talking of Evereska and what it is suffering, he is talking of Vala and what she is enduring. I say he is doing this to save her."

Storm raised a cool gaze to the giant's face and asked, "Why would that be wrong?"

Aris scowled and spent a moment trying to think of an argument, then gave up and looked away without answering.

Storm looked back to Galaeron and remained just as silent.

Finally, he could bear her scrutiny no longer.

"So you'll do it?" he asked.

Instead of answering his question, Storm asked one of her own, "I want to be clear on this. If your shadow takes you, you're asking me to kill you?"

Galaeron nodded.

Storm shook her head. "No, Galaeron. If you want this, you must say it."

"When . . ." Galaeron's throat went dry, and he had to stop and start again. "When, not if—because I am losing the battle even here—but *when* my shadow takes me, I want you to kill me. More than that, I want you to promise me now that you will. I've brought enough evil into this world through folly and accident. I have no wish to cause it directly."

"If that is what you want, I promise," Storm replied. She stood and turned to Aris. "What about you, my large friend? Will you go with Galaeron?"

"Him?" Galaeron asked, also standing. "This doesn't involve Aris. There's no need for him to return to Shade."

Storm did not look away from the giant.

"Aris goes everywhere with you, Galaeron," she said, "and he has vowed to avenge Thousand Faces. If he suddenly remains behind when you set off to fight the phaerimm, what will the Shadovar think?"

"She's right," Ruha said. "They would grow suspicious, and that suspicion would spoil your plan. This must be done right . . . or not at all."

Galaeron dropped his head. He had nearly killed Aris once already, during their escape from Shade when he had succumbed to his shadow self and used the giant to lure a blue dragon into an ambush. Had Storm not answered Ruha's call for help, Aris would have died, and this time there would be no one to call for help. If matters went wrong—even if they went right—it might well be the death of them both.

Galaeron shook his head.

"Then we won't do it." He raised his gaze, met Aris's eyes, and said, "This is not something I would ask of you. You have already done more than I could expect even of an elf friend, and I will not see you killed."

"You think that is why I don't like your plan? Because I fear for my life? That is an insult worse than any your shadow has ever spit out."

Aris's big fist crashed down on the table, smashing it to pieces and sending splinters and shards of goblet flying in every direction.

"You saved my life at Thousand Faces," the giant continued. "It is yours to spend."

A tense silence settled over the courtyard. Galaeron was so shocked by the giant's uncharacteristic show of anger that he did not dare look up to apologize.

Finally, Storm rose.

"I guess that settles it, then," she said. She used her hands to brush the wine off her leather armor. "We'll look for you tomorrow, after dawn."

CHAPTER FIVE

15 Flamerule, the Year of Wild Magic

To Malik's astonishment, Escanor was still glowing when he dared enter the presence of the Most High. The prince could be seen from fifty paces away, first as a dim, pearly ball floating beneath the copper flicker of his distinctive eyes, then as a luminous cage of ribs encasing a kernel of pulsing light. A wave of stunned whispers followed him across the throne room, and as he drew closer Malik could see that Escanor was actually staggering. The mantle of shadow that usually served him as a body was bleeding away in wisps, bestowing on him a rather gauzy and serpentine appearance.

Escanor stopped at the foot of the dais, his glow illuminating half a dozen younger princes who were coming up behind him. Though none were in as sorry a condition as Escanor, they had gone with him to attack the Chosen on the High Ice, and three were bleeding shadow from lesser wounds.

Escanor bowed and would have fallen over, had one of his brothers not braved the ghostly light to lend him a hand.

"I apologize for appearing before the Most High in this condition," he said.

"As well you should," Hadhrune said. "It is an insult."

"Indeed," Malik agreed, standing in his customary place just above Hadhrune. Having grown tired of the seneschal's jealousy over his position as Telamont's most trusted advisor—and weary of the constant assassination attempts—Malik had decided to try a strategy of alliance to placate the man. "If the Most High wanted us to see his face, he would show it to us himself . . . though I must admit I am curious to see it myself."

He did not even cringe at this last part of his statement. Much of the reason the Most High valued Malik's advice so highly was the curse placed on him by the harlot Mystra, which always compelled him to tell the truth when he spoke. Telamont Tanthul rarely chastised him for the embarrassing slips that this caused him—and sometimes even seemed to find them amusing.

But not today. A set of icy talons sank into his shoulder, and a cold voice whispered into his ear.

"Your curiosity on that count would kill you, my behorned friend, and slight a prince of mine again and you shall have it satisfied."

Malik's mouth grew as dry as dust. "I meant no offense, Most High . . ." He struggled to end there, but the truth welled up inside him and spilled from his mouth of its own accord. "At least to you, for I have always felt secure in your protection and completely free to insult whomever else I desired."

The Most High removed his icy talons, patted Malik's shoulder, and said, "And now you don't."

Telamont slipped past and descended the stairs toward his son. Knowing it would be suicide to stand higher than the Most High, Malik followed him down the stairs. The Most High stopped on the bottom step, leaving Malik, Hadhrune, and the rest of the throne room attendants to scramble for places on the floor. In the glow of Escanor's wounds, the sycophants looked ghoulish and wrinkled, with hollow cheeks and sunken red eyes. Only Telamont himself seemed immune to the light and remained hidden in the shadows beneath his cowl.

Taking advantage of the light—he always tried to make the best of every situation—Malik risked a surreptitious glance at his wounds. Though cold spears of anguish still pierced his shoulder where the Most High had grasped him, there were no holes in his flesh, nor any blood on his robe.

Telamont asked, "You engaged the Chosen, my son? They did this to you?"

Keeping his head bowed, Escanor nodded and said, "That is so, Most High."

Telamont's platinum eyes shone brighter in the darkness that was his face.

"Good." He lifted a murky sleeve, motioning Escanor to his feet, and continued, "Rise and tell me how many you killed."

Escanor's shadows seemed to grow even thinner as he stood.

"I fear the answer is none, Most High," he said, his coppery gaze remaining fixed on the floor. "We were defeated."

"Defeated?" It was Hadhrune who asked this. "*Seven* princes of Shade?"

Escanor's eyes swung toward the seneschal. "The Chosen are formidable enemies."

"Which is why I advised the Most High to send seven of you," Hadhrune countered, "and an entire company of the Gate Guard."

Though the effort of defending himself drained Escanor, none of his brothers seemed eager to leap to his defense.

"Your plan did not take into account . . . the quickness of the Chosen. They fling magic as easily as you do aspersions."

Hadhrune responded with a smile—the predatory smile of a hunter in pursuit of crippled prey.

"They are only human," he said. "How could their spellcraft be quicker than that of a shadow lord?"

"That is a mystery to me," Escanor replied, sounding more sincere than sarcastic. "Next time, perhaps you should lead the assault and tell us."

"There will not be a next time," Telamont said in that low even tone that Malik had learned to associate with cold rage. "We cannot afford one."

"Unfortunately, I doubt the choice is yours," Malik said. He had long ago discovered that times like these were when he stood to gain the most with the Most High, since everyone else was too busy cowering in fear to curry favor. "Now that the Chosen have seen how powerless you are to stop them, they will certainly return to roll up the shadow blankets faster than you can lay them."

Telamont whirled on Malik, his platinum eyes shining brightly enough to see by.

"We are not powerless!"

"N-n-no, of course n-not," Malik stammered. "Only, after the losses Shade suffered in Tilverton, you will be if you lose a company of warriors each time you try to stop the Chosen from stealing one of your shadow blankets."

One of Telamont's murk-filled sleeves reached out, and a tendril of shadow knotted itself into Malik's robe and picked him up by the lapels.

"Why must you always be right, little man?"

Malik shrugged and thought it might be wiser to say nothing, but that was never an option when Telamont Tanthul wished an answer. He lasted only a breath before the Most High's will forced him to speak.

"It is my curse, Most High," he said—but of course there was no stopping there. "It is my design always to tell you what you wish to hear—but since that is rarely what is true, before I know it I am foolishly blurting out the things your other advisors are too wise to say."

"Too wise," Escanor asked, glaring pointedly at Hadhrune, "or too cowardly?"

Telamont's glance darted in the prince's direction.

"Careful, my son. You are one of those Malik is talking about."

He lowered Malik back to the floor, then slipped a murky hand through Escanor's ribs and grabbed the prince's still glowing heart.

"Interesting. Tell me about the spell that did this."

Escanor's gaze shifted to the hand in his chest.

"It was the silver fire." His voice was shaky. "It burned through my spell-guard—"

"No." Telamont pulled his arm away, and a glowing palm appeared at the end of his sleeve. "Silver fire is raw Weave magic. If that's what this was, we would be spinning into a dimensional vortex right now."

"Really?" Malik gasped.

He had witnessed enough combat to know that when raw Weave magic contacted raw Shadow Weave magic, the result was a rip in the fabric of reality. It was just such an accident—when the magic bolts of Galaeron Nihmedu's Tomb Guard patrol met one of Melegaunt Tanthul's shadow bolts—that had ripped the Sharn Wall and released the phaerimm in the first place.

"Then you must be . . ." Too late, Malik realized the risk he was taking by revealing that he realized Telamont's true nature. He tried to hold his tongue, but the curse compelled him to finish what he had started. ". . . living shadow magic!"

The Most High's murk-filled cowl turned in Malik's direction.

"Not living, exactly." A faint crescent of purple appeared where a human's smile would have been, and Telamont finished, "No need to feel bad about blurting it out. You were never going to leave here anyway."

"Most High?" Malik looked around as though searching for a door, but of course there was no escape into anything but the shadows. "That is hardly needed! I can keep a secret as—"

"The *enclave,* worm," Hadhrune said. "He means you will never leave Shade Enclave."

"Just so," Telamont said. "I find your advice too . . . *necessary* . . . to let you go."

"Is that all?" Malik sighed in relief. "Then we are in agreement. Why would I wish to leave Shade? I have everything I desire here—Villa Dusari, the ear of the Most High, a stable for my beloved horse and plenty to feed her. I would be a fool to leave all this!"

For once, there was nothing more for his curse to compel him to say.

"How very pleased we are," Hadhrune said, running his thumbnail across his palm. "I am sure the princes are as delighted as I am."

"The only delight that matters is mine," Telamont said. "I will be delighted when someone tells me what to make of this."

He held up his glowing hand.

"Obviously a form of false magic aura," Hadhrune said. "Commonly used in bazaars and such places to make plain weapons appear enchanted."

Telamont remained silent, and when Hadhrune did not add anything more, he turned to Malik. Resolved to jeopardize his position no further that day by being the bearer of bad news, Malik tried to remain silent as well.

Then he found himself saying, "We have a saying in Narjon, where I was once an esteemed merchant: if someone fills your oil jar with sand, it is not because he wishes to give you sand."

Telamont and the princes remained silent and continued to look at him.

"Have you no scale cheats in Shade?" Malik asked, exasperated. "It means someone is trying to deceive you. Whoever created this false aura wishes you to believe his spell is silver fire—"

"Phaerimm!" Telamont and Escanor growled the word together.

"That would explain the swiftness of their spellcasting," Hadhrune said, turning to Escanor. "It surprises me that you failed to see it in the field."

"Had you ever *been* in the field, perhaps you would—"

"Enough," Telamont said in that cold, dangerous tone again. "You are both to blame."

He raised an arm, and with a flick of his sleeve sent Hadhrune crashing into Escanor. They went tumbling across the throne room floor locked in an embrace of pain. Telamont waited until they had vanished into the shadows before turning to the rest of his princes.

"Let that be a lesson to you," he said. "In all things, you succeed or fail together. If one fails me, all fail me."

The princes' eyes dimmed with fear, then somehow speaking in flawless unison they said, "We understand, Most High."

Telamont glared at them for a moment, then finally waved a sleeve in the direction Escanor and Hadhrune had tumbled.

"See to your brother's wounds and your own. This war is too close to lose another prince."

The princes bowed and retreated into the shadows, leaving Malik and the other attendants alone with Telamont. The Most High placed a sleeve around Malik's shoulders, turned him toward the dais, and started to ascend back to his throne.

"It pleases me that you are happy here, Malik."

"Very happy," Malik said. "Except for the frequent attempts on my life, perhaps."

"Ah, yes," Telamont sighed. "Hadhrune."

Malik waited for the Most High to say he would no longer have need to worry or that something would be done about that, but they continued to climb in silence until they came to the step where Malik normally stopped.

Telamont kept his arm around Malik's shoulders, guiding him onto the throne platform itself. This drew an astonished murmur from the attendants below, but the sound faded to silence as the Most High took his seat and stared into Malik's eyes.

"Hadhrune was not so different from you once—if you will forgive being compared to an elf."

Malik's jaw fell at this revelation, for he had never seen enough of Hadhrune's shadow-swathed face to note either arched eyebrows or pointed ears.

"There was a time when he served me as well as your counsel does now," Telamont continued. "I tell you this so you will know that I reward those who aid me with eternal loyalty, even after they have lost their usefulness and become a burden."

Malik inclined his head. "I am honored that you would treat me so."

"I *could*," Telamont said, his voice again assuming that dangerous coldness, "were this debacle not your fault."

"*My* fault?" Malik broke into a cold sweat. "How have I caused this, Most High?"

"This happened because we did not anticipate the phaerimm's plan. We did not anticipate their plan because we do not have the knowledge my son Melegaunt passed on to Galaeron. We do not have Galaeron because he is still in Arabel."

Telamont sank back into his throne and continued, "Did you not tell me that if we sent Vala to be Escanor's bed slave, Galaeron would return to Shade and try to rescue her?"

"I may have said, er, uh—" Compelled by Mystra's curse to tell the exact truth, Malik stammered to a stop then was forced to continue, "I *did* say that was the surest way to draw him back in a rush. I have no dou—er, a reasonable belief—that my plan will still work . . . eventually."

Telamont's eyes grew white and icy. "*Eventually*, my patience will come to an end. One might even say that it is waning now."

A lump the size of a fist appeared in Malik's throat, but he still managed to say, "Indeed?"

Telamont remained silent.

Malik found that he had another question, a question he desperately did not want answered but which was rising up inside him like his stomach after a meal of bad fish. He clamped his mouth shut and swore he would not open it, that he would choke on the words before he allowed them to spill forth.

But his will was no match for that of the Most High, and he soon heard himself asking, "What happens when your patience has gone?"

"Then Vala will pay for her treachery in helping Galaeron escape," Telamont pronounced.

"That would certainly be a great waste of womanly flesh." As fond as Malik was of Vala, he was less worried for her than he was relieved at not hearing his own name. "But a waste that matters little to me, as I am quite sure the only thing I would ever find in her bed is a quick death."

"That might be preferable."

Again, Malik found himself asking a question he did not really want answered.

"Preferable, Most High? To what?"

"To taking her place," Telamont answered.

"Take her place?" Malik exclaimed. "But I am a man!"

"And if you want to stay that way, I suggest you make good on your plan."

Malik felt the blood leaving his head and knew he was close to fainting, which was hardly something that would inspire the Most High's confidence. Knowing from his long experience as a merchant and a spy that the best way to cover a weakness was to bluff, he forced himself to meet Telamont's gaze.

"You must know that in my service to Cyric, I have suffered a hundred injuries worse than that." It was as true a statement as any he had ever made. "If you wish to inspire me, you must do better than that."

The murkiness beneath Telamont's cowl stilled with shock.

"You dare demand a boon?"

"When the risks are great, the reward must be even greater," Malik said. "That is the first rule of business taught to me by my wise father."

Telamont remained motionless for several moments, staring at Malik in disbelief. Finally, the purple crescent of a smile appeared beneath his eyes.

"As you will, then," he said. "Bring me Galaeron Nihmedu, and you shall name your price. Fail . . . and I shall name mine."

CHAPTER SIX

16 Flamerule, the Year of Wild Magic

Even had there not been a giant-sized gap in the caravan between Galaeron and Ruha, the group of wealthy citizens holding a farewell party at the city gate practically announced that Aris of Thousand Faces was leaving town. The Arabellans had turned out in their finest splendor, many standing in silk-draped wagons beside their latest acquisitions—masterpieces in granite and marble, bought the day before at give-away prices. All eyes were fixed on the long line of riders and draft animals coming down the street, and as soon as the onlookers saw the unexplained space where the invisible giant was walking, they raised sparkling flutes of champagne in silent tribute.

"I'd say your idea worked, Ruha," Galaeron said quietly. "Had we hired a crier to stroll the streets all night, we couldn't have spread our 'secret' any faster."

"Yes, I have always found that the surest way to proclaim a thing is to say it should not be repeated," Ruha said. "I only hope it did not pain Aris to part with so many works so cheaply."

"Why should that pain me?" Aris whispered. "Their owners will enjoy the pieces all the more, and I don't have to carry so much gold."

"There are plenty of Arabellans who would've been happy to shoulder the burden for you," Galaeron said. "The way they hoard the stuff, one would think they eat it."

As the front of the caravan reached the gatehouse, the caravan master slipped out of line to pay the gate tax. The bursar held himself primly upright and made a show of tallying each draft animal as it passed through the gate.

His guards stood at strict attention, their gazes fixed on the opposite side of the archway and their halberds posted at full-arm. Though Cormyrean officials were reputed to be generally honest—at least by human standards—they were no more prone to perpetual diligence than other men, and Galaeron realized that Aris's well-wishers were not the only ones who had come down to see them off.

When their turn came to pass under the archway and be counted, Galaeron glanced into the arrow loop behind the guards and found a familiar cascade of golden hair shining in the depths of the gatehouse. He dipped his head in acknowledgment. The hair moved closer, and Princess Alusair's familiar face appeared on the other side of the loop. Her eyes were red and glassy, though it was impossible to say whether from weeping or exhaustion.

"Thank you." Galaeron mouthed the words without speaking them aloud. "Your kindness has lit my heart."

Alusair smiled. "And your courage mine." She also spoke the words silently. "Sweet water and light laughter, my friend."

"Fare you well." Galaeron did not give the traditional "Back soon" reply, for they both knew he would not be returning to Cormyr. "May your realm prevail and your people know peace."

Galaeron could not be certain Alusair saw enough of this last wish to understand, for she vanished behind the edge of the arrow loop as the caravan continued forward. They passed beneath the spikes of the iron portcullis and clomped across the drawbridge onto the beginning of the High Road.

Once they were outside the city walls, a small army of beggars—farmers and craftsmen rendered destitute by the ravages of the Goblin War—emerged from the tents and ramshackle huts of Pauper's Town to beg alms. Aris slipped sacks of gold to Galaeron and Ruha, who tried to avoid calling attention to their friend's generosity by proclaiming, "Here's a copper for you," and pressing the gift firmly into the supplicant's hand each time they passed out one of the gold coins.

The strategy proved even less effective than their "effort" to sneak out of town undetected. Whenever the astonished beggars—especially the children—opened their hands and saw what they had been given, they could not help crying out in delight. Soon, Galaeron and Ruha were surrounded by a moving throng, many of whom noticed the giant-sized gap between them and guessed the true identity of their benefactor.

They reached the small bridge that separated the marshaling fields from Pauper's Town, and the press of beggars brought the caravan's progress to a near standstill. The curses of drivers behind Galaeron and Ruha began to grow both in volume and vehemence but were drowned out by a steady chorus of,

"Ilmater's blessing on the Generous Giant," or, "Thanks to the Tall One!"

It was in the middle of this madness that a slender hand wearing two silver rings reached up for a coin. Clasped around the wrist above the hand, hidden almost out of sight inside the cuff of a purple sleeve, was a silver bracelet bearing the skull-and-starburst symbol of Cyric, Prince of Lies. Galaeron ran his gaze up the sleeve to a silver-trimmed collar, where he found himself looking into the sunken eyes of a hollow-cheeked woman with ropy blond hair.

"I have had a vision," she hissed. "One you love—"

Galaeron pressed a coin into her hand and said, "Here's your copper. Take it and go."

She let the coin drop in the dust, nearly felling Galaeron's horse as a knot of beggars dived beneath its hooves to retrieve the offering.

"Listen to me, elf!" Her hand grabbed his reins and brought his progress to a stop. "You must return to Shade. I saw the Seraph in a dream—"

"I don't know what you're talking about," Galaeron said. He pulled his boot free of the stirrup and planted his foot in the center of her chest. "This caravan is bound for Iriaebor."

He started to push her off—and found the tip of a stiletto sliding up under the armor on his calf. The sensation of cold steel pricking his leg caused a dark fury to rise inside Galaeron. Leaving the half empty sack of gold to slide off his saddle and spill on the ground, he reached across his body and grabbed the hilt of his sword.

"Shade," the woman hissed. "Go, or she will die."

Galaeron's heart began to pound like a Vyshaan war drum. Though he desperately wanted to ask the woman about her vision, he held his tongue and drew his sword half out of its scabbard. Even had he thought he could trust a Cyricist, he would never have risked his plan by telling her that Shade was exactly where he intended to go.

"You have mistaken me for someone else, Madam," Galaeron said. "Now, step back or lose your head."

The woman's eyes turned black and sun-shaped, with long tongues of darkness wagging around the edges.

"Believe."

She sank her stiletto a quarter of an inch into his calf, and Galaeron's blade rasped free of its scabbard almost of its own will. The woman raised her chin and waited with eerie calmness as it arced toward her collarbone.

"Believe!"

Galaeron's attack came to a sudden end as his forearm struck a huge, invisible hand.

"No," Aris's voice rumbled down from above.

"Leave her be, friend," Ruha called from the other side of Aris. "The mad cannot be blamed for their madness."

"Nor the messenger for the message," the woman added. Her voice was gravelly and multifold, as though there were a hundred people speaking at once. "Go."

The black suns faded from her eyes. Leaving her stiletto hanging from Galaeron's calf, she stumbled back and fell into the throng of beggars fighting over the coins he had let fall. Aris's grasp slackened, and Galaeron lowered his blade, his hand trembling so badly he could barely slip the tip into its scabbard.

"My friend, what is it?" Ruha asked. "Why are you so frightened?"

"More startled than frightened," Galaeron said. He reached down and plucked the woman's dagger from his calf, then displayed the bloody tip. "A message from our friend the cuckold. He wants to see us."

Ruha's dark brow rose, and Galaeron tossed the dagger over the beggars into an empty place in the field. When he turned to urge his horse forward he saw that it was hopeless. The road ahead was blocked by at least a hundred paupers—all with their hands out, praising Aris's generosity—and the little bridge was occupied by two dozen caravan guards on their way back from the marshaling fields.

Once they were clear of the bridge, the guards began shouting at the paupers to clear the road, using their shields and the shoulders of their big war-horses to enforce their demands. Galaeron did his best to remain patient. Whether or not the message had truly come from Malik, it only served to heighten his concern for Vala. His feelings for her were not as spiritual as the love for Takari that he had denied all those years on the Desert Border South, but only because a human and an elf could never come together like two elves could.

Nevertheless, Galaeron did love Vala—if not as deeply as Takari, then at least as strongly—and it had tormented him to remain comfortable in Arabel while she served Escanor as a bed-slave. Not a day had passed that he did not dream of returning to free her. If only she could hold on until he got himself captured.

When the guards began to grow impatient with the paupers and slap at them with the flats of their blades, Aris hit upon a helpful solution and began to fling handfuls of gold away from the road. It took two throws before the beggars realized what was happening and fled, all yelling Aris's praises and pleading for him to throw a handful their way.

Once the road was clear, the guards moved quickly to secure the caravan, thundering past on both sides and barking orders to get moving. Five of their number peeled off and came up beside Galaeron and Ruha, placing themselves so that any beggars returning for more handouts would have to go through them first.

The largest, a hatchet-faced woman in a helmet and dusty fighting leathers, came alongside Galaeron and waved them across the bridge. The guard's voice was as familiar as it was biting.

"Well done, elf. I doubt there's a deaf man or blind woman within a league of here who doesn't know you're sneaking out of Arabel."

Galaeron took a closer look. The speaker's gaunt features softened into those of Storm Silverhand, the hair that looped out from beneath her helmet turning silver and silky, the thin-lipped mouth growing full and shapely.

"This wasn't part of the plan." Fearful of betraying the identity of his guards, Galaeron was careful to avoid the honorific one usually showed the Chosen. "The gratitude of the paupers took us by surprise."

"Oh, well that's fine then," growled the rider behind her. "How comforting to know things just *slipped* out of control."

They started across the bridge. Galaeron glanced over his shoulder to find the visage of an old horse-faced guard yielding to the black beard and frowning features of a man who could only be the renowned elf-friend, Khelben Arunsun.

Galaeron decided not to mention the message from Malik. The Chosen appeared less than enthusiastic as it was, and the last thing he wanted was to give them an excuse to change their minds.

"I apologize for the mistake," he said. "I should have realized how gold would affect—"

"Galaeron is not to blame," Aris said, his voice booming down out of the empty sky. "I am the one who wanted to give them the gold."

"Will you be quiet up there?" Khelben demanded. "At least *pretend* you're trying to sneak out of here unnoticed."

"I apologize," Aris said, his voice a low rumble that made the bridge planks quiver beneath the horses' hooves, "but you mustn't blame Galaeron—"

"There's no need to blame anyone," said a third guard. Riding opposite Galaeron on Ruha's far side, she had only one arm and a voice similar to Storm's. "No one should be condemned for sharing with the hungry."

As she spoke, Galaeron began to see through the illusion guarding her identity and realized that this had to be Khelben's consort, Laeral Silverhand. There was a tiny arm growing from the stump of the one she had lost in the Shaeradim, but even this did not detract from her beauty. She was, if anything, even more lovely than her sister, with a warmth and charm alien to Storm's brusque manner—or perhaps it merely seemed so to Galaeron because Storm never bothered to hide the dislike she bore him.

Khelben was silent a moment, then said, "You're right, of course." He sighed heavily. "Again."

This drew a laugh from the last two guards, and Galaeron recognize the same silver in their voices as in Laeral and Storm's. He hazarded a glance in their direction, and as he began to see through the illusions, he recognized in their sparkling eyes and silver hair two more of Storm's sisters. The slimmest of the two, and the most feminine in her carriage and manner, could only be the celebrated Lady of Silverymoon, Alustriel Silverhand. The other, a more imposing figure as powerfully built as a man, had to be the mighty Dove Falconhand—Harper, Knight of Myth Drannor, and friend to the elves.

The Chosen had not only answered Galaeron's call for help, they had answered it in strength. If Khelben seemed tense, it only made sense. With Elminster still missing with the Simbul, and ghostly Syluné more or less confined to her farm in Shadowdale, the only available Chosen they had not brought was the Dark Sister, Qilué. Given his limited experience with drow during his days in the Tomb Guard, Galaeron was just as glad.

They left the bridge and rushed to catch the head of the caravan, which was stopped in the marshaling field while the captain of the guards grouped the draft animals by swiftness and burden and assigned personnel to watch over them. He placed Galaeron and Ruha with a group of lightly burdened riders, and at Storm's magically enhanced suggestion, assigned the five Chosen to watch over them.

Once the captain had moved on, the Chosen gathered their horses in a tight circle around Galaeron, Ruha, and the still invisible Aris.

"Here's my plan, Galaeron," Khelben said. "We're going to make a few—"

"Darling?" Laeral interrupted. "Aren't you forgetting who thought of this in the first place?"

Khelben scowled but said, "All right." He turned back to Galaeron. "Your plan's a sound one, but we're going to—"

"Pardon me," Alustriel said. "But I'd prefer that someone who's actually been inside the city does the planning."

Khelben rolled his eyes. "Very well." He turned back to Galaeron and said, "We all like your ideas."

"Very impressive," Dove said.

Khelben nodded almost reluctantly then continued, "But there are some things we should bring to your attention."

He stopped to check for the others' approval.

Storm whirled her hand to urge him on. She glanced back toward the rear of the caravan, which was already coming across the little bridge.

Khelben looked irritated but he said, "First, you won't be able to eat until we're inside the city."

Galaeron raised his brow and said, "I hadn't thought of that."

"We didn't think you had," Alustriel said, "but I'm sure you understand. The journey will be unpleasant enough as it is."

"I don't think I could ride for more than a few days without eating anyway," Galaeron agreed. "We'll put that part off as long as we can."

"My thoughts exactly," Khelben agreed. "Second, you may have noticed there are five of us."

"I can do it instead," Aris said. "I'm larger."

"Actually, we were thinking of splitting the group into two teams," Laeral said. "As insurance."

Though Galaeron was reluctant to ask Aris to assume any more risk than he already was, he knew better than to argue. The giant had made his feelings on the subject clear when he smashed the table in their courtyard.

"Splitting is a good idea, if Aris is willing," Galaeron said.

Khelben smiled. "Good," he said, "then we're all agreed."

"Not quite." Galaeron raised his hand, and avoiding Ruha's gaze, said, "Ruha can't come with us."

"That is not your decision," Ruha replied. Her tone was angry, though not surprised. They had spent most of the night arguing the point, finally letting the matter drop only because the time had come to join the caravan. "This has nothing to do with Evereska."

Galaeron ignored her and fixed his gaze on Storm.

"The Shadovar need me," he said, "and they value Aris, but Ruha is nothing to them but a problem. If she comes with us, there's every chance the Shadovar will put her to death."

"That is my risk, not yours," the witch said, running her gaze from one Chosen to the next. "He is trying to protect Malik. Malik saved his life, and now the foolish elf believes they are friends."

"That is true," Aris said, "but it is also true that Hadhrune believes you broke his command and tried to kill Malik. If you return, it will be just as Galaeron says."

The five Chosen gazed at Ruha expectantly.

When the witch merely looked away, Dove Falconhand said, "I think you should stay behind, Ruha. Your presence might endanger the mission."

"Or save it," Ruha argued. "You cannot know that yet—and what will become of Malik? I have hunted the dog too long to let him live like a Sheikh in their palaces."

"If we are successful, there may no longer be a Malik to concern yourself with," Storm said. "If we fail, he will come out sooner or later. Cyric is too cruel to leave him there in comfort for long."

Ruha said nothing more, but the angry look she flashed Galaeron left little doubt about whose life she thought he had just saved. A dark voice inside whispered that she was an ungrateful hag who deserved the death she would find in Shade, but Galaeron closed his mind to those shadowy thoughts and reminded himself that she had good reason to hate the little man. He was a remorseless killer who had single-handedly saved the Church of Cyric and restored the mad god to power, and he was undoubtedly working to spread his god's influence throughout the city of Shade. That he had saved the lives of both Galaeron and Aris many times while they traveled together mattered not at all. That had been an alliance of convenience, and Galaeron knew as surely as Ruha did that Malik would not hesitate to betray them in the name of his god.

Galaeron considered again whether to tell the Chosen about the message he had received from Malik but was deterred by the fury in Ruha's eyes. Given the number of Chosen who had come and the courtesy they had shown him in the strategy session, he felt sure that they intended to follow through on the plan no matter what. But Ruha would seize on any suggestion of betrayal by Malik as an excuse to accompany them into the city. Galaeron had no doubt at all about what would become of her if she fell into Hadhrune's hands. For the witch's own good, it would be better for him to keep the secret.

Or so Galaeron told himself.

CHAPTER SEVEN

16 Flamerule, the Year of Wild Magic

Once the captain had the caravan arranged to his liking, he gave the order to depart. Like some thousand-legged millipede, the line came alive and began to snake its way westward along the High Road. Galaeron and Ruha rode in silence on opposite sides of their invisible friend, Galaeron struggling to ignore the dark thoughts continually welling up in his mind, the witch glaring at him over her veil.

Aris, suffering from the fatal honesty that was the curse of his race, tried several times to reason with her, to make her see they were trying to protect her as much as they were Malik. Ruha heard only the part about protecting Malik and chastised the giant for serving an evil god. That was the end of any conversation for the rest of the day. They ate their lunch in cold silence, Khelben urging Galaeron and Aris to gorge themselves and build up what stores of fat they could. They did as the archmage suggested, and though the giant's presence was a very open secret in the caravan, Storm renewed the invisibility spell on him. They spent the rest of the day feeling lethargic and uncomfortable, until the caravan master finally called a halt. It was already late in the afternoon, with the sun sinking low over the Storm Horns and the road ahead vanishing into its golden glow.

No wonder, then, that no one sounded the alarm before the dragons were on them. The creatures came straight out of the sun, the big one in the center sweeping low over the center of the caravan, its mere presence panicking mounts and men alike, sending guards diving for roadsides and horses crashing headlong into the woods south of the road. The great beast did not breathe fire, gas, or anything else, nor did it devour any horses or snatch screaming men in its claws. It did little more than swing its long neck from one side of the road to the other, its great head passing slowly over each knot of cowering riders.

Blinded as he was by the brilliant ball of the setting sun, Galaeron did not realize for a moment that the dragon had no flesh or hide. It was all bone, with an empty cage of ribs large enough to hold Aris, and blue stars burning in the depths of its hollow eyes.

"Malygris!" Galaeron gasped. "They're coming for us *now!*"

"Into the woods!" Khelben shouted as he reined his horse into Galaeron's and forced him to turn toward the forest. "Aris, duck and run!"

The invisible giant went thumping toward the woods, his big feet flattening the brown grass as he ran. Ruha and the others led the way after him, and soon they were galloping away from the road in a loose circle.

They had traveled no more than thirty paces before the low *whumpf* of pulsing wings sounded over their heads, then a wall of blue scales dropped out of the sky to block their way. The dragon was an old one, close to two hundred feet from nose to tail, with fangs as long as swords and claws that could grasp a war-horse around the withers. It swung its head in their direction and opened its jaws to display the ball of lightning crackling in its gullet, then did nothing at all.

That was the frightening part, at least to Galaeron. The thing knew who they were or they would have already been dead.

"Back!" Khelben ordered.

As one they wheeled their mounts around and started back toward the road—only to stop an instant later when the third dragon crashed down in front of them. As long as the one behind them, it was perhaps a ton or two lighter, with a long, sinuous body and a bristly fence of spines down its back.

Like the other one, it opened its mouth to reveal the ball of lightning crackling in its gullet.

Surrounded as they were by Mystra's Chosen, some part of Galaeron realized they were in no trouble. Any single one of his companions could have slain both dragons with little more than a word and a flick of the wrist, but that was a hard thing to remember while staring into a mouthful of fangs as tall as an elf. Knowing there was a second dragon coming up from behind made it all but impossible to remain calm.

Drawing his sword, Galaeron turned to the closest Chosen—it happened to be Storm—and yelled, "Do something, you useless scold!"

"What would that be, milord?" asked Storm, who had already drawn her own sword. She pushed the weapon uselessly into the air. "I'm not here to fight dragons."

She set her heels to her horse and raced off. No sooner had she gone than the rest of the Chosen scattered, behaving more or less like typical caravan guards. Galaeron started after Khelben, and the dragon bounded in front of him. He wheeled around, his mount stumbling as it bounced off Aris's invisible leg, and started after Alustriel.

The other dragon landed on its haunches a hundred feet ahead, one claw stretching in Galaeron's direction. Black fear welled up inside Galaeron. He felt the Shadow Weave flowing into him and found his hand dropping the reins so he could cast a spell. In his terror, he almost didn't stop himself.

But the beast was only trying to capture him, and the dread he felt was only its natural aura of panic. If he allowed himself to succumb, his plan would fail. Evereska would fall. Vala would die. Galaeron forced his hand down again and fumbled for the reins, but he was already turning the horse by pressing a knee against its shoulder.

Ruha streaked past beside him and called, "Keep going!"

The witch flung sand into the air and shouted in the Bedine tongue. A thick cloud of dust whirled up to engulf the dragon's head, and its talons closed on air. Galaeron caught the reins and jerked the panicked horse back toward the mountain of blue scales ahead.

The dragon let out a crackling bellow and sweeping its long neck around in great serpentine arcs tried to shake free of the swirling dust. The cloud followed wherever its head went.

Ruha galloped under the undulating neck and streaked for the woods. The beast roared in frustration, sent a blue bolt of lightning cracking over her head, and swung back in Galaeron's direction.

A tremendous bang echoed across the plain, and Aris appeared beside the dragon's dust-swaddled head, his largest stone-shaping hammer grasped in both hands. He brought the tool down again, staggering the beast and sending a ripple rolling down its neck.

Galaeron dodged past a wildly lashing claw. He saw the giant raising his arms for another blow.

"Enough!" he called. "Run!"

Aris brought the hammer down anyway, this time drawing a dull thud as it cracked the dragon's skull. Galaeron ducked under a madly undulating neck and was nearly unhorsed by the edge of a flailing wing. He glanced back to see Aris vaulting over the dazed beast's back. The giant shouldered aside a wing-buffet and rushed after Galaeron.

The dragon's dust-engulfed head bobbed uncertainly around, and Galaeron heard a telltale sizzle rising from the thing's throat.

"Watch your—"

A blinding fork of energy danced out from the dust cloud, but Aris was already diving for cover beneath the dragon's wing. The bolt struck half a dozen paces behind the giant, spraying dirt and burning grass fifty feet into the air. Aris emerged beneath the other side of the wing and rolled to his feet, then raced for the woods in great booming strides.

Galaeron looked forward again to find the forest looming ahead like a wall. Ruha and two of the Seven Sisters had already dismounted and were crouching down among the drought-stunted leaves. He angled toward them. The witch rose and pointed at the sky behind him. Not waiting to see whether she was casting a spell or shouting a warning, he broke hard in the opposite direction. He felt a deep throb in his stomach as a pair of huge wings beat the air behind him.

A pair of enormous rear claws tore into the ground beside him, then the second dragon crashed to its forefeet and spun after him. Galaeron heard the shriek of Ruha's magic bolts and the twang of a couple of bowstrings, but knew the attacks would not even distract the beast. He pulled his feet free of the stirrups and hurled himself from the saddle, flinging his sword off to the side and tucking into a forward roll.

At that speed the impact felt like it would break bones clear down to his ankles, but Galaeron came up on his feet and somehow ran two steps before falling victim to his momentum. He tumbled headlong across the meadow. The dragon's scaly belly flashed over his head twice then there was only dusky sky and dusty ground.

Galaeron came to a rest sprawled on his back and gasping for breath, staring back overhead at a wall of blue scales. He heard his horse scream and saw its body spin through the air off to his right, then he felt his own body erupt in pain as he began to slide across the ground. He raised his chin and saw Dove and Storm dragging him by his ankles.

"Well acted, elf," Storm said. "I thought that 'do something, you useless scold' was an especially brilliant touch."

Galaeron was in too much pain to tell whether she was mocking him or actually believed he had been performing for the dragon. They reached the forest, where the undergrowth added to Galaeron's humiliation by slapping him in the face with leaves and twigs. The sisters dragged him another fifty paces to where Ruha was waiting. Finally, they stopped and pulled him to his feet, drawing a series of wheezy groans as he struggled to return the wind to his lungs.

Khelben Arunsun burst through the trees on his horse, then dismounted and sent the beast on its way with a slap.

He took one look out into the field, and asked, "Can you run, elf?"

Galaeron glanced behind him. The second dragon, the one that had just missed snatching him from his horse, did not seem to realize where he had escaped to. It was spinning in a slow circle, ripping up huge tufts of grass and sending small boulders bouncing across the ground as it searched for his hiding place. Still engulfed in Ruha's dust cloud, the other one had gone mad with rage. It was feeling its way down the road on all fours, smashing and shredding any living thing it touched. Already it was smeared to the elbows with blood, and it was closing fast on a screaming tangle of horses and handlers.

Seeing the situation, Galaeron nodded to Khelben and managed to croak, "Perhaps not fast . . . but I can run."

"Sure you can," Storm scoffed. "You can't even talk."

Taking his far arm by the sleeve, she bent down and hoisted him onto her shoulders. Khelben nodded his approval, then led the way deeper into the forest.

"Wait!" Galaeron wheezed.

The archmage didn't even slow down. "What is it?"

Though the pain was starting to subside, being slung across Storm's shoulders was doing nothing to put the air back in Galaeron's chest.

"The . . . caravan!" he said. "It's . . . it's being shredded."

"Yes, and it's our fault," Khelben said. "Very unfortunate."

"I think Galaeron is asking if you couldn't do something," Ruha said.

Dove glanced over at Galaeron and asked, "You really aren't asking if we could slay those little lizards, are you?"

"This is no time for ridiculous questions," Storm added. "Maybe you've noticed we were taken by surprise?"

"I noticed," Galaeron replied. Either his breath was returning, or his rising anger was giving him strength. "We can't just let them die."

Khelben stopped and said, "I thought you wanted to destroy Shade." His voice was sharp with impatience, but there was a softness in his expression that seemed to indicate he understood what Galaeron was asking—and why. "I thought you wanted to save Evereska."

"I do," Galaeron said, "but you can save those people, too."

Seeing that he had finally recovered his breath, Storm dropped him to his feet. Khelben stepped over, eyes burning with anger, and glared down at him.

"The Chosen cannot save everyone on Toril." His tone was as anguished as it was resentful, as though it pained him to state this obvious fact. He waved a hand in the direction of the screaming caravanners and continued, "You chose, elf. Those few, or the thousands in Evereska and the dozens of thousands across the rest of Faerûn who will perish if we reveal ourselves and your plan fails."

"But it's our fault," Galaeron said. He was beginning to feel very small and naive. "There must be a way without you revealing yourselves."

"If there was, don't you think we would have done it?" Storm demanded. "You insult me, elf. I wouldn't do it again."

She turned and started through the woods, more or less toward the last place Galaeron had seen Aris.

Khelben lingered long enough to explain, "The deed itself would betray us. How many caravan guards do you know who could defeat Malygris and two old blues?"

"None."

"That is the problem," Khelben said. "I assume you are choosing Evereska?"

With the screams of the distant caravanners ringing through the trees, Galaeron could barely bring himself to nod, but he did.

"I thought as much."

Khelben cast a last glance in the direction of the road, then turned and started after Storm. Dove motioned Ruha after him then took Galaeron by the hand and followed.

"It is a hard lesson," Dove told him, "but one you must learn if you ever hope to live with the power you carry." Though they were running at a near sprint and taking care to do it without rustling leaves or cracking twigs, Dove's words came as easily as if they had been strolling in the gardens of her house on Evermeet. "Babes may be born into this world innocent as rain, but they have blood on their hands 'ere the end of their first year. We all do."

"A comforting . . . thought," Galaeron said. Though he was as accustomed to running long distances as anyone, he had to concentrate to remain silent in both breath and step. "Are you trying to make me glad I have no children?"

"I am trying to help you. Even if you eat only fruit and never set foot on the ground, you cannot live without killing. Something dies that you may live, even if only the worm that will never hatch in the apple you ate."

"I understand the laws of nature," Galaeron said. "I am still that much of an elf."

"But not a wise one," Dove replied. "And wise you must become, lest you smother Faerûn in evil through your good intentions."

She could not have distracted Galaeron more had she sank a dagger into his chest. He caught his foot on a root and crashed to the ground, causing the entire group to stop and whirl around. Khelben cocked his brow, Storm scowled and shook her head, and Galaeron could not read Ruha's expression behind her veil.

"I beg your leave," Galaeron said as he scrambled to his feet. The others resumed their run, and he grabbed Dove's hand to hold her back. "I am listening."

Dove's expression turned to one almost of pity.

"And still you do not hear," she said as she squeezed his hand until something popped inside. His whole arm erupted into pain. "You have a lot of blood on your hands, Galaeron. The powerful always do."

Galaeron raised his throbbing hand. Though he had not seen Dove cast any spells or felt her use any magic, it had turned the color of an open wound. He was so shocked that he barely noticed the broken bone sticking up under the skin behind his index finger.

"I . . ." Galaeron did not know quite what to say. He was still too confused to be angry, and even his shadow seemed too stunned to react. "I don't understand."

"No?" Dove shrugged, then started after the others, adding, "When you do, the hand will heal."

Galaeron took a moment to set the break then, bones still throbbing, he set off after the others.

The injury proved a useful distraction. As he grew accustomed to the pain, his ire began to rise, and with it his shadow. It took only a dozen steps before he grew so consumed fighting the darkness inside that he no longer heard the screams coming from the road. The thought occurred to him that this was what Dove had intended, though he doubted the pain of a simple broken bone could ever make him forget the anguish of those they were abandoning.

A few hundred steps later, they came to a small stream where Aris was waiting with Alustriel and Laeral. The two sisters had filled five small vials with water and set them out on a flat boulder along the bank. Four of the vials were already gleaming with a silver aura of magic, and Alustriel was saying a spell over the last. Khelben and the rest of the Chosen went to the boulder and waited for Alustriel to finish.

Aris noticed the way Galaeron was holding his hand and frowned in concern.

"You hurt yourself. Maybe I can—"

"Quiet!" Dove hissed. "The dragons are coming."

Aris peered up into the forest's darkening canopy and said, "I don't see—"

Ruha held a finger to her veil and whispered, "Listen."

Aris fell silent. Galaeron listened and heard nothing but the distant murmur of panicked caravanners crashing through the dusky woods. It took him a moment to realize that Dove was talking about what they *couldn't* hear. There were no chirping crickets, no hooting owls, no more screams from the road.

A faint rustle drifted down through the treetops. Galaeron thought at first that a breeze was coming up, but the rustle continued to grow and soon became the distinct hiss of air rushing over scales. A dragon-shaped darkness appeared to the north and came sweeping through the woods toward them. Galaeron and most of the others scrambled for cover, Alustriel lingering to complete her spell and Aris kneeling beneath the boughs of a great oak. The hissing grew louder, and the darkness came nearer, meandering back and forth, as vast as a lake, swallowing everything in its path.

Alustriel finished her spell in a hushed whisper, then took up the last vial and lay down in the shadows along the stream bank. Galaeron kept his gaze turned upward, but the canopy was too thick for him to see anything except a tiny smear of sky and a handful of the evening's first stars. The hiss swelled to a whooshing, then the edge of a wing blocked even that small light.

They were plunged into darkness, and Galaeron waited in frozen silence, the throbbing of his broken hand forgotten. He counted one heartbeat, two, a dozen, then two dozen. Finally, the rushing faded to a hiss, and the darkness swept away to the south. He started to breathe again without realizing that he'd ever stopped, and a lone cricket began to chirp somewhere beyond the creek.

Khelben emerged first, going straight to the boulder to pick up a potion. By the time the others had arrived, he already had the cap off and was raising it to his lips.

Before he could drink, Alustriel caught him by the wrist and said, "Hold there." She took the vial from his hand and passed it to Laeral. "Perhaps you have no care whether you drink a man's potion or a woman's, but we do."

Khelben raised a brow. "There's a difference?"

Alustriel nodded and said, "A pair of bosoms would look as strange on you as a beard would on me."

She selected another vial that looked just the same and gave it to him. Once Alustriel had passed out the rest of the potions, Khelben raised his hand as though making a toast, and the Chosen drank the magic down.

The effect was swift, but not instantaneous. By the time they finished their potions, the Chosen had shrunk to the size of elves. They continued to diminish before Galaeron's eyes, their fingers growing so small they had to grasp the vials in their whole hands. Alustriel produced two green pills from somewhere within her cloak. Though they could not have been much smaller than peas, in her fingers they looked more the size of Cormyr's purse-hogging gold lions.

"Swallow this when you are ready to be rid of us," she said. "There is no hurry except that imposed by your hunger . . . but in the Lady's name, don't eat! There are some ways I never wish to pass."

Galaeron reached down to take the pills and said, "Have no fear of that. I doubt Aris and I will be dining at any banquets."

Galaeron turned to pass the pill along and found the giant staring south into the forest, his brow drawn into a deep furrow.

"Aris?"

"The dragon—it's coming back," the giant whispered. "Ten seconds, perhaps twenty."

Galaeron passed Aris's pill up—he had to tug on the hem of the giant's tunic to get his attention—then looked back to the Chosen. They were still waist-high.

A faint hiss drifted down through the treetops, and a familiar darkness appeared in the woods ahead.

"We're not going to make it," Galaeron whispered.

Khelben looked up at Ruha. The witch paled—at least what little could be seen above her veil—but nodded and began to rub her hands together. Galaeron started to protest, but was reminded of the difficult decisions they had already made when his hand started to throb again.

By the time he turned to say his good-byes, Ruha was already racing away from them. She murmured a word of magic, and the sound of her whispering feet began to reverberate through the forest. A soft pulse sounded down through the leaves as the dragon flapped its huge wings, then its black shadow abruptly turned and swept off in pursuit of the fleeing witch.

"Fare you well, my brave friend," Galaeron whispered.

"You won't be rid of her that easily, elf," Storm said. She stood only about as high his knee, and her voice was little more than a tinny hiss. "Ruha spent her childhood dodging blue dragons. She'll be there waiting when Shade falls."

"I pray so," Aris whispered. He looked down, then kneeled and extended a hand. "I think I can do it now, if you're ready."

"I don't think we'll ever be ready for something like this," Khelben said, stepping onto the giant's palm, "but if you can do it now, the sooner the better."

Aris tipped his chin back, then dangled Khelben over his open mouth.

"And remember not to chew!" Khelben ordered.

Aris dropped him headlong into his gullet, then made a sour face as he struggled to swallow without closing his mouth. For a moment, Galaeron thought his friend would choke and send Khelben flying through forest, then the archmage's black boots finally vanished into the giant's gaping mouth.

Aris made a loud gulping sound, then lowered his hand again.

Laeral and Storm exchanged uneasy glances, and Storm waved her sister forward.

"By all means."

"You're too kind," Laeral said with a grimace, then she stepped onto Aris's palm.

She had grown just enough smaller that the giant was able to gulp her down without gagging, and Storm went down even easier. That left only Alustriel and Dove, who—at ankle height—were still too large for Galaeron to swallow.

While they waited, Dove turned to Alustriel. "You're sure we won't suffocate?"

"That's what the water breathing magic is for." She looked up at Galaeron and added, "You will remember to drink lots of water."

Recognizing it as an order and not a question, Galaeron merely nodded.

"And we won't be digested?" Dove pressed.

"We're Chosen," Alustriel said. "A little stomach acid isn't going to hurt us. And I *do* have protection—"

The flicker of a far-off lightning bolt flashed through the forest, followed almost instantly by a muffled crackle. Galaeron glanced over and saw the distant glow of a burning tree.

"What now?" he asked. At about twice the size of his thumb, Alustriel and Dove were still too large for him to swallow—at least without chewing first. "It has to be coming this way."

"There's only one thing *to* do." Alustriel waved a tiny arm, and the five vials shattered into sparkling dust. "If you wait here, the dragon will know you want to be caught."

The steady throb of wings beating air sounded from the direction of the burning tree and began to grow rapidly louder, and the dragon's dark shadow sailed through the forest in their direction.

Galaeron snatched both Chosen up in his good hand and shouted, "Run, Aris!"

The giant spun and crashed off to the west. Trying to keep hold of the shrinking Chosen without suffocating or crushing them—in his panic to escape the dragon for a few moments longer, the absurdity of that concern did not strike him—Galaeron turned southward and sprinted along the bank of the stream. He was making it more difficult to capture them both, but he had to try as hard as he could to escape. A dragon that old would know if he tried to make it easy.

The dragon's shadow arrived to the terrific rushing of leaves as the trees shuddered beneath the buffeting of its wings. Galaeron stopped—more from terror than conscious will—and dropped behind a fallen log. The beast passed overhead so closely that he could smell the odor of fresh lightning still clinging to its scales and hear the high branches scraping its belly. He thought for a moment that it would take him before he could swallow the Chosen, but it continued on westward, chasing the crashing steps of Aris.

Galaeron opened his mouth to sigh in relief and found himself panting for breath. The dragon plunged into the forest with a horrific sound of crashing and splintering, and Aris bellowed in shock. The cry changed to one of pain and fear, then rose into the air.

And that was all. The giant was gone, just that fast.

Galaeron remained motionless, half-expecting to hear Aris's body come crashing back into the trees when the dragon realized it still didn't have him. When the giant's cries only grew more distant, he finally stood and looked down at Alustriel and Dove. They were about half the size of his thumb now, small enough that even an elf could swallow them.

"Aris was taken," he reported, "but I think it missed—"

The leaves shuddered with a sudden rushing as something settled in the treetops, then the trees began to groan and creak beneath some great weight. Galaeron was seized by such an aura of cold terror that his shadow rose inside him and set his mind whirling in a black tornado. Slowly, he raised his eyes, and above the treetops he saw what looked like black, bare limbs curving across the few visible wedges of starlit sky.

Galaeron stood there, frozen in terror and confusion, trying to understand what he was seeing. An enormous black cord of bare vertebrae snaked across a smear of open sky a dozen paces to his right, bringing into view a fleshless, horned skull as large as a rothé.

The skull slowly rotated around until Galaeron found himself looking into the burning blue star of a huge, lifeless eye.

Galaeron! Alustriel's voice came to him inside his head, slicing through the black fog of fear that was clouding his mind. *Now!*

Even in his dragon-inspired panic—and this was the worst he had ever experienced—Galaeron knew better than to raise Malygris's curiosity by swallowing the Chosen in front of him. Instead, acting as much by instinct as by plan, he spun on his heel and fled, bringing his hand to his lips as he ran and sucking the pair into his mouth.

A huge claw crashed down above him, bringing with it a torrent of leaves and splintered wood and trapping him in a cage of bony talons.

"Not so fast, elf," Malygris said. "You are the one I have been searching for."

Galaeron swallowed and felt the Chosen sliding down his throat. With any luck, he had remembered not to chew.

CHAPTER EIGHT

16 Flamerule, the Year of Wild Magic

Keya Nihmedu stood in the first rank of the Company of the Cold Hand, trembling in the rumble and the flash of the attack, her head tipped back as she watched sheet after sheet of crimson blast magic roll across Evereska's flickering mythal. The city's archers answered by darkening the sky with their arrows, and elf battle mages stood spaced along the Meadow Wall, barraging the demolished terraces of the Vine Vale with crackling bolts and arcs of acrid flame.

But, aside from the wall of bugbear mind-slaves behind which the phaerimm were hiding, nobody was dying. The thornbacks themselves were hovering at the edge of spell range, defended from Evereska's assaults by missile guards and spell shields, and they were even more careful to keep their ragged army of beholders and illithids scattered far up the vale where no arrows and few spells could do them harm. The elves were just as safe behind their mythal. While it stood, no attack—magic or otherwise—could cross the Meadow Wall to harm anyone inside.

For perhaps the thousandth time in the past two days, Lord Duirsar strode by in front of the Company of the Cold Hand, his wrists crossed behind his back and his gaze fixed on the distant rank of phaerimm. The events of the last months had aged him as elves do not age, turning his long hair more gray than silver and stooping his shoulders beneath the weight of his worries.

"I see what they're doing, Lord Commander," Duirsar said to a tall moon elf—the acclaimed Kiinyon Colbathin—who was striding along at his side. "It's going to work."

"The mythal has held all these months, Lord Duirsar, even when it was cut off from the Weave." Attired in the battered but once-elegant armor of an Evereskan high noble, Kiinyon looked as care-worn and stressed the high lord himself. "It will hold until Lord Commander Ramealaerub arrives."

Duirsar spun on Kiinyon, wagging a bony finger in his face.

"*If* Ramealaerub arrives, Lord Commander—if," he said. "Even if he does, it may not be in time."

Kiinyon did not argue the point. At last report, Ramealaerub's army had still been camped in the Vyshaen Barrows, awaiting guides from Evereska. Unfortunately, sending guides by foot was impossible, and those who tried to teleport made it only as far as the vale's boundary before falling to ground in a bloody spray, no doubt intercepted by the same phaerimm magic that prevented inbound supplies and reinforcements from entering Evereska via its translocational gates.

Duirsar turned and studied the phaerimm.

"They are wearing us down, Lord Commander, draining our defenses."

"They are *trying*, milord. That is not the same as doing." Kiinyon glanced back at the long line of young runners bringing casks of fresh arrows down from the city and said, "It would take a decade to deplete Evereska's supply of arrow wood, and with the Weave available again, there is no need at all to worry about our magic."

"You know what I am worried about, Lord Commander—and it is not arrows or lightning bolts," Duirsar replied, glancing up at the flickering mythal. "I think the time has come for the lion to leave his den."

Kiinyon scowled in Keya's direction, and she realized she was nodding in agreement. She stopped but held his gaze until duty compelled him to turn his attention back to Lord Duirsar.

"Milord, that's what the enemy wants," Kiinyon said. "They are trying to draw us out where we will be vulnerable to their attack."

"Or exploiting our temerity to exhaust the mythal." Duirsar continued to study the sheets of magic crashing across the surface of the mythal and said, "In all my centuries, I have never seen it waver like this. The mythal needs our help, Kiinyon."

The lord commander looked up, shielding his eyes against the flashing magic, and said, "We are doing all we can. At least our archers and our battle mages are holding them at a distance. Imagine the damage the thornbacks could do, were they free to stand beside the mythal itself."

Keya had to bite her tongue to maintain the silence expected of a soldier in the ranks. Kiinyon Colbathin was one of the greatest spellblades Evereska had ever known—almost the equal of her own father, who had fallen saving the life of Khelben Arunsun—but he was an under-confident, and therefore timid, general. It would be wrong to blame Kiinyon for Evereska's inability to break the siege, though he had certainly not hesitated to blame her brother Galaeron for prompting it, but it was no exaggeration to say that his only clear strategy seemed to be holding out until someone from outside arrived to save them.

Lord Duirsar remained silent for a long time after Kiinyon spoke. Keya thought he might actually be trying to imagine what possible difference it would make if the phaerimm *were* standing at the mythal.

When he lowered his gaze she saw more anger in his face than uncertainty, and she knew that he was growing as frustrated with his lord commander as she and the rest of Evereska. Duirsar stared at the ground and seemed to be debating something, then raised his gaze and looked straight at her.

"What say you, Keya?" he asked.

Keya knew better than to let her astonishment show, or to hesitate for fear of offending Kiinyon. Khelben Arunsun had been her house guest for much of the siege, and during that time she had spent enough time in the company of both elves to know that Lord Duirsar expected an answer when he asked a question and that Kiinyon would only hold her reply against her if he thought she was being less than honest. Cautious though the lord commander might be in his strategy, he was faithful in his duty and loyal to his city, and if that meant being embarrassed in front of the High Lord, then so be it.

Keya took all the time she dared to consider her answer—thinking fast was no easy task with the battle thunder crashing overhead—then she inclined her head in deference.

"If Evereska's army crosses the Meadow Wall to meet the phaerimm spell to spell, it will not return," she said. "Milord Colbathin is correct in this much. Our losses were heavy enough when we had an army of Shadovar and two Chosen fighting at our sides. Without them, our casualties would be total."

Though accustomed enough in matters of state to hide his feelings behind a mask of indifference, Lord Duirsar was too exhausted and nerve-racked to conceal his surprise. He studied Keya as he might a crouching wolf, his eyes narrowed and his brow raised.

But it was Kiinyon himself who demanded, "And in how much am I mistaken, Swordlady?"

Keya dipped her head in the lord commander's direction and said, "In fighting not to lose, milord. We cannot break the siege by conserving our forces. We must summon our resolve and fight to win."

Seeing the look of apprehension that came to the lord commander's eyes, Keya turned back to Duirsar, whose wry smile suggested that he understood exactly what she was saying.

"Continue, Lady Nihmedu."

Keya felt a secret thrill at being called by her hereditary title. At just over eighty, she was still a decade too young to assume the title formally, and being addressed by it by Evereska's high lord was a token of his respect.

Daring to raise her head and speak more forcefully, she said, "For too long we have been trusting others to do what we must do for ourselves. No one can break this siege but us."

"Then we are doomed," Kiinyon said. "Without help, we are no match—"

"When are you going to understand, Lord Commander?" Keya interrupted. "There *is* no help."

"Mind your tone," Kiinyon ordered. "Lord Duirsar asked for your opinion. He did not give you leave—"

"I have heard you calling to Khelben and the others," Keya continued, growing ever bolder. "Have they come? Have any of the Chosen?"

Kiinyon frowned at her insolence, but said, "They will."

"Before the mythal falls?" Duirsar asked. "I have been calling to the Chosen, as well. Only Syluné answers, and just to send word that the others cannot come."

The despair that came to Kiinyon's face almost sank Keya into despondency as well.

"Our situation is not hopeless," she said, as much to herself as to Kiinyon. "We have resources and have only to use them."

"How?" Lord Duirsar asked. "Until you tell me that, you have told me nothing at all. If we dare not cross the Meadow Wall to meet them, and we cannot win by standing behind it, what are we to do?"

"Make them pay," Keya said. "If they want to attack the mythal, we must make them pay to do it."

"Again, I ask how?"

"With these," said Kuhl, one of the two humans flanking her in the company's front rank. Burly and black-bearded, he was about as big as a rothé and woollier than a thkaerth, with a swarthy round face and hands the size of a plates. He stepped forward holding his glassy darksword in hand. "We sneak out there with the Cold Hand and start cutting them down, one at a time."

"And we keep doing it until they all leave or they're all dead," added Burlen, the human standing to her other side. "Or until there aren't any more of us to go back."

"That's the way we do it in Vaasa," Kuhl said.

Keya smiled up at her mountainous friends, then nodded to Lord Duirsar and said, "We teleport out there in small strike teams, hit hard, and come back."

Duirsar smiled. "And we see how determined *they* are, for a change."

"Risk the darkswords?" Kiinyon asked, shaking his head. "Every one we lose out there is one we won't have in Evereska if they—"

The lord commander was interrupted first by the crackling roar of an erupting fireball, then by a chorus of anguished screams. Keya and the others spun toward the sound and were astonished to see a battle mage and his escorts rolling on the ground in flames, a wagon-sized ring of smoke above them rapidly contracting around a breach in the mythal.

Before the hole could close, a crimson sphere came streaking across the Meadow Wall in their direction. Lord Duirsar flung up his hand, raising a spell-guard with enough speed to convince Keya that the rumors about him being one of Evereska's secret high mages were true. The fireball flattened against the mystic shield and crackled into nothingness, leaving only a faint orange glow to mark where it had struck.

Duirsar watched only long enough to be certain that the mythal had sealed itself again, then turned to back to Kiinyon and said, "I would say that decides the matter, wouldn't you?" Without waiting for a reply, he turned to Burlen and Kuhl. "Teams of six? Four warriors and two battle mages?"

Unhappy at being left out of the planning and quite sure she was the only one who understood why the high lord was suggesting those particular numbers, Keya said, "That will be fine, milord—one mage to teleport and one to cast a decoy."

"Decoy?" Burlen asked.

"So you have time to attack," Duirsar said, nodding his approval to Keya. "Otherwise the phaerimm will be on you before you can recover from the afterdaze."

"Recover?" Kuhl scoffed. "We aren't going to be there that long. Just give us mages who can get us out as quick as they get us in—and the teams should have three warriors, not four."

"Only three?" Duirsar asked. "I don't understand."

"I do," Kiinyon said.

He flashed a smile at Keya—as close to an apology as she would ever receive from the great hero, she knew—then he set about organizing the Company of the Cold Hand into trios. Though the company had less than twenty darkswords borrowed from the Vaasans who had fallen when the phaerimm escaped their prison, Kiinyon had close to a hundred of Evereska's finest spellblades to choose from. The darkswords had been forged by the archwizard Melegaunt Tanthul over a hundred years earlier and passed down from parent to child for four generations, and they would freeze the hand of any wielder not of the owning family. To get around the problem, for each sword, the Company of the Cold Hand had five warriors who passed the sword from hand to hand as their fingers grew too numb to hold onto it.

For these attacks, there would be only one wielder for each sword, so Kiinyon was free to chose the most experienced and powerful spellblades available. When he came to Keya and the two Vaasans, the only three members of the company who could hold their darkswords as long as they wished, the lord commander at first assigned Burlen and Kuhl to separate trios. When Keya insisted on being assigned to a group as well, they insisted on teaming with her.

"Dex is already mad as a dragon about her taking his darksword," Burlen explained.

As Dexon's lover—or more precisely, the mother of his unborn child—Keya had become a member of his family and able to hold his darksword without freezing her hand. With Dexon still struggling to recover from the wound he had received in the last big battle, she had taken his sword and rushed off to join the fight when the phaerimm began to attack. Dexon had chased her down Treetop and halfway across the Starmeadow screaming for her to bring it back and stay there were he could defend her. Keya half expected to see him come hopping out into the meadow at any moment, dragging his spell-withered leg along and yelling all the time that they had to protect her. Humans were strange that way, believing they could hoard what they loved like gold and keep it safely hidden away in their vaults.

Lord Duirsar returned with seven of Evereska's most powerful battle mages, most of them instructors in the Academy of Magic—when there had still been such a thing. Kiinyon explained the plan, then arranged five of the teams into a triangle, with the wizard in the middle and the three warriors ringing him, facing outward. The sixth team—Keya's—he arranged in a square, taking the fourth side himself.

"You're sure this is going to work?" Kiinyon asked.

"Like grease on ice," Kuhl answered. "When we get there, just keep hold of my belt with your free hand and swing with your sword hand."

"Very well."

Kiinyon drew his borrowed darksword and signaled the attack. Keya heard the battle mage start his spell, then there came a dark eternity of falling. Her stomach rose into her chest, and she grew weak and dizzy and cold. A dead silence filled her ears, and she felt nothing but her own heart hammering fast and hard in her chest—and she was somewhere else, the ground rumbling beneath her feet and her eyes and nose burning with the brimstone stench of Hell.

"Swing!" shouted a familiar gruff voice.

Reminded of the sword in her hand, Keya swung even as her mind struggled to make sense of her smoky, fire-blasted surroundings. She hit nothing, but heard off behind her shoulder the wet slap of a sword cleaving flesh and spun instinctively toward the sound, bringing her darksword around in a vicious backhand.

This time, Keya hit something and felt her blade bite deep. Blood, hot and sour-smelling, splashed her across the jaw and throat. A squealing whirlwind filled the air with dirt and ash, then golden bolts of magic appeared from nowhere and began to ricochet off her spell-turning bracers. Some of them came bouncing back past her head, deflected by identical bracers worn by all the warriors in the Company of the Cold Hand.

Keya glimpsed an expanse of thorny scales and finally recalled where she was and what she was doing there. She reversed her blade and brought it back across the phaerimm's body, this time stopping at the end of the stroke to plunge the tip in deep.

The creature screamed again in its windy language. Its tail came arcing up at her face, the barbed tip already dripping with its paralyzing poison. Kiinyon reached past her shoulder, catching the attack on his borrowed darksword and flicking the barb away before it could strike. Keya thanked him by bringing her own weapon, still plunged deep into their foe, down the length of its serpentine body.

The phaerimm pulled itself off her blade by floating a few feet backward. Keya thought it would teleport to safety, until Burlen's darksword came tumbling past and split the thing the rest of the way through. It fell to the ground in a pile of blood and entrails.

Burlen extended his hand toward the sword. It rose out of the gore and tumbled back into his grasp, then Kuhl's big hand grabbed Keya by the belt and pulled her back into position.

"Time to go."

Realizing that she had released her own grip, Keya started to reach back for Burlen's belt—then heard someone cry out from above.

"Keya?" The voice was so weak and hoarse as to be unrecognizable, but it was speaking Elvish. "Can that be you?"

Keya looked up the vale, and two terraces above, saw a half-starved wood elf scout peering through a gap in a wrecked wall. Over her shoulders and head, she had a makeshift camouflage tarp covered with withered grape vines, but Keya could see enough of the scout's face to tell that her red-rimmed eyes were as sunken as a banshee's and her lips cracked and bloody with thirst. A hundred paces behind her, a mixed company of beholders and illithids were rushing down the vale to investigate.

"It's time!" Burlen urged. "Grab hold."

"Wait!" Keya called as she started toward the elf. "She needs help."

"No time," Kuhl said. Still holding her by the belt, he lifted her back into the fighting square. "We kill and run."

Keya tried to break free, but the Vaasan's grasp was too powerful.

"I can't just leave her!"

"And you won't help her by getting yourself killed," Kiinyon said. To the battle mage, he added, "Get us there and I'll—"

The battle mage cast his spell, her stomach rose into her chest, and there came that cold eternity of falling. A dead silence filled her ears and she began to feel queasy, then she was someplace not too different, the ground still shaking beneath her feet and the stench of brimstone still burning her nostrils.

Keya felt the weight of the darksword in her hand, and recalling the last time they had teleported, she began to swing.

Her sword hit nothing, but a familiar elf voice cried out, "What are you doing, you bear-stinking oafs? Hold your blades!"

The Vaasans had picked up enough Elvish to realize that they were being addressed, and Keya glanced over her shoulder to find an exhausted wood elf glaring up at them. Even as haggard as the elf was, Keya recognized the brown eyes and cupid's bow smile as those of her brother Galaeron's favorite scout, Takari Moonsnow. Lying on the ground and covered to the shoulders in dirt and withered grape vines, it looked as though Takari was crawling up out of the ground, a sight that only added to the confusion of Keya's afterdaze.

"Takari?" Keya gasped. "What are you doing here?"

A rumbling cloud of black fume appeared two terraces down and began to rain tiny spheres of magic. As the balls struck the ground, they exploded into crackling sprays of fire, lightning, or hissing green fog. Keya felt her knees weaken as she realized how close the strike had come—how close *she* had made it come—to the spell sprays.

"Good thing you moved!" Takari said.

The withered grape vines rolled aside and Takari emerged from beneath the camouflage tarp. She was protected by little more than a ragged suit of leather perforated in so many places it could no longer be called armor. Nor was she wearing any magic—not the boots of secret passing given to all rangers who served Evereska, nor even a pair of spell turning bracers or one of the mind-shielding helms Evermeet had sent to equip the elven army.

Keya motioned Takari into the group as a rosy glow fell over them. She turned to see the pink cone of a magic-killing ray illuminating them from the great central eye of a beholder on the next terrace. With the beholder were another half-dozen of its kind and twice that number of mind flayers.

"Lolth's fangs!" Kiinyon cursed. "Over the wall!"

Keya had no chance to obey. Kuhl was already lifting her by her belt, wrapping her into an arm the size of a thkaerth and diving over the wall. Keya barely had time to turn the blade of her darksword away before they came down on the other side, Kuhl crashing to the ground like a magic-felled rothé and Keya landing atop him as light as a feather. Burlen flashed past overhead and smashed down beside them in a heap of clattering armor.

"Stay low!" Kiinyon yelled from somewhere beyond Keya's feet. "Ready your magic bolts."

"Magic bolts?" the battle mage gasped. "We need to leave . . . and now!"

"Do it!" Kiinyon ordered. "Kuhl, Burlen, watch our backs."

It sounded to Keya like the lord commander was preparing for a holding action instead of a fast retreat, but after coming so close to causing a disaster just moments earlier, she knew better than to question the order. She slipped off Kuhl barely in time to avoid being crushed as he rolled to his stomach and crawled off across the terrace.

The pink radiance of the magic-killing beam vanished, and the mordant smell of rock dust began to fill the air as the beholders swept their disintegration rays back and forth across the wall. Keya readied her magic bolts, then lay listening to the sizzle of dissolving stone as she awaited Kiinyon's order. He seemed to take forever, though perhaps it only felt that way because she knew the phaerimm who had assaulted their previous position would know where they were and would be moving up to attack.

Finally, in a surprisingly calm voice, Kiinyon said, "Beholders only. Three, two, now."

Timing her move so she came up behind the sweep of the disintegration ray, Keya peered over the top of the smoking wall and loosed her spell at the second beholder in line. Three golden bolts streaked from her fingertips, striking the central eye and causing it to erupt in a bloody spray. The creature screeched in pain and began to spray the beams of its remaining eyes haphazardly along the length of the wall.

Rising alongside Keya, Takari fired five bolts into the first beholder in line and dropped it on the spot. Kiinyon and the battle mage destroyed the rest of the creatures, the wizard spreading his attacks among three of the eye tyrants and leaving nothing but starbursts of red gore, Kiinyon's magic splitting both targets cleanly down the center.

"Cover!" the lord commander ordered.

Keya and Takari dropped behind the wall side-by-side, then heard the heart-stopping rip of a fire storm erupt behind them. Recalling that Takari had no magical protection, Keya turned to throw herself in front of the wood elf. She found herself looking down the throat of a fiery spray of tiny red spheres. A handful of the flickering spheres—it could have been three or thirteen—came arcing in her direction, then encountered the magic of her spell-turning bracers and ricocheted off in a smoking meshwork of flame.

Keya landed lightly on her side and knew instantly by the stench of burned leather and charred flesh that she had not prevented all of the fiery balls from getting through. She sprang to her feet facing the direction of attack, trying through smell and guesswork to place herself in front of the wounded wood elf.

"How are you back there?"

On the terrace below, she saw a pair of phaerimm moving behind the half-ruined wall opposite her, floating away from each other with only their arms and toothy mouths exposed. There was no sign of Burlen or Kuhl, though Keya knew better than to worry about that. The Vaasans had an uncanny knack for remaining unseen, even in the barest ground, until they attacked. Keya thought it had something to do with the darkswords, but if so, it was a trick Dexon had not yet taught her.

When Takari did not answer, Keya asked again, "You alive back there?"

"Do I sound dead?" Takari's voice was thin with pain. "How are you doing that?"

"What?"

A wave of ash and dust began to roll up the terrace toward them. Keya knew that, whatever was coming, she could not shield Takari from it by standing in front of her.

Keya started, "On my—"

Way ahead of her, Takari landed on Keya's back and slipped an arm over her collar to hold on. Keya could feel the other arm hanging limply against her back.

"The darksword," Takari said. "How come it isn't freezing your hand?"

Keya glanced down at the weapon in her hand but was spared the necessity of explaining her circumstances as the wave arrived with a low, barely audible rumble.

"Jump it!" Kiinyon yelled.

Keya took three running steps and leaped.

Though Takari was small for a wood elf and Keya's muscles were hardened by half a year of military service, she was still not strong enough to carry them both over something that was nearly as high as her chest. At the last minute, she decided her only hope was to dive.

The wave caught Keya just below the hips. Though her bracers protected her from the magic itself, the momentum of the impact numbed her legs and flipped her high into the air. Takari's arm slipped free, and the Green elf went tumbling away. The world flashed past in a whirling kaleidoscope of blue sky and blackened ground, gray terrace wall and flickering orange mythal. Keya felt the darksword fly from her hand, then she crashed down flat on her back and felt the air leave her lungs in a single pained howl.

A deafening boom sounded from somewhere above her. Keya craned her neck around and saw the wall she had just left erupting into the air. She watched in dazed fascination as the dry-laid rocks—each the size of an elf's head—separated from each other and flew off in their own directions.

As the stones finally reached the top of their arcs, it occurred to her that what went up usually came down—and that the gray shapes rapidly growing larger in the air above were going to come down on her. Keya rolled to her side and wrapped her arms around her head, then counted one, two, three nearby thuds before the first crashing thump struck her pauldron.

Keya's shoulder exploded into limp agony, and only the fingers clasped behind her neck prevented it from flopping away and leaving her head exposed. Her thigh went sore and useless as a stone struck it. Another glanced off her back and sent bolts of throbbing fire shooting into her temples and down to her feet. She tried—unsuccessfully—not to scream and told herself that the pain was a good thing, that as long as she could feel she could still walk—or run, given where they were.

Keya took two more strikes—one on her rump and another in the ribs—before the stones finally stopped raining down. Her father had managed to drill enough tactical sense into her that she knew the phaerimm would not have launched a shock attack if they did not intend to follow it up with a rapid advance, so Keya allowed herself only one attempt to draw the wind back into her chest—it was as unsuccessful as her effort to leap the wave—before she rolled to her hands and knees and spun toward her attackers.

She found them halfway across the terrace, their barbed tails dripping poison and their jagged teeth showing in the smiles atop their slug-shaped bodies. Dexon's darksword was nowhere in sight, but Takari lay a dozen paces farther down the terrace, twisting about in a pained daze, one shin canted at a wrong angle and the bones of her shoulder showing through the hole the first phaerimm attack had burned in her armor.

To Keya's astonishment, the battered wood elf somehow managed to draw her sword and swing herself into a kneeling position. The phaerimm paid Takari no attention whatsoever, but the sight inspired Keya to extend a hand and call to the darksword as Dexon had taught her, by imagining the feel of the hilt in her hand.

A moment later, the darksword came tumbling into Keya's hand from somewhere behind her. Only six paces beyond Takari, the phaerimm stopped and began to whistle to each other in their strange language of winds.

"Takari, I'm right behind you," Keya called. She did not advance toward the wood elf for fear of prodding the phaerimm into action. "If you can drag yourself back to me."

"Yes . . . I can do that."

Takari's voice had assumed a strange distance, and Keya cursed silently, knowing that one of the thornbacks had taken control of the Green elf's mind. Where were the Vaasans? They were supposed to be protecting the rear . . . and what were Kiinyon and the battle mage doing?

The last question, at least, was answered by a string of mystic syllables and the deep knelling that always accompanied the summoning of a large amount of iron. Keya turned and saw what looked like a rusty square cloud fluttering down on the terrace above. She did not even notice the charging illithids until they saw the shadow and looked up and began to screech in panic. The wall slammed down an instant later, so close that Keya felt a rush of displaced air and heard the crackle of bursting illithid skulls.

A handful of the fastest illithids escaped being crushed and spun on the battle mage, their tentacles flailing in his direction as they attempted to stun him with their mental blasts. The attacks were no more effective against his helmet's magic mind guard than would have been a phaerimm's attempt to make a mind-slave of him. As the battle mage leveled his hands in their direction, Keya glanced back at Takari and found her half a dozen paces away, sword in hand and still dragging herself up the terrace. Behind her, the phaerimm continued to float, content to let the wood elf do their work for them.

Disturbed by their calm, Keya hazarded a glance in Kiinyon's direction and found him surrounded by lemure corpses, no doubt summoned by the phaerimm to prevent him from casting his escape magic. Another trio of the little devils appeared as she watched. With the darksword now stored securely in its scabbard, Kiinyon felled two with a kick and a dagger slash, but the third escaped and circled around to attack from behind.

Keya had little doubt that the renowned spellblade would be able to drop that one as quickly as the others, but the phaerimm strategy was working. Translocational magic was too complicated—even for someone of his skill—to cast while fighting hand-to-hand, and the thornbacks had more beholders and illithids rushing in from all sides. They had to do something, and fast.

Keya started forward, stretching a hand out as though to help Takari to her feet. The wood elf's gaze was still blank as she reached out to accept Keya's hand, but her sword remained down by her thigh, ready to strike.

Takari's grasp felt cold and clammy as it closed on Keya's. Something like alarm flashed in the depths of her brown eyes, then her hand clamped down hard. With surprising strength for one so battered, Takari jerked Keya down. The wood elf's blade came up in a smooth arc that, had it not met Dexon's darksword on the way, would have come down on Keya's neck.

As it was, the darksword sliced through Takari's blade as smoothly as it did phaerimm scales. The blade tumbled away harmlessly, flashing like a trout in a forest stream. Keya planted a foot in Takari's chest and pushed her to the ground, then stepped forward and sent her darksword spinning toward the nearest thornback.

A trio of screeching lemures appeared in front of the phaerimm. They were instantly sliced in half by the tumbling blade, but served their purpose by absorbing enough energy to send the darksword spinning to the ground. Both phaerimm turned to rush for the sword—and Burlen and Kuhl appeared behind them, rising from behind the far terrace like thieves stepping from an alley.

They hurled their swords as one, taking the astonished phaerimm so completely by surprise that Keya doubted the creatures ever knew what had killed them. The thornbacks simply sank to the ground half a dozen yards shy of Keya's sword and lay there with the Vaasans' weapons in their back.

"It's about time," Keya said. "What took so long?"

"An argument," Burlen answered. "Kuhl doesn't think we ought to be using you for bait."

He summoned his darksword back to his hand, and Kiinyon finally yelled for them to come running. Keya turned to see the black rectangle of a dimensional gate flickering in the air beside him. She summoned Dexon's darksword to hand, then cautiously removed her foot from Takari's chest and looked down to find the elf studying her with a look of utter astonishment.

"Are you all right?" Keya asked. "Ready to go home?"

Takari nodded, but seemed unable to take her eyes off of Dexon's darksword.

"You've got to tell me how you can do that!"

CHAPTER NINE

17 Flamerule, the Year of Wild Magic

Even for dragons, the flight to Shade was a long one. Galaeron hung in Malygris's grasp through the night and all the next day. At dusk he finally saw the city, a distant diamond of umbral murk floating low over the purple mirror of Shadow Lake. As always, it was swaddled in wisps of black fog, giving it the appearance of a lone storm cloud or a mirage. The swirling specks of a hundred or so vultures wheeled beneath it, in constant pursuit of the garbage that fell like rain from its refuse chutes. There were also larger specks, shaped like tiny crosses and circling the city in the tight formations of veserab patrols.

Malygris raised his head, and Galaeron's skin suddenly began to prickle and his hair stood on end. A deep crackling erupted a few yards above his back, and the air began to dance with silvery flashes. He craned his neck around and saw an enormous ball of blue lightning blazing inside the dracolich's empty cage of ribs. Malygris opened his jaws, and the lightning shot up his throat in a blinding white fork of energy that left Galaeron struggling to blink the glow from his eyes.

As Malygris announced his triumphant return to Shade, a terrible sense of fear and loneliness settled over Galaeron. His plan was a sound one, or the Chosen would never have agreed to the attempt, but it was also one that demanded more strength than he was sure he possessed and sacrifices that were not his alone to make. The last time he had glimpsed Aris, the giant had been hanging by his shoulders, chin resting on his chest and his captor's talons sunk deep into his flesh. Given Anauroch's heat and the dragons' refusal to stop for water, there was every reason to believe that Aris would be suffering from sun stroke in addition to whatever injuries he had endured during his capture.

Not for the first time, Galaeron cursed himself for listening to Storm. He was beginning to question just how much Aris's absence would really have raised the Shadovar's suspicions. Having seen how callously the Chosen spent mortal lives, it was easy to believe they were risking his friend's life for only modest benefit. If Aris were to die on behalf of the plan, Galaeron's resolve would be so weakened by guilt he would succumb to his shadow self.

In fact, he was starting to think that this was exactly what they wanted, that they had some other secret plan to save Faerûn that did not involve saving Evereska. Wouldn't that be just like the Chosen? Maybe they had quietly struck a bargain with the phaerimm to subvert the city defenses from the inside, so the thornbacks could attack from the outside and destroy their mutual enemy. It was just as well, then, that Galaeron had remained silent about the message from Malik. The little man might prove useful yet.

As they crossed Shadow Lake, Shade swelled from a tiny diamond of murk into a more nebulous form that might have been a solitary thunderhead on the verge of bursting, or a plume of ash drifting across the sky from some nearby volcano. A patrol of veserab riders came out and took flanking positions to either side, their jittery mounts hissing and spewing black fumes as they felt the fear aura that surrounded all dragons. Paying the escort no attention at all, Malygris continued onward until the black haze filled the entire sky ahead, then he dived to the bottom of the cloud and entered the dark murk there.

Once inside the cloud, the enclave itself grew visible, a huge capsized mountaintop honeycombed with utility passages and ventilation shafts. Malygris began to circle the crags of the overturned peak in an ever-growing spiral, his fear aura keeping the ever-growing colonies of bats and birds at a cautious distance. Even the jewel-eyed sentries who stood constant watch from their hidden crannies shrank back out of sight as the dragon passed.

Though the city could be departed in any number of the usual mundane ways—flying, translocational magic, even jumping—circling up from the bottom was the only way to enter. Even then, those seeking entrance had to come only at dusk, when the hidden city grew briefly visible. Any other approach would lead the unfortunate traveler through the plane of shadow to any one of a thousand planes it touched. It was, Galaeron knew, a defense the Shadovar considered unbreachable by any army on Faerûn and one that made them feel invulnerable enough to treat the rest of the world as no self-respecting lord would his dogs.

At last, they neared the top of the mountain, where the great Cave Gate already hung open, its huge mouth an ebony hollowness opening into an even darker wall of black stone. Malygris seemed to take great delight in extending his wings and clacking both sides of the portal with the yellowed bone tips. A properly awed murmur rustled through the depths of the cavern as he swooped to a stop at the rear of the vast Marshaling Plaza and banged down with Galaeron pinned to the floor beneath his huge talons.

A pair of similar crashes from nearer the mouth of the cave confirmed that the dracolich's companions had landed behind them.

Holding Galaeron down so tightly that his face scraped along the floor, Malygris pushed him forward.

"I bring gifts fitting to my splendor," Malygris said. His tone was surprisingly deferential, at least for a dracolich. "Here are the warmbloods you have been seeking."

"So I see." The voice was sibilant and pervasive, like a whisper rolling into the cavern from some distant passage. "It should not surprise me that dragonkind has succeeded where my own princes have failed. You are to be complimented, Malygris. This is most excellent."

The speaker was Telamont Tanthul, Most High of Shade and father of the Thirteen Princes. But even had the shadow lord not spoken, Galaeron would have sensed his presence in the chill stillness of the air—and in the cold fear that held the cavern in its grasp. Even Malygris, who as the Blue Sovereign of Anauroch need not bow to any other, lowered his skull in respect.

Without being audibly prompted, the dracolich spoke again. "Matters went as I knew they would, of course. The two-legs cowered in my shadow, and the ones we sought fled into the forest." The dracolich pricked Galaeron with the tip of his talon and added, "Though these mammals thought to hide their giant with their pitiful wizardry, they were fools. Their magic is nothing to mine, and the mere attempt revealed to us who we were seeking."

Galaeron's stomach suddenly went cold and queasy, and it had less to do with the Chosen being carried inside it than with simple fear. If Telamont's willpower could master even that of a dracolich, what chance did Galaeron have of hiding his betrayal? When the Most High's attention turned to him, the truth would become a breath held too long, and the harder he tried to keep it inside, the more desperate he'd grow to release it. His only chance was to confess all and claim the plan had been Storm's idea, that the Chosen had forced him to—

No.

That was his shadow speaking. The idea had slipped up on him so smoothly, felt so natural that he had almost accepted it as his own. But if he betrayed the Chosen, he would also be betraying his loyal friend Aris, and that one thought served as a lifeline back to his true self.

The Most High remained silent, and more words spilled out of the dracolich's mouth.

"My worshipers have spies in every city of Faerûn," Malygris continued. "When they informed my priests that the giant was selling all of his stone whittling, I knew the ones you desired would soon leave the city."

"As did we," Telamont replied. His voice was cold and calm. "Yet you acted while my sons planned and fretted. Shade is in your debt."

"Indeed," said a silken voice Galaeron recognized as that of Yder Tanthul, the Sixth Prince of Shade, "but one wonders at how easily this 'secret' was discovered. Our agents were watching as they left Arabel. Starting a beggar's riot does not seem a very secretive way to leave a city."

"You challenge me, shade?"

There was an alarming crackle in Malygris's voice, and Galaeron was almost crushed as the dracolich shifted his weight forward.

"As a courtesy to your lord," the dracolich continued, "I will suffer your insult this once. But your stink offends me. Be gone."

"Be *gone*?" Yder fumed.

Galaeron wished he could reach the little pill Alustriel had given him. Even a dracolich did not speak to a prince of Shade in such a manner, and he thought the coming clash might provide just the diversion he needed to disgorge the Chosen and escape into the city.

But Yder said no more, and after a moment of staring across the floor through Malygris's talons, Galaeron realized that the prince had indeed gone.

"Yder means no offense, Mighty One," Telamont said in a tone that was soft, and almost hypnotically soothing. "He is only a few centuries old and not yet capable of appreciating the full depth of a dragon's cunning. He stands in awe of your magnificence."

"Then it pleases me to let him live," Malygris replied. "Consider it a gift."

"You honor me too much, my friend. Is there a gift you desire in return?"

The air grew as cold and as still as ice. The hem of Telamont's dark robe—all Galaeron could see of the shadow lord—drifted forward.

"There is nothing," Malygris said. "The honor of your friendship is all I seek."

"That you have."

An expectant silence descended between the pair, then Malygris finally said, "But Techora is making demands on me."

"And Techora is?"

"The new one sent by the Cult of the Dragon," Malygris explained. "I mention this only because her petitions often interfere with our friendship."

"This is the seventh in as many tendays," the shade replied. It was a statement of fact. "One might think you are simply trying to escape the bargain you struck with the Cult of the Dragon."

"It is hardly my fault that the priests they send are all rude and foolish," Malygris rumbled. His talons tightened until Galaeron let out an involuntary groan. "Should I tolerate ineptitude among my servants?"

"No more than I." Telamont's tone was almost resigned. "Yder will see to her. That shall be his atonement gift to you. What defenses does this one bear?"

"Only the usual protection amulets," Malygris said as he raised his claw, freeing Galaeron, "and the mammal is not even as powerful as the others. The cult is beginning to run out of priests."

"That would be good," Telamont said. "Not that I have ever been displeased with the splendor of *your* gifts, Malygris."

The dracolich spun around in a great clatter of bones, nearly crushing Galaeron with a carelessly placed rear foot and upending a dozen of Telamont's bodyguards with his long tail.

"How could you? They came from a dragon."

Malygris sprang into the air and departed the Marshaling Plaza over the heads of his two assistants. Telamont motioned for Prince Clariburnus to keep watch over Galaeron, then exchanged gifts with the other two dragons, promising to undermine the walls of an annoying castle for the one that had captured Aris and to reroute a caravan trail closer to the lair of the other.

As the agreements were made, Galaeron had a chance to see that while Aris had suffered no wounds worse than the talon punctures in his shoulders, the heat and thirst had taken its toll. The giant lay on the floor half conscious, with glassy eyes, a flushed face, and limbs as white as chalk. His hands were trembling and his breath was coming in fast, shallow pants.

"Aris needs water," Galaeron said. He was surprised to find his own throat swollen and raw from thirst. "We haven't had any since last night, and the desert—"

"He can wait," Clariburnus replied. "After the trouble you two caused us, I hope he chokes on his tongue."

"I am sure that would make the Most High very happy," mewled a familiar voice. "Especially after he has waited all this time for you to recapture them."

The dumpy form of Malik el Sami yn Nasser pushed between the waists of Clariburnus and Brennus and stepped into view. Dressed in a gray tunic with a tabard of black shadow over the top, he seemed an unwitting parody of the imposing forms of the two princes—especially with his weary, bloodshot eyes and his cuckold's horns proudly displayed atop his head.

Malik turned and called back between Clariburnus and Brennus, "Go and fetch a few barrels of water, and hurry. If the giant is harmed, I will see to it that the Most High has your heads."

To Galaeron's amazement, half the troop turned and scurried to obey. Any doubt that Malik had meant his message to lure Galaeron into a trap vanished at once.

"I see you've come up in the city," Galaeron said.

"No thanks to you."

The little man came forward, and brushing aside the black pike Clariburnus put out to keep him from getting too close, stood over Galaeron.

"How could you leave Vala to suffer so long? Your cruelty nearly got me killed!"

Putting aside for the moment how one might be connected to the other, Galaeron asked, "Then she's still alive? Your message said—"

Clariburnus used the pike to push Malik away. "It is not this lizard's place to discuss the slave of a prince."

Malik shrugged, spread his hands, and said, "He is right. Perhaps, if you please the Most High, he will intervene and let you see for yourself all the terrible things that Escanor has been visiting upon her at night."

Galaeron would have smiled at Malik's cleverness, had the answer itself not filled his head with so many terrible images. The bones in his broken hand began to throb, and he thought of the crimson stain Dove had placed on it and how he would explain that to Telamont Tanthul.

The water arrived, and without leaving any for Galaeron, Malik led the soldiers carrying it over to his friend Aris. Clariburnus seemed to take delight in watching Galaeron lick his lips as he watched the little man trickle it down the giant's throat. Finally, Telamont Tanthul returned from his gift-making, and seeing where Galaeron's attention was fixed, motioned him to his feet.

"Come, you must be thirsty as well—and curious about your friend's condition."

He waited for Galaeron to rise, then placed an icy sleeve across Galaeron's shoulders and started toward the giant.

"I'm sorry for the difficult journey," Telamont continued. "It was my intention to bring you here in a more pleasant fashion, but you know dragons . . . I fear Malygris and his consorts may have been somewhat rougher on you than necessary. That young blue you killed in the Saiyaddar?"

Galaeron nodded, scarcely able to believe that the Most High was speaking to him as though he had just returned from a short trip outside the enclave.

"It was one of theirs," the Most High explained, just as they reached Malik and the water barrels and stopped. "To tell you the truth, you're lucky you made it here at all. They kept giving us beholders and asabis and demanding that we help hunt down the murderers."

Galaeron's throat grew even drier. Blue dragons were not particularly family oriented, but he had talked to enough of them while serving along the Desert Border South to know that it offended their sense of magnificence to have a warmblood kill a wyrm of their own line.

"Then I'd say we were very lucky," he said.

"We arranged something," said the Most High. He lifted an empty sleeve and pulled an ebony dipper out of the shadows, then filled it with water and passed it to Galaeron. "They really can't tell the smell of one moon elf from another, and it was a simple matter to sneak the hide into a camp one night."

Galaeron found the water going down the wrong passage and choked, spraying it out in a cone of silvery droplets.

"You didn't!"

"What choice did you leave me?" Telamont said. His voice had assumed that cold levelness it acquired whenever he struggled to contain his temper. "They kept bringing gifts, and I could hardly tell them it was you."

Galaeron looked at the empty dipper and wondered if he dared fill it again. Having tasted water, he could think of little except his thirst, but he had seen Telamont in moods like this and knew how risky it could be to presume in his presence.

On the other hand, what was the worst the Most High was going to do? Certainly not kill him, and angering him might make it easier for Galaeron to resist his will. He refilled the dipper and drank.

Telamont watched, platinum eyes burning with fury, but his empty sleeves folded calmly in front of him.

When Galaeron had finished, he asked, "Good?"

Galaeron met the shadow lord's gaze and smacked his lips.

"Have another." Telamont took the dipper and refilled it, then passed it back and said, "I insist."

Galaeron found himself gulping the water down like a drunkard breaking a long abstinence. Once the dipper was empty, Telamont took it and refilled it.

"You left Arabel with a caravan bound for Iriaebor, did you not?"

"That's so, but we were bound for Evereska." Galaeron told the lie quickly, trying to get it out before Telamont's will began to press down on him and force the truth. "To join the fight against the phaerimm."

Telamont passed the dipper back to Galaeron, and again he found himself gulping the stuff down as though it might evaporate before he could finish.

"That is what our agents suggested, and yet Yder's point troubles me. What was it he said?"

Before Galaeron could answer, a pair of yellow eyes appeared in the darkness behind Telamont.

"That starting a beggar's riot does not seem a very good way to sneak out of a city."

Yder's gaunt face took form around his golden eyes, then he emerged from the shadows and stood at father's side.

"I also thought it strange," Yder added, "that they announced their departure by selling all of the giant's work."

Yder glanced over at Aris, who lay stretched out on his back, unaware of his surroundings, with Malik kneeling astride his chest dribbling dippers of water onto his cracked lips.

Telamont refilled Galaeron's empty dipper, and Galaeron began to gulp it down. He was no longer thirsty—he could already feel Alustriel and Dove sloshing around inside, banging off the walls of his stomach—but he could not stop himself from gulping it down as he had all the others.

"Had they needed the coin for their journey," Yder continued, "I would put this down to necessity."

"But if they needed the coin, why give it all to the beggars?" Clariburnus asked. "Something here stinks like the sulfur pits of Carceri."

Telamont refilled the dipper. Though Galaeron's stomach was already so bloated it ached, he found himself reaching for it.

"It does sound odd, does it not?" The Most High pulled his hand away and asked, "Perhaps you care to explain it?"

Again, Galaeron forced the lie out before Telamont's will had a chance to compel the truth. "The statues earned more than we expected."

His fingers touched the dipper's handle, but Telamont did not let him take it.

"Is that so?" Telamont asked.

He released the dipper, and Galaeron began to pour more water into his swollen stomach. He was already in pain, but his mind insisted that he was as thirsty as before. Stopping was out of the question.

Telamont waited until Galaeron was finished, then refilled the dipper and held it in front of him. Though Galaeron felt like he might vomit up what he had already swallowed at any moment, and spill Alustriel and Dove on the Most High's feet, he wanted that water. He ached for it in the way he ached to touch the Shadow Weave, in the way a suffocating man aches for air.

"There was too much," Galaeron said. "We couldn't carry it."

Telamont continued to hold the dipper away, but remained silent. His will began to press down on Galaeron, and this time Galaeron could think only of how thirsty he had been crossing the desert and how much he wanted that water, of how badly his stomach hurt already, of how good it would feel when he drank that last dipper and finally grew so full he had to bring up everything he had swallowed.

He heard himself saying, "Besides, Prince Yder is right. We wanted to be captured."

This drew a smirk from Yder and a flash of interest from the Most High. Telamont allowed Galaeron to take the dipper, then watched with the purple shadow of a smile as the contents vanished down the elf's throat. Galaeron felt water sloshing in his throat, and his jaws began to ache.

Telamont took the dipper and refilled it, and Galaeron found his hand reaching for it yet again. Telamont held the handle away and remained silent. The weight of his will was crushing, and Galaeron could think of nothing but his aching jaws, his bloated stomach, and his overwhelming thirst.

"We came to rescue Vala," he said.

"You see?" Malik was up and sliding off Aris's chest, flinging water in all directions as he gestured with his dipper. "My excellent plan worked!"

Telamont remained silent and continued to hold the dipper out of reach. Galaeron felt the shadow lord's will crushing down on him, trying to force out the rest of the truth. He clenched his jaws and thought only of Evereska and his loyal friend Aris, of how the giant and the Chosen were risking so much to help—and there was his mistake. A dark voice arose inside him, reminding him of the blood on the Chosen's hands, telling him they could not be trusted, whispering of necessary trade-offs and secret bargains with the phaerimm.

Galaeron's mouth began to open, and it seemed to him that it belonged to someone else, to the dark being inside—

And Malik was at the Most High's side.

"Anything I want," he said. "That was our bargain."

"If *you* brought me Galaeron Nihmedu," Telamont said. "As I recall, Malygris did that."

The weight of his will diminished, and Galaeron's mouth became his own again.

"It was *my* message that lured him out," Malik said. "If I had not sent word telling him to come and save Vala, he would still be hiding from your magic in his Arabellan bolt hole."

"Be careful who you argue with, little man."

Telamont grew distracted enough to let the dipper drift into reach. Still possessed by his thirst, Galaeron snatched the handle and began to drink . . . and knew his stomach had reached its limit. Even as he drained the last of its contents, he began to gag.

"This is not some back alley flea market," Telamont continued, paying no attention to Galaeron's discomfort. "And I am no trader in trinkets."

"Nor am I some idiot dragon who can be bought off with your unkept promises," Malik retorted.

This was too much for the Most High. Telamont's sleeve lashed out in Malik's direction, and the little man tumbled away into the shadows. Three heartbeats later, a loud thud sounded from the gloom high up in the vaulted ceiling. A long breath echoed down afterward, and a softer thump from a dark corner.

Galaeron drained the last drops in the dipper and felt the contents of his stomach starting to rise. Realizing there was no fighting his own body's reflex, he flung the dipper aside and covered his mouth with both hands, then began a frantic search for someplace he could expel the Chosen where the Most High and his princes would not see.

The blow that Telamont had struck Malik would have been enough to kill most men, much less the impact against the wall that had followed, or the long fall that had followed that. Yet even as Galaeron was pushing past Clariburnus with both hands over his mouth, Malik was limping out of the darkness, one impossibly twisted arm raised in Galaeron's direction.

"Ask him," Malik said. "Ask him if he did not receive a message from me that Vala's life was in grave danger, and if he did not allow himself to be captured so he could save her life."

There was an instant of silence then Telamont said, "As you wish . . . but I warn you, my patience is at an end."

Galaeron felt a familiar burden settling over him, but this time, the Most High would need to be patient. By then, Galaeron was leaning over Aris's leg, ejecting a watery torrent down between the giant's knees. He saw a pair of silvery flashes come splashing out and disappear into the shadows beneath Aris's huge thighs. He continued to vomit a foul-smelling bile, and the weight of Telamont's will vanished.

"I think we will leave the question unanswered for now, Malik." The Most High sounded a little queasy himself. "The fact of Galaeron's return matters more than who is responsible. Name your price—but do not presume too much."

"Me? Presume too much?"

Malik's delight was evident even over sound of Galaeron's continued retching.

The little man thought for a moment then said, "I am not the type to ask for much, er, much more than I think I can get. All I want is my friend Aris."

"The giant?" Telamont asked. "You wish me to spare his life?"

"Yes, that is what I wish," Malik said. "And to have him as my slave, since I am very sure you do not want him running loose in your city again . . . and since his statues will bring an even greater profit if I have no need to share."

"I see." Telamont began to chuckle. "You may have the giant—and with him, the responsibility to see that your slave does Shade no harm."

Galaeron finally stopped retching. Wiping his mouth, he turned to see a very battered Malik standing a few paces away, examining the giant from head to foot.

A cold sleeve settled on Galaeron's shoulder, and he turned to find Telamont standing beside him.

"Come, Galaeron, let us return to the Palace Most High," Telamont said as he guided the elf toward the Marshaling Plaza's gloomy exit. "After such a difficult journey, I am sure you must be starving."

CHAPTER
TEN

1 Eleasias, the Year of Wild Magic

No hammer had ever felt so heavy in Aris's hand, nor any stone as unyielding—nor any work more forced. He was standing at the Black Portal inside his master's new church—Malik's Temple of the One and All—cutting a three-level relief of Cyric's sun-and-skull sigil above entrance. It was a perfunctory piece without heart, and given the egg-shaped corona surrounding the skull, badly flawed. He told himself that this was what came of slave labor, of forcing an artist to execute someone else's vision, but he knew better. The truth was that he lacked strength. With not a single opportunity since his arrival in Shade to expel Khelben, Laeral, and Storm from his stomach, he had refused to eat, and the long fast had left him too dizzy, weak, and blurry-eyed to do a good job.

Aris's guards—three of a dozen Shadovar -warriors hired by Malik to keep constant watch over him—made approving noises from below. Like most of their fellows, this trio acted more like assistants than keepers, passing him tools and running to fetch water kegs whenever he grew thirsty. They also heaped praise upon everything he did, even on the shape studies he made before beginning a new work. Aris did not know whether this was something they genuinely felt or that Malik had instructed them to do in the hope of keeping him happy and productive. In any case, the adoration had grown so ludicrous that the shape studies had to started to disappear when he was finished with them. He had started to shatter the roughs before discarding them, lest the guards—or, more likely, Malik—sell them as Aris originals. Even slaves had their standards.

Finally, he stepped back into the narthex to study his work and banged his skull on the rib of a ceiling vault. His head began to reel, and he had to brace himself against a column. His hammer, which he had not even realized he had dropped, clunked to the floor and sent a flake of marble as large as a vulture skittering down the arcade.

A guard peered out from around the column behind which he had dived for cover, his sapphire eyes shining like blue stars in his dark face.

"Aris?" The wispy voice belonged to Amararl or Gelthez—Aris could never tell one Shadovar from another. "Are you all right?"

Aris nodded but continued to lean against the column.

"You're sure?" This guard was bold enough to step over beside Aris's knee and ask, "Do you need a keg of water?"

"No, I am well." He flicked his free hand in the direction of the sun-and-skull relief and said, "Though it would be hard to tell from that."

"What are you talking about?" asked the first guard. "It's not beautiful, exactly, but compelling—*very* compelling. And those empty eyes . . ." He shuddered. "I can almost see the dark suns burning in them."

Aris pushed off the column and leaned forward, studying the eye sockets.

"You do not think the left eye is pear-shaped?" the giant asked."

The guard craned his neck to study the dark sigil.

"Maybe a little."

"Or the other one too large?" asked Aris.

"Larger than the other one," said the third guard. "But it only adds to the effect—and places it firmly in period."

"In period?" Aris scowled down. "What period?"

"Your Slave Period," the first guard said. "While your excellence of detail has slipped under Malik's output pressures, it's widely acknowledged that under bondage, your work has raised grimness to a level of the sublime."

"There's quite a debate raging among the princes as to whether this is your best work or your worst," said the second guard. "The Most High has yet to decree."

"What do you think?" asked the third. "It would be interesting to hear the artist's opinion."

"My opinion is that your princes know nothing about art," Aris grumbled. He started to retrieve his hammer, then suddenly realized there was a reason his keepers behaved more like assistants than guards. Trying to suppress a smile, he placed his hands on his knees and stooped down so he could speak quietly. "But I am flattered to know you think so highly of my work."

"Indeed," said the first. "Were it not for the chance to watch you, do you think anyone would work for what Malik is willing to pay?"

Now Aris *did* smile. "Is that why you were taking my shape studies?"

"Not exactly." The guards cast nervous looks at each other, then the second one continued, "We took a handful for ourselves—it's the only way someone less than a lord can afford your work—but Malik claimed most."

"He was offering them as gifts to anyone who joined his church," said the third guard.

"Why am I not surprised?" Aris growled. "After all I taught him, he knows better than to show a rough!"

The Shadovar shared smiles, then the first one said, "He certainly knew you would not like what he was doing. You should have seen his face when we told him you had started breaking them."

"I thought his eyes would pop out of his head," the second chuckled. "He actually lay on the floor beating it."

"Yes, I would have liked to see that."

Of all the betrayals Malik had perpetrated on him, Aris considered distributing his shape studies to be the worst. But he had more immediate problems to worry about, namely finding a few moments of privacy so he could swallow Storm's pill and free the Chosen—before he starved to death. Kneeling on the floor so he could speak even more softly, he fixed his gaze on the first guard, who seemed to be more or less the leader of this trio.

"Gelthez, it is not fair that Malik profits so much from my work," Aris said, "while he pays you a starving wage."

"Amararl," the guard corrected. He shrugged. "There are many things in this world that are not fair."

Aris winced inwardly and forced himself to continue in a casual manner. "That's so, but it's also true that friends must do what friends can to make the world better for each other. I think I'll make a piece for each of you, if you would like that."

The mouths of all three dropped open.

"There's nothing I would treasure more!" gasped Amararl.

"It's true what the Arabellans say," the second guard added. "Your heart is as big as you are."

The third guard was not so enthusiastic.

"What would Malik say?"

"Malik may own me, but my work is mine to give."

"I am certain he would feel otherwise," said the third guard. "And the Most High would agree. Whatever a slave makes, a master owns. That is a law as old as Shade itself."

"How unfortunate." Aris sighed heavily. "That is a strange law. No giant would ever honor it."

Aris left the statement to hang and retrieved his hammer, but continued to kneel on the floor and pretended to study his work. Just as he taught Malik the basics of sculpting, Malik had taught him the principles of negotiation. If his plan was to succeed, he knew that the guards themselves would have to suggest the critical illicit step.

It took only a moment before the first guard, Amararl, turned to the third. "Malik wouldn't have to know, Karbe."

"Of course he would have to know," Karbe said, his amber eyes flashing in anger. "He is the Seraph of my lord Cyric, the One and All! We could no more deceive him than the Most—"

The objection came to a strangled end as a dagger tip—it belonged to the second guard, Gelthez—erupted from Karbe's chest. Aris cried out in shock, but Amararl reacted by clasping his hand over the mouth of the dying Shadovar and pushing him back onto his attacker's blade. Gelthez finished the murder with a quick back and forth flick, then withdrew the weapon and let his victim collapse to the ground.

"I was so tired of listening to all that babble about 'The One,' " Gelthez said. "He was about to drive me as mad as his god."

Amararl kicked the corpse to be certain it was dead, then nodded and looked up at Aris and said, "I think we can work something out."

Aris could not stop staring at the corpse. Though he had seen plenty of death in battle, this was the first time he had ever been present at—no, been *involved* in—a murder.

"You killed him!" Aris gasped.

"Don't worry about him, Aris." Gelthez knelt over the body and wiped his dagger on its cloak. "He converted. It is no less than he deserved."

"Converted?" Aris asked. "From what?"

"That is not important. Now, what is it you want?" Amararl asked. "We may not have—"

They were interrupted by the muffled voice of someone approaching the Black Portal.

"As you can see, Prince," Malik was saying, "all of the sculpting is being done by my slave Aris—when he is not busy on his statues, of course."

Amararl and Gelthez looked to each other, their jewel-colored eyes sparkling with alarm.

"*Prince?*" Gelthez mouthed.

Their gazes dropped to the corpse between them, and Amararl mouthed some curse Aris did not understand.

"And should you decide to become a member of Malik's Temple of the One and All," Malik continued, "you will receive a discount of a quarter of the price on any of Aris's works you purchase."

The sound of Malik's feet scuffing the stairs came through the portal. Aris glanced outside, but saw only the murky facades of the buildings across the square.

"A discount?" It was the wispy voice of Prince Yder. "That does not seem much of a gift for the prestige I would bring by converting."

Gelthez grabbed Karbe by the arms and started to drag him away, but the spreading pool of blood made vain any hope of concealing the corpse. Aris pushed the body back to the floor, then motioned the two Shadovar aside.

"Of course, the discount is only on purchases made *after* you become a worshiper of the One." Malik's voice grew more distinct as he neared the top of the stairs. "Once you have announced your conversion, it will be my pleasure to make a gift to you of any work you desire."

"You are too kind." Yder's voice was even colder and more sibilant than usual. "I shall look forward to touring Aris's studio."

Outside, the crown of the prince's head was just rising into view. Aris stood and dropped his hammer on Karbe. It hit with a resounding thud, obliterating all evidence of the murder in a spray of blood and bone.

The conversation outside fell silent.

Aris dropped to his rump with a crash far louder than the sound the hammer had made, then braced his head in his hands. There was no need to pretend he was dizzy. His head was already reeling from rising and coming back down too fast.

Malik rushed through the Black Portal. On his heels followed Yder, with a dozen gold-armored escorts close behind him. All eyes instantly fell on the mess beneath Aris's hammer.

"What is this I see?" Malik gasped.

Gelthez was quick with the answer, "Aris did it!"

Aris glanced over and saw the Shadovar, trembling in fear of Yder, drawing his sword.

"Yes, that's what happened." Amararl stepped to Aris's other side. "He grew dizzy and dropped his hammer. It happened to land on Karbe."

"Is that so?"

Malik studied the mess beneath the stone hammer and the pool of blood spreading across the dark floor. When he saw the chip Aris had dislodged earlier, he marched across the narthex, his eyes bulging and his finger wagging.

"Look what you have done to my floor, you clumsy giant!" He stopped and stood in the divot. "If you would eat as I have commanded, you would have the strength to keep hold of your tools!"

Yder and his escorts followed Malik across the narthex.

"Aris is not eating?" asked the prince.

Malik cringed at his slip, then turned to face the prince. "It is nothing to concern yourself with." He tried to stop speaking there, but his face twisted into the bitter mask it made whenever Mystra's curse forced him to clarify a lie of omission. "He will certainly perish if he does not eat soon, but that will only increase the value of the pieces you purchase before he is gone."

Yder stepped past Malik to where Aris was sitting. Tall even for a prince of Shade, he barely had to tip his head back to meet Aris's gaze.

"Aris, why are you starving yourself?"

Afraid the prince would force an answer with the same magic Telamont used, Aris looked away and said the first thing that came to mind—well, the second, since the last thing he wanted to do was admit the truth.

"The food is not to my liking."

"What?" Malik said. "Have I not offered to prepare anything your heart desires? Have I not brought whole boars from your own home in the Greypeak Mountains and roasted them under your nose, only to see the entire beast vanish down a rubbish chute when you could not be enticed to eat one bite?"

Aris's mouth watered at the mere memory of the smell.

"I have never been fond of swine." His stomach growled its protest of the lie, but he added, "I am more fond of yaddleskwee."

"For the thousandth time," Malik demanded, "how can I serve yaddleskwee when you refuse to say what it is?"

This drew a sharp-fanged grin from Yder.

"I see," he said. "I think I know what this 'yaddleskwee' is."

Aris gulped, sincerely hoping the prince did not. A favorite of fire giants, yaddleskwee was the food he most hated in the world. Somehow, he had just never developed a taste for pickled beholder brains.

"You do?" Malik asked.

Yder nodded. "It is not that difficult to figure out." He raised his gaze back to Aris and said, "You refuse to eat because you are unhappy with Malik as a master."

Aris breathed a sigh of relief, and nodded. "He was once a friend—"

"As I am still! Had I not asked the Most High to make you my slave, who knows what would have become of you?" Malik paused there, fighting against his curse, then continued, "Though I doubt your fate would have been much worse, for Shade values your art too highly to execute you out of hand."

Aris ignored the protest and said, "But now he betrays me at every opportunity." Aris glared down at Malik, and allowing the bitterness of his tone to give voice to his very real anger, said, "And he betrays my art."

"Betray your art? Ungrateful giant! How many times must I save your life before you show thanks?"

Malik met Aris's glare with a fierceness born of his own injured feelings—then he seemed to recall the prince he was trying to impress and grimaced, no doubt mortified at how badly matters were going. He took a breath and composed himself, then turned to Yder.

"Pay no attention to the prattling of a temperamental artist, Prince Yder. I will deal with my slave later—and I assure you he *will* eat." Malik shot Aris a look of pure venom, then dared to touch the prince's elbow and gestured toward the nave. "For now, however, allow me to show you the rest of the temple."

Yder remained where he was and said, "I think not." He glared down at the hand on his arm until Malik removed it, then looked back to Aris. "It pleases me to hear you are unhappy in Malik's service."

Malik's eyes widened in alarm and he said, "If you think you can steal my slave—"

"Silence." Yder's hand was on Malik's throat, squeezing until it appeared the little man's eyes would pop from their sockets. "When I wish to hear your obscene voice again, I will break something and let you scream."

Given the shade of purple Malik's face was turning, Aris doubted the *Seraph* could have protested had he dared try.

Aris asked, "Why should a slave's feelings interest a prince of Shade?"

Yder's yellow eyes glimmered in amusement.

"Because it would have been a great waste to eliminate you," he said, "and now I know you will not—"

The sentence ended in a screech as Malik drew the dagger he kept hidden beneath his robe and brought the curved blade up into Yder's wrist.

The prince's hand opened, and Malik wasted no time gathering his wits or getting his breath back. He fled through the nave and vanished into the darkness between two columns.

Yder flung his arm forward, and showing no apparent concern for the hand flapping at the end of his bleeding wrist, cried, "After him!"

Yder's escorts swept past in a dark rush, leaving Aris alone with his two guards and the prince. It was only a moment before the temple was filled with shouted commands and the chime of blades probing beneath black pews. Though Aris could not decide whether he was glad for Malik's escape or sorry for it, he was not worried about what happen to the little man once he was caught. The *Seraph* had an uncanny—Ruha insisted god-given—ability to vanish the instant he was out of sight.

Still trying to figure out *why* Yder was chasing Malik, Aris asked, "You did not come here to convert?"

"Hardly."

Finally paying attention to his injury, Yder grabbed his flopping hand and pressed it back to his wrist. The bleeding ceased immediately, and black shadows began to swirl over the wound.

Yder continued, "It was bad enough when the worm stole the ear of the Most High, but this—" he rolled his eyes across the temple's vaulted ceiling—"this could not stand. It is good you were not a part of it."

Aris glanced up at the relief he had been working on and wondered how much the prince really knew about what he had been doing.

"You're no Cyricist, I mean," Yder said. "Your disappearance would have been difficult to explain."

Aris asked, "And Malik's won't?"

"No one will notice. You will finish his temple, but Malik will become a recluse, never to be seen by anyone except his personal servants—personal servants who are loyal to the Hidden One."

Aris did not have to ask who the Hidden One was. Though Shar had no temples in Shade—at least none he had ever noticed—the Mistress of the Night was popular enough in the city that Aris, gifted with the acute ears of most giants, seldom went more than a few hours without overhearing a whispered prayer to her.

At length, one of Yder's escorts emerged from the nave and dropped to a knee.

"High One, the blasphemer has vanished."

"Vanished?"

Yder glanced over to Aris's guards, who, already trembling in fear of their own fates, could only shrug and shake their heads. His golden eyes deepened to stormy brown, and he looked back to his escort.

"You have used the Hidden One's Gift?"

"We have, and still we could not find him," the warrior said. "He must have escaped."

"Escaped?" Yder's voice was cold and level. "How did you let that happen?"

The escort's gaze remained fixed on the floor.

"It is a mystery—" this was a favorite phrase of Shar's worshipers—"the exits remain blocked, and we've searched every vestibule and chapel."

Yder cursed under his breath, and it dawned on Aris how much the prince was risking. Malik had bragged many times about his relationship with Telamont and how his strategy to lure Galaeron back to Shade had earned the Most High's undying gratitude. If only half of what the *Seraph* claimed was true—and Aris knew that Mystra's curse prevented him from telling a lie—then all Malik need do to save himself was reach the Palace Most High and report what had happened. If Yder survived Telamont's wrath at all, his political base would be greatly weakened.

Having learned the hard way from Malik's treachery, Aris thought he saw a way to turn the situation to his advantage. He could not volunteer the information too readily. Malik had taught him that the surest way to manipulate someone was to remind him of his problem, then let him think you knew a way to solve it.

"I may know where he went," Aris said.

Yder spun on him. "And you remain silent?"

"It didn't occur to me that you would want the opinion of a slave."

"You are a slave by the Most High's decree," Yder said. "There is nothing I can do about that."

Aris shrugged. "It was also his decree that Malik be my—"

In a movement as smooth as a sliding shadow, Yder leaped into Aris's lap and had the tip of a black sword pressed to his throat.

"If I am to be suffer once for defying the Most High, I may as well suffer twice."

"There's a trapdoor under the altar." Aris began to wonder if he had played the game a little too well, and added, "Gelthez can show you."

Yder turned his yellow eyes on the guard.

Gelthez's jaw fell. "T-t-trapdoor?" He continued to stammer for a moment, then finally seemed to understand what Aris was doing to him. "He's lying!"

"Go look. You open it by pressing on the left corner of the base stone."

Aris had no idea whether this was where Malik had fled, but having built the secret door himself, he did know that Yder would find the passage.

"If Gelthez refused to open it for you," the giant added, "perhaps it's because he has converted."

"Converted?" Gelthez gasped. He reached for his sword and spat, "Liar!"

Yder's escort caught the guard's arm before it could reach his scabbard, then slipped behind him and pressed a dagger to his back.

Gelthez turned to Yder with a look of desperation.

"You cannot listen to him, my prince. He is a murderer! He killed Karbe."

Yder stepped off Aris's lap and said, "I thought that was an accident."

"No, it was—"

"I wasn't talking to you," Yder said.

When he turned to Amararl, it was all Aris could do to keep from smiling. Amararl had no choice except to back up Aris or admit that he had lied earlier.

"The hammer was dropped, my prince," he said. "It did not look intentional to me."

This was enough for Yder, who nodded to the escort and said, "Take him and see. If he shows you how to open the door, spare his life."

The escort bowed, and still holding his dagger at the man's back, turned to leave.

"Send a company to the temple treasure vault," Yder said. "I'll join you there after I see to the giant."

"The treasure vault, my prince?" the escort asked.

"Where else would Malik lay a secret tunnel?" Yder said.

Aris's heart fell. He had Amararl in his hold just as Malik had taught him, but that would do him no good with a prince of Shade standing there.

Yder glared at Amararl and said, "Why did you not tell me about this trapdoor, guard? Are you also a Cyric-worshiper?"

"Never, my prince!" Amararl spat on the floor and said, "That is all I have for the Mad One."

Yder remained silent, awaiting his answer.

"I—I knew nothing about the door," Amararl said. "I was not guarding the giant when he built the altar."

The prince looked to Aris, who confirmed the claim with a nod.

"Gelthez was with a different group that day," Aris lied. He was beginning to think he had spent too much time in Malik's temple; the lies were beginning come as easily as his own breath. "That was when Malik converted them."

"You will give me these names, giant."

Aris shrugged noncommittally, then finally saw how he was going to get what he wanted.

"If you like, but they will be no good to you if you do not beat Malik to his treasure vault."

Yder's eyes brightened in alarm.

"He has escape magic there?"

"He doesn't need it," Aris said. "He has a blessing from his god that helps him hide. That's how he—"

Aris had no need to finish. Yder was already rushing into the nave, calling back over his shoulder for Amararl to stand watch on the slave.

No sooner was the prince out of sight than Amararl braced himself against a black column and sank to the floor, his legs trembling and his brow dripping with sweat.

"Well done, giant," he said. "What is it you want?"

"Nothing that will get you in trouble," the giant replied. Feeling nearly as relieved as the guard, Aris started for a dark corner. "Only a few minutes alone."

CHAPTER ELEVEN

1 Eleasias, the Year of Wild Magic

Malik pulled himself up inside the false coffer in his treasure vault and kneeled there in the cramped darkness, his breath coming heavy and fast, his throat raw and aching where Yder had nearly crushed it. An alarming rasp and rattle was building behind him as his pursuers scurried up the tunnel, and even with the gifts of stealth and endurance bestowed on him by the One, he would need to hurry if he wished to stay ahead of them. It would not be easy, not when every gasp of air fanned the anguish burning in his crushed gullet, but he had to reach the palace before Yder and inform the Most High of the prince's treachery. In circumstances such as these, a ruler's findings were always dictated by the one who arrived first.

Voices began to whisper up the tunnel, and Malik knew he would be doing well to gather even the bags containing his most valuable gems before they entered the vault behind him.

"Accursed giant!" he hissed. Only Aris knew about the secret tunnel, as Malik had made him construct it secretly at night, when everyone assumed he would be sleeping. "Why am I vexed with friends who never think of anyone but themselves?"

Vowing that the giant would pay for his selfishness, Malik released the latches that held the coffer closed. Using his back to lift the lid, he rose to a crouch. The vault was dark, quiet, and enormous. Save for perhaps two dozen coin boxes and gem bags, it was also mostly empty. Building a temple was expensive—even when wealthy converts donated much of the material in exchange for Aris's statues—but Malik had no doubt the investment would prove worthwhile. Once the interior frieze work was completed, he planned to start charging a hefty fee to come and stand in the narthex. Any who wished to see the sublime work in the rest of the temple would be required to convert—a process that would require a substantial offering as proof of the novice's sincerity.

A Shadovar helmet thunked into the low lintel where the tunnel crossed the treasure vault's foundation. Reminded of the urgency of his situation, Malik slipped out of the coffer and lowered the lid as quietly as possible. The latches clicked softly as they reengaged, and he began to fumble for the magic lamp he kept on the floor at the corner of the coffer.

Instead of the smooth loop of a lamp handle, his hand found what felt like the scuff-roughened toe of a veserab-hide boot. Malik's mouth went instantly as dry as dust, and he reached for the curved dagger hidden inside his cloak. A strong hand caught him by a horn and lifted him off his feet. A second hand, still shaky because of the tendons Malik had slashed but more than strong enough to hold him motionless, clamped hold of his wrist.

"Not this time, my behorned friend," said Yder's hissing voice. "Not even you surprise me twice."

The prince bent Malik's hand back until he screamed and let the dagger fall free.

"The One will not stand for this!" Malik warned. He thought for a moment that Mystra's curse might actually permit the threat to stand, but soon heard more words tumbling from his mouth. "He will certainly punish me terribly for allowing you to interfere with the completion of his—"

The prince released Malik's wrist and brought his fist up. The blow drove Malik's jaws together with a tooth-shattering crack, and he had just enough time before sinking into darkness to wonder what would have happened to him had Yder hit him with his good hand.

✡✡✡✡✡

Wet, pale, and tiny, the Chosen looked like a trio of newborn whelps—like a trio of *stillborn* whelps, as motionless and silent as they were. Worried that the fall to the vestry floor might have been too long for such small creatures—even on his hands and knees, the distance was more than six feet—Aris reached down and nudged Khelben with the nail of his index finger.

Nothing happened, except that Khelben flopped onto his back.

Aris placed a fingertip on Khelben's chest and felt nothing. Of course, given their size differences, searching for a heartbeat was akin to a human feeling for the pulse of a locust.

"Wake up," he whispered. "You *must* be tougher than that—you're Chosen!"

When Khelben remained motionless, Aris sighed and rolled first Storm, then Laeral onto their backs. When neither moved, he placed them side-by-side and checked for signs of life as he had with Khelben.

"Hey—watch those fingers!" warned a tiny female voice.

Raising his brow in surprise, Aris put his hands down and lowered his head to within a yard of the floor, now squinting in an attempt to keep the Chosen in focus at such a close distance.

"My apologies," he whispered. "I was only feeling for a—"

"We know what you were feeling for," chuckled a second tiny woman. "And I thought an artist would be different!"

Aris turned his head from side to side, trying to get a better view of the three figures stretched out beneath his head. None of them seemed to be speaking or moving, but considering that they were Chosen, that meant very little.

"Up here, big fella," said the first voice. "Beside you."

Aris turned in the direction of the speaker and found himself looking into a pair of tiny, ivory-colored blurs. He leaned away, and the blurs slowly resolved themselves into the beautiful faces of Alustriel Silverhand and Dove Falconhand. Still only half the size of his thumb, the two Chosen were dressed in flowing black cloaks that, as they hovered beside him, gave them the appearance of some sort of shadow sprites.

"Where did you come from?" Aris gasped.

"We've been keeping an eye on you," Dove said, chuckling at his surprise.

"This is no time to play games," Aris complained. He glanced down the passage to make certain that his guard, Amararl, was still out in the nave as he had promised—and to be sure that there were no other Shadovar approaching the vestry. "Yder is here with a small army."

"I'd call it more of a strike team," Alustriel said. "When we realized where it was going, we thought we'd better tag along and see what was happening."

"A good thing we did, too," Dove said. "This is the first time we've found you alone."

"It's the first time I've *been* alone—as you can see." Aris waved a hand at the motionless Chosen on the floor. "Was it too long? I didn't eat anything, but I don't think anyone expected it to take this long."

Alustriel's voice grew reassuring. "They'll be fine, as soon as I wake them."

She flew down to the floor and kneeled beside Khelben, then began to slap his face and whisper his name into his ear.

"They went into a magical hibernation." Dove explained. She hovered near Aris's head, watching down the passage with him. "After the third or fourth day without food—earlier, if they refused to drink water you'd already drunk—their bodies would have started to draw on the Weave to sustain them. Even a giant could not have withstood that much magic flowing through him for very long, so they used a spell to shut down."

"Like bears when the snow comes."

"Something like that. Except there's still been a little magic flowing through your body. It gave you the strength to work at Malik's tempo, but it's also done some damage—affected your coordination and perception, made it difficult to do things that should be easy." Dove pointed at a lopsided likeness of Cyric on the wall. "As soon as you burn off the last of that energy, you're going to fall asleep for a very long time. Before that happens, you should eat. Eat as much as you can keep down."

"As much as I can keep down?" Aris's mouth began to water at the prospect. "When can I start?"

"Soon," Dove laughed. "but first, keep watch while I remind the Blackstaff where he is."

She gestured at the floor, where Khelben's eyelids were fluttering and his chest rising at regular intervals. Alustriel had moved on to Laeral.

Khelben's eyes opened. He took one look at the images of madness decorating the vestry and scowled in alarm.

"You had better hurry," Aris said. "One look at these walls, and he's liable to think he's gone to the Nine Hells."

Dove was already dropping to his side. She pulled her hood back and let her silver hair spill free, then took Khelben's arm.

"Now don't start hurling spells around," she said. "There's nothing to worry about."

"Of course there's something to worry about—" Khelben pushed himself into a seated position—"can't you see what Aris has been carving?"

Out in the nave, Amararl peered into the vestry passage with a beetled brow.

Aris looked down at the five Chosen, gestured in the direction of the nave, and said, "My guard's patience is coming to an end."

"Let's risk a few moments longer, in case we have need of your knowledge," Khelben said. He turned to Dove and Alustriel. "What progress have you made? Given that the city still floats, I take it you have not destroyed the mythallar."

"We haven't even found it," Dove confirmed. "Asking Galaeron's help is out of the question. He's been locked inside the Palace Most High since we arrived, and we can't go inside."

"Dare not go inside," Alustriel corrected. "It seems to be a nexus in the Shadow Weave. The closer we approach, the weaker our connection to the Weave. If we were to enter. . . ."

"No use in getting ourselves killed," Khelben agreed.

"But we have made this," Dove said as she produced something from inside her cloak. It was so tiny that it took a moment for Aris to recognize it as a folded sheet of parchment. "This shows most of the city, save for what's within the walls of the Palace Most High."

Khelben took the parchment and began to open it.

"Maybe Aris can help us," he said.

"I fear not. I've never been to the mythallar." Aris peeked out into the nave and found Amararl starting toward the vestry passage. "I should go, before—"

"I said *help*." Khelben spread the parchment on the floor and continued, "Even if you don't know where it is, you have a better idea of where to search than we do."

Aris regarded the parchment dubiously. Though it had opened to the width of Khelben's arm, it was little larger than a thumbnail to him.

"How can I read a map I can barely see?" he asked.

"Try," Dove said.

Aris glanced back to find Amararl coming down the side aisle toward the vestry, then he sighed and stooped down to obey. The instant his eyes fell on it, the image floated off the parchment and began to expand, growing so large he could barely take in all he could see.

Amazed, Aris diligently studied the map, systematically running his gaze along each street and down every service passage. It didn't take him long to realize that the image was adjusting itself to his scrutiny, sliding past beneath him to keep centered the object of his attention, growing larger or smaller depending how long his eyes remained fixed on a certain area.

Amararl's voice came down the passage, "Aris?" He sounded more worried than demanding. "What are you doing in there? What's that light?"

"Our bargain was for privacy!"

Though the voice that boomed this sounded like Aris's, it was from Alustriel's tiny mouth that the words came.

"Our bargain was for a few minutes of privacy," Amararl corrected. "It has been ten—and I heard voices."

"Echoes," Alustriel retorted. "The temple is filled with Yder's warriors."

Amararl considered this a moment, and said, "Warriors who will be returning soon. If you're not here, I'll say you ran off."

"And I that you allowed me to," Alustriel said. "Therefore, I suggest you return to your post. Tell me when you hear someone coming."

"I'm your guard, not your servant!"

"There is no difference, now," Alustriel shot back. "Unless you wish to meet the same end as Gelthez or Karbe."

She raised her tiny hand and flicked her fingers in a spell, then said in her normal voice, "Never mind him, Aris. We can still hear if he sounds an alarm, but now he can't hear or see anything in this room."

Aris spent another five minutes studying the map, then finally looked through the translucent image at the Chosen below.

"I just don't know," he said. "If I had to guess, I'd say it was inside the Palace Most High."

"That was our first thought too," Dove said, "but during the battle Galaeron described, the phaerimm were using magic. Unless they've learned to tap into the Shadow Weave—"

"We've seen no sign of that," said Laeral, who was standing with her sister Storm at Khelben's side, "but it still doesn't mean you don't have to go through the palace to reach it."

"Yes, it does," Storm said. "The phaerimm got there."

"With the aid of a malaugrym," Dove pointed out. "It might have been able to sneak them through the palace."

"Would *you* trust your life to a Malaugrym?" Storm countered. Without waiting for a reply, she continued, "If the phaerimm can get there, so can we."

"If we can find it," Laeral said. "If Galaeron can't help us—"

"We'll have to ask Vala," Khelben finished.

"Her, I can help you find," said the giant.

Aris shifted his scrutiny to the great plaza of gloom sculptures that surrounded the Palace Most High, then slowly moved his gaze along the edge until he came to a huge, many-spired mansion with a procession of flying buttresses and a long tunnel of barrel vaults.

"You will find her here, somewhere inside Escanor's palace."

The Chosen studied the map from below for a moment then Khelben said, "It would be nice if any of us had actually met her. The Shadovar were obviously trying to lure Galaeron back with all those rumors about her being Escanor's slave. What if they're just that—rumors?"

"A good point," Storm agreed. "Vala and her men *were* in service to Melegaunt, and I have it on good authority that she slew three phaerimm for them in Myth Drannor."

"Vala and her men served Melegaunt in order to keep an oath their ancestors had sworn," Aris said. "Their duty was discharged when Shade returned."

"But that does not mean she is Escanor's slave," Storm pressed. "Ruha said that it was her choice to remain with the prince."

"So Galaeron would escape before his shadow took him," Aris said. Storm's aspersions were beginning to irritate him, and he let it show. "She loves Galaeron as a crane loves its mate. If she is with Escanor now, it is not by her choice."

Storm raised her brow at his tone, but shrugged and gave a little nod. "If you say so, Aris."

"I do," he said. "If you wish her help, all you need do is say you are friends of Galaeron's."

"Good," Khelben said. He began to fold the parchment, and the map went dark. "That's just what we'll do. My thanks for your help, Aris. We'll try to fetch you before the city falls, but that may be—"

"We are all risking much," Aris interrupted, "but only Galaeron's sacrifice is certain. If you value that, save Vala first. The rest of us are here by choice."

"If that is what you wish, my friend." Khelben met his eye and nodded. "We will do what can be done."

✡✡✡✡✡

Malik awoke to the sound of snakes hissing into both ears. Judging by how he felt, they had bitten him a dozen times, a hundred times. His head throbbed and his back ached. There were pins of light piercing his eyes and rivers of fire coursing through his veins, and he had a bladder that felt like two gallons of wine in one gallon of space. The snakes were about to draw him into quarters. They had him by each wrist and each ankle, and they were all pulling in opposite directions. His arms were ready to pop from his shoulders and his legs to divide what no man ever wished to have divided.

As Malik's head began to clear, the hissing grew softer and more distant, and he realized it was not snakes hissing into his ears. It was voices, the whispering voices that filled the throne room of Telamont Tanthul.

If he was in the presence of the Most High and in so much pain, there could only be one explanation.

Yder had beat him to the palace.

"It is not true!" Malik screamed. "Whatever the prince says, it is all a terrible lie!"

For once, his curse did not compel him to say more, and the whispering quieted. A strange sloshing sounded beside him. Malik opened his eyes and saw white fire in his brain. He closed them again, and the fire went away.

"Why do you torment me like this?"

He tried to turn toward the sloshing and found his head held motionless by a strap across his brow.

"I have done nothing wrong!"

"Oh, but you have, Seraph," hissed a cold voice—a familiar cold voice. "You have stolen from the Hidden One."

"Stolen?" Malik cried. "What have I stolen . . . aside from a few dozen coins from the pockets of worshipers in my own temple?"

"The worshipers themselves," the voice said. "You have stolen the Lady's faithful."

Malik was greatly relieved to recognize the voices as Prince Yder's. If Yder was doing the speaking, then they would not be in the Palace Most High, and it could not be Telamont Tanthul who had ordered the terrible punishment.

A pair of cold fingertips pulled Malik's eyelids open. The brilliant fire returned, but this time the white fire was only a silver light as blinding as the sun, and there was a chasmal darkness in the center—with two blazing eyes and a heart of cooling embers.

"The Lady is angry, Malik."

As Yder spoke, Malik's eyes grew accustomed to the pain, and he discerned a pair of huge hooked horns crowning the head of the dark figure above him.

"In-d-deed," Malik stammered. "I can see that for myself . . . though in truth I must say she does not look very ladylike to me."

This caused a strange murmur of gasps and chuckles to spread outward behind Yder. There followed a moment of silence, and Malik had the sense that his captor had turned away to glare at his followers.

"Make a joke of your own god if you wish, little man," Yder said, "but when you make fun of the Hidden One, it is the Lady who laughs."

The prince's fingers pressed down until Malik thought his eyeballs would burst.

"Who was joking?" Malik cried.

The murmur that followed this was even louder than the first. Yder's hand came away from Malik's head.

"Silence!"

The command was muffled, as though the prince had turned his back when he spoke it. Malik blinked the spots from his eyes and again found himself staring at the dark figure overhead. It was a ghastly demon as large as Aris and as black as night itself, with long curving talons at the end of outstretched arms.

Yder returned his attention to Malik and said, "Mock the Hidden One again, and I shall pull your brains out by your own antlers."

The prince grabbed Malik by one of his horns, and a dark hand appeared on the hooked horn of the figure overhead.

Malik bit his own cheek, lest he cry out in astonishment and give the prince an excuse to do as he threatened. The monster above was certainly his own shadow, but that gave him no hint of relief. Melegaunt Tanthul had once summoned the wretched being to serve as a guard, and the accursed thing had made clear it would like nothing better than throttling Malik with its own hands.

"You are learning, Seraph," Yder said. "Perhaps this will not be as difficult as I feared."

"Not difficult would be good," Malik agreed. "I am a captive in the temple of Shar the Ni—?"

Yder struck him a blow that returned his thoughts to their muddled state.

"Do not speak the Hidden One's name!"

"I am only trying to be certain," Malik complained. "How do you expect to convert me, if you will not tell me who it is I am to worship?"

For the first time, Yder's face came into view. He was wearing the black skullcap and purple mask of the high priest.

"You would convert?" he asked.

Malik's chest began to grow cold and tight, as it had when Fzoul Chembryl had asked a similar question in the hidden temple of Iyachtu Xvim. At the time, he had been weak from torture and assured only of a life of impoverishment in servitude to a mad god, and nothing would have pleased him more than to find protection in the church of some other deity. But that had been before he understood how impossible it was for him to betray the One, and before he had established what promised to be—in addition to the altar that would give Cyric control over the Shadow Weave—the wealthiest temple in all Faerûn.

"Convert?"

The tightness in Malik's breast became a smashing weight. The heart beating—slurping—in his chest was not his own, but a rotting mass of curd that, in a fit of the deranged genius of the mad god, the One had plucked from his own body and traded for Malik's mortal—though far healthier—heart. Since that day, the mere thought of betraying Cyric brought crushing agony. It was all Malik could do to continue speaking.

"Certainly I will convert." His chest felt as though someone was standing on it. "I will convert you and all of your followers to the Church of Cyric, the One and All!"

The weight vanished.

Yder's fist came from nowhere, catching Malik in the side of the mouth. Two teeth came loose and got caught in his throat. Malik began to choke.

"Trifle with me all you wish," Yder said. "The goddess relishes your blood on her altar."

Malik's only answer was a cough. He grew dizzy from lack of breath, and the world started to close in around him. He fought to stay conscious, summoning his anger by imagining his wealth in the hands of Prince Yder and his filthy Sharists.

"Nothing to say?"

Yder struck him again, and Malik's mouth grew so full of blood that it bubbled over his lips and spilled down his cheeks onto Shar's altar.

"That is good, Seraph," Yder said. "You are learning to please the Lady."

Unable to do anything else, Malik stared at the monstrous shadow hanging above him. A purple crescent appeared where the traitorous thing's mouth should have been—a smile. It thought he was going to choke to death.

Malik continued to cough.

"You *will* convert, Seraph," Yder said. "All you control is how long it takes."

"The Hidden One rules all," said someone behind the prince.

A chorus of whispers filled the chamber as Shar's worshipers repeated the paean. Had he not been so busy coughing and choking, Malik would have laughed. He might die upon Shar's altar or even rot upon it, but he would never convert. That was the one thing he did not control at all.

Malik's vision narrowed to a black tunnel, then went completely black. Yder's voice came to him from far away, demanding that he pay attention and not insult the Hidden One by closing his eyes upon her. The prince's cold fingertips settled on his eyelids and pulled them open, and that was the last thing Malik felt before sinking into a soft bed of unconsciousness.

The next thing was the heel of a large hand slamming him between the shoulders, and the icy fingers of another one dangling him upside down by his ankle.

"Breathe, you craven little ranag!"

The hand struck Malik again. The teeth upon which he had been choking flew from his lips, along with a mouthful of blood and bitter-tasting bile. He started to gasp and cough at the same time, two conflicting actions that left him helplessly hiccuping for breath.

"Did you really think you could escape that easily?" Yder demanded. "The Hidden One will not be deprived of her pleasure."

Malik opened his eyes and was blinded by the same painful radiance as when he had returned to consciousness before.

"And I am most thankful for that," Malik said, "though I know it is likely to cost me a month of terrible agony!"

Knowing Yder would interpret his gratitude as progress toward a conversion, Malik would have liked to stop there and enjoy the reward any good torturer would bestow on him as incentive for further progress—but Mystra's curse would not allow it.

"Now I can finish what I have started by converting you and your followers to the Church of Cyric—" Malik tried to bring his hands up to cover his mouth, but found his wrists manacled together behind his back. The words continued to spill out—"so that I may spare my soul the danger of having to present itself at the Shattered Castle after I have failed to seize control of the Shadow Weave for the One, as he instructed."

Yder shook with such a rage that the chains binding Malik's wrists began to jingle. Malik cringed and tried to guess whether he would lose fewer teeth by clenching his jaw or leaving it to hang slack, but the blow never came. Instead, the prince remained silent and continued to hold him upside down, allowing Malik a few precious moments to study his surroundings.

They were, as Malik had guessed from the altar, in a temple to Shar—though it was certainly far from what he had imagined such a place would look like. While the walls were covered with the expected images of mysterious women and dark disks limned in purple flame, the chamber itself was blindingly bright, so much so that the shadows dancing on the walls seemed more real than the worshipers standing motionless in long rows of pews. There were easily a thousand Shadovar there, all submerged to their knees in a glimmering pool of mirror-bright fluid. As thick and viscous as quicksilver, the liquid was slowly flowing out toward the edges of the chamber, where it gathered at the walls and vanished down the drainage pits in lazy whirlpools.

Malik recognized the liquid instantly. It was the same thing that he and his friends had found inside the Red Butte in Karsus, spilling out of the Karsestone that Galaeron had used to summon Shade back into the world.

The prince hoisted Malik by the chain between his manacles, forcing his arms up and back until he thought his shoulders would break.

"In my centuries," Yder said, "I have learned a few things about pain."

Malik felt sick to his stomach. Though the One had blessed him with the ability to suffer any amount of agony and still have the strength to perform his duties as Seraph, that did not mean he was immune to pain. Quite the contrary. It seemed to him that he always felt pain more acutely than those around him—and usually a great deal more of it.

As Yder turned back toward the altar, Malik was not all that surprised to find himself looking at a luminous white boulder about the size of a horse. There was a jagged fissure down the center, and from this crack poured a steady flow of the silvery liquid that had filled the temple.

The stream was, Malik knew from his earlier adventures in the Red Butte, the last whole magic in the world. Seventeen centuries earlier, a mad Netherese archwizard named Karsus had tried to steal the godhead of Mystryl, the goddess of magic at that time. It had been a terrible mistake. The Weave had filled Karsus to bursting and killed him on the spot, and it had split into the Weave and the Shadow Weave. The luminous white boulder was Karsus's heart—all that remained of the mad archwizard—and the silver magic pouring from it was all the remained of the original, unsplit Weave.

Though Cyric's rancid heart began to slush so hard that Malik could barely hear himself think, he forced himself to remain calm. The Karsestone, as they had dubbed the boulder, was undoubtedly an artifact of untold power, but it seemed to Malik that for Shar's worshipers to tolerate its bright light inside their hidden temple, it had to be something more—something much more.

"The Karsestone!" Malik gasped as though he had just realized what he was looking at, for it was important to his plan that Yder did not realize how much Malik understood about what he was seeing. "That seems an odd altar for followers of the Nightsinger."

"Shadow is born of light," Yder said.

The phrase was repeated by a thousand whispering voices as Yder hoisted Malik onto the stone and laid him facedown.

"All the same, so much bright light must be a great insult to your goddess . . . unless the Karsestone is the source of the Shadow Weave, of course." Malik swore a silent oath, for it been Mystra's curse that compelled him to add such a clumsy probe, then he hastened to add, "Or the one you worship here is not really Shar, but some other Hidden—"

Malik's face smashed into stone as his tactic succeeded in angering the prince and distracting him from the gaff.

"I told you never to call the Hidden One by name."

"My apologies," Malik said. His voice sounded rather nasal, for his nose had been shattered and was pouring blood down over the Karsestone. "I only meant that this is certainly the last place the Most High would look for his stolen Karsestone."

"What makes you think it is stolen?" Yder asked, not quite able to keep the smugness from his voice.

Ever wary of the Seraph's ability to escape, the prince pinned Malik's neck to the stone with one hand while he removed the chain from the manacles and attached it to a ring hanging from an iron post alongside the altar. Malik didn't know whether to be glad his plan had worked or ashamed it had taken so long for him to see the true nature of things.

For the Shar worshipers to tolerate the Karsestone's brilliance in their temple—and, more importantly, for the goddess not to strike dead the ones who permitted it to be there—the boulder had to be of inestimable value to the Nightsinger. Malik no longer doubted that much—it was the source of the Shadow Weave, as Mystra's curse had caused him to blurt out, or something that she wished to keep hidden from the other gods.

More terribly, if Shar considered Shade a safe place to hide such a thing—and if Telamont Tanthul truly had given the Karsestone to Yder for the Hidden One's temple—then she had to feel secure in her control of the city. For Shar to feel secure in her command of the Shadovar, she had to control the Shadow Weave itself.

"The spiteful hag!" Malik cried. "She has commanded it all along!"

"Curse her now all you wish, Malik."

Yder spun him around then flipped him onto his back and fastened another chain to his second manacle.

"Before this is done," the prince added, "you will sing her praises."

"And you will lick the offal from my boots!" Malik shot back. "The Shadow Weave is Cyric's by right! Am I not the one who saved the life of that fool Galaeron so he could betray his word to Jhingleshod and steal this stone?"

It was his own anger that compelled him to say this and not Mystra's curse, but he knew it was a mistake the moment the words spilled from his mouth. Yder's yellow eyes turned as bright as the sun. He bared his ceremonial fangs and bent so low that Malik feared the prince would bite his nose from his face.

"Is that why you came here?" he demanded. "To steal the Hidden One's crown?"

Malik said nothing and looked away.

"Answer!" Yder commanded. "Answer, or I will feed you to your own shadow."

The prince pulled his head aside so that Malik could see his shadow's hateful eyes glaring down at him. No longer did the monstrous thing seem dependent on Malik for its form. It looked as thick and as solid as any giant he had ever seen. Malik looked away on the pretext of meeting Yder's angry gaze.

"Do you think I am afraid of my own shadow?" he demanded. "I am favored of the One. I have seen a thousand things that were a hundred times worse . . . though never any who know all the wretched things I have done in my life."

"Look!" Yder grabbed Malik's aching jaw and forced him to stare up into his shadow's angry eyes. "You have seen the trouble Galaeron's shadow has brought on him. What do you think yours would do, were I to let it inside you?"

"Why should I fear such a thing?" Malik squeaked. "If a shadow is all the things I am not, this one is undoubtedly as charitable as I am selfish, as trustworthy as I am corrupt, as brave as I am craven. My shadow would only make me all the things that women desire and men admire."

"What of Cyric?" It was the shadow that asked this question—and that flashed a brutal purple smile as it did so. "How would he feel about a Seraph who was all those things?"

The blood went cold in Malik's veins, and he swung his gaze to Yder.

"What was your question again?"

CHAPTER TWELVE

1 Eleasias, the Year of Wild Magic

In the dim light of the cell, the link was easier for Vala to feel than to see, even with skin numbed by cold and calluses. She worked her foot up the chain until she felt pit-roughened metal, then pinched the loop between her toes and lifted it toward her mouth. Even flexible as she had grown over the past couple of months, she could not bring it all the way to her face. Once the chain went taut, she used her leg muscles to pull herself closer. She let her toes slide down one link then spit a mouthful of saliva onto the pitted surface.

Vala had her doubts about whether she could actually spit her way to freedom, but with her hands manacled behind her back and no other tools to work with, it was the best she could do, and it gave her something to focus on when she was not being abused by Escanor or his retainers. She could not just sit there in the dark, waiting between sessions. She had to keep trying, to know she was at least attempting to escape.

Besides, when she had started, there had been no pits in the link at all. Vala let the chain go slack, then wrapped her toes into it and began to jerk downward against the eye hook that secured it to the wall. A hundred times, then find the link and spit. If she just kept working at it, something would give. The hook would loosen in the wall, or the link would grow rusty and break, or a guard would think she had lost her mind and grow careless enough to let her kill him. *Something* would happen. It had to, if she was ever to see her son again.

A voice whispered, "Vala?"

Vala hit the end of the chain and was back on the floor before she realized she had jumped. She spun on her seat, her legs cocked for thrust kicks, and found no one there.

Great, she thought. Something *has* happened. I've started to hear things.

"We're not going to hurt you," the voice said.

Vala squinted toward the voice and saw nothing but murk, then a tiny man in black robes hopped onto her foot. She wasn't just hearing things. The man—the *delusion,* she corrected herself—had an unruly black beard and dark eyes, but his face and arms were too light to be Shadovar.

"No need to cower, my dear," he said. "We're friends of—"

Vala flicked the figure off her foot and heard it hit a wall with a real-sounding thud. She *was* cowering, frightened of her tortured mind's own phantasms.

"I won't let this happen," she said to herself. Vala straightened her shoulders and raised her chin—but she did not lower her leg. "Go away!"

"Softly, child!" This time the voice was female, and it came from over near the door. "Mind the guard."

Another voice, on her other side, began what sounded like a spell. The bearded figure returned, this time flanked by two female figures with flowing silver hair, and Vala realized that, phantasms or not, they were all around her. There could be hundreds of them out there in the dark, swarming over the floor. Thousands, maybe, an army of dark little shadow faeries come to feast now that her flesh was suitably battered and bruised. She screamed. She could not help herself, the sound just erupted as she let out her next breath.

The shadow faeries cringed and looked toward the door, and in the next moment Vala was silent. Her mouth remained open and her throat continued to vibrate, but there was no more sound.

The male faerie looked toward the door and asked, "The guard?"

"Still thinking about it," the female voice whispered. "He's curious, but not alarmed."

Vala could see her, another silver-haired faerie down on the floor, peering around the corner of the archway.

"Keep an eye on him," the male said.

Followed by the two silver-haired females, he circled toward Vala's head. They were joined by a third female, which fluttered over from behind Vala and settled on the floor next to them. Vala tried to spin around to bring her feet toward them but one of the females made a motion with a sliver-sized wand, and she found herself unable to move.

"I'm sorry we frightened you," the male said. "Clearly, your ordeal has taken more of a toll than we imagined."

Had Vala been able to talk, she would have suggested that they change places and see what kind of toll being a Shadovar slave took on him.

"Can you stop screaming?" asked one of the women. "We have some questions."

Vala grew aware of her aching jaw and realized that her mouth continued to gape open, that her throat was raw from screaming. She clamped her mouth shut and glared at the black-clad faeries beside her. They certainly looked solid enough.

The woman nodded, made a dismissive gesture, and a whimpering, rasping sound came to Vala's ears. It took a moment to identify the source as her own throat.

"Good," the man said. He held his hand out and moved it in a placating motion that made Vala want to kick him. "We're friends of Galaer—"

"Galaeron?" Vala finished for him.

She brought her breath under control. Phantasms or not, she could not have these faeries telling Galaeron that she had whimpered when they came for her.

"He sent you?" she asked.

The women looked at each other. They looked uncomfortable.

"What's wrong?" Vala demanded. "Is he hurt?"

"We wouldn't know," the man, whose manner was gruff, said.

One of the faerie women stepped in front of the male and said, "Galaeron is on a mission of the utmost importance to all of Faerûn."

"As are we," said the second woman, also stepping in front of the male. "Perhaps it would help if we introduced ourselves. I am Storm Silverhand."

"I'm Dove Falconhand," said the woman at the door.

"I am Alustriel Silverhand," said the woman who had cast the spells. She motioned at the last woman, who was still standing beside the black-bearded man. "This is our sister Laeral."

"And that would make me Khelben Arunsun." The faerie man pushed his way between the two women who had stepped in front of him. "Now that you're properly awed, maybe you'd care to answer a question or two and help us save the Heartlands."

Vala scowled down at the male, quite certain that she had lost her mind.

When she didn't say anything, Khelben rolled his eyes and turned to the one who had introduced herself as Alustriel.

"How can she not know who we are?" he asked. "Is Vaasa so backward?"

"We know of the Chosen even in Vaasa," Vala said. "We also know the difference between flesh and phantasm. Why would the five of you show up in my cell, the size of dolls, unless I were mad?"

"Because we need your help," Alustriel said. She stepped over and placed a hand on Vala's jaw. Her touch felt real enough, solid and warm. "We must find the mythallar, and you're the only one who can help."

"Trouble!" hissed the woman by the door. "The guard's coming."

The faeries vanished as quickly as they had appeared, leaving Vala alone in her cell.

"Wait!" She felt more isolated than ever—and more certain that she was losing her mind, more frightened. "Don't!"

The guard appeared in the doorway, a hulking shadow lord with ruby eyes and filed teeth. Vala thought he was Feslath, one of Escanor's favorites.

"Don't what?" Feslath demanded. "Who are you talking to?"

Though his Shadovar eyes could see in the dark as easily as Vala could see in daylight, he did not even bother glancing around the cell. He knew as well as she did that there was no one in the room, that her mind had finally snapped.

"I asked a question, slave."

Vala glared at him and refused to answer. She was not worried about revealing the presence of her visitors—the delusions were hidden safely inside her mind—but she could not obey, not even in this. Once she started to surrender, it would grow easier and easier, until she finally belonged to them in spirit as well as body.

"You defy me?"

Feslath grinned and took the whip off its hook. He did not even need to look to find it.

"As you like. Assume the position."

Vala was supposed to turn her back and bow her head so her eyes would be protected.

Instead, she glared straight into Feslath's eyes and said, "Go suckle a veserab."

The whip caught Vala across the chest almost before she had finished the curse. Refusing to give him the satisfaction of a scream, she clenched her jaw and took the next strike in silence as well, but the third caught her across the ribs and forced an involuntary gasp. Feslath, in particular, was a master of the technique and delighted in forcing her body to emit the sounds her mind held in check.

The next lash caught her across the previous one, and Vala began to grow dizzy. The assault would not end until she fell unconscious. Praying that he would keep landing his strikes on top of each other, she glared into his eyes and watched his arm draw back.

A dark-cloaked figure rose behind Feslath and caught his arm by the wrist. Feslath's eyes flared red, and he spun around to find the butt of a large black staff crashing into the side of his head. His knees buckled, and he melted to the floor like a suit of empty silks.

Khelben Arunsun, standing fully six feet tall, kicked the shadow lord in the ribs—hard—to make certain he was unconscious, then came to kneel beside Vala.

"You could have answered him," he said.

Vala shook her head, and vaguely aware of her gaping jaw, gasped, "You *are* real."

Khelben nodded, but made no move to undo her manacles.

"Does that mean you'll help us?" he asked.

Vala shook the chain by which she was attached to the wall.

"Does that mean you'll get me out of here?" she asked in return.

Khelben's face grew impatient.

"We'll come back for you, but our mission depends on secrecy and surprise. We can't take you along now without the risk of drawing attention to ourselves."

Vala considered this a moment then pointed her chin at Feslath's fallen figure.

"You're already running that risk," she said. "And no offense, but if you're going after the mythallar, I don't like your chances of getting back here to rescue me before this rock hits the ground."

"The fate of Faerûn itself hangs in the balance!" Khelben's voice was deep and righteous. "You would bargain for your own life?"

"I have a son who needs a mother." Vala didn't flinch at Khelben's angry scowl, but added, "I am not the one who is bargaining."

"She has a point, Khelben."

Dove and the other three Chosen appeared on the floor between them, still no more than a hand high.

Dove continued, "We promised Aris—"

"We will keep our promise," Khelben insisted, "without risking our mission."

"You're sure our mind wiping magic will work on a Shadovar?" Alustriel asked. "They are not beings of the Weave."

"Even if it does, there will still be the lump on the guard's head to explain," Storm said. "He'll wonder how he got it, and that in itself might give us away."

"I know a way it won't matter," Vala said, seeing her chance.

Khelben looked to her and raised his brow.

Vala explained her plan, and when she finished, Khelben continued to study her with narrowed eyes.

"This will work," Vala said. "It stands a better chance than your memory-stealing magic."

"Alustriel's memory-stealing magic," Khelben corrected. "That's not what worries me."

"Then what does?" Laeral asked.

"Vala," he said plainly. "It's not as though she's helping us out of the goodness of her heart. If Galaeron couldn't tell us where to find the mythallar, how do we know Vala can? She might be lying so we help her escape."

"Galaeron returned to the Palace Most High via Telamont's magic," Vala said. "I *walked* home."

Khelben continued to look doubtful.

"What if I were lying?" Vala asked. "Would you leave me here to fall with the city?"

"Of course not," Alustriel said. "We promised Aris we wouldn't."

"Then why should I lie?"

Finally, Khelben smiled and said, "I suppose you're right at that, aren't you?"

Khelben dragged the unconscious guard over to Vala and laid him at her feet. While she used the heel of her foot to make it look as though *she* had knocked him unconscious, Khelben removed the keys from his belt and undid her manacles. Once she was free, Vala wrapped the chain around his throat and began to choke him. None of the Chosen watched this part. They clearly wished there had been another way.

Not Vala. She had only to think of the beatings she had suffered at Feslath's hands for this small vengeance to seem not nearly enough. The thought sent a chill down her spine, and she found herself wondering if it was only magic-users who could let their shadows inside.

Once the guard was dead, Vala took his equipment and dressed herself in his clothes, and Khelben shrank himself back to the size of the others. She stuffed all five of the Chosen into her pockets, and aided by spells of invisibility and silence, crept down the stairs to the base of the confinement tower. Here, she had to kill two more guards, the first when he turned toward the opening door, the second while he was struggling with the dying body she had shoved into his arms. Leaving the bodies inside the stairwell behind the locked iron door, she used the second one's cloak to wipe the blood off the floor, then tossed it into a garderobe and left the area.

From there, it would have been a simple matter to descend the back stairs and vanish into the city. Instead, Vala entered a servant's passage and traversed the back of the great palace. Though she passed a constant stream of maids, pages, and butlers, she remained concealed from both eye and ear, for the magic of the Chosen was powerful enough to remain effective even after combat had been joined.

A quarter hour later, Vala emerged from the servant's passage into the dusky lobby outside the prince's private wing. The great anteroom doors were closed and guarded, as they had been since his return from the battle on the High Ice, and for a moment she despaired of making her plan work. There was no other way into the wing—at least that she had ever seen—and even invisible, she could not best a dozen of Escanor's shadow lords.

But, as Vala had hoped, the prince's duties could not be ignored even when he lay half-dead in his bed. It was not long before a courier approached the great doors bearing a shadow-filled message bottle. Vala fell in on his heels, following so closely that when a guard ordered him to stop three paces from the doors, she had to dodge around his side to keep from running into him. The guard took the message bottle and dismissed the courier, waiting until he had vanished down the corridor before he turned and knocked softly on the door.

Vala stood at the guard's side for a seeming eternity, barely daring to exhale lest her breath tickle the hair on his arms. Finally, a steward opened the door just far enough to lean out and take the message bottle. It would probably have been wise to wait for a serving maid or some other domestic whose duties would require opening the door more than a shoulder's width, but there was precious little time to make the decision, and Vala knew that the deaths in the confinement tower would not go unnoticed for long. She dropped to her haunches, pivoting around in front of the guard, and duck-walked sideways through the narrow opening, trying so hard not to step on his heels that the closing door caught her foot.

The guard called something to the chamberlain, who was already a step away, then shoved with his shoulder. Vala's foot seemed to fold along the length, but the heavy door bounced back enough for her to pull her foot into the room after her.

The door clicked shut, and Vala dropped to her seat, at once sighing in relief and opening her mouth in an unvoiced scream of pain. It would have been nice to set aside one of the weapons in her hand and check for broken bones, but such indulgences killed more warriors than they saved. She rolled to her knees and came up facing the interior of Escanor's large anteroom, where half a dozen clerks sat attending to the prince's private business.

Vala started across the chamber on her hands and knees, angling for the dark corridor that led deeper into the prince's inner sanctum. There, she had to slip under the crossed glaives of another set of guards.

Once inside the murky passage, she rose and put some weight on her foot. The pain was dull and general, more like a bad bruise than a break. She took a few steps. Finding the foot would support her, she continued through Escanor's private study into his dressing room, and passing another pair of guards and a small clique of servants at each stage, from his dressing room into his large and opulent bedchamber.

Escanor lay alone in his bed, little more than a man-shaped shadow cleaving to a cage of black ribs. His beating heart was visible inside, still glowing faintly with the light of the Weave flames that had nearly consumed him. He was attended on one side of the bed by a servant and on the other by a black-robed priestess wearing the purple mask of Shar. Two of Escanor's battle lords were standing at the foot of the bed. Vala's darksword was on display in a rack above the prince's headboard, locked behind a pair of crystal doors.

Vala! Khelben's voice came to her inside her head. *In the name of the Weave, what are you doing?*

Vala did not answer. She had not told the Chosen about this part of her plan, but it was as necessary to their success as finding the mythallar. She stepped over to the foot of the bed, and in a single spinning stroke, slashed the throats of both guards.

The men had barely fallen before the priestess raised her hands and began a wispy prayer to her hidden goddess. Vala cut this short by lashing out with the whip in her other hand. The cord wrapped itself tightly around the woman's throat, and the prayer ended in a strangled gasp as Vala jerked the priestess off her feet. The servant started for the door, his jaw working in shock, but emitting only strangled gasps. She spun past the end of the bed, bringing her sore foot up in a hook kick that caught him square in the nose with the hardest part of her heel. He flew off his feet so hard that the back of his head hit first and made a sickening crack on the stone floor.

Giving up on her spell, the priestess charged blindly forward, using one hand to pull against the whip around her throat and the other to slash her dagger blindly through the air. Vala waited for the next stroke to sweep past then she stepped forward and snapped the outside of her hand into the hinge of the woman's jaw. The priestess went instantly limp, her eyes rolling back in her head and the dagger slipping from her hand.

Vala dropped the whip and turned back to the bed. In Escanor's shadowy eye sockets were a pair of copper flames, faint and flickering as he struggled back to consciousness.

Vala! If you're counting on us to help you kill—

"Quiet."

Though Vala spoke the word aloud, she heard the word only in her mind. She started forward toward the display case. The flames in Escanor's eyes brightened, and she knew the prince was returning to his senses. She hurled her sword, reached for her dagger, and leaped onto the bed.

A wisp of shadowy arm rose through the covers. Her tumbling sword ricocheted upward and smashed a crystal door, and something hit her in the chest like one of Aris's hammers. She fell off the bed backward and landed face-down on the floor.

"Guards!" Escanor's voice was barely a croak, but a croak loud enough to cause a stir out in the dressing room. "Help!"

Vala raised her hand and called silently to her darksword. She heard the tinkling of shattered crystal, and the weapon came sailing over the foot of the bed. The hilt slipped into her palm like the hand of an old friend. The blade was trailing a wisp of shadow where it had brushed Escanor's body.

You have your sword—time to go! Storm urged. *Out onto the balcony.*

Vala rolled sideways to her knees and came up with her arm cocked to throw. When she saw Escanor swinging out of the opposite side of the bed, she did just that. The blade caught him between the shoulder blades, slicing through two ribs and the faintly pulsing heart.

The prince died without a scream. His ribcage simply dropped to the floor in two pieces. The guards from the dressing room rushed into the chamber to find the cleaved heart dissolving into a cloud of shadow.

"*Now* it's time to go."

Again, Vala heard her words only in her own mind. As the guards rushed to their dying prince, she called the darksword back to her hand. She would have liked to stay and find the magic ring given to her by Corineus Drannaeken in the catacombs beneath Myth Drannor, but a search of that magnitude was out of the question. She raced toward the double doors and leaped into the air—then barreled into two more guards as they came rushing in.

Vala planted one foot on each of their shoulders—she was aiming for their throats, but had not jumped high enough—and she managed to drive enough of a seam between the startled Shadovar for the rest of her body to pass through. She thumped down on her side with her head barely a sword's length from either one, then she gathered her feet beneath her and dived forward, rolling across the balcony in a series of somersaults. The guards shouted the alarm and blindly clinked their swords on the stone only inches behind her.

At last, Vala came to the end of the balcony and found the balustrade blocking her path. She finished one more somersault, gathered her feet beneath her, and sprang over headlong.

Vala was within a dozen feet of the street before a magic hand finally reached out to stop her fall.

Next time, young lady, we won't catch you, Khelben warned. *That was nothing but a vengeance killing.*

"So it was," she said, "and if I hadn't done it, no one would have believed my escape was my own. Not after the things that devil did to me."

Vala's feet touched the street, and she started toward Shade's lower warrens at a sprint.

✡✡✡✡✡

The Vaasans sat together on one side of the table, laughing and dribbling and whacking each other on the back mightily as they ate and drank and described the day's combat to their jealous comrade, Dexon. To listen to the men talk, battling phaerimm was no more dangerous than stalking forest rothé, save that the phaerimm made it all much more exciting by hunting back. Had Takari not been along and seen for herself the humans' deadly effectiveness that day—and many others—she would have believed the wine was stretching their tongues.

But it had all happened just as they described, and they had indeed added three tails apiece to their belts. Armed with Dexon's darksword, Keya Nihmedu had claimed two for her own growing collection. Takari had taken only one, but that was with nothing but her own elven steel. Had she been wielding a darksword of her own, she would have killed more phaerimm than anyone.

Takari took the ewer and refilled it from the wine cask in the scullery, then stopped in the doorway and eyed the two healthy Vaasans from behind. With their massive shoulders and braided black hair, they looked more like thkaerths to her than humans, but she had spent enough time fighting at their sides to know that neither man was entirely the brute he seemed. She had seen Burlen risk his life several times to protect Keya without ever allowing her to notice, while Kuhl had returned from one patrol with a litter of orphaned raccoons tucked inside his cloak.

After a moment of deliberation, Takari settled on Kuhl and came up behind him with the ewer. They always stopped to wash the blood and soot off in Dawnsglory Pond before returning home to Treetop, so she knew that Kuhl was both a little leaner and less woolly than Burlen. It was still going to be like wrestling a bear, but she saw no reason to make it any more distasteful than it had to be.

"More wine, Kuhl?"

Without waiting for an answer, Takari pressed herself to Kuhl's burly back and reached around his shoulder to refill his goblet.

She was wearing only the thinnest of shifts, so she knew he could feel her as well as she could feel him, but he only nodded and voiced his thanks without so much as a glance in her direction. Seeing that Dexon's goblet was almost empty, Takari took the opportunity to make her point more clearly by plastering herself to Kuhl's shoulder as she stretched forward to refill it. Lingering there rather longer than was necessary, she turned and smiled.

Kuhl looked away, a crimson flush rising up his cheeks.

Burlen pushed his goblet toward the ewer and said, "I'll take another swallow myself, if you don't mind."

Takari banged the ewer down and peeled herself off Kuhl's shoulder.

"Why should I mind? I'm sure you can pour."

This drew a roaring laugh from Dexon and a hurt expression from Burlen. Kuhl's face grew even redder. Takari wondered whether all humans were as dense as the one she had picked, or if there was something about Kuhl she did not understand. She had seen him casting hungry looks her way as they bathed.

Takari circled around to Kuhl's other side and found Keya Nihmedu studying her with a thoughtful frown. After learning how Keya had acquired the ability to hold Dexon's darksword—by allowing him to get a child on her—Takari had made the mistake of asking whether the other Vaasans had families at home. Keya seemed to have guessed her plan.

Takari ignored the condemnation she sensed in the younger elf's gaze and pulled a chair close to her quarry.

She ran a finger up Kuhl's forearm, and his brow grew shiny with human-smelling sweat.

"I'd like it if you showed me how you did that rollover on the bugbear today," she said.

A expectant silence descended over the room, and Dexon and Burlen studied Kuhl with wolfish grins.

"It was a good move," Keya broke in. She kept her gaze fixed on Takari. "Maybe you could show us all tomorrow."

"Now would be better for me," Takari said.

She had spent a tenday and a half praying to the Winged Mother to make her ready, and she could sense by the warmth in her womb that she was. It had to be this evening. She rested her fingers on the inside of Kuhl's meaty elbow and applied a little pressure.

"You can show the others tomorrow," she whispered.

Kuhl seemed to melt under her touch, but was somehow still oblivious to what she was suggesting.

"I can show you now. It won't take long," he said, rising and gesturing at the floor. "Lie down and be me, and I'll get on top and be the bugbear."

Dexon cringed and said, "I don't think this is something I want to see."

"Nor I," Keya agreed. "Takari, this isn't fair—"

"*Fair*?" Takari interrupted. "Galaeron made his choice when he left me in Rheitheillaethor and ran off with Vala. If I decide to try a human, too, that's no business of his—or yours."

Keya's mouth fell open, and Takari could see by the confusion in the younger elf's eyes that she had succeeded in muddling the issue. Whatever Keya had guessed, she could not know whether Takari was using the human for pleasure, revenge, or access to a darksword.

"Uh, Takari?" Kuhl asked. "What do you mean, 'try a human?' "

"What do you think I mean?" Takari rolled her eyes and said, "I've seen the way you stare at me when we bathe."

Kuhl looked guilty. "You have?"

"It's hard to miss," Takari said.

"It's all right?" Kuhl gasped. "I thought it bothered elves when we peeked."

"It is a little unsettling, to tell the truth," Takari said. Seeing the look of confusion that came to Kuhl's eyes, she decided that it would be best to state the matter as plainly as possible. "I'm giving you a chance here to do more than stare, Kuhl. Are you interested or not?"

"Interested."

"Good."

Takari took him by the wrist and started for the contemplation, but they were quickly intercepted by a disapproving Keya Nihmedu.

"Kuhl," she said, "you do realize she's using you?"

A grin the size of the crescent moon spread across Kuhl's face and he said, "I sure hope so."

He picked Takari up and slipped past Keya at a near charge, and a moment later Takari found herself wrestling the bear. The experience was not as unpleasant as she had feared, in large part because it was over so quickly.

The second time lasted a little longer. She was surprised to find that she was no longer disgusted at all, save for near the end when he really did start growling like a bear.

The third time, she actually started to enjoy it, and that was when Lord Duirsar's messenger flew in through the open window. Oblivious to what was happening, the snowfinch began to flit around their heads, chirping and tweeting as though the world were coming to an end.

"Manynests," Takari gasped. "Not . . . now!"

The bird landed on her shoulder and shrieked into her ear. The mood vanished instantly, and Takari extended a finger.

"Bird, this had better be good."

Manynests broke into a long series of whistles.

"What?" Takari asked. "When?"

She freed herself of Kuhl's embrace and swung her feet onto the floor. The snowfinch peeped in reply, then chirped a query.

"Of course!" Takari said, rising. "Tell him we'll meet them at the Livery Gate."

Kuhl propped himself on an elbow and asked, "Meet who?"

She snatched Kuhl's weapon belt off the floor and tossed it to him without touching the darksword's hilt. She didn't want Kuhl to know why she had bedded him, not until she knew the seed had been planted.

"The phaerimm," Takari replied. "They've breached the mythal."

✡✡✡✡✡

Somewhere in the Palace Most High, Galaeron hung swaddled in velvet murk, immobile, able to breathe and scream but no more. Shadovar voices hissed in the distant gloom. Shadow seeped into his pores, permeating him with every breath, doubt and suspicion and anger steadily darkening his heart. How long he had been there was impossible to say. No one ever came to feed him or give him water or attend to his broken hand, or even to ask if he was ready to cooperate, but he never seemed to grow hungry or thirsty, or have need to answer nature's call. He hung there suspended in the moment, a throbbing pain-filled moment without beginning or end, without limit of any kind.

It seemed to Galaeron that the mythallar should have been destroyed long before, that the Chosen should have found it and sundered it, and brought Shade crashing down into the desert. Maybe they had. Trapped as he seemed in a single moment, how would he know? Or maybe he had been there only an instant after all. Maybe all his thoughts since Telamont hung him there had rushed through his mind in a single instant, and Khelben and the others were still awaiting their chance to escape into the city.

Or perhaps the Chosen had abandoned him, wherever here was, content to believe the shadow inside him would never escape to darken Faerûn. That would be just like them, to sacrifice an individual for the sake of the many—as long as that individual was not one of *their* number. Galaeron thought back to his capture and recalled how quick they had been to abandon the caravan, how cleverly they had arranged things so that none of them had been called upon to make the ultimate sacrifice. The cowards would not hesitate to leave him there alone to suffer for all eternity.

And that was exactly what Galaeron—the *real* Galaeron—would want, he reminded himself.

His shadow had all but taken him. Every thought contained a hidden doubt, every emotion was colored by suspicion. It would not be long before he yielded. He had only to grab a handful of shadowstuff and use its dark magic to cast a spell, and he would be free to seek his vengeance on all who had wronged him. Telamont had said as much when he'd imprisoned him, had promised that that was how Galaeron's struggle would end, that all Galaeron controlled was *when* it ended.

Galaeron believed him. If the timing was all he could control, then control it he would.

The hissing of the distant voices faded to silence, and the air grew heavy and chill. Galaeron's heart climbed into his throat, and he began to search the darkness ahead for the burning disks of Telamont's platinum eyes.

The air only grew colder and more still.

"You are stronger than I thought, elf," the Most High's wispy voice hissed into Galaeron's ear. "You are beginning to anger me."

Galaeron smiled. He tried to turn toward the voice, but his whole body seemed to pivot with him, and Telamont remained just beyond his peripheral vision.

Galaeron had to settle for speaking into the shadow.

"At least there's that," he said.

"Oh, there is more," Telamont said. "Much more. My son Escanor is dead."

Galaeron started to say something spiteful then realized that to express such malice to a grieving father—even *this* grieving father—would be to invite his shadow in.

"I'm sorry to hear that."

A deep chuckle sounded beside Galaeron's ear.

"Lies are of the shadow, too, elf."

"It was compassion—not a lie."

Galaeron's thoughts were racing. Had the city fallen and Telamont come to take vengeance? Did he see a way to use his son's death to force Galaeron completely into shadow? Or was he simply there to take out his anger on Galaeron?

"Whatever I may have thought of Escanor," the elf said, "whatever I would have liked to do to him myself—I'm sure you loved him."

Telamont was quiet for a moment, not using his will to press for an answer as usual when he fell silent, but genuinely seeming to contemplate Galaeron's words.

"Perhaps I did, at that," the Most High said. "What a pity Vala was not so charitable as you."

A cold knot formed in Galaeron's stomach. Telamont's cold presence pressed closer to him.

"She escaped her cell," the Shadovar said. "She killed him in his sick bed."

The knot in Galaeron's stomach grew as heavy as lead.

"Did his guards . . . ?" He could barely bring himself to voice the question, "Is she dead?"

"That would make you angry, would it not?"

A cloaked form coalesced in the murk before Galaeron. With the Most High already whispering into his ear, it took Galaeron a moment to realize that the figure in front of him also belonged to Telamont.

"I could tell you she is, and you would fly into a rage." Telamont's eyes grew bright and angry, but his voice continued to whisper into Galaeron's ear, "And with rage would come your shadow. It would claim you for all time."

"Then she's not dead." Nor had the mythallar been destroyed, Galaeron realized. Had Shade fallen, Telamont would be more interested in killing him than claiming him. "You don't know where she is."

"And with hope comes strength," hissed the disembodied voice. "The strength to defy me. What am I to do?"

He fell silent, and the air grew heavy with expectation.

Fearing that one answer would lead to another and another until he betrayed their plan, Galaeron tried not to answer. Telamont remained silent, and his will pressed down on Galaeron all the more fiercely. Eventually, he could resist no more, and the words tumbled out of their own accord.

"Tell me the truth."

The purple crescent of a smile appeared in the hood beneath Telamont's eyes.

"The truth? What is 'truth,' really?" Telamont's voice whispered into Galaeron's other ear. "The truth is that she will be."

The lump in Galaeron's stomach began to grow lighter. Vala was still alive.

"If you catch her."

"*When* we catch her," Telamont corrected. "Where can she go? It's a thousand feet to the ground."

He paused, and Galaeron feared for a moment that Telamont meant to force an answer that would betray the attack on the mythallar, but Telamont had something else in mind.

"She will be caught. My other sons are tracking her even now."

Galaeron fought not to smile. He had said nothing about the Chosen yet, and if the princes were busy searching for Vala, they would not be watching the mythallar. Perhaps they had even helped her escape to create a diversion. That would be just like those cowards, to sacrifice a helpless woman so they wouldn't have to risk their own lives. It occurred to Galaeron that he might save Vala's life by warning Telamont about their plan. That was what those traitors deserved.

"You do not care?" Telamont asked. "I thought you loved this woman. I thought she was the reason you betrayed us."

Telamont grew quiet, and again the weight of his will slowly crushed Galaeron's resolve.

At last, Galaeron admitted, "That's true. I do love her."

"A pity, then," Telamont said. "The things that will happen when we recapture her. . . ."

He fell silent, leaving Galaeron to imagine the horrors that would be visited on her. Given the punishment Vala had suffered just for aiding in his escape, he could not bear to think of the death she would meet after killing a prince of Shade. He began to feel Telamont's will pressing down on him, compelling him to speak what he was thinking. Time and again, Galaeron found himself ready to blurt out his plan, to reveal how he had tricked Telamont into bringing the Chosen into Shade.

Somehow, he resisted. Deep down inside, part of him wanted to believe it was honor that stopped him, that something inside him was strong enough to resist the will of the Most High of Shade. But the truth was that he had again fallen into the grasp of his shadow self, and it simply did not believe Telamont could be trusted.

Every time Galaeron started to say he would trade Shade's life for Vala's, or that he could deliver five Chosen in exchange for her freedom, his shadow refused. It reminded him that Telamont had once offered to teach him how to control his shadow—as if that could be done—and of how badly that bargain had turned out. It reminded him of how powerful the Most High was. Galaeron had only to hint at the attack on the mythallar and Telamont would begin to pressure him for answers. The Shadovar would know everything within minutes, Vala would be condemned to a lingering death anyway, and Galaeron would be left with nothing for his betrayal.

For once, Galaeron's shadow self was right. Telamont had done nothing but betray him. Telamont deserved what was going to happen to his city. All of the Shadovar did. And Vala? He wanted to save Vala, but he could not do it by yielding to Telamont.

Finally, Telamont said, "Love is not as strong as I imagined." The pressure did not relent, but his voice came from the hooded shape before Galaeron's eyes. "You do not wish to save Vala?"

"I would do anything to save Vala," Galaeron said, "but I am no fool."

"No?" Telamont's voice sounded like cracking ice. "Then you know she will not escape."

"And you know I can help you."

A dark voice inside Galaeron screamed for him to hold his tongue, that he was a fool if he thought he could bargain with Telamont Tanthul.

Galaeron ignored the voice and continued, "The phaerimm continue to trouble you. Take me to the world-window. When I see her at home in Vaasa, I'll help you with them again."

Telamont drifted closer, until Galaeron could see nothing in front of his face but two platinum eyes. He forced himself to hold the gaze, and eventually he saw that the eyes were silver coronas burning around two disks of shadow blacker than darkness. The pressure of his will grew crushing, and still Galaeron did not look away. Finally, the shining coronas flickered with something like amusement, and Telamont drew back a little.

"Love is not as strong as I imagined."

The Most High's eyes resolved themselves back into disks, and his dark form began to melt back into the darkness.

"But hope . . ." the shade said. "That is so much stronger."

The crushing burden of his will remained. Galaeron waited, expecting the compulsion to answer some unspoken question to arise inside him at any moment. There was only the intangible weight—and a different pressure, rising from inside, a feeling that was closer to fear and uncertainty, perhaps grief. Finally, when the shape of Telamont's body had dissolved back into the darkness and there was only the pale light of his fading eyes, it was this pressure that forced Galaeron to break his silence.

"Wait!" Galaeron said. "What about Vala?"

"I accept." The eyes vanished, but Telamont's voice hissed from the darkness all around, "If you wish to save her, you have only to grasp the shadows and free yourself."

Before Galaeron could object, voices began to hiss again in the distant gloom, and the crushing weight of Telamont's will was gone. Galaeron found himself torn between pride in having matched wills with the Most High and apprehension over his comment about hope. What had he meant about hope being so much stronger? Probably, it was just some ploy to make Galaeron yield to the Most High's will, to surrender himself to shadow, but there had been something about the way it was said that made him feel otherwise, a note of revelation in Telamont's voice that suggested a flash of insight. His tone in agreeing to trade Galaeron's cooperation for Vala's life had been one of ridicule, as though he knew the offer would never be accepted.

A dark voice whispered that Telamont was playing him for a fool. There was only one way to escape, and Galaeron refused to use it. Half the Shadovar in the enclave had to be laughing at him at that very moment. Galaeron resisted this line of thought by reminding himself of what happened the last time he used the Shadow Weave, of how he had alienated Vala and nearly gotten Aris killed. If Telamont had provided an easy escape, it was because it was no escape at all. Galaeron had sworn an oath never to use shadow magic again, and it was an oath he intended to honor.

Galaeron occupied himself for what seemed the multiverse's next eternity, arguing back and forth with the dark voice inside his own head, knowing there was only one escape and knowing as well that a fate worse than death awaited him if he took it. Had he been confident that he would know when the Chosen shattered the mythallar and the city fell, perhaps he would have had the fortitude to wait.

As it was, the uncertainty was more than he could bear: the fear that Shade would crash into the sands of Anauroch and be fifteen centuries buried with him still there in that dark moment wondering if his plan would ever succeed, wondering if Vala would live to see her son again, wondering if Takari had ever forgiven him for the selfish fear that had made him turn her away. The image of a black, drop-shaped body appeared his mind and began to grow larger. The thing had three bulbous protrusions that, considering the fang-filled mouths at the end, might have been heads. A trio of arms, each ending in three hands with a single eye in the palm, sprouted from its body in three unlike places. The phantasm—for he had no doubt that that was what it was—reminded Galaeron vaguely of the sharn he had freed when they destroyed the first lich Wulgreth.

I have been looking for you, Elf.

Galaeron's jaw dropped. For once, his shadow self seemed too stunned to take advantage of the situation, and he experienced a moment of internal silence that he had not enjoyed since making the mistake that had allowed his shadow to invade him in the first place.

What, no "hi ho, old friend?" the sharn asked. *No, "well met, Xrxvlayblea?"*

"W-hat, uh, how . . . ?"

"That will do, I suppose."

The sharn—Xrxvlayblea—was floating in the shadows before Galaeron, all ton and a half of him, or it, or them, or however one referred to a blob of three-headed . . . stuff. It waved the eyes in several of its palms over Galaeron.

"Y-you're real?" Galaeron stammered.

One of the heads shot up close to Galaeron's face and spewing drool from its fangs, snapped, "Did I not say I would return to repay the favor you did me in Karsus?"

"You did," Galaeron gulped.

"Now is when you need me most, is it not?"

Galaeron managed a nod.

"Of course it is," another head spat. "Or I wouldn't be here."

Galaeron shook his head and wondered if he had begun to hallucinate.

"There you have it, then," the third head said. "You're ready now. Favor repaid."

The sharn turned and started to float away into the shadows. Galaeron tried to pull an arm free and found that he was as stuck as ever. He debated the wisdom of talking to a hallucination. A dark voice asked what could it hurt, and he decided nothing.

"Wait!"

The sharn stopped, but did not turn.

"Ready for what?" Galaeron asked.

"Ready to do what you were not ready to do then," the sharn replied.

Galaeron frowned. "But I'm still caught."

"Whose fault is that?" asked one of the heads—from behind, it was impossible to see which. "You'd better get unstuck."

"You don't understand," Galaeron said. "I can't use the Shadow Weave. I swore an oath."

"An oath?"

The sharn swung back around and shoved two palms in Galaeron's face so it could stare at him eye-to-eye.

"Why'd you do a witless thing like that?" it asked.

"I've been having a shadow crisis," Galaeron explained. "When I use the Shadow Weave, my shadow self takes over. The next time, it may be permanent, so I vowed not to cast any more shadow magic."

"Breaking a vow is bad business." The eyes in the palms blinked, and it said, "But don't be angry with the Shadow. That's what he wants—and it's not his fault, anyway. You made a promise you can't keep."

The sharn turned and started to float away again.

"That's it?" Galaeron cried. "That's your big favor?"

One of the heads twisted around to glance back over its body.

"Look, I'm not here to tell you how to live your life. You can do it now, or you can do it later, when it doesn't matter. Your choice. Favor repaid."

"One more question," the second head added, "and you owe me."

"You don't want that," the third head said. "Really."

"No," Galaeron said. "I'm sure I don't. My thanks, and fare you well."

"No doubt of that," the sharn said, and it vanished into the whispering gloom.

More than a hundred heartbeats passed before the dark voice inside suggested that maybe they should ignore the sharn, that maybe it had been an illusion conjured up by Telamont Tanthul to trick him into using the Shadow Weave. Maybe, after all, they should hang there in the murk for a while longer. Galaeron realized that maybe his shadow self was saying the opposite of what of it truly wanted, that maybe it really wanted him to escape and was just suggesting the opposite because it knew he would do the opposite of *that* . . .

"Maybe," Galaeron said. He closed his eyes, then grasped a handful of shadow and closed his fist as well. "And maybe not."

CHAPTER THIRTEEN

2 Eleasias, the Year of Wild Magic

To Aris's dismay, elegance had not returned with strength. With Malik gone, the giant found himself secretly in the service of Prince Yder. He stood over the High Altar in Malik's Temple of the One and All, cutting a relief of Shar's Black Moon around the oblong skull-and-starburst he'd done when the temple still belonged to Malik.

He could hardly ask for better working conditions, even were he a free giant. He had only to ask, and whatever he wanted to eat or drink would be brought from any far corner of Faerûn. A company of assistants attended to his every need, and he worked at his pleasure and was free to do whatever he wished at other times. He was not even much of a captive, as he was free to wander the city of Shade at will—so long as he did not mind an escort of several armed shadow lords.

His tool control had returned to normal after he'd slept off the effects of hiding the Chosen in his body, and the Dark Moon was cut shallowly enough so that it did not draw attention to itself. Still, there was something intrinsic to the goddess's hidden nature that he was not quite conveying. A viewer had only to look at Cyric's skull-and-starburst to see that it floated inside Shar's Dark Moon, and that would not do at all. She was more subtle than that, more mysterious.

Aris stepped away to gain some perspective, barely noticed as he sent a dozen attendants scrambling for cover, and decided he would have to rethink the whole thing. He dropped his hammer and chisel into the tool bag on his belt and backed out of the chancel area.

"Go to my workshop," he said, motioning the attendants toward the door in the north transept. "Bring a stack of sail canvases and a barrel of sketching charcoal."

The attendants rushed to obey, leaving only four shadow lord guards who did their utmost to remain quiet and out of sight. Yder had apparently ordered them to avoid reminding Aris that he was a captive, but it made no difference. He always knew they were behind him. He could *feel* them there, just out of sight.

A throaty rasp came up the nave's center aisle as someone pushed open the Black Portal. Aris waved an absentminded hand in the direction of the sound and kept his attention fixed on the object of his frustration. A pair of guards rushed off to send the visitor away. There followed the hiss of whispered conversation, then a scuffle, a few syllables of magic, and the clatter of armored bodies hitting the floor.

"What's wrong with you oafs?" Aris snapped, too absorbed in aesthetics to register anything but an annoying disturbance. "Can you not see I'm trying to think?"

The other two guards were already stomping down the aisle to intercept the intruder. This time, the incantation ended in a sharp crack. The flash of lightning lit the chancel, and at last Aris saw the solution to his problem. The entire High Altar would become the Dark Moon, with the upper hemisphere forming a semicircular back panel at the rear and the lower hemisphere descending down into the choir. The trick would be to get the right foreshortening where the level changed, and to find a way to round the staircase toward the bottom. Growing ever more excited, Aris dropped to his knees and began to search his belt bag for a nubbin of sketching charcoal.

"Difficult to tell who's the slave here and who are the guards." The voice registered vaguely as a familiar one. "You weren't this difficult back in Arabel."

"Do you have something to sketch with?" Aris lowered a hand without looking. "I must get this down while I still have it in mind."

"Aris!" the voice barked. "Leave it. You're done here."

"Done?"

Scowling at the interruption, Aris shook his head and found Galaeron standing at his side. The elf looked much as he had when they were separated at the Cave Gate, save that his face was lined with fatigue and his eyes veiled behind a glossy darkness.

"Galaeron . . ."

Aris could feel the details of his idea slipping away even as he spoke, but he was so happy to see his old friend alive that he didn't care . . . much.

"What are you doing here?" he asked.

"What do you think?" Galaeron retorted. "I escaped."

"Escaped? From the Palace Most High?"

Galaeron nodded. "I had to use the Shadow Weave," he said, looking back down the main aisle of the nave, where Aris's four guards lay in various forms of death. "I'm sorry."

Aris's heart went out to his friend.

"You have not failed anyone." He laid two fingers on the elf's shoulder and said, "I am proud you did not yield before this."

"I didn't yield," Galaeron said. "I chose. Telamont is after Vala."

Aris went hollow inside.

"Then he knows?" asked the giant.

"Knows?"

"About the Chosen," Aris said. "They couldn't find the mythallar, so I sent them to Vala."

A shadow descended over Galaeron's face.

"The Chosen must have freed her," he said. Galaeron motioned Aris to his feet and turned toward the Black Portal. "I gave them away. That's what he meant."

Aris rose, but made no move to follow.

"What who meant?"

"The sharn," Galaeron answered as he continued down the aisle. "He appeared to me in the Palace Most High. He said he had come to repay the favor he owed us, and told me I had a choice to make."

"And?"

"And he left, and I made my choice," Galaeron replied. "I couldn't bear the thought that Telamont would capture Vala again, but now I see he was talking about more—much more."

Seeing that Galaeron was not going to wait, Aris caught up to him with a single step. He plucked Galaeron off the floor and held him at head height.

"The sharn from Karse came to you in the Palace Most High?"

"Isn't that what I just said? Put me down. We need to go find Vala and the Chosen."

Aris continued to hold Galaeron and said, "The sharn left you there to free yourself? He left you and told you to use the Shadow Weave?"

If Galaeron saw the reason for Aris's alarm, he showed no sign.

"The sharn was warning me," the elf said. "Telamont had just been there, trying to convince me to use the Shadow Weave to save Vala. When I refused, a strange look came over him. Telamont said hope was stronger than he had imagined and left."

"That was what the sharn was warning you about?"

Galaeron shook his head and replied, "I think Telamont knew I was defying him because I expected something to happen soon. It must have dawned on him that Vala had help escaping, because he left in a hurry. We have to find the Chosen and warn them."

"All very plausible," Aris said. "But the sharn left you there with no way to escape except to use the Shadow Weave."

Galaeron shrugged and said, "I had to accept the inevitable, and I'm the stronger for it."

He peeled Aris's thumb back and slipped free, landing on the floor in an easy crouch.

"Who is stronger?" Aris asked, a little frightened by how easily Galaeron had broken his grasp. "How can you be certain it was the sharn you saw and not some trick of Telamont's?"

"Because we beat him," Galaeron replied, starting toward the Black Portal again. "My shadow and I matched wills with Telamont Tanthul, and we beat him."

"Galaeron, listen to yourself," Aris said. He stepped over the elf, then spun and stooped down to block his way. "Telamont Tanthul has been trying to trick you into yielding to your shadow since the day we arrived in Shade. You finally do it, and suddenly you're stronger than he is?"

"Yes," Galaeron said simply. "The Shadovar thrive on deception and subterfuge, I know that, but the biggest fraud they ever committed on me was when Melegaunt tricked me into fighting my own shadow. He filled me with doubt, and doubt made me weak."

"And now you are sure," Aris said, filling his voice with mockery and mistrust. "Now you are strong."

"Now I am whole," Galaeron snapped back. "That makes me strong. I have no time to explain it now."

He whispered a mystic word and waved his hand at Aris's foot, and the foot started to slide across the floor.

"I am going to the mythallar," Galaeron said, stepping under Aris toward the Black Portal.

"Wait!" Aris turned, growing ever more suspicious, and said, "Back in Arabel, you told me you didn't know how to find the mythallar."

"Not on this plane."

Galaeron pressed a palm to the Black Portal and spoke a few words in ancient Netherese. The door dissolved into shadow mist.

The elf turned to Aris and said, "I hope you'll come with me. One way or the other, I don't think Shade will be safe for you very much longer."

Aris's mind was whirling with suspicions, foremost among them the fear that Telamont was using Galaeron to reveal Vala and the Chosen to the Shadovar. But for that to be so, Galaeron could not be under the Most High's sway, for if he were Telamont would have only to ask to learn what he wished to know.

"I'll come," he said, stepping toward the shadowy portal, "but first you must promise that when this is done, you will never touch the Shadow Weave again. You can still be saved."

"I was inviting you, Aris, not begging," Galaeron said in a voice that held both scorn and patience. "I don't need to be saved from anything."

Galaeron turned and stepped through the Black Portal, leaving Aris alone in the Temple of the One and All, alone and feeling angry and abandoned. He could not decide whether it was Galaeron who had just departed or Galaeron's shadow—or someone Aris did not even know. The elf's parting rebuke had left him feeling both resentful and hurt, and such rudeness simply was not like his friend. It made Aris want to retreat into his work, but of course that was foolish. If Galaeron's plan worked, it would all be rubble in a few minutes anyway, and if the plan failed, the last thing he wanted to do for the next few hundred years was devote his talent to hiding Dark Moons in the sacred sculpture of other deities. Besides, whether or not he still knew the elf, Galaeron was his friend, and no matter how strange they became, one did not desert one's friends as they went off to fight Telamont Tanthul and the Princes of Shade—at least stone giants did not.

Aris followed Galaeron through the Black Portal and into the shadow mist. The air grew frigid, and the floor turned as soft as snow.

Aris called into the blackness, "Galaeron?"

He took another tentative step, doing his best to continue in a straight line.

"Where are you?"

When no answer came, Aris decided he had waited too long. The shadows were no place to become lost. He turned around and retraced his steps exactly.

Three steps later, he remained in the dark.

Perhaps his first two steps had been longer than he thought. Holding his arm before him, Aris took another step forward.

"Galaeron!"

A small hand pressed itself to his kneecap and the elf whispered, "Quietly, my friend."

Aris's sigh was anything but soft.

"I thought you'd left me behind."

"I have too few friends to leave them wandering around the Fringe alone," Galaeron replied. He pulled on the leg of Aris's trousers, guiding him forward. "We must be careful. I don't know who else might be watching."

"Watching?" Aris whispered.

Galaeron stopped, and the black mists ahead slowly grew translucent. Aris saw that they had stopped just inside the Shadow Fringe. Ahead lay a large crater lined in obsidian, with no apparent seams and a surface as smooth as the interior of a glass bowl. Standing near the bottom, spaced at equal intervals along the inner wall, were Khelben and the four sisters. They held their arms outspread, fingertips pointing toward their comrades to either side, so that they formed a great ring around the interior. Within this circle lay a disk of gray opalescent light, which they were slowly walking toward the bottom of the basin.

Vala was nowhere in sight. Nor were Telamont and his princes.

Aris kneeled at Galaeron's side and stooped down to whisper, "Perhaps they did not find—"

Galaeron made a motion, and the rest of Aris's sentence vanished into silence.

The mythallar is beneath that dimensional portal, Galaeron's voice said inside his head. *Vala is here somewhere, you may be sure.*

Aris was about to ask whether Telamont was also there when, about a quarter of the way around the crater, the dark figures of all ten surviving princes emerged from the Shadow Fringe. They did not step from the obsidian lining so much as they peeled themselves out of it. They began to slide silently down the wall. Aris reached for his tool pouch for something to throw and started to rise, but Galaeron put out a restraining hand.

The Chosen will have foreseen this.

The princes were almost upon the Chosen when they struck an invisible barrier and came to an abrupt stop, tiny forks of golden energy crackling outward around each impact point. They leaped to their feet, wailing in pain and shock, and scrambled a few steps up the wall then stopped there, bleeding dark mist into the air. Three of them collapsed again almost immediately and melted back into the Fringe. The others hurled globes of shadow magic toward the bottom of the crater. The balls hit the barrier and erupted into huge black sprays, then rained back down in tiny beads of darkness that skittered across the invisible surface like drops of water on a hot frying pan.

While the others continued to assail the barrier, the gaunt figure of Prince Lamorak conjured a shadow disk. He and his brother Malath stepped aboard and floated out toward the center of the crater, their fingers working madly as they twined strands of shadowsilk into the shape of a small hand axe.

Aris grabbed one of his chisels but before he could pull it from his tool bag to throw, a bolt of golden magic streaked down from the opposite crater rim to blast Lamorak's shadow disk into shards. Malath pitched headlong into the invisible barrier and fell instantly limp, his body first melting into a black puddle, then coming apart and skittering across the surface in steaming black globules. Lamorak hit on his back, screamed once, and managed to bounce himself into the air. He vanished with the sharp crackle of a teleport spell.

Aris looked across the crater toward the source of the golden bolt and glimpsed a swirl of Vala's golden hair as she dropped out of sight behind the rim. Though he had never seen her cast a spell, it was not a wild guess to think that one of the Chosen might have loaned her a ring or wand capable of hurling the magic bolts. Unfortunately, Aris was not the only one who had spotted her. Yder and Aglarel scurried after her, their lanky limbs oddly spiderlike as the princes ascended the slick wall.

Aris glanced down and was relieved to find his friend staring after Vala, his elf brows arched high in concern. Still, Galaeron made no move to go after her. Recalling how, while facing a similar situation under the influence of his shadow self on the Saiyyadar, the elf had nearly gotten him killed by using him to bait a dragon into an ambush, Aris grabbed Galaeron's shoulder and urged him after her.

Galaeron pulled free of Aris's hand.

They would have foreseen that. We must wait here in the Fringe for what they did not foresee.

Aris started to ask angrily what that might be, but Galaeron's spell kept him silent. He could only wait and watch as the Chosen, ignoring the princes' ever more frantic efforts to penetrate the mystic barrier, continued to walk the dimensional portal toward the bottom of the basin. Yder and Aglarel reached the rim of the crater and disappeared over the top. The basin began to tremble and fall away beneath them.

Aris's jaw dropped. The Chosen had done it—Shade was falling. He snatched Galaeron up. Determined not to become separated from the others whatever the elf said, he jumped into the basin—but landed in the same place he had been, with the basin continuing to fall away below him.

When we are needed, Galaeron hissed. *Not before.*

✡✡✡✡✡

How long he had lain chained on Shar's altar, Malik could not say. All he knew was he had grown so weak with hunger that his belly had lost the strength to rumble, that his tongue was so swollen with thirst he could not have drunk if someone had given him water, that his ears had become so inured by the constant hissing of the Hidden One's worshipers that the sudden silence left him feeling deafened and dizzy.

He had the sensation of floating—a sensation that only grew stronger when his shadow on the ceiling started to shrink and loom ever darker, when the stream of silver magic pouring from the stone began to swirl around him in beads as large as his head, and especially when the confused forms of Shar's worshipers began to tumble through the air and bounce along the shadow-stained ceiling.

So weakened by thirst and hunger was Malik that for a few moments, he was too confused to comprehend what he was seeing. Had he finally died and begun his journey to the Shattered Castle, or had the harlot Shar suddenly granted all her worshipers the ability to fly? Or perhaps it was an hallucination. Perhaps all the hardships he had endured on behalf of his god Cyric had finally taken their toll, leaving him as demented and mad as once his god had been.

Then Malik hit the end of his chains and felt his withered hands nearly slip free of one of the manacles, and he knew what had happened. The One had answered a prayer. Finally, Cyric had taken mercy on his poor servant and raised a finger to help in the impossible mission he had assigned him, and soon the Sharites would pay for all of the torment and abuse they had heaped upon him while he lay chained to their goddess's stolen altar.

"Your doom is upon you!" Malik yelled through the floating swirl of silver beads. "Cyric has come for me at last, and he shall take a terrible vengeance on you."

"Fool!"—the voice that hissed this came from his own shadow, lying flat upon the ceiling not a dozen paces above him—"Nothing could be farther from Cyric's mind than your misery."

"You cannot know that!" Malik said, more for his own comfort than because he believed his shadow needed to know. "You are nothing to him." He meant to stop there, but felt more words welling up as Mystra's curse compelled him to speak the full truth. "Except another torment for me!"

This drew a purple smile from the shadow, which said, "The one service I am happy to perform for your lying god, but that does not change the truth of what is happening. The city is falling."

"Falling?" Malik shrieked. He noticed that other voices were beginning to join him. "With *me* in it?"

"A pity, is it not?" the shadow asked.

"More than you know."

In this, Malik was telling the truth, for Cyric was fond of telling him the fate that awaited him if he ever failed in one of the divine missions assigned to him. It took only an instant for the thousand promised torments to flash through his mind, for in his infinite wisdom, the One had made Malik memorize them until he knew them all as well as his own name.

But there was no way to avoid it. The city was going to crash into the desert, and he was going to die along with everyone else, no doubt crushed beneath the Karsestone, since he was still chained to it . . . and that was when Malik saw how he would save himself.

Once before, when Cyric had sent Malik to fetch a sacred book from inside the Keeper's Tower at Candlekeep, the One had told him he had only to call the name of the One and All three times once he had succeeded in his duty and he would be rescued. Given that Yder had called the Karsestone the crown of his goddess Shar, and given that it was also the only remaining source of the ancient whole magic in all of Faerûn—perhaps even Toril itself—it seemed reasonable to suppose that he who controlled the Karsestone might also control the Shadow Weave.

The stone might be, Malik realized, just like a crown. If not actually the source of Shar's power over the Shadow Weave, it was at least a symbol of it, and he had learned in Calimshan that he who controlled the symbol soon owned the power.

When the city's true caliph had lost his crown to a ring of thieves, the master of the thieves had audaciously set the crown on his own head and challenged the caliph to take it back. Try as he might, the old man never succeeded, and it was not long before the city revered the thief as the new caliph.

And so it would be with the Karsestone, Malik believed. No—he *knew*. There could be no other reason the goddess of shadows would permit an artifact of such blazing light to serve as the High Altar in her holiest of temples.

Seeing that he had floated to within five feet of the ceiling—and that his shadow was little larger than he himself, but as black as obsidian—Malik closed his eyes. He had no idea how long it would take the city to crash into Anauroch, but they had been falling for a full five or ten breaths, and they had to hit soon.

"I have it, Mighty One! I have the Shadow Weave chained right here on my back!"

When Mystra's curse did not compel Malik to add anything more, or even to clarify that it was just a symbol, he decided his plan was going to work and called, "Cyric, the One, the All!"

Nothing happened. He floated so close to the ceiling that he could not see anything except his shadow's smirking face.

"How pitiful you are," it said. "It shames me to know I spring from your image. Even if Cyric could hear you, do you think he would answer?"

"*If* he could hear me?" Malik screamed. "What do you mean *if*?"

"What do you think I mean?" the shadow retorted. "This is the temple—"

The explanation came to an abrupt end as Malik touched the ceiling and came into contact with his shadow. The red eyes winked out and its shape grew more squat and less monsterlike. Malik experienced a rush of cold magic as it reattached itself to his body.

"Thish is justh what you desherve!" With his face pressed against the stone ceiling, it was impossible to speak clearly. "You will be with me when I fathe the One'sh anger!"

The ceiling lifted away from his face, and Malik thought for a moment that his shadow had been wrong, that Cyric had come for him after all. Then he heard splashing, and screaming, and all around him he saw Shadovar flailing their arms and beads of silver magic assuming teardrop shapes as they plummeted back toward the temple floor.

Closing his eyes, Malik yelled again, "Cyric, the One, the All!"

Nothing happened, except that a steady roar began to build beneath Malik. No sooner had he identified the sound as the Karsestone's steady stream of magic pouring into the pool below than the roar exploded into a thunderous splash, and the air shot from his lungs as his back slammed into the Karsestone. He bounced once and felt his legs come free as the shackle bolt holding his feet came out, then he felt bones snapping in one hand as it was pulled through the closed manacles.

For a moment, Malik thought it would end there, that everything would go black and he would awaken on the Fugue Plain, abandoned to the rough mercy visited upon all the faithless wretches who displeased their holy masters by the thieving god of the dead, Kelemvor.

But that was not to be. Still attached to the Karsestone by his one unbroken hand, Malik rolled off to the cracked side and caught the spray of magic full in the face. Before he could close his mouth and twist away, he swallowed three huge gulps, and of course they went down the wrong passage and immediately filled his lungs.

Malik expected to drown—and quickly—but this was magic. It coursed through his lungs into the rest of his body, filling him with renewed vigor. The weakness brought on by his hunger and thirst vanished, and the hand he had just broke began to heal—though with the fractured bone still unset, it felt like Aris had driven a chisel through it. Malik gathered his legs beneath him and turned to find the temple filled with battered Shadovar, some floating facedown in the silver magic and some sloshing toward the exit arches as fast as their dark legs would carry them.

A pair of fanatical Shar worshipers saw him standing beside the Karsestone and started to rush it, yelling that this was the doing of the infidel thief. It was at that very moment that the ceiling vaults gave way beneath the strain of the sudden stop and began to shower down into the temple. The largest worshiper was crushed beneath a section of a stone rib as long as Aris was tall, and the other vanished behind a screen of falling debris.

Making good use of his Cyric-given ability to vanish, Malik ducked beneath the surface of the silver pool to hide. The surviving fanatic arrived a moment later, hacking into the water with his black sword and swearing that he would mount Malik's horned head on his wall. Though it would have been a simple matter to follow the last manacle chain down to Malik's hand itself, the One's magic prevented the worshiper from seeing this. Malik came up behind him, reaching around to draw the Shadovar's dagger from his belt. He used the worshiper's own weapon to open his belly.

A long section of wall collapsed behind Malik. The whole temple tilted, and he found himself being dragged along behind the Karsestone as the current carried everything in the room toward a huge whirlpool in the corner. He had just enough time to realize that he was about to be dragged down one of the drainage pits he had noticed upon his first awakening in the chamber.

Malik felt for a moment like the city had begun to fall again, but then his manacle chain went slack, tight, and slack again as the Karsestone hit something, bounced, and began to roll. He found himself first flying wildly through the air, then watching the stone fly past over his head, then being jerked along behind it before he finally slammed into it face first and came to a rest.

Compared to the crash and roar of the initial fall, the chamber seemed eerily quiet. That did not mean silence. The air was filled with the wailing and groaning of the injured, the staccato splashing of debris and people falling into viscous pools of magic, and the steady gurgle of the magic stream still pouring out of the cracked Karsestone. Malik slowly picked himself up, and discovering he had survived more or less intact, he turned to see where he had landed.

He lay propped against the wall of one of the workshop caverns where the Shadovar made their shadow blankets. To his right lay the huge, comb-like loom they used to weave the shadowsilk into cloth, and to his left lay the hundred-yard slit they used to provide the light they needed to create shadow. Most interesting to Malik, however, was the shallow tin pan directly in front of him. Tipped at a steep angle because of the city's tilt, the pan was easily a hundred paces square, but no more than a fingernail's thickness in depth. At the far side—several dozen yards higher than Malik's head—was a long collection trough still containing some of the silver magic that had once distributed evenly across the trough.

A tremendous rumble shook the loom cavern, then it slowly righted itself. The silvery magic from the Karsestone spilled into the tin pan and began to spread toward the far corners of the room. The sun drifted briefly across the mouth of the light slit, then vanished behind the top edge and sent a narrow wedge of shadow shooting across the pan. Where the shadow came into contact with the spreading sheet of whole magic, it bonded instantly into a wafer-thin triangle of shadow blanket.

"They use whole magic!" Malik gasped, suddenly understanding what he was seeing. "They need the Karsestone to make their blankets."

The city continued to tilt, going a little past center and tipping in the opposite direction. Realizing that whatever he had learned, it would do him no good if he did not survive to tell Cyric, Malik leaped to his feet. Sometimes pushing, sometimes pulling, and sometimes being swung along himself, he began to guide the Karsestone toward the sun slit along the right side of the room.

Given his usual luck, Malik thought he would probably manage to push the Karsestone out into the desert just before the entire Shade Enclave came crashing down upon them.

✡✡✡✡✡

Dark as Galaeron's heart had grown, it had nearly torn apart as he and Aris watched Aglarel and Yder vanish over the basin rim in pursuit of Vala. After the abandonment of the caravan at Eveningstar, he had no illusions about the Chosen's willingness to risk one for the good of the many. That he was also willing to take the same risk—and with someone he loved—struck him as neither good nor evil, only necessary. That events had proven him right made him feel neither vindicated nor culpable, only sorrowful. He finally understood what Dove and the others had been trying to tell him that day—or so he believed, as his hand had finally healed and returned to its proper color—that the Chosen already carried their shadows inside, that it was not possible to bear so much responsibility and power without darkening one's own spirit.

"Ready yourself, Aris," he said. Galaeron spoke normally, for there was no longer any chance that the Shadovar would overhear him. "We are needed."

Through the thickening shadow fog rising from the battle below, the Most High was barely visible, a ghostly figure standing at the edge of the Chosen's melted defense barrier. He was staring down into the bottom of the basin, where the mythallar sat amid the fuming tatters of the dimensional portal Khelben and the others had been lowering over it when he finally revealed himself by spraying a wave of shadow fire across their overhead protection.

The battle after that had been as fast as it was furious, with the five remaining princes diving straight through the black flames to attack. In the few moments it took for the barrier to burn away enough for Galaeron to see what was happening, the dimensional portal was destroyed, the Chosen were engaged by the princes, and the city stopped falling—at least temporarily. The obsidian mythallar was a truncated sphere no more than a hundred feet high, but with ghostly shapes gliding about inside and the same dark aura as the first time Galaeron had seen it.

The fight raging around the mythallar was both fierce and wild, with shadow balls and lightning bolts crashing against spell shields, silver blades clanging against black, feet and fists flying too fast for an eye to follow. Fearful of creating more dimensional rifts like the one that had sucked Elminster into the Nine Hells, both sides were avoiding the use of pure magic. Even so, in half a dozen places there were alarming whirls of shadow-filled air, two of which seemed to be drawing spells into their spinning hearts and growing larger as they fed on the magic.

Galaeron pointed at the broad-shouldered figure of Prince Clariburnus, who was being steadily beaten back by a blinding flurry of blade and foot attacks from Dove Falconhand.

"See if you can take Clariburnus from behind," he told Aris, "and tip the balance in our favor."

Aris hefted his giant hammer and replied, "I'll distract him at least, but it worries me that we see only the princes and the Most High." The giant gestured at Telamont, who was holding his palms out toward the damaged mythallar, no doubt controlling the flow of the Shadow Weave to steady the city, and asked, "Where is their army?"

"Anywhere but here," Galaeron replied.

It didn't take a wild guess to know that the Shadovar would not want to run the risk that one of their soldiers would meet a stream of the Chosen's silver fire with a shadow bolt. The resulting tear in the world fabric might well suck the entire enclave into a plane more hellish than the one they had just escaped.

Aris grunted, and asked, "Do I want to know what you will be doing?"

Galaeron pointed at Telamont and said, "I'll be keeping the Most High busy."

Aris's eyes went wide.

"Has your shadow made you insane?" he gasped. "You're no match—"

"A bloodfly is no match for a rothé, but which one does the biting?" Galaeron motioned Aris forward and said, "You will emerge behind Clariburnus."

Aris regarded Galaeron with a skeptical expression.

"Be careful, my friend. I have not yet given up on you."

Galaeron smiled and said, "Then it must be true, what the *sy Tel'Quessir* say—there is nothing more stubborn than a Stone Giant." He laid a hand behind Aris's knee and pushed. "Hurry, before those fools open another hell mouth."

Aris lurched forward, stumbling out of the Fringe. Galaeron remained behind long enough to see him emerge from the basin's obsidian wall a few paces behind Clariburnus, his great hammer already arcing down toward his target's head. The prince sensed the attack at the last instant and twisted away, but the distraction was all Dove Falconhand needed to drive her own attacks home. Flinging magic with one hand and swinging steel with the other, she first dispelled the Shadovar's blade guard, then sank her magic sword to the hilt in his abdomen. He stumbled back under Aris's legs, letting out a throaty howl that was audible even above the battle din. The prince took his vengeance by slashing his black sword behind Aris's leg.

The giant's knee buckled, and that was as long as Galaeron dared watch before leaping out of the Fringe. He came out directly behind Telamont, kicking with both feet, calling a bolt of black lightning with one hand and swinging his stolen sword with the other.

The Most High did not flinch. He did not even look. He merely stepped out of the way. As Galaeron sailed past, he swung the sword and flung the lightning. As soon as his black blade touched Telamont's robe, it shattered. The lightning bolt fizzled an inch from his hand, then Galaeron found himself hanging motionless before his target, staring into a pair of flickering platinum eyes.

"Elf!" the Most High barked. In his anger, Telamont almost balled one of his wispy hands, and the city trembled as his control over the mythallar slipped. "How did you get free?"

Galaeron smiled—it seemed the Most High did not know all that happened in his palace.

"In the most unexpected way possible . . ."

Galaeron opened himself to the Shadow Weave and felt its cold magic come flowing into him from every direction.

"I took your advice."

Galaeron turned his palm outward and unleashed a bolt of pure shadow magic. The attack seemed to take Telamont by surprise, if only because he had not been prepared to see Galaeron calling upon the Shadow Weave. Unfortunately, it also had next to no effect, casting only a short-lived cloud over the Most High's face before it vanished into the darkness beneath his cowl. The city seemed to fall once more—for just a heartbeat—then the Most High caught it again.

"You have yielded to your shadow, I see," Telamont said. "It will not be long before you are able to return the information Melegaunt worked so hard to collect."

"I can recall it now," Galaeron said, "but you wouldn't be wise to count on me for favors—and 'yielded' is not the word I would have used. I have joined with my shadow, but my will remains my own."

Telamont's platinum eyes flashed, and Galaeron's limbs spread outward. He spun around until he was hanging upside down over the battle. Aris lay on the floor of the basin, bleeding from three different wounds and writhing in pain. The Chosen were faring far better. Though both Dove and Storm were pouring blood from rents in their armor, only three princes remained in the basin. Prince Mattick was giving ground under a furious assault of blade and spell.

All Galaeron had to do was keep Telamont's attention focused on him instead of the fight. He tried again to open himself to the Shadow Weave, but all he felt this time was a spongy presence through which no magic would pass.

"Is something wrong, elf?" Telamont asked. "Perhaps your will is not your own, after all?"

In the basin below, Prince Mattick had dropped to a knee beneath the furious onslaught of magic coming from Alustriel and Laeral. Dove and Khelben were driving his brother Vattick away from him and would soon be in a position to finish him with a blow from behind.

"My will is enough mine to vow you shall never have the knowledge Melegaunt passed to me," Galaeron said. "And if you doubt I have the strength to keep my oath—"

"Your strength I do not doubt. You resisted your shadow far too long." Telamont's voice was wispy and cold. "A pity, really. Had you surrendered to it as I urged, I could have saved you as I did Hadhrune. Now, you are useless to me. I will be forced to wring the knowledge from your worthless mind . . . just as I have your foolish hope for defeating my princes."

As Telamont spoke these last words, the princes Aglarel and Yder emerged behind Alustriel and Laeral. Aglarel caught Alustriel from behind with a vicious overhand strike that cleaved her a foot and a half through the shoulder blade before she could teleport away in a wailing spray of crimson blood.

Khelben glimpsed Yder from the corner of his eye and aiming his black staff over Laeral's shoulder blasted him with a storm of meteors that sent him tumbling halfway up the basin wall.

That left Mattick free to counterattack. He rose, wielding an oversized black sword in one hand and flinging a spray of winged black spiders from the other. The spiders swarmed Khelben's head in a droning black cloud, but it was the sword that proved most deadly, hacking Dove's leg off at the knee. She fell cursing and saved herself from a deadly second blow by unleashing a long ribbon of silver fire.

Mattick escaped a certain death only by flinging himself off to one side and bowling Khelben over by rolling into his legs. In the meantime, Dove's silver fire was burning through the shadowy fog above the basin, and Galaeron glimpsed a curving sweep of a sandy lakeshore far below. It took him a moment to register what he was seeing, and he realized why the mythallar was so difficult to find except through the shadows. The basin was in what had once been the top of the mountain but was now the bottom of the city, resting upside-down and looking straight down upon the desert below.

The hole in the clouds closed as quickly as it had opened, and Dove teleported to safety as well. Only Khelben, Laeral, and Storm remained, with the five Shadovar princes closing in around them and relentlessly herding the trio toward a whirling cyclone of shadow-filled air. There was Aris, too, still writhing on the floor, slowly sliding toward the middle of the basin on a sheet of his own crimson blood. No one was paying him any attention, and Galaeron quickly looked back to Telamont, lest the Most High sense the hope growing in his heart and do something to stop the clever giant.

Galaeron found even that strategy fraught with peril. Sliding down the basin wall behind Telamont was Vala, holding one hand clamped into a fist so she could point a star-shaped ring at the Most High's back. In the other she carried her darksword, her arm cocked and ready to throw at the first sign that he knew she was there.

Desperate to keep his mind on something else—and terrified that Telamont had already sensed his thoughts—Galaeron looked back to the Chosen.

"Use the silver fire!" he shouted. "It is the only—"

"Silence, you fool!" Telamont said. "Would you destroy Faerûn rather than let us have a place—"

He too fell silent as, to Galaeron's amazement, Khelben raised his hand and loosed a stream of the shimmering magic fire at Telamont. Crying out in rage and disbelief, Telamont had no choice but to lift both hands and raise a spell shield before him. Freed of the Most High's grasp, Galaeron plummeted toward the bottom of the basin and barely had time to cry out a spell of soft falling before the air erupted into whistling white sparks and cracking lances of black lightning. He brought his legs around beneath him and landed atop the mythallar itself—just in time to turn and see Vala come tumbling into Telamont from behind.

What happened next was impossible to say. He saw Telamont's shadowy feet fly, Vala's sword arc, and a black arm whip into the crackling air. All of them dissolved into shadow. The blow of a tremendous hammer shook the mythallar, and Aris cried out in triumph. Something like a volcano exploded beneath Galaeron's feet, and he found himself tumbling through air as black and as thick as tar.

He smashed into an obsidian wall and tumbled to his feet only to have his legs fly out from beneath him as the basin swung up beside him. He went somersaulting down toward the edge then came to a sudden stop, then went cartwheeling back toward the center. Three times he glimpsed the mythallar, chipped and pouring shadow fume out into the basin, with Aris wedging his legs beneath one side and still hammering at it with his sculpting hammer, before he hit it and stopped.

"Aha, Galaeron!" Aris cried. "It is an unworkable stone, but not too hard to flake!"

"I think—" the basin pitched wildly in the other direction, and Galaeron barely kept himself from tumbling away by grabbing hold of the giant's tool bag—"you have done enough!"

Aris stopped hammering long enough to ask, "What else is there to do?"

Galaeron saw Vala go tumbling by—and sweep Vattick off his feet to leave a severed Shadovar leg in her wake—before she vanished into the black mist and began to scream a savage Vaasan war cry. Galaeron plucked a handful of shadowstuff from the blackening air and shaped it into a pair of spiders. One of these he passed to Aris with instructions to swallow, and the other he gulped down himself. Two quick incantations later, and they were both scrambling across the basin on all fours, their hands and feet sticking to the slick surface as though coated with paste.

They found Vala and the last three Chosen in desperate straits, unable to keep their feet and caught inside a ring of Shadovar princes. Aglarel hurled a shadow ball at Storm, who barely managed to swing her legs around in time to take the attack in the thigh instead of her chest. The orb drilled a fist-sized hole through muscle and bone that clearly left her unable to fight, yet she did not teleport away as had the other Chosen when they grew too wounded to fight. Khelben leveled his staff at the prince who had wounded her, but the only thing that shot from the end was a laughable drizzle of yellow light.

Galaeron touched a finger to his temple, then used his shadow magic to speak to Aris in his thoughts

They're helpless! he explained. *The shadowstuff is smothering their magic.*

Aris nodded then pointed to Aglarel and Yder, and hefted his hammer.

Good, Galaeron sent. *Go.*

They sprang forward together, Aris catching the two princes by surprise, smashing their helms and sending them somersaulting across the basin floor before they vanished into the black mists. Galaeron caught Mattick from behind with a shadow bolt that sent him tumbling headlong into the Chosen's midst, where Laeral and Khelben quickly proved that they were not entirely helpless by planting their daggers at least twice in every unarmored inch before the prince beat a hasty retreat by dissolving back into the shadows.

That left Brennus, Clariburnus, and Dethud attacking from behind. A pair of dark bolts caught Khelben in the shoulders and sent him sliding across the basin toward Aris, while a shadow claw extended from Dethud's forearm to close around Laeral's throat and start dragging her back toward the Shadovar's ranks. Galaeron leaped forward to attack, but Vala was already hurling her darksword into the prince's chest. The weapon sank to the hilt, then dropped to the floor as Dethud retreated into the shadows.

Vala called the weapon back to hand and started to charge Brennus but was knocked from her feet as that basin made another wild swing. Her hip had barely touched down before she was back on her feet and starting forward.

Galaeron caught her by the arm and said, "It's done."

"Not yet." She turned and pointed up the basin wall into the black mists and said, "I got one of his arms, but Telamont's still up there."

A pair of dark disks came hissing across the basin and would have slashed their heads off, had Aris not knocked them off their feet before it arrived. Galaeron rolled to his knees and counterattacked with a flight of shadow arrows.

Brennus blocked them easily and sent the dark shafts streaming back in their direction. Aris took two in his arm, and Vala one in her shoulder, and three more nicked Galaeron along one side of his neck and arm.

"It's done," Galaeron said. They were the most difficult words he had ever been forced to say, and also the surest. He took Vala's arm and shoved her back toward the three battered Chosen. "We aren't going to win this."

Aris refused to retreat.

"But the mythallar—"

"Is cracked," Galaeron said. "Perhaps that will be enough to bring the city down."

Aris turned and hurled his hammer at the heart of mythallar.

Clariburnus waved his hand and sent the tool somersaulting away, then Brennus sent a bank of black fog rolling toward them. Galaeron raised a wind spell that he hoped would send the fog rolling back toward the princes, but Brennus dispelled it with a gesture. Storm began to choke on the fumes, and it occurred to Galaeron that he was learning something else about power, that sometimes the most difficult part of wielding it was knowing when it was not enough.

"We've done as much as we can."

Galaeron motioned for the wounded giant to gather up Storm and the other Chosen, then he grabbed hold of Vala and shoved her into the others.

"Well said, elf," Khelben replied. He stretched a hand behind Vala's back to clasp Galaeron on the shoulder. "You're learning."

Another shadow bolt came hissing into the group to catch Storm square in the back. Laeral's arm lashed out to catch her sister under the arm, then the basin tipped precariously in the opposite direction. Only Aris's sticky appendages and long reach kept the group from tumbling across the basin and becoming separated again.

"All right!" Laeral cried. "Galaeron, will you please get us out of here while there's still something left to get out of?"

CHAPTER FOURTEEN

2 Eleasias, the Year of Wild Magic

Ruha sat wedged in a shady cleft high in the Scimitar Spires East, watching the Shade Enclave slowly sink toward the purple waters of Shadow Lake. Enormous as it was and swaddled in black shadowstuff, the enclave resembled a storm cloud crashing down from on high, complete with sheets of silver lightning illuminating jagged sweeps of misty curtain and mysterious, half-heard roars rumbling out from its hidden heart. Veserab riders were descending from the city in masses of swirling wings, and hordes of shadowalkers were beginning to emerge from dark places all across the nearby hills. This increased the likelihood that she would be forced to flee before she found her friends—and Malik—but Ruha was glad to see so many Shadovar escaping alive. As terrible as were the calamities they had unleashed on Faerûn with their shadow blankets, she had no thirst for vengeance. The death of an entire city would do nothing to bring back the hordes who had already perished.

The enclave—or rather, the black cloud surrounding the enclave—dropped an abrupt five hundred feet, sending scores of veserabs tumbling through the air and bringing the city approximately level with Ruha's hiding place. Though it was difficult to see much through the billowing murk, every so often she glimpsed a crag of stone cliff sweeping past, or an expanse of black wall plummeting down out of the shadows only to suddenly reverse direction and vanish back into the gloom.

Shade was wobbling, Ruha realized, as though someone were struggling to keep it aloft. She could only guess what that meant for her friends, but it could not be good. Certainly, they were not the ones attempting to save the city.

"Storm?" Ruha said aloud. "How fare you? I am here."

Knowing the Weave would carry no more than a few words to Storm's ear, Ruha stopped there. Several more times, a craggy cliff emerged from the black mists and swept past. Each time, the stony face seemed a little hazier and indistinct, as though she were looking through a denser fog—or more of it. Despite this, she quickly began to recognize the features of the cliff and realized that the city was no longer sinking.

Someone was saving it.

"Storm?" Ruha called again. "Khelben? Are you there?"

When no response came she tried Laeral, then Alustriel, and finally she received an answer.

The battle went badly, and I cannot contact them either. Even coming to Ruha through the Weave, Alustriel's voice sounded weak and full of pain. *I was wounded and forced to leave. Is Shade still . . . ?*

It stopped sinking. Ruha replied using Alustriel's spell. *What that means, I don't know.*

Dove was injured as well, Alustriel reported. *I hesitate to ask, but—*

I'll learn what I can, Ruha offered.

The rumble of a collapsing building—or perhaps several of them—sounded somewhere inside the enclave, then a huge cascade of rubble tumbled out of the cloud and splashed into Shadow Lake.

The situation here is unsteady, Ruha sent, *you may not hear from me for some time.*

Thank you, Alustriel said. *Be careful. Dove and I will return as soon as we are well enough to help.*

Ruha watched until the rubble had stopped splashing into the lake, then she drizzled a little saliva on her hand. She had not used her magic for fear of alerting a Shadovar patrol to her presence, but Alustriel's request rendered that fear irrelevant. The Shining Lady would never have asked for help, were she not worried that Galaeron's plan had gone terribly wrong. Ruha made a wiping motion in the air before her, at the same time using the elemental magic favored by desert witches to cast a spell of clear seeing.

The shadow mist grew transparent, so long as she looked straight ahead. For the first time, she saw Shade unmasked. The city of grand palaces and imposing edifices that had seemed so breathtaking was gone. In its place hung a jumbled mountain of shabby tenements and dilapidated mansions, collapsing one after the other as the enclave lurched about like a camel on the deck of a storm-tossed ship. Even the overturned peak upon which it rested was flaky disintegrating shale instead of hard granite.

Pouring down the face of the mountain was a stunning thread of silver liquid, not so much falling into the lake as stretching down through the surface. Whether it actually touched bottom or continued through it down into the heart of the Phaerlin was impossible to say, but Ruha knew by how the strand remained tight from top to bottom that it was not falling water. She followed its shining line up to the source and discovered that it came from a cleft in a red, heart-shaped boulder lodged in a horizontal fissure about halfway up the mountain.

Swinging about beneath the boulder, affixed to it by some means not apparent at that distance, was a pudgy little shape with a pair of tiny nubs rising from the top of his head. Ruha needed no more magic to recognize what she was seeing. She knew a pair of cuckold's antlers when she saw them.

✡✡✡✡✡

It was Malik's accursed fortune that the Shadovar had to be the worst smiths on this plane or any other. He was hanging with his feet braced against the lower lip of the sun slit, trying to pull the Karsestone—which stood a full head higher than he was tall—through an opening that rose only to his chin. One of the links in his manacle chain had opened. The gap was not large, but given his strength and his pitiful condition even that much was a comment on the sorry state of Shadovar metalworking.

"Cyric!" he called.

He continued to pull, but kept a careful eye on the link.

"The One—"

The cleft swept upward as the city began another of its wild oscillations. For perhaps the hundredth time, Malik found himself tumbling down toward the opposite corner. He could think of nothing but the weak chain, of what would become of him if the link opened and he went tumbling into the lake below. Drowning would be the least of it. Thirsty as he was, it might even be pleasant. Afterward, though, the things that would happen to his spirit if he failed Cyric and died . . . that he could not even bear to contemplate.

The free manacle struck him in the head, and the chain jerked him along upside-down. He slammed into the upper lip of the sun slit and flipped down in front of the tumbling Karsestone just in time to catch a long spray of whole magic straight in the face. He began to cough violently, then the boulder was rolling onto his chest. Ribs crackled, his breath left him in a scream, and the stone stopped. On top of him.

Malik cursed and kicked and shoved, but the thing would not budge. It was wedged in place against the ceiling of the slit, which meant he had somehow—at last—dragged it into the opening.

He craned his neck to the side, and through the cascade of silvery magic pouring down over his face, he glimpsed a ragged notch in the upper lip of the sun slit. Malik began to believe he might really succeed in stealing the stone. That he would no doubt be killed in the process was an unpleasant consequence, but in his service to Cyric, he had suffered many things far worse.

The pain was beyond belief, and it was impossible to draw breath, but Malik had long ago learned to ignore minor inconveniences such as those. He hooked his heels over the lip of the opening and pulled. The Karsestone slipped a little—and more weight settled on his chest.

Maybe that meant there would be more room at the top. Malik pulled harder with his legs. Something snapped in his chest. He pulled harder *and* shoved with his arms. Nothing moved, but he did grow dizzy from lack of air. Thus reminded that the stone was laying on *him*, he saw that if he could only get out from beneath it, there would be room for it to fall completely on its side and slide out into the empty air.

Lacking any other means of extracting himself, Malik straightened his legs and began to swing them back and forth in a widening arc, trying to work first his hips free, then the rest of his body as well. Behind him, the roar and crash of screaming Shadovar and tumbling stone rose and faded in time to the wild oscillations of the enclave. The Karsestone pressed more heavily as the slit swung downward. Malik's vision closed in, and stars began to appear around the edges of the darkening tunnel. The rush of oblivion filled his ears, then the slit reached the apogee of its swing and started back down.

The weight all but vanished. Malik flung his legs down in the direction they were traveling and felt his hips slip out from beneath the boulder. He rolled to his side and pushed, hard, and was free.

The Karsestone rocked toward him.

"Devil rock!"

Malik pushed off and pivoted on his hip, whirling out of its path and back into the loom chamber. The Karsestone settled on its side, rocked to the right, rocked to the left, and slipped over the edge.

The manacle stretched Malik's arm out full, and he thought his hand would pop free of his wrist. Instead, he flew out the sun slit after it and found himself following the Karsestone down through a swirling cloud of veserab riders. The boulder struck glancing blows to two beasts and sent them tumbling and hissing away, then finally caught one square between the wings. The impact slowed their fall just long enough for a little slack to develop in the chain that connected Malik to the stone. The rider slipped past, bloody and twisted on one side and the mount broken and screeching on the other, then the purple waters of Shadow Lake grew visible no more than a thousand feet below.

Malik smiled.

"Cyric!" he screamed. "Hear me now, Cyric, the One—"

When he cried the last word, no sound came from his mouth. The lake continued to come up beneath him, though with the ferocious wind filling his eyes with tears, it was all but impossible to see. He tried again and remained as mute as a tortoise. He cursed Shar, thinking she was only trying to protect her prize, then glimpsed a dark shape angling down to intercept him. Thinking it was only an alert Shadovar lord, Malik reached for his stolen dagger—and instantly found himself engulfed in a web of sticky magic strands.

In a web of sticky strands of *Weave* magic.

Malik stopped falling, and wailed more in frustration than pain as the Karsestone stretched his manacle chain taut—again—and jerked his shoulder out of its socket. He thought the terrible strain would tear off his arm. Instead, the boulder stopped falling, and he found himself staring out a small gap down his manacle chain to the open link. The gap was as wide as a dagger blade and growing before the one eye that could see it.

Malik tried to see who had captured him, but the magic web held his head too tightly for it to turn. It hardly mattered. He knew without looking who it was. She had a gift for arriving when he most needed her to be somewhere else. They turned and started across the lake toward the Scimitar Mountains.

"Where are your manners, Malik?" Ruha called. "Will you not thank me for saving your life?"

The opening in the link continued to grow, and in his fury it barely registered that Ruha had annulled the magic that had silenced him earlier. "Meddling Harper witch!" Malik cried. "Can you not see that I am robbing the Shadovar of their greatest power?"

"And giving it to Cyric, I am certain," Ruha surmised, relieving him of the compulsion to add this himself. "I think the rest of us will be better served with the Karsestone in the hands of the Chosen—and you standing before a Harper court."

"You may as well murder me here!" Realizing that he could speak again, Malik tried again to say, "Cyric, the—"

Again, his words began to spill silently from his mouth. They passed out from beneath the city's shadow, but Malik could see that the chain would never hold until they reached shore. The open link was straightening before his eyes. He tried to call out, hoping that if he could warn Ruha she would at least save the stone until he could steal it later, but the only thing to leave his mouth was his silent, anguished breath.

The link lost its last bit of curve, and the Karsestone plummeted free. Malik and Ruha shot skyward, but only long enough for Ruha to regain control and start down after the falling stone.

"You heel-biting cur!" Ruha stormed. "What have you done?"

Even had he been able to speak, Malik would not have bothered to defend himself. He was too busy trying to mark the place the stone would enter the water. Flapping along behind the diving witch as he was, that was an impossible thing in its own right. He saw little more than flashes of dark water and streams of fleeing veserabs.

"Kozah's breath!" Ruha cursed.

She pulled up sharply, and suddenly. As Malik swung beneath her he had a view of nothing but water. A giant waterspout was rising up to meet the Karsestone, seven watery fingers stretching out to entwine it. Perhaps the One had heard after all. Or so Malik prayed.

The silvery fingers closed around the boulder and pulled it down into Shadow Lake, leaving behind a huge black whirlpool. Malik prayed that it had been Cyric's hand that had taken the crown of the Shadow Weave and that consequently he would not be left to languish forever in the hell of his god's displeasure.

But it was not to be. As the stone vanished into the lake's murky depths, a glistening purple eye appeared in the heart of the whirlpool and winked at him.

Malik knew better than to hope the eye belonged to Cyric. The One never sent signs, except when he was angry.

✡✡✡✡✡

Head spinning with afterdaze, Galaeron arrived clasping Vala's hand, his other arm looped around Aris's knee, his eyes aching in the brilliant sun. Crackles, bangs, and half-muffled roars rumbled out of the sky while off in the distance an erratic din of booming splashes rolled across a broad expanse of water. There was trouble over there, and it slowly came back to Galaeron that he and his companions were the cause. Aris groaned, stumbling forward, and crashed to a knee, spilling an armload of bloodied humans as he put a hand out to catch himself.

A glimpse of black beard was all it took for Galaeron to recall where he was and how he had come to be there. Instead of turning to check on the injured Chosen, he looked back and was disappointed to see the murk-swaddled city still hovering a thousand feet in the air, engulfed in swirling clouds of veserabs and releasing a steady rain of debris down into the lake. There were no obvious signs of pursuit, though anyone powerful enough to recapture Galaeron and three Chosen would come by shadow, not air.

As Galaeron studied the enclave, he noticed a thin line of darkness running between the lake and the city. It was near the shore and so faint as to be almost invisible but also straight and unwavering. As he watched, the lower end moved out toward deeper water, slicing through the purple waves without leaving a wake. Shade itself remained where it was. Galaeron spent a few moments observing, trying to puzzle out what he was seeing. Veserabs circled around it, and debris bounced off it as though it were a solid rope, yet it was as transparent as a pale shadow. Through it he could see passing Shadovar, falling boulders, and even the mountains on the lake's far shore.

Galaeron finally gave up guessing, and seeing that the enclave was not going to sink any lower, he turned back to his companions. Laeral was handing Aris his third flask of healing potion, and the wounds Khelben and Storm had suffered were already closing. Khelben held a vial out to Galaeron and motioned at the gashes in his neck.

"You may as well take care of those before we return."

"Return?" Aris asked. The flask Laeral had given him slipped from his hand and shattered on the stony ground. He appeared not to notice. "To Shade?"

"That's where the mythallar is," Storm replied. She stood and tested her wounded leg. It nearly buckled beneath her, but that did not stop her from nodding approvingly. "I'll need a quarter hour, no more."

In what seemed another life, Galaeron would have been impressed by how quickly the Chosen healed. Having seen what he had seen and knowing how quickly any Shadovar warrior—especially the princes—could heal themselves, he knew his companions to be woefully overmatched.

But it was Aris who objected.

"Has that silver fire melted your brains? We can't return to Shade without Galaeron's magic, and look at him!" Hardly seeming to notice the two shadow arrows still lodged in his shoulder, the giant waved a huge arm in Galaeron's direction. "He's going to have a terrible time getting back to normal as it is. You can't ask him to use more shadow magic."

"Aris, there's no 'normal' to get back *to*. I've told you that," Galaeron said, wondering how he would ever make the giant understand that shadow and light were only illusions. Once one accepted the truth of that, everything became light . . . and everything became shadow. "I was not all good before, and my shadow was not all bad."

"You could have fooled me," Aris said. "Or perhaps you have forgotten what happened in the Saiyaddar?"

"Of course not, but that happened because of the struggle, not because of my shadow. It's the refusal to yield that causes the crisis."

"It was the crisis that Telamont was trying to exploit," Laeral surmised. "He wanted to make you fear your shadow so you would keep struggling and remain unbalanced until he could take control."

"To some extent, yes," Galaeron agreed, "but the struggle *is* necessary. You need to build strength. The shadow is very strong, and I think it would overwhelm you if you accepted it too soon."

"I understand—better than you can know." Laeral said. She cast a private glance at Khelben then looked back to Galaeron. "Once you're ready, accepting your shadow will make you stronger and better."

"Stronger, yes, but better?" Galaeron asked. "I don't know. Strength overcomes weakness, so the strengths in my shadow have overcome some weaknesses in my character, and the strengths in my character have overcome most of the weaknesses in my shadow. So I feel whole—but that hardly makes me a paladin. The world is a darker place than I knew before, and I'm the darker for seeing that. It's not something I'd describe as better."

Sympathetic expressions came to the faces of all three of the Chosen, and Khelben said, "We can't know what you're going through, Galaeron, but I'm sure we share this much. There are times when we all wish we could go back to, uh . . . the way we were before, but the door only opens one way."

"And even were it possible to go back, I would still use any magic necessary to return us to the city," Galaeron said. As thankful as he was for the understanding and comradeship the Chosen were extending to him, he was also convinced that it was folly to do as they asked. "If we return now, we accomplish nothing but our own deaths. The princes heal as fast as the Chosen, and there are more of them than of us."

"Which is why we must strike now, and quickly," Storm said. Her eyes were locked on Galaeron, fixing him in place like a snake pinned beneath an eagle's claw. "This is your plan. Will you see it through or not?"

"Not if it means losing three of Mystra's Chosen," Galaeron said. "Impotent though you may be, you are the only hope Faerûn has, and I will not—"

"Impotent?" Khelben grumbled. He stepped closer, all trace of his earlier camaraderie vanished. He raised his famous black staff as though he meant to rap Galaeron on the brow with it. "I will teach you impotent!"

Galaeron stood unflinching, ready to take whatever blow the wizard cared to deliver, if that would make him and the other Chosen listen.

Laeral spared him the necessity, catching Khelben by the arm and dragging him back a step.

"He has a point, my love. Telamont will not have failed to notice our helplessness once the mythallar was cracked."

"All the more reason to strike now." Khelben's glare slid from Galaeron to Laeral as he said, "Before he expects our return. If we are as 'impotent' as the elf claims, surprise may be our only chance."

"And if we fail, we have no chance," Aris countered.

" 'We?' " Storm echoed. "I doubt there is any sense in your risking your life as well, my friend. Your size is nothing but a hindrance, and your strength will do us little good."

"Little good?" Aris boomed. "Did you not notice that I am the one who cracked the mythallar? You are not returning without me, I promise you that."

Though it did not escape Galaeron's notice how smoothly Storm had shifted the topic to *how* they would return from *whether,* he turned a deaf ear to the argument and glanced toward Vala. She had remained on the fringes of the argument, silent and withdrawn, watching him the entire time in the blunt Vaasan way. Her green eyes remained as enigmatic as the emeralds they resembled.

Galaeron would have given anything to know what she was thinking. Did she consider him weak for yielding to his shadow? Or was she under the misconception—as he had been—that it was a sacrifice necessary to save Faerûn? He considered it a given that she hated him for abandoning her to Escanor. After all that had befallen her—and Telamont had described it to him many times while he was a prisoner in the Palace Most High—he did not understand how she could stand to look upon his face without drawing her sword, but the choice had been hers. She was the one who had hurt him in order to save him, and if her plan had worked she had only herself to blame.

Galaeron knew what he saw in Vala's eyes: anger. She had given so much to protect him. It could only seem to her that he had thrown her sacrifice back in her face, that he had returned to Shade without a thought to what she had done and become the thing she had so desperately tried to prevent.

She was right. Though he had certainly hoped to free Vala, it was Evereska and Faerûn he had come to save. The Chosen would never have agreed to help him otherwise, and he could see how right they would have been. Vala was a mere afterthought, one even Galaeron would have forsaken for a slight increase in their chances of success.

None of that changed his love for her—or how he wished he had spoken to her about it when there was still a chance she would listen.

Galaeron grew aware of a heavy silence and realized the others were looking at him.

Without taking his eyes off Vala, he said, "You know the Shadovar better than anyone here. What do you want to do?"

"What I want is to end this and go home." Vala's gaze finally left Galaeron's. She turned to face Khelben and said, "What I think—"

Vala pulled her darksword and spun back in Galaeron's direction, her arm drawing back to throw.

Startled by just how badly he had underestimated her anger, Galaeron opened himself to the Shadow Weave. He swirled his hand before his body and hissed a wispy Shadovar spell, and a shadowy disk of protection sprang into existence between him and Vala.

Vala dropped her gaze and scowled, and it was only then that Galaeron realized she had been looking past his shoulder. Khelben took advantage of the distraction to slip to her side and catch her by the crook of the elbow.

"No need, my dear," he said. "It's Ruha."

Vala squinted into the sky above Galaeron and said, "So it is. She really should wear some other color."

Galaeron turned to see Ruha's black-cloaked figure sweeping down from the sky, her *aba* and veil flapping wildly in the wind and a familiar figure dangling from a manacle chain attached to her wrist.

"Aha!" Aris boomed, yelling in Malik's direction. "Let us see how you like life in bondage!"

Ruha circled them once, losing altitude, then let Malik slam down and dragged him half a dozen steps across the rocky ground before alighting gently herself.

She bowed in Storm's direction, and pinning Malik's neck to the ground with her foot, touched her fingers to her brow.

"Well met, my friends. Have you conversed with your sisters?"

Storm cast a quick glance in the direction of the other Chosen then said, "Not since our defeat in Shade."

Thinking that no one was paying attention to him, Malik snaked his free hand out to reach for a rock. He found three throwing daggers—Galaeron's, Vala's, and Ruha's—planted in the ground around his wrist and quickly withdrew the offending arm.

Ruha continued the conversation without pause.

"I am pleased to say they both survived. When they could not reach you in the customary ways, Alustriel grew worried and asked me to investigate."

"How long before they're ready to attack the mythallar again?" Khelben asked. Turning to Galaeron, he added, "They'd make a big difference, especially if we're willing to risk the silver fire."

"Fight? In the shadow harlot's den?" Malik cried. "I will cut my wrist off before I allow you to drag me back there!"

"Your wrist is safe for now." Galaeron met Khelben's gaze and said, "There is no point in fighting on their ground. Better to attack the shadow blankets directly and draw them out as the phaerimm were doing."

"It hardly matters to you, Malik," Ruha said. She pulled him to his feet, jerking his hand away from Vala's dagger just as his fingers brushed the hilt. "If I am not needed here, I ask leave to return Malik to the justice of Twilight Hall, while I still have him chained to my wrist."

All three Chosen inclined their heads with expressions that suggested they would be just as happy to adjudicate the matter themselves and be done with it there.

Storm said, "An excellent plan, and I think enough magic remains here for us to see you safely sped along your way."

"To Twilight Hall?" Malik's fear was evident in the way his voice cracked. "I'll be murdered!"

"Only after you are found guilty of a few of your crimes," Khelben answered. "And the word is 'executed'."

"Executed or murdered, it is all the same!" Malik cast a plaintive gaze in Aris's direction and said, "Will you just sit by and let them do this to someone who has saved your life so many times?"

"I will be glad to describe how you saved me," he said, "and also how you enslaved me so you could use my shape studies to grow your church!"

For the first time, a look of despair came over Malik's round face. He seemed to consider his options for a moment then turned to Khelben with a wild-eyed gaze.

"I can tell you how to destroy Telamont Tanthul in a single strike!" He remained silent only a moment before his mouth began to twitch, and more words spilled out. "Of course, there is every chance that you will destroy all of Shade and half of Anauroch with him. . . ."

Even a prospect that terrible was not enough to keep Khelben from cocking his eyebrow.

"You know I can never lie," Malik reminded him.

"We're listening," Laeral said.

Malik's bulging eyes appeared to focus on the tip of Ruha's boot as he planned what he would say next. Given what he had already told them about the pitfalls, Galaeron could not believe the Chosen were even interested in hearing the suggestion.

Finally, Malik looked back to Khelben and said, "What good will it do me to save the world if I am not here to see it?"

Ruha dropped a knee into the middle of his back and used a cuckold's antler to pull his head up, then wrapped the chain connecting their manacles around his neck.

"What makes you think I would ever let you tell them something that would destroy Anauroch?" Ruha asked. "I would rather see you dead and stand before the judges of Twilight Hall myself!"

She tightened the chain until he began to gasp. "Ruha!" Khelben shouted. He seemed as surprised as Galaeron was by the witch's behavior. "Let him speak."

"Never!" she replied, pulling until Malik's eyes began to bulge. "If you want to know—"

Ruha's exclamation came to an abrupt end as Storm plucked her off Malik's back.

"Harper hag!" Malik croaked. "I ought to tell them just for spite!" Again, his face contorted into a conflicted mask, and he added, "Except that after what happened in Shadowdale, I know no Chosen would ever be foolish enough to fling a bolt of silver fire into a being of pure shadow essence."

Galaeron did not realize Ruha's threat had been a ruse until he saw her exchange congratulatory glances with each of the Chosen.

Laeral said, "Not very helpful, Malik."

"Actually, we've already tried silver fire," Storm said. She didn't explain that the attack had only been a ruse designed to buy time for Vala. "Telamont blocked it with a shielding spell."

"Though that hardly matters," Khelben added. "I no longer have much influence with the Harpers anyway."

"Harpers?" Malik screeched. "I am talking about Ruha."

"In exchange for revealing that Telamont Tanthul is pure shadowstuff?" Galaeron scoffed. He was beginning to understand the game the Chosen were playing. "You'll have to do better than that if you want me to set you free."

"There is no use listening to him, Malik," Ruha warned. "*That* will never happen."

The anger in Ruha's eyes was convincing, and it occurred to Galaeron that the others might not realize he had joined their game.

"Perhaps not while you live," Galaeron said, keeping his tone even. He dropped his hand to the hilt of his sword. "It makes no difference to me."

Malik's eyes lit like a pair of torches.

"Kill her?" asked Malik. He considered the situation for a moment, then grew doubtful. "You are too much of a coward. You would never do such a thing."

"To save Evereska?" Galaeron responded. "What do you think I *wouldn't* do?"

It did not escape Galaeron's notice that Khelben, Vala, and all the rest were inching in his direction—nor did it escape Malik's. He considered the proposal only a moment.

"You have already won!" Malik blurted. "There is no need to destroy the mythallar or even to slay Telamont." He would have stopped there, but for Mystra's curse. "They cannot make their shadow blankets without the magic of the Karsestone, and the Karsestone is gone!"

"What?" This from Vala, who was finally beginning to seem interested in the discussion. "Gone how?"

"Into the lake," Ruha explained. "It was attached to his other wrist and fell free. A waterspout reached up to take it."

"It was Shar's hand," Malik explained in a dismal voice. "She has had control of the Shadow Weave all along."

This was enough to make Galaeron draw his sword and press the blade to Ruha's throat. Storm and Vala drew their own blades and stepped over to defend the witch, and it was not clear to Galaeron whether they were warning him off or just supporting his act. In fact, he was no longer sure that he was acting. Doing his best to seem as though he might be worried about the possibility of fighting two of the best swordswomen in Faerûn, Galaeron kept his blade pressed to Ruha's throat.

"Before I set you free," he said to Malik, "tell me how you know all this."

Malik eagerly recounted how, while chained to the Karsestone in Shar's hidden temple, he came to the realization that it was the symbol of her control over the Shadow Weave. Then he told of how, when the city began to fall, the stone had pulled him down into one of the looming chambers, and of how hard he had struggled to steal the stone for Cyric so that he would one day rule the Shadow Weave—and perhaps the Weave itself, since if there was any god capable of putting the two back together, it was the One and All.

By the time Malik finished, Galaeron was not only sure that the *Seraph* was telling the truth, but also that he had correctly interpreted everything he'd seen. Even Khelben seemed convinced.

"I'm willing to grant that Shar caught the Karsestone," Khelben said, "and even that the stone is the symbol of her control over the Shadow Weave, but if the Shadovar need it to create more shadow blankets, I don't see what's to stop her from returning it."

"Nothing," Galaeron answered. "Except that Shar is the goddess of *unrevealed* secrets. After Prince Yder allowed the *Seraph* of an arch rival to not only discover the Karsestone's role and location, but to come so close to stealing it, I am sure she will find a safer place to hide it."

"And let the Shadovar suffer for their sins," Laeral said. "I agree."

This drew a broad smile from Malik, who looked up at Galaeron and said, "I am waiting."

"I would do many things to save Evereska," Galaeron said. "and one of them is lie."

"Lie?" Malik screeched. "The One will punish you for this—though I will surely be the one who suffers in your place! After the many times I have saved your life, how can you do this to me?"

"Because it is necessary."

Though Malik had never done anything to hurt Galaeron and it pained the elf to betray an old friend, he lowered his sword. He stepped back, and with the little man still hurling invectives at his back, he turned to Storm.

"It seems our plan worked for most of Faerûn, if not Evereska," he said. "I thank you for trying."

"As we thank you," Khelben said, slapping a hand on Galaeron's shoulder, "but we are not done yet. Did I not overhear you telling Telamont that you now have a complete understanding of the phaerimm?"

Galaeron nodded, not daring to believe Khelben would say what he hoped Khelben was going to say.

"You did."

Khelben glanced over his shoulder toward Shadow Lake, where the erratic torrent of debris falling from the gloom-cloaked enclave had finally dwindled to a sporadic rain. Instead of fleeing the city, most veserabs seemed to be trying to find a safe route back, and even the crash of collapsing buildings was growing more intermittent and muted.

"Laeral, Storm, what say you?" he asked. "Have we done enough damage here?"

"Not enough," Storm said, "but all we can."

"Yes," Laeral said. "I think it is high time we returned to Evereska."

She held out her arms, inviting Galaeron and the others to join hands with her for an instantaneous return to the Shaeradim. Aris kneeled down and extended a pinky for her to hold, but Vala made no move to join the circle. Galaeron was surprised—and perhaps just a little relieved—to discover he had a sinking feeling in his chest. If his heart was breaking, then sorrow could not be a weakness his shadow had overcome. He went to stand close to Vala.

"I know it's a lot to ask," Galaeron began, "especially after what I put you through, so I won't. If you want to come to Evereska with us, you and your sword are more than welcome."

Vala grunted what might have been acceptance, refusal, or simply an acknowledgment of the question, then said, "One thing. Were you watching when Yder and Aglarel chased me out of the mythallar?"

Galaeron nodded.

"And you didn't come after me?"

Galaeron shook his head.

"Why not?"

"Because I wanted to destroy the mythallar, and I knew our chances would be better if Aris and I remained in hiding until Telamont showed all of his tricks." Galaeron swallowed, then added, "And because I knew you could take care of yourself."

"*Knew,* Galaeron?" she asked.

"Hoped, anyway."

Vala pushed her upper lip into a half-hearted sneer, then shrugged and smiled.

"At least you're honest." She grasped his hand, stepped over to Laeral's teleport circle, and said, "Of course I'm coming. Do you think I'd dare go back to Vaasa without my men and our darkswords?"

CHAPTER FIFTEEN

2 Eleasias, the Year of Wild Magic

After Ruha departed for Twilight Hall with Malik chained to her wrist, Khelben used his sending magic to advise Lord Duirsar of their imminent arrival. The spell failed. Nor did he receive any reply when he tried to contact Kiinyon Colbathin, and when Galaeron tried to contact Keya, the only response he experienced was a fleeting impression of terror. The six of them wasted a few more minutes hazarding uninformed guesses as to how the phaerimm might be interfering with communication magic based on the Shadow Weave as well as the Weave. Able to imagine only dire scenarios, they finally concluded that they simply could not know what was happening and divided themselves into two traveling groups.

A few moments later, Galaeron was lying between Vala and Khelben on a sooty terrace high in the Vine Vale, staring down a staircase wasteland into the crater-pocked pasture inside the Meadow Wall. The once-lush grass was gone, burned off or blasted away by battle magic or withering beneath the rotting corpse of one of the thousands of elf warriors scattered across the field. In the center of the meadow, the marble cliffs of the Three Sisters were speckled around the base with stars of soot and sprays of crusted blood. Atop the hills themselves, curtains of black fume were rising out of the great bluetop forest, coalescing into a single dark cloud that left visible only the lowest reaches of Evereska's majestic towers.

As Galaeron watched, a leaden light erupted in the woods beneath the Groaning Cave, and a deafening crack reverberated across the entire vale and echoed off the looming cliffs of the High Shaeradim. As Galaeron blinked the flash from his eyes, he noticed a ring of falling trees expanding outward, their crowns all pointing away from the center of the explosion. By the time the blast played itself out, the circle of destruction was more than a mile across.

"It is safe for Laeral and Storm to come ahead with Aris," Galaeron said. He spoke without turning to look at Khelben. "You can be sure there are no phaerimm within a mile of us."

"That's awfully quick to be so certain of their positions," Khelben observed. "We haven't been here a minute."

"A minute is all I need," Galaeron said. He rose to his knees and waved a hand in the direction of the burning city. "The phaerimm are down there, looting Evereska of its magic."

"And their servants?" Khelben asked. "All it takes to sound the alarm is a beholder or even a gnoll."

"The phaerimm think they have won," Galaeron explained. "They will have their servants with them, carrying their plunder and helping to claim and defend their new lairs."

"They have no fear of a counterattack?" Khelben asked.

"At the moment, they fear us less than they fear each other." Though the words were Galaeron's, the knowledge came to him in the form of a strange half-thought, closer to a premonition or a feeling than something he actually remembered. "They will know how preoccupied Faerûn has been with the problems caused by Shade, and how impossible it would be for anyone to send an army against them."

"True as that may be," Khelben said, "it does not always require an army to defeat one."

"They are certainly worried about the Chosen," Galaeron said, picking up on Khelben's meaning, "but I doubt they have a choice in the matter. It is not in the nature of the phaerimm to work together. Now that the prize is in hand, everyone must claim his share or watch another steal it from beneath him."

As Galaeron explained this, the tiny shape of a stick figure elf tumbled out of the smoke cloud, hit the edge of the cliff summit, and pinwheeled all the way down into the meadow. Had the mythal been functioning properly, it was not something that would have happened. A protective spell would have caught the victim and lowered him—or her—gently to the ground.

The death made Galaeron wonder what had become of his sister, Keya. The last he had heard, she was doing well with her pregnancy and also as a warrior, joining Vala's men on hunting forays and claiming half a dozen tails for her own belt, but that had been before the mythal fell. Could she be one of the bodies lying down in the meadow or perhaps the one he had just watched plummeting out of the smoke? He longed to try another thought sending, but knew that would be foolish. Assuming she remained alive, there was a good chance that she was fighting at the moment, and the distraction of an unexpected thought popping into her head might well prove fatal. Galaeron could only hope that the moment of fleeting terror he had experienced the first time meant she was still alive—and that his intrusion had not changed that.

"How long will the phaerimm remain at each other's throats?" Khelben asked.

"A tenday, at least," he answered, "but not much longer. Their internal squabbles are swift and deadly."

"A tenday." Khelben's discouragement was hard to miss. "What then?"

"By then, they will have settled matters and prepared their individual defenses." Galaeron did not like the drift Khelben's questions were taking. "They will be impossible to root out."

"The Shadovar did it at Myth Drannor," Khelben countered.

"At the cost of their other ambitions in Faerûn," Vala pointed out. "And there were only a few dozen at Myth Drannor. Here, there will be hundreds."

Khelben sighed and said, "We have lost Evereska." His fist thudded into the ground, raising a small cloud of ash and dust. "It will be all we can do to contain them in the vale."

Though Galaeron did not share Khelben's despair, he remained silent, ordering his thoughts and summoning to mind all he knew about the situation in Evereska. He had an inkling that matters were not as hopeless as Khelben thought, but whether that feeling was due to Melegaunt's wisdom or his own need to undo the terrible mistakes that had led to the fall of the LastHome, he could not say.

Vala laid a warm hand on his forearm and said, "I'm sorry, Galaeron. You did everything you could."

Galaeron started to say that he had not yet done everything, but he was cut off by the soft crackle of a teleport spell. He glanced over his shoulder to make certain the new arrivals were who they expected and saw a gray cloud rising two terraces above. Laeral and the others lay on the ground, spitting soot and blinking confusion from their eyes.

"Hold your spells, miladies," Khelben called to his fellow Chosen. "We're safe enough for now."

The sound of Khelben's voice seemed to draw Laeral out of her afterdaze. She glanced into the bottom of the valley, and her face fell.

"Goddess help us!" she gasped. "We're too late."

"I think not," Galaeron said, finally convinced that the inspiration he felt was more than his own desperation.

He rose and motioned for Laeral to bring the others down, then took a length of shadowsilk from his pocket and began to wrap it around his little finger, fashioning it into a small cone.

"We have come just in time."

Khelben rose to his knees and pulled Galaeron back down.

"Have patience, elf. We'll save as many *Tel'Quess*ir as we can, but first we must plan."

"The best way to save my people is to kill the phaerimm in their city."

Galaeron went back to fashioning his cone.

Laeral and Khelben exchanged knowing glances, and Khelben said, "This isn't your fault, Galaeron. It was Melegaunt who freed the phaerimm, not you."

"That's right," Storm said. Having recovered from her afterdaze, she was jumping down onto the terrace with Galaeron and the others. "We know how the Shadovar think, now. They planned all along to make the phaerimm everyone else's problem. I'd bet my hair that Melegaunt breached the Sharn Wall where he did on purpose. What better way to lure the phaerimm out of Anauroch than to offer them Evereska's mythal?"

"If it was indeed an accident, it worked to the Shadovar's advantage," Galaeron agreed. He finished his cone and carefully removed it from his finger, then set it aside on a stone. "But I am no innocent in this. I was warned many times about Melegaunt, and still I brought Shade into the world."

"You can't blame yourself," Aris said. He was sitting on the back wall of the terrace, leaning over to cup a hand beneath one of the thousand springs that had once watered the terraces of the Vine Vale. "They would have found another way."

Galaeron raised a hand to forestall more forgiving words, and said, "I'm not seeking absolution . . . nor am I speaking out of guilt."

"Then out of vengeance." Laeral phrased this as a fact, not a question. She glanced at Storm, then added, "I know how I would feel, were my sister down there and I unable to contact her."

"If I was seeking vengeance, I would not want your help." Galaeron could see they were still afraid his shadow might be influencing him, and he had no doubt it was. That did not mean he was wrong. "I am talking about victory, not retribution. Hear me out. If you don't like what I say, I'll not hold it against anyone who chooses to remain behind."

Khelben scowled, clearly unhappy with having someone else assume the leadership. Still, he listened patiently. When Galaeron finished, his frown turned thoughtful, and he looked to the other Chosen.

"What do you think?"

"Simple plans are the best," Storm said. "This one is simple, I'll give it that."

"Perhaps too simple," Laeral said. "What's to stop the phaerimm from seeing through it?"

"The arrogance of the phaerimm themselves," Galaeron answered. "They won't believe anyone capable of defeating their spells of clear-seeing."

Leaving the others to consider the merits of his plan on their own, Galaeron started to fashion another cone out of shadowsilk. After a moment, Aris removed a stone from the terrace wall and shaped it into a small bowl with two quick strikes of his hammer, then filled it with soot from a charred log and used the spring to moisten it. When he began to smear the resulting paste up his legs in thick black stripes, Vala cocked a doubtful eyebrow.

"You're a little large for camouflage," she said. "Don't you trust Galaeron's magic?"

"I trust Galaeron," Aris replied. He glanced at Galaeron and gave a grim nod. "But given who we are going to attack, I think it wise for one of us to use no magic. Besides, stone giant camouflage is better than you know. The number of times you have walked past one of us and not known it would surprise you."

"Nothing surprises me anymore," Vala said. She dipped her hand in the bowl and leaped up on the terrace behind Aris. "Bend down, and I'll do your neck before we go."

"Then you've decided to go as well?" Laeral asked.

"Have to. My men and our darkswords are down there." She peered around Aris, looked down at Galaeron, and added, "And I really need to see how this turns out."

Her words made Galaeron ruin the shadow cone he was pulling off his finger. She was probably alluding to the promise she had made to slay him if he ever fell completely under the sway of his shadow, but there was a warmth in her tone that made him hope that she might forgive him, that there might still be room in her heart to love him.

Continuing to hold Vala's gaze, Galaeron began to wrap the shadowsilk around his little finger again. At the same time, he whispered the incantation for a spell of thought sending and began to speak to her in his mind.

Vala.

Her jaw dropped, and her sooty hand came off the back of Aris's bald skull.

Before we go, I want to apologize for leaving you behind, Galaeron said. *I'd understand if you never forgive me, but I hope you can.*

Vala's eyes softened.

There's nothing to forgive. The choice was mine, and I knew what could happen. She returned to camouflaging the back of Aris's head, adding, *But I am torn up, Galaeron. Inside.*

Galaeron's heart sank. *I see. I didn't mean to intrude. Please forgive—*

There's that word again, Vala interrupted. *I don't blame you—that's not what I mean. But since Khelben and the others helped me escape, I've been filled with this . . . I haven't felt anything good. I just want to go home and drink mead in front of the fire. Alone.*

What about Sheldon? You must want to see him.

Galaeron felt ashamed of himself. He had allowed Vala's usual stoic bearing to lull him into thinking she had somehow emerged whole from her enslavement. He had been thinking only of how her ordeal affected him, not of what it might have done to her.

Not like this, she replied. *Not all broken inside.*

You won't always be broken, Galaeron said. *I'll stand by you for however long it takes. I wish I'd told you this before, Vala. I do love you.*

Vala gave him a wistful smile.

Now you tell me. Now that your shadow made you.

Galaeron didn't realize they had become an object of attention until Vala's eyes grew self-conscious and her gaze darted away. Khelben cleared his throat, and either ignoring the looks that had been passing between the two or pretending he had not noticed, he stepped in front of Galaeron.

"You are quite certain the phaerimm will not be able to detect or dispel your magic?" he asked.

"They would have to use the Shadow Weave," Galaeron said, "but we must be wary of beholders. They could undo us with their antimagic rays."

"Beholders we can handle," Storm said.

Khelben sighed, then said, "Very well. If you are determined to pursue this foolish plan of yours, it seems we have no choice except to come along to protect you. How soon can you be ready?"

In answer, Galaeron slipped the last cone of shadowsilk off his finger and pressed it to Khelben's chest.

"Hold that there."

Khelben did as instructed, and Galaeron drew on the Shadow Weave to cast a spell. The black cone expanded to a full ten feet in length, engulfing the Chosen in a stocking of darkness. Galaeron fashioned a barbed tail at the narrow end and four crooked arms at the wide end, added some teeth and other details to create the head-disk, and he found himself looking at what appeared to be a shadow-swathed phaerimm.

"An excellent likeness," Aris complimented. "Though the elbows are too far down the arms, and the tail barb should curve a little more."

Galaeron made the necessary corrections and a few more when Vala, Laeral, and Storm added their opinions. When everyone agreed the likeness was true, he stepped back and spoke a final word to set the shape.

"In Evereska, we should try to stay in the wooded areas where shadows won't seem out of place," Galaeron said. "I assume you can use your own magic to fly and speak the phaerimm wind language."

Khelben replied with a whistling gust of wind and floated into the air.

"Good," Galaeron said. "Avoid using your silver fire. If the phaerimm see it, they will know you are here."

"What about wands and rings?" Laeral asked.

"The shadow mask will conceal their use, as it will your voices and gestures," Galaeron said, "but you must careful not to fling any spell components outside your disguise. The phaerimm do not need components, so if they see you using them. . . ."

"Understood," Storm said, stepping forward. "Me next. I always like fighting with four arms."

Galaeron pressed a shadow cone to her chest and repeated the spell he had used to disguise Khelben, then did the same for himself and Laeral. Finally, he turned to Vala.

"Since you're not a spellcaster, it would be best to disguise you as a mind-slave."

Vala rolled her eyes and tried to make light of the suggestion, but the hurt was plain in her eyes.

"Don't enjoy it too much."

"Not at all," he assured her. "If you think you could hold a blank look—"

"Galaeron, just do it."

Galaeron flattened a small disk of shadowstuff in his hand and carefully molded it over her face. When he cast his spell, Vala's complexion darkened by half a dozen shades. Her eyes grew glassy and vacant, and her expression fell dead and still. It pained Galaeron to see her even in this counterfeit bondage. It reminded him of how selfish and deluded he had been during his shadow crisis and of all she had sacrificed to save him. How he would ever repay her, he could not begin to imagine.

"Are we all set then?" Khelben asked. "I've opened a door to the woods at the base of Cloudcrown Hill. Unless you've a better idea, I thought Lord Duirsar's palace the ideal place to open our campaign."

"There is no better idea," Galaeron said. He turned to find a magic door shimmering at the downhill edge of the terrace. "The phaerimm are sure to be fighting over the plunder there."

"I thought as much." Khelben waved a slender phaerimm arm toward the door. "Storm and Laeral have departed."

Not bothering to ask why Khelben had asked for an opinion if he had already sent the two sisters through, Galaeron started toward the shimmering door. He made it only one step before Vala caught him by his collar—she probably thought she was holding onto one of his disguise's four arms—and pulled him back.

"Wait."

She spun him around and stood there staring at him with her vacant eyes. Finally, she asked, "Where do I kiss?"

Galaeron leaned forward and pressed his lips to hers. It felt a little like kissing a zombie, at least until he closed his eyes, and even then it remained tentative and reserved—at least by Vaasan standards.

When they finally finished and Galaeron caught his breath again, he asked, "For luck?"

"Just in case," Vala corrected, drawing her darksword. "I wouldn't want a Shadovar's fist to be the last thing that ever touched my lips."

She stepped past Galaeron into the magic door and vanished with a crackle.

Galaeron followed Vala into the portal. He had grown so accustomed to teleport magic that he was no longer bothered by the breath-taking cold or the eternal instant of falling, but that did not prevent him from being dazed when he finally felt the ground beneath his feet again. The air was filled with sluggish rumbles and long, unintelligible howls. A crimson ball of fire was rolling toward him in slow motion, with orange tendrils curling out from its flanks in listless swirls.

Galaeron dived out of the way and found himself floating among the enormous trunks of a majestic bluetop forest, four spindly arms waving in front of his face. The sight reminded him that he was supposed to be impersonating a phaerimm, though exactly why still remained a mystery to him. While the open woods around him felt familiar, there was something that did not seem quite right, as though he turned a corner and found himself in an unexpected room.

The fireball was still coming, slowly. Behind it, a fork of lightning flickered into existence and slithered through the trees like a crooked white snake, then exploded through a bugbear's chest and twisted off in pursuit of a mind flayer. The attack was answered by ten golden bolts, flying along in a tight wedge formation that angled toward their moon elf target at about the speed of a flock of migrating geese.

Galaeron floated out of the fireball's path. Crouching behind a freshly split boulder about fifty paces distant, he saw a much-battered bladesinger still holding up the smoking hand that had hurled the spell. More offended by the attack than concerned about it, he pulled a few strands of shadow-silk from his pocket and hurled them in the bladesinger's direction, hissing an incantation. The elf was instantly wrapped in a cocoon of sticky black shadow.

Galaeron! the familiar voice of Laeral Silverhand sounded inside his mind. *There's no need to defend yourself. You can fly faster than that spell's coming.*

A pair of shadow-swathed phaerimm emerged from the trees behind him, Vala close on their barbed tails. As soon as Galaeron saw the emptiness in her eyes, he recalled their plan and saw that something had gone terribly wrong.

This isn't Cloudcrown Hill, he objected.

No—we're at the Groaning Cave, Vala replied. *I recognize it from when we came during my first visit.*

Galaeron looked over his shoulder and saw the cave less than a hundred paces up the hill. A small company of elf warriors was gathered on the entrance veranda, crouching behind the stone balustrades and using the high terrain to fire arrows and spells down on the bugbears and illithids in the forest below. Like everything else in this strange battle, their attacks seemed to be in slow motion, the arrows floating rather than flying to their targets and the spells less flashing across the sky than simply advancing.

Galaeron drifted out of the path of two arrows coming toward him, then heard a soft crackle as Aris arrived in the wood. The fireball had already passed by and was in the process of exploding into the hillside behind them. Galaeron grabbed the giant by his arm and pulled him forward so the back blast wouldn't burn him.

Khelben appeared an instant later, in the middle of a slowly wagging tail of flame. He floated there in the fire for a moment, afterdazed and no doubt finding it even more difficult than had Galaeron to adjust to his new surroundings. Galaeron shoved Aris's arm toward Vala, then he floated over and pulled the Chosen out of the fire.

"Where are we?" In his confusion, Khelben neglected to use thoughtspeech. "This isn't—" He caught himself and switched. *Cloudcrown Hill!*

We came out on the other side of the city, Laeral informed him, *near the Groaning Cave.*

Worse than that, Galaeron said. *We came out in the past.*

How can that be? Storm demanded. She reached behind Galaeron and batted an arrow aside. *It can't happen.*

It did, Galaeron replied. *A little after we arrived in the Vine Vale, this whole wood was leveled by an explosion. And now—*

It's still standing, Vala finished. *I saw the blast, too. Somehow, we got here before the trees fell.*

A fork of lightning snaked down from the cave mouth and caught Storm square in the center of her phaerimm disguise. The blast drove her to the ground but seemed to cause her no injury. Khelben and Laeral lifted their head-disks toward the source of the attack, and that alone was enough to send several dozen elves scrambling away in slow motion.

These disguises have one drawback, Vala sent as she rushed to take cover behind a fallen bluetop. *They work!*

She vanished over the trunk. Galaeron and the Chosen followed, and a moment later they were taking shelter in the crook of a massive limb. Aris came and stood behind them, his camouflage working so well that had Galaeron not been directly under the giant, he would never have seen him.

I should have realized something like this would happen. Khelben's tone was apologetic. *We've already seen what comes of mixing Weave and Shadow Weave.*

We have, agreed Storm, *but not this time. If this had something to do with shadow magic, how could Aris be here? He has no shadow magic.*

That's true, Laeral said. *Whatever went wrong, it happened when Khelben opened his magic door.*

"The mythal!" Galaeron was so excited that he forgot himself and said this aloud. *It had a defense against teleporting!*

Not 'had,' Khelben replied. *Evereska's mythal still has a bite.*

So it sent us into the past? Vala asked.

Arrows began to sink into the trunk of the fallen bluetop at sporadic intervals.

And it relocated our exit portal, Laeral said. *We're lucky the mythal was weakened, or the displacement might not have been so minor.*

If this is minor, Vala said, *I don't want to see major.*

The comment brought to mind the strange blast that had leveled the woods around the Groaning Cave shortly after Galaeron and the first group arrived in the valley. He turned to look at Khelben.

Khelben? Do you remember that big blast we saw after we arrived?

The gray light? he replied. *Of course.*

Well, Galaeron said, *that happened here.*

It was impossible to say what happened beneath Khelben's disguise, but all four of phaerimm arms stopped moving, and his tail dropped to the ground.

Time! he gasped. *We're moving through it faster than everyone around us—*

And when we catch up . . . Laeral let the sentence trail off.

What? Aris asked. He had vanished so completely into the forest that Galaeron had forgotten he was there. *I don't understand.*

Trouble, Storm said. *Really big trouble.*

It seemed to Galaeron that the arrows were starting to thunk into their tree trunk more rapidly. He peered up toward the Groaning Cave and saw the archers moving a little less torpidly now, sending their shafts down the hill with a speed that could almost be described as flying rather than drifting. A battle mage caught sight of him and stretched out a finger to send a lightning bolt in his direction.

Galaeron used his shadow magic to send a thought message to the man.

Hold your attack! I am Galaeron Nihmedu, an elf and a friend.

The mage grabbed his head and stumbled back. *Ooouuuuuuut offfffff myyyyyyy heeeeeeeeeeeeeeeeaaaaaaaaaaaaaaaaaaddd, monnnnnnnnnnnssssssssssssssterrrrrrrrrrrrrrrr!*

The mage followed his order by stumbling back to the balustrade and completing his spell. The lightning bolt shot down the slope far faster than previous ones, almost too fast for the eye to follow. Galaeron barely had time to roll aside and cry a warning before the bolt was there.

Storm rose into its path and took the bolt full in the body.

Storm! Galaeron cried.

The bolt sank into Storm's body and vanished with no stench of charred flesh and not even much of a crack. She settled back behind the tree trunk and let out a satisfied belch.

Don't concern yourself, Galaeron, Laeral said. *Storm can eat lightning all day.*

A little gift from my sisters when I went to fight Iyachtu Xvim, Storm explained. *Now, don't you think we ought to get away from here? Far away from here?*

What could it hurt? Khelben replied.

For one of the Chosen, you don't sound all that confident, Vala observed.

It's not a matter of confidence, Laeral said. *It all depends on whether the temporal displacement wave is centered on us or our point of arrival.*

Huh? Vala asked.

She means run! Galaeron said.

He lifted Vala to her feet and shoved her into the woods in the direction opposite the elves who were attacking them. Khelben and the other Chosen rose into the air and floated along beside her, using their magic and their bodies to deflect the barrage of attacks that rained down from the veranda of the Groaning Cave. Before following, Galaeron took a moment to dispel the shadow web he had cast on the bladesinger.

Leave . . . this . . . place . . . now! he urged, spacing his words so the elf would be more likely to comprehend. *Big danger!*

The bladesinger pulled out of the dissolving shadow web looking more confused than alarmed but quickly took the advice when a beholder and his escort of bugbears came charging after him from the phaerimm side of the battle. Galaeron sent a similar warning to the elves on the veranda outside the Groaning Cave. Their only answer was a shimmering sphere of force that closed to within a dozen paces before Galaeron noticed it and fled his hiding place. A dull rumble sounded behind him a moment later, and he looked back to see the bluetop erupting into a spray of splinters. The ball expanded almost swiftly enough to catch him. Time was definitely moving faster.

Galaeron caught up to the others and followed close behind, dodging silver snakes of lightning and using his magic to turn arrows with wind spells or shadow shields. Aris ran alongside at a distance of twenty paces, slipping through the woods as stealthily as any ranger. As long as the companions kept moving, they had little to fear from their elf attackers, who clearly found it impossible to hit targets that must have seemed mere blurs. Though there were bugbears, illithids, and beholders aplenty in the wood, they were too busy fighting to pay any attention to a shadowy band of "phaerimm."

The companions had little trouble leaving the area of the cave, only to discover that the battle in the rest of the forest was just as fierce and twice as confused. There seemed to be no clearly drawn ranks or objectives, just random clusters of elves and mind-slaves and the occasional phaerimm attacking each other with spell and steel, sometimes from a hundred paces distant, sometimes standing toe-to-toe. All too often, the battles were between elves and elf mind-slaves, the former reluctant to strike killing blows and the latter all too eager. Whoever the combatants were, they seemed to be moving faster, their lightning bolts flashing through the wood faster than Galaeron's eye could follow, their arrows whizzing past too swiftly to deflect.

Whenever possible, Galaeron urged the warriors to flee and used his magic to free the elf mind-slaves. It was this last good deed that complicated their flight, when six phaerimm appeared behind a rank of advancing bugbears and began to whistle at them in Winds.

"Yoooou!" The phaerimm's challenge was slow and trilling, but not so slow it was difficult for Galaeron's speech magic to understand. "Explain yourselves."

Realizing no one else would understand the importance of responding with an accusation, Galaeron floated forward to confront the phaerimm.

"You stole . . . my slave." Though Galaeron had not intended it, the wind spell he was using to modulate his speech ripped through the forest like a cyclone, tearing leaves from the trees and assailing their challengers with sticks. "I . . . demand a gift!"

"A gift?" The six phaerimm drifted a few paces back, clearly buying the space to begin a spell battle. "Who are you? Why do you whistle so fast?"

"Who dares ask—"

That was as far as Galaeron got before three tongues of silver fire shot out to engulf the three closest phaerimm.

"No time!" Khelben yelled in Common, already flinging a handful of rainbow dust on the ground beneath the phaerimm. "We've got to keep going!"

Galaeron was already hurling a shadow ball at the nearest surviving phaerimm, while Vala had drawn her sword and was cocking her arm to throw. Though the forest time had nearly caught up to their time, enough of a difference remained for Khelben and Galaeron to unleash their spells before their foes reacted. The shadow ball caught its target at an oblique angle and drilled a head-sized oval through half the length of its body. The phaerimm collapsed in a limp heap, its life spilling out onto the forest floor in a steaming heap.

Khelben's prismatic wall was not so effective. It sprang up beneath the phaerimm as he had obviously intended, but the thing floated through its defenses in a spray of gem-colored flashes and counterattacked with a black disintegration bolt. Khelben took the bolt square in the chest and smiled, then stretched two of his arms in the creature's direction.

In the meantime, the last phaerimm had loosed a flight of magic bolts at Vala. To Galaeron's horror, she stood her ground and hurled her darksword at her attacker.

"Vala!"

Galaeron stretched out a hand to raise a shadow shield in front of her, but even with time on his side, he was not that fast. The bolts struck home.

"No!"

Vala staggered from the impact and dropped a foot back to brace herself. She raised her fist, pointing her ring in the phaerimm's direction and shooting the same flight of golden bolts back at her attacker.

The darksword arrived first, opening the thing from lip to tail. It trilled wildly and vanished in a silver dazzle of teleport magic. The golden bolts sizzled off into the forest to draw an anguished cry from some elf warrior

Galaeron had not even seen. Vala opened the same hand and called her sword back without lowering her arm.

Khelben's phaerimm refused to retreat so easily. A wall of flames sprang to life between it and its attackers and set the forest instantly ablaze. Unable to see, Khelben elected to save his spell, and the whirling disk of shadow that Galaeron sent spinning through the barricade cut nothing down except a long swath of bluetops—and perhaps the half a dozen elves whose voices he heard screaming in panic and rage.

Balls of flame as large as a beholder began to sizzle off the fire wall in the direction of Galaeron and the Chosen. Galaeron barely managed to pluck his shadow off the ground and throw it up in front of him, and even then the heat was enough to singe his hair as the crackling orbs struck his silhouette and vanished into the shadow plane.

Unable to react quickly enough, Khelben caught one of the spheres full in the chest and erupted into flame. He floated calmly to the ground, where he remained until Laeral, who caught two spheres in the chest without emitting so much as a wisp of smoke, covered his body with hers and smothered the fire.

As this happened, Storm was streaking headlong into the flames. She took three of the fireballs square in the head-disk and laughed, then plunged headlong through the burning wall . . . and was too late.

Aris had already emerged from the woods on the other side of the burning wall. He stooped down and wrapped his big hands around the phaerimm—it was at the near end of the fire barrier, not where Galaeron had expected at all—and squeezed until it popped. Storm was left with nothing to do but dispel the phaerimm's magic and extinguish the flames.

Galaeron rushed to Khelben's side and asked, "How bad—?"

"It isn't," Khelben growled. His disguise remained that of a shadow-swathed phaerimm, so it was impossible to see how badly he was hurt. "We don't have time. Those phaerimm were *fast*. The time streams must be converging."

"Right," Laeral said. "Let's go."

Aris and the three Chosen turned to start through the woods again, and Galaeron was about ready to start after them when he realized that Vala was neither ahead of them nor behind.

"Wait!"

Storm stopped and twisted her head-disk around to look at him.

"Wait? We don't have time to—"

Galaeron flew over to where he had last seen her and noticed a set of boot prints—a set of *big* boot prints—on the ground.

"They took her!"

"They?" The three Chosen gathered round and began to curse as one. "Of all the black fortune!"

"That's human," Galaeron said. "Male and large. Very large."

"Vaasan," Khelben growled. He looked into the woods, and in Common yelled, "Kuhl! Burlen!"

Their answer came in riotous motion as a dozen elf warriors sprang out from behind tree trunks, under logs, beneath piles of dead leaves, and rushed to attack. Only the slim advantage of their faster-moving time stream spared Galaeron and his fellow Chosen from being chopped into a dozen pieces each by the darkswords that had once belonged to Vala's slain company of warriors.

"Up!" Galaeron cried in Common. "Watch yourselves!"

As he yelled the warning, he was already rising above the reach of his attackers. Khelben and the other Chosen followed, but poor Aris found himself surrounded by half a dozen elves tossing their glassy black swords from hand to hand.

The elves below Galaeron and the Chosen drew their arms back to throw.

"Hold!" Galaeron cried, speaking Elvish. "I am Galaeron Nihmedu, a citizen of Evereska, once a Tomb Guard prince patrolling the Desert Border South, who resides in Treetop in Starmeadow, son to Aubric Nihmedu and brother to Keya Nihmedu of the Long Watch, friend to—"

"Strange how you do not look much like an elf," said a familiar—though much hardened—female voice.

A young moon elf of little more than eighty appeared from behind the trunk of a bluetop, her turquoise hair tucked up beneath an ostentatious battle helm that could only have been made by the Gold elves of Evermeet. Her gold-flecked eyes were shot through with red lines, and her cupid's bow smile had gone straight and grim with worry, but Galaeron would have known his sister had she looked a hundred times more drained. His heart drummed in joy.

"Keya! You're alive!"

Keya narrowed her eyes in suspicion and said, "So it seems, for now."

There was a slight drawl as she spoke, just enough to suggest the slower passage of forest time. She reached behind a tree and pulled Vala into view, and Galaeron was astonished to see that someone had actually taken Vala's darksword and bound her hands in elven rope.

"Where did you come by this mind-slave?" Keya asked. "Tell me that, and we will let you live—so long as you swear to leave Evereska and never return."

"You are not a very good liar, Keya." He dispelled the masking magic that made him look like a phaerimm, then drifted down toward the ground, adding, "But neither you nor Evereska has anything to fear from us."

"Hold there, you devil!" Keya ordered. "Any lower, and I'll give you the death you deserve for impersonating my brother."

This drew a snicker from Vala, which drew an angry glower from Keya.

"Keya!" Khelben snapped in Elvish. "He *is* your brother. Release Vala and flee this area—now!"

"Do you think I take orders from worms?"

To demonstrate that she did not, Keya hurled her darksword. Even with the faster speed of his time stream, Khelben barely had time to pivot out of the way and let the weapon tumble past. Two dozen archers suddenly appeared from their hiding places, arrows nocked and arms drawing their bows back to fire. Storm and Laeral were already casting spells of paralyzation. Keya's entire company froze where they were, bows half flexed and swords half raised.

Khelben retrieved Keya's darksword from the tree where it had lodged itself, then flew down to her. Burlen stepped into view from behind the tree where Vala had been held, his own arm rising to throw his darksword.

Galaeron stopped him with a shadow web.

Khelben nodded his thanks, then flipped the weapon around and shook the hilt in Keya's face.

"You are trying my patience, young lady. We have reasons for our appearance, and no time to explain them to you now."

A loud crackle sounded from the direction of the Groaning Cave. Galaeron glanced back and saw a tiny brilliance flickering down through the bluetop boughs.

Khelben continued to lecture Keya, "When we release you and your company, you are going to take it on faith that I am telling you the truth and flee this area—"

"Uh, Khelben?" As Galaeron spoke, he was watching the tiny sphere of brilliance expand above the trees. "There isn't going to be—"

"Starmeadow!" Laeral yelled, already laying a portal on the ground in the center of the elven company. "Teleport!"

Storm was already shoving paralyzed elves into the circle. Khelben took one look at the expanding circle of light and cursed, then wrapped his arms around Keya, Burlen, and two more elves, and vanished. Galaeron sprang to Vala's side, grabbing her bound hands, and started back toward Laeral's teleportation circle.

Vala jerked him back, nearly pulling him off his feet.

"Not without my sword!"

Back near the Groaning Cave, crooked forks of light began to dance down through the trees, and the war rumble there fell into a sudden silence. Galaeron stepped around Vala and found her sword leaning against the tree. He snatched it up and cut her bindings—no other blade would have severed the elven rope—then handed the weapon back to her.

"*Now* can we go?"

Galaeron grabbed her wrist and turned toward the teleportation circle and ran headlong into a small wood elf with doe-brown eyes, an impish smile, and a bared long sword.

"Well met, Galaeron," she said. "*Still* rescuing Vala, I see."

Galaeron's jaw fell. "T-Takari?"

Takari smiled and said, "So you *do* remember."

Galaeron surprised her with a heartfelt embrace, and she surprised him by returning it just as warmly.

"I was afraid I'd never see you again," he said.

A long, deafening crackle sounded from the direction of the Groaning Cave, and a column of leaden light appeared in the forest in front of the veranda.

Vala appeared beside them.

"Break it up, you two!" She slid an arm between them and used a deft elbow to force Takari back, then said, "No offense, but we've got to go."

Takari glanced at the offending elbow as though she might remove it, then smiled sweetly and said, "No offense taken."

She glanced back in the direction of the brightening column of light, then turned and waved at what appeared to be a pile of leaves.

"Come along, Kuhl! We'll let Galaeron teleport us out of here."

CHAPTER SIXTEEN

2 Eleasias, the Year of Wild Magic

Galaeron arrived in a tangle of arms both human and elf, Vala clasping his shoulders on one side, Takari tucked against his ribs on the other, Kuhl standing opposite, encompassing them all in a great bear hug and glaring down as though he wasn't quite convinced that Galaeron's transformation from phaerimm to elf was a return to true form.

The air reeked of brimstone and charred flesh, and it resounded with booms and cracks and wails. Still struggling with teleport afterdaze, Galaeron recalled he had been somewhere else trying to flee some impending cataclysm. The air had smelled the same there, and the battle din had been just as loud. He began to fear they had not escaped after all, that they were about to suffer the consequences of whatever terrible event they had been fleeing.

Galaeron glanced up at the canopy of a bluetop forest and cringed at the familiarity of it.

"I think the mythal rebuffed—"

He was about to say "my teleport spell" when a leaden brilliance filtered through the wood. He was jolted by a tremendous concussion—a concussion that erupted in the pit of his stomach and blasted outward. His palms and soles went numb, his eardrums thumped, and pain filled his head.

He found himself on his hands and knees with Vala, Takari, and Kuhl, thinking they were all going to die and wondering why the mythal had interfered with his magic when it normally deflected translocational spells only when they crossed its perimeter. Of course, Galaeron had used shadow magic. Months before a healthy mythal had prevented Melegaunt from touching the Shadow Weave, but in its weakened state, it had not obstructed any of the shadow spells Galaeron cast outside the Groaning Cave.

This was as far as Galaeron's thoughts went before it occurred to him that he had already survived the shock wave. The roaring in his ears was actually a deafening silence, he realized, and the ground beneath him had not shuddered once with the impact of a falling bluetop. He rose to his knees, glancing around, and saw that while the wood was familiar, it was not the one beneath the Groaning Cave. The undergrowth had been allowed to offer shelter to the birds and animals, and the terrain was not as steep.

Perhaps they had reached Starmeadow after all. Galaeron started to rise . . . and was pulled back down by Kuhl's meaty paw. The Vaasan used fingertalk to call for silence, then slipped back into the underbrush as stealthily as any elf. When Vala and Takari did the same, Galaeron dropped to his belly and followed, then turned and peered through a bush.

Starmeadow lay directly ahead, its small expanse layered in acrid fume and its lush grasses blackened from battle. At the far end, Dawnsglory Pond had turned pink with spilled blood and was still boiling from some blast of magical heat. Bodies both elf and otherwise lay strewn along the far side, where the Chosen and the Company of the Cold Hand had been attacked while still dazed. Like Galaeron and his companions, those out on the battlefield were already starting to recover and rise. Both sides seemed to have been unprepared for the fighting, with the elves and their allies caught out in the open and the phaerimm and their mind-slaves strewn haphazardly along the meadow edge adjacent to Galaeron and his companions.

An elf in tattered armor picked up a darksword and used it to lop off the tentacled head of a mind flayer. A phaerimm floated up and countered with a black ray that left a melon-sized hole in the warrior's chest. Another elf sprang up, catching the sword before it hit the ground, and charged the killer. The battle burst into full rage, silver bolts and white flashes tracing brilliant streaks through the air, flames bursting up from the blackened ground, heads and chests and bodies rupturing from no visible cause. Even the mythal exerted itself to join in, pelting Evereska's enemies with a hail of slushy pellets that dissolved on their shoulders and had no effect except to make the elves fight harder.

Galaeron thought of Keya and wanted to charge out onto the field to find her, but the calmer part of him—the darker, more cunning part—held back. Foolish heroics would accomplish nothing except a foolish death, and Keya needed him alive. The entire Company of the Cold Hand needed him, as did Khelben and the other Chosen, as did all of Evereska. He was the only one who understood the phaerimm, who knew how to defeat them.

He had to work toward his purpose and trust his sister to keep herself alive. To do anything less was to betray the warrior spirit in her . . . and that of Evereska herself.

Galaeron found the Chosen near Dawnsglory Pond, still in their phaerimm disguises and hurling spells back into the main body of the Company of the Cold Hand. At first, he thought they were just trying to protect their identities and escape until they could execute his plan. It took a moment of careful observation before he realized that their spells were all flash and thunder, and that they were carefully positioning themselves to catch the phaerimm in a flanking attack. Seeing they could do even better, he backed deeper into the underbrush, then motioned for the others to arm themselves and follow.

Kuhl moved more like a forest cat than the cave bear he so resembled, and the four companions slipped around the phaerimm flank guard. Galaeron sprang out of a bush behind an illithid, and the thing's heart stopped beating before it realized someone had driven a sword through it. As Galaeron was dropping back out of sight, Takari's death arrow droned past his head and killed the illithid's beholder partner, then Vala and Kuhl charged out of the underbrush to attack four astonished bugbears. The closest pair raised their battle-axes to block. The Vaasans' darkswords slashed through the thick oak shafts like bread, then opened the throats of both creatures. The second pair of bugbears, alarmed as well as stunned, thought better of fighting and turned to roar the alarm.

It was a bad mistake. Galaeron hurled a dark bolt, Takari fired two more death arrows, and the Vaasans threw their darkswords. Only Vala targeted the nearest one, but her black blade sank to the hilt between the monster's shoulder blades. He took three more steps, then crashed to the ground in a lifeless heap. The other bugbear fell where he was, head lost to Galaeron's magic, heart burst by Kuhl's darksword, legs shriveling around Takari's black arrows.

The first sign of a counterattack came when a huge bluetop trunk burst into flaming splinters. A terrific cracking echoed down through the boughs, and Galaeron looked up to find what seemed an entire sky of leaves and trunk crashing down toward him. He flicked a wad of shadowstuff up at it and shouted a word in ancient Netherese. A web of dark strands appeared overhead, anchoring itself to surrounding trees to catch the falling bluetop.

The swirling crackle of meteor stones reverberated through woods from somewhere ahead. Galaeron dived behind the nearest bluetop and glimpsed a smoke trail bending toward him as the pebbles adjusted course. They struck the tree with a series of staccato bangs. He scrambled forward and peered around the other side of the trunk and almost lost his head to a black ray.

He rolled back in the other direction and was flash-blinded by a fork of oncoming lightning.

Galaeron dropped flat and bit dirt as the bolt cracked past overhead. With time passing at the same rate for everyone, he was no match for a phaerimm. He pulled back, readied a shadow shield, and barely had time to raise it before the undergrowth parted a dozen paces away and a thornback head rose into view.

Vala emerged behind it, ran her darksword down the length of its back, and disappeared back into the brush just before a beam of green radiance disintegrated the foliage where she had been standing. Takari's bow sang, and the ray vanished. Vala leaped up, waving a severed phaerimm tail in Galaeron's direction, and started through the forest again.

Before following, Galaeron said, "Khelben, they're trapped between us. We're coming from the opposite end."

By the time he rolled out from behind the tree, Kuhl had already killed a second phaerimm rushing to aid the one that Vala had slain. Galaeron returned to his place in the battle line, and they sneaked through the undergrowth, slaying several more bugbears and two more illithids before Takari threw her voice into the trees overhead and gave a warning bird whistle.

A conflagration of fireballs and lightning bolts streaked up toward the sound, setting two bluetops ablaze and showering the forest floor with burning boughs and broken limbs. Galaeron followed one of the spells to its source and spied what appeared to be a cone-shaped log standing suspiciously upright in the heart of big honey bramble about twenty paces ahead. He sent a flight of shadow arrows streaking toward the log, then dived for cover and started rolling. He was helped along the way by several concussion waves and a wall of magical heat.

By the time Galaeron stopped, the forest ahead was disintegrating into splinters and flame. He came to his knees and found an illithid stumbling in his direction, its tentacled head looking wide-eyed back over its shoulder. Galaeron barely had time to draw his sword before the thing ran onto the point and impaled itself. He finished the job with a few blade flicks, then shoved the illithid away.

The situation was much the same along the rest of the battle line, and Galaeron had no doubt that it was because the Chosen were behind the enemy, attacking. The phaerimm mind-slaves were blindly fleeing the inferno, running headlong into Vala and Kuhl. The Vaasans were taking a terrible toll, spinning and whirling, cutting in two any monster that came within reach of their darkswords and using their pommels to knock unconscious the occasional elf mind-slave.

But there were only two of them and easily a hundred mind-slaves. Dozens slipped past and crashed off through the brush. Takari did her best to stop the monsters, emptying her quiver into their backs and slowly working her way forward so she could conserve arrows by plucking once-fired shafts out of dead bodies. Galaeron used shadow bolts to cut down a pair of bugbears and a beholder angling toward her back, then Takari felled a fleeing illithid, and there were no more enemies.

The patter of falling rain sounded behind Galaeron. He turned to find a small torrent deluging the battle line, dousing the fire and filling the wood with billowing steam. The storm would do nothing to save the trees already burning, but it would at least prevent the flames from spreading. When a trio of phaerimm emerged from the steam cloud, Galaeron found himself preparing a shadow bolt. He knew by how the forest murk seemed to cling to their bodies that they were the Chosen, but that didn't prevent him from cringing. The disguise was more convincing than he had realized, and he suddenly understood why it had been so hard to convince Keya of his identity back at the Groaning Cave.

"A sad thing to lose so many bluetops," Khelben said, twisting his head-disk around to look back toward the battle line. "Most are older than I am."

"Evereska has been invaded," Galaeron said. "The trees must pay along with the rest of us."

Takari's jaw dropped in outrage. She started to rebuke him for saying such a thing, then reconsidered and simply cast an accusing look in Vala's direction.

Vala shrugged and said, "Don't look at me. I'm not the one who told him to embrace his shadow."

"I'm not saying we should let the forest burn," Galaeron retorted. "Only that we should remember what will become of Evereska's forests if we let the phaerimm take Evereska."

"Sometimes the lesser of two evils is the only good possible," Laeral agreed. She started toward the edge of the meadow. "Let's see if Keya needs help, shall we?"

✡✡✡✡✡

But the Company of the Cold Hand had the situation well in hand. Without their phaerimm masters to guide and intimidate them, most of the mind-slaves had already lost interest in fighting and started to withdraw. It required only a couple of thunderbolts from the flank to turn the retreat into a rout, and Evereska's forces were alone in the field only a few minutes later.

Keya gave orders to gather the wounded and retrieve the darkswords, then waved Aris out of his hiding place on the opposite side of the meadow and came over to join Galaeron and the others. With a battle-jaded face and worry lines in her brow as deep as field furrows, she looked immeasurably older and grimmer than when Galaeron had last seen her, but stronger as well. With Burlen at her back, she stopped and gave Vala a warm—though weary—embrace, then stepped back and studied her brother.

There was a hardness in her eyes that made Galaeron worry she blamed him for what had happened in Evereska, and he began to fear their reunion would be less than a joyful one. He was more than willing to accept responsibility for his blunders, but the thought that his mistakes might drive a wedge between him and his sister was more than he could bear. It was bad enough that the war he started had taken their father from them; that it should also destroy the little that remained of his family would be a punishment worthy of Loviatar.

Finally, Keya dropped a hand to her protruding belly and said, "You heard, I suppose?"

Wondering what her pregnancy had to do with his mistakes, Galaeron replied, "Storm told me."

"Well, what are you waiting for?" Keya moved her hand back to the hilt of the darksword hanging in her scabbard and said, "You might as well say it and be done with it."

Galaeron frowned, puzzled.

"What is there to say?"

Keya cringed, but tightened her lips and visibly began to gather herself. "I know this isn't something you expected, but I'm over eighty years old. I can make my own decisions—and it's not like there was anyone here to ask."

"Ask," Galaeron repeated. "About what?"

Vala nudged him the back with her elbow. "The baby."

"You rothé!" Takari hissed. "Have you gone completely human?"

Finally, Galaeron realized that Keya did not blame him for what had happened in Evereska, that she was not even thinking about the war. She was frightened, not angry, and she only wanted the same thing from him that he wanted from her. He started to laugh, which only made Keya set her jaw.

"Is that all you're worried about? What *I* think?" Galaeron asked. He took her by the shoulders. "I can't tell you how happy that makes me!"

Now it was Keya who looked puzzled.

"Why wouldn't I care what you think?"

Before Galaeron could answer, Takari interposed herself between the two.

"Galaeron is very happy for you," she said, "and he thinks Dex will make a wonderful father . . . for a human. Right, Galaeron?"

"Of course," Galaeron said. "I only thought—"

"And Keya is happy to have you back," Takari said. "No matter what the Golds say, she knows this isn't your fault. Isn't that true, Keya?"

"Even the Golds know the Shadovar tricked you," Keya said. "They've been planning this for centuries."

Takari nodded to Burlen and said, "Let's get out of here before the phaerimm come back to finish the job."

"Come back?" Galaeron repeated. "That's the one thing we don't have to worry about. No phaerimm survivor is ever going to admit he was defeated."

Keya and Takari exchanged looks, then Keya said, "Galaeron, they *always* come back."

"They're determined to wipe out the Company of the Cold Hand," Takari added, "but we're making them pay."

"Determined?" Galaeron did not like the sound of that. "You mean they're still fighting an organized battle?"

Burlen scowled down at Galaeron and grumbled, " 'Course they're organized. You want to kill a wolf pack, you'd better be more organized than they are."

"So they're *all* working together?" Galaeron asked. This felt wrong to him, contrary to all Melegaunt had learned about the phaerimm during his century of spying. "None are fighting over Evereska's magic? None are trying to claim the best lair?"

Keya said, "They're too busy hunting us." She turned to Burlen and said, "Have the war mages lay some death wards. We'll rendezvous at the Floating Gardens to plan our next strike."

Burlen had barely turned to pass the order along before the Company of the Cold Hand began to melt into the woods. Keya took Galaeron by the hand and, motioning for the others to follow, started through the forest toward the back side of Dawnsglory Pond.

"Glad homeagain, brother—such as home is these days." Keya threw a disgusted scowl in the direction of the Chosen, then quietly asked, "Why the phaerimm costumes? We almost killed you."

"My idea," Galaeron said. "I expected the phaerimm to be at each others' throats by now. We were going to fan the flames, make it look like they were killing one another and stealing each other's plunder. We'd hoped to start an all-out battle between them."

They reached the near bank of Dawnsglory Pond. Keya paused to send Takari to scout ahead with Kuhl and Burlen, and Vala decided to go along. As they had vanished into the undergrowth, Keya looked back to Galaeron.

"What made you think they'd fall for something like that?"

"I was wondering the same thing," Khelben said, speaking over their shoulders. He and the Silverhand sisters remained disguised as phaerimm. "Clearly, Galaeron's source was mistaken."

"No. The information was correct. That's why Telamont wanted me back."

"It would not be the first time the Shadovar have fooled you—or me," Laeral said, laying a pair of spindly phaerimm hands on his shoulders. "They are never playing the game we think. That's what makes them so hard to defeat."

"Or maybe something's changed," Storm added. "Whatever. But these disguises have served their purpose. If the phaerimm are coordinating their efforts, I doubt we're going to fool them again—and, to tell the truth, I'm tired of dressing like an overgrown slug."

"As am I," Laeral agreed. "The next time I'm attacked, I'd rather it not be by elves."

Galaeron dispelled the disguise magic but remained convinced that the information Melegaunt had worked so hard to gather would not simply grow outdated. There was something about the situation he did not yet understand.

They started through the forest after Takari and the other scouts, and Galaeron said, "Keya, hunting the Company of the Cold Hand can't be the only thing the phaerimm are doing in Evereska. What else are they doing?"

"That we know about?" Keya replied. "For one, they're keeping Lord Duirsar and Kiinyon Colbathin trapped in the palace on Cloudcrown."

"Alone?"

Keya shook her head. "Lord Duirsar has a circle of high mages from Evermeet, and Zharilee is there with what remains of the Long Watch."

"How do you know all this?" Khelben asked, walking along on Keya's far side. "I've tried to reach both Lord Duirsar and Kiinyon with magic and heard nothing back."

"The phaerimm have besieged the palace with an antimagic shell," Keya reported, "but Manynests comes and goes as he pleases."

"They're holding Lord Duirsar prisoner?" Galaeron asked.

"Isolating him," Keya corrected. "They couldn't breach the palace wards, so they prevented him from leaving."

"More likely the High Mages," Laeral observed. "If the Company of the Cold Hand is giving them trouble—"

"That's it!" Galaeron burst. "The high mages!"

"What about them?" Khelben asked.

Instead of answering, Galaeron stopped and took his sister by the shoulders.

"You said 'for one thing,' the phaerimm were keeping Lord Duirsar trapped," he said. "What are the other things?"

"Aside from the fighting you'd expect in any battle, there's really only one other thing," Keya said. "About ten of them have gathered at Hanali Celanil's statue. We haven't tried to penetrate their security perimeter, but Manynests says they're using a lot of magic."

"I'll bet they are," Khelben said.

Keya appeared perplexed by this remark, but Galaeron had a feeling he knew exactly what Khelben meant.

"That's where the mythal was cast?" Galaeron gasped. This was a secret so closely guarded that, aside from Lord Duirsar and the city's high mages, only Evereska's most loyal friend among the Chosen would be privy to it. "At the statue of Hanali Celanil?"

"I doubt there was a statue there when it was cast," Khelben said. "And I wasn't there, you understand."

"But that's what you've been given to understand," Galaeron concluded. Conviction and excitement began to well up inside him as half-formed thoughts raced through this mind, fitting all the pieces of the puzzle into place. "That would explain why they haven't fallen into quarreling yet."

"It does?" This from Aris, who had been creeping along behind them. "They're feeding off the mythal?"

"Not feeding," Galaeron said. "Feeding would cause fights."

"Dismantling, then," Khelben said, following the line of Galaeron's reasoning. "They're taking it apart spell by spell."

"So the magic will return to the Weave?" Keya asked. "Why would they do that?"

"Because the magic *won't* return to the Weave," Storm said. "It's not raw anymore. It can't."

"The magic will stay here, inside the boundaries of the old mythal," Laeral explained. "It'll infuse the whole area."

They came to the path that led from Dawnsglory Pond up to Starmeadow Tower. Hearing Takari's all-clear warble, they crossed to Goldmorn Knoll and traversed the slope, the woods more open and therefore more dangerous.

Once the entire group was safely across, Khelben looked down over Keya's head and said to Galaeron, "It seems the phaerimm have learned to share. That hardly sounds like the creatures you claimed you could have warring with themselves inside a day."

"It doesn't," Galaeron agreed, "but if they have learned to share, it's only because a leader has emerged who is strong enough to dictate terms."

"If a strong leader has emerged among the phaerimm," Laeral said, "we dare not let them have Evereska."

Storm nodded and made a fist, which she touched lightly to Galaeron's shoulder.

"Not if we value the rest of Faerûn, we don't."

✡✡✡✡✡

The snowfinch was up in the tree again, peering down through the bluetop boughs at the ring of phaerimm hovering around the statue of the elf goddess. It did not peep either in alarm or complaint and in fact seemed to be spying on their progress, but Arr did not dare blast the feathered nuisance. The SpellGather had finally found a thread of loose magic and was about to pull the first spell from the mythal, and the last thing she wished to do was disrupt their concentration.

Even with Zay and Yao, and eight more of the finest spell artists of her race—or any other—working nonstop since they entered the city, her plan had yet to yield a breath of magic. Already, two young softthorns had violated the WarGather's edict against plunder-taking, and she had been forced to promise Tuuh a service gift to hunt them down and pin their skins to the GatherStone as a warning to others. And now there was talk of four longbarbs at the Cave-that-Taunts attacking their own kind shortly before the killblast.

The members of the WarGather were beginning to doubt her plan, especially her ability to prevent loot-taking. She could sense that much in their frequent inquiries about the SpellGather's progress and in the gusts with which they warned one another away from the great armory at the Academy of Magic. Her plan had to start freeing the mythal's magic soon, or the WarGather would dissolve around her. Arr had no illusions about what would befall her then. She had promised too many gifts, and forgiveness was not a virtue of the phaerimm.

Ryry emerged from the forest behind Arr and floated to her side.

"How goes it?" Ryry asked.

"You shall have your spell crown," Arr gusted. "What news from the Cave-that-Taunts?"

"After the killblast, now it is calling us flatworms," Ryry reported. "It claims the spell was its doing."

Arr found herself curling her tail. She forced it straight again, then decided that had to be a lie. Who had ever heard of a cave that could cast spells?

"Then I am certain," Arr began, "that you asked why it killed so many elves along with our dozen and a half."

"Of course."

Several of the SpellGather phaerimm began to work their four arms over each other as though pulling a long rope. Arr put a hand out to silence Ryry and went still as stone, praying that they finally had a thread, even a small one, to demonstrate the progress she had promised the WarGather.

The finch peeped.

The arms of the spell artists fell motionless one after the other, and they returned to pluck at the strand they had found. Arr gnashed her pointed teeth and checked again to see if there was any magic on the bird, but it seemed as null as a rock. Another peep like that, she vowed, and it *would* be a rock, and she didn't care how many days of concentration the spellcasting shattered.

Calming herself, Arr turned her attention back to Ryry and asked, "What was the cave's reply?"

"It had none," Ryry answered smoothly. "Its claim was a lie, I am sure."

"No doubt," Arr answered. It was almost certainly Ryry who was lying—to cover for her oversight—but Arr would only alienate a fellow member of the WarGather by making the accusation. "It is an insult that a hole in the ground speaks our language."

"Indeed."

"What of the four betrayers?" Arr asked.

"They are not betrayers."

Ryry's thorns bristled with pride. Arr waited in stillness, for she had learned the value of allowing allies their moment.

"They are impostors," Ryry said at last. "Impostors who escaped the killblast and fought with the blackswords at the Starmeadow."

"There was a fight at the Starmeadow?"

"Only just completed," Ryry said. "I have sent a killtroop, but you know how quickly the blackswords vanish after they attack."

Arr was still thinking about the betrayers.

"Impostors?" she asked, openly skeptical. "And no one saw through their magic?"

Ryry grew less proud of herself. "They may be shadow pullers," she said. "One of the softhorns who survived saw dark bolts."

"Dark bolts?" Arr repeated. "Did our spies not say Shade had fallen?"

"Nearly fallen," Ryry corrected. "The Chosen have somehow anchored the city over the north end of the lake, but Shade is now stable. It isn't going to fall, not until we bring it down ourselves."

Arr was so shocked she nearly let herself sink to the ground. Tricking the Chosen into destroying Shade for them had been a cornerstone of her plan, but somehow the Shadovar had prevailed. Could it be true? *Could* the Shadow Weave be stronger than the Weave?

"Arr?"

Arr did not realize she had let herself sink again until she found herself looking up at Ryry. She used her tail to push herself back into the air.

"Why was I not told of this earlier?"

Ryry angled her thorns back in anger and replied, "If Xayn fails to abide by his promise, I am not to blame."

"Xayn?" Arr repeated, finally getting hold of herself. "The blackswords killed Xayn this morning. It is nothing to concern ourselves about."

Ryry's stillness was an accusation.

Arr gestured at the statue of the elf goddess.

"The SpellGather has loosened a strand," she said. "It would take all the princes of Shade to stop us now, and they sent only four."

Ryry brought her four hands together over her dished head and quoted Arr's oft-repeated refrain, "Together, all things are possible." She steepled her sixteen fingers into a single pyramid, causing the finch overhead to take wing and flee. "Is there a way I can be of service?"

"Yes." Though it would mean the promise of another service gift, Arr pointed after the bird and said, "Kill that finch."

CHAPTER SEVENTEEN

2 Eleasias, the Year of Wild Magic

You're sure this plan will work?" Takari asked. "I don't think anyone was all that impressed with the last one."

"There are no sure things," Galaeron said, "but it has a chance."

"A *good* chance?" Vala asked.

They were hiding among the musty-smelling roots dangling beneath the Floating Gardens of Aerdrie Faenya, waiting in the mucky water of a knee-deep nourishment pond. Aris and the Chosen had already left for Cloudcrown Hill to rescue—fetch was more accurate—Lord Duirsar and the high mages. Galaeron had once again assumed the likeness of a phaerimm, and the entire Company of the Cold Hand had vowed they were ready to lose fingers—or even entire hands—to the cold of their borrowed darkswords.

Galaeron turned his head-disk toward Vala and held her gaze.

"A better chance than you had in Myth Drannor. That turned out well enough."

Vala rolled her eyes. "I only had to kill six phaerimm," she said. "We're talking ten here—all at once."

Manynests, just returned from his spying mission and perched on Keya's shoulder, chirped an urgent correction.

"Twelve," Keya translated for those who did not understand peeptalk, then frowned at Galaeron. "I don't see how you can do it."

"I don't have to," Galaeron explained. "I only have to kill the leader. After that, the WarGather will fall apart."

"That we understand," Vala said, taking Galaeron's four-fingered hand. "It's the part where you don't live I'm having trouble with."

"That *we're* having trouble with," Takari added.

She came around to Galaeron's other side and slipped her hand through the crook of one of his spindly arms. The Vaasans scowled—Vala at Takari, and Kuhl at Galaeron—and Kuhl rested a hand on the pommel of his sword. Their jealousy meant nothing to Galaeron. He loved Takari as much as he did Vala, and if that angered someone, it was no concern of his. He covered Takari's hand with his own.

"I'll be all right," Galaeron said. "You'll be right behind me."

"We have to fight through a ring of beholders and illithids," Vala reminded him.

"That's going to take time," Keya added. "Why don't you shadowalk a dozen of us in there—"

"Because we'd be lucky to last a breath," Burlen said, cutting her off. "*We* won't look like a phaerimm, remember?"

Though Galaeron knew Burlen was more concerned with protecting the mother of Dexon's child than assuring their success, he mouthed a silent thanks to the Vaasan. His plan depended on timing. The Company of the Cold Hand had to clear the defenses around the SpellGather before Aris arrived with the Chosen and the high mages. It would take time to do what Galaeron intended, and Keya and the others would need to set a defensive ring of their own before the phaerimm pulled themselves together to counterattack.

Khelben's voice sounded inside Galaeron's head, *We're in position, with a clear view of the statue hill.*

Good—we'll leave now, Galaeron replied.

He looked up at Manynests and sent the little snowfinch ahead with a tweet, then used his two free arms to wave the others forward.

They followed Manynests to the shore and left the dangling roots behind, stepping out from beneath the overhead gardens into a thick hedge of dusk-blossom. The snowfinch took his leave with a merry chirp and climbed above the hedge toward Cloudcrown Hill—then wheeled around and came diving back, squealing in alarm.

Thinking an owl or a hawk was after their courier, Galaeron flung a strand of shadowsilk into the air behind Manynests and spoke a two-syllable incantation. He realized his mistake when a silver lightning bolt cracked through the hedge crest and snaked its way out across the nourishment pond, leaving a mile-long tunnel of scorched root ends in its wake.

In the next instant, the phaerimm that had cast the spell came streaking over the hedge into the shadow net. The strands could not be broken, but

Galaeron was not prepared for the shock—and was probably not strong enough to hold it even had he been—and the net slipped free.

The astonished thornback tried to swing around to see what had caught it, but lost control of its flight and rolled sideways into the mass of roots beneath the floating gardens. It tangled quickly and hung there in the air, howling gusts of frustration and stirring the water below into a froth. The three Vaasans reacted first, Vala and Burlen charging through the hedge to meet the oncoming attack, and Kuhl splashing into the pond to finish off the trapped phaerimm.

Keya sprang into action almost as quickly, ordering half her company southward in a flanking action and sending the other half through the hedge to support Vala and Burlen. As surprised as he was impressed by the commander his little sister had become, Galaeron prepared a dark bolt and turned to hurl it before the phaerimm teleported out of its predicament.

But this one had no intention of leaving. It thrust two hands through the shadow net, and a shimmering mirror of magic appeared before it and sent the black dart sailing back at Galaeron. He pivoted out of the way and heard a muffled crackle as the missile slammed into the ground behind him. A third hand waved in Kuhl's direction, and the Vaasan went tumbling across the pond. He slammed headlong into Takari, who had been trying to sneak around for a clean flank shot, and they both splashed into the water and did not rise again.

Galaeron was already flicking an obsidian sliver into the air. He yelled a word of command, and the sliver grew as long as his arm and began to spin, blurring into a large black disk. It shattered the phaerimm's mirror and severed one of the arms that had been holding the shield. Slicing a tunnel through the root tangle, it vanished.

When the injury did not cause the phaerimm to teleport away, a cold lump formed in Galaeron's stomach. He began to fear that the WarGather had somehow learned of their plans and was already mounting an assault to stop them, but if so, why send only one assailant over the hedge?

Galaeron rolled a thread of shadowsilk into a wad. Before he could speak the mystic word that would expand the tiny orb into a shadow ball, the phaerimm was pelting him with golden darts of Weave magic. When the bolts dissipated harmlessly against the spell-guard Laeral had placed on him, the thornback switched instantly to dispelling magic. The spell-guard began to flicker and flash.

Galaeron hurled his shadow sphere, only to see the phaerimm stick an arm through the net and open an extradimensional portal in its palm. The black orb grew elongated, then curved toward the hand and vanished like a hawk down the gullet of a hungry dragon.

A new flight of magic bolts shot back at Galaeron. The first three dissipated against the flickering spell-guard, but the fourth burned through and sent him tumbling back through the air. The fifth and sixth landed, pinning him against the duskblossom hedge and burning thumb-sized holes in his body. Though his phaerimm disguise prevented even him from seeing where they landed, a searing pain shot through his thigh, and his shoulder went numb.

Keya screamed her rage and sent her darksword tumbling past Galaeron's head. The phaerimm raised a hand and deflected the attack with a blast of force.

Takari rose out of the pond beneath it and plunged Kuhl's darksword up into the thickest part of its body. The thornback filled the root thicket with roaring gales of pain and finally teleported away.

Or, rather, *tried* to teleport away.

An instant after it vanished, it reappeared outside Galaeron's shadow net, scattering across the pond in precisely diced squares. Takari caught much of the spray square on and emerged with a cube of phaerimm flesh hanging from the end of a thorn lodged in her shoulder. Not seeming to notice, she charged over to the hedge still holding Kuhl's darksword and slipped through to the other side.

Keya rushed to Galaeron's side.

"How bad?"

"Not bad," he said. "I'll survive."

"You'd better." Keya extended her hand, and Dexon's darksword flew back into her grip. "The baby's going to need an uncle."

She smiled and slipped through the hedge to join the others. It was not until she was gone that Galaeron realized what he had seen.

Takari had been holding Kuhl's sword. Her hand did not look cold.

No wonder Kuhl had been unhappy to see him.

Galaeron looked back into the pond and saw the Vaasan floating on his back, a pink cloud halloing his head where a long gash was pouring blood into the water. Kuhl's head had been propped on a log. His chest was rising and falling at regular intervals, and his eyes were already beginning to flicker open. Leaving the Vaasan to awaken on his own, Galaeron flew over the hedge. He nearly lost his leg when a warrior of the Cold Hand rose from the other side, and mistaking him for the enemy, reached for his borrowed darksword.

"Spare your fingers," Galaeron said in Elvish. "I'm *our* thornback."

The elf flushed with embarrassment. He let his weapon slip back into its scabbard.

"Sorry for the mistake, Lord Nihmedu."

Though hardly the first time Galaeron had been addressed by his formal title since returning to Evereska, it made him feel more remorseful than respected. Lord Nihmedu was his father. That he carried the title now only reminded him that his mistake had cost his family as dearly as his city.

Galaeron acknowledged the warrior's politeness with a dip of his head-disk, then continued across the garden's formal access path into the open woods beyond. The fighting there was over as well, with Vala and the others poking around the bushes in search of stragglers. From the looks of things, the fight had not been a difficult one. There were no more than a dozen mind-slaves scattered among the trees, most of them bugbears. Galaeron saw only two beholders and a single illithid.

Whatever the attack was, it was not the preventive strike he had feared. Galaeron extended a finger and whistled. Manynests dropped out of the bluetops, whistling nonstop about how close he had come to being blasted into feathers and how fast he had flown to avoid it.

Galaeron let the bird peep himself out, then said, "Now you must fly to Cloudcrown Hill. Khelben is expecting you, and he'll worry if you don't show."

Manynests peeped a question.

"I know I'm bleeding," Galaeron said, "but there's no need to worry him about that. The attack continues as planned."

Manynests peeped another question.

"Yes, I did see how fast you flew," Galaeron said, "but no, I don't think all the thornbacks are after you now. They have other quarry to hunt. Now, off with you."

Galaeron raised his hand and launched the finch, which vanished into the forest canopy.

"Takari!" an angry bellow erupted from the hedge behind Galaeron.

Galaeron twisted around to see Kuhl's burly form pushing through the duskblossoms. A steady cascade of blood was pouring out of his head wound, concealing his sunken eyes behind a red curtain and filling his bushy beard with thick, steaming crimson. Somehow, he saw through the torrent clearly enough to locate Takari, who was using his darksword to poke through the snarled stems of a giant bell-bramble.

"Thief!" Kuhl staggered forward, his hand rising to call his darksword. "My sword!"

Takari's knuckles whitened as she fought to hold the weapon.

"Let me use it a while. You can barely walk."

"Elven trollop!" Kuhl continued forward, not seeming to realize that in the case of a wood elf, at least, that was a little like calling a snake a reptile. "It was never me you wanted. I see that."

"That's not true." Takari wrapped her second hand around the hilt. "I wanted you, too, sometimes."

She began to back away. Though it looked like she was retreating, Galaeron was astonished to see Takari holding the darksword tip down, grasping the hilt in a double-hand stack and keeping a half-open stance. She was *trying* to look helpless and unprepared, inviting Kuhl to charge.

And charge Kuhl did, leaping forward with all the power and speed of a wounded rothé. Even flying, Galaeron knew he would never intercept the man in time to save his life. Instead, he flicked a strand of shadowsilk in Kuhl's direction and spoke a quick incantation, catching him in the same shadow net he had used to tangle the phaerimm.

The net appeared around Kuhl a mere three steps from Takari, and his momentum carried him forward another two before he crashed to the ground. Worried that Takari would go ahead with her plan anyway, Galaeron used the trailing line to pull the kicking Vaasan safely out of harm's way.

Kuhl rolled around so he could face Galaeron.

"And *you* are her panderer!" the Vaasan shouted. "This was your—"

Galaeron pinched his fingers together and uttered a spell, and the Vaasan fell silent. He handed the trailing line to the warrior who had addressed him as Lord Nihmedu with instructions to keep Kuhl safe but bound, then turned to deal with Takari.

Vala was already handling the matter. She had crept up behind Takari—no easy feat—and plucked the wood elf off the ground. Vala wrapped a burly arm clear around her body and grasped her sword arm just above the elbow. With her feet off the ground, Takari had no way left to defend herself except drop the darksword and cast a cantrip, and she was not dropping the sword.

Vala wrapped her thick fingers around Takari's wrist and slowly twisted it back toward the thumb, and the darksword dropped free. She passed her captive to Burlen with instructions to choke her unconscious at the first sign of trouble, then she picked up Kuhl's sword and used it to slash open the shadow net holding Kuhl.

"Here's your sword," she said, returning the weapon. "Put it away and get that cut attended to, and don't even *look* in her direction."

"But she—"

"Kuhl! I'll take care of it." Vala shoved him toward the hedge, then turned granite-hard eyes in Galaeron's direction and said, "We need to talk."

None to happy to see Kuhl free and Takari restrained, Galaeron dipped his head-disk in agreement.

Vala led the way to a small hollow where they could speak privately.

"I should have known this would happen." Her tone was angry, but not accusatory. "You'll have to take one of them with you."

"Why?" Galaeron asked. He was still unhappy with—and a little suspicious of—her decision to free Kuhl and restrain Takari. "Because you're jealous of her?"

"You think this is about you?" Vala rolled her eyes. "Get over yourself. Takari is carrying Kuhl's baby."

"I realize that," Galaeron said, "but I am not enough of a human to be jealous—"

Vala brought a hand up and managed to find Galaeron's head through his disguise and cuff him—more or less gently—above his ear.

"Are you listening?" she demanded. "We can sort that out later, if we live long enough. We've got a problem with Takari and Kuhl."

"That much was apparent," Galaeron said, finally overcoming his initial reaction to how she had handled Takari. "Perhaps you should explain the rest."

"Thank you," Vala said.

Before she could begin the explanation, Keya appeared at the edge of the hollow and came down to join them.

"I sent Burlen to watch Kuhl and put an elf in charge of Takari."

Keya was informing, not asking permission, and Galaeron was again impressed with the commander she had become. Her arrangement was both more secure and likely to raise less resentment in the rest of the company.

"I think they're really ready to kill each other," Keya continued. She turned to Galaeron. "And you're not helping matters. I know you and Takari have a past, but do you have to rub Kuhl's nose in it?"

"That's not the real trouble," Vala said. Even she did not question Keya's leadership; she simply turned to include the young elf in the conversation. "Kuhl's darksword has a history."

"A history?" Galaeron asked. "They all have histories."

"Not like this," Vala said. "Most of our darkswords have passed through the hands of five or six warriors, eight at most. Twenty-two have carried Kuhl's sword."

"Twenty-two?" Keya gasped. "That's one every five years."

"The bearers are lucky to carry it that long," Vala said. "The first was Yondala, who took the weapon up to defend her child from a flight of saurians. After, her husband began to grow jealous of the power she wielded.

One morning, we found her floating in the marsh, and Gromb had the sword. When it was determined that he had killed her in her sleep, he tried to escape Bodvar's justice and used the darksword to slay two more warriors. The weapon was given to their eldest son, but he died a year later when a rock fell on his head while he was playing with his brothers."

"And Bodvar let the family keep such a sword?" Keya gasped.

"It was not his to take, and it would have come back the instant some relative of Yondala's stretched a hand out and called to it."

Nor would they have dared destroy the weapon, Galaeron realized. Even he could not say what would happen if one of the blades was broken—nor how Melegaunt would have reacted. He nodded to Vala.

"You're right, we can't have them together—especially not during the battle."

"I'll dismiss Takari from the Cold Hand," Keya said. "She can go back to the Hidden Caves to help Dexon guard the children."

"If you dismiss her from the Cold Hand, you can't tell her to do anything," Galaeron said. "Do you really think she'd stay away from the battle?"

"Not likely," Vala said. "One of them must go with you."

"That's almost a death sentence," Keya objected. "Galaeron will be lucky to survive with his shadow magic."

"We will all be lucky to survive, no matter where we are," Vala replied, "and one of them is sure to die if we do anything else."

Keya considered that, then nodded.

"Galaeron should choose." She turned to him and continued, "Whoever it is will be fighting at your side. You should choose the one who will help the most."

Galaeron knew that Keya's suggestion—no, her order—made sense, but it felt like she was asking him to choose between Takari and Vala. He had already done that once, during the battle with the second Wulgreth, when he had been forced to chose between saving Vala's life and protecting Takari. He had saved Vala, and Takari had been terribly injured, and he did not ever want to make a decision like that again.

If he took Takari, he stood a good chance of losing her forever. If he took Kuhl, Vala would know he was saving Takari's life at the expense of one of her followers. While Vala had already made clear she would consent to the decision, he doubted she would ever forgive him for it.

Galaeron looked back to Keya and asked, "Who's doing was this situation? Did Takari pursue Kuhl, or Kuhl—"

"That has nothing to do with your decision," Keya said. "Choose the one who'll be the most use to you."

"Kuhl's wound is not serious," Vala said, "and he will have his darksword."

"But Takari has fought at your side for twenty years," Keya said. "She will know what you are going to do before you do it."

Keya's argument made clear which choice she believed he should make—and Galaeron knew she was right. Even without Kuhl's darksword, Takari would be better at watching his back, and he would be better at watching hers.

"Keya, you've grown too wise for one so young." Galaeron closed his eyes, then said, "Takari."

Keya laid a hand on his arm. "She's the best choice, Galaeron."

"We'll start the shadowalk from here," he said. "It will give us time to prepare."

"As you wish. I'll send her along."

Before leaving, Keya stretched up to kiss his cheek, but missed because of the phaerimm disguise and got his chin instead.

"Soft songs, my brother."

"And light laughter, my sister," Galaeron said. "Father would have been proud."

"Of both of us."

Her eyes grew glassy and wet. She turned away and wiped them, then disappeared over the rim of the hollow.

Vala grabbed hold of Galaeron's ears, no doubt misled by his magic disguise into thinking she had taken him by his hands.

"No need to worry about your sister, Galaeron. Dexon has Burlen and Kuhl looking after her. I'll be there, too."

"Then she'll be fine, I have no doubt," Galaeron said. "As long as my plan works."

"It will—*I* have no doubt."

Vala leaned in, finding Galaeron's lips the first time, and kissed him long and hard—Vaasan hard. He wrapped his real arms around her waist and held her there until he began to grow dizzy from lack of breath.

When he finally let go, she stepped back and studied Galaeron with a raised brow.

"Never thought I'd do that."

Galaeron frowned in confusion, then realized she could not see his expression and had to ask, "What?"

Vala made a sour face and said, "Kiss a phaerimm."

She started after Keya, but stopped atop the hollow to look back over her shoulder.

"But I'm glad I did—and I'd have done it anyway, even if you had chosen Kuhl."

"Would you have?"

The question slipped out before Galaeron realized he was truly asking it, but he did not try to attenuate the doubt it implied. When it came to offending others, even those he loved, his shadow had made him fearless.

Vala's tone grew serious, though not angry. "I understand about Takari—I truly do."

Galaeron felt as though a knot in his chest had come undone.

"I'm glad," he said. "Thank you."

"No reason to thank me. I'd never want you to do something that cold for me. I know I wouldn't for you."

Vala drew her sword and turned toward the Company of the Cold Hand.

✡✡✡✡✡

Soot-starred and smoke-shrouded though it was, Cloudcrown Palace was the finest example of Evereska's naturist architecture that Aris had yet seen. From the slope below, where he was hiding in the trees at the edge of what remained of the forest that had once covered all of Cloudcrown Hill, the palace resembled a stand of bluetops packed so closely together that the huge boles had grown into each other. The scaling on the bark was so expertly done that even his practiced sculptor's eye would not have known it was stone, save for the handful of places where an enemy spell had actually penetrated the defensive magic and cratered one of the ancient towers.

The antimagic shell the phaerimm had erected around the palace was functional but artless, a bell-shaped dome of shimmering translucence that soared up from beneath the ground and vanished from sight a thousand feet or more overhead. Aris knew it had to continue far higher and curve inward to cover the tower pinnacles, but even his eyes were not keen enough to see a variation so subtle at such a great distance.

The thornbacks themselves were standing watch on the slope above, hiding among the tangles of blast-toppled trees that covered the hillside. So far, Aris located only three on this side of Cloudcrown, spaced at even intervals in a semicircle just out of arrow range. Their mind-slaves—and more than a few of their fellow phaerimm—lay scattered over the killing zones beneath the palace's hidden arrow loops, a decomposing testament to the ferocity of the battle that had ended in stalemate.

The undulating speck of a tiny finch rounded the palace wall at what would have been treetop height, had there been any trees still standing, then disappeared in the direction of the statue of Hanali Celanil. Though Aris had not yet visited that particular work, he had been assured by everyone who had that it was among the city's finest. Rumor had it that it was also as old as Evereska itself, which would make it one of the few surviving examples of high elven religious art from the Pre-Netheril period.

Something sharp pricked his knee, and he looked down to see Storm Silverhand slipping her dagger into its scabbard. She did it without looking, for she was scowling up at him with a worried expression.

Red eye? Her fingertalk was as fast as Galaeron's, which made it difficult to follow. *That's the sigil.*

Sigil? With his long fingers, Aris suspected his reply seemed to Storm like he was drawling or stuttering. *There's a sigil?*

Fur the tackle!

Storm pointed at the palace, and Aris finally realized what she was trying to remind him of. Manynests' departure was the *signal.*

Sorry, he signed. *I'm a little nervous.*

What's to be nervous about? Storm replied. *This plan has to be better than the last one.*

That should make me feel better?

Aris removed the two largest hammers from his tool belt, and fixed his eye on a nose-shaped burl about twenty feet off the ground. The hardest part of his job would be keeping that knot in sight. If he went to the wrong one, Galaeron's plan would fail.

An immense roar erupted on the opposite side of the hill, and fans of gold and crimson blast magic spread across the sky behind the palace. The three phaerimm rose from their hiding places and stirred the air into a tempest as they hurled questions back and forth, but none of them showed any sign of departing their posts. Heart rising into his throat, Aris raised his hammers and prepared to make a run he knew he could not survive.

Storm laid a restraining hand on his knee.

Aris looked down to find her shaking her head. She raised a single finger, then looked back up the slope.

The battle continued to rage on the other side of the palace. The hill shuddered beneath their feet and sheets of flame licked around the walls of the palace, and still the phaerimm remained on post. Aris cocked his brow. They had only a minute or two before the thornbacks realized that all of the noise was being made by just two Chosen. After that, it would be only seconds before they realized the attack was a diversion and returned to his side of the palace.

As the largest target on the hill, Aris knew what would become of him if he was still on the battlefield then. He wouldn't even mind—not much—except that would mean that Galaeron's plan had failed. Evereska's art would be lost forever.

Storm took her hand from Aris's knee. Aris nodded, she nodded back—and two of the phaerimm flew off toward the other side of the hill.

Storm's jaw fell. She closed it, then flashed the quick fingertalk sentence: *Told you so!*

She pointed at the last phaerimm, her finger darkening to black as she whispered an incantation so softly even Aris couldn't hear it.

The last phaerimm left his hiding place and raced after his fellows.

For a moment, Aris was too shocked to react. There was nobody between him and the burl. All he had to do was run up there, reach through the antimagic shell, and knock a hole in the wall. Then Lord Duirsar and Kiinyon Colbathin and the High Mages and the Long Watch would start pouring out on their ropes, leaping across the antimagic shell into the battle-torn meadow, where Storm would by then have laid a teleport circle that would take them straight to the statue of Hanali Celanil that Aris wanted so desperately to see.

"What are you waiting for?" She pulled a packet of amber dust from inside her cloak, raised her arms so Aris could pick her up and carry her up to the palace, and said, "Plans don't work any better than this."

CHAPTER EIGHTEEN

2 Eleasias, the Year of Wild Magic

Galaeron and Takari arrived at the statue of Hanali Celanil to find a small circle of phaerimm using all four hands to pull golden strands of magic off the hem of the goddess's gown. They were feeding the threads out behind them, filling the air with a shimmering snarl of loops and whorls so dense and bright that it was difficult to see the thornbacks themselves. Where the tangle touched the ground, it passed through the paving stones as sunlight passes through water, leaving the impression that the great statue stood upon the surface of a dark, still pond rather than a courtyard of granite cobblestones. Galaeron counted twelve phaerimm pulling thread, with a thirteenth watching from beneath a tree at the edge of the plaza.

"That's the one Manynests told us about." He did not bother with fingertalk. Though the phaerimm could undoubtedly eavesdrop into the Shadow Fringe where he and Takari were hiding, they could not do it without using Weave magic—and in the Shadow Fringe, Weave magic would shine like a beacon light for Galaeron. "I'm fairly sure that's their leader. It's the only one we absolutely have to kill, so if something goes wrong—"

"Nothing's going to go wrong, now that you've come to your senses and decided to bring me along." Takari let a hand drop the hilt of her borrowed darksword. "I only wish Keya would've given me Kuhl's sword. That one I can hang on to."

"Kuhl's sword is not Keya's to give," Galaeron said. "And Kuhl has need of it himself."

It was the fifth or sixth time he had reminded her of that, and his patience was giving way to alarm. There was a dark familiarity in the way that simple fact kept eluding her, in how every conversation seemed to return to Kuhl's darksword.

"Our need is greater." She pointed at the phaerimm leader and said, "You said yourself we absolutely have to kill that one."

"That is what *we* absolutely have to do. Kuhl and the others have to destroy the defensive perimeter—absolutely. If they fail, our success means nothing."

As he spoke, Galaeron looked Takari full in the eyes. Though hardly veiled in darkness, the irises were shot through with tiny streaks of shadow. She had to be told; it was her only chance of controlling her hunger for the sword.

"Takari, I didn't come to my senses. We thought it best to keep you away from Kuhl and his darksword."

"What?" she asked. "Why would you keep me away from something that is mine by right?"

"Because it isn't yours by any right. You only think it is because you've been shadow touched."

"Shadow touched!" Takari objected. "I *earned* that sword!"

"It's an heirloom. How could you earn . . ." Galaeron let the question trail off as he realized what Takari was saying. He looked at her stomach, which had not yet begun to bulge, and asked, "You did that on purpose?"

Takari raised her chin and said, "Of course it was on purpose. Do you think I would lay with that rothé by accident?"

"Of course not, but neither did I think you had done it to steal his darksword."

"'Steal' is such a human word," Takari said, rolling her eyes. "I just wanted to use it and maybe keep it after he died."

"After you killed him," Galaeron corrected. He turned to keep an eye on the tree branch. Manynests would be arriving soon. "You always meant to keep it."

"How do you know what I meant—"

"I know a shadow when I see it, Takari," Galaeron said.

The phaerimm leader sent an angry gust whirling across the cobblestones, and the SpellGather began to pull threads twice as fast. That would be word of the attack on Cloudcrown Hill. Galaeron did not have much time to convince Takari of her peril. The way she was thinking, once the battle started she would run down to take the darksword from Kuhl.

"There's a shadow in your eyes," Galaeron continued. "You wanted a darksword for yourself, and Keya showed you how to get what you sought."

"That doesn't mean I was going to kill him," Takari retorted. "Humans have short lives—especially around here—and I'm patient."

"Maybe that was what you intended, before you touched the sword, but you were going to kill him at the Floating Gardens."

"He was charging me!"

"You could have scrambled up any of a dozen trees. I saw how you were standing, Takari—and the way you held the sword. It was a double-hand stack."

"You don't know how quick Kuhl can be," Takari said. "I had to defend myself."

Galaeron risked turning his attention from the phaerimm long enough to lock gazes with Takari.

"When he grabbed for the sword, you were going to fall and let the blade swing up in his groin." There was no accusation in his voice, only insistence and certainty. "It would have looked like an accident."

Takari met his gaze for only a moment before her eyes flicked away, her defenses finally starting to crumble. She retreated to the edge of the Shadow Fringe and peered out through snarl of magic threads.

"Hanali's gown is starting to look ragged," she said. "If we don't attack the SpellGather soon—"

"You can't ignore this, Takari," Galaeron interrupted. "Think back to when you borrowed Kuhl's sword at the Floating Gardens. You took the time to turn him face up."

"I didn't want him to drown." She sounded as though she were remembering, not explaining. "He's not so bad, for a human."

"But after you borrowed the sword. . . ."

"I didn't *borrow* it. You can't borrow what's already . . ." Takari let the sentence trail off, then raised a hand to her mouth and turned to look at Galaeron again. "And now I want him dead!"

"It's the sword. That one carries a curse." Galaeron took her by the arm and gently pulled her away from the Fringe edge. "It opens you to your shadow."

"My shadow?" Takari gasped. It was the first time Galaeron could recall seeing true terror in her eyes. "Will I turn into one of *them*?"

"That will depend on how you react, I think," Galaeron said. "I'm not sure, but I do know you mustn't take Kuhl's sword from him again. If you fail in that, you'll have to kill him, and if you kill him, you *will* be lost."

"Great." Takari's eyes slid away from his, focusing somewhere beyond his shoulder. "Manynests. . . ."

Galaeron turned around to find the little bird flying into the tree above the phaerimm leader's head. In his beak, he carried something pointed and twice as long as he was.

"What's that he has?" Takari asked.

Galaeron twisted a few strands of shadowsilk together at the top, then uttered a spell and began to whisk himself with the brush end.

"I don't know," he said. "It's not part of the plan."

Manynests landed on the lowest branch over the phaerimm's head-disk. He stretched his neck forward, letting out a sharp chirp, and released what he was carrying. The pointed end dropped first, spinning slightly so that the long spine rising along one side of the shaft grew visible.

"It's a tail barb!" Takari gasped.

The barb hit the phaerimm on the rim of the mouth and bounced off its missile guard. The creature puffed in surprise and tipped forward to retrieve the barb. It held the thing over its open mouth for a moment, then raised its head-disk toward the branch where Manynests sat scolding it in peeptalk.

"*Ithinkthat'soursignal.*" Galaeron's words came out in a rush, for the spell of speed he had cast upon himself had already taken effect. "*Remembertheplan.*"

Without awaiting a response, Galaeron floated to the edge of the Fringe and sent two dark bolts hissing into the phaerimm leader. The first burned a fist-sized hole through the middle of its chest and sent it wobbling back into the tree trunk. The second clipped it along the rim of its mouth, gouging a long furrow along the side of its head-disk and lopping an arm off at the shoulder.

Takari's booted feet landed squarely in Galaeron's back as, executing her part of the plan, she caught him with a flying drop kick that sent him tumbling tail-over-arms out into the courtyard. He did not pass through the strands of Weave magic so much as they passed through him, burning like nettles and engulfing him in a crackling halo of green sparks. That was not part of the plan. He glimpsed the leader of the phaerimm wrapped around the base of the tree. Its three remaining arms rested limply on the ground and black gore oozed from the hole in its body. Galaeron brought himself to a halt and spun to face Hanali's statue.

The members of the SpellGather had stopped pulling magic and were already starting to drift away from the circle. Galaeron pointed two arms back toward the shadow from which he had emerged. Takari was already retreating into the shadows, her legs and the tip of her borrowed darksword just disappearing into the Fringe as planned. Galaeron gestured wildly in her direction, his arms throwing off huge sheets of green sparks as they sliced through the air.

"After her!" He used his magic to howl in Winds, "She's getting away!"

Whether it was his accent or the sweeping lines of green sparks, the phaerimm were not falling for it. They raised their arms in his direction, and even with his speed magic, Galaeron barely had time to raise a shadow shield before a hundred golden bolts came streaking in his direction. He huddled down behind the circle and tried not to scream. The hiss of the approaching bolts rose to a sizzle, and the sizzle to a roar, and the roar to a deafening crash as the missiles reached his shield and vanished down into the shadow plane. The crash disappeared into a ringing silence that left the ground shaking and Galaeron's eardrums throbbing, his nostrils tingling with the rainwater smell of spent magic.

Galaeron did not wait. He flipped the shield around and dived through it into the shadows, and even then he was very nearly caught by the storm of fire magic and disintegration rays that converged on the place he had been kneeling. He remained a moment to see if any of his attackers would be foolish enough to pursue him into the dark circle, then he closed it behind him and streaked through the shadows back to Takari's side.

"That plan worked about as well as a pixie ladder," Takari said. "I don't think they were fooled by your disguise."

She was peering out into the courtyard, watching two trios of phaerimm work their way toward the shadow where she and Galaeron stood watching. "It doesn't look like it," Galaeron replied, "but my plan did work."

Galaeron dispelled the illusion magic that made him look like a phaerimm, then took an arrow from Takari's quiver and began to rub it with shadowsilk.

"Really?" Takari sounded more than doubtful, she sounded distrustful. "I don't see that."

"They stopped attacking the mythal, didn't they?"

Galaeron plucked a death arrow from her quiver and rubbed the head with shadowsilk. He uttered a piercing spell and passed the missile back to her.

Takari nocked the arrow and raised her bow, but turned to Galaeron before firing and tipped her head back, lips slightly parted.

"In case this one doesn't work either—"

"It *will* work."

Galaeron took another arrow from her quiver, and Takari rolled her eyes.

"Same old Galaeron." There was genuine disgust in her voice. "Won't ever give a wood elf a chance."

She set the tip of her arrow on the closest phaerimm, which was no more than twenty paces away, and pulled the bowstring back.

Galaeron laid his free hand over her draw arm.

Takari turned, her expression one of irritation.

"I do love you," Galaeron said.

Takari's jaw dropped. Had Galaeron not tightened his grasp, she would have let slip the arrow.

"You're only saying that because we're about to die."

Galaeron shook his head, then looked back to the approaching phaerimm. They had closed to fifteen paces. He cast another piercing spell on the arrow in his hand.

Takari ignored the thornbacks and continued to study Galaeron.

"You always did have a lousy sense of timing," she said, "but I'll take what I can get."

She loosed her arrow, and the shaft took its target square in the body. Galaeron's shadow magic allowed it to penetrate the phaerimm's missile guard and sink to the fletching. The thornback squalled in pain and teleported away, though not so quickly that Galaeron failed to notice the black disintegration crater forming around Takari's arrow.

The five survivors attacked with a veritable spell-storm of flames, meteor stones, lightning, and half a dozen other kinds of magic death. As the spells entered the shadow where Galaeron and Takari were hiding, they were funneled through a shadow door that opened on the opposite side of the courtyard, and the phaerimm were blasted from behind by their own spells.

Two died instantly, and two more teleported away to safety. Galaeron handed the death arrow to Takari. She nocked and loosed it into the remaining thornback even as it flicked its fingers at their hiding place. Galaeron's dimensional door shimmered once, then crackled out of existence. By then, the phaerimm who had dispelled it lay motionless on the ground, a black hole expanding around the arrow buried in its head-disk.

Galaeron grabbed Takari's hand and guided it to his belt.

"Hold tight," he said.

"You can be sure."

He turned and raced into the deep shadows. Though his power was great enough to keep at bay most of the lesser creatures they were likely to stumble across on such a short journey through the Deep, Galaeron was careful to keep moving and moving fast. Shadow-touched though she was, Takari was still enough a creature of the Weave that Galaeron could feel her radiating heat against his back . . . warm and distinct . . . and if he could feel it, so could the shapeless mouths that preyed on the hapless visitors who wandered too far from the Fringe.

They had traveled about a dozen heartbeats when a terrible gurgling growl erupted in the distance behind them. Takari stopped, her hand pulling on Galaeron's belt as she turned to look over her shoulder.

"Keep moving!" he warned. "Or it'll be us next."

"What is it?" Takari asked.

"Its guarding our back trail," Galaeron answered. "That's all that matters."

A lightning bolt crackled in the distance and fell silent. There was no flicker of light, not even a faint one, and Galaeron knew that had they been looking straight into the bolt, they would have seen nothing. So deep in shadow, light vanished almost at its source. The shadow monster growled again, then died with an agonized wail.

"That can't be good," Takari said.

"We can do our own dirty work," Galaeron said. "The attack will slow them down. The sound will draw things that even phaerimm don't want to run into."

"What about us?" Takari asked.

"We don't want to run into those things either." Galaeron pulled her toward the Fringe and added, "That's why we went first."

Once they were out of the Shadow Deep, Galaeron came up behind the tree where Manynests had alighted. He stopped in the Fringe. Though they could not see into the courtyard from the their vantage point, any phaerimm still lurking in the area were less likely to come poking around in the shadows. He cast his piercing magic on another death arrow and returned it to Takari.

"Use that only if a phaerimm comes for us," he said. "Let me borrow the darksword."

Takari unhooked her scabbard, but did not hand it over.

"Where are you going?" she asked.

"To surprise our pursuers," he said, drawing the darksword from the scabbard. "This shouldn't be difficult, but you know what to do if I don't come back."

Though the hilt began to chill his hand, the cold no longer caused him any discomfort. Like Melegaunt, Telamont, and Hadhrune, he was part of the shadow.

"Yeah," Takari said. "Die."

"I meant check the leader," Galaeron said. "Be certain it's dead."

Takari shook her head in mock despair and said, "I know what you meant, Galaeron." She started to turn away, then changed her mind and grabbed Galaeron behind the neck. "First, you prove you weren't lying. First you prove you love me."

She pulled his head close to hers and kissed him long and hard, a kiss born of two decades of longing, a kiss that would no longer be denied. Though he knew their pursuers would be coming up fast, Galaeron let himself melt into it, let his spirit and his lips and his tongue touch Takari's as he never had before. They joined as only elves can join, and Galaeron felt what she had always known, that they were spirit mates, that they belonged together no matter what the heartache and loneliness and sorrow brought down on them by their destiny. Nothing remained to keep them apart—nothing except their human lovers.

Takari sensed this as soon as Galaeron did, of course, and she was the first to pull away.

Galaeron would not make her ask.

"I still love her," he said.

He was not admitting anything Takari did not already know, but he had to say it aloud. He owed her that much—and himself, too.

"I'd have to be blind to miss that," Takari said. She smiled—a little sadly—and glanced down at her belly. "I have a few entanglements of my own."

Galaeron kissed her again—briefly—and slipped back into the shadows. Once he was alone, he had no fear whatsoever of the unseen creatures who haunted the Deep. He was as much a part of the darkness as they were, and anything powerful enough to find and stalk him would also be intelligent enough to sense the power he bore. This wisdom was also born of the gift Melegaunt had passed to him, as was his knowledge of the phaerimm, and the ways of the Shadow Deep, and the lore of shadow spells, and who knew how many other dark Shadovar secrets. As far as Galaeron could tell, the only part of Melegaunt's experience that the old archwizard had failed to pass along was what to do with so much power and how to wield it wisely. Melegaunt likely had never known or—if he had—cared.

Twenty steps later, the Fringe lay well out of sight. Galaeron stopped to wait. There was no need to hide, nor anyplace to do so had he wished. In the Deep, there was only shadow, and in the hands of those who knew the art, shadow could be shaped into whatever was needed or desired.

Soon, Galaeron sensed a fiery presence approaching along the path he and Takari had taken. Though it was impossible for an elf—or any creature enclosed within a skin—to perceive shape, he felt by the intensity of the thing's heat and its apparent size that it was a phaerimm. He waited long enough to be certain only one creature remained, then he raised a wall of shadow in front of himself and waited.

While far from lost, the phaerimm was obviously frightened. In the vain hope of keeping shadow monsters at bay, it was talking softly to itself, using its powers to stir the shadows into a constant whirl. The thorn-back also had half a dozen spells prepped and ready to cast—Galaeron could feel the scorching nodules of Weave magic hanging from its body.

He allowed it to pass, then dismissed his shadow wall and stepped out behind it.

The nervous phaerimm reacted quickly, encasing itself in a cocoon of fire and launching a volley of magic darts. The blow caught Galaeron in the shoulder and sent him tumbling back head over heels—not a safe way to travel in the Shadow Deep, even for him. A pair of jaws opened beneath him and tore into his calf, trying to drag him down into some hidden lair. He brought his darksword down alongside his leg. It felt like cutting air, but the mouth opened and he pulled free.

The phaerimm was faring worse than he. Galaeron could feel it a dozen paces ahead and off to one side, stirring the silent shadows into a froth as a pack of shadow creatures—some flying and some slithering—manifested all around and pulled in six directions at once. The thornback was defending itself as well as it was able, but its teleport spells would not work and its other spells were ineffective. No matter how many creatures it destroyed, more formed to take their places. No matter what kind of armor it covered itself in, their shadow fangs and dark claws tore through. An arm came off, then the tail, and finally a long strip of thorny hide.

Galaeron would have left the creature to its fate, save that Melegaunt's wisdom had taught him better than to count a phaerimm dead until it lay disemboweled and burning on the ground. Moving back toward the tree where he had left Takari to avoid attracting a pack of his own attackers, he prepared a volley of shadow arrows and sent them hurling into his entrapped foe.

The impact caught both victim and tormentors by surprise. The phaerimm literally came apart, pieces flying in the dozen different directions that it was being pulled. The angry shadow creatures—those that had not been pinned in place by a dark arrow—melted back into the darkness and came undulating in Galaeron's direction.

Galaeron opened a shadow door and stepped through, emerging into the relatively safe world of the Fringe. For a moment, he was lost to the afterdaze and did not know where he was. Then, as the flash and flicker of war magic began to filter up through the trees from the slope below, he recalled that he was in the middle of a battle and that it was his job and Takari's to make certain the statue of Hanali Celanil was free of phaerimm when Khelben and the Chosen arrived with the High Mages, and that Takari should have been waiting for him right there in the Fringe.

"Takari?"

Galaeron glanced around the Fringe, finding nothing, and limped out onto the hillside. He was dizzy and sore, his arm so weak he could barely lift it.

"Takari!"

The only answer came in the form of a series of excited peeps from the tree above his head. Galaeron raised his chin and found the familiar white face of Manynests peering down at him.

"She did what?" Galaeron gasped. Takari was not the type to leave her post, not even when she was shadow touched. "That can't be right."

Manynests answered with a sharp chirp, then pointed his beak down the hill.

"What about the leader?"

Manynests chirped a question.

"The phaerimm leader," Galaeron said. "The one you dropped the barb on."

The finch peeped angrily.

"All right, the one you *attacked*," Galaeron said. "What did she do about that phaerimm?"

The bird's answer caused Galaeron to limp around the tree as fast as he could move. There were no phaerimm in the courtyard surrounding the statue—at least at first glance—and there was nothing where the leader should have been, save for a puddle of steaming black blood.

"She let it go!" Galaeron cried. "Takari left her post!"

Manynests dropped out of the tree. He landed on one of the darts still protruding from Galaeron's shoulder. He twilled a long question, then cocked his head and looked down the hill toward the battle.

"No," Galaeron growled. "I really don't think Kuhl needed her help."

CHAPTER NINETEEN

2 Eleasias, the Year of Wild Magic

Whether the caustic taste in her mouth was ash or fear, Keya Nihmedu could not say. She knew only that her tongue had gone as dry as a flame, that it had become impossible to tell the shuddering of the ground from her own trembling, and that the child in her belly would be lucky to see the world with its own eyes. Burning bluetops were crashing all around her, horse-sized boulders were tumbling down the slope in a ceaseless cascade, and the air was hot enough to bake acorns. The Cold Hand's objective had sounded simple enough when Galaeron explained it back under the Floating Gardens, but she was hoping he had a backup plan.

Crawling on her belly, Keya crept along beneath the upper slope of the trail cut to where Vala was taking shelter with Kuhl and Burlen. Unlike her elves, who were either lying flat on their bellies keeping a watch up the slope for tumbling boulders or blindly arcing arrows up in the general direction of the enemy, the Vaasans were sitting with their backs to the battle. They were sharing sticks of jerked thkaerth meat and laughing and shoving each other in the shoulder, though they had made concession enough to the fighting to remove their swords from their scabbards and leave them lying at their sides within easy reach.

As Keya approached, Vala removed a stick of dried meat from their rations bag and offered it to her.

"No, thank you," Keya shouted to make herself heard over the battle roar. "I don't have much stomach for thkaerth lately."

Though she hoped the Vaasans would think this was because of her pregnancy, the truth was she simply could no longer stand the sight of cooked meat; it reminded her too much of the burned bodies that lay scattered and unburied throughout all of Evereska. Trying to look as unconcerned as the Vaasans, she drew herself up beside Vala and removed her sword from its scabbard.

"What do you think?" Keya asked. "Concentrate our spellcasters and try to mount a breakthrough?"

Vala replied, "That would only make them easy pickings for the phaerimm."

"What phaerimm?" Takari asked. "Manynests didn't say anything about phaerimm."

"Manynests is a bird. What he can't see doesn't exist for him. But they have one." Vala jerked her thumb over her shoulder and said, "Up there."

Burlen leaned in front of Vala, looking Keya over with a concerned expression, and held out a piece of jerked thkaerth.

"You sure you don't want one?" he said. "You need to keep your strength up."

Keya waved him off and continued to address Vala. "How do you know where the phaerimm is?"

Vala cast a pointed gaze in the direction of a line of charred bodies and said, "The best thing we can do right now is wait."

A sonorous rumble sounded from above and quickly began to grow louder. Keya started to roll to her stomach so she could crawl up the bank to see what was coming. Vala extended an arm and stopped her, pushing her flat against the slope before lying back herself. The rumble built to rhythmic crashing, then suddenly went silent. A rothé-sized boulder tumbled off the rim of the slope and sailed over their heads, bouncing off the far side of the trail and vanishing into the woods below.

"Mind-slaves aren't very bright," Vala said. "Sooner or later, the bugbears will run out of boulders, and the beholders will knock down the last bluetop. *Then* we attack."

"We don't have that long," Keya objected. "According to Galaeron's plan, we should be taking out the perimeter defense now, before Khelben and the others arrive with the high mages. Otherwise, the mind-slaves will turn and counterattack—"

"Then *that's* when we'll take them," Vala interjected. "Or maybe when Aris gets here. If he can hurl a few boulders back up the hill, we might be able to break their line."

"What we can't do is attack into the teeth of their defense," Burlen said. "We'll just get the Cold Hand wiped out, and who will there be to stop the counterattack?"

Keya glanced past Vala and Burlen to Kuhl, and asked him, "What do you think?"

Kuhl's expression merely darkened, and he looked away.

"He agrees with us," Burlen said. "Pay no mind to his manners. He's letting his sword do his thinking."

Burlen reached out and slapped his companion in the back of the helmet. Kuhl's scowl deepened, but he looked away and continued to remain silent.

"Plans are good," Vala said, drawing Keya's attention back to the matter at hand. "Once the spell-flinging starts, they aren't worth the breath it took to speak them. We have to wait for our opportunity—"

She was interrupted by a gusty howl they all recognized as the screech of a wounded phaerimm.

"There's your thornback!" Keya called. She rolled to her stomach and began to shimmy up the bank. "While we sit here talking, someone is killing it."

She stuck her head above the rim just far enough to look up the shattered hillside. Fallen bluetops crisscrossed the slope, blast craters pocked the ground, and curtains of fire poured gray fume into the air. Fifty yards above, a long rank of mind-slaves peered down from behind a meandering breastwork, hurling boulders and magic, anything they could down upon the company of the Cold Hand. There were dozens of bugbears and maybe ten beholders, reinforced by a trio of illithids and a handful of vacant-eyed elves, but the wounded phaerimm was nowhere to be seen. The instant it suffered a serious wound, it had no doubt teleported to safety.

The dark dash of an elven death arrow flashed out of a bluetop behind the enemy breastwork and disappeared into the trenches. A beholder rose briefly into view, its sharp-toothed mouth twisted into a grimace of pain. Keya had just enough time to identify the Tomb Guard's distinctive black-feather fletching on the butt of the arrow before the Cold Hand's battle mages blazed the creature into a red spray.

A thick human hand grabbed her by the ankle and pulled her back down the slope.

"Get down!" Vala snarled. "Dexon will have my head if I let some beholder burn that pointy-eared head off your shoulders!"

Keya was about to protest when a purple ray droned past above, cutting a deep furrow in the rim of the slope, coming within a finger's width of disintegrating her skull. Her heart hammered in her chest so hard that she thought it would break a rib, but she managed to retain enough control of her wits to point her darksword up the slope.

"T-T-Takari!"

"Takari?" It was Kuhl who growled, "Where?"

"In a tree," Keya gasped. "Behind the enemy. I saw her arrow—"

"Which tree?"

Kuhl crawled to the rim and peered through the furrow that had nearly cost Keya her life.

"I don't see her," he said.

"Kuhl, she isn't after your darksword," Keya told him. The last thing they needed was to renew the fight over his ancestral weapon. "Takari's trying to help us break through."

"She's coming for my sword!" Kuhl insisted. He glanced away from the furrow long enough to scowl in Keya's direction. "And you—you're a thieving vixen just like her. The phaerimm took Dexon's leg, but you're the one who's stolen his sword—and his manhood."

There was a time when the raw rage in Kuhl's voice would have sent Keya fleeing, but now it only filled her with cold anger.

"Kuhl, I will overlook the affront to me because it is easy to see how your sword might be more powerful than your mind," she said, "but insult my husband's manhood again, and you will die choking on yours."

Keya glared at the Vaasan until she saw enough of the anger fade from his eyes that she felt certain there would be no need to make good on her threat. She glanced over at Vala, who only shrugged and spread her hands. Keya frowned and nodded toward Kuhl. Vala looked away, thinking, then a veil of sadness seemed to fall over her face. She nodded and crawled up the slope next to Kuhl.

With the burly Vaasan safely under control, Keya turned her thoughts back to the battle. She hazarded a glance over the rim and saw that whatever Takari was doing up there, her attacks were having an effect. A patrol of a dozen bugbears that had been dispatched up the hill to hunt her down lay scattered across the slope, some lying motionless with smoking holes through their torsos, others flailing about trying to pull long elven arrows from their backs. Several beholders were sweeping the forest canopy with their disintegration rays, reducing the number of attacks coming down the hill above Keya as well as raining boughs and limbs on the slope.

Keya slid to the bottom of the embankment and used fingertalk to order the Company of the Cold Hand to assemble behind her, leaving only the archers and every third battle mage to hold their current lines. Within moments, a long stream of warriors began to crawl along the base of the embankment. Keya issued her orders to the first arrivals, along with instructions to pass them along, then she crawled back up to join Vala and the Vaasans.

Vala had her arm across Kuhl's shoulders and was whispering something into his ear that Keya could not hear.

"Another arrow!" Kuhl growled, pointing. "There she is."

Kuhl started to rise and charge up the hill, but Vala caught him by the belt.

"Not yet, Kuhl," she said, pulling him back down. "That's what she wants, isn't it?"

Kuhl considered a moment then nodded.

"Vala!" Keya gasped. "What are you doing?"

Vala whirled on her with an expression that could only be described as demonic.

"You want to use this or not?" she demanded. "Because Kuhl's the only chance we have to get there anytime soon."

As Vala spoke, Burlen continued to speak to Kuhl from the other side.

"She wants you to charge out there alone, doesn't she?" Burlen asked. "She wants you to get yourself killed."

"I won't," Kuhl replied. "She doesn't know. She'll never get my sword."

There was a darkness in his eyes that Keya had never seen there before, something cold, monstrous, and terrifying risen to mask the laugh-lined face she had come to consider that of one of her human brothers.

"What doesn't she know?" Keya asked.

"You'll see," Vala said. "It's Kuhl or Takari now. There's nothing we can do about that, except decide whether we're ready to use it. Are you?"

Keya glanced along the embankment in both directions and saw a long line of warriors in position to charge up the hill. To an elf, their faces were pale and their knuckles white from squeezing their sword hilts, but their jaws were set and their eyes fixed on Keya, awaiting the command to charge.

"Ready when you are," Keya said. "May the gods forgive us."

"It's not the gods we should ask," Vala replied.

She placed a hand on Kuhl's shoulder then raised her head and pointed into one of the bluetops still standing behind the mind-slaves' breastwork.

"There she is, Kuhl," said Vala.

"None of this is your doing," Burlen added. "The pointy-eared vixen seduced you."

"That's right," Vala added. "She let you get a child on her on purpose." As she spoke, Kuhl started to darken—not only his expression, but his face and hands, his eyes, and even the huge ranger's cloak Lord Duirsar had presented him. "All Takari wanted was your sword."

"Oh, she wanted the child, too," Keya said, catching on to what the

Vaasans were doing. "The *sy Tel'Quessir* sell their half-human children to pay for wine."

Vala and Burlen dropped their jaws, and Keya thought for a moment she might have taken the fib too far.

Kuhl turned soot-black, blurring around the edges like a shadow or a ghost, and he let out an angry wail. He rose and did not bound over the embankment so much as soar over it, and the slope instantly above exploded into a roaring tempest of death as the defenders hurled all manner of missiles and magic down upon him.

Thinking it had been the Vaasans' purpose to goad Kuhl into drawing the first wave of enemy attacks, Keya raised her hand to call the charge. Vala caught her arm and pulled it down.

Wait. Vala spoke in elven fingertalk—the only speech that would not be drowned out by the crash and roar of battle. *Let him get a little ahead of us.*

Ahead of us? Keya retorted. *There can't be anything left of him.*

But when she peered over the rim of the embankment, she saw that there was. Through a wall of smoke and flame twenty paces thick, Keya saw Kuhl's black silhouette still weaving and twisting up the hill. Lightning blasts passed through his shadowy form without slowing him down. Magic bolts glanced off him, trailing long wisps of black murk. Disintegration rays struck his dark aura and dissolved. Boulders he always managed to duck or dodge, spears he deflected and slipped, arrows stuck only in the strongest parts of his armor. It was as though he had become half phantom and half rothé, a creature of the shadows that could be seen but never stopped. Keya watched in awe until he vanished into the thickening smoke, then turned to Vala and raised her own darksword—or rather her husband's.

Can this sword do that? she asked.

No!

And never try! It was Burlen who added the explanation, *He's given himself to his sword. It can't be undone.*

The roar began to abate as Kuhl continued his charge, and Vala looked up the hill and spoke a single syllable. She didn't shout or use fingertalk, but Keya didn't need words to understand her meaning. She brought her arm forward then rose and charged over the rim of the embankment.

✡✡✡✡✡

From Takari's perch high among the rustling bluetops, the charge of the Cold Hand looked the stuff of songs. Through the smoke and flame came a golden-helmed tide of elf spellblades, words of mystic power pouring out of their mouths, forks of silver and gold flashing from their fingertips, swords glinting in their hands and armor gleaming on their breasts. The mind-slaves met the onslaught with a tempest of ray and rock, hurling boulders, flinging death bolts, spraying fire. Still the elves came, bounding over blast craters, scrambling across fallen bluetops, leaping through fire curtains and falling by the dozens but never wavering, never dropping for cover, never slowing.

Leading the charge was a shadow-cloaked bear of a man, out ahead by twenty paces or more, twisting and turning, taking magic blasts full in the chest, eyes shining like bronze embers, darksword in hand, burly legs carrying him up the wrecked hill at a speed no elf message runner could match.

Kuhl.

Swaddled in murk though he was, Takari would have known the slope of those huge shoulders from a thousand paces distant, would have recognized among an army of men the grace with which her paramour carried his mighty frame. As humans went—as *males* of any sort went—he was a magnificent example, ferocious when there was need and kind when there was not, always brave and never boastful, a lover who knew how to give *and* take.

Takari could not be sorry for how she had used him—or she would never have known him as the gentle giant he was—but she was sorry for what had come between them, for the curse that had turned her simple plan into a deadly rivalry.

But the fault lay with Kuhl, not Takari. He should have warned her about the curse before he lay with her—and never mind that she had told him not to worry about children. She had not said there wouldn't be any, only not to worry about them. Even after the mistake had been made, all the stupid rothé had to do was share. Had he only been strong enough to lend her the sword, everything would have been fine and there would have been no need to—

Takari did not grasp what she was about to do until she found herself staring down the length of an arrow at Kuhl's chest. The shaft was marked with black fletching, of course, for she had only two death arrows remaining. The rest of her quiver she had exhausted trying to soften up the mind-slave defenses for Keya. But even had there been another choice, she knew better than to think she would have found anything else on her bowstring. It had been the curse that nocked the arrow, and the curse wanted Kuhl dead.

Takari released the tension on her bow slowly, but deliberately did not move her aim away from Kuhl. There had to be another phaerimm down there somewhere or the mind-slaves would not be fighting so hard, and Kuhl was in the most danger. Having seen how slyly the curse worked, she would be stronger than it was and protect Kuhl from afar. She was not some base human whose will could be dominated by a sword.

The shower of death ebbed as more mind-slaves fell to the onslaught of elven spells, and as they exhausted their supply of boulders and magic. The charge gathered speed, with an ever-growing number of Cold Hand warriors pouring up the hill from behind, pressing those in front onward and taking their places when they were struck down. Twice, Kuhl was attacked by spells powerful enough to have come from a phaerimm, but each time Takari traced the flash trail back to mind-slave mages. Through a break in the smoke, she glimpsed Keya dancing up the slope with Vala and Burlen pounding along at her heels, then a pair of beholders found her hiding place and began to attack the base of the tree with their disintegration rays. She slipped around the trunk out of their view, then raced along a limb and jumped into another tree.

By the time Takari found a new hiding place, Kuhl had crashed into the enemy lines and was whirling his way down the entrenchment, his darksword opening bugbear bellies left and right, his feet sweeping legs from under elf mind-slaves, his boot heels crushing the skulls of fallen illithids. Somehow, his free hand had tangled itself in a snarl of beholder eyestalks, and he was swinging the eye tyrant around like a shield, catching bugbear axes and elven swords on its leathery body.

Takari was alarmed—and a little repulsed—to find herself feeling a secret thrill of delight. Though Kuhl showed no sign of slowing down, he had to be hurting. Even through the finest Evereskan armor, the bugbear blows alone would be powerful enough to snap bones and crush skulls. Kuhl would soon fall, and she would have only to stretch out her hand—

No.

Takari did not dare speak the word aloud—not with two beholders hunting her—but she did think it. She was stronger than the curse. She was a wood elf, who knew what was important in life (dancing, honey wine, and jolly company)—and what was not (power, wealth, and authority). She would help Kuhl—if only she could find a way—and they would share the sword.

Kuhl's helmet came flying out of the melee, its chinstrap broken and its gaudy gold brim buckled by the impact of a bugbear axe. Takari thought that it was done then, that Kuhl would fall beneath the feet of his attackers and vanish.

But the Vaasan bear fought on, reaching the back of the trench and scrambling out onto the hillside. He spun on a knee and lopped the heads off a trio of pursuing bugbears. He smashed a foot into the face of an elf mind-slave and sent him tumbling back into the breastwork. He was free, with no living enemies within a dozen paces of him.

Instead of turning along the back of the trench to attack the enemy's flank, Kuhl started up the hill into the forest. Takari thought he intended to slay her two hunters, but he ignored the beholders—who did not seem to realize she had escaped their attack and were busy searching for her body in the tree they had toppled—and he angled toward her new hiding place. Though it seemed impossible he could have seen her move when the beholders had not, his angry bronze eyes went straight to the bough on which she was perched. It had to be the darksword. The weapon could feel her desire for it, and it was leading him to her. Takari might be stronger than the sword's curse, but Kuhl was not. He'd kill her, if she didn't kill him first.

That was nonsense. Kuhl was too heavy to move through the forest canopy like a wood elf. All Takari need do was stay high in the bluetops, out on the bough ends where Kuhl could not follow. What was it that Galaeron had told her? That she had opened herself to her shadow, and that if she killed Kuhl, she would be lost to it. Takari believed him. It was already working hard to claim her, to trick her into murdering the father of her child.

Would it be murder if he died in battle?

The question came to her in her own voice, but so wispy and cold that it sent a chill down her spine.

No one would ever know.

So startled was Takari that at first she didn't see the illithid climbing out of the entrenchment behind Kuhl. She was preoccupied with the voice, wondering whether someone was eavesdropping on her thoughts or her shadow had already grown strong enough to speak. Of course, this distraction was exactly what the voice had intended. By the time she saw what was happening, the illithid had run a dozen steps toward Kuhl, and its mouth tentacles were extending in his direction. Angered by this manipulation, Takari did not think, hesitate, or even consciously aim. She simply drew her bowstring and let fly.

The angle was not a particularly difficult one, at least not for a Green elf ranger who had spent her whole life making exacting shots. The arrow zipped down in Kuhl's direction, passing a dozen feet over his head but still close enough to make him duck, and it planted itself in the center of the illithid's mouth tentacles. The creature flew off its feet backward and crashed to the ground as still as a statue and immediately began to shrivel inward.

How Kuhl reacted, Takari never saw. The deafening boom of a magic blast rumbled up from the forest floor behind her, and she knew without looking that something powerful had found her hiding place. She jumped for a clump of leaves low on the adjacent tree, her stomach rising into her chest and limbs spread to slow her descent, one hand still clutching her bow.

As Takari crashed into the boughs, she was slapped in the back by the giant hand of a blast concussion. It pushed her deep into the tangle of twigs and leaves facefirst, but she caught a fistful of a branch with her free hand and hooked her legs around another limb as thick as a Vaasan arm.

Takari thought her descent would stop there, but she felt the limb shudder and suddenly found herself falling, staring up at the splintered end of a branch. She had just enough time to wonder why she hadn't heard it break, then she slammed down on the forest floor and was instantly buried beneath a snarl of leafy boughs.

It took only an instant for Takari to realize why she had not heard the limb shatter and that listening for the enemy would do her no good. Her ears were ringing like a halfling dinner bell. She pushed out from beneath a log and found her last arrow still in her quiver. Takari cautiously climbed for the top of the tangle.

Her shoulders ached, and her legs felt half numb, but everything moved when she told it to. It was only a moment before she poked her head up to find Kuhl less than a dozen paces away, striding purposefully in her direction. Behind him were the two beholders that had been hunting her, making good use of his preoccupation to float up close for a sure kill.

Takari pushed herself up onto a somewhat steady branch and nocked her last death arrow. Kuhl narrowed his bronze eyes and broke into a sprint, cocking his sword arm to throw and inadvertently blocking her shot at the beholders. She found her aim drifting to his chest—then she jerked it up and away.

"No." More loudly, she yelled, "Kuhl, go left!"

Reacting perhaps by instinct or perhaps because he realized that the arrow would already be on its way if it was meant for him, he stepped left—and threw the sword anyway.

Takari cursed his human weakness, set the point of her arrow on the big central eye of the nearest beholder, and let fly. She watched only long enough to see her shaft pass beneath Kuhl's sword, then she dropped back into the tangle of boughs . . . and heard a sickly thump behind her.

A howling wind tore at the trees, and Takari knew before she turned to look that Kuhl had not thrown at her, but that he had found the phaerimm she had been hunting.

Ears still ringing, Takari scrambled out the back of the bough tangle and found the phaerimm lying motionless on the ground, opened down the center where Kuhl's tumbling darksword had split it open. The sword itself lay a few paces beyond the dead thornback, so coated in gore it was barely recognizable.

Takari stretched her hand out, preparing to call the darksword to her grasp. She thought of Kuhl, and waited. He would need the sword to meet the second beholder behind him, and if he had to fight her for it . . . but the sword did not fly to his hand. It did not even rise, or wobble.

Go ahead—it's yours now, the dark voice inside whispered. *The beholder is coming.*

"Be quiet!" Takari hissed.

She turned her palm up and called the darksword to her hand.

With the beholder coming, what choice did she have?

CHAPTER TWENTY

2 Eleasias, the Year of Wild Magic

The grim expressions on the high mages' amber faces as they examined the tattered hem of Hanali Celanil's stone cloak told Galaeron all he needed to know. The phaerimm had undone too many of the mythal's ancient spells for his plan to work. Before they could proceed, the circle would have to repair the damage—provided they were willing to make the sacrifice for a city that was not even their own.

Not waiting for the high mages to announce the conclusion themselves, Galaeron turned to Lord Duirsar and the others waiting with him in the shadow of the great statue, and said, "Milord, the phaerimm have done too much damage." To make himself heard over the battle roar coming from the slopes below, Galaeron nearly had to shout. "The high mages need time to do a high casting, and that means we must be prepared to defend them."

"If time is all we need, we have this battle won already," said Kiinyon Colbathin. Like Lord Duirsar and every other Evereskan in the courtyard, Kiinyon was dressed in a full suit of much-dented battle armor that—by the smell of him—he had not shed in the better part of a tenday. "Young Lord Nihmedu's plan has proven an excellent one. We have only to send the Long Watch down the slope, and we'll have the enemy trapped."

"For how long?" asked Storm. She was standing behind Lord Duirsar, towering over his shoulders with Khelben and Laeral. "Any victory here will be short-lived until we repair the mythal. The phaerimm have tens of thousands of their mind-slaves scattered across Evereska, and I'd bet my hair that most of them are on their way here right now."

"All the more reason to move swiftly," Kiinyon replied.

He turned toward the back of the courtyard, where the Long Watch was forming into battle ranks as they emerged from Laeral's teleport circle. He summoned the company commander forward, then turned back to Storm and said, "Once we seize the breastworks, it will not matter how many mind-slaves the phaerimm send against us. Galaeron's plan is an excellent one, and I'm confident we can hold long enough to see it through."

"Yes," Lord Duirsar said, making a point of casting an approving nod in Galaeron's direction, "you may well have saved us."

"Not so easily as Master Colbathin suggests, I fear," Galaeron said. "The mind-slaves below are not the danger."

"They are," Kiinyon declared. The commander of the Long Watch—a young Gold elf female named Zharilee—arrived at his side, and he turned and spoke to her. "When the Cold Hand drives the mind-slaves out of their entrenchment, they will have no place to retreat but here. The Long Watch will prevent that, descending through the forest to fall on them from behind. The enemy will be trapped between two of our companies, and it will be a simple matter to seize the entrenchment for our own use."

He nodded and waved Zharilee away to execute his order. Galaeron bit his tongue to keep from calling Kiinyon—a former commander who had spent two decades making Galaeron's life as a Tomb Guard as miserable as possible—a fool.

Instead, Galaeron said, "It's the phaerimm I'm concerned about. They can teleport into the courtyard as easily as we can."

"Didn't you say that they wouldn't do that?" asked Storm. " 'Without their leader, they'll be too disorganized and busy thinking of themselves to counterattack.' I'm *sure* you said that."

"I did." Galaeron felt the heat come to his face but continued in a sure voice, "And without their leader, that would be so."

Khelben winced, closed his eyes, and said, "Don't tell me—"

"The leader survived."

Galaeron did not explain what had happened, in large part because he didn't know. Takari might have ignored his order and gone straight after Kuhl's sword, or she might have gone around the tree to finish the leader off and discovered that he was already gone.

"But it was injured?" Laeral asked.

"Yes," Galaeron said. "Very badly. It was unconscious for a time."

"Then it won't return," Kiinyon said. He glanced over his shoulder and nodded approvingly as the Long Watch filed down the hill. "These phaerimm are cowards at heart. Hurt them once, and they run for cover."

"Normally, yes."

As he spoke, Galaeron's mind was racing. With Kiinyon having committed the Long Watch to battle, any attempt to recall them would be noticed by the enemy, and it wouldn't take the phaerimm long to puzzle out why. If Galaeron wanted to foil the counterattack, he would have to find a more subtle way.

"This one was the leader," he continued. "It will have too much at stake to give up. It'll be back with all the help it can muster."

Kiinyon shook his head and started to chide Galaeron for contradicting him, but Lord Duirsar raised a silencing hand.

"How can you know this?" he asked Galaeron. "You speak as though you've lived among the phaerimm."

"Not exactly," Galaeron said.

Though he knew the dim view his fellow Evereskans were likely to take regarding the source of his information, he explained without hesitation how Melegaunt had passed on his knowledge before dying—and how he had been forced to yield to his shadow before he could retrieve it. The tale evoked an expression somewhere between revulsion and pity from Lord Duirsar and plain revulsion from Kiinyon Colbathin.

"So you're telling us your information comes from the Shadovar?" Kiinyon asked. The last of the Long Watch was disappearing into the forest, and the sound of their first attacks could already be heard rolling up from the far side of the courtyard. "Milord, Galaeron's intentions have always been good, but his naivete has made him a pawn of the Shadovar from the start."

Khelben started to defend Galaeron, but Lord Duirsar cut him off by speaking directly to Kiinyon.

"Master Colbathin, did you not say just a moment ago that Lord Nihmedu's plan was an excellent one?"

Kiinyon scowled but nodded.

"Then I suggest we listen to him."

"Thank you, milord," Galaeron said. Though the relief he experienced was for Evereska, he did not try to hide the triumph he felt. "I'm sure Master Colbathin will find he was correct in his first assessment of my plan."

"I wouldn't be too impressed with myself," Kiinyon said. His eyes looked as dangerous as those of any beholder. "I'll recall the Long Watch."

Galaeron caught him by the elbow. "It's too late for that."

Kiinyon glared down at the hand on his arm as though he would bite it off.

Galaeron continued to hold it.

"This is what we must do now . . ."

He explained his idea, emphasizing how important it was that the Chosen save their silver fire until the mythal had been repaired, then he asked, "Any questions?"

"Only one," Khelben said. "What if we're not quick enough?"

"Then the high mages die and we continue the fight for Evereska without them . . . or the mythal," Lord Duirsar said, drawing his ancient sword. "So I suggest we be quick enough."

Lord Duirsar asked the high mages to begin their repair of the mythal at once, and Galaeron spent the next few minutes positioning his 'troops' in the shadows around the statue. He would have liked to have Aris there with them, but they had already decided the giant would be most useful supporting Keya and assigned him to join the Cold Hand after departing the palace. Galaeron thought he could hear Aris's boulders crashing into the enemy entrenchment already, but with the battle roar below, it was impossible to be certain.

Once the others were arrayed in their hiding places along the edge of the courtyard, Galaeron stepped into the shadow of the statue itself. He took one last glance around. Seeing that Lord Duirsar, Kiinyon, and the Chosen were all safely concealed within the Fringe, he descended into the shadows himself. The phaerimm were surely wary of such hiding places, but there would be a moment after they arrived when their caution would not matter. It was then that Evereska would be won or lost, Galaeron finally redeemed or forever vilified.

The high mages had already encircled Hanali's statue and begun their work. The two assistants stood to either side of the goddess, their palms turned down, drawing from the ground the golden strands of Weave magic the phaerimm had released earlier. Their dulcet voices were raised in intonation, each singing a separate spell of support, yet weaving their words together in musiclike harmony.

The leader stood behind the goddess, casting a protection spell so ancient the words barely seemed Elvish. As he sang, he was taking the Weave strands from his two assistants and plaiting them back into the hem of Hanali's cloak, slowly restoring it to its original flawless condition. With every fiber he restored, the mage grew a little wispier and more translucent, as though weaving himself into the mythal. Though Galaeron was hardly privy to the secrets of elven high magic, he had heard whispers of spirit-binding during his time at the Academy of Magic, and he knew what he was seeing. The leader would become a part of the mythal, watching over Evereska for all time.

The high mages continued their work for what seemed an eternity, slowly weaving the magic back into the mythal and restoring the statue to its original state. Galaeron concentrated on watching for phaerimm but found his attention drifting to their work more often as time passed. They wove in the most powerful magic first—the spells of imprisonment and foresight and meteor storms—and saved the simpler magic for last. By the time they had worked their way down to relatively minor magic like detection spells and dimensional locks, the leader was so translucent it was possible to look through him to the far side of the courtyard.

Only a few ragged edges remained to repair on Hanali's cloak, and the battle in the entrenchment was raging ever louder, suggesting that mind-slave reinforcements were already starting to pour in from the rest of Evereska. Galaeron knew Kiinyon and the others would be wondering if he had been wrong about the phaerimm counterattack after all, but the long wait only convinced him that the leader had more influence than he had believed. Even for the phaerimm, it took time to gather resources—and the longer they took, the more they were gathering.

The high mages were down to their last magic—simple spells of soft falling and true striking—when half a dozen phaerimm crackled into existence around the statue. Teleport-dazed though they were, they arrived attacking, spraying the courtyard with golden bolts of magic and long tongues of flame. Most of the attacks were blind and found no target at all, but one flurry did strike a supporting mage. Her spell shield flashed silver and dissipated, drained by the power of the attack, and one missile penetrated to burn a thumb-sized hole in her shoulder.

The mage continued her incantation without missing a syllable.

Galaeron and the other two elves were already leaping from their hiding places, each rushing to attack the nearest phaerimm and hurling his most powerful death spell at the next closest. Galaeron sent a dark bolt hissing through the torso of his first thornback and glimpsed Lord Duirsar's falling to a black death ray that could have taken a giant. Then he was on his second target, slashing his darksword down the length of its thorny body. The creature vanished in a twinkle of teleport magic, leaving behind a pool of black blood.

More crackles sounded around the courtyard as a second wave of phaerimm arrived flinging magic and fire. Galaeron raised a shadow shield to cover his back, then hurled a flight of dark bolts at the first thornback he saw and charged the second. A scything blade appeared out of nowhere and came swinging at him from the side. He blocked with the edge of his darksword, cleaving it down the center, and turned back to find Storm Silverhand stepping out of the shadows behind his attacker. Dispelling its blade guard with one hand and swinging her sword with the other, she lopped the phaerimm's tail off about a third of the way up its body—then came staggering in Galaeron's direction as an errant fireball ricocheted off her shoulder and went raging into the forest.

Eyes flashing, Storm whirled on her attacker and charged. The battle became a mad melee of spell, blade, and claw. A female voice shrieked in pain. Galaeron spun around to see the high mage who had been wounded earlier falling to the ground. Where once there had been a leg she had only a smoking wound, but she was still singing her alarm spell and feeding golden strands of Weave to the leader.

Galaeron rushed to help, but Kiinyon was closer. Hurling a flight of magic bolts at her attacker, the legendary spellblade sprang to her side and caught her under the arm. His bolts dissipated harmlessly against the phaerimm's spell shield, but by then Galaeron was flinging a shadow net over it from behind. The startled thornback tried to teleport away and exploded into a thousand fleshy cubes.

Kiinyon pulled the mage to her feet, holding her up so she could finish the spell and shielding her with his own body. A trio of lightning flashes streaked in from all sides, and Galaeron knew the phaerimm were recovered enough from their teleport afterdaze to mount a concerted attack.

The first bolt overloaded Kiinyon's spell shield and drew a startled curse. The second caught him square in the chest, melting through his armor and setting him on fire at head, hands, and feet. The third bolt caught the high mage square in the back and slammed her headlong into the side of Hanali's leg. Her body didn't even go limp; it burst into flames and flew apart.

The spell songs of the other two high mages fell out of harmony, and the leader's hands began to fumble as he struggled to continue weaving. Though they were also under attack, it was not as heavy as on Galaeron's side of the statue, and Laeral and Khelben were doing a good job of keeping it that way.

Racing the last five steps to Hanali's feet, Galaeron flung a shadow sphere into the head-disk of one of the mage's attackers and hurled his darksword through the torso of the second, then he stepped over Kiinyon's body and turned his palms toward the ground. He was no high mage, but the alarm spell was not difficult, and he had seen enough of how the circle harmonized to stand in.

Galaeron began to sing.

The surviving high mages faltered. The leader turned his translucent head toward Galaeron and studied him for a moment, then looked back to his weaving. Galaeron feared the two mages would not accept him into their circle but they adjusted their pitch to blend with his more sonorous voice and continued their spells.

Galaeron felt a slight impact as a flurry of spells struck him in the back and disappeared into his shadow shield. His heart raced with the knowledge that he was standing there motionless while a bevy of phaerimm hurled magic at him, but he forced the fear from his mind and gave himself over to the song he was creating with the high mages. He began to twist his fingers through the gestures of the alarm spell, drawing the magic up out of the ground as he had seen the dead mage do.

The strands came up dark and cold.

Galaeron's voice quavered, but when he hesitated to pass the shadow magic over, the leader reached over with a translucent hand and took the first black thread. As the mage plaited the strand into the hem of Hanali's cloak, his eyes darkened, becoming a pair of murky orbs floating in a transparent face. He reached over and took the next strand from Galaeron's hand.

A three-armed phaerimm flew up beside the statue where its attacks wouldn't be blocked by the shadow shield protecting Galaeron's back. It plunged its tail barb into his belly. So absorbed in the spell song was Galaeron that it barely registered that this was the leader or that it was pumping its poison into him. He felt his feet leave the cobblestones, but that troubled him no more than did the distant pain burning in his belly.

Lord Duirsar was there, beating the phaerimm back with spell and blade. Galaeron continued to sing. He was one with the high mages, concerned only with the casting. The leader reached up and took the next strand from Galaeron with an invisible hand. This time, when he plaited the thread into Hanali's cloak, he followed it in.

Galaeron came to the end of his song, and his belly erupted in pain. He did not realize that the casting was finished and he had been released from the spell until he saw Lord Duirsar below him, fighting the phaerimm leader toe-to-tail, driving it back with flashing steel and pelting it with bolt after bolt from a magic ring. Storm was rushing to the elf lord's side, one hand raised to hurl her own spells, the other still carrying her sword.

Galaeron reached for his shadowsilk but knew even as tried he would not succeed. The phaerimm's poison had left him paralyzed and floating helplessly above the ground. As he watched, two more phaerimm appeared at Storm's back, spraying fire and lightning blindly and lashing out with their tails. He shifted his eyes in the opposite direction and saw that the situation was much the same in the rest of the courtyard, with Khelben and Laeral standing back-to-back and wary phaerimm pelting them from a distance.

Newly repaired though it was, the mythal remained exhausted and starved from the abuse it had suffered since the start of the phaerimm invasion. It mustered itself enough to send a single golden meteor streaking down into the courtyard. The orb blasted only one of the phaerimm that had just teleported in behind Storm, leaving the other to tumble off smoking and teleport away.

The boom was loud enough to draw the attention of everyone in the courtyard. Lord Duirsar narrowly blocked a tail barb when he spun around to see what had caused the sound. Storm, who had been much closer to the explosion, was left picking herself up off the cobblestones.

"Storm!" Galaeron had to hiss the words between clenched teeth, but he knew that as one of the Chosen, she would hear. "The mythal is whole! Use the silver—"

The phaerimm leader gestured in Galaeron's direction, and even his muttering grew silent. Lord Duirsar took advantage of the opening to pour a flurry of magic bolts into the thornback's torso and send it tumbling away, then Storm turned and loosed a stream of silver fire into the base of Hanali's statue. Khelben and Laeral followed her lead an instant later, and the statue began to glow with a bright silver light.

The glow faded as quickly as it had appeared. The phaerimm leader hurled a black death ray at Lord Duirsar that the elf lord sent ricocheting off with a spell mirror. Taking a cue from their leader, the other phaerimm renewed their attacks, and Galaeron began to think that he had failed Evereska again, that his idea had been disastrously misguided and even the unadulterated magic of the Chosen's silver fire could not provide the burst of energy the mythal needed to defend Evereska. Fighting through his disappointment and pain, he opened himself to the Shadow Weave and prepared to loose a shadow blast. He had no control over his own movement, but if a phaerimm happened to pass—

A rain of golden meteors came streaking down from the sky, crackling, sizzling, and leaving a long trail of black smoke in their wake. The first one struck the phaerimm leader, blasting the creature into a spray of sparkling nothingness and laying Lord Duirsar out on the ground next to it. The next three landed in a semicircle around Khelben and Laeral, leaving the two Chosen slumped back-to-back, their eyes as round as coins and their jaws hanging slack. Two more crashed down behind Storm, who flinched a little and looked around to see if there was anything left to kill.

It took only four more strikes in half as many seconds before there wasn't anything left to kill. The rest of the phaerimm—the few who had survived—teleported away, and the meteor shower began to spread outward from the statue, seeking targets in other parts of the city. Galaeron saw perhaps another dozen strikes before the rain grew erratic and dwindled away, leaving the sky streaked with the smoky trails of their descent.

No, not smoke. Smoke trails grew crooked and feathery as they dissipated in the breeze. The streaks remained straight, narrow, and dark.

"Are those what I think they are?" Storm asked.

Galaeron looked down to see Storm below him. She had a coil of elven rope she had taken from Kiinyon's belt and was busy tying a slip knot. He would have asked her what she thought the stripes were, except that he remained both paralyzed from the phaerimm leader's poison and silenced by its magic. It was probably just as well—he really didn't want to be the one to say they were shadows.

Storm finished her knot, then deftly tossed the loop up over Galaeron's feet.

"Well, Galaeron," she said as she began to pull him down, "when you save a city, you certainly leave your mark."

✡✡✡✡✡

For the third time in as many hours, the Chosen poured their silver fire into the base of Hanali Celanil's statue. A silver blush rolled up the goddess's imposing figure, then slowly faded as the ravenous mythal drew the raw magic into itself. Moments later, a swarm of golden meteors crackled down from the sky, each streaking toward a distant part of the city where some enemy of Evereska's lay hiding from the mythal's justice.

Galaeron supposed that most of those enemies were still phaerimm, but the last time the meteors had fallen, he had seen them strike beholders and illithids, even a bewildered bugbear who looked more interested in fleeing the city than conquering it. Once the mythal might have shown mercy on a hapless mind-slave as much a victim of the phaerimm as Evereska's own citizens, but no longer. The renewed mythal concerned itself only with who was an enemy to the city and who was a friend, and it destroyed enemies and protected friends.

Considering the stripes of shadow that remained behind every time a meteor descended, Galaeron half expected the next golden ball to land on him, but the mythal had finished with the courtyard surrounding Hanali's statue, and even with the hill below. No attacks had fallen anywhere near the hill since the second wave, when its deadly barrage had broken the counterattack on the captured entrenchment and sent the phaerimm mind-slaves fleeing for the far corners of the city. With reinforcements pouring up the hill by the dozens, victory was only a matter of waiting and consolidating, of carefully expanding the areas of elf control each time the mythal struck.

Galaeron should probably have felt proud, but in truth he was simply restless. After the mythal's initial strike, Laeral Silverhand had attended to his stomach wound, and finding no phaerimm egg planted inside, pronounced him likely to survive but in need of rest. Storm had trickled a healing potion down his throat, then tied him down to a tree root to wait for the phaerimm's paralysis poison to wear off, and there he had been stuck, wondering what had become of Vala and Aris, of Keya and her Vaasan friends, and most of all, what had happened between Takari and Kuhl and their sword.

It was another quarter hour before Galaeron could move his fingers, and a quarter hour after that before he had control enough to untie Storm's torturous knots. By the time he succeeded, Lord Duirsar was holding a meeting with the Chosen, the commanders of the city's surviving companies, Aris, and anyone else likely to play an important part in the events to come.

Galaeron coiled the rope and hung it on his belt, then straightened his armor and started across the courtyard to join the others. Storm's healing potion had proven remarkably effective. Though he had felt the phaerimm's tail barb sink deep, the wound caused him little discomfort as he walked, and when he looked down, he was surprised to find the puncture already closed.

As Galaeron approached, his sister Keya was the first to notice. Without excusing herself from the circle kneeling in front of Lord Duirsar, and apparently not caring that she was bringing the meeting to a dead stop, she leaped to her feet and rushed across to him with her arms spread wide.

"Brother!"

Keya threw herself into Galaeron so hard that he stumbled back and would have fallen, had she not closed her arms around his shoulders and caught him.

"You're well?" she asked.

"Well enough," Galaeron laughed. He pried himself loose and held her at arm's length. "And you?"

"Not a scratch."

Keya did a twirl to demonstrate, though she was so crusted in dirt and blood that it was barely possible to tell she was female.

"I'll take your word for it. And what of the others?"

"We lost Kuhl," said Vala, coming to join them. She smiled grimly. "Everyone else made it."

"I'm sorry for Kuhl's loss." Galaeron took her hands, then said quietly, "And glad to see you still here."

"Then how about showing it?"

Vala kissed him deep and hard, drawing a hearty and somewhat astonished laugh from the others in the crowd. She held the kiss just long enough to be scandalous, then released him and nodded over her shoulder at Takari.

"And showing it not just to me," Vala said.

Not quite sure what to make of Vala's remark or Takari's unaccustomed meekness, Galaeron went to Takari. He was hardly surprised to find Kuhl's darksword in her scabbard, but when he looked into her eyes, the shadow was gone. There was sorrow and guilt, perhaps, but no darkness.

"Galaeron, I'm sorry," Takari said, hardly able to look him in the eye. "I didn't mean to leave my post, but it was already gone when I went around the tree, so when I heard the Cold Hand trying to attack . . ."

"It's all right."

"I thought I should go help," she continued. "It was probably just the curse. . . ."

"Whatever it was, Takari, you did the right thing," Galaeron said, taking her hands. He didn't know what had happened with Kuhl's sword and wasn't sure he ever wanted to, but he could see by the clearness in her eyes that she had not been taken by her shadow. "I'm just happy you're still here."

Takari smiled that carefree cupid's bow smile that he remembered from all those years on the Desert Border South.

Galaeron could not resist. He kissed her as hard as Vala had kissed him, though this time the crowd's astonishment took the form of a shocked murmur rather than a hearty laugh. It didn't matter to Galaeron. He loved Takari and Vala both, and he had made so many mistakes so much worse on the way to saving Evereska that he really didn't care what they thought. He would not curb his feelings to please anyone—he had learned that much at least.

"Ahem," said Lord Duirsar's familiar voice. "If I might intrude."

Galaeron and Takari parted—reluctantly—and he bowed to the elf lord.

"Thank you. Now that you seem to be feeling better—" Duirsar drew a nervous chuckle from the assembly by turning to them and arching one of his gray eyebrows—"it occurs to me that with the death of Kiinyon Colbathin, Evereska has need of a new Master of the Defenses."

"Galaeron would make a fine commander," said Laeral Silverhand. "He has already saved the city once."

"Hear, hear!" cried Dexon, limping up behind Keya on his still-withered leg. "I can tell you, your young cubs are already recounting the tales of how he lured the phaerimm to their deaths."

As the Vaasan spoke, Keya, Zharilee, and the other commanders of the elven companies were kneeling on the -cobblestones. They drew their swords and turned the tips toward Galaeron, then touched them to the ground in a gesture of loyalty. Even the high mage from Evermeet, the one whom Galaeron had joined in repairing the last strands of the mythal, dropped to a knee and inclined his head.

It did not escape Galaeron's notice, however, that it was only the humans who were actually voicing their approval. With the exception of Takari and his sister Keya, the elves were reluctant to meet his eyes, and many of them seemed unable to keep their gazes from straying toward the shadow-striped sky.

"What say you, Galaeron?" Lord Duirsar laid a hand on Galaeron's shoulder. "Will you lead the defenders of Evereska—what few of us remain?"

"Milord, I don't know what to say."

Instead of kneeling to accept the appointment, Galaeron turned and looked into the eyes of the high mage. There he did not find even the uncertainty and apprehension that filled the eyes of the others—only revulsion, fear, and mistrust. Of all the elves there in the courtyard, the high mage had felt the touch of Galaeron's shadow most clearly, and it was in his eyes that Galaeron could read his future in Evereska. He inclined his head to the mage not in bitterness or anger, but acknowledgement and acceptance, then turned back to Lord Duirsar.

"Lord Duirsar, I will, of course, serve Evereska until we have seen the last of the phaerimm and their mind-slaves driven from the Shaeradim."

He glanced in Takari's direction and allowed his glance to linger there until he saw realization dawn in her eyes, then he turned to face Vala.

"But I have given my word to Vala that I would see the darkswords we have borrowed returned safely to their families in Vaasa."

Duirsar's jaw dropped, and a murmur of disbelief rustled through the assembly. No elf dared refuse Lord Duirsar—at least no elf who was a citizen of Evereska.

"Galaeron!" Vala hissed. "There's no need—"

"I am an elf," Galaeron cut her off. His eyes darted toward the high mage. "I keep my promises."

Even Vala could not miss the gratitude and relief in the high mage's expression.

"I hope you understand, milord," Vala said. "It is a matter of some importance to my people that the weapons be returned by the one who borrowed them."

Taken aback though he was by Galaeron's refusal, Lord Duirsar was nevertheless wise enough to recognize a graceful out when it was offered. He nodded courteously and smiled.

"It was rude of me not to think of that. I'm quite certain we'll be able to find someone else." He paused for a moment then turned to Keya and said, "And what of you, young Lady Nihmedu? Will we be needing to find a new commander for your company as well?"

Dexon limped forward, as completely oblivious to the proper etiquette as only a Vaasan could be, and growled, "With your permission, Milord, we'll be making our home here—as long as you can stomach me, that is."

Lord Duirsar turned to Vala and asked, "Would that be agreeable to the Granite Tower?"

"He's free to do as he pleases," Vala said. She reached out and pinched Dexon's swarthy cheek. "As long as he gives the baby a Vaasan name."

"At least the first one," Keya promised.

"Very well, then," Duirsar said, turning to Dexon. "Then it would be our honor to 'stomach you' for the rest of your life, my friend."

Dexon grinned and engulfed Lord Duirsar in a bear hug.

While the elf lord endeavored to extract himself, Vala turned to Takari and said, "And you're free to do as you please, too."

Takari frowned. "Free?" she asked. "Of course I'm free. I'm Sy'*Tel'Quess*."

"Let me put this another way," Vala said. "As the bearer of Kuhl's child and his darksword, you have a home with us in Vaasa."

"With you?" Takari said. She smiled broadly and came over to stand with Vala and Galaeron. "We're all going to Vaasa to live in the Granite Tower . . . together?"

"If you like, yes."

Vala glanced at Galaeron as though looking for rescue, but of course he only smiled and used fingertalk to thank her. She went pale, but quickly collected herself and took Takari by the arm.

"We have some very interesting customs in Vaasa," Vala said, narrowing her eyes at Galaeron. "Our men sleep in the snow."

EPILOGUE

3 Eleasias, the Year of Wild Magic

No sooner had Shade Enclave stopped wobbling than the summons came to Malygris, the Blue Suzerain of Anauroch. Though it took a mighty act of will to resist the call of the Most High, the dracolich lingered atop his perch, watching to see if the thread of shadow that ran between the enclave and the dark lake beneath would dissolve, or if the capsized mountain would rise to its former place high in the sky. When neither happened, Malygris deigned to answer. Lifting his boneless magnificence off the peak where he'd been resting, he flew into the city.

Before entering the cave where the Most High always met him, Malygris took a turn over the enclave and found that the magnificent metropolis had degenerated overnight into a drab city of hovels and tenements. The Palace Most High, whose grandeur had awed even him, was in the light of Anauroch's sun little more than a barren field, with a freestanding arch to mark the entrance and a handful of stairwells leading down into the ground.

When Malygris finally entered the Cave Gate, he found Telamont Tanthul waiting with a pile of freshly decapitated heads large enough to hold a dragon. The stench was awful, but that would change with a decade of curing. Though he tried not to show it, Malygris was impressed. The next time the accursed Cult of the Dragon priests came to his lair with some errand, he would enjoy watching their faces when they looked upon his new nest.

Malygris was so grateful that instead of forcing the Most High to come to him as usual, the dracolich landed in front of the shade. The platinum glow of Telamont's eyes seemed less bright, but there was another sign of his weariness.

"You were occupied, Mighty One?" Telamont asked.

"That is none of your concern." Malygris raised his horny snout bone toward the pile of heads and asked, "You have gifts?"

The Most High nodded and waved an empty sleeve toward the heap. If he realized his confidence was being tested, he showed no sign.

"The Cult of the Dragon," said he shade.

Malygris's jaw dropped.

"The *whole* cult?"

"Only the fools who knew of your bondage," Telamont clarified.

"All? You're sure?" Malygris asked. He could hardly believe what he was hearing. "I am free?"

Telamont inclined his head.

"Did you not tell me it was impossible to free me of the Cult?"

"It was *then*," Telamont answered. "We acted when we could be certain."

"And when your need was greatest," Malygris said, turning toward the cave mouth. "You may deliver the heads to my lair."

He spread his wings, but found himself unable to launch. The weight of Telamont's will pressed down on him so hard he thought it might crush one of his minor wing bones, and he found himself speaking thoughts he had intended to keep private.

"I have seen the true face of Shade, and I am no longer awed."

Malygris tried to stop there, but Telamont's will forced him to continue, "The Chosen mammals are peeling your blankets from the High Ice, and the strength of the other warmblood realms will soon return. It will not be long, I think, before your city crashes into the lake or flees back into the shadow."

"You are mistaken, my friend, but I will not hold it against you."

Telamont pointed at the floor by his feet, and Malygris found himself clattering over to lay his magnificent chin on the cold stone. He thought instantly of the amulet the cult priests used to control him, but it was not hanging from the Most High's neck. Telamont Tanthul had his own magic.

"Shade is here to stay."

"Shade is here to stay," Malygris found himself repeating.

"We have many enemies, but we are accustomed to enemies."

"We have many enemies—" Malygris tried to resist saying "we," but the will of the Most High was as heavy as all of his coin piles together—"but we are accustomed to enemies."

"Shade will prevail as it always prevails, by hiding in the darkness and striking from the shadows."

Malygris's resistance crumbled, and he found himself repeating the words of his own will.

"Shade will prevail as it always prevails, by hiding in the darkness and striking from the shadows."

"Good," Telamont said. He raised his sleeve and wrapped five tendrils of cold shadow around Malygris's nose horn. "Together, we will triumph."

When he spoke this time, Malygris believed what he was saying.

FORGOTTEN REALMS

MARK SEHESTEDT

Chosen of Nendawen

The consumer, the despoiler, has come to Narfell. His followers have taken Highwatch and slain all who held it–save one.

Book I
The Fall of Highwatch

Book II
The Hand of the Hunter
November 2010

Book III
Cry of the Ghost Wolf
November 2011

Vengeance will be yours, the Master of the Hunt promises.
If you survive.

FORGOTTEN REALMS®

Award-winning Game Designer

BRUCE R. CORDELL

Abolethic Sovereignty

There are things that we were not meant to know.

Book I
Plague of Spells

Book II
City of Torment

Book III
Key of Stars
September 2010

". . . he weaves a tale that adds depth and breadth to the FORGOTTEN REALMS history."
—Grasping for the Wind, on *Stardeep*

A DUNGEONS & DRAGONS® NOVEL

Wizards of the Coast®